WISSENSCHAFT UND KUNST

Herausgegeben von
SABINE COELSCH-FOISNER
DIMITER DAPHINOFF

Band 38

CATERINA PAN

Popular Theatre in Early Modern England, Germany and Italy (1570–1640)

A Study in Intercultural Theatricality with an Analysis of *Engelische Comedien und Tragedien* (1620)

Universitätsverlag
WINTER
Heidelberg

Bibliografische Information der Deutschen Nationalbibliothek
Die Deutsche Nationalbibliothek verzeichnet diese Publikation
in der Deutschen Nationalbibliografie;
detaillierte bibliografische Daten sind im Internet
über *http://dnb.d-nb.de* abrufbar.

Gedruckt mit Unterstützung der
Österreichischen Forschungsgemeinschaft.

Die Reproduktionsrechte der Abbildungen liegen bei den Autoren.

UMSCHLAGBILD
Pieter Brueghel the Younger, *A Village Festival
in Honour of St Hubert and St Anthony* (1632).
© The Fitzwilliam Museum, Cambridge.

ISBN 978-3-8253-4949-3

Dieses Werk einschließlich aller seiner Teile ist urheberrechtlich geschützt.
Jede Verwertung außerhalb der engen Grenzen des Urheberrechtsgesetzes ist
ohne Zustimmung des Verlages unzulässig und strafbar. Das gilt insbesondere
für Vervielfältigungen, Übersetzungen, Mikroverfilmungen und die Einspeicherung
und Verarbeitung in elektronischen Systemen.

© 2023 Universitätsverlag Winter GmbH Heidelberg
Imprimé en Allemagne · Printed in Germany
Umschlaggestaltung: Klaus Brecht GmbH, Heidelberg
Druck: Memminger MedienCentrum, 87700 Memmingen

Gedruckt auf umweltfreundlichem, chlorfrei gebleichtem
und alterungsbeständigem Papier

Den Verlag erreichen Sie im Internet unter:
www.winter-verlag.de

To my 'itinerant' family and friends

"A thing of beauty is a joy for ever" (Keats)

"Hoc erat in votis: […] auctius atque
di melius fecere. Bene est."
(Horace)

Acknowledgements

The present study is the revised version of my PhD thesis, which I completed in November 2021 at the University of Salzburg as a member of the Doctorate School 'Cultural Production Dynamics'. In 2020, my PhD project was awarded the Young Investigators Award of the University of Salzburg. The publication was made possible thanks to the generous funding of the Österreichische Forschungsgemeinschaft.

My gratitude goes to my advisor, Univ. Prof. Dr. Sabine Coelsch-Foisner, for this longed-for opportunity. Special thanks also to the many institutions and experts who have helped me in my research: Dr. Elizabeth Harding from the Herzog August Library in Wolfenbüttel, Dr. Silke Wagener-Fimpel from the State Archive of Lower Saxony, Walter Steinmetz, librarian at the Cistercian monastery of Rein near Graz, and Friedrich Simader from the Austrian National Library in Vienna. I would also like to thank Univ. Prof. Dr. Johann Hüttner, Univ. Prof. Merle Tönnies and Dr. Christopher Herzog for their kind suggestions.

I would never have embarked on this long journey without the encouragement and constant support of my dear family and friends, to whom I am immensely grateful: my parents, my sister, Anna and Juli, my grandparents, my parents-in-law, Nadia, Francy, Sara and Vincenzo. Last but not least – Daniel, Valentino and Amalia.

Salzburg, June 2023

England produces many excellent musicians, comedians, and tragedians, most skilful in the histrionic art; certain companies of whom quitting their own abodes for a time, are in the habit of visiting countries at particular seasons, exhibiting and representing their art principally at the court of princes. [...] their skill procured them so much favour, that they returned home greatly rewarded, and loaded with gold and silver. (Erhard Celius Eques auratus Anglo-Wirtembergicus. 4to. Tubingae 1605, p. 229. Quoted in Latin and translated by Albert Cohn, *Shakespeare in Germany in the Sixteenth and Seventeenth Centuries: An Account of English Actors in Germany and the Netherlands and of the Plays Performed by Them During the Same Period.* Wiesbaden: Dr Martin Sändig oHG., 1967 [1865], p. LXXVII).

We can be bankrupts (say the players) on this side and gentlemen of a company beyond the sea. (*A Rod for Run-awayes.* By THO. D., London, 1625, quoted in Cohn, op. cit., p. XCVI).

Contents

Introduction 1

1. Theoretical Framework 15
   1.1. Early Modern 'Popular' Culture and Theatre – A Definition 17
   1.2. Adaptation as Intercultural Process in the Renaissance 23
   1.3. Intercultural Theatricality: Inter-Theatricality, Recognition and
        Reader-Response Theory 29

2. Early Theatricality in-between Popular Orality and Erudite Literacy 33
   2.1. Ritual and Lay Theatre: Mummers' Plays, Mysteries, Morality Plays
        and Interludes 37
   2.2. Fools and Clowns from the Middle Ages to the Renaissance 44
   2.3. Tradition and Innovation in the Emerging Professional Theatre 50

3. Commedia dell'Arte in Italy and Northern Europe 55
   3.1. The Art: Origins and Maturation 60
   3.2. The Skills: Masks and Characters 64
   3.3. The Trade: Troupes, Actors and Repertoire 75

4. Elizabethan Theatre and the Italianate Influence 85
   4.1. Professional Companies: From Courtly Patronage to Public
        Entertainment 88
   4.2. The Making of a Play: Italian and English Parallels 93
   4.3. Shakespeare and Commedia dell'Arte – A Brief Survey 99

5. The English Comedians in Germany and Austria 107
   5.1. The Four Phases of Influence 113
   5.2. The First 'Ambassadors': Kemp, Browne & Co. 123
   5.3. Browne's Successors and the Continental Repertoire 133

6. Intercultural Theatricality in *Engelische Comedien und Tragedien* 155
    6.1. The Religious Plays: *Esther* and *Von dem verlornen Sohn* 162
    6.2. Fantastic and Pastoral Comedies: *Von Fortunato, Von eines Königes Sohne* 175
    6.3. Comedies with 'Types': *Von Sidonia und Theagene, Jemand und Niemandt* 190
    6.4. The 'Shakespearean' Tragedies: *Von Julio und Hyppolita, Von Tito Andronico* 204
    6.5. The Clown's Domain: *Pickelheringspiele* and *Singspiele* 223
    6.6. The Parameters at Work in the Collection 240

7. The German and Austrian Stages as Competition and Melting Pots 251
    7.1. *Der Jud von Venedig* – Synthesis beyond the 1620 Collection 252
    7.2. English and Italian Traces in Duke Heinrich Julius, Jacob Ayrer and Andreas Gryphius 263
    7.3. Arlecchino, Pickelhering and Hanswurst/Kasperl – Rivals or Brothers? 277

Conclusion – A New Perspective on Early Modern Popular Theatre 287

Bibliography 293

List of Illustrations 305

List of Abbreviations and Glossary 307

Introduction

To embark on the study of any topic in the early modern period is to humbly accept a constant unravelling in a vast and hazy field. Speculations, contradictions and a lack of sources are inevitable hurdles along the way but make the journey all the more interesting. In my work, I aspire to give an overview of the historical development of early modern popular theatre from 1570 to 1640, giving special attention to wandering troupes to demonstrate the importance of 'intercultural theatricality'. Aware that any transnational or transcultural approach bears the problematic view of nations and cultures as "static fields, between which objects, people and ideas move", as George Oppitz-Trotman warns,[1] I prefer to speak of *intercultural theatricality* along the lines of Julia Kristeva's intertextuality and consider European culture as a network of shared knowledge rather than as a combination of single nations.[2] Intercultural theatricality sees theatre as an adaptation and competitive emulation within an intangible, shared network of written and oral exchanges of which few vestiges have survived in present-day knowledge.

The broader 'European' perspective is given by the contextualisation of the first professional forms of performance for a large audience after the Middle Ages in Italy, England, Germany and Austria – a north-south cross-section of central Europe. Apart from personal affinities with these countries, as I have Italian and Austrian roots and have studied English and German literature, the choice is motivated by their geographic proximity and the lively cultural exchange among them.

The time span can be explained as follows: in mid-sixteenth-century Italy, Commedia dell'Arte companies became established and toured southern Europe

---

[1] George Oppitz-Trotman, *Stages of Loss: The English Comedians and Their Reception* (Oxford: OUP, 2020), p. 23.

[2] The term *theatricality* has been used in many different ways in different fields of research. In theatre studies, it denotes the conscious reference to artifice and mimesis on stage as opposed to realism and believability. As Thomas Postlewait and Tracy C. Davis put it, "theatricality has been used to describe the gap between reality and its representation." Tracy C. Davis and Thomas Postlewait, ed., *Theatricality* (Cambridge: CUP, 2003), p. 16. Similarly, for Ragnhild Tronstad it is the "metaphorical relationship between the theatre and the world." Ragnhild Tronstad, "Could the World become a Stage? Theatricality and Metaphorical Structures", *SubStance* 31.2:3 (2002), pp. 216–24, p. 216. In the field of semiotics, Roland Barthes said: "What is theatricality? It is theatre-minus-text, it is a density of signs and sensations which is constructed on stage starting from the written argument." Roland Barthes, *Critical Essays*, trans. Richard Howard (Evanston, IL: North Western UP, 1972), p. 26. My use of the term takes the text into account but goes beyond the dimension of drama and intertextuality mentioned in the previous definitions in order to focus on the intercultural relationship between early modern performance cultures.

from 1565 onwards, reaching their apogee in the second half of the seventeenth century.[3] Theatre in England was first professionalised in the 1580s and flourished until the closure of theatres at the beginning of the Puritan Interregnum in 1642. The fruitful combination of different national sources and practices was made possible thanks to their intrinsically itinerant nature and was later exported to, and highly influential for, other European countries, especially Germany. While London was witnessing Shakespeare's breakthrough, some of his fellow actors ventured abroad to seek fortune there. First the clown Will Kemp arrived in 1585, then Robert Browne and his troupe toured the European continent several times from 1592 onwards, until the Thirty Years' War put an end to their travels. As Gerhart Hoffmeister explains, "England's contribution to the foundation and development of German literature in the 1600s falls far behind the impact of French, Spanish and Italian contributions – with the exception of the theatrical activities and influence of the English actors who played on the Continent."[4] France and Spain had an important role in mediating classical culture between Italy and England but will only be touched on marginally, as they were virtually unvisited by English itinerant actors[5] and therefore go beyond the scope of this study. For a similar reason, the Netherlands are included only in part, since they were an important first stop for troupes from England but did not host Commedia dell'Arte companies, as Willem Schrickx asserts.[6] The major focus lies in the joint influences of English and Italian wandering theatre on the German stage. In the course of this work, I use the term 'German' to refer to German-speaking territories of the time. Unless otherwise stated, this includes Austria. I exclude Switzerland because it was rarely toured by English and Italian itinerant companies.

In England and Italy, professional theatre developed at almost the same time, with similar features in the field of popular culture. Italian companies reached England in the late sixteenth century, first as musicians and acrobats, then with the influential repertoire of the Commedia dell'Arte. Shortly after that, the English Comedians started touring the Continent. Moreover, culture travelled through texts: according to extant theatre plays, translations by Renaissance scholars of

---

[3] Walter Hinck documents the Commedia dell'Arte company of the Gelosi in Linz and Vienna in 1565, from where they moved to southern Germany, France and England. See Walter Hinck, *Das deutsche Lustspiel des 17. und 18. Jahrhunderts und die italienische Komödie: Commedia dell'Arte und théâtre italien* (Stuttgart: Metzler, 1965) p. 65. In the following chapters, I will not italicise *Commedia dell'Arte* but use the Italian way of writing it in capital letters, even though some English studies also accept the spelling in lower case letters.

[4] Gerhart Hoffmeister, "The English Comedians in Germany", in Gerhart Hoffmeister, ed., *German Baroque Literature* (New York: Frederick Ungar, 1983), pp. 142–58, p. 142.

[5] One exception is Robert Browne's tour to Lille and Fontainebleau in 1604. See chapter 5.2.

[6] See Willem Schrickx, *Foreign Envoys and Travelling Players in the Age of Shakespeare and Jonson* (Wetteren: Universa, 1986), p. 119.

Greco-Roman drama, erudite comedies or pastoral plays in a similar style must have been available to playwrights along with romances, collections of tales, popular chapbooks, and historic and religious texts. While research has been done on single theatre histories, the contribution of itinerant actors in transporting plots, genres and performance practices as well as reviving popular elements otherwise overlooked by 'high culture' has not been sufficiently explored. It should be noted that the distinction between 'high' and 'low' culture was very fragile in the Renaissance, a time when scholars suggest there was a "collapse of boundaries".[7] Looking at textual, artistic or cultural materials, the popular and the erudite have much in common as far as theatre is concerned.

The following intertextual reference from Jacques's monologue beginning with "All the world's a stage, / And all the men and women merely players" in *As You Like It* (1599) is an example of how a characteristic feature of a mask of the Commedia dell'Arte, Pantalone, was inserted into one of the most famous speeches in Shakespearean theatre. The vision of life as a sequential process is taken from the morality play and enriched with the metatheatrical *theatrum mundi* metaphor, which compares the progression of ages to acts of a play. The sixth age is described thus:

> And so he plays his part. The sixth age shifts
> Into the lean and slippered pantaloon,
> With spectacles on nose and pouch on side;
> His youthful hose, well saved, a world too wide
> For his shrunk shank, and his big manly voice,
> Turning again toward childish treble, pipes
> And whistles in his sound. Last scene of all,
> That ends this strange eventful history,
> Is second childishness and mere oblivion,
> *Sans* teeth, *sans* eyes, *sans* taste, *sans* everything.[8]

Senility wears a distinctive "lean and slippered pantaloon, / With spectacles on nose and pouch on side". The footnote to the Arden Shakespeare edition explains that a pantaloon is a pair of "baggy trousers worn by an old man over his emaciated calves, hence the name for the stock comic personage in the Italian *Commedia dell'Arte*."[9] No such footnote was available or even necessary to a popular

---

[7] See Chris Barker, *Cultural Studies: Theory and Praxis* (London et al.: Sage, 2003), pp. 63–9. The term *Renaissance* from *la rinascita* (rebirth) first appeared in Giorgio Vasari's *Vite de'più eccellenti architetti, pittori, et scultori Italiani* (1550/1568). The Renaissance "collapse of boundaries" entails an open fruition of culture (following the early modern mutual adaptation to different contexts) but also a new creation of borders and increasing distinctions in the Baroque period.

[8] *As You Like It*, 2.7.158–67.

[9] *The Arden Shakespeare As You Like It*, edited by Juliet Dusinberre (London and New York: Routledge, 2006), p. 229.

audience in Shakespeare's London. The use of a Commedia dell'Arte figure as epitome of senility reveals how well known the Italian tradition[10] was at the end of the sixteenth century in England. Or, perhaps, it merely demonstrates that the popular imagery connected to the representation of elderly people on stage was so common to different countries that a pantaloon immediately indicated old age in various cultures. Such tiny textual instances are apt for suggesting how deep-rooted shared knowledge was, and how easily it escapes notice if one is not aware of the interconnectedness of traditions but turns the attention to intertextuality alone.[11] Evidently, both culture and knowledge travelled, not only on the page but also on the stage, where they reached wide audiences and shaped new tastes.

Taking a closer look, the following questions arise: where did the common elements come from? How did touring theatre companies make use of shared knowledge to shape their audiences' expectation and how were they creatively received? Determining what we know of this intangible, shared heritage presents many difficulties due to our lack of oral records. Still, attempting to investigate these aspects might reawaken an interest in a communal European popular culture and in how aesthetics was (and still is) influenced by different national and cultural trends.

The phenomenon of intercultural theatricality, of which adaptation is a vital component, can be retraced particularly well on the pre-Baroque German stage,

---

[10] The term *tradition* follows Thomas Pettitt's definition: "A tradition is characterised essentially by its mode of performance, comprising dialogue, gesture, action, movement, interaction between performers and between performers and audience, all related to a particular physical environment, and evolved in a particular social and cultural context." "English Folk Drama and the Early German *Fastnachtspiele*", *Renaissance Drama*, New Series 13 (1982), pp. 1–34, p. 8.

[11] Numerous references to Commedia dell'Arte 'types' synthetised with more humanised and individualised Shakespearean characters can be found in *The Taming of the Shrew* (references to Pantaloon in 1.1.45 and 3.1.36, and to extemporising and mother-wit by Petruchio in 2.1.257–8), the tragicomic *The Merchant of Venice* (Gratiano is a Dottore-like character with the same name as the mask in Commedia dell'Arte), *Hamlet* (wise Polonius can be compared to a Dottore), *Twelfth Night* (when Malvolio describes those who laugh at the jokes of the fool Feste thus: "no better than fool's zanies" 1.5.84) and *A Midsummer Night's Dream*, where the "Bergamasque dance" is mentioned as well as the fact that "man is but a patched fool" 4.1.204. The footnote to the *New Cambridge Shakespeare* edited by R. A. Foakes informs us that Bottom here refers to fools who seem to have worn "parti-coloured coats rather than patched in the sense of patchwork. The visual effect was similar enough for 'Patch', the name of the famous fool of Cardinal Wolsey, to become a common term for a fool probably assimilating at the same time an Anglicisation of the Italian 'pazzo', 'a foole, a patch, a madman' as John Florio defines the word in his Italian-English dictionary, *Queen Anna's New World of Words* (1611)." *The New Cambridge Shakespeare: A Midsummer Night's Dream*, ed., R. A. Foakes (Cambridge: CUP, 1995), p. 113. Moreover, Puck and Ariel, from *A Midsummer Night's Dream* and *The Tempest* respectively, echo the Zanni's mischievous wit and acrobatics. For more literary references to the Zanni, see the *OED* (1989) under the heading 'zani'.

rarely appreciated enough for what it is: the melting pot of English and Italian, and later also French and Spanish, tendencies. Contrary to Oppitz-Trotman's assertion that the English Comedians could not "benefit from ongoing contact with an audience with whom they might share – even speculatively – common experiences and concerns",[12] I argue that playwrights and actors relied on a shared knowledge, which connected them to their audiences thanks to an intangible legacy of the past. Returning to these common roots sometimes entailed a step *backwards* in the development of theatre in favour of mutual understanding.

While studies of Shakespearean drama and travelling companies in Europe were intensively pursued in the late nineteenth and early twentieth centuries, interest in this topic has progressively faded. Recent research has set its focus on the histories (in the plural form) of world theatre and European theatre,[13] international adaptations of Shakespeare's plays,[14] and performance in Shakespeare's London – for example E. K. Chambers's comprehensive *The Elizabethan Stage* (1923) or Andrew Gurr's *The Shakespearian Playing Companies* (1996). Similarly, there has been an abiding interest in Commedia dell'Arte, in which Vito Pandolfi, Sirio Ferrone, Allardyce Nicoll, Robert Henke, and Wolfgang Thiele are just a few experts.[15] Combining the two research areas, Kathleen Marguerite Lea's comparative study *Italian Popular Comedy: A Study in the Commedia dell'arte 1520-1620, with Special Reference to the English Stage* (1934) investigated points of contact between Commedia dell'Arte and Shakespeare, which

---

[12] See *Stages of Loss*, p. 261.

[13] E.g. Phillip B. Zarrilli and Gary Jaz Williams, ed., *Theatre Histories: An Introduction* (London and New York: Routledge, 2006); and Manfred Brauneck, *Die Welt als Bühne: Geschichte des europäischen Theaters* (Stuttgart: Metzler, 2007).

[14] In 2022, the Arden Shakespeare showed new interest in the Continental adaptations of Shakespeare by publishing a new English translation of four plays of the English Comedians' repertoire, namely *Der Bestrafte Brudermord* ('Fratricide Punished' based on *Hamlet*), *Romio und Julieta* (*Romeo and Juliet*), *Tito Andronico* (contained in *Engelische Comedien und Tragedien* of 1620) and *Kunst über alle Künste, ein bös Weib gut zu machen* ('An Art beyond All Arts, to Make a Bad Wife Good' also called *Die Böse Katharina* (1672), i.e. 'The wicked Catherine', a rendition of *The Taming of the Shrew*). See *Early Modern German Shakespeare: Hamlet and Romeo and Juliet. 'Der Bestrafte Brudermord' and 'Romio und Julieta' in Translation*, edited by Lukas Erne and Kareen Seidler (London: Bloomsbury, 2022); and *Early Modern German Shakespeare: Titus Andronicus and The Taming of the Shrew. 'Tito Andronico' and 'Kunst über alle Künste, ein bös Weib gut zu machen' in Translation*, edited by Lukas Erne, Maria Shmygol, and Florence Hazrat (London: Bloomsbury, 2022).

[15] See Vito Pandolfi, *La Commedia dell'Arte: Storia e testo* (Florence: Ed. Sansoni Antiquariato, 1957); Sirio Ferrone, *La Commedia dell'Arte: Attrici e attori italiani in Europa (XVI-XVIII secolo)* (Torino: Einaudi, 2014); Allardyce Nicoll, *The World of Harlequin: A Critical Study of the Commedia dell'Arte* (Cambridge: CUP, 1963); Robert Henke, *Performance and Literature in the Commedia dell'Arte* (Cambridge: CUP, 2002); Wolfgang Thiele, ed., *Commedia dell'Arte: Geschichte – Theorie – Praxis* (Wiesbaden: Harrassowitz, 1997).

were strikingly ignored by Geoffrey Bullough's monumental analysis *Narrative and Dramatic Sources of Shakespeare* (1966). However, all previous studies tend to focus on one or at the most two countries, overlooking the potential of giving a 'European' perspective, not only as history of literature, but as literature at work. Alberto Martino tried to fill a gap in research concerning the presence of Italian comedians in central Europe with a collection of essays[16] which, again, leaves out itinerant players from other nations in that area. Other than historic investigations, a resurgence of Commedia practices in contemporary theatre was carried out by Artemis Preeshl, who introduced masks and sight gags of the "living theatre", as she calls it, in her staging of Shakespeare's plays from 2005 onwards.[17]

As to research into the English itinerant companies in German-speaking lands, it was long obfuscated first by the priority of building up a national literature in the Baroque, and then by a preoccupation with Shakespeare's works rather than with how they reached the European continent.[18] It was the Romantic author Ludwig Tieck who sparked the interest in the English Comedians but also initiated the ambivalent attitude of scholars towards their merits, as a quote from his *Deutsches Theater* (1817) shows:

> Als in London die *Theater* blühten und selbst im Auslande berühmt waren, gingen zuweilen Schauspieltruppen nach den Niederlanden, um dort zu spielen, und ohngefähr um das Jahr 1600 (vielleicht einige Jahre früher), treffen wir in Deutschland wandernde Schauspieler an, die unter dem Titel der Englischen Comödianten herum reisen, um unseren Landsleuten eine, wenn auch nur schwache, Vorstellung von der Höhe der englischen *Poesie* und von der Vortrefflichkeit der dortigen Schauspielkunst zu geben.[19]

A central question that shall be investigated is how 'weak' the impression of the English 'excellence of performative artistry' on the Continent really was and why it was perceived as such. Based on the material collected by Tieck, in 1865 Albert Cohn published his seminal *Shakespeare in Germany in the Sixteenth and Seventeenth Centuries: An Account of English Actors in Germany and the Netherlands*

---

[16] Alberto Martino and Fausto De Michele, ed., *La ricezione della Commedia dell'Arte nell'Europa centrale 1568–1769: Storia, Testi, Iconografia* (Pisa and Rome: Fabrizio Serra Editore, 2010).

[17] See Artemis Preeshl, *Shakespeare and Commedia dell'Arte: Play by Play* (London and New York: Routledge, 2017).

[18] For this reason, I prefer to avoid the old-fashioned denomination *strolling players*, as it implies a qualitative interpretation.

[19] Ludwig Tieck, ed., *Deutsches Theater* (Berlin, 1817), vol. 1, p. XXIII. Translation: 'At a time when theatres blossomed in London and were famous even abroad, troupes of actors went occasionally to the Netherlands to perform there, and around the year 1600 (or maybe a few years before) we meet itinerant players in Germany who travelled around under the name of English Comedians to give our countrymen an impression, albeit a weak one, of the heights of English poetry and the excellence of performative artistry there.'

and of the Plays Performed by Them During the Same Period, followed by several historical reconstructions by Julius Tittmann (1880), Elisabeth Mentzel (1882), Johannes Meissner (1884), Karl Trautmann (1884–7), Wilhelm Creizenach (1889), Emil Herz (1903), and Willi Flemming (1931).[20] Due to the scarcity of primary sources scattered among hardly accessible archives, some editorial inaccuracies and qualitative (mis)interpretations that marred these studies were perpetuated from Cohn and Mentzel up to E. K. Chambers, until recent research uncovered and amended them.[21] In 1985, Jerzy Limon's study *Gentlemen of a Company: English Players in Central and Eastern Europe, 1590–1660* made available new documents about the travels of the English Comedians in eastern Europe. His findings about the Baltic route, i.e. Poland, the Czech Republic and territories formerly German like Danzig,[22] are illuminating but give little attention to the performed plays, presumably the same repertoire presented in Germany; nor does he connect the presence of Commedia dell'Arte players, who even reached Russia, to the English Comedians as I do for Germany and Austria. The same applies to Willem Schrickx's deeply researched account *Foreign Envoys and Travelling Players in the Age of Shakespeare and Jonson* (1986), which dug up relevant historical records but does not analyse the plays staged by the English Comedians in the Spanish Netherlands and Germany, and completely ignores Commedia dell'Arte companies. Other than that, there have not been great discoveries of records since Ralf Haekel found two unknown letters by the English Comedian Robert Browne in 2004.[23]

I experienced the problematic question of sources myself, as my expectation of combing through old archives for possibly relevant materials was disappointed.

---

[20] See Albert Cohn, *Shakespeare in Germany in the Sixteenth and Seventeenth Centuries: An Account of English Actors in Germany and the Netherlands and of the Plays Performed by Them During the Same Period* (Wiesbaden: Dr Martin Sändig oHG., 1967 [1865]); Julius Tittmann, *Die Schauspiele der englischen Komödianten in Deutschland* (Leipzig: Brockhaus, 1880); Elisabeth Mentzel, *Geschichte der Schauspielkunst in Frankfurt a.M.* (Frankfurt a.M.: Völkers, 1882). Caveat: as the inaccuracy of Mentzel's reconstructions has repeatedly been proved, I shall not refer to her text in my study but adduce it here as important contribution to the research area. Johannes Meissner, *Die englischen Comoedianten zur Zeit Shakespeares in Österreich* (Vienna: Carl Konegen, 1884); Wilhelm Creizenach, *Die Schauspiele der englischen Komödianten* (Berlin, Stuttgart: W. Spemann, 1889); Emil Herz, *Englische Schauspieler und englisches Schauspiel zur Zeit Shakespeares in Deutschland* (Nendeln: Kraus Reproduktion, 1977 [1903]); and Willi Flemming, ed., *Barockdrama*, vol. 3, *Das Schauspiel der Wanderbühne* (Leipzig: Reclam, 1931).

[21] For a critical analysis of the major studies about the English Comedians see George Oppitz-Trotman's introduction to *Stages of Loss*.

[22] See Jerzy Limon, *Gentlemen of a Company: English Players in Central and Eastern Europe, 1590–1660* (Cambridge: CUP, 1985).

[23] See Ralf Haekel, "Neue Quellen zur Geschichte der Englischen Komödianten in Deutschland", *Shakespeare Jahrbuch* 140 (2004), pp. 180–5.

Whereas Tieck and Cohn could freely rummage through lists of plays, municipal records and manuscripts surrounding the English actors, nowadays these delicate sources are locked away from the public. The numerous archives I contacted (Berlin, Dresden, Frankfurt, Cologne, Vienna) all replied that they were slowly digitising their whole inventory in reverse chronological order and had not yet reached the time before 1700; at most, they could provide documents with precise shelf marks, i.e. already known data. Thus, for the historical part, my research was impeded, and I had to content myself with using formerly documented materials, mostly of administrative nature like licences, bills and lists of plays. Occasional discoveries of new material give reason to hope that possibly there is room for further research about the historical context once the digitisation is over.

Given the precarious situation of new historical evidence and the meticulous quality of earlier studies of scholars with privileged access to archived materials, I rely on their historical reconstruction and add an unprecedented reading of the English Comedians' repertoire that considers international traditions at work within the context of popular culture. For this purpose, I travelled to the most important cities visited by the English Comedians, starting with Wolfenbüttel, their first stop. From first-hand research at the State Archive of Lower Saxony, I found a sustained interest in the fate of the actor Thomas Sackville, who stayed in the surroundings conducting the trade of cloth merchant and never returned to England.[24] Apart from that, the legacy of the English players in Wolfenbüttel persists in literary documents accessible in the nearby Herzog August Library. Founded in 1572, it holds a vast number of ancient manuscripts and valuable editions, such as the original print of the first collection of German plays associated with the English Comedians: *Engelische Comedien und Tragedien* ('English Comedies and Tragedies') of 1620.

In 1975, Manfred Brauneck reprinted the collection in an annotated edition with a short commentary as *Spieltexte der Wanderbühne*. Still, for a long time the subject did not find great attention in research, especially not in the actors' home country, England. This might be due to the fact that the English Comedians' repertoire was only partly translated into English by Albert Cohn[25] and later by Ernest

---

[24] Around 1900, the archivist Paul Zimmermann collected all the extant traces of Sackville's life in Lower Saxony and published a few essays on the subject. At the State Archive of Lower Saxony, I was shown Zimmermann's notes and letters in running 'Kurrent' handwriting, documenting his research.

[25] In *Shakespeare in Germany in the Sixteenth and Seventeenth Centuries* (1865), Albert Cohn translated six German plays by the English Comedians and their imitator Jacob Ayrer into English, namely Ayrer's *Sidea* and *Phaenicia* (1618), *Von Julio und Hyppolita* and *Von Tito Andronico* (from the 1620 collection *Engelische Comedien und Tragedien*), a version of *Hamlet* (published in 1710) and an adaptation of *Romeo and Juliet* (published in 1848).

Brennecke[26] to show the garbled form in which the works of Shakespeare entered mainland Europe and became part of the foundation of theatre there, almost one hundred years before his name was actually known to the audience.[27] Nor have any of the other secondary sources I rely on been translated into English. As they are so old and rare that they obtain a historical value themselves, even German scholars struggle to get hold of them. For these reasons, whole fields of inquiry have either been forgotten or ignored in England until very recently.

In the last ten years, more and more experts have devoted themselves to the English Comedians in the fields of theatre history, history of literature and studies on transcultural exchange, and this reprisal of scholarly discussion speaks for the relevance of the topic. Peter Brand in collaboration with Bärbel Rudin drew new attention to the biography of the impresario Robert Browne (2010); Joel B. Lande studied the role of the (English) fool in the birth of German literary drama in *Persistence of Folly* (2018); and George Oppitz-Trotman's *Stages of Loss* (2020) tried to uncover the socio-economic reasons for the long underestimation of the English Comedians in German-speaking lands.[28] The greatest gap in research remains a combination of currents, a bringing together of the findings about how Italian itinerant theatre influenced English drama *and* of how Elizabethan plays with an Italianate influence were exported to Germany and Austria, where they met with Italian Commedia dell'Arte troupes and mingled with pre-existing forms of performance to create new hybrids. Even the two major studies tackling early modern plays in Germany in relation either to the English Comedians, namely Gustaf Fredén's *Friedrich Menius und das Repertoire der englischen Komödianten in Deutschland* (1939), or to Commedia dell'Arte, i.e. Walter Hinck's *Das deutsche Lustspiel des 17. und 18. Jahrhunderts und die italienische Komödie* (1965), follow the usual binary approach England–Germany, and

---

[26] Ernest Brennecke re-translated some of the plays already present in Cohn (*Titus Andronicus* and *Hamlet/Der bestrafte Brudermord*) and added a new translation of *Peter Squentz* by Andreas Gryphius, *Der Jud von Venedig* (an adaptation of Shakespeare's *Merchant of Venice*) and *Tugend- und Liebesstreit* (based on *Twelfth Night*). See Ernest Brennecke, *Shakespeare in Germany: 1590–1700. With Translations of Five Early Plays* (Chicago and London: University of Chicago Press, 1964).

[27] As Joel B. Lande argues, until the 1760s Shakespeare was a "nonentity in the German-speaking world". *Persistence of Folly: On the Origins of German Dramatic Literature* (Ithaca and London: Cornell UP, 2018), p. 25.

[28] See Peter Brand and Bärbel Rudin, "Der englische Komödiant Robert Browne (1563–ca. 1621): Zur Etablierung des Berufstheaters auf dem Kontinent", *Daphnis: Zeitschrift für Mittlere Deutsche Literatur und Kultur der Frühen Neuzeit (1400–1750)* 39 (2010), pp. 1–119; Joel B. Lande, *Persistence of Folly*; and George Oppitz-Trotman, *Stages of Loss: The English Comedians and Their Reception*.

Germany–Italy, instead of a threefold one.[29] Likewise, the promising study *Transnational Connections in Early Modern Theatre* edited by M. A. Katritzky and Pavel Drábek (2019) did not look into this comparison.[30] In the latest analysis of the repertoire associated with the English Comedians, *Die Englischen Komödianten in Deutschland* (2004), Ralf Haekel reads their texts against the background of the Renaissance doctrine of affections and comes to the conclusion that their function was primarily didactic and closer to the morality play than to Elizabethan drama.[31] This interpretation offers crucial insights but – again – does not take other forms of itinerant theatre into consideration on the grounds that the English Comedians' plays were not characterised by fixed social 'types' like those of the Commedia dell'Arte;[32] a thesis that shall be questioned in this work.

The present study of German plays performed by the English Comedians explores the mutual influence, called intercultural theatricality, at work in texts and performances with the help of parameters to identify to what extent different European traditions like Elizabethan theatre and Commedia dell'Arte interfered with and modified each other. This will be achieved by studying the plays exported, adapted and performed by the major English companies in Germany (headed by Browne, Green, Sackville, Webster, Spencer) and contained in the

---

[29] See Gustaf Fredén, *Friedrich Menius und das Repertoire der englischen Komödianten in Deutschland* (Stockholm: Palmers, 1939) and Walter Hinck, *Das deutsche Lustspiel des 17. und 18. Jahrhunderts und die italienische Komödie: Commedia dell'Arte und théâtre italien* (Stuttgart: Metzler, 1965). Fredén only acknowledges the Italian influence on one play of the 1620 collection *Engelische Comedien und Tragedien*, namely *Von Sidonia und Theagene*, but does not go into detail; and Hinck focuses more on the vague Italian and English influences on the German clown than on the English Comedians' repertoire and its impact on German playwrights.

[30] See M. A. Katritzky and Pavel Drábek, ed., *Transnational Connections in Early Modern Theatre* (Manchester: Manchester UP, 2019). Still, the study is valuable for points of contact among other European countries, e.g. Spain, the Netherlands and France.

[31] See Ralf Haekel, *Die Englischen Komödianten in Deutschland: Eine Einführung in die Ursprünge des deutschen Berufsschauspiels* (Heidelberg: Winter, 2004). In particular, he states: "Für die Englischen Komödianten ist kennzeichnend, das [sic!] ihr Theater kein Typentheater, wie das der italienischen Commedia dell'Arte, sondern ein Affekttheater war, das maßgeblich durch zwei zeitgenössische Diskurse geprägt ist: durch den Fortunadiskurs, nach dem das Schicksal der Figuren organisiert ist, und daran anschließend durch den Affektdiskurs, der die Handlungen der einzelnen Figuren bestimmt." Ibid., p. 12. Although he repeatedly speaks of Pickelhering's improvised *lazzi* and of numerous other points common to the English Comedians and Commedia dell'Arte, like the fact that their professional ensembles were active at court and in the towns with a repertoire based on "Kombinatorik" i.e. combination of scenes and plays, Haekel sticks to the thesis that the alleged absence of 'types' contravenes a comparison between the two forms of theatre.

[32] Throughout this study, I will use the literal translation 'types' for the *tipi fissi* of Commedia dell'Arte, meaning stock characters with specific physical, psychological, social and linguistic traits and recognisable costumes, masks and props.

first and most important collection of plays attributed to them: *Engelische Comedien und Tragedien* (1620/24). Apart from comedies and tragedies, the collection contains less considered but rewarding genres such as the *Pickelheringspiele* (Pickelhering plays or farces) and *Singspiele* (literally: song play/drama, i.e. musical comedies or jigs), which combined pantomime and music and had a far-reaching impact on German and Austrian comedy.[33] Although the second collection of plays before 1640, *Liebeskampff* (1630), would still belong to the time frame, its content will only marginally be touched on as it no longer represents the English influence but is the product of a variety of adapted sources from Italy and France. Instead, I have added another play not contained in the 1620 collection, *Der Jud von Venedig*, performed in 1626 and held at the Vienna State Library in a manuscript version of 1680–90, because it constitutes a fine example of synthesis between Italian, English and German sources. What appears undeniable is that travelling played a crucial role in the creation and reception of popular theatre.

In the first chapter, I establish a practicable theoretical framework to capture the essence of early modern popular theatre. Firstly, it must be clarified what the term 'shared network of exchanges' circumscribes. Since no single theory fully encompasses the topic, a combination of theories will be used to reconstruct the material conditions favourable for theatre prior to the outbreak of the Thirty Years' War. More precisely, intercultural adaptation theory (J. Sanders, L. Hutcheon, G. Genette), reader-response theory (W. Iser) and concepts of reception theory such as the "horizon of expectations" of the audience (H. R. Jauss) and *ghosting* (M. Carlson) are associated with discourses on popular culture in relation to folklore, and/versus high culture. Hereby a particular interest lies in how the carnivalesque (M. Bakhtin) modelled the professional figure of the clown.

---

[33] In my use of the term *farce*, I follow the definition given by the Encyclopaedia Britannica: "a comic dramatic piece that uses highly improbable situations, stereotyped characters, extravagant exaggeration, and violent horseplay. The term also refers to the class or form of drama made up of such compositions. [...] Antecedents of farce are found in ancient Greek and Roman theatre, both in the comedies of Aristophanes and Plautus and in the popular native Italian fabula Atellana, entertainments in which the actors played stock character types – such as glutton, graybeard, and clown – who were caught in exaggerated situations." <https://www.britannica.com/art/farce> (last accessed 9 March 2020). In this study, the genres of *Posse, Pickelheringspiel, Singspiel* and other terms like *Volksbuch* will be left in German to underline the specific character of these terms in the German context. English translations given in brackets and single inverted commas only partly consider the whole genetic development of the genres, their peculiar features and the connection to the native culture. Similarly, Italian terms will only be translated where there is a true equivalent in English, otherwise they will be left in the original. In general, all translations are mine, unless differently stated.

The second chapter offers a structured report of secondary sources about the origins of popular performances in order to give attention to early forms of intercultural theatricality. A study of its major representative, the fool professionalised as the clown, sheds light on the cultural background in which Commedia dell'Arte and Elizabethan drama later thrived and merged with pre-existing theatrical forms known in Germany and Austria before the advent of the English Comedians.

Chapters 3 to 5 investigate the political, cultural and social context in which itinerant theatre became professionalised between 1570 and 1640. The historical background will describe the almost parallel development of the first official companies in Italy (chapter 3) and England (chapter 4): Commedia dell'Arte arose from a mixture of medieval carnival traditions and popularised erudite drama, while Elizabethan drama merged Renaissance Humanism[34] with popular culture. Also, this part outlines how the emerging professional theatre was exported by itinerant players to German territories in different phases until the Thirty Years' War (chapter 5). There is historical proof of the impact of the English Comedians on German literature and theatre culture; and the influence of the Commedia dell'Arte on English literature appears visible from the analysis of exemplary dramas written and performed in Germany and Austria. But their common roots and similar development are still open to discussion and require textual proof.

Chapter 6 represents the core of this study with the analysis of the collection of plays associated with the English Comedians on the German stage, *Engelische Comedien und Tragedien* of 1620. A helpful methodological starting point to approach any play is to break it down into its components: plot; structure and arrangement of scenes; characters and motifs; and paraverbal elements (staging, sound, movement). For each aspect, I set up a different parameter – 'memorialisation', 'hybridisation', 'adaptation' and 'visualisation'[35] – to systematise the adaptation process at work in this collection and exemplify the dynamic

---

[34] The terms *Humanism* and *humanist* follow Nicholas Mann's definition: "The term *umanista* was used in fifteenth-century Italian academic slang to describe a teacher or student of classical literature and the arts associated with it, including that of rhetoric. The English equivalent 'humanist' makes its appearance in the late sixteenth century with a similar meaning. Only in the nineteenth century, however, and probably for the first time in Germany in 1809, is the attribute transformed into a substantive: *humanism*, standing for devotion to the literature of ancient Greece and Rome, and the humane values that may be derived from them." Nicholas Mann, "The Origins of Humanism", in Jill Kraye, ed., *The Cambridge Companion to Humanism* (Cambridge: CUP, 1996), p. 2.

[35] The parameters are indebted to Sabine Coelsch-Foisner's research project "ARGE Kulturelle Dynamiken" of the Österreichische Forschungsgemeinschaft, <http://kulturelle-dynamiken.sbg.ac.at/> and the studies she edited, *Memorialisation* (Heidelberg: Winter, 2015), *Theatralisierung* (edited with Timo Heimerdinger; Heidelberg: Winter, 2016), and *Visualisierung: Bildwissen – Wissensbilder* (edited with Christopher Herzog; Heidelberg: Winter, 2020).

development of German popular theatre as synthesis of Elizabethan drama, Commedia dell'Arte and local performance cultures like Shrovetide plays.[36]

Parameter 1, 'memorialisation', concerns the plots and investigates how authors of the early modern period received and selected material from international literatures to craft the dramatic text. These borrowings were rarely acknowledged and, if recognised, accepted as *ghosting*,[37] which means that in this context 'memorialisation' does not always entail a conscious tribute to a previous source.

Parameter 2, 'hybridisation of content, form and style', is closely linked to memorialisation due to the versatility and ubiquity of dramatic recycling in the Renaissance. Authors usually pillaged and reassembled subject matters from a variety of sources and genres – for example *novelle*, biblical and historical narrations. The way these segments, particularly from Commedia dell'Arte and Elizabethan drama, were adapted to the German and Austrian stages comes into focus here.

Parameter 3, 'adaptation of themes, motifs and characters' explores the recurring character types[38] and situations derived from various international sources that appear on the early modern popular stage, such as the hen-pecked husband, intrigue plots, mistaken identities, cuckold husbands, sly servants and many more.

Parameter 4, 'visualisation, sound and movement' refers to staging, acting styles and para-verbal communication. Especially when actors and spectators speak different languages, other acoustic and visual elements, such as stage design, props, playing apparel, etc. must assist mutual comprehension. Due to their sensory nature, they act as vessels of meaning and are understood and remembered more easily, which leads back to memorialisation and hybridisation.

Chapter 7 is devoted to the legacy of the itinerant players from England and Italy in German and Austrian theatre. Firstly, the analysis of a play beyond the 1620 collection, *Der Jud von Venedig*, provides insight into the amalgamation of a Shakespearean plot with Commedia dell'Arte patterns. Then, the works of three of the most important German imitators of the English Comedians show how

---

[36] The only attempt at methodically analysing most of the plays of this collection has been undertaken by Gustaf Fredén in *Friedrich Menius und das Repertoire der englischen Komödianten in Deutschland* (1939). Although he provides a profoundly researched comparative reconstruction of the sources used in the English Comedians' plays, his study is more preoccupied with stylistic and linguistic cues which might prove the identity of the possible editor, in his view Friedrich Menius, than with tracking the international currents which worked on the collection according to parameters as I do. Moreover, Fredén wrote in German, so his insights are not available to an English-speaking readership.

[37] A term coined by Marvin Carlson in *The Haunted Stage: The Theatre as Memory Machine* (Ann Arbor: University of Michigan Press, 2011).

[38] The interrelation between literary characters recycled partly (just their names and attributes) or completely is called "interfigurality" by W.G. Müller. See Wolfgang G. Müller, "Interfigurality: A Study on the Interdependence of Literary Figures", in Heinrich F. Plett, ed., *Intertextuality* (Berlin and New York: W. de Gruyter, 1991), pp. 101–21.

long-lasting their impact was in drama.[39] Thirdly, in terms of theatricality, the figure of the fool as representative of popular culture and popular theatre, e.g. in the Viennese *Volkstheater*, exemplifies the vital contribution of international components to shaping national forms of popular theatre.

An intercultural view of the European influences will foster our understanding of the interrelations between theatrical traditions that have always been considered as separate despite their common cultural context. Additionally, a new reading of *Engelische Comedien und Tragedien*, which celebrated the 400th anniversary of its publication in 2020, could boost interest in this valuable example of mutual exchange among Italian, English and German popular theatre.

---

[39] In this respect, Ruth Gstach's recent edition of the German play *Die Liebes Verzweiffelung* by the Austrian itinerant player, Baroque poet and, later, Capuchin monk Johann Martin, better known as Laurentius von Schnüffis (1633–1702), written between 1655 and 1662 and performed between 1660 and 1690, offers valuable insights into the legacy of the English and Italian influence on the German *Wanderbühne*. See Ruth Gstach, *Die Liebes Verzweiffelung des Laurentius von Schnüffis: Eine bisher unbekannte Tragikomödie der frühen Wanderbühne; Mit einem Verzeichnis der erhaltenen Spieltexte* (Berlin and Boston: W. de Gruyter, 2017). It will briefly be discussed in chapter 5.3. of this book.

1. Theoretical Framework

Wandering troupes represent a fascinating phenomenon within the Europe-wide boom of theatrical activity in the sixteenth and seventeenth centuries. As long as they remain on the margin of national literature, however, their achievement cannot be fully appreciated.[1] Many scholars such as Manfred Brauneck or Kathleen M. Lea acknowledge the cultural cross-fertilisation between Italy and England, England and Germany, and Italy and Germany, but none has combined the three countries toured by itinerant companies to actually prove this threefold influence on a textual level. The innovative aspects in the approach of intercultural theatricality are, firstly, to broaden the scope of early modern theatre to a more 'European' level and show in the plays how Italian, English and German elements of plots, characters, motifs, etc. met and merged on the popular stage. A second aspect is to illustrate that intercultural theatricality worked not only on the high level of Renaissance erudition but was also fostered by wandering troupes immersed in a system of shared knowledge which persisted from antiquity and the Middle Ages throughout the early modern period.

Shared strategies of theatre production and perception – such as the clown, elements of the morality play and the Everyman theme – permeate early modern theatre. In this period, popular entertainment and art theatre amalgamated to establish what would become 'canonised' theatre. In a relationship of constant exchange, popular productions appropriated the classical models of erudite drama and were at the same time taken up by professional theatre. A more widespread perspective including both the ancient and the medieval roots of early modern theatre is apt for showing that its genesis transcended nationalism and spread among different people and countries not only through travelling texts but also through travelling individuals – especially actors – in the role of mediators and 'translators' (in the literal sense of 'bringing something across').[2] This permeation presupposes a common basis of shared knowledge and traditions at the heart of the intercultural adaptation. I prefer to call such exchange a 'network of shared

---

[1] For centuries, the marginalisation of English Comedians in Germany was also due to an unfavourable prejudice against their allegedly inferior skill. According to George Oppitz-Trotman, the opinion of scholarship regarding the English Comedians has been biased by the general fear that itinerant theatre ideologically entailed a loss of control, identity and morals. See the introduction to *Stages of Loss*. For instance, Willi Flemming claims that the English Comedians were devoid of a cultural tradition and just buffoons on a basic level. See *Barockdrama*, vol. 3, *Das Schauspiel der Wanderbühne* (Leipzig: Reclam, 1931), p. 12.

[2] Translation is a phenomenon studied at length by Susan Bassnett, e.g. in *Translation Studies* (3rd ed. London and New York: Routledge, 2002).

knowledge' rather than just 'popular culture', by which I mean a form of lore progressively erased by the nationalisation and literarisation (meaning 'the transformation of something into literature') of an elite culture.

This chapter seeks a description of what popular culture and theatre mean in the early modern period and of the mechanisms of adaptation and recognition at work in the process of intercultural theatricality. This will be done in the form of a structured report of other critics' research findings, from which I draw my own definitions and conclusions. The next chapter shall present some examples of this (oral) popular culture recognisable in early theatricality. One instance is the figure of the fool, who presents universal and recurring characteristics from archaic cultures, antiquity and the Middle Ages, to the early modern and Baroque period (and to some extent up to the present day). It is therefore no coincidence that the first travelling players made use of clown figures, music and dance to overcome the cultural, linguistic and logistical challenges connected to performing in a country virtually devoid of a national theatrical tradition. Since the clown had already been a crowd-pleaser in medieval drama and on the Elizabethan stage, he was readily exported.

Intercultural theatricality, of which adaptation and recognition of popular elements are essential components, provides the critical framework within which I reconstruct the socio-historical context of the wandering troupes active in German-speaking countries. These concepts also form the basis for the parameters – memorialisation, hybridisation, adaptation and visualisation – which are elaborated to analyse the English Comedians' repertoire in the 1620 collection and to retrace the derivatives of the fruitful Anglo-Italian amalgamation on the German stage. As George Kernodle states: "We have argued about what the Shakespearean stage was like; but we have looked neither at the traditions of visual arts which shaped that theatre nor at the other theatres of the time which showed different solutions to the basic problems – different combinations of the basic patterns."[3] He argues that the link between medieval theatre and Elizabethan drama can be found in the continuity of artistic and pictorial conventions inserted into the scenography, but these "basic patterns" can be easily transferred to ambits such as intertextuality and intercultural theatricality. Basic patterns have made up modern theatre at least since the Renaissance and must be considered in terms of diachronic and synchronic influences anchored in a relationship of dialogue with popular culture as a network of exchanges.

A particularly interesting example is the case of Shakespeare, who can be classified neither as a Renaissance scholar nor as a plebeian entertainer. Contemporary research on Elizabethan plays and their adaptations cannot omit their immersion within a festive culture and folk customs nor overlook the processes of reinvention, adaptation and appropriation of recycled elements that coexist alongside the high-culture status. The amalgamation of different sources, from antiquity to

---

[3] George R. Kernodle, *From Art to Theatre: Form and Convention in the Early Modern* (Chicago: University of Chicago Press, 1944), p. 1.

folklore, proves the creative potential of new forms of popular theatre in the emerging European market, seemingly opposed to a 'high' culture for the elites. However, since the Renaissance 'high' culture drew on similar sources, this dichotomy shall be questioned.

1.1. Early Modern 'Popular' Culture and Theatre – A Definition

Before entering the complex field encompassing the popular in the early modern period, it is necessary to briefly narrow down what is meant by *early modern*. Both the early modern period and the Renaissance are loose indications for cultural, social and political advancement over centuries and cannot serve as a precise period or aesthetic designation without further specification. Especially in the transition from the late sixteenth to mid-seventeenth century, multiple currents like *Renaissance* and *Baroque* coexist and converge. For Gerald Gillespie:

> Renaissance has remained a quite general label covering the aggregate of humanist literary interests and subjects, and not just neoclassical currents, in Europe from the late fifteenth well into or even beyond the sixteenth century. It applies to both vernacular and Neo-Latin writings, and the various national languages were affected by Renaissance impulses originally spread from Italy.[4]

From this quote it appears evident that Renaissance culture, influenced by Humanism and Italy, reaches well into the sixteenth century, although the turn of the seventeenth century brought along a new stylistic and cultural orientation in central Europe, for which the term *Baroque* is widely accepted. Associations range from "theatrical", "irrational", "tense" and "dynamic" to "excessive", "outrageous", "disordered" and "unnatural" in Gillespie's words.[5]

The Renaissance and the Baroque have so many elements in common that a strict separation is almost impossible. This is also due to the fact that not all European countries moved in the same cultural direction at the same time. The Baroque originated in Italy in the early seventeenth century as a new opulent form of producing works of art (music, theatre, literature, architecture) which consciously broke the rules set up by the Renaissance, without ever completely disregarding them. This innovative style soon spread within Europe with different forms. In the German context, for example, the preoccupation with topics around death and *vanitas* was foregrounded by the atrocity of the Thirty Years' War. In England, the term *Baroque* started to be used only in the late seventeenth century and mainly applied to architecture.

A shared aspect of the Renaissance and Baroque period in all these countries, for Leonard Forster, is the bilingual Latin and vernacular culture, whereby Latin

---

[4] Gerald Gillespie, "Renaissance, Mannerism, Baroque", in Gerhart Hoffmeister, ed., *German Baroque Literature* (New York: Frederick Ungar, 1983), pp. 2–24, p. 5
[5] Ibid., p. 12.

was increasingly replaced by national languages as they became codified for literary use.[6] While Latin texts addressed a wider public of educated men throughout Europe, the often-illiterate populace in the single countries were left out of this circulation of 'high' knowledge; however, this does not imply they had no knowledge at all. The same genres found in Latin literature were recorded in the vernacular as well. And then there was the whole aspect of 'lower' popular heritage and folklore, often connected to the vanishing oral culture and illiteracy.

Turning now to the terminology of *popular culture*, Robert Shaughnessy attempts to delimit the vast and often blurred semantic field connected to the word *popular*:

> The 'popular' is itself hardly a singular or uncontested term or frame of reference: seen from some angles, it denotes community, shared values, democratic participation, accessibility, and fun; from others, the mass-produced commodity, the lowest common denominator, the reductive or simplified, or the shoddy, the coarse, and the meretricious.[7]

Due to the wide scope of the adjective *popular*, which alters depending on the context and theoretical background, a brief and clear definition is virtually impossible. It is a necessary choice to concentrate on those aspects that apply to the early modern period without sparking off a complex debate between folk and popular culture. An equally necessary step is to question the dichotomy between high and low implied in the more negative connotations.

In this context, Stuart Hall distinguishes between the "market definition" and "anthropological definition". The first sees *popular* as commercially successful but also associated with manipulation and debasement of a not clearly defined 'people's culture'; the second involves the denotation 'of the people', unfortunately mostly connoted as plebeian or vulgar as opposed to an elite culture.[8] The easiest structural principle of the *popular* seems to be its distinction from anything that is elitist or highbrow because it entertains the masses, produces financial gain and is therefore less respectable.

John Storey's discourse on the popular offers a helpful starting point for moving away from the qualitative judgements contained in the previous quotes. He distinguishes between popular culture 1) as culture liked by the people, 2) as made

---

[6] Leonard Forster, "Neo-Latin Tradition and Vernacular Poetry", in Hoffmeister, ed., *German Baroque Literature*, pp. 85–108, p. 88.

[7] Robert Shaughnessy, ed., Introduction to *The Cambridge Companion to Shakespeare and Popular Culture* (Cambridge: CUP, 2007), pp. 1–5, p. 2.

[8] See Stuart Hall, "Notes on Deconstructing the Popular", in John Storey, ed., *Cultural Theory and Popular Culture: A Reader* (Hemel Hempstead: Prentice Hall, 1998), pp. 442–53, p. 445. Similarly, for Raymond Williams *popular* has many meanings: 1) "well-liked by many people"; 2) it can be described in the contrast between high and popular culture; 3) used to describe a culture "made by the people for themselves"; 4) it can refer to the mass media imposed on people by commercial interests. See Raymond Williams, *Keywords: A Vocabulary of Culture and Society* (London: Fontana Press, 1983 [1976]), p. 237.

by the people (agents), 3) as manipulative mass culture (consumers), 4) as a residual category synonymous with inferior culture, 5) as social construction trespassing across the division into 'high' and 'low', 6) as postmodern culture in which popularity is a question of quantity not quality, or as 7) as popularity in the sense of political struggle and negotiation in British cultural studies.[9] Although all the points, aside from the last two, can be applied to early modern popular culture and theatre "as social construction trespassing the division into 'high' and 'low'", one reference is missing – notably that of a shared knowledge. It can be found, however, in François Laroque's definition of the *popular* in Elizabethan times:

> […] the epithet *popular*, which the Elizabethan elite and educated classes often associated with the somewhat vague idea of vulgarity and ignorance, on the contrary betokened a very specific and living culture […] that was rooted in a basic fund of primitive religion and that expressed an indefatigable curiosity in the material side of everyday life and an insatiable appetite for it. Such a culture is a complex, contradictory and virtually unclassifiable mixture, at once an art of living and a world vision, incorrigibly down-to-earth and materialistic, yet, at another level haunted by superstition. In the Elizabethan period it was thanks to the clown of the public theatres that this culture was represented and diffused even in the heart of major cities, so that fashion, mutual influences and a desire for popularity abetting, it came to provide the inspiration for some of the greatest scenes created by Shakespeare and his contemporaries.[10]

This passage contains both the "idea of vulgarity and ignorance" and the "living culture […] rooted in a basic fund", of which the clown is a central spokesman. It also refers to the "mutual influences" at work in a culture that was not just 'low' but as inspiring for Elizabethan drama as 'high' culture.

To bypass the multiple connotations of the term *popular culture*, I prefer the concept of a 'shared network of knowledge', which includes the heritage, reprisal, promulgation and combination of pre-existing materials of popular lore, rituals, beliefs, legends, songs, characters, etc. (summarily betokened as popular culture) visible on the early modern stage. This network also encompasses elements of 'high' Renaissance culture, religion and literature, rooted in popular culture and either popularised in oral culture or elaborated by scholars and writers in the realm of literacy. Delving more deeply into how this "contradictory and virtually unclassifiable mixture" of shared knowledge works, folklore theories about tradition, orality and enactment can offer helpful suggestions.

According to Roger D. Abrahams:

> *Folklore* is a collective term for those traditional items of knowledge that arise in recurring performances. […] For folklore to work effectively in a performance there must therefore be a consonance between the situation that has arisen, the item that is called

---

[9] See John Storey, "Discourses of the Popular", in Sabine Coelsch-Foisner and Dorothea Flothow, ed., *High Culture and/versus Popular Culture* (Heidelberg: Winter, 2009), pp. 1–16, p. 5.

[10] François Laroque, *Shakespeare's Festive World: Elizabethan Seasonal Entertainment and the Professional Stage*, trans. Janet Lloyd (Cambridge: CUP, 1993), pp. 49–50.

forth, and the enactment. The performer must recognize the situation when it arises, know the appropriate traditions, and be able to perform effectively. Just as in any personal interaction, the enactment must evince understanding of the decorum involved in the social system in which both performer and performance exist. Such concerns of appropriateness may be regarded as both constraining and liberating. The performer must pick an item that is not only on the appropriate theme and calls for the proper level of dictions and has a message which is pertinent, but it must have internal characteristics that make an appropriate comment on the situation, and this it must do judiciously and economically.[11]

Abrahams describes folklore as a genre or performative form in its own right, whereby the term *genre* comprises "certain patterns of expression [...], traditional forms and the conventional contents of artistic representation, as well as the patterns of expectations which both the artist and the audience carry into the aesthetic transaction."[12] The "traditional items of knowledge" (or "basic patterns" as Kernodle calls them) reflect this sense of communality present in my idea of a network of shared knowledge. It is their recurrence and consonance within different contexts and social systems that make elements of the folk or popular so malleable, long-lasting and transferrable throughout centuries and cultures. Moreover, the performative aspect of narratives as well as the 'role' taken up by a performer in a given situation ties in with theatre and drama based on pre-existing sources and traditions. From here it is only a step towards conceptualising popular culture as a network.

In general, a culture's mythology can also be understood as a body of traditional narratives perpetually reinterpreted in new contexts. For Roland Barthes, the process of appropriation intrinsic in mythical concepts is an expansive metalinguistic and communicative relocation in a new social and cultural geography.[13] Similarly, folklore tales are considered multidimensional communicative acts in which performance, text and context combine and are inseparable from each other. If one parameter is changed, processes of adaptation are necessary, for instance, to fit the text to the context or the performance. Therefore, adaptation is a key element for the survival and transformation of simple, oral folk or popular forms in an emerging literary and more complex performance culture like that of early modern Europe. For Julie Sanders, folklore and fairy tales serve as "cultural treasuries and repository of archetypes", which often present personal and civic rites of passage similar to myths but with a specific set of signifiers and symbolic systems, used and reinterpreted by many authors like Shakespeare.[14] This medley of classical

---

[11] Roger D. Abrahams, "The Complex Relations of Simple Forms", in Dan Ben-Amos, ed., *Folklore Genres* (Austin and London: University of Texas Press, 1976), pp. 193–214, p. 195.

[12] Ibid., p. 193.

[13] Roland Barthes, *Mythologies*, trans. Annette Lavers (London: Vintage, 1996 [1972]), p. 119. See also Herwig Gottwald, *Mythos: Mythisches in der modernen Literatur* (Heidelberg: Synchron, 2004).

[14] Julie Sanders, *Adaptation and Appropriation* (London and New York: Routledge, 2006), p. 82.

mythology and folklore magic can be found not only in myths, legends, fairy tales and ballads (like that about the legendary sixteenth-century hero Robin Hood), but also in Elizabethan drama and its adaptation on the German stage. An example of this is *Othello*, where the classical tragic hero Othello faces magic and a Vice-like demonic character, Iago.[15] Sanders adds that other elements are not as common in myth as in folk tales, such as dysfunctional structures and the transgression of established social, cultural, geographical and temporal boundaries.[16] It is precisely this transgression – often associated with the clown and the carnivalesque – that makes popular lore adaptable to new circumstances and apt for travelling.

Finally, Peter Burke's definition of popular culture as "a system of shared meaning, attitudes and values, and the symbolic forms (performance, artefacts) in which they are expressed or embodied",[17] succinctly expresses the concept of a shared network. In particular, the embodied nature of popular culture leads back to orality and physical performance and makes a separation between popular culture (be it a "basic fund", "traditional items of knowledge" or a network of shared knowledge) and theatre arduous.

The denomination *popular theatre* (encompassing both the dramatic/textual and the performative sphere) as we know it in English comes from the French *théâtre populaire*, first mentioned by Jean-Jacques Rousseau in 1758.[18] From a historical perspective, itinerant players have often been associated with the rearward terminology of *street theatre* or *popular theatre*, although both carry specific meaning connected to different literary movements and ages (for example political Street Theatre in the 1960s or popular theatre as *Volkstheater* in the Viennese tradition).[19] In recent years, street theatre has been reintroduced as a modern and

---

[15] Like Milton's Satan, Iago envies Othello's fortune and seeks revenge for his own ill-treatment. A 'devilish' trait is that he despises patient acceptance of injustice as a Christian virtue and counts himself among those who plot against their exploiters: "IAGO [...] Others there are / Who, trimmed in forms and visages of duty, / Keep yet their hearts attending on themselves / And, throwing but shows of service to their lords, / Do well thrive by them, and when they have lined their coats, / Do themselves homage: these fellows have some soul / And such a one do I profess myself." (*Othello* 1.1.48–54). For Robert Watson, Othello is an "inclusive Everyman" figure, both "animal and angel, Christian and pagan, black and white, soldier and lover, foreigner and patriot." Robert Watson "Tragedy", in A. R. Braunmuller and Michael Hattaway, ed., *The Cambridge Companion to English Renaissance Drama* (Cambridge: CUP, 1997), pp. 301–51, p. 338.
[16] Sanders, *Adaptation and Appropriation*, p. 83.
[17] Peter Burke, *Popular Culture in Early Modern Europe* (New York: Harper & Row, 1978), p. 9.
[18] See Joel Schechter, ed., *Popular Theatre: A Sourcebook* (London and New York: Routledge, 2003), p. 3.
[19] A contrastive comparison between people's theatre and popular theatre can show similarities and differences between the terms. In the German tradition, people's theatre under the name of *Volkstheater* has become an independent genre from the early 1830s, meaning any performance "for the people" (*Volk*). Thus, the emphasis is placed more on the recipients as on the content or the precise genre of the literary product. See Thomas Schmitz, *Das Volksstück* (Stuttgart: J.B. Metzler, 1990), pp. 4–5.

independent theatre practice, but in reality, it is arguably the oldest form of theatre in existence and deeply rooted in popular culture. Before theatre became professionalised as a trade or economic venture in the Renaissance, it was initially connected to popular festivities on the streets, be it carnival, Christmas or public celebrations, often without a specific stage area, author, script or even a paying audience. The increasing social distinction connected to the idea of 'people' is also present in later categorisations, which include the already discussed aspects of economic success and a large audience.

Although these definitions appeared centuries later and do not directly refer to Renaissance popular theatre, they can still be applied to the popular theatre performed by the travelling players as a financial enterprise. They too wanted to make a living from their acting and thus needed to suit the taste of as many spectators as possible, both in exclusive courts and in inclusive town squares. In popular culture, material and economic power was itself the driving force, whereas the influence of Renaissance scholars was designed for a small erudite group and not for the masses. For this reason, David Mayer stresses the importance of the large audience in determining popular theatre in the early modern period: it was mainly aimed at a wide range of spectators in an emerging market, a broad and varied group of people for which a binary distinction into 'high' and 'low' would be oversimplified. In his words, one could deem "popular" that "drama produced by and offered for the enjoyment or edification of the largest combination of groupings possible in that society",[20] to which I just want to add its immersion in a shared network of knowledge and exchange.

Jürgen Hein's distinction between *Volkstheater* as "institution" or as "intention" can give further insights. The institution is interested in the relationship between production and reception, while the intention refers to the attitude of the play towards the people.[21] Depending on what idea the playwright has of the 'people' who are the addressees of the play, the content and form will change. *Volkstheater* as institution targets most of the population and the development of the productions is intrinsically connected to the development of the audience. This can also be observed in the English Comedians' adaptation of plays and modes of performance. For them, popular theatre was not an institution per se, it was part of the larger institution of theatre they had experienced in England and were now exporting abroad as a novelty to suit their audiences' taste. Their plays contributed to a new intention on the part of the performers and playwrights and established a new institution of theatre, namely that of popular theatre and later the people's

---

[20] David Mayer, "Towards a Definition of Popular Theatre", in David Mayer and Kenneth Richards, ed., *Western Popular Theatre* (London: Methuen, 1977), p. 263.

[21] Jürgen Hein, "Das Volksstück. Entwicklung und Tendenzen", in Hein, *Theater und Gesellschaft: Das Volksstück im 19. und 20. Jahrhundert* (Düsseldorf: Bertelsmann-Universitätsverlag, 1973), p. 2–28. See also Hugo Aust, Peter Haida and Jürgen Hein, ed., *Volksstück: Vom Hanswurstspiel zum sozialen Drama der Gegenwart* (Munich: C.H. Beck, 1989).

theatre in Vienna, whose origins lead back to the English Comedians and Commedia dell'Arte.

In summary, the sharing, adapting and recycling inherent in the very nature of oral popular culture as a network can be recognised both in Renaissance culture and in the professionalisation of popular theatre as a commercial venture to entertain the masses with material pillaged from various sources. The leading principles of this process shall now be investigated in order to understand how cultural transposition worked for the wandering troupes and which consequences it had.

1.2. Adaptation as Intercultural Process in the Renaissance

Adaptation is a fundamental trait of the network of shared knowledge and a distinctive feature of intercultural theatricality, no matter if the 'sharers' were representatives of Humanism or popular performers. The theory of adaptation postulated primarily by Julie Sanders, Linda Hutcheon and Gérard Genette aids the reconstruction of the context in which the plays of my corpus were produced on the basis of pre-existing texts of various genres and then transposed onto the stage. It also shows that imitation and emulation were common practices at all levels of education, from Renaissance grammar schools to popular entertainment. A novelty in my approach is to combine adaptation theory with reception theory to illustrate why the exportation of English plays (influenced by other international sources) was so successful among the German-speaking audiences.

According to Julie Sanders, the term *adaptation* "signals a relationship with an informing source text or original" despite reinterpretations and generic changes, while *appropriation* entails a "more decisive journey away from the informing source into a wholly new cultural product and domain."[22] Therefore, appropriated texts are not always as clearly acknowledged as in the adaptive process. Both terms belong to the field of intertextuality associated with Julia Kristeva but also to the post-colonial notion of "hybridity" – in Homi Bhabha's words: how things and ideas are "repeated, relocated and translated in the name of tradition."[23] The whole of literature is a web of echoes, parallels, points of comparison, themes, tropes and patterns reiterated and taken up throughout the centuries in different cultures. Thus, previous works of literature are the material for new literary texts in a process of constant reframing and rebuilding with the same substance. This idea is present also in the concept of emulation, wherefore drawing inspiration from a source is never just copying it but creating a new eclectic product which bears some resemblance to the original and is at the same time an original in its own right. To enable innovation, one must accept differences and change.

---

[22] Sanders, *Adaptation and Appropriation*, p. 26.
[23] Homi K. Bhabha, "Cultural Diversity and Cultural Differences", in Bill Ashcroft, Gareth Griffiths, and Hellen Tiffin, ed., *The Post-Colonial Studies Reader* (London and New York: Routledge, 1995), pp. 155–7, p. 157.

Sanders sees adaptation as a) a transpositional practice, for example from one genre to another; b) an editorial practice such as trimming or pruning a text; and c) an amplificatory procedure involving adding, expanding and commenting. All three aspects usually aim at making a text that is removed in time or space relevant and accessible to new audiences. The process of an older text being brought "up to date and closer to its own audience (in temporal, geographic, or social terms)" is called *proximization* by Genette.[24] Compared to Sanders, Genette gives a more detailed description of his concept of *transtextuality* or the textual transcendence of a text i.e. "all that sets the text in a relationship, whether obvious or concealed, with other texts."[25] Since in his view any text is a hypertext grafting itself onto an earlier text that it imitates or transforms, called hypotext, adaptation is an omnipresent procedure in literature. After all, to adapt, from the Latin *adaptare*, simply means 'to make fit' to new audiences, times, places, ideologies and cultures.

Appropriation has two different forms as well: if the original is still recognisable in the appropriated version, Sanders speaks of "embedded texts" and "interplay". If the interplay between appropriation and source gives way to productive new meanings, application and resonance, she defines it as "sustained appropriation".[26] The latter can even raise the questions of intellectual property, plagiarism or homage if the indebtedness is not acknowledged but evident despite changes.

Both forms of inspiration and transformation depend on other sources for the provision of a shared body of storylines, characters and ideas upon which authors and actors can vary, on the premise that the audience[27] participates in the interplay of similarity and difference to appreciate the reshaped product. In other words, a 'communality of understanding' is necessary for adaptation to work effectively.

Similarly, Linda Hutcheon points out that "we use *adaptation* to refer to both a product and a process of creation and reception" and therefore suggests the need

---

[24] Gérard Genette, *Palimpsests: Literature in the Second Degree*, trans. Channa Newman and Claude Dobinsky (Lincoln: Nebraska UP, 1997 [1982]), p. 304.

[25] Ibid., p. 1. A similar opinion of intertextuality as coexistence of texts is held, inter alia, by Harold Bloom in *Anxiety of Influence: A Theory of Poetry* (2nd ed. Oxford: OUP, 1997). He suggests six different ways of relating to previous texts, i.e. *clinamen* ("poetic misreading or misprision proper"), *tessera* ("completion or antithesis"), *kenosis* ("discontinuity with the precursor"), *daemonization* ("a movement towards a personalised Counter-Sublime"), *askesis* ("self-purgation"), and *apophrades* ("the return of the dead"). See Bloom, op. cit., pp. 14–15. Imitation practices in the Elizabethan period are investigated in Sabine Coelsch-Foisner, ed., *Elizabethan Literature and Transformation* (Tübingen: Stauffenburg, 1999).

[26] See Sanders, *Adaptation and Appropriation*, pp. 18–32.

[27] I prefer the term *audience* for its etymological connection to *audire* – hearing, rather than Sanders's 'readership', which would be misleading for mainly illiterate recipients immersed in an oral culture. See Sanders, op. cit., p. 45. I will treat the argument of audience response phenomenologically rather than as a scientific analysis or historical classification, which would be a demanding task that other scholars have confronted.

for a "theoretical perspective that is at once formal and 'experimental'".[28] This clarification is vital for my study: in the development of a popular theatre tradition in Germany and Austria both the productive and receptive aspect of adaptation combine to create new hybrid forms. Sharing also means producing as soon as something is adapted, translated or transposed. For Hutcheon the difference between adaptation and appropriation depends on the degree of indebtedness and explicit reference to the original. In her definition, *adaptation* is:

> 1) an acknowledged transposition of a recognizable other work or works;
> 2) a creative and an interpretive act of appropriation/salvaging;
> 3) an extended intertextual engagement with the adapted work.
> Therefore, adaptation is a derivation that is not derivative – a work that is second without being secondary. It is its own palimpsestic thing.[29]

Derivation and *palimpsest* are relevant terms to explore the transposition and intercultural exchange at work between England, Germany and Italy in the early modern period, when oral and literary dissemination co-existed.

In Renaissance culture, adaptation, imitation and emulation play a major role. As the classical models represented the highest standard, grammar schools encouraged their students to follow them as closely as possible. Erasmus from Rotterdam and Roger Ascham were eminent promoters of the imitation training which consisted of reading and comparing authors to tease out similarities and variations, i.e. to retrace the imitation and amalgamation in their works, and then to imitate them in turn. It might therefore be said, as does Janet Clare, that Renaissance drama owes its origins to this rhetorical training of imitation, poetic translation and acknowledged borrowings.[30] Since copyright or originality of the product were considered less important than they are nowadays, authors and playwrights were not frowned upon for mingling the best parts of plots, characters, morals and style, as long as their imitation contained traces of emulation. This concept is beautifully illustrated in Seneca's metaphor of bees collecting nectar from the "choicest flowers" to convert it into something new and sweet: honey.[31] In the process of emulation, the essence of the flowers is still maintained, meaning that the source cannot be left out, but the product is a transformed version (or derivation) which makes the connection to the original hardly retraceable. In this sense, the 'original' invention refers to the choice of materials moulded to a new purpose (adaptation) and often embellished (emulation). A direct imitation or mere translation without inventiveness would not meet the requirements of emulation.

---

[28] Linda Hutcheon, *A Theory of Adaptation* (London and New York: Routledge, 2006), p. XIV.
[29] Ibid., p. 8.
[30] See Janet Clare in *Shakespeare's Stage Traffic: Imitation, Borrowing and Competition in Renaissance Theatre* (Cambridge: CUP, 2014), p. 4.
[31] See Seneca, Epistle 84.

An art in-between orality and textuality like early modern theatre represents a fascinating instance of how imitation and emulation interact. In the sixteenth century, theatre scripts were considered working documents, mostly anonymous collections of single parts/scenes or commodities owned by the companies. Therefore, actors also took the liberty to alter the texts, which often derived from a collaborative process or teamwork. Because of this practice, the printed text in most cases represented one of many possible pillaged or pirated versions, and stage performances were more important than the text. Especially in the case of Shakespeare and Elizabethan drama, appropriation and adaptation had a wide-reaching and productive echo. Immersed in a culture in which narrative patterns were circulated on stage with little regard to origins or authors, Shakespeare himself was an active adaptor, imitator and appropriator from a variety of sources: antiquity, folklore, history, contemporary productions. Geoffrey Bullough's meticulous source-spotting categorised Shakespeare's sources into direct sources (for instance Ovid or Italian *novelle* directly re-contextualised with minor alterations to the plot), analogue sources, translations, possible sources, probable sources and supplements or amplifiers to sources.[32] Due to the richness of sources and themes Shakespeare and his contemporaries drew from the network of shared knowledge common to the recipients, dramatic adaptations of their plays could easily travel and have an impact on European literatures and theatricality. Seen in this light, adaptation works as collaboration or negotiation across time, cultures and languages.

In the following section, I want to give a detailed account of Genette's terminology revolving around intertextual transposition as it gives further insights into adaptation. Some of the terms he uses will be included in my operational toolkit to analyse the 1620 collection of plays associated with the English Comedians. In *Palimpsests*, Genette takes up Kristeva's idea of intertextuality in his broader concept of *transtextuality* and defines it as one of five possible types of transtextual relationships, of which *hypertextuality* is the most useful for this study. Hypertextuality is literature "in the second degree", a text derived from a pre-existing text which it either transforms (directly) or imitates (indirectly) with ludic, satiric or serious intent.[33] In his view, transposition is the most important hypertextual practice, which can be subdivided again into many different forms. Translations are the transposition from one language to another, for instance.[34] Then, there are

---

[32] See Geoffrey Bullough, *Narrative and Dramatic Sources of Shakespeare* (London and New York: Routledge, 1966).

[33] It seems necessary to list the other transtextual relationships apart from *hypertextuality* according to Genette: 1) *Intertextuality* is the "copresence" between two texts or more (e.g. quotations, plagiarisms or allusions); 2) *Paratextuality* is the relationship that binds the text "within the totality of the literary work, to what can be called its *paratext*" as would be a foreword, illustrations, secondary signals, etc.; 3) *Metatextuality* is usually simply termed *commentary*, i.e. any critical examination of a text; and 4) *Architextuality* is a taxonomic category, a declaration of a genre. See Genette, *Palimpsests*, pp. 3–7.

[34] Ibid., p. 213.

quantitative transformations which alter the text more than a translation because they either reduce or augment its content.

Reduction comprises excision, concisions and condensation. *Excision* refers to the suppression or amputation of single words or larger parts of a text. Another form of excision is *expurgation*, a reduction with an edifying function, in other words a form of censure.[35] Censure was also well known to actors and playwrights both in England and abroad, where high-ranking support came at a price and plays were always controlled by municipal authorities or royal officers.

In contrast to the practice of cutting, trimming and pruning inherent to excision, *concision* happens when abridged versions of a text appear without the suppression of any significant part and are formulated in a new way. For this reason, concise versions are works in their own right, while excisions are not.

The third type of reduction, *condensation*, is different from concision and excision because it does not operate directly on the hypotext to reduce it but creates an autonomous synthesis from memory. The result of this mental operation can be a didactic summary, an abridgement, or a digest, i.e. a scaled down and condensed version of the model. The latter type is the most similar to the kind of adaptation at work in the collection of plays by the English Comedians for the German stage at the turn of the seventeenth century.

More precisely, a few German adaptations contain direct quotes from the English original; therefore, we can speak of literal translation or excision in the way Genette means it, because both work directly on a hypotext. More commonly, the itinerant players scaled down the model to an audience-friendly, extremely reduced and simplified rendition. They also made use of summaries, another form of condensation. This happened frequently before 1608, when the first plays started to be performed in German; prior to this development, the German-speaking clown would explain the plot in-between acts, as Albert Cohn asserts.[36] Since these adaptations are a mixture of free translations, excision (reduction of textual material for practical reasons or due to censure) and concise abridged versions of English plays played from memory and not on the basis of a written text, they clearly are a peculiar mixture of transpositional processes.

Reduction is not the only transpositional procedure described by Genette and adopted by the English Comedians. In fact, texts can also be augmented, either by *extension* (adding elements to content) or by *expansion* (a stylistic dilation such as doubling the length of each sentence). Since these two practices often go together, they can be termed *amplification*.[37]

If addition and suppression are combined, the result is *substitution*, which means that narrative structures, characters or linguistic extrapolations might be taken from one text and inserted into another. This phenomenon occurs in the

---

[35] Ibid., pp. 228–37.
[36] See Cohn, p. XVI.
[37] See Genette, p. 254.

Anglo-German plays too, especially when Pickelhering scenes were inserted into the play instead of the original subplot, which was mostly just suppressed.

A further manifestation of transposition is *transmodalization*, i.e. "any kind of alteration in the mode of presentation characterising the hypotext." If it involves a shift from one mode (in his sense the term comes close to *genre*) to another, Genette speaks of *intermodal transmodalization*, while a change of the internal functioning within the same mode, i.e. from drama to drama, is called *intramodal transmodalization*.[38] An example in the English Comedians' repertoire would be changing the outcome of a play from tragedy to comedy as happens in *Von Julio und Hyppolita* compared to *The Two Gentlemen of Verona*.

Dramatisation and narrativisation are antithetical instances of *intermodal transmodalization* and are very important for the parameters of memorialisation and hybridisation used in this study. Most playwrights drew their inspiration from a variety of sources from different ages, nationalities and genres. In the transition from epic to drama in particular, less importance was given to diegetic instances like the narrator or the chorus, and the distribution of dramatic speech was altered. While native forms of German lay drama were still characterised by narrative structures, the English Comedians introduced a lively mimetic performance (*mimesis*) instead of narration (*diegesis*), a well-received novelty.

A modification in diegesis, for Genette, can lead to both *naturalisation* (a change of nationality, probably close to Sander's concept of *appropriation*) and *proximization*, i.e. bringing the diegesis or mimesis up to date and closer to the audience in temporal, geographic and social terms.[39] The English Comedians' proximization was so effective that it led to a naturalisation of Elizabethan repertoire on the German stage. In fact, the recipients soon demanded a customised national tradition.

A further form of psychological or pragmatic transformation is the revaluation of a character thanks to a more significant or attractive role in the value system of the hypertext.[40] This is what happened with the clown in the English Comedians' transpositions of plays. As adaptations frequently chose the point of view of marginal or offstage figures to shed new light on a plot, the clown was revalued from comic character of sketches to protagonist of the English Comedians' repertoire. In the new value system of the German stage, he was highly appreciated for mediating between actors and audience and was given increasingly more importance over his original role in Elizabethan drama.

Although they were probably unaware of it, the English Comedians were making use of adaptational strategies known to them from the Renaissance context and transferring them to the stage. With this in mind, the following subchapter explores the way meaning is created in theatre, in which – compared to reading – the dimension of performance is added to the bare text.

---

[38] Ibid., p. 277 and p. 284.
[39] Ibid., p. 304.
[40] Ibid., p. 312.

1.3. Intercultural Theatricality: Inter-Theatricality, Recognition and Reader-Response Theory

In Renaissance culture, the basis of imitation, emulation, adaptation and appropriation appears to be intertextuality. This interaction of texts ranges from verbal echoes or rearranged material for different audiences to expanding the source and identifying it as "cultural otherness".[41] Intertextuality alone, however, does not give enough consideration to the intercultural effort made by the wandering troupes when they exported their repertoire. Therefore, in my concept of intercultural theatricality I associate the more theatre-specific notion of "inter-theatricality", presented in Janet Clare's study *Shakespeare's Stage Traffic*, with recognition and Wolfgang Iser's reader-response theory. The aim is to shed light on to the way aesthetic response is produced in the special case of performers from a different cultural background to their audience.

The term *inter-theatricality* was framed by Clare to better describe the early modern "stage traffic" operating amongst companies and playwrights, audiences and plays.[42] Like intertextuality, inter-theatricality entails adaptation as the revisioning of one or more texts for a new occasion in political and aesthetic terms. In this case, dramatic texts and context are interwoven as in any intertextual ambit, but the aspect of dramaturgy (i.e. adapting a story to actable form) and the performance event are added.[43] The intellectual pleasure at the core of any adaptation is the recognition of the changes made to the source. But what is recognition and how does it work? And how were adaptation theory and recognition beneficial to the early modern wandering troupes?

The dynamics of recognition and the interplay between expectation and surprise are addressed in Marvin Carlson's concept of *ghosting*. He argues that theatre as the retelling or re-enacting of stories uses the textual and visual memories of the spectator (for example knowing the plot, having already seen a different

---

[41] The term *intertextuality* was coined by Julia Kristeva and discussed by Roland Barthes and many others, in particular Stephen J. Lynch in *Shakespearean Intertextuality: Studies in Selected Sources and Plays, Contributions in Drama and Theatre Studies* (Westport, CT and London: Greenwood Press, 1998), who uses the phrase "cultural otherness" on p. 86.

[42] See Clare, p. 23. The expression *stage traffic* is borrowed from the title of her study, *Shakespeare's Stage Traffic*.

[43] Ibid. Clare cites a fascinating case of a contemporary of Shakespeare reflecting on recognition. On 2 February 1602, John Manningham, a student of Law at the Middle Temple, wrote in his diary that he attended Shakespeare's *Twelfth Night* and found it "much like the *Comedy of Errors*, or *Menaechmi* in Plautus, but must like and near to that Italian called *Inganni*." *Diary of John Manningham, of the Middle Temple and of Bradbourne, Kent, Barrister-at-Law, 1602–1603*, edited by John Bruce (London, 1868), p. 18. This exceptional recognition of hypotexts does not reflect the knowledge of most spectators but gives a good example of the awareness of intertextuality and inter-theatricality. See Clare, p. 144.

staging, remembering an actor in a different role etc.), whose recognition of "recycled" material is an essential part of the reception process.[44] Thus, memory and intertextuality/inter-theatricality not only combine in the mind of the spectator, but can also be used by the playwright to recycle narratives and characters or to play with the audience's associations. In its double nature of process and product, adaptation is closer to emulation than to imitation, because it adds to the original.

This double nature is mentioned in Hans Robert Jauss's reception theory too, when he explains that recognition in adaptation can be a productive aesthetic experience (*poiesis*) on the part of the author, and a receptive aesthetic experience (*aisthesis*) for the recipient. The necessary pre-condition for recognition to work is a similar "horizon of expectations" (*Erwartungshorizont*) or "intersubjective system of reference". He argues that this dialectical relationship between the readers or spectators and a new product can be constructed by various – mainly linguistic and literary – approaches:

> First, through familiar norms or the immanent poetics of the genre; second, through the implicit relationships to familiar works of the literary-historical surroundings; and, third, through the opposition between fiction and reality, between the poetic and the practical function of language.[45]

Although in the early modern period the transposition relating to intertextual adaptation was rarely acknowledged and appropriation was common, a learned audience would easily recognise it. All they needed was a degree of imitation close enough to the original to allow parallels and references – such as genre poetics, familiar works and the function of language listed by Jauss. Even commoners in Shakespeare's times would recognise plots and characters seen in other plays or references to a shared "intersubjective system of reference".

Things become more complicated when these backgrounds vary. In the case of the itinerant players relocating English plays to Germany, sometimes the process of understanding was less immediate and gratifying due to a different cultural context. For international audiences immersed in the knowledge system of the Renaissance, the approaches mentioned by Jauss would certainly have worked effectively. Similarly, the illiterate audiences of the travelling actors had their own popular, religious and folkloristic knowledge that could help them understand the action on stage. The English Comedians facilitated mutual understanding by considering the spectators' cultural context and shared pre-knowledge, which partly coincided with that of the London audience thanks to their immersion in a common popular culture. As shall be argued, the unprecedented success of the English repertoire in Germany lies in the creative amalgamation of many different (literary

---

[44] Marvin Carlson, *The Haunted Stage: The Theatre as Memory Machine* (Ann Arbor: University of Michigan Press, 2011), pp. 3–5.

[45] Hans Robert Jauss, "What is and for what purpose does one study literary history?", lecture at Constance held in April 1967, p. 24, quoted in Robert C. Holub, *Reception Theory: A Critical Introduction* (London and New York: Methuen, 1984), p. 60.

and oral) sources to create a hybrid most suited to the audiences' taste and expectations. The initial difficulty for the actors was to detect the points of contact between the cultures to make their plays accessible. In other words, they had to find a form or code that would at once meet and shape the audience's world.

Regarding codes, the transfer of Wolfgang Iser's phenomenological reader-response theory to theatre helps us to better understand the process of adaptation. Iser states that the message of literary works is transmitted in two ways: the reader receives it by composing it with a code that often arises during the process itself. Contrary to the face-to-face communication for example in a dramatic performance, the text cannot adapt to the reader because of an asymmetry in interaction and a lack of a common situation (called "no-thing" by Iser). The readers are therefore expected to overcome a degree of indeterminacy, since no text is ever fully identical to the world or experiences of the recipient, and to actively fill the narrative blanks or gaps.[46] A combined guidance of the dramatic set up, orchestrated by the author (the so called "guided projection of the reader's imagination"), and the suggested ambiguity which leaves space for personal interpretations ("schematised views") make an aesthetic response possible.[47] In offering these keys of interpretation, the writer or actor must be aware of the audience's expectation and the context of reception to evoke an aesthetic response in the form of an active participation in inferring and closing the gaps.[48] This leads back to the general conditions to be considered in order to reach an audience – even more so for adaptations.

Indeed, "an adaptation, like the work it adapts is always framed in a context – a time and a place, a society and a culture; it does not exist in a vacuum", as Linda Hutcheon declares.[49] Thus, adaptators must deal with the reality of reception to find resonance. This process of bringing a content closer to the audience is still a common feature of most theatrical representations today (apart from epic theatre and other post-modern genres that tend to disrupt identification), otherwise the

---

[46] The relationship between the text and the readers' experience can be as follows: if the text contradicts their expectations, the recipients classify it as "fantastic", whereas if it merely echoes reality, it is considered "trivial". As a result, indeterminacy can lead to reflection or criticisms, depending on which aspects of reality the readers perceive in the text. See Wolfgang Iser, "Indeterminacy and the reader's response in prose fiction", in J. Hillis Miller, ed., *Aspects of Narrative* (New York: Columbia UP, 1971), pp. 1–45. The vague use of *determinacy* and *indeterminacy* was later criticised by Stanley Fish's reader response criticism but the categories of "fantastic" and "trivial" are still useful.

[47] "Schemata" are primary and conventional codes of the text that instruct the readers about the secondary codes leading to interpretation. The effort on the part of the recipient is to select these important elements scattered throughout the text in a foreground-background relation, focus on one theme at a time and simultaneously connect it to the total combination of themes, termed "horizon". See Wolfgang Iser, *Der Akt des Lesens: Theorie ästhetischer Wirkung* (München: W. Fink, 1976), pp. 155–64.

[48] See Wolfgang Iser, *Prospecting: From Reader Response to Literary Anthropology* (Baltimore and London: The Johns Hopkins UP, 1993), pp. 5–33.

[49] Hutcheon, op. cit., p. 142.

pleasure of understanding, recognising and empathising inherent to any aesthetic experience can hardly be achieved. On the one hand, this may involve changing the time and place in the process of adaptation, for example in an attempt at updating a plot; on the other hand, the adaptation can be transcultural, implying a change of language and alterations in the cultural associations. Both forms were necessary for the English Comedians; especially the transcultural adaptation, which was made more complex by the encounter with many traditions and cultures, for example the Commedia dell'Arte in Germany and Austria. Just as the authors selected the best source texts and combined them in an effort of emulation, the actors picked the most suitable plots, characters and styles to create a hybrid that would resonate with their audiences. In doing so, they went beyond intertheatricality because they had to resort to intercultural strategies for evoking a response in their audience.

To conclude, intercultural theatricality is the most useful approach to the dynamics of adaptation and recognition because it is multidirectional and context-related. Within this framework, the parameters of memorialisation, hybridisation, adaptation and visualisation account for the historical and theatrical dimension implied in adaptation as well as the audiences' expectation and response. Adaptation theory and its relationship to recognition and response shall now be applied to examples of early theatricality within the popular context.

2. Early Theatricality in-between Popular Orality and Erudite Literacy

The network of shared knowledge was at work well before the early modern period. In ancient Rome, rural fertility rituals with comic figures like Pappus, as well as physical and explicitly sexual elements were absorbed in the *Saturnalia* (ritual festivities to honour the god Saturn) and later in the comedies of Titus Maccius Plautus (254–184 BC). Even if the popular beliefs and customs were ridiculed or enjoyed little consideration, they were adapted from the oral to the written sphere and thus survived. During the Middle Ages, these same elements reappeared in a Christian guise in mummers' plays and mysteries, or in folk drama like hero combat plays, sword dance ceremonies, Morris dances and wooing plays.[1] In Renaissance England, the relationship between the popular medieval heritage and a national renewal of the classical world was even more multi-layered: not as tightly connected to academia and literature but deep-rooted in theatre. This versatile continuation of popular themes contributed to a revival of drama at a highbrow literary level and beyond. In fact, it was the familiarity with humorous characters and physical references known from quotidian life that made complex plots from classical literature accessible to a large audience, and it was on these features that the first early modern theatre companies based the staging of ancient, biblical and contemporary sources.

The subsections of this chapter retrace some instances of popular performances, such as mummers' plays, mysteries and moralities, and performers, like the clown, that worked as a foundation for professional touring companies in the late sixteenth and early seventeenth century. As an introduction, the model of theatrical development by Anna Baesecke describes the transition from non-verbal mimicry to spoken/written drama. Next, the difference between theatre and drama will highlight the oral and popular roots of performance before the literary tide of the Renaissance took over. As will be shown, the creation of early modern theatricality was always in-between orality and literacy and entails an interplay of popular and erudite culture. In particular, the popular and the literary influenced each other, merged and adapted to the tastes of the audience.

---

[1] See Thomas Pettitt, "English Folk Drama and the Early German *Fastnachtspiele*", *Renaissance Drama, New Series* 13 (1982), pp. 1–34, p. 4, for a more detailed description of English folk drama. The disguised performers of folk plays usually enacted a death and resurrection sequence, reminiscent of seasonal rituals intended to "ensure the return of spring and fertility after the winter's dying back." Dennis Kennedy, ed., *The Oxford Encyclopaedia of Theatre and Performance* (Oxford: OUP, 2003), p. 476. For Kennedy, the functions of this non-naturalistic entertainment in the Middle Ages and in the early modern period were to build or maintain a feeling of community, to preserve or undermine social hierarchy, or to channel disruptions into socially acceptable bounds. Eventually, these forms of entertainment were outlawed by episcopal decree or surpassed by professional theatre (see ibid.).

Baesecke's evolutionary theory of the development of any drama from its origins to the present understanding of the term provides a good starting point to retrace the gradual development of plot, performance and acting space.[2] The first stage is called 'non-verbal pantomime[3] or dumb show' (my translation of *Mienenspiel*), a simple imitation of those elements of reality able to elicit fear, pleasure and awe by means of gesture without a real situation or story. The second phase is the 'pantomime of a dramatic situation' (*pantomimische dramatische Situation*) with a group of performers involved in the transformation of reality through gesture and movement in a delimited space. Usually, fundamental human experiences such as conflicts and fights are represented. The third stage is the 'pantomime of a dramatic process' (*pantomimischer dramatischer Vorgang*), which entails the combination of various situations to create an experience or plot, but still limited to non-verbal language. As soon as verbal language is used in the fourth phase, called 'dramatic process' (*dramatischer Vorgang*), the spoken word is foregrounded in comparison to gesture, facial expressions and proxemics. Fifthly, there is the 'dramatic performance' (*dramatische Vorführung*), in which the audience is aware of the theatrical illusion, meaning a second reality on stage, similar, but not equal, to everyday life. Space is divided into separate areas for performers and spectators, as if to underline the division between reality and illusion. The last stage of dramaturgical complexity, namely 'drama as we understand it nowadays' (*das Drama im heutigen Sinne*), is a heightened imitation of reality so close to reality that the illusion can be broken or interrupted without losing the participation of the audience. In summary, the major and most important transition from early forms of mimicry to drama, in Baesecke's view, is the use of language.[4] She then argues that the lack of linguistic knowledge on the part of the English Comedians is to blame for the low quality of their plays, which never reached the highest stage of development in Germany. Instead of following this questionable thesis, the model can serve different purposes.

Firstly, although this abstract and theoretical approach to the step-by-step progression of drama does not refer to any tradition in particular and does not account for sudden upsurges in quality and quantity, like those witnessed in sixteenth-century England, it can still be a valid tool for understanding the cultural context. In fact, even significant increases in talented actors, playhouses and playwrights and a change of taste in the audience, however rare and difficult to comprehend,

---

[2] See Anna Baesecke, *Das Schauspiel der englischen Komödianten in Deutschland* (Halle: Dissertation, 1935), p. 10. The translations of her German concepts are mine.

[3] *Pantomime* in this context does not refer to the type of musical theatre developed in nineteenth-century England for family entertainment during Christmas and New Year. Later, pantomime became synonymous with slapstick comedy, a participatory form of theatre based on folklore tales enriched with gags and ridiculous violence, as Jeffrey H. Richards explains in *The Golden Age of Pantomime: Slapstick, Spectacle and Subversion in Victorian England* (London: Tauris, 2015), p. 35. Instead, the archaic pantomime is closer to modern pantomime including dancing and singing.

[4] See Baesecke, *Das Schauspiel der englischen Komödianten in Deutschland*, p. 15.

require certain pre-conditions. A flourishing intellectual activity and thriving entertainment need a long period of peace, favourable socio-economic conditions and the interest of rulers in fostering cultural output. These circumstances can explain even fortunate constellations like boosts of productivity in literature, but perhaps not always in gradual steps as clearly defined as in Baesecke's model.

Secondly and more importantly, if we accept the idea of intermediary phases that lead to the establishment of fully developed and literary dramatic art, it is also plausible that these phases can be repeated or reversed if necessary or desirable. That is precisely what the English Comedians did. Since their first audiences could not understand all that was said on stage, they had to return to earlier, preverbal phases of the development of drama to meet the linguistic and aesthetic understanding of their German spectators. In particular, the analysis of plays will show that they resorted to a combination of popular and learned (i.e. classical) elements that were used effectively in England but were not yet as unified and amalgamated in Germany. It seems that once they found the right 'formula' to adapt to their audience in the 1590s, the upsurge of theatrical production was very fast and only stopped by the outbreak of the Thirty Years' War in 1618.

So where was this formula anchored? The smart move of the English Comedians was to return to a combination, not a separation of 'high' and 'low'. If the transition from pre-verbal mimicry to drama was shaped by an increasing use of language, as Baesecke suggests in her evolutionary theory,[5] it can be argued that the replacement of literature over orality as cultural medium contributed to a marginalisation of the popular in a similar way as happened with mimicry. Still, theatre cannot do without physical expression completely, nor can the popular be completely erased by literarisation. In Renaissance culture, the invention of print went hand in hand with a redefinition of culture as philologically learned and *written*. This influenced education and parts of society towards a new ideology of conscious separation between 'high' intellectual culture in Latin, and 'plebeian' popular culture in the vernacular. Nonetheless, this distinction was not clear-cut and allowed many intermediate and hybrid forms between the poles.[6] Amalgamation is an essential concept for understanding the development of (Renaissance) theatre and the various influences acting upon it.

On the one hand, in the early modern period there was the revival of the Greco-Roman cultures. The humanists' interest in reconstructing ancient Greek and Roman theatre was not limited to philology and the study of the texts. It also paid attention to the architectural and cultural space designated for drama and interpreted the rediscovered plots written for an audience some centuries ago, which

---

[5] Ibid., p. 10.
[6] Hybrid forms in-between 'high' and 'low' are, for example, the common humanist trope of the Ship of Fools, which satirically presented follies/vices in a sort of carnival masquerade but also reflected on the idea that true wisdom lies precisely in the awareness of one's foolishness. See for instance Erasmus of Rotterdam's *Moriae Encomium*, translated as *Praise of Folly* (1509), or Sebastian Brant's *Ship of Fools* (1494).

frequently lacked contextual information or practical instructions on how to understand or put them on stage. In other words, Humanism supplied the theoretical basis for drama but the practical aspect of theatre as performance had to be sought elsewhere, and contemporary forms of playing suggested themselves.

On the other hand, the medieval vernacular morality plays and mysteries, which arose from a still tangible substratum of pagan rituals, continued to be performed even in Shakespeare's day.[7] This means that for a long period, at least until the guild system was abandoned, mysteries and moralities existed in parallel with Renaissance theatre. The difference was that ever since archaic festive celebrations, oral transmission was the rule for semi-professional popular performers, to which Peter Burke counts "ballad-singers, bear-wards, buffoons, charlatans, clowns, comedians, fencers, fools, hocus-pocus men, jugglers, merry-andrews, minstrels, mountebanks, players, puppet-masters, quacks, rope-dancers, showmen, tooth-drawers, and tumblers."[8] For this reason, written records are rare and only saved a small part of this oral culture from oblivion.

Although the transition from orality to literacy connected to the professionalisation of theatre in Renaissance Europe tends to disguise, forget or disavow the popular origins of drama, the popular could never be completely supplanted. Especially in aliterate cultures (i.e. cultures without a writing system) and predominantly illiterate ones, theatre thrives on orality and "scripts", i.e. patterns of doing, not modes of thinking, according to Richard Schechner.[9] He explains that since the Renaissance and the concomitant extensions of literacy, "the ancient relationship between script and doing was inverted. In the great tradition of the west the active sense of script was forgotten, almost entirely displaced by drama" in the sense of written text.[10] However, the dramatic text can only be understood in performance and the dramatic speech itself is full of action. Therefore, a limitation of drama to the text does not recognise a whole tradition of the popular, nor does it consider the function of oral genres as a bridge to written literature. In fact, many elements of popular culture like folk songs and folktales, mystery plays, chapbooks, and seasonal festivals such as Midsummer also survived thanks to

---

[7] For instance, Andrew Gurr states that in 1571 the mayor of the city of Chester vehemently clung to the traditional Corpus Christi processions – an important heritage from the Middle Ages – rather than allowing itinerant troupes of "dangerous vagabonds" to perform in the city. See *The Shakespearian Playing Companies* (Oxford: Clarendon Press, 1996), p. 37.

[8] Burke, *Popular Culture in Early Modern Europe*, pp. 15–16.

[9] Richard Schechner, *Performance Theory* (London and New York: Routledge, 2003 [1988]), p. 64.

[10] For Schechner, *drama* is "a written text. Score, scenario, instruction, plan, or map", *script* is "all that can be transmitted from time to time and place to place; the basic code of the events", *theatre* is "the event enacted by a specific group of performers [...] the manifestation or representation of the drama and/or script", and *performance* is "the whole constellation of events [...] that take place in/among both performers and audience from the time the first spectator enters the field of the performance [...] to the time the last spectator leaves." Ibid., p. 71.

written texts. And from this repository of archaic cultures that changed and reappeared over the centuries, writers would draw inspiration for their works, keeping the popular alive in new forms.

In this context, Baesecke argues that a distinction between drama and theatre is misleading, since the very origin of dramatic situations can be found whenever mimic elements of play, dance and ritual are shared by a number of people.[11] The dramatic process, she states, is the representation of conflicting forces in various theatrical situations with a special, codified language. In the case of a small audience with the same sociological background, simple gestures, allusions or direct hints are enough for them to participate in the creation of an illusion of reality. With larger audiences, the participation might not be as straightforward, therefore an explicit transformation, for example with masks, costumes, etc., is necessary to overcome the distance between spectators and players.[12] In other words, the bigger the common network of shared knowledge, the easier the comprehension.

The more one looks at it, the more fragile the distinction between high/literate and low/oral appears. Their co-existence might be indebted to common roots, from which they developed in different directions, maintaining and reviving elements of oral and popular culture in a new context. Professional theatre was reborn in the early modern period, after it had virtually ceased to exist concurrently with the fall of the Roman empire. But this does not mean that theatre had died altogether during these centuries. The following chapter will demonstrate how rituals, "scripts" and dramatic performances survived and cross-pollinated theatre as 'playing' and drama as 'play' within a network of shared knowledge.

2.1. Ritual and Lay Theatre: Mummers' Plays, Mysteries, Morality Plays and Interludes

With the model of Baesecke in mind, this section investigates the popular precursors of early modern professional theatre. The indebtedness of the Renaissance to the Greco-Roman world was certainly at the core of the rebirth of drama. However, it was only *one* component, a revival of a long forgotten and almost lost heritage. The other vital constituent was ritual and lay religious theatre immersed in popular culture, which was equally influential for the professional stage. First, I want to show how the aspect of performance was present in the ritual and religious sphere well before the conscious perception of theatre as illusion within precise social, aesthetic and architectonic conditions. Next, the use of space and ritual elements will be discussed to explore the continuity between archaic/medieval forms of participatory performances and the wandering troupes acting on streets and marketplaces. Finally, early instances of intercultural theatricality like mummers' plays, mysteries and moralities in England will help to trace back common roots among the different national currents (for example Elizabethan drama,

---

[11] See Baesecke, *Das Schauspiel der englischen Komödianten in Deutschland*, p. 3.
[12] Ibid., pp. 5–7.

Commedia dell'Arte, German Baroque theatre). These will be described and compared in the subsequent chapters of this work.

Many scholars like James George Frazer, Richard Schechner, Roger D. Abrahams or Robert Weimann[13] share the opinion that drama and performance originated from serious categories of play, such as ritual and magic. As Baesecke's model suggests too, the mimetic representation of nature or religion in rituals entails many features of the dramatic performance: both shaman/priest and actor are liminal beings in-between the worlds who take up roles as personae by means of masks, costumes, conventional gestures and repeated words and actions. As Philip Zarrilli explains, the ecstatic and magical experience crossing the borders of the human and of reality, time and space is believed to have effects on the community and is often shared with an audience taking part in the ritual.[14] This happens in religious celebrations as well. For example, in every Catholic mass the whole community partakes in the re-enactment of Jesus Christ's sacrifice, whose body is transfigured into bread and wine. The sensory experience of being part of a performance is detectable even in the etymology of the word *theatre* (from the Greek *thea* designating "a place from which to observe or see")[15] and should justly direct the attention towards the perception and the actions rather than merely towards the text. This calls even more into question the distinction between drama and theatre mentioned earlier. A new distinctive category that enters here is that of *space*, in particular the difference between acting space and viewing space.

From the earliest periods, the link between drama and religious experiences in open spaces directly involved the democratically seated or, even better, standing spectators. In archaic, non-verbal pantomime (stage I in Baesecke's model), the worlds of reality and mimesis were likely to blur, also because there were no walls or architectural structures separating the action from the beholders. Playing on the same level meant that everybody was involved. As soon as there was a delimited space for action, pantomime could present dramatic situations (stage II) or whole dramatic processes (stage III) even without words. From the Middle Ages until well into the early modern period there were no real theatres apart from temporary elevated platforms (Latin: *mansiones*) with a common floor area (*platea*) set up in the open spaces of cathedrals for special religious celebrations like Easter. A detail from Pieter Brueghel the Younger's 1632 painting of a village fair shows the closeness of audience and actors on a precarious booth stage.

---

[13] James George Frazer, *The Golden Bough: A Study in Comparative Religion* (London: Macmillan, 1890); Schechner, *Performance Theory*; Roger D. Abrahams, "The Complex Relations of Simple Forms", in Dan Ben-Amos, ed., *Folklore Genres*; Weimann, *Shakespeare und die Tradition des Volkstheaters*.

[14] See Phillip B. Zarrilli, "Performance and theatre in oral and writing cultures before 1700", in Phillip B. Zarrilli and Gary Jaz Williams, ed., *Theatre Histories: An Introduction* (London and New York: Routledge, 2006) pp. 1–38, pp. 32–7.

[15] Samuel Weber, *Theatricality as Medium* (New York: Fordham UP, 2004), p. 3.

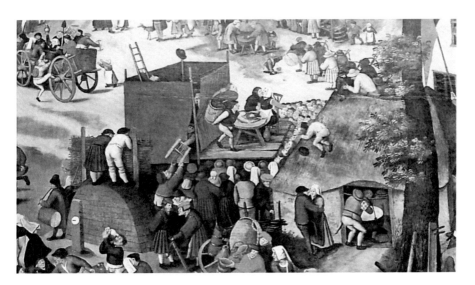

Figure 1: Detail from Pieter Brueghel the Younger's *A Village Festival in Honour of St Hubert and St Anthony* (1632). The Fitzwilliam Museum, Cambridge.

According to Susan Bennett, this open use of space granted a more active participation than after the establishment of private theatres in the seventeenth century, which separated the fictional from the real sphere by means of a twofold barrier: a social one in the form of admission prices set to limit the social composition of the audience, and a physical one, since in playhouses the pits were replaced by stalls, in which spectators would passively sit in the dark and no longer react to the performance.[16] In the case of wandering theatre, this separation was not as drastic; neither in the social sense, because itinerant companies entertained both courtly audiences and the lower classes in market places, nor in a physical one, given that the unusual location on the streets permitted a greater freedom of movement and interaction. This is precisely where the continuity from archaic to early modern performance can be found: in popular forms of theatre, on the streets, in marketplaces or on improvised booth stages surrounded by the audience on the same level. The recipients' role was vital for those performers economically dependent on a favourable audience, but this audience first had to be found and made accustomed to a newly emerging form of theatre between religious ritual, political event, mere entertainment and socio-economic practice. Once the spectators were used to dramatic processes foregrounding words over gesture and movement (stage IV), proper dramatic performances could ensue, in which the space between reality and illusion was not only physical but also mental (stage V). In this respect, performers could consciously break the illusion on stage by moving back and forth from the world of the stage to that of the spectators.

[16] See Susan Bennett, *Theatre Audiences: A Theory of Production and Reception* (London and New York: Routledge, 1990), p. 4.

Seen in this light, the ritual-religious sphere and the organisation of space are essential for reconstructing the first forms of not fully conventionalised drama. Like the ritual, theatre is a collective activity with a performative aspect. Despite the demonisation and virtual abolition of theatre by the Catholic Church in Western Europe by the sixth century AD, dormant elements re-emerged precisely in liturgical drama, as John Coldewey argues.[17] The history of Christ and the whole religious liturgy lend themselves to dramatisation and were eagerly used as indoctrinating devices for example with guild-sponsored Corpus Christi plays and representations of the Passion in the vernacular.

A first example of English vernacular drama with ritual elements can be found in the mummers' plays, an outgrowth of ancient fertility celebrations still extant in the Middle Ages, which were combined with Christological tropes. Closely associated with the medieval sword dance meant to symbolise the reawakening of the Earth from the 'death' of winter, this form of drama presented the central theme of death and resurrection of the hero, usually Saint George in England. As Robert Potter explains, seasonal and pagan religious rituals like Morris-dancing and Robin Hood skits, which were often better known than the Bible, were reflected in the four-part structure of the mummers' plays, of which, unfortunately, no text prior to the eighteenth century exists.[18] These parts include: 1) an address to the audience in the Prologue; 2) the introduction of the two champions, Saint George and the Bold Slasher, who boast and fight until one of them is wounded or killed; 3) the healing and resurrection of the wounded, brought about by a doctor and his impudent and clownish servant operating a mock-beheading; and 4) a comic conclusion with a final address to the audience, followed by dances and a collection of money (*quête*).[19] Although festive games derived from pre-Christian folk rituals like the mummers' play were presented even at court at Christmas and during the carnival revelries, amateur players of folk drama were still seen as separate from more 'serious' lay performers connected to special religious occasions such as mysteries (from the Latin *ministerium* or *officium*, or from the French

---

[17] John C. Coldewey, "From Roman to Renaissance in drama and theatre", in Milling and Thomson, ed., *The Cambridge History of British Theatre*, vol. 1, pp. 3–69, p. 7.

[18] See Robert Potter, *The English Morality Play: Origins, History and Influence of a Dramatic Tradition* (London and New York: Routledge, 1975), p. 12.

[19] Ibid., p. 15. An early form of mysteries are the Easter plays. Originally written in Latin, the liturgical *Quem-quaeritis* trope of the Angel announcing Christ's resurrection was progressively developed as scenes in vernacular, like the oldest fragment at the Muri Cloister in Switzerland (thirteenth century) or the Redentinian Easter Play (1464) testify. From these combinations of liturgy and drama later ensued the more elaborate Passion Plays, subdivided into various days or cycles, e.g. the Passion Play of St. Gallen (fourteenth century), that of Alsfeld (1501) or that of Bolzano (1514), and the Low-German cycles of Hamburg and Hildesheim. Later, these sacred representations had a far-reaching echo not only in German-speaking countries but also in England and France. See Dieter Wuttke, "Harlekins Verwandlungen", in Georg Denzler, Norbert Glatzel and Jacob Lehmann, ed., *Commedia dell'Arte: Harlekin auf den Bühnen Europas* (Bamberg: Bayerische Verlagsanstalt, 1981), pp. 52–66, p. 55.

mystère/métier meaning craft). This Continental phenomenon filtered into the national tradition through travelling actors immersed in oral culture rather than translations, at least until the invention of print.[20]

In fourteenth-century mysteries, distinguished guild members were annually appointed by civic authorities to perform vernacular liturgical dramas with a written biblical basis during the Corpus Domini processions. Each guild would perform episodes of the history of salvation most fitting their trade with pageants and cycles of scenes. Like a sort of living storybook, the bakers prepared the Last Supper, the goldsmiths were responsible for the apparition of the Three Wise Men or Magi, and the shipbuilders would set up Noah's Ark. As we know from the many cycle manuscripts from York (with 48 pageants), Chester (25), Wakefield (32), Beverley (36), Newcastle and Norwich (12 each) and Coventry (42 miscellaneous pageants of touring companies),[21] these representations contain pagan, burlesque and grotesque elements connected to popular culture, which seem to clash with the pious intent. One might deduce that the more the scriptural dramas were removed from the church to the marketplaces, the more creative freedom of expression was granted. Again, the space of performance influenced form and content. For example, both the Chester and the Wakefield pageants about the Deluge feature the so-called 'hen-pecked husband motif'. In a comic incident alien to the Bible, Noah's lazy wife does not help with the preparations and stubbornly refuses to board the Ark because she wants to chat with her gossip friends or to continue spinning respectively. The marital conflict inserted into the religious performance inevitably ends with a comic exchange of blows for the audience's amusement. At the end of the Chester pageant, the wife gives in to her husband's "frankishfare" (i.e. nonsense) and "being conquered she deals a slap", as the Latin

---

[20] In this context, the main features of English folk drama like the mummers' plays connect to the German *Fastnachtspiele*, as Pettitt proves in his essay "English Folk Drama and the Early German *Fastnachtspiele*". For instance, both were seasonal performances for Christmas and carnival and were presented exclusively by male amateurs in disguise. See Pettitt, op. cit., p. 8. In my view, some commonalities between German and English forms of folk drama may also be traced in Commedia dell'Arte, e.g. the use of masks and the immersion in the carnival festivities. Pettitt argues that numerous fifteenth-century German Shrovetide plays feature wooing characters like in the English wooing play (ibid., p. 6). They could be compared to the later Innamorati scenes of Commedia dell'Arte. Others present the 'miraculous' healing of a wounded fighter thanks to a doctor as in the hero combat plays (ibid.). Since the doctor, his humorous servant and the scatological cures he proposes almost turn the spectacle into a farce, they come close to the Dottore of Commedia dell'Arte. There is a further group of *Fastnachtspiele* including a series of boasts by young men about their strength and sexual abilities which echo the sword dancers in England (see ibid., p. 7) and, I would add, the conceited Capitano of Commedia dell'Arte.

[21] See Coldewey, "From Roman to Renaissance in drama and theatre", in Milling and Thomson, ed., *The Cambridge History of British Theatre,* vol. 1, pp. 3–69, p. 50.

stage direction says.[22] This motif was so successful that it recurred over centuries and can be found in the Pickelhering plays of the 1620 collection as well. Returning to the connection between early forms of drama and rituals, it is interesting to underline that the imitation or simulation of sacred content in a profane style can also be *desecrating*, literally: to make something sacred *un*sacred; even more so when the acting space was removed from the liturgical context. Thus, the physicality and self-conscious theatricality present in later mysteries with farcical byplays undermined the sacredness of the ritual.[23]

The development from ritual drama to increasingly lay theatre was particularly relevant for the non-cycle plays, which according to Simone Ebelsberger fall into three sections: saint plays, biblical or secular history plays, and morality plays.[24] Fifteenth- and sixteenth-century saint plays, as the name suggests, dramatised the life, miracles, conversion and death of saints, and were usually put on for the saints' feats in parishes, whereas biblical or secular history plays presented edifying moral stories.[25] Similarly, morality plays such as *Mankind* (1465–70) and *Everyman* (1495), which thrived in the fifteenth century in conjunction with Corpus Christi mystery cycles, aimed at making the spectators repent of their sins and convert to a pious life, as Everyman does with the help of Good Deeds. Since moralities did not involve the whole community as performers in costly pageants, attention could be focused on complex contents and characters instead. Moralities progressively took the place of mysteries as the power of the Church and of medieval guilds decreased and Humanism occasioned a versatile anthropocentric representation of the human condition.[26]

---

[22] Original text "*Et dat alapam victa.*" From *The Chester Pageant of the Water-leaders and Drawers of the Dee concerning Noah's Deluge*, in Ernest Rhys, ed., *Everyman and Other Old Religious Plays with an Introduction* (London et. al.: J. M. Dent & Sons, 1909), p. 33.

[23] In the *Wakefield Second Nativity Play*, the evangelic narration of the Adoration by the Shepherds at Jesus' birth is almost completely eclipsed by the prank of Mac who steals a sheep. His bossy wife suggests hiding it in the cradle and pretending it is their new-born baby to avoid suspicion. The comic climax is reached when she even swears to the doubtful shepherds: "I pray to God so mild, / If ever I you beguiled, / That I eat this child, / That lies in this cradle." The audience would laugh at the irony, knowing that the 'child' is actually a sheep meant for eating. The play ends with a beating of the thief Mac before the birth of Jesus is announced. See *Wakefield Second Nativity Play*, in Rhys, ed., *Everyman and Other Old Religious Plays*, p. 67.

[24] Simone Ebelsberger, '*Everyman' und 'Jedermann': Die Wirkungsgeschichte eines mittelenglischen Morality Plays* (Salzburg: Dissertation, 2002), p. 36.

[25] Ibid.

[26] *Everyman* is a good example for the continuity of popular elements within an international shared network of knowledge. For instance, one of the oldest plays performed by citizens in Vienna was *Homulus* (1553), an adaptation of the English morality play *Everyman*, which had been translated first into Latin by the Dutchman Diesthemius and then published in German by Jaspar von Gennep in Köln in 1539. See Johannes Meissner, *Die englischen Comoedianten zur Zeit Shakespeares in Österreich* (Vienna: Carl Konegen, 1884), p. 24. The story of Everyman was rewritten in Latin as *Hecastus* by the Dutch

The main characters of moralities were usually allegories of abstract concepts such as good and evil with specific functions: Virtue, Mercy, Hope, Faith or Jesus fight against Mischief, Vices or the Devil to obtain the universal human figure's soul. It was usually Vice who came into conflict with Virtue and initiates the dramatic struggle, referred to as *Psychomachia* (battle of spirits or soul war) after the first medieval allegory by the Latin poet Prudentius (fifth century AD).[27] In this juxtaposition of characters with clear moral roles, the distinction into 'high' and 'low' in both linguistic, social and religious terms reoccurs. In *Mankind*, for example, the vices Mischief, Nowadays, New Guise and Nought are farcical, bawdy characters, close to the audience as they move between *platea* (audience on the ground) and *locus* (elevated stage, scaffold or pageant waggon), directly address the spectators and even collect money during the play (lines 457–70).[28] Their irreverent pranks and scatological songs recall the plebeian Lord of Misrule, less fearful than the devil Titivillus and laughed at by the spectators for example when Mankind beats them off with his shovel (378–400). Despite being the actual agents of the plot and idols of the public, they must yield to Virtue/Mercy, a flat and moralising character, but win the favour of the audience, which sympathises with them and laughs at their misfortune. In this respect, Vice certainly shares points in common with the fool or clown, presented in the next subchapter.

As we have seen, both the comic byplays of mysteries and the evil tempter Vice transformed into laughingstock progressively reversed the pious moralistic intent into a farce of moral ideals. A similar effect of entertaining through desecration can be found in the genre of the interlude.[29] Interludes were initially created as a

---

scholar Joris van Lanckvelt aka Georgius Macropedius, and then translated into German as *Ein comedi von dem reichen sterbenden menschen, der Hecastus genannt* ('A comedy of the rich dying man called Hecastus') by Hans Sachs in 1549, with the addition of new Reformatory ideals. The medieval heritage lived on until the twentieth century, as Peter Potter explains, when W.B. Yates (*The Hour Glass*, 1900), George Bernard Shaw (*Man and Superman*, 1905), Hugo von Hofmannsthal (*Jedermann*, 1911), T.S. Eliot (*Murder in the Cathedral*, 1935), and Bert Brecht (*The Caucasian Chalk Circle*, 1948) reworked the Everyman theme in modern terms. For a detailed analysis see Potter, op. cit, chapter 10. And especially in Salzburg, Everyman is summoned on stage every year for the famous Festival.

[27] See David M. Bevington, *From Mankind to Marlowe: Growth of Structure in the Popular Drama of Tudor England* (2nd ed. Cambridge, Massachusetts: Harvard UP, 1968), p. 9.

[28] The references to the lines are taken from the online translation of the original text by the Utah Valley University <https://web.archive.org/web/20160724104710/http://research.uvu.edu/mcdonald/3610/mankind.html> (last accessed 7 June 2020).

[29] The *Encyclopaedia Britannica* defines interlude as an "early form of English dramatic entertainment, sometimes considered to be the transition between medieval morality plays and Tudor dramas. Interludes were performed at court or at great houses by professional minstrels or amateurs at intervals between some other entertainment, such as a banquet, or preceding or following a play, or between acts. Although most interludes were sketches of a nonreligious nature, some plays were called interludes that are today classed as morality plays", <https://www.britannica.com/art/ interlude> (last accessed 3 March 2019).

humanistic alternative to popular communal and festive plays in the fifteenth and sixteenth centuries. While early Tudor interludes used classical sources combined with the conventions of moralities to educate the audience at court or at school, on a lower social level interludes were introduced as musical skits between the acts of miracle and morality plays or during feasts. Though maintaining the character constellation and symmetry of moralities, the absence of allegorical abstractions and didactic aims turned the serious content into a lively and realistic parody of society, as David M. Bevington argues.[30] Thus, the comic stage intermingled popular elements with religion to reflect upon the meaning of good and evil in everyone's life and upon the distance between representation and reality, theatricality and mimesis. Elizabethan drama cleverly inserted the episodic interludes into the plays as subplots[31] and interlinked the serious themes of moralities with the laughable stock characters and the slapstick of clownish farces.

In summary, theatrical continuity originated from a constant integration and reflection of different elements: the ritual and religious sphere involuntarily supplied the basis for the first semi-professional performances outside of the church. Combined with other forms of entertainment which thrived on streets and in marketplaces, such as ballad singers, jugglers, etc., the vital lymph of theatre as performance was created. Oral and popular culture thus served not only as a repository of characters and stories, from which Renaissance playwrights would draw, but also as a theatrical counterpart to drama as bare text. A fine example of how popular elements contributed to early theatricality is the genesis of the clown – a most adaptable and at the same time surprisingly unchangeable character, whose presence so well connects the 'high' with the 'low', the present with the past, the street with the court, the body with the mind, and the serious with the comic from antiquity to Renaissance and beyond.

2.2. Fools and Clowns from the Middle Ages to the Renaissance

The terms *clown* and *fool* are often used synonymously. Not surprisingly, the German word *Narr* does not distinguish between fool, clown and jester, as if to underline the similarity of the terms.[32] Generally, *clown* and *fool* discern two comic figures identified rather by their function than by a specific name. While the fool's

---

[30] See Bevington, *From Mankind to Marlowe*, p. 9.
[31] See Potter, op. cit., p. 124 for examples of subplots recalling interludes in Shakespeare, such as the conspiracy of Vice disguised as Virtue in *Richard III* and *Macbeth*; the initiation of the naive hero in *Julius Caesar* and *Troilus and Cressida*; the formal confession and repentance of a hero in *The Taming of the Shrew*, *Richard II*; the unmasking and punishment of disguised Vice in *Twelfth Night* and *Othello*.
[32] In England, *jester*, *buffoon* and *merry-councillor* are ambiguous terms denoting both the court fool and the unattached buffoons, which were rather found in interludes. In Elizabeth's entourage, the courtly fool Somers was soon eclipsed by the professional clown Tarlton. See Welsford, op. cit., pp. 20–4.

real or simulated madness afforded nobles at court a chance to laugh of unspeakable truths, for François Laroque the clown was "one of the foremost representatives and spokesmen of popular culture"[33] as art and profession. For this reason, this character deserves attention in a study about popular theatre.

In the clown – be it the rustic clown, the witty fool or the refined jester – gesture, acrobatics, dance and song predominated over facial expression and the word, and the centrality of the unruly body became a key element of subversion. In this context, Mikhail Bakhtin's concept of the *carnivalesque* is useful for its connection to traditional festivities and for the idea of reversal. Based on this theoretical background, the present section aims at giving a short outline of the genesis of the clown and his evolution in the Middle Ages and the Renaissance and at pinpointing the premises on which the English itinerant players could count when they started touring Germany. As Elizabethan theatre and Commedia dell'Arte had taught them, they established the clown as principal mediator, reconnecting to earlier forms of popular entertainment common to their German audience. Here actual instances of a shared network, which have only been conceptualised in theory so far, begin to appear.

According to Bakhtin, the carnivalesque spectacle creates a parallel world on the borders between life/reality and art/imagination by means of bodily degradation, exaggeration and ambivalence. In this sense, the clown embodied the triumph of the "carnivalesque vision of the world", which is composed of three fundamental elements: firstly, the setting of the world upside-down ("parody" or "uncrowning") also known as reversal; secondly, the predominance of material and physical preoccupations connected to a "grotesque realism"; and thirdly, ambivalence through the co-existence of contraries (for example life-death, affirmation and negation, naivety and forthrightness) to which absurd wordplays and culinary puns are connected. The clown's speech revolved around the sphere of the body; he lacked inhibitions about his voracious appetite for both food and sex, and his verbal obscenities from the "material bodily lower stratum" drew attention to the limits of the world of high-minded lyricism.[34] Despite the apparent poverty of popular language, the dialectical expressions left space for disrespectful distortion, scatological or sexual *sous-entendus*, improvisation and satiric allusions. In word and deed, the popular nature of the clown appeared in his down-to-earth humour with frequent references to sex and bodily functions. This legacy of the ritual value of fertility rooted in popular culture made the clown a universal character, also because physical instincts do not distinguish between social classes. What derived from the clown's ambivalent and grotesque confusion was, on the one hand, a universal laughter made possible when actors and audience are at the same level; on the other hand, a suspension of laws, order and social barriers following an inside-out logic. His connection to the carnivalesque thus made the

---

[33] Laroque, *Shakespeare's Festive World*, p. 42.
[34] See Mikhail Bakhtin, *Rabelais and his World*, trans. Hélène Iswolsky (Bloomington, Indiana: Indiana UP, 1996 [1940]), pp. 2–24.

clown the active agent of subversion and restoration in a metamorphosis from order to disorder and back to order.

Ever since antiquity the carnivalesque has been quintessential of comic characters. Still, the supposition that the figure of the clown may derive from the ancient mime of the Latin rural satire and comedy has not been proved conclusively, because the continuity was too often interrupted and is not retraceable with sufficient approximation. There are just some vague structural and stylistic similarities between the Roman *mimus*, the character of Vice in medieval moralities, and the clown of the early modern period, which support the argument of a 'genealogy'. These shared aspects entail: 1) a predilection for costumes with recognisable props, 2) the frequent use of puns and wordplays in prose and metre, 3) a physical acting style, and 4) the alternation of drama and dance, and comic and serious content. As Robert Weimann explains, in ancient mime shows the most simple-minded of all characters called *Stupidus* was a favourite with the audience who enjoyed his constantly being hungry and craving for food as well as his ridiculous costume with pointed headgear and a club as a phallic symbol.[35] These same attributes are found in a personage familiar to the German audience of the seventeenth century – the fool Kasperl, who was a close relative to Hanswurst,[36] Pickelhering and Zanni/Arlecchino, as will be shown in chapter 7. In fact, this puppet or actor could easily be recognised by a pointed hat, a club and a colourful dress, which coincide with the description of the *Stupidus*. Added to the exterior parallels, there were probably also similarities in their roles, as the mime, the mischief-maker in moralities and the clown all presented an excessive physicality and a constant preoccupation with bodily matters, which connected them to the carnivalesque.

But where did these features, common to itinerant popular clowns, come from? Apart from the Roman origins, the clown's genesis in theatre includes an amalgamation of ancient satiric traditions, medieval *jongleurs* and amateur folk players. The figure of Vice from the morality play has often been considered the precursor of the clown for his riotous behaviour and his free speech, which, however, were ultimately defeated in the name of morality. Artemis Preeshl suggests that the clown "evolved from its roots in Vice to the bossy Italian *buffone* (stand-up performer) of the late sixteenth century, who came of age in the three-dimensional witty fool in Shakespeare's mid-to-late comedies and tragicomedies."[37] This hint is appealing because it brings together popular entertainers from different national backgrounds and points at an intercultural network of exchanges. In a liminal po-

---

[35] See Weimann, op. cit., p. 46.
[36] In the German area, the clown Hanswurst was known from the fifteenth century, but it was the Austrian actor Anton Stranitzky (1670/6?–1726), who made him the protagonist of the Old-Viennese *Volkstheater*.
[37] Artemis Preeshl, *Shakespeare and Commedia dell'Arte: Play by Play* (London and New York: Routledge, 2017), pp. 33–4.

sition between court and street, the fifteenth-century Italian *buffone*, a proto-professional figure close to the English jester, connected spectators of higher and lower social extraction, contaminated traditions and subverted forms and customs, as Daniele Vianello argues.[38] The disenchanting topsy-turvy world he created with laughter and obscenity made him the interpreter of social injustice, presented tongue-in-cheek to amuse but also to express criticism. Playing the fool, the actor showed how foolish civilised society was, provided that the audience was willing and able to recognise the blurred reflection of reality on stage.

In light of these general historical considerations, it is time to see how the early modern clown came into being and what distinguishes him from the fool. Subversion is still a key element in understanding the historic development from country bumpkin and court jester to clown and fool on stage. In Enid Welsford's definition, the fool was "the man below the average human standard but whose defects have been transformed into a source of delight", an amphibian between reality and imagination, and a bystander who makes everyday life comic on the spot thanks to improvisation.[39]

Initially, the fool's role was connected to the Feast of Fools during the medieval Christmas revels and the carnival preceding Lent. As François Laroque explains, in these celebrations secular Lords of Misrule were dressed in improvised regalia and appointed to lead the amusements at court and in local communities with songs and dances.[40] Their function was to subvert societal and cultural norms in a relatively ordered way, for example by means of music and acrobatics, before returning to the usual order. This procedure is similar to the carnivalesque experience that joined ancient Roman mimes to medieval mummers, and fools and jesters to the clown.

In Renaissance England, the distinction between fool and clown became increasingly connected to their spheres of action. In sixteenth-century courts, the fool was the only figure to brave royalty's wrath by speaking veiled insults and unspeakable truths so elegantly that he got away with it. His wordplays and double meanings did not cause rebellion but masked complex messages with funny puns and movements.[41] On a popular level, the Lord of Misrule's ballads and jigs

---

[38] See Daniele Vianello, *L'arte del buffone: Maschere e spettacolo tra Italia e Baviera nel XVI secolo* (Rome: Bulzoni editore, 2005), pp. 37–9.

[39] Enid Welsford, *The Fool: His Social and Literary History* (London: Faber and Faber, 1935), pp. IX-XII. From this excellent survey of the fool from antiquity to the Renaissance in Europe, I have extracted only some information relevant for the professionalisation of theatre and of the clown in Shakespeare's day.

[40] See Laroque, *Shakespeare's Festive World*, p. 50.

[41] For this reason, Erasmus considers the fool a truth-teller, whose insight is disguised as insanity, and praises foolishness in his *Moriae Encomium* (1509). Not only humanists celebrated the fool; he was also the protagonist of many collections of pranks, like the tales around Till Eulenspiegel, a legendary German jester, who presumably died in 1350. Welsford explains that Till Eulenspiegel's pranks were later dramatised by Hans Sachs and translated into English by Copland between 1548 and 1560. The name Eulenspiegel

(initially not only a dance but also sung exchanges of rhymed couplets including satire, libel, scurrility and lively dances) were readily transferred onto stage at the end of each performance, as was the figure of the fool. However, as Diana Henderson argues, the subversive potential still needed control since identification with the fool as representative of the populace was likely to become unruly.[42] This could happen when the foregrounding of the body was seen as a metaphor for the people as the nation's body and the audience members recognised the inequality and unhappiness they were victims of.[43] For this reason, the Master of Revels became a regulating and censoring institution to avoid excessive misrule during festivities or upheavals in theatres.

On the Elizabethan stage, the clown assumed the main features of the festival fool such as his amusing naivety, carnivalesque reversal and physical functions of the body, and presented them either as solo entertainer or in the role of the fool. Festival fools would at the same time imitate laughable rustic idiots and entertain the audience with witty speeches. This double nature of wisdom and idiocy typical of the foolish figures led to the increasing – though questionable – distinction between 'natural fool' and 'artificial fool'.[44] Welsford states that the Elizabethan clowns Richard Tarlton and Will Kemp made the 'natural fool' a successful personage and at the same time a persona, i.e. their alter ego.[45] Then again, the 'artificial fool' appeared prominently in Shakespeare's plays between 1598 and 1605, as Touchstone in *As You Like It* or as Feste in *Twelfth Night*, shaped by the actor Robert Armin (1568–1615). Instead of one persona, he developed the worldly-wise fool, i.e. an artist with the ability to change quickly between multiple personalities, from rustic Zanni to trained motley.[46] These examples show that the Shakespearean clown was a product of amalgamation, in which Sara Romersberger recognises Vice questioning the hero, the rabble-rouser Lord of Misrule, and the philosophic court jester.[47] In other words, he derived his force

---

was translated into Howleglass, a literal rendition of the German *Eule*/owl and *Spiegel*/mirror, looking glass. This character then influenced the figure of Robin Goodfellow also known as Puck, like in Shakespeare's *A Midsummer Night's Dream*. Welsford also lists other "mythical" fools like Marcolf (a Latin imaginary fool, whose deed were translated into English in 1492), and Bertoldo (an invented Italian and French buffoon who later influenced Commedia dell'Arte). See Welsford, op. cit., p. 50.

[42] See Diana E. Henderson, "From popular entertainment to literature", in Shaughnessy, ed., *The Cambridge Companion to Shakespeare and Popular Culture*, pp. 6–25, p. 13.

[43] See ibid.

[44] For a discussion on the German *Naturnarr* vs. the *Kunstnarr* or *Schalksnarr* see Edgar Barwig and Ralf Schmitz, "Narren, Geisteskranke und Hofleute", in Bernd-Ulrich Hergemöller, ed., *Rändergruppen der spätmittelalterlichen Gesellschaft* (Warendorf: Fahlbusch, 2001), pp. 239–69.

[45] See Welsford, op. cit., p. 243.

[46] See ibid., p. 251.

[47] See Sara Romersberger, "Shakespeare's clown connection: Hybridizing Commedia's Zanni", in Judith Chaffee and Oliver Crick, ed., *The Routledge Companion to Commedia dell'Arte*, pp. 312–20, p. 315.

from a network of exchanges between the popular and the erudite, sublimated in professional performances and literature.

Was there then a substantial difference then between fool and clown? From Welsford's account the medieval fool was the precursor of the clown as professional figure on stage. Still, ambiguity remains since the fool populated the stage too. A useful disambiguation among these two figures on the border between art and reality is to consider the clown as comic intermediary between audience and stage, a sort of popular 'insider' in the sense that he was immersed in the world of the audience and often spoke to them directly or entertained them with themes and problems from real life. By contrast, the fool as dramatic character took up a distanced position of 'outsider'. According to Peter Thomson, the fool was more involved in the play, but always as a quizzical character who belonged neither to the world of the audience, like the clown, nor to the realm of fiction.[48] From this angle he philosophically questioned the relationship between reality and fantasy.

Nonetheless, the terms continued to be used synonymously: in Shakespeare's day, the clown as dramatic persona identified a variety of roles, from court fool to rustic. The spheres of action of the fool and the clown thus cannot easily be separated, as the following extract from *An Apology for Actors* (1612) shows. In it, Thomas Heywood sums up the function of the clown as holding up a mirror to provide a double reflection: on the one hand, the representation reflects reality; on the other hand, it triggers a mental reflection in the audience able to recognise their own faults and reform.[49]

> And what is then the subject of this harmless mirth? Either in the shape of a clown, to show others their slovenly and unhandsome behaviour, that they may reform that simplicity in themselves, which others make their sport, lest they happen to become the like subject of general scorn to an auditory.[50]

The edifying effect of the clown's "harmless mirth", mentioned in this quote, was unusual for the time. In fact, dancing and clowning, the grotesque and the parodic were often criticised by Puritans and moralists who failed to recognise the pivotal metatheatrical role fools and clowns played in Renaissance theatre.[51] For this reason, the process of ennobling the art of comedy was felt to be necessary on the

---

[48] See Peter Thomson, "Clowns, fools and knaves: stages in the evolution of acting", in Milling and Thomson, ed., *The Cambridge History of British Theatre*, vol. 1, pp. 407–23, p. 417.

[49] The metaphor of theatre as reflection or mirror of reality was common in the Renaissance. For instance, Hamlet says that the purpose of playing "was and is, to hold as 'twere, the mirror up to nature" (*Hamlet*, 3.2.22–3).

[50] Thomas Heywood, *Apology for Actors: In Three Books, from the Edition of 1612, Compared with That of W. Cartwright, with an Introduction and Notes* (London: Shakespeare Society, 1841), p. 34.

[51] For example, the Puritan Philip Stubbes wrote about the negative teachings derived from playhouses in *Anatomy of Abuses*: "[…] if you will learne to contemne GOD and al his lawes, to care neither for heaven nor hel, and to commit al kinde of sinne and mischef

part of actors in England (and Italy), who in the early sixteenth century started to distinguish between the 'vile buffoon', dishonouring the profession and abusing his body, and the 'honest comedian', i.e. a skilled and educated craftsman able to entertain and amuse the audiences without discredit, as Leo Salingar argues.[52] As this ennoblement went hand in hand with literarisation and the movement away from oral popular culture, the physical, violent, earthly, buffoonish and acrobatic became typical traits of the clown, while the philosophic, critical, elegant, witty and sardonic belonged to the stage fool. This way, both clown and fool continued to entertain large audiences, subdividing among themselves the primordial features inherited from the mime, the buffoon, the Lord of Misrule, Vice of morality plays and many other carnivalesque popular figures.

With the secularisation and professionalisation of theatre, the double nature of idiocy and wisdom was either connected to two different figures, like the two Zannis of Commedia dell'Arte (one witty and astute, one dull and boorish), or to the professional clown as entertainer for the masses, superseding the fool. This development took place during Shakespeare's career, when clowning was becoming more and more controversial, and the first touring companies started to leave England. In the English Comedians' adaptations, the musing melancholic fool was rare while the clown with his non-verbal skills became the more exportable and vendible product. The fact that the company managers of Commedia dell'Arte troupes and of the English Comedians in Germany usually played the clown shows how important this character was for the first professionals: he was the darling of the audience, the representative of the people and the mediator of content and thus constituted the core of entertainment, as we shall see. Therefore, in the chapters about the itinerant players I will mainly use the term *clown* to refer to the central professional entertainer of early modern popular theatre. This humble figure with a long tradition rediscovered by Renaissance culture was further developed in the Baroque period, when the transition from popular to erudite, amateur to professional, oral to literary theatre in Italy and England, as well as their mutual influences and their impact on the German stage, took place.

2.3. Tradition and Innovation in the Emerging Professional Theatre

This subchapter discusses the transition from amateur to professional theatre in England to see, in broad terms, how the popular worked together with the 'high' Latinate culture of the socio-political elites. It presents instances of the cultural

---

you need to goe to no other schoole, for all these good Examples, may you see painted before your even in enterludes and playes." Philip Stubbes, *The Anatomy of Abuses* (London, 1583). Digital version <https://www.bl.uk/collection-items/the-anatomy-of-abuses-by-philip-stub bes-1583#> (last accessed 8 February 2021) L 9v.

[52] See Leo Salingar, *Shakespeare and the Traditions of Comedy* (Cambridge: CUP, 1974), p. 16.

amalgamation at the basis of early modern theatre and introduces the detailed historical analysis of similar developments in Italy and German-speaking countries presented in the following chapters. Special emphasis will be given to the clown as mediator between the worlds of reality and fiction, of erudite and popular culture, and to how the professionalisation of theatre affected his development.

Dramatic performance as we understand it today (stage V in Baesecke's model) started to be established only from the late Middle Ages, as has been expounded, and more predominantly in the Renaissance, when theatre became professionalised. On the Continent, the records of full-time actors playing together in organised companies start from the mid-sixteenth century: in Spain, Lope de Rueda founded a troupe in 1540; in Italy, the first documented contact between professional actors dates from 1526, when Francesco Nobili's (also known as Cherea) touring company exported adaptations of classical pieces by Plautus and Terence while the first practitioners of Commedia dell'Arte met in Padua in 1545; next, France and England followed in 1552 and 1576.[53] According to Susan Bennett, "if the nature of the audience changed, then so did the cultural status of the theatrical event."[54] The core of this transformation arguably resides in the early modern rediscovery of ancient theatre in conjunction with the professionalisation of old forms of staging and acting. These two components amalgamated and spread throughout Europe via the printing press but also thanks to the itinerant players performing at courts and on the streets.

In England, the evolution from lay troupes of morality players to regular actors was slow. Only by the 1580s is it possible to speak of professional players and playwrights, like Kyd and Marlowe, although the public appeared indifferent to the writers' names. The essence of theatre, for Leo Salingar, was the actor giving life to the text but also adding himself to it, and indeed Shakespeare himself throughout his professional life "was first of all an actor."[55] Similarly to the Commedia dell'Arte, subject matter and play were intended as something belonging to everyone, of common knowledge and fruition, not limited to a certain dramatist or drama. This shared network was indebted to sources newly acquired from Greek and Latin on the one hand, and to the lively popular heritage on the other hand. As printing increasingly influenced the way drama was written and performed, the whole trade of working on stage became fixed, controllable, and thus 'respectable'. At least this was true of official troupes, while popular theatre still maintained a close connection with orality and the involvement of the audience. 'High' and popular culture thus cross-fertilised each other and contributed to the creation of an official form of theatre.

The first philological current of the Renaissance, Humanism, and its rediscovery of ancient drama had a deep impact on Tudor England. On the one side, mum-

---

[53] See Manfred Brauneck, *Die Welt als Bühne: Geschichte des europäischen Theaters*, vol. 1, p. 430.
[54] Bennett, *Theatre Audiences*, p. 3.
[55] Salingar, *Shakespeare and the Traditions of Comedy*, p. 261.

mers wandering from town to town started to expand their repertoire in the marketplaces under the influence of farces, biblical and mythological plots and popular 'evergreens' like the clown. On the other side, scholars explored classic rhetoric and subject matters – such as revenge and stock characters like the braggadocio *miles gloriosus* in the eponymous Plautian comedy – and shaped various genres by merging late antique prose, the Arcadian lyricism of pastorals, and Renaissance novelistic literature. Cultural amalgamation increased the popularity of mixed genres, like the tragicomedy – later criticised as 'impure' dramatic form by Martin Opitz and Johann Christoph Gottsched[56] – and of mixed sources from ancient Rome and Greece, but also from performances nearer in time and space, for example, the moralities. Thus, the popular tradition of theatre was raised to an intellectual sphere but also continued to entertain the masses.

In this context, the already-mentioned Everyman theme of the moralities is useful for tracing the intersection of a popular subject into a Renaissance world view. In Marlowe's version of the *Faustus* material, the protagonist is no longer a medieval allegory of human fate and frailty, like Everyman, but is the self-willed master of his own destiny. In numerous scenes, good angels or a symbolic old man try to make Faustus repent whenever he is in doubt (*The Life and Death of Doctor Faustus*, 1.1.73, 2.3.12 and 5.1.36) but his thirst for knowledge is so strong that he gives in to the bad angel and the devil. Not even Mephistopheles' almost moving account of his own fall from grace can shake Faustus's "manly fortitude", at least until the end, when it is too late.[57] The early modern Faustus represents the humanist's search for knowledge on a sophisticated level while the role of Mephistopheles appears as a parodic rendition of Vice, whose power is limited to burlesque sorcery, for example when he plays a trick on the horse-courser and sells him a horse that vanishes as soon as it touches water (4.1.). As distinct from Everyman, Faustus is damned as a bad example, but also admired for his tragic stature. These changes demonstrate how Elizabethan playwrights mingled popular and humanist elements towards the creation of a national theatre – respectful of the classics but also indistinctly aware of its own popular past, as this popular component contributed to making the plays palatable to a large audience.

As a matter of fact, the first permanent theatres in England were more dependent on the spectators' popular taste than on patronage as their principal source of income. Diana Henderson speaks of a "socio-cultural mingle-mangle" of the

---

[56] See for instance Martin Opitz, *Buch von der deutschen Poeterey* (1624), edited by Richard Alewyn (Tübingen: Niemeyer, 1963), p. 20.

[57] "FAUSTUS. Where are you damned? MEPHISTOPHELES. In hell. FAUSTUS. How comes it then that thou art out of hell? / MEPH. Why, this is hell, nor am I out of it. / Think'st thou that I, who saw the face of God / And tasted the eternal joys of heaven, / Am not tormented with ten thousand hells / In being deprived of everlasting bliss? / O Faustus, leave these frivolous demands, / Which strike a terror to my fainting soul! FAUSTUS. What, is great Mephistopheles so passionate / For being deprived of the joys of heaven? / Learn thou of Faustus manly fortitude, / And scorn these joys thou never shalt possess." *The Life and Death of Doctor Faustus*, 1.3.75–88.

Elizabethan period when she describes the Shakespearean audience as "hungry for words *as* performance" and the authors' "self-conscious artistry in melding once 'elite' reading matter with popular stage antics."[58] This shared knowledge or "mingle-mangle" can hardly be separated into categories of 'high' and 'low' as it was a network of materials from multiple sources and in multiple forms. A representative of this hotchpotch culture in-between popularity and erudition, orality and literacy is the early modern clown, who underwent a peculiar development with the professionalisation and literarisation of theatre in this period. A short excursus on the clown Richard Tarlton (died 1588) shall exemplify this evolution.

Of humble origins but extraordinarily talented, Dick Tarlton managed to be solo entertainer, jester at court, company player, many aristocrats' favourite, and star of the city all in one. Peter Thomson argues that his success was connected to a manifest adherence of his persona to the underclass.[59] Like the Zannis of Commedia dell'Arte, he presented himself as rustic immigrant to London and thus wove his personality into a recognisable stage persona. Further points in common with Commedia dell'Arte were the use of improvisation in his songs and rhymed responses, collected after his death in *Tarlton's Jests* (1611), and his characteristic visual appearance with a drum, as can be seen in the image below.[60]

Figure 2: Richard Tarlton with his pipe and tabor inside the majuscule letter 'T' accompanied by the verse: "The picture here set down, / Within this letter T, / Aright doth shew the form and shape / Of Tharlton unto thee", in John Scottowe, *Alphabet*, around 1592.

---

[58] Diana E. Henderson, "From popular entertainment to literature", in Shaughnessy, ed., *The Cambridge Companion to Shakespeare and Popular Culture*, pp. 6–25, p. 18.

[59] See Peter Thomson, "Clowns, fools and knaves: stages in the evolution of acting", in Milling and Thomson, ed., *The Cambridge History of British Theatre*, vol 1, pp. 407–23, pp. 409–10.

[60] For a thorough analysis of *Tarlton's Jests* see Richard Preiss, *Clowning and Authorship in Early Modern Theatre* (Cambridge: CUP, 2014), ch. 3.

From 1575 to 1583, Tarlton became a member of the Sussex's Men, one of the first professional companies in England, and later switched to the Queen's Men. Even in this position, his repertoire on stage continued to draw on oral culture: ballads, parodies and comic jigs, presented as dramatic dialogues with lewd connotations, dance, music and acrobatics. This unique combination shaped the early modern clown figure who played with improvisation, reversal, reflection and illusion by stepping out of his role like Vice did in the morality play.

Although this versatility was not suitable for literary Renaissance drama, increasingly tied to the written text and less to the oral performance, Shakespeare and his contemporaries were too astute to renounce such a precious habit and therefore inserted the clown or fool as a literary character. Soon, every company had its own clown for the jigs – the short afterpieces with song and dance involving sexual misadventures and cross-dressing, which became a standard conclusion to any play until they were inserted as subplots into the plays around 1600.[61] Other popular elements re-introduced on the professional stage were, for instance, the fairies and mythological figures from folklore, which often appeared in connection with clownish characters in the subplots. Instances of blending the clown and magical beings are the jester Robin Goodfellow or Puck in *A Midsummer Night's Dream* and witty Ariel in *The Tempest*. Thus, the frowned-upon comic and folk elements of oral culture found their way back into drama.

These examples demonstrate that the transition from popular to Renaissance drama was gradual and characterised by amalgamation, adaptation and innovation of various traditions. However, the effect of placing literacy before orality was to increment the successful delivery of comic lines planned by the author and to diminish the autonomy of the actor. In a certain sense, the playwrights regulated the subversive potential of the player just as the Master of Revels censored the Lord of Misrule. As the next chapter shows, Commedia dell'Arte went through a similar process in the transition from orality to literarisation.

---

[61] See Thomson, "Clowns, fools and knaves: stages in the evolution of acting", in Milling and Thomson, ed., *The Cambridge History of British Theatre*, vol 1, pp. 407–23, p. 412.

3. Commedia dell'Arte in Italy and Northern Europe

The following chapters investigate the socio-historical context in which Italian and English popular theatre developed between 1570 and 1640 and how these products of amalgamation influenced the German and Austrian stages. In chronological order, I start with Commedia dell'Arte, the most famous form of Italian popular theatre, as it was the first to spread into Europe, both as art, skill and professional trade. In particular, the connection to Renaissance erudite comedy (*Commedia erudita* or *sostenuta*) is a fine example of the amalgamation of 'high' and 'low' on the popular stage and its successful relocation in a new cultural context abroad. Subsequently, chapter 4 describes the professionalisation of theatre in England to find parallel developments between Italy and England in the so-called Italianate influence.[1] Finally, chapter 5 outlines the condition of drama and theatre in Germany before the advent of the wandering troupes, especially from England, and the impact they had on indigenous theatre production of the time. As an exemplary case study, the collection of plays associated with the English Comedians, *Engelische Comedien und Tragedien* (1620), will be analysed in chapter 6.

In a comparative perspective, the questions addressed to reconstruct the cultural background of theatricality in Italy, England and Germany are: How were the itinerant companies organised? Where, how and why did they travel? What difficulties did they face? How did recycling of material and negotiation of meaning work both for Italian and English troupes to meet the audience's taste abroad? And who shaped this taste, the actors or the spectators? Apart from a historical reconstruction, I am interested in the interactive processes of creation and reception connected to theatre and theatricality; in how far travelling called for the active intervention of the company in adapting pre-existing topics both on the stage and on the page with a variety of strategies; and how this permeation into different cultures and levels of education may be attributed to a shared network. It is useful to start with the development of each 'national' form of theatre to detect intercultural points of contact that suggest a mutual influence.

Beginning with Italy, the many nuances of Commedia dell'Arte will be addressed as follows: firstly, the meanings of the name and its salient characteristics; secondly, its development from the origins to the seventeenth century; thirdly, the skills required for this 'art' and its masks, in other words the performative dimension; and fourthly, the organisational and economic aspects in the wake of the professionalisation of popular theatre. Being a commercial venture, Commedia

---

[1] The term *Italianate* is borrowed from Artemis Preeshl, who speaks of Italianate culture to describe the influence of Italy on early modern English literature and drama. See *Shakespeare and Commedia dell'Arte*, p. XIV.

dell'Arte companies toured and adapted their repertoire for a diverse audience before the plays were fixed as literary drama. My aim is not to give an exhaustive picture of Commedia dell'Arte but to present a summary of major studies on the topic,[2] focussing on those aspects that will be useful in discovering similar occurrences of intercultural theatricality.

Commedia dell'Arte is the most common name used for a specific form of theatre with stock characters and masks, which flourished between 1550 and 1750.[3] It can be translated literally as comedy of skills, or as Kathleen Lea affirms: "'comedy of the profession' – apparently an Italian invention of the sixteenth century – stands for improvisation, the recurrence of masked characters, professional players, and the appeal to a popular audience."[4] In this sense, Commedia dell'Arte belongs to popular theatre in terms of what it depicted and to whom it appealed, as Mazzone-Clementi argues.[5] The popular element in production and reception was thus deep-seated in the very nature of this theatrical style, which spread quickly from Italy throughout Europe and Russia, influencing the greatest playwrights of the era. The name appeared posthumously in the eighteenth century, when a scientific interest in the topic was kindled; earlier denominations are *Commedia a soggetto* (comedy tied to a subject matter, an invitation to 'go with the subject'), *all'improvviso* (improvised comedy following the principle of 'anything goes'), *a braccio* (*extempore*, literally: at arm's length), *Commedia di Zanni/Gratiani* (taking up the names of some masked characters), but also negative definitions such as *commedia mercenaria* (mercenary comedy).[6] The different names are ascribable to the disparate records and opinions about this style of performance, unified only in time under the umbrella term Commedia dell'Arte,

---

[2] My historical reconstruction of the socio-cultural context of Commedia dell'Arte is indebted to Kathleen Marguerite Lea, *Italian Popular Comedy: A Study in the Commedia dell'arte 1520–1620, with Special Reference to the English Stage* (New York: Russell & Russell, 1962 [1934]); Vito Pandolfi, *La Commedia dell'Arte: Storia e testo* (Florence: Ed. Sansoni Antiquariato, 1957); Sirio Ferrone, *La Commedia dell'Arte: Attrici e attori italiani in Europa (XVI-XVIII secolo)* (Torino: Einaudi, 2014); Robert Henke, *Performance and Literature in the Commedia dell'Arte* (Cambridge: CUP, 2002); Wolfgang Thiele, ed., *Commedia dell'Arte: Geschichte – Theorie – Praxis* (Wiesbaden: Harrassowitz, 1997); Roberto Tessari, *Commedia dell'Arte: La Maschera e l'Ombra* (Milan: Mursia, 1981); Allardyce Nicoll, *The World of Harlequin: A Critical Study of the Commedia dell'Arte* (Cambridge: CUP, 1963); and Konstantin Miklaševskij, *La Commedia dell'Arte o il teatro dei commedianti italiani nei secoli XVI, XVII e XVIII*, trans. Carla Solivetti (Venice: Marsilio, 1981 [1914]).

[3] Kathleen Marguerite Lea, *Italian Popular Comedy* (subsequently abbreviated to *IPC*), vol. 1, p. 2.

[4] Ibid., vol. 1, p. 3.

[5] Carlo Mazzone-Clementi and Jane Hill, "Commedia and the Actor", in Joel Schechter, ed., *Popular Theatre: A Sourcebook*, pp. 83–9, p. 84.

[6] See Karl Riha, *Commedia dell'Arte: Mit den Figurinen Moritz Sands* (Frankfurt a.M.: Insel, 1980), p. 53.

which does not necessarily mean it has to be comic, as originally the word *commedia* referred to theatre in general. All definitions contain characteristic elements, concisely summarised in Roberto Tessari's overview: it had mercenary origins (*mercenaria*) and presented masked men and women on stage (*Zanni/Gratiani*), challenging the classicist revival of Greco-Roman theatre. Although the popular heritage from the archaic mimes survived in a residual subculture, it was devalued for being different from official 'learned culture'. An additional feature was the refusal to adhere rigorously to a written text (*a braccio, a soggetto*) and the exaltation of gesture and orality over literacy. The simple but engaging plots derived their force from clearly codified comic 'types' or fixed characters, which came to life thanks to the illusion of spontaneous performing (*allo improvviso*).[7] A detailed description of the constituents will give a more complete picture of this extraordinary form of theatre.

In the transitional period from the Renaissance to the Baroque, Commedia dell'Arte affected many European currents with its attention to gesture, posture, position and spacing. Originally presented on the streets by travelling mountebanks, Commedia dell'Arte soon captivated the courts and palaces due to its universal appeal to all social classes and to its distinctive collective style based on the collaboration of actors with fixed roles and masks. Proud of their position and craft, the professional comedians popularised a new form of comedy in-between learned drama and street entertainment. However, as Tessari argues, criticism from academics, clergymen and civic authorities did not cease for a long time and the comedians were disregarded as vulgar contaminants of eminent sources or mercenary vagabonds causing fights and promoting immorality. Considerable concern was due to the impromptu and carnivalesque nature through which Commedia dell'Arte eluded the control of any author and consequently of authority in general.[8] At the same time, the natural and free style of acting obtained approval, as the only 'fixed' element in Commedia dell'Arte was the skeletal plot called *canovaccio* i.e. a 'canvas' awaiting to be decorated in a continuum between improvised playing and scripted drama. This document usually contained a list of characters like Pantalone and Zanni, props (also called *robbe*, i.e. things, such as ladders, a purse, etc.) and salient turns in the summarised action outline; the rest was enriched by the actors. Therefore, Commedia dell'Arte represents a peculiar form of theatre, neither fully mimetic nor literary, although both aspects are present in its two most important characteristics in my eyes: physicality and improvisation.

Physicality points to the professional virtuosity in gesture, proxemics and acrobatics rendered necessary by the use of masks that hide eyes and nose. The inhibited facial expressions required compensation on two levels: 1) non-verbal body movement, which conveyed meaning via what Wolfgang Thiele calls "écriture corporelle"; and 2) verbal polylingualism, since each character spoke a

---

[7] See Roberto Tessari, *Commedia dell'Arte: la Maschera e L'Ombra*, p. 30.
[8] Ibid., p. 23.

distinctive dialect called *generico*.[9] Often the comic effect of physicality surpassed that of verbal language, especially abroad, where Italian was not spoken. Through both means of communication, the main goal was to provoke laughter with burlesque *intermezzi*,[10] for example with funny *lazzi* (miniature comic business involving acrobatics or magic tricks and sometimes vulgar pranks). One example of a *lazzo* is the renowned *Dialogo in terzo* in which Zanni or Brighella have to deliver a love message from one lover to the other and always mangle the words in order to create equivocal and vulgar phrases.[11] Initially unconnected to the main plot, these episodic sketches later evolved into slapstick subplots incorporated into the action on stage, as Artemis Preeshl explains.[12] A similar use of the interlude or jig can be observed in the early plays of the English Comedians in Germany and shows a closeness between Commedia dell'Arte and dramatic practices in England, as will be shown.

A further component of Commedia dell'Arte was improvisation, made possible by the predominance of orality over a written dramatic text. Since extemporisation depended upon flexibility within a rigid structure of plot and characters, it was not completely unconnected to drama and dramaturgy and should not be mistaken for creation *ex nihilo*. The structured plot was given by the *canovaccio* with the narrative pillaged from many sources such as *novelle*, ancient comedies, folk tales, historical episodes or contemporary erudite comedy. Moreover, structured character constellations provided the framework in which the plot could be carried out. Due to the fixed 'types', each with their specific mask, dialect and speech genres always played by the same actor, each performer had a vast repertoire of oral texts, situations and gestural routines to draw from on stage. In this, the players were aided by a tendency of Commedia dell'Arte towards a symmetrical arrangement of parts or patterns of scenes with recurring themes. For this reason, Louise George Clubb compares the practice of improvisation to a combinatory

---

[9] Wolfgang Thiele, "Commedia dell'Arte: Stegreiftheater aus Italien und Frankreich", in Georg Denzler, Norbert Glatzel and Jacob Lehmann, ed., *Commedia dell'Arte: Harlekin auf den Bühnen Europas*, pp. 1–20, p. 19.

[10] According to Elisabeth Fritz, the seventeenth-century *intermezzi* are short comic scenes or sketches in-between acts that can take the forms of 1) farces; 2) improvisation after the style of Commedia dell'Arte; 3) monologues; 4) spiritual *intermezzi*; 5) mythological and allegorical *intermezzi*; and 6) dances. By contrast, *intermedi* ususally consisted in ballets, arias and short scenes of serious content during courtly representations. See "Intermedi e Intermezzi (dalle origini fino all'anno 1768, circa)" in Alberto Martino and Fausto De Michele, ed., *La ricezione della Commedia dell'Arte nell'Europa centrale 1568–1769: Storia, Testi, Iconografia*, pp. 371–402, p. 378.

[11] See Anna Maria Testaverde, ed., *I canovacci della Commedia dell'Arte* (Torino: Einaudi, 2007), p. 756.

[12] See Preeshl, op. cit., p. 35.

composition of modules, for example of characters or actions, called "theatregrams".[13]

The centrality of improvisation granted an endless variation of the same stock without having to constantly change the repertoire or the place of performance. However, it caused both the rise and fall of the Commedia dell'Arte because a well-balanced combination of repertoire, individuality and spontaneity, which was the key to a successful performance, needed both talent and training. According to Allardyce Nicoll, the level of instruction and professionality of the players was disparate and caused great rivalry, so educated actors like Flaminio Scala and Francesco Andreini provided written models for their colleagues to follow. Thanks to their solid knowledge of the classics and scripted Commedia erudita (learned comedy), they committed themselves to elevating the ill-reputed entertainment by turning it into a literary art once they were retired from the stage.[14] When the oral tradition of Commedia dell'Arte became literate and took up the structure and content of Roman drama, *novelle* and Commedia erudita, the performers started to deny its popular origins by distinguishing between *commedianti virtuosi* ('virtuous' professional actors who became playwrights or used their play scripts) and *ciarlatani comici* (extemporising charlatans and buffoons).[15] In the time of the first generation of actor-playwrights, the boundary between the terms could easily be crossed from either side, because even the literary *canovaccio* structure still allowed for improvisation. By contrast, with the regulator Carlo Goldoni (1707–93) this permeability slowly ceased, as ordinary scripted theatre put an end to the popular form of Commedia dell'Arte. Goldoni's apparent revival of the Commedia dell'Arte masks, 'types', *scenari* and themes tied the actor to a fixed written text in such a way as to make improvisation impossible. In his view, this was done to aid the less proficient actors on the one hand and to respond to a change of taste in the audience on the other hand.[16] Throughout his oeuvre, Goldoni's reform was gradual and moved from the *canovaccio* structure with improvised parts to an increasingly literary character comedy centred on bourgeoise virtues and problems, according to the new ideals of the Enlightenment. By 1750 he had abandoned the use of masks, reduced the number of dialects and left out the former protagonist of the plot, the servant, in favour of moralistic realism in the French manner of Molière. The playwright Carlo Gozzi (1720–1806) refuted Goldoni's reform and tried to maintain improvisation in his magical comedies based on fairy tales. His merit was to introduce this typically popular

---

[13] Louise George Clubb, *Italian Drama and Shakespeare's Time* (New Haven and London: Yale UP, 1989), p. 249. In her view, this modular composition was shared by Elizabethan dramatists and Italian Commedia dell'Arte.
[14] See Nicoll, p. 33.
[15] See Lea, *IPC*, vol. 1, p. 311.
[16] Goldoni's reform started with the metatheatrical play *Il teatro comico* (1750), harshly criticised in Venice but well-received in Vienna, where Gottsched had already set a new standard for theatre. See the introduction to Goldoni's *Il teatro comico*, 1750 (Milan: Mursia, 1969).

genre to European theatre but by foregrounding the literary form, Gozzi equally destroyed the extemporising aspect.[17]

Thus, the ascent, acme and decline of the original form of Commedia dell'Arte took place in little more than a century, from the mid-sixteenth to the mid-seventeenth century, and coincided with the replacement of the vital energy of extemporisation and orality by literary *scenari*[18] with little inventiveness on the part of the performers. As Pierre Louis Duchartre states, "the success of the Commedia dell'Arte depended almost entirely on the acting rather than on the scenarios."[19] Still, had it not been for these *scenari*, we would only have a few pictorial records and first-hand descriptions of Commedia dell'Arte, making a reconstruction of its theatre practices almost impossible. Literarisation at the same time jeopardised and preserved oral culture. In the case of Commedia dell'Arte, the amalgamation of erudite and popular culture was particularly relevant and will be explored in the next section about its origins and development.

3.1. The Art: Origins and Maturation

There are many theories about the obscure origins of Commedia dell'Arte. For scholars like Kathleen M. Lea, Karl Riha and Konstantin Miklaševskij, it originated in Roman comedy.[20] Henning Mehnert suggests an ancestry in late medieval Italian mysteries or *sacre rappresentazioni*, i.e. dramatisations of the saints' lives and biblical stories still performed in sixteenth-century Italy,[21] while Max Kommerell claims it developed from improvised representations at court in continuation of Hellenistic mimic drama exported from Byzantium to Venice, where it merged with the carnival farce.[22] Benedetto Croce interprets the emergence of the trade of Commedia dell'Arte, called "teatro buffonesco" (i.e. a performance based on bodily expressions rather than on poetry and literature), as a sociological

---

[17] See Pandolfi, *La Commedia dell'Arte: Storia e testo*, vol. 4, for a detailed comparison between Goldoni and Gozzi.

[18] As Anna Maria Testaverde explains in the introduction to *I canovacci della Commedia dell'Arte*, initially *scenario* was a synonym for *canovaccio*. After Basilio Locatelli's academic collection *Della Scena de' Soggetti Comici* (1628/32) appeared, the term *scenari* identified more elaborate *canovacci* closer to drama. See Testaverde, ed., op. cit., p. XXVI.

[19] Pierre Louis Duchartre, *The Italian Comedy: The Improvisation Scenarios, Lives, Attributes, Portraits and Masks of the Illustrious Characters of the Commedia dell'arte*, trans. R. T. Weaver (New York: Dover, 1966 [1929]), p. 30.

[20] See Lea, op. cit. vol 1., p. 225; Riha, op. cit., p. 54; and Miklaševskij, op. cit., p. 20.

[21] See Henning Mehnert, *Commedia dell'Arte: Struktur, Geschichte, Rezeption* (Stuttgart: Reclam, 2003), p. 23.

[22] See Max Kommerell, *Dichterische Welterfahrung: Essays. Betrachtungen über Commedia dell'Arte* (Frankfurt a.M.: Vittorio Klostermann, 1952), p. 163.

answer to the needs of the people in a specific social and cultural context.[23] Combining these views, Vito Pandolfi asserts that its origin is a mystery, not ascribable to any preceding phenomenon, but relatable to 1) Latin popular theatre; 2) carnival festivities and masks; 3) a vulgarised or even parodied form of Renaissance erudite comedy in Italy; 4) the professionalisation of theatre to please a popular audience with fixed 'types' and a mimetic, everyday language; and 5) a legacy of the *commedia popolare* and the *buffoni* tradition.[24] Without discarding any of these possibilities, it is safe to say that it was a collective form of theatre rooted in the past, with 'old' plots and stock characters presented in a new and lively acting style. Since all these theories give insights into the signature traits of Commedia dell'Arte, they will briefly be presented one by one.

The hypothesis of Commedia dell'Arte as continuation of Roman popular comedy ties in with the idea of a network of shared knowledge. One of the arguments in favour of this assumption is the use of fixed comic characters called 'types' both in Roman comedy and in Commedia dell'Arte, as Wolfgang Thiele affirms.[25] The comedies by Plautus and Terence, modelled on the Greek author Menander, featured fixed characters such as the *adulescens,* a young man in love with a prostitute, slave or eligible woman, i.e. the *virgo*. The youth was usually aided in his pursuit of love by a clever slave, and hindered by an old man (*senex*), who was often burdened with an irate wife, the *matrona*. Other personages were the pimp or slave dealer *leno*, the blustering but coward soldier *miles gloriosus* and his *parasitus*, a liar concerned primarily with his own appetite.[26] The resemblance of the ancient model with the description of the Commedia dell'Arte characters or 'types', presented in the next subchapter, seems to corroborate this thesis.

Luigi Riccoboni (1676–1753), lead comedian in Paris, was the first to support the idea of a classical heritage in his *Histoire du théâtre italien* (1731) to ennoble this often-criticised form of art.[27] For example, as early as 1584 Niccolò Rossi considered the bawdy and mercenary entertainment of Commedia dell'Arte unworthy of the name 'comedy' because of its remote similarity to Atellan buffooneries.[28] The ancient *Atellanae* were semi-improvised Latin farces of rural Rome

---

[23] Benedetto Croce, "Intorno alla Commedia dell'Arte" in *Poesia popolare e poesia d'arte* (Bari: Giuseppe Laterza e figli, 1957), p. 503 and p. 510.

[24] See Vito Pandolfi, *Il teatro del Rinascimento e la Commedia dell'Arte* (Rome: Lerici Editore, 1969) pp. 147–9.

[25] See Wolfgang Thiele, "Commedia dell'Arte: Stegreiftheater aus Italien und Frankreich", in G. Denzler, N. Glatzel and J. Lehmann, ed., *Commedia dell'Arte: Harlekin auf den Bühnen Europas*, pp. 1–20, p. 16. Another common point, he adds, is the use of masks. Initially of cultic origin, the mask could confer a different and magic identity or role to its wearer. In later Greek and Roman theatre, actors used clay masks also for making emotions clear and as a resonating-body around their head to augment the voice.

[26] Ibid.

[27] See Luigi Riccoboni, *Histoire du théâtre italien* (Paris: A. Cailleau, 1731).

[28] See Niccolò Rossi, *Discorso sulla commedia* (Vicenza, 1584): "Né commedie io nominerò giammai quelle che da gente sordida e mercenaria vengono qua e là portate,

with four mimes – Maccus, Pappus, Dossenus and Bucco.[29] There were also four 'types' in the original Commedia dell'Arte: Arlecchino and Brighella (the two Zannis), Pantalone and Dottore, as noticed by the famous eighteenth-century Venetian playwright Carlo Gozzi (1720–1806). Following in the footsteps of Riccoboni, he pointed out that the value of this dramatic form is ascribable precisely to the correspondence between the characters of Commedia dell'Arte and the *fabula Atellana*: "Maccus, a Protean fool or Harlequin; Bucco, a garrulous clown or Blockhead; Pappus, a miserly, amorous, befooled old man; Dossenus, a moralising charlatan."[30] Moreover, like Commedia dell'Arte, the proto-literary improvisation of the Roman mimes dealt with everyday problems, family intrigues, erotic motifs and political criticism, as Manfred Brauneck explains.[31] Although Pandolfi dismisses this classical descent as unfounded,[32] there are correspondences which suggest a continuation of popular entertainment from antiquity to the Renaissance, albeit with interruptions.

One such interruption was the fall of the Roman Empire, when the Church gained more power and virtually stopped professional theatre in Italy until the advent of Commedia dell'Arte. Before that, wandering *joculatores* presented farcical sketches with masked characters during public festivities like the carnival in Venice. For this reason, A. K. Dshiwelegow claims that Commedia dell'Arte as such began in the fourteenth century, when it emerged from correlated forms of popular entertainment provided by the *saltimbanco* (mountebanks, jugglers and acrobats), *cantastorie* (storytellers and ballad singers in octaves) and *buffoni*.[33] More specifically, Daniele Vianello argues that the Italian *buffone* was not a prototype of Commedia dell'Arte but an autonomous and parallel form of professional comedian. In fact, while the *buffone* took up many roles as a single person and used dialects to differentiate between the characters in his monologues, Commedia dell'Arte actors presented a variety of 'types' characterised by different dialects and engaged in improvised dialogues.[34] The common use of oral tools of characterisation, though in different forms of delivery, makes a connection to the *buffoni* tradition plausible but difficult to document because of its immersion in oral culture.

A more retraceable path would be to consider Commedia dell'Arte a vulgarised form of Renaissance erudite comedy developed as professional popular theatre in

---

introducendovi Gianni Bergamasco, Francatrippa, Pantalone e simili buffoni, se non volessimo assomigliare ai Mimi, alle Atellane e ai Panipedi degli antichi", quoted in Tessari, op. cit., p. 1.

[29] See Riha, op. cit., p. 52.
[30] Carlo Gozzi, *The Memoirs of Count Carlo Gozzi*, trans. John A. Symonds (London: John C. Nimmo, 1890 [1797]), p. 38.
[31] See Brauneck, *Die Welt als Bühne: Geschichte des europäischen Theaters*, vol. 1, p. 230.
[32] See Pandolfi, *La Commedia dell'Arte: Storia e testo*, vol. 1, p. 11.
[33] See A. K. Dshiwelegow, *Commedia dell'Arte: Die italienische Volkskomödie* (Berlin: Hensche, 1958), p. 42.
[34] See Daniele Vianello, *L'arte del buffone*, pp. 39–55.

Italy. The relation of Commedia dell'Arte to classical and medieval histrionic styles makes it a hybrid influenced by its direct dramatic predecessors, Commedia erudita and Commedia villanesca. Without these pre-existing traditions, Commedia dell'Arte would arguably not have come into existence as theatre in-between 'high' and popular culture.

On the one hand, there was the Commedia erudita or learned comedy, modelled after the principles of antiquity and enriched with idealised, satiric and moral themes connected to the court, academia and the Church. In the second phase of the Italian Renaissance, Ludovico Ariosto (1474–1533) merged the plots of *novelle* with the structure and comic characters of the Greco-Roman drama, like Angelo Poliziano had done before him, but opted for a new form: the lively octaves taken from the Italian storytellers and ballad singers (*cantastorie*), as Leo Salingar explains.[35] Thus, the Italian Commedia erudita, a literary form of drama with allusions to ancient culture, a complex language, sumptuous set designs and double plots was developed between the fifteenth and sixteenth century.

On the other hand, there was the Commedia popolare or villanesca (folk or popular comedy), which consisted of popular performances by artisans and guilds with roots both in the Middle Ages and in Roman comedy but not yet refined or cohesive enough to have stock characters and a fixed structure.[36] It was established as a dramatic genre in the sixteenth century by Angelo Beolco (1496–1541), better known by the name of his stage character, the peasant Ruzante. In his satiric monologues, Beolco reworked plays by Plautus in the style of Commedia erudita with elements of popular performances like the *buffoni*'s use of dialects. For this reason, Brauneck advances the view that this adaptation of Commedia erudita by a practitioner foreshadowed the creation of Commedia dell'Arte, most importantly for his 'invention' of a 'type'.[37] Whereas nobles and aristocrats were amused by the parody of a stereotyped peasant facing famine, war, exploitation and poverty, spectators of lower social extraction could empathise with Ruzante's misfortunes. The use of a local character with a specific dialect was later taken up in Commedia dell'Arte.

Bringing together these different theories sheds new light onto the amalgamation of currents inherent in Commedia dell'Arte. The first documentation, such as contracts, accounts like the *Dialoghi* by Massimo Troiano (1568)[38] and collections of plays, dates from its heyday in the seventeenth century and presents the

---

[35] See Salingar, *Shakespeare and the Traditions of Comedy*, p. 184.
[36] See Pandolfi, *La Commedia dell'Arte: Storia e testo*, vol. 1, for a collection of extant texts belonging to this tradition and comprising buffoonish monologues, sung ballads, *contrasti* (contrasts/back-and-forth) and *frottole* (literally fib, a humorous narrative in monologic or dialogic form).
[37] See Brauneck, *Die Welt als Bühne*, vol. 1, p. 431.
[38] See Massimo Troiano, *Dialoghi di Massimo Troiano: ne quali si narrano le cose più notabili fatte nelle nozze dello illustriss. & eccell. Prencipe Guglielmo 6. conte Palatino del Reno, e duca di Bauiera; e dell'illustriss. & eccell. Madama Renata di Loreno* (Venice: Bolognino Zaltieri, 1569).

acting style as finished product shaped by a few official troupes, without considering its far-reaching origins. Still, there is a clearly visible but intangible connection to ancient mime, medieval folklore, mountebanks, and the erudite theatre of Renaissance scholars. In Lea's words, Commedia dell'Arte was a "compromise between the two manifestations of the dramatic instinct during the Renaissance"; the academics' rendering of classical drama in the form of learned comedy and the indigenous rustic mimicry and parody.[39] Therefore, it should not be deemed a corruption of Commedia erudita but a synthesis of divergent and stratified currents like the *buffoni* tradition and carnival festivities, able to adapt flexibly to other cultural contexts, shape them and be influenced in return.

Being a product of amalgamation, it was the nature of Commedia dell'Arte to wander, to become naturalised in many European countries and to always change according to time, place and audience. The centres of its rapid development were Venice, Rome and Naples, before it became an international vogue. As soon as the first professional Commedia dell'Arte troupes started touring Germany, Austria, England, Spain and France in the mid-sixteenth century, their style and technique inspired the actors and playwrights of the countries visited. To better understand the working mechanisms of Commedia dell'Arte and its expansion throughout Europe, the next subchapter illustrates its central protagonists – the masked and unmasked 'types' – before turning to the commercial and entrepreneurial side.

3.2. The Skills: Masks and Characters

In 1560, most companies consisted of ten actors and actresses with precise roles ranging from parents and lovers to servants and ruffians. From this fixed stock, improvisation had its source. Usually, the personages appeared in couples with regular relationship patterns: two *vecchi* or old men – Pantalone and Dottore, two Zannis or servants, two or more pairs of *innamorati* or lovers, eventually a *Capitano* (soldier), a *servetta* (young maid), a magician, and an older woman, wife or courtesan. Each *tipo fisso* (fixed 'type') was recognisable by its costume or mask, linguistic and gestural peculiarities mirroring local or social stereotypes, and specific psychological traits. Carlo Mazzone-Clementi distinguishes them according to three levels of characterisation: firstly, the *maschere* or popular comic masks like Zanni, Dottore and Pantalone; secondly, the *parti gravi*, semi-serious or poetic characters such as the Innamorati, the only 'literary' characters without a mask; and thirdly, the *parti ridicole*, i.e. funny roles – *Capitano, servetta*, Courtesan.[40] Later, the *parti meridionali*, 'types' from the South of Italy such as the Neapolitan Pulcinella, were added to the original *parti settentrionali* from the

---

[39] See Lea, *Italian Popular Comedy*, vol. 1, p. 229.
[40] See Mazzone-Clementi and Hill, "Commedia and the Actor", in J. Schechter, ed., *Popular Theatre*, pp. 83–9, p. 85. Commedia dell'Arte characters will not be italicised in further references but written in upper case letters because proper names are capitalised in Italian.

North, making Commedia dell'Arte a truly national Italian comedy, as Walter Hinck asserts.[41]

The way the characters interacted on stage was as fixed as the individual characteristics of each. Ludovico Zorzi visualises the conventional interplay upon which a *canovaccio* was based as follows: eight fixed parts (four comic masks – the *vecchi* or old men and two servants, called the first and the secondary Zanni – and four serious parts mirroring them), around which additional movable characters like the Maid, the Courtesan, the Capitano or the Magician gravitated.[42] The asymmetry given by an uneven number of dramatis personae generally left out the villain, braggart or *deus ex machina* with heightened comic or dramatic effect.

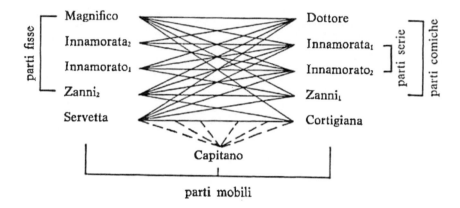

Figure 3: Typical structure of a *canovaccio* with the (a)symmetrical arrangement of characters and masks taken from Ludovico Zorzi.

As the diagram shows, the structure in which improvisation took place was linked to the number of closely intertwined characters on stage, ideally two 'types' with set combinations. These couples cooperated or argued in a responsive way, meaning that each utterance aimed at provoking a response. To facilitate the seemingly spontaneous interaction, the characters were associated with specific speech genres, which in Robert Henke's classification encompass: 1) *tirate*, i.e. long monological lamentations, accusations or eulogies of the *vecchi*; 2) lyrical amorous dialogues between the Innamorati drawn from Petrarchism with its catalogue of beauties and natural metaphors; 3) funny *lazzi* or self-contained digressions with elaborate word plays based on puns or absurd logic, and *burle*, practical jokes typical of the Zannis; and 4) the *bravure* of the Capitano, i.e. highly rhetorical,

---

[41] "Denn zu einer wahrhaft nationalen Komödie wird die Commedia dell'Arte dadurch, daß sie sich mit den Typen auch deren Sprache aus Städten und Landschaften bis hinunter nach Neapel zusammenholt." Walter Hinck, *Das deutsche Lustspiel des 17. und 18. Jahrhunderts und die italienische Komödie: Commedia dell'Arte und théâtre italien*, p. 12.

[42] Ludovico Zorzi, "Struttura → fortuna della 'Fiaba' gozziana", *Chigiana, Journal of Musicological Studies* XXXI (1974), pp. 25–40, p. 38.

ostentatious reports of his heroic deeds.[43] The manners of speaking gave each actor an opportunity to show the character's peculiar traits and rely on a repertoire of similar situations.

Returning to the connection between the popular and orality, Commedia dell'Arte provides an intriguing example of 'literate orality' or 'oral literacy'. In fact, the mimetic speech genres rested upon written mediums such as *centoni* or *cibaldoni* (commonplace books) with speeches to be learned by heart. But even the literate style was orally mediated and reflected a conversational style close to the audience's everyday language. Another aspect pointing at orality is the fact that this form of popular theatre started as improvisation and was then fixed as a literary text. The characters and plots were derived from an authorless oral tradition and, although some editors like Flaminio Scala claimed paternity to the *canovacci* they collected, in *Discorso sopra l'arte comica, con il modo di ben recitare* (1608) Pier Maria Cecchini (1563–1641) admitted that it was mostly 'stolen' material in disguise, in line with the practice of imitating and emulating of the Renaissance.[44] Moreover, since the fixed 'types' were well known to the audience and were expected to behave according to their usual patterns, the plot was usually secondary and merely a frame in which the characters would develop. In other words, theatre was more important than drama. This form of characterisation gave way to a particular pleasure of meeting the actors "half-way", in Allardyce Nicoll's words, because the spectators did not need an exposition of the play or an introduction to the unchangeable 'types' already seen in previous plays.[45] Amy Drake argues that as in modern-day sitcoms the effect of Commedia dell'Arte arises from the presentation of a closely intertwined group of characters well known to the audience in advance but facing new challenges in each play with a more or less predictable selection of actions and reactions.[46] Recognition in this case relies on

---

[43] See Henke, *Performance and Literature in the Commedia dell'Arte*, p. 15 and pp. 32–4.

[44] Pier Maria Cecchini wrote: "usar astuzia [...] acciò che il furto paja patrimonio, et non rapina" ('make use of shrewdness [...] so that the theft may appear property and not robbery', my translation). *Discorso sopra l'arte comica, con il modo di ben recitare* (1608), quoted by Ferruccio Marotti and Giovanna Romei in *La Commedia dell'Arte e la società barocca* (Rome: Bulzoni editore, 1991), p. 83. According to Robert Henke, Cecchini wrote the first substantial treatise about Commedia dell'Arte, in which he addressed issues of technical nature such as the need for more logic, decorum, verisimilitude and structure instead of focussing only on the farces. Moreover, he had the merit of introducing the Neapolitan 'type' of Pulcinella in 1632. See Henke, op. cit., pp. 198–202.

[45] Allardyce Nicoll, *The World of Harlequin: A Critical Study of the Commedia dell'Arte*, p. 35.

[46] For example, Amy Drake compares the character constellation of the American sitcom *The Big Bang Theory* to Commedia dell'Arte patterns. Sheldon recalls the pedantic Dottore, Howard the braggart Captain, Leonard and Penny the Lovers, Raj a Pedrolino in search of his lady and Stuart a modern-day Brighella with a comic-bookstore instead of an inn. See "Commedia dell'Arte Influences on Shakespearean Plays: *The Tempest, Love's Labor's Lost*, and *The Taming of the Shrew*", *Selected Papers of the Ohio Valley Shakespeare Conference* 6:3 (2013), pp. 11–30, pp. 24–5.

a pre-existing system of references, deduced from observing known characters contending with unknown situations, which worked equally well in the past as it does today.

It seems appropriate to give a short description of the single characters, before comparing Commedia dell'Arte plots to English and German plays. Whenever possible, references to English authors are added to give a broader understanding of their international influence and reception. The main sources about Commedia dell'Arte are the collections of *canovacci* and *scenari* with pictorial records like that by Flaminio Scala (1611) and Basilio Locatelli (1628/32) as well as treatises by practitioners, for example Francesco Andreini (1608) and Andrea Perrucci (1699),[47] which appeared, however, almost half a century after the first performances. These theatrical documents, presented in the next section, are the basis of the studies by Kathleen Lea, Pierre Louis Duchartre and Robert Henke, to whom my description of the characters is indebted.[48]

Innamorati (Lovers)

The role of the lovers or Innamorati was of vital importance for the romantic plot and the intrigues connected to it. It was around these poetic characters that all the other parts revolved. Usually, the *capocomico* (leading player) would write the dialogues and play the male lover (*comico innamorato*), called either Flavio, Fabrizio, Cinzio or Lelio, while his wife or sister would take up the female counterpart with fanciful names like Angelica, Ardelia, Aurelia, Flaminia, Lucinda, Lavinia or Isabella.[49] Apart from sudden changes of mind, frantic tantrums and jealous outbursts, the lovers did not present any individual personal trait; as the name says, they were primarily defined by being in love. According to their social status, their amorous passion was earnest and verbally refined in a high-flown Tuscan. The predominant element of romance in Commedia dell'Arte and the rhetoric of wooers were a legacy of the Commedia erudita and for this reason the young and graceful Innamorati were dressed elegantly and did not wear a mask like the *maschere* and most *parti ridicole*. Their speech genres may be defined as literary in a double sense, as Kathleen Lea suggests: because they referred to literature, in particular Petrarchan poetry and its amorous language, and because the *concetti* or conceits to embellish their jealousy, rejection, night and ladder scenes,

---

[47] Flaminio Scala, *Il teatro delle favole rappresentative overo la Ricreatione Comica, Boscareccia e Tragica, / Divisa in cinquanta Giornate* (1611); Basilio Locatelli, *Della Scena de' Soggetti Comici* (1628/32); Francesco Andreini, *Le bravure del Capitano Spavento* (Venice 1607/1618); Andrea Perrucci, *Dell'arte rappresentativa premeditata, ed all'improviso* (1699).

[48] Kathleen Lea, *IPC*, vol. 1; Pierre Louis Duchartre, *The Italian Comedy: The Improvisation Scenarios, Lives, Attributes, Portraits and Masks of the Illustrious Characters of the Commedia dell'arte*; Robert Henke, *Performance and Literature in the Commedia dell'Arte*.

[49] Giovanni Treccani, *Enciclopedia italiana delle Scienze, Lettere ed Arti* (Rome: Istituto della Enciclopedia Italiana, 1950), p. 943.

mutual disdain, unhappiness and wooing were usually written in advance and collected in commonplace books.[50] Despite their poetic and at times tragic sentiments, even the semi-serious lovers were not above buffoonery. When their declarations of everlasting love sounded too narcissistic and extravagant, the bawdy tones of Zanni/Arlecchino and Servetta provided a comic response ("uncrowning" or "parody" to use Bakhtin's terms)[51] in the manner of the Nurse in *Romeo and Juliet* or Emilia in *Othello*.[52] This common point between Commedia and Shakespeare introduces the Zannis.

From the Zannis to Arlecchino

The Zannis, two servants from Bergamo, are not only the protagonists of the Commedia dell'Arte but also those with the most complex derivation. As Vito Pandolfi explains, they spoke the dialect of Bergamo for a historical reason: many poor peasants from the mountains around Bergamo sought work as porters in Venice and other wealthy cities of northern Italy in the sixteenth century. Their Venetian nickname was Zanni, a dialectal version of the name Gianni/Giovanni, and they were ridiculed for their thick accent and primitive ways, later transferred to the stage.[53] Artemis Preeshl argues that in the plays the abused servants could seek revenge and fool their masters in a reversal of power.

> In commedia, illiterate peasants who were not well-versed in Venetian served abusive masters. Too poor to change their jobs, the Zanni punished their masters with slapstick onstage. With too many foreigners in Italy, the comici told the story through broad gesture and sight gags that helped to transcend linguistic barriers.[54]

This quote pinpoints three main features of the Zannis: the socio-cultural background involving a certain degree of criticism, the function of carnivalesque reversal and the physical acting style. The fact that servants subverted an established order and created havoc is indeed an instance of the carnivalesque experience. In addition, the Zannis' involvement with the body, their social position and their use of dialect as language of the people for ambivalent, scatological or satiric allusions and songs all tie in with what Bakhtin calls "grotesque realism"[55] and made the

---

[50] See Lea, *IPC*, vol. 1, p. 105.
[51] See Mikhail Bakhtin, *Rabelais and his World*, p. 22.
[52] Referring to *Othello* Richard Whalen points out that it is a synthesis of the main characters of Commedia dell'Arte, all condensed in one play: "Commedia dell'Arte was at the height of its popularity in Italy in the late 1590s, when the Shakespeare plays were being written. Among the principal stock characters in *Commedia dell'Arte* were the Zanni, the secondary Zanni, Pantalone, the Capitano, Pedrolino, the innocent woman, and her lady-in-waiting or maid. These seven stock characters are mirrored in the seven principal characters in *Othello*." Richard Whalen, "Commedia dell'Arte in *Othello*: A Satiric Comedy Ending in Tragedy", *Brief Chronicles* 3 (2011), pp. 71–108, p. 115.
[53] See Pandolfi, *La Commedia dell'Arte: Storia e testo*, vol. 1, p. 98.
[54] Preeshl, *Shakespeare and Commedia dell'Arte*, p. 29.
[55] See Bakhtin, *Rabelais and his World*, p. 23.

Zannis representatives of the people in ways cognate with the (English) clown. In particular, the emphasis on kinesics was the Zannis' speciality and a key factor in making Commedia dell'Arte comprehensible to diverse audiences, at home and abroad. The same solution worked for Italian actors in England and later for the English itinerant players in Germany, where gesture played a more important role than language.

Why were there two Zannis? In *Dell'arte rappresentativa premeditata, ed all'improvviso* (Naples 1699) the Italian amateur actor and poet Andrea Perrucci explains that the two servant characters mirrored the two old men with contrasting and complementary features. The first was astute, swift, witty, clever, keen on scheming, disillusioning, fooling and cheating, while the second was similar to the Plautian parasite: dumb, buffoonish, nonsensical, and unable to distinguish his right from his left hand.[56] Both the sly fox and the acrobatic, degraded simpleton were required for different functions: the witty servant would attend to the plot with his intrigues while the other played the awkward booby. For this reason, the speech genres appointed to the Zannis were imbued with physicality and practical jokes (*burle*) meant to interrupt the main action with interchangeable miniature farces (*lazzi*) about revenge, disguise, parody of supposed death, stealing, etc. Soon, the two Zannis made their way up to a proper personality with a myriad of names to distinguish their opposite character traits: Arlecchino, Brighella (a scheming knave, often an inn keeper wearing a thief-like moustache, a jacket and a pair of trousers trimmed in green, a green hat and a dagger),[57] Pedrolino (an imbecilic clown, usually a secondary Zanni to Brighella or Arlecchino), Truffaldino, Triviello, Stoppino, Fritellino, Francatrippa, Scapino and later, after 1632, Pulcinella and Coviello from Naples.

Costumes were another way of differentiating the two sides of the Zannis. The earlier simple white dress of the Zannis was taken over by Brighella and the Neapolitan Pulcinella, while Arlecchino obtained the typical patchwork suit and a black leather mask. Initially, this mask was made of wood rather than leather and left the eyes uncovered under exaggerated eyebrows and grotesque bumps similar to the worn-out horns of a devil.[58] Like Vice in the morality play,

---

[56] Freely translated from Anton Giulio Bragaglia, ed., *Andrea Perrucci: Dell'arte rappresentativa premeditata, ed all'improviso* (Florence: Edizioni Sansoni Antiquariato, 1961 [1699]), vol. 3, p. 215. The facsimile is available online on the website of the Biblioteca nazionale of Naples, <http://vecchiosito.bnnonline.it/biblvir/perrucci/ indice.htm> (last accessed 17 May 2020).

[57] See Duchartre, op. cit., p. 23.

[58] Many scholars argue in favour of the popular origins of Arlecchino. For Miklaševskij, the name might derive from the folkloristic figure of (H)erlenkönig in German and Scandinavian mythology or from Alichino, a devil in Dante's *Inferno* Canto XXI and XXII (see *La Commedia dell'Arte o il teatro dei commedianti italiani nei secoli XVI, XVII e XVIII*, p. 51). Others, like Lea, state that the word *Herlequin* pronounced 'Harlequin' existed in France before the Italian travellers arrived in the sixteenth century and denoted a "reveller associated with the charivari and the comic devils of the miracle and mystery plays whose

Arlecchino functioned as an agent of the plot, but his devilish traits were attenuated by his comic dexterity.

In the course of time, Arlecchino started to merge the characteristics of both Zannis in one personage: intelligent, resourceful, cowardly, full of mockery, voracious, bibulous and lazy. This refinement was fostered by skilled and capable actors who shaped the role according to their personality. For example, the famous comedian Alberto Naseli, better known by his stage name Zan Ganassa, greatly contributed to the progression from Zanni to Arlecchino not only in Italy but also at the court of Charles IX of France and of Philip II of Spain in 1572. Being of Bergamasco origin, he combined his own regional speech with Baroque elements of gesture and costume and gradually dispossessed Arlecchino of the devilish medieval characteristics recalling Vice and other popular figures, as Henning Mehnert asserts.[59] After Zan Ganassa, the first actor unquestionably known as Arlecchino was Tristano Martinelli, who visited London in 1573 and 1578 with his wife Angelica and his brother Drusiano.[60] His emblematic costume made of colourful patches recalled the playful resourcefulness of the courtly jester, but also witnessed the character's socially subordinate position, which explained his never satisfied hunger. Still, he made up for it with his slyness and could generate comedy alternatively through naivety or satiric criticism of his superiors.

By the seventeenth century, Arlecchino prevailed over his colleagues and became the right-hand man of his master Pantalone, with whom he shares the props of dagger and purse in many pictorial records. One example is a detail from the famous late-sixteenth-century frescos of the 'Narrentreppe' by the painter Alessandro Padovano at the Castle of Trausnitz in Landshut (Bavaria).[61]

    antics and licence of speech recalled his devilish ancestry." *Italian Popular Comedy*, vol. 1, p. 75. The medieval diabolical features were later humanised in the Renaissance. Probably Commedia dell'Arte companies touring France from 1571 took up the name of the legendary Harlequin, which appears as Arlecchino only after that date, as Enid Welsford claims in *The Fool: His Social and Literary History*, p. 89.

[59]   See Mehnert, *Commedia dell'Arte: Struktur, Geschichte, Rezeption*, pp. 11–12. To one of Zan Ganassa's company members, Stefanello Bottarga, stage-name of Francesco Baldi, we owe the earliest collection of Commedia dell'Arte *scenari* called *Zibaldone* ('Medley') of 1580. In it, particular attention is given to Naseli's character Zanni and his *burle*, which, however, are not described in detail. See Alberto Martino, "Fonti tedesche degli anni 1565–1615 per la storia della Commedia dell'Arte e per la costituzione di un repertorio dei *lazzi* dello Zanni", in Martino and De Michele, ed., *La ricezione della Commedia dell'Arte nell'Europa centrale 1568–1769*, pp. 13–68, p. 47.

[60]   While Tristano Martinelli was certainly the more talented comic actor, Drusiano was primarily a manager and organised various tours through Europe with the major Commedia dell'Arte companies of his day. In fact, he was associated with the Confidenti in Spain 1587, served the Duke of Mantua with the Uniti in 1595, and visited France with the Accesi in 1600. These companies will be presented in the next subchapter.

[61]   For a detailed description of the frescos see Nicole Schalbach, "Prime rappresentazioni della Commedia dell'Arte. La Scala dei Buffoni e il fregio del soffitto dello studiolo del duca Guglielmo nel Castello di Trausnitz a Landshut", in Martino and De Michele, ed., *La ricezione della Commedia dell'Arte nell'Europa centrale 1568–1769*, pp. 403–26.

Figure 4: Pantalone and Zanni/Brighella singing a serenade. Detail from the north-west wall of the 'Narrentreppe' (1575–9) at Trausnitz Castle (Bavaria).

Pantalone dei Bisognosi / Il Magnifico

Pantalone dei Bisognosi, ironically meaning 'of the needy' although he was notoriously rich and greedy, is often presented centre stage with Arlecchino in pictorial representations.[62] His name recalled the Venetian saint Pantaleone and due to his

---

[62] For information about the visual records of Commedia dell'Arte see the excellent study by M. A. Katritzky, *The Art of Commedia: A Study in the Commedia dell'Arte 1560–1620 with Special Reference to the Visual Records* (Amsterdam: Rhodopi, 2006).

Venetian origin, Pantalone used the dialect of Venice to reprove, persuade, command and offer advice. He also used to hold long patronising or invective speeches (*tirate*), which were often memorised in advance and could begin and end at any time, if improvisation so required. The name Pantalone may also derive from the red pantaloons worn by the character, as in Jacques's monologue from Shakespeare's *As You Like It* (2.7.158–67). Alternatively, he was called *Magnifico* (magnificent) as either a respectful epithet or an ironic comment on his avarice.

This stock character was probably connected both to the Roman mime character Pappus, a lecherous, old miser, and to the *senex* (old man) of Latin comedy and Renaissance Commedia erudita, as Mehnert argues.[63] With these personages he shares lustfulness and stinginess, negative traits personified in the social stereotype of an elderly, rich and petty Venetian merchant and counsellor. Apart from a beaked mask and a goatee, which are emblems of an almost devilish rapacity, Pantalone usually wore a red woollen bonnet, a long black coat or robe over red tights and elegant pointed Turkish slippers. In addition, a short phallic knife and a visible purse symbolised his lust and desire for money.

In the early representations, Pantalone is not depicted as excessively old; quite the contrary, he sings and dances gaily with his servant Zanni. It was in the later development of Commedia dell'Arte as character comedy for the bourgeoisie that he took up the roles of old father and husband. As a father, he usually pretended to care for his children's virtue and moral integrity, when in fact he was only preoccupied with his own sexual adventures and wealth. If he had a son, he constantly worried about his offspring's dissolution of the patrimony. If he had a daughter, she was frequently a ward with a large dowry he was not willing to give to any suitor. Moreover, in the role of the foolish old suitor, he badgered younger women like the courtesan, the Innamorata or the maid (Servetta), with little success. These premises made Pantalone an easy prey to the intrigues of his servants or the Innamorati, who often foiled his plans. Since the help of his servant Zanni and of his friend the Dottore was mostly useless, in the end the rejected Croesus must, of course, admit defeat to appeal to a popular audience.

Other characteristics associated with the old man were more positive or serious to allow variations: he could be a lovable or frantic father, lover, husband and master, but in most cases, he played the incorrigible eavesdropper, gullible, jealous coxcomb, or duped miser. This unflattering representation of a rich Venetian merchant was in line with what Pandolfi describes as "bourgeois satire" rooted in Commedia dell'Arte. In fact, the Innamorati were a distorted depiction of Petrarchism, the Capitano functioned as a satire on the military and the Dottore was a parodied version of the humanist scholar.[64] As can be seen, Commedia dell'Arte encompassed all aspects of quotidian life, turning them on their head in a carnivalesque reversal for comedy's sake but also with a whiff of social criticism.

---

[63] See Mehnert, op. cit., p. 24.
[64] See Pandolfi, *Il teatro del Rinascimento e la Commedia dell'Arte*, pp. 175–80.

Dottore / Gratiano

Closely connected to Pantalone was the second *vecchio*, Dottore. Both the title and his byname Balanzone, from *balanza* /scale, i.e. a symbol of justice, indicated his profession as a lawyer. Sometimes he was also called Gratiano, after a twelfth-century lawyer and erudite who, in Sirio Ferrone's view, might have served as a parodied model for the character.[65] The fallen humanist had a peculiar speech genre consisting either of incorrect Latin quotations to glorify his fragmented classical erudition, or the dialect of Bologna, a city famous for its university. Whether his malapropisms (*spropositi*) are due to a superficial and outdated scholarly education or to plain ignorance is not clear; anyway, the macaronic Latin had been a predominant comic feature of the character ever since Commedia erudita.

The Dottore wore a black costume with a very large hat and often carried heavy books to represent the learned but stupid and boastful 'type' of the pedantic charlatan. Everything in his gesture and appearance revealed his vacuous ridiculousness and verbal extravagance, which he displayed on stage by giving unrequited advice to Pantalone in a highly codified oral virtuosity called *gratianatoria*. These nonsensical monologues (*tirate*) were full of wordplays, illogical conclusions, misunderstandings, Latin blunders and ill-quoted references to the classics.[66] Due to the complexity and outward erudition of the speech genre, his parts were written in advance in commonplace books and then memorised to be used at the actor's discretion, as was the case for the Capitano.

Capitano

In the sixteenth century, there were two hyperbolic military characters on the Commedia dell'Arte stage: the bravo and the Capitano. The first was a destitute soldier reminiscent of Ruzante, who performed the basest deeds for money. By contrast, the Capitano was ridiculous but always followed noble ideals.

The Capitano is a direct offspring of Plautus' *miles gloriosus,* a boastful, pretentious and conceited soldier of fortune full of bravado. His costume featured a military dress of the period – often Spanish, to parody the soldiers occupying large parts of Italy – with an oversized weapon and "a mask with a long thin nose and a bristling moustache resembling iron spikes", as Duchartre describes it. His evocative names – Capitan Spavento (fright), Fracassa (smash), Spezzaferro (iron breaker), Terremoto (earthquake), Rinoceronte (rhinoceros), Coccodrillo (crocodile) – revealed the pettiness of the character.[67] Due to an outsized ego, the military would-be hero produced a series of self-representations which clashed with his pusillanimity and turned him into a laughingstock.[68]

---

[65] See Sirio Ferrone, *La Commedia dell'Arte: Attrici e attori italiani in Europa (XVI-XVIII secolo)* (Torino: Einaudi, 2014), p. 42.
[66] See Lea, *IPC*, vol. 1, p. 27.
[67] Duchartre, *The Italian Comedy*, p. 24.
[68] See Henke, op. cit., p. 24. Henke also explains that the comic force behind the Capitano character was the incongruity between word and deed, boasting and fact, just as in

In the asymmetrical character constellation of Commedia dell'Arte, the braggart was alone or sometimes accompanied by a servant called Trappola (trap). As Hinck points out, the name Trappola referred to the metaphorical trap the servant laid to the naive captain by asking him to narrate his heroic deeds and encouraging him to exaggerate even more.[69] While the Capitano's speech genres ranged from unrealistic *bravure* (boasts) to *ingiurie* (insults) and *minacce* (threats), his servant's impertinent asides directed at the audience exposed the character's vanity. Some examples of the Capitano's absurdity and extravagance connect him to the lying Baron von Munchhausen and the braggart Vincentio Ladislao, protagonist of a play by Duke Heinrich Julius, described in chapter 7.2.

In the early *scenari*, the Capitano was a soldier, close to the bravo, involved in adultery or turned out to be the lost son of either Pantalone or Dottore, but in the course of time he developed his own comic personality owing to the actors impersonating him. One of the most famous Captains was the multilingual actor and playwright Francesco Andreini (1548–1624), who spent a year as a slave in Turkish galleys in his youth and learned several languages, as Henke explains.[70] This personal background was woven into his stage character, for example when the Capitano makes ridiculous references to Spain and the Spanish language. Once retired, in 1607 Andreini published the hyperboles of the Capitano under the title *Le bravure del Capitano Spavento* ('The Brags of Captain Fright-All') to be preserved for future players.[71] Again, literarisation went hand in hand with the professionalisation of Commedia dell'Arte and had an impact on every single character.

Servetta (Franceschina)

Like many other stock characters of the Commedia dell'Arte, the 'type' of the waiting maid (*servetta* or *fantesca* in Italian) was already present in the Commedia erudita but mainly as an attendant to her lady and not as an autonomous personage with sweet diminutive names like Colombina, Corallina, Diamantina, Ricciolina, Pasquetta, Smeraldina and Franceschina.[72] This 'movable' part did not wear a

---

Shakespeare's Falstaff. There is no evidence of whether Falstaff was known directly to the Commedia dell'Arte troupes. One can only observe similarities between the characters: both were the target of numerous pranks due to their unfulfilled desire for most women on stage, although they were convinced to be heartthrobs (ibid.).

[69] See Walter Hinck, *Das deutsche Lustspiel des 17. und 18. Jahrhunderts und die italienische Komödie*, p. 112: "Weit entfernt davon, sich nur mit Geduld zu wappnen und den Bravaden zuzuhören, deren Hohlheit er am ehesten durchschaut, hat Trappola seine heimliche Lust daran, seinen Herrn zu noch gewaltigeren Gedankentaten anzutreiben und – wenn die Erinnerungs-, d.h. die Einbildungskraft einmal zum Atemholen ansetzt – mit eigenen Erfindungen weiterzuhelfen."

[70] See Henke, p. 175.

[71] Ibid., p. 176. A second volume of *Bravure* followed in 1618, and the two parts were reissued together in 1624. Moreover, in 1612 Andreini published *Ragionamenti fantastici, posti in forma di Dialoghi rappresentativi* ('Fantastic discourses in dialogic form').

[72] See Treccani, *Enciclopedia italiana delle Scienze, Lettere ed Arti*, p. 943.

mask, spoke Milanese, Tuscan or even Neapolitan and functioned as an advisor, messenger, meddler and female counterpart to the Zanni.[73] She was often admired for her beauty and sharp tongue, and was always on the lookout for a suitable husband, usually Arlecchino. With their outspokenness and practical jokes Arlecchino and Franceschina mirrored and parodied their young Innamorati employers while at the same time they fooled their old ones, Pantalone and Dottore. Of course, ultimately everyone complied, and the plot ended merrily with the archetypal rite of passage from old to new. It is not a coincidence that Franciscina (sic!) is the maid's name in the German adaptation of Shakespeare's *Merchant of Venice*, i.e. *Der Jud von Venedig* analysed in chapter 7.1.

In summary, each mask embodied a stereotyped social role with specific character traits, a speaking name, a costume that indicated the character's position, an individual speech genre and a dialect. This array of versatile comic elements lent itself to improvisation and enjoyed great success throughout Europe thanks to the wandering troupes who adapted their acting style to suit different contexts.

3.3. The Trade: Troupes, Actors and Repertoire

The art, skills and masks of Commedia dell'Arte drew their force from a unique amalgamation of Commedia erudita, antique models and popular elements like the *buffoni* tradition. As soon as the form became established, it quickly turned into a commercial venture expanding even abroad and becoming 'fixed' in written texts. This interplay of professionalisation, literarisation and touring is the focus of this section.

There are several business models connected to popular theatre in early sixteenth-century Italy, which show the importance of orality in a pre-literary society and reflect the numerous influences that shaped Commedia dell'Arte. For Robert Henke the trade of entertainment could assume the following forms: 1) the "piazza tradition" of mountebanks and *buffoni* or *cantastorie* (minstrels or ballad singers) who addressed the audience's oral memory of tales, songs and ballads. This model echoes the popular roots of Commedia dell'Arte and was similar to 2) the "oral agreement" between *buffoni* and sovereigns to obtain a licence, as opposed to 3) the democratic written contract in "fraternal companies". The ensuing developments witnessed a dignification of the players owing to 4) "court patronage", which encouraged travelling with letters of recommendation and passports. There were also independent performances in city halls or assembly rooms called 5) "*stanze* performances". Other ways of entertaining extra-courtly crowds were the mercantile 6) "proto-bourgeois models" of entrepreneur-based companies for the public market. If the manager was at the same time the leading actor of the company with shared rights, it is more correct to speak of 7) the "*capocomico* model", soon the most successful touring concept, which moved away from the streets and

---

[73] See Miklaševskij, op. cit., p. 55.

became subordinate to courtly power.[74] All these forms provide an idea of the continuum between mountebank spectacles and honourable professional companies determined by orality rather than written texts. However, with the professionalisation of theatre, written texts like contracts, promptbooks and, later, drama, gained increasing importance.

The first documented Commedia dell'Arte contract between members of a professional Italian theatre company dates from 1545 under the guidance of actor-dramatist Ser Maphio dei Re, aka Zanin in Padua.[75] This departure from civically or clerically funded amateur theatre represents a capitalistic innovation which combined the oral agreement with the democratic fraternal company led by a *capocomico*, to use Henke's terms.[76] At the same time, the "piazza tradition" was elevated to a courtly level and ready to expand onto the national and international public market. The official agreement included the exact duration of the tour, the extent of profit-sharing with deductions for common expenses and the chores of each member of the company, with a double function. On the one side, it guaranteed financial support for the actors and reinforced the mutual dependence and unity within the troupe, which was vital for improvisation. On the other, it provided a certain degree of security and protection which paved the way for the development of other similar contracts between professional actors throughout Italy and encouraged touring.

Initially, as in the case of the first itinerant players in England, the Commedia dell'Arte troupes consisted of twelve actors and were organised democratically without aristocratic patronage, although they increasingly adapted their repertoire to the courts, as Sirio Ferrone points out.[77] The practical, social and political difficulties tied to an itinerant life were regulated in a cooperative way, and each member had precise responsibilities such as obtaining a licence, replenishing the stock of plays and props or making sure the performance was well accepted.

In time, patronage became a key element for the companies' economic survival in Italy. Even if courtly productions were subdued to the taste of the duke, it was more profitable to play for a small noble audience than for a large public in hired rooms or on the streets, also due to the strict licensing policies and the high taxes imposed by the civic authorities. Although censure was part and parcel of the theatre business as in Shakespeare's day, the transitory nature of the shows for an audience of commoners allowed a greater freedom of expression, and actors got away with staging bawdier material. Still, the main aim of a company was to be considered respectable in order to have access to the courts in Italy and abroad.

As Roberto Tessari argues, a way of ennobling the profession was to turn the business into a 'brand' with a recognisable denomination connected to artistic and

---

[74] Henke, *Performance and Literature in the Commedia dell'Arte*, p. 10.
[75] See Pandolfi, *Il teatro del Rinascimento e la Commedia dell'Arte*, p. 139.
[76] See Henke, op. cit., p. 10.
[77] See Sirio Ferrone, *Attori, mercanti, corsari: La Commedia dell'Arte in Europa tra Cinque e Seicento* (Torino: Einaudi, 2011 [1993]), p. 78.

moral values that underlined their interest in culture rather than in commerce.[78] While in the first half of the sixteenth century troupes were named after their leading actor, from around 1560 companies with descriptive fanciful names flourished after the model of the established literary, scientific and scholarly Academies like the Intronati in Siena or the Accademia Fiorentina. The most important companies were the Comici Gelosi ('The Zealous Comedians', a name derived from their motto, *Virtù, fama ed honor ne fèr gelosi* 'We are zealous of attaining virtue, fame and honour') and the Confidenti ('The Confident').[79] Despite the shifting number of ten to fifteen members and frequent re-organisations, their success depended on the internal unity necessary for improvisation and consolidated through family ties. In 1574 the Gelosi and Confidenti merged to become I Comici Uniti ('The United or Union of Comedians') for two years and then split up again in 1577, when Flaminio Scala became the leader of the Gelosi, substituting for Drusiano Martinelli.[80] He was followed by Francesco Andreini, who dissolved the Gelosi in 1604 after his wife and co-actress Isabella's death.[81] A part of the company continued as the Fedeli ('The Faithful') under his son Giovan Battista Andreini aka Lelio at the Mantuan Gonzaga court and performed in Prague and Vienna between 1627 and 1629. The rest of the troupe became the Accesi ('The Enlighted/Enflamed') and travelled to Vienna and Linz under Pier

---

[78] See Tessari, p. 67.

[79] See Riha, p. 56. He adds that the Compagnia dei Gelosi was one of the first Commedia dell'Arte companies. The renowned Arlecchino performer Alberto Naseli aka Zan Ganassa visited Mantua (1568) and Ferrara (1570) and reached Lyons in 1571 as well as Spain in 1574, where he played at the Corral de la Pacheca in Madrid at the presence of Lope de Vega. The members of Ganassa's company who did not follow him, established a new troupe called the Gelosi, soon the most renowned Italian travelling company. They acted in Milan in 1658, in northern Italy until 1571, in Blois and Paris from 1577 to 1579, where they might have met English actors. They were back in Italy in 1603 and again in France in 1604.

[80] See Pandolfi, *Il teatro del Rinascimento e la Commedia dell'Arte*, pp. 340–7.

[81] Isabella Andreini (1562–1604) was perhaps the most famous Commedia dell'Arte actress, so celebrated in the role of Innamorata that she served as a template for this role in Flaminio Scala's collection of *scenari*. But she was also a highly educated member of scholarly Academies, writer and playwright of numerous dialogues and rhetorical disputes on the role of the Innamorati, on comedy, tragedy and other genres. These texts were posthumously collected by her husband Francesco Andreini in 1616 and issued by her colleague Flaminio Scala in 1621. See Vito Pandolfi, *Isabella comica gelosa: Avventure di maschere* (Rome: Edizioni moderne, 1960) for a detailed biography and bibliography. According to Kathleen McGill, Isabella Andreini worked hard to dispel the prejudice of being a 'public woman' because of her 'immoral' profession. At the head of a theatrical dynasty, her career paved the way for the later rise of the operatic prima donna. With her most famous role as crazy Isabella in *La Pazzia D'Isabella* ('Isabella's madness') in 1589 she contributed to the gradual development of the *amour fou* theme in a feminine ambit. In that case, folly became comic, and the shrew would be cured from her 'insanity' by means of punishment and taming (as in Shakespeare's *Taming of the Shrew*). See Kathleen McGill, "Women and Performance: The Development of Improvisation by the Sixteenth-Century Commedia dell'Arte", *Theatre Journal* 43.1 (1991), pp. 59–69.

Maria Cecchini aka Fritellino, who was even given a peerage by Emperor Matthias in Innsbruck in 1614, as Alberto Martino records.[82]

Ever since its emergence, Commedia dell'Arte was an itinerant form of entertainment for practical reasons: vagrancy granted independence from the control of a single patron and offered more opportunities to perform the same repertoire to diverse audiences.[83] Italian troupes travelled more continuously than their English colleagues because Italy lacked a great urban and cultural epicentre comparable to London with its stable theatres for a large public. From the 1570s, many companies regularly toured Europe for financial gain, often following the routes of previous actors who were not yet part of Commedia dell'Arte.

First, the Commedia dell'Arte troupes moved from court to court in northern Italy, giving performances for the civic audience as well. Then, the major itineraries between 1560 and 1630 went across the borders. As Walter Hinck explains, Linz and Vienna were the first stops of the Gelosi in 1565; other Commedia dell'Arte troupes performed in Bavaria (1568), Prague (1624, 1628) and again Vienna (1568–9, 1614, 1660), where the highly estimated Giovanni Tabarino was court actor from 1568 to 1574.[84] As Italian comedy and culture were part of a patrician upbringing at any European court, Commedia dell'Arte troupes like the Confidenti and the Accesi entertained noble audiences proficient in the Italian language throughout the sixteenth and seventeenth centuries. In the course of time, *intermezzi* with 'types' and extemporised scenes made their appearance even in German Baroque operas and Jesuit drama, proving the naturalisation of the foreign influence, especially in the genesis of the later *Wiener Volkstheater*. However, it was still a pleasure for the few, at least until the Commedia dell'Arte repertoire become accessible to the masses through puppet theatre in German.[85]

Apart from that, France hosted Commedia dell'Arte actors from 1571, especially due to the presence of Italian patrons such as Caterina and Maria de' Medici. The 1615 performance of the Confidenti under Flaminio Scala in Paris paved the way for the *Comédie italienne* and its impact on Molière (1622–73).[86] Other coun-

---

[82] See Alberto Martino, "Fonti tedesche degli anni 1565–1615 per la storia della Commedia dell'Arte e per la costituzione di un repertorio dei *lazzi* dello Zanni", in Martino and De Michele, ed., *La ricezione della Commedia dell'Arte nell'Europa centrale 1568–1769*, pp. 13–68, p. 25.

[83] See Ferrone, *La Commedia dell'Arte: Attrici e attori italiani in Europa (XVI-XVIII secolo)*, p. 62.

[84] See Hinck, *Das deutsche Lustspiel des 17. und 18. Jahrhunderts und die italienische Komödie*, p. 65.

[85] In 1658, Pietro Aggimondi started staging Commedia dell'Arte plays for a wide public in the Judenplatz in Vienna with marionettes called *bambozen/bambocci*.

[86] Alberto Martino recounts that Molière saw the *Comediens Italiens* at the Petit-Bourbon in 1658 and at the Palais-Royal between 1662 and 1673 and was so impressed by the actor Tiberio Fiorilli playing Scaramouche that he inserted him in his plays. See *Die italienische Literatur im deutschen Sprachraum: Ergänzungen und Berichtigungen zu Frank-*

tries visited were England from 1572 and Spain from 1574 onwards. Tessari indicates further successful tours in France, Austria and Germany, where the Commedia dell'Arte players most likely encountered the English Comedians, with stops in Dresden, Nördlingen, Nuremberg, Stuttgart, Regensburg, Augsburg, Frankfurt, Cologne and Strasbourg, Danzig, Warsaw, Denmark and Saint Petersburg.[87]

Given the European dimension of the touring circuit, it may not be a coincidence that the first detailed written account of a Commedia dell'Arte performance and the oldest extant *scenario* corresponding to it refer to Germany. On the occasion of Duke Wilhelm V's wedding to Renate of Lothringen, on 8 March 1568 the Fleming Orlando di Lasso and the Neapolitan Massimo Troiano organised a "Commedia all'improvviso all'italiana" in three acts.[88] Since the performers were musicians and amateurs, we cannot properly speak of a touring troupe or even of professional Commedia dell'Arte actors. Still, the lengthy account of the event written by Troiano himself (*Dialoghi* in three books published in Munich in 1568 and in Venice a year later) is a valuable source of metatheatrical information about the actors and the plot.[89] In 1575 the duke had a great staircase decorated with Commedia dell'Arte scenes and characters called Fools' Staircase as a synonym for professional comedians. Although the frescos at Landshut-Trausnitz castle do not represent the scenes described by Troiano, the *Narrentreppe* is an important pictorial record of the deep impact Italian popular theatre had in Germany.[90] Soon, more plays with Commedia dell'Arte 'types' started to appear, like the Neo-Latin comedy *Turbo* (1616) by the Protestant scholar Johann Valentin Andreae, the first play to include a servant with the French name of Arlecchino, Harlequin.[91]

Rutger Hausmanns Bibliographie (Chloe, Beihefte zu Daphnis. Amsterdam: Rodopoi, 1994), p. 407.

[87] See Tessari, op. cit., 66.
[88] See Vianello, *L'arte del buffone*, p. 123, and Lea, *IPC*, vol. 1, p. 6.
[89] "FORTUNIO: The Excellent Messer Orlando di Lasso was the Magnifico, Messer Pantalone di Bisognosi; Messer Giovanni Battista Scholari da Trento, the Zanni; Massimo played three parts, the prologue of the awkward rustic, the lover Polidoro, and the Spanish desperado, called Don Diego di Mendozza. Don Carlo Livizano was Polidoro's servant, and the Spaniard's man was Gregorio Dori from Trento. The Marquis of Malaspina took the part of Camilla the courtesan who was in love with Polidoro. Ercole Terzo was her servant, and there was also a French servant." Massimo Troiano, *Dialoghi*, translated by Lea in *IPC*, vol. 1, p. 7.
[90] As the frescos are too fragile to be shown to the public, the castle of Trausnitz offers a virtual tour, <https://www.burg-trausnitz.de/deutsch/burg/narren.htm> (last accessed 26 October 2020).
[91] For a detailed analysis of the play see Walter Hinck, *Das deutsche Lustspiel des 17. und 18. Jahrhunderts und die italienische Komödie*, ch. 3, and Ralf Böckmann, *Die Commedia dell'Arte und das deutsche Drama des 17. Jahrhunderts: Zu Ursprung und Einflussnahme der italienischen Maskenkomödie auf das literarisierte deutsche Drama* (Nordhausen: Traugott Bautz, 2010), ch. 7.3. This evidence confutes Joel B. Lande's argumentation that Commedia dell'Arte was not at the core of German comic theatre because

Alongside contracts, letters and historical records, the sphere of written records surrounding Commedia dell'Arte also includes the literarisation of the repertoire. The main sources documenting this process are Vito Pandolfi's monumental study in six volumes *La Commedia dell'Arte: Storia e testo* (1957) and the collection *I canovacci della Commedia dell'Arte* edited by Anna Maria Testaverde (2007), which contains all the works by Flaminio Scala (1611), Basilio Locatelli (1628/32),[92] Ciro Monarca,[93] and the abbot Placido Adriani (1734–9),[94] as well as miscellaneous anonymous texts collected by seventeenth-century scholars and held at the Corsinian Library in Rome (1621–42),[95] the Vatican Library, the Correr Library in Venice and the National Library in Florence. In the analysis of the English Comedians' plays in Germany I will return to these collections to pinpoint commonalities.

These theatrical documents are not play texts, as the actors of Commedia dell'Arte were skilled in playing semi-improvised scenes loosely summarised in a schematic *canovaccio*. Instead of precise lines for each character, the *canovaccio* contained an outline of every turn of the plot, usually structured in one dominant

  Harlequin made his first regular appearance a century after the English Comedians' arrival and, even then, mediated via France and not directly through the itinerant companies. See *Persistence of Folly*, p. 40.

[92] *Della scena de' sogetti comici* by Basilio Locatelli in two volumes (1628 and 1632, held at the Biblioteca Casanatense of Rome) is an important collection of plays with a preliminary discourse to the reader in each volume. Locatelli was not an actor like Scala but an amateur scholar close to the Roman Academies who wanted to render pre-existing *scenari* 'civilized' by means of a theoretical apparatus. He argues that unnecessary buffoonery must be avoided in literary plays and left to the mercenary public players. This sharp distinction between academic and street culture already marked the death of Commedia dell'Arte as popular theatre. Nonetheless, the 103 collected *scenari* (60 comedies, 20 farces, 12 tragicomedies, 8 pastorals, one heroic play based on *Orlando Furioso* and 2 tragedies) give a good overview of the contemporary dramatic genres and plots. Francesco Andreini, Andrea Perrucci, Pier Maria Cecchini and Nicolò Barbieri aka Beltrame were famous editors too, but not reformers and regulators like the later playwrights Carlo Gozzi and Carlo Goldoni.

[93] Ciro Monarca is a pseudonym of the anonymous author of *Dell'opere regie* ('Royal works'). Under the influence of the Spanish *siglo de oro*, this mid-sixteenth-century collection of 48 *scenari* was based on the repertoire of the Florentine companies and focussed on historical themes, tragedies inspired by Spanish and Elizabethan drama, and episodes from romance like *Orlando furioso*. See Alberto Martino "Fonti tedesche degli anni 1565–1615 per la storia della Commedia dell'Arte e per la costituzione di un repertorio dei *lazzi* dello Zanni", in Martino and De Michele, ed., *La ricezione della Commedia dell'Arte nell'Europa centrale 1568–1769*, pp. 13–68, p. 50.

[94] Placido Adriani's manuscript collection at the Augustan library of Perugia bears the title *Selva, ovvero zibaldone di Concetti Comici* ('Multitude or miscellany of comical concepts').

[95] Among the Commedia dell'Arte texts at the Biblioteca Corsiniana in Rome, there is the famous anonymous collection of 100 *scenari* entitled *Scenari più scelti d'Istrioni* ('Choicest *scenari* of the comedians') in two volumes, which belonged to the Cardinal Moritz of Savoy and has been in possession of the library since 1736.

and one secondary romantic plot of love, intrigue and mistaken identities. Later, more precise and defined *scenari* emerged. They included not only the list of characters and props (*robbe*), the subject matter and the salient moments, but also the style of conversation, grouping, gestures and stage directions the actors had to follow, being allowed only to fill the blank spaces in-between with extemporisation. It should be noted that the *canovacci* contained merely the plot of a play, written exclusively for professionals or amateurs, and were not meant to be read by the audience. In a tradition based on a combination of orality and physical performance, theatre could never be just a text for reading; nor was it desirable to stage a play the same way over and over again. To facilitate the mise-en-scène, *scenari* were frequently accompanied by commonplace books with stock scenes, jokes and speeches composed by the players or adapted from other plays. Moreover, they were enriched by iconographic details about the scenography, costumes and masks of the time.

Apart from the already mentioned actor-playwright Francesco Andreini, who published *Le bravure del Capitano Spavento* (Venice, 1607/1618) and the literary remnants of his wife Isabella's roles and speeches as a model for future actors, his colleague Flaminio Scala (1552–1624), director of the Gelosi, also felt the need to memorialise the ephemeral oral performances through literarisation. For Henke, Scala's *Il teatro delle favole rappresentative overo la Ricreatione Comica, Boscareccia e Tragica, / Divisa in cinquanta Giornate* (1611) stands out among the almost a thousand mostly anonymous *scenari* compiled between 1611 and 1734 as "ideal macrocosm of theatrical archetypes"[96] as well as the first appearance of Harlequin within the framework of a printed play.[97] The 'Theatre of the Represented Fables or Fairy Tales or the Comic, Woodland/Pastoral and Tragic Recreation Subdivided into 50 Days' contains 48 *canovacci*: 39 comedies based on love intrigues, one tragicomedy, one tragedy, one pastoral and others of mixed genres. Each skeletal plot is introduced by a short summary called *argomento* and a list of dramatis personae and props. The characters are then arranged as they enter, and there is a short description of what they do to unfold the plot, but the lines are left to the actors. Every company would therefore give a different delivery of the same *canovaccio* and, even within one company, every performance would be slightly different depending on the actors' interpretation.

Unlike Andreini, Scala did not focus on his character alone but collected the most successful plays performed by his company; and unlike Basilio Locatelli's academic collection *Della Scena de' Soggetti Comici* (1628/32), which aimed at 'civilising' the plots, Scala provided other practitioners with a pool of 'real' plays. The fact that he presented himself as a deliverer of already existing scenic material performed during his career was in line with the authorless tradition of Commedia dell'Arte, although, by printing them, he laid claim to a sort of copyright of ideas.

---

[96] Henke, *Performance and Literature in the Commedia dell'Arte*, p. 187.
[97] Nicoll, *The World of Harlequin*, p. 1. Henry F. Salerno translated Scala into English as *Scenarios of the Commedia dell'Arte: Flaminio Scala's 'Il Teatro delle favole rappresentative'* (New York: New York UP, 1967).

The novelty admired by his contemporaries was that this oral treasure could become a printed text without unnecessary additions and alterations, preserving the oral nature and the possibility of extemporising.[98] This made the collection unique and independent from conventional written drama, until 'proper' playwrights like Carlo Goldoni responded to the audiences' desire for a refined entertainment in a literary style by setting up new rules which relegated Commedia dell'Arte to the page. Still, Scala's choice of leaving out the Zannis and the *lazzi* already indicates a movement in the direction of literary ennoblement, later pursued by Locatelli and Goldoni.

As Scala's collection shows, the genres could range from comedy, tragicomedy and tragedy to dramatised mythological tales and romances. According to their content, Nicoll subdivides Commedia dell'Arte comedies into cuckolding comedies, romance comedies (concerned with passion, jealousy and friendship) and intrigue comedies (featuring disguise, mistaken identities, cross-dressing etc.).[99] One might add the pastoral comedy as a further subgenre, which connects Commedia to the 'high' culture of the Academies but also heightens the comic effect of magic. The *Leitmotiv* common to all genres is generally the love story between the Innamorati, hindered by the old men and aided by the servants as in the Plautian and erudite comedy.

An example of a hybrid genre favoured by Commedia dell'Arte is tragicomedy, which borrows elements from romance, pastoral, farce and Commedia erudita. Giambattista Guarini, author of the tragicomedy *Il Pastor Fido* ('The Faithful Shepherd', Venice 1590) with a preliminary compendium called *Compendio della poesia tragicomica* (1601–2) was the initiator of the trend.[100] Soon, both the literary model for and the theoretical apology of tragicomedy were readily accepted abroad. England recognised it as 'mixed mode' also owing to John Fletcher's translation of Guarini in 1610, as G. K. Hunter states.[101] Even before that, many of Shakespeare's plays such as *Hamlet, Othello, Measure for Measure, All's Well That Ends Well* and *Twelfth Night* already count as tragicomedies, which were so in vogue at the time. Points in common between English drama and Commedia dell'Arte like these hybridisations are the topic of the next chapter.

---

[98] See the eulogistic introduction to Flaminio Scala's collection written by his fellow actor Francesco Andreini.

[99] See Nicoll, *The World of Harlequin*, pp. 127–41.

[100] In his *Compendio*, Guarini gives the following definition of tragicomedy: "A tragi-comedy is not so called in respect of mirth and killing, but in respect of its want of deaths, which is enough to make it no tragedy, yet brings some near it, which is enough to make it no comedy, which must be a representation of familiar people, with such kind of trouble as no life be questioned, so that a god is as lawful in this as in tragedy, and mean people as in comedy." Translated by John Fletcher in the preface to *The Faithful Shepherdess* in Fredson Bowers, ed., *The Dramatic Works in the Beaumont and Fletcher Canon* (Cambridge: CUP, 1976), p. 250.

[101] See G. K. Hunter, "Italian Tragicomedy on the English Stage", *Renaissance Drama* 6 (1973), pp. 123–48, p. 130.

To conclude this short overview of Commedia dell'Arte the following points need to be stressed: the key to the early and immediate success of the *Commedia all'italiana* resides in its easily recognisable 'types', derived from Roman characters and Renaissance erudite drama. Common sources interlinked academic and popular comedy in Italy, and Commedia dell'Arte often accentuated the dramatic effectivity of neoclassical plots or *novelle*. As a product of amalgamation tied to orality, physicality and improvisation it could easily adapt to new circumstances when the established troupes started to travel for economic gain. Overcoming linguistic and logistic difficulties, Italian wandering troupes achieved resounding success in the noble and popular environments of their host countries thanks to a common basis of understanding rooted in popular culture. For instance, the Commedia dell'Arte characters representing universal human traits were certainly helpful in the exportation process and had a far-reaching echo throughout Europe. In the course of time, Commedia dell'Arte developed independently from Italian actors and underwent a similar 'backwards involution' witnessed in the English itinerant players. Since the audiences abroad were unaccustomed to this form of theatre and not immersed in the same context as the actors, touring companies had to reduce the spoken parts and rely on visual slapstick and physicality. At court, where Italian was comprehensible, the acting style witnessed a refined and literary appropriation of the 'arte' as drama; at the same time, for large public audiences, the 'commedia' developed as parallel, oral and popular theatre. Thus, the two components of popular orality and erudite literacy, which are at the core of this form of theatre, contributed to its significant impact abroad. Once the literarisation process took over, Commedia dell'Arte could more easily be relocated to other European countries, albeit in a simplified and trivialised form. For this reason, it lends itself as a visible example of intercultural theatricality: in England, the Italianate influence left traces in Elizabethan theatre and, in later centuries, the characteristic qualities of Commedia dell'Arte were reduced to pantomime and puppetry like the Punch and Judy characters.[102] Moreover, the literature and dramaturgy of German popular theatre and, later, of the Viennese *Volkstheater* are deeply indebted both to English and Italian popular theatre. By focussing on Commedia dell'Arte and its relationship with English and German drama, I do not intend to argue that it was the only influence but want to stress the points in common and the merit the touring companies from Italy and England had in fostering professional theatre in Germany and Austria.

---

[102] As Miklaševskij argues, Pulcinella's black and white costume was taken over by the French Polchinelle or Pierrot, and the name Pulcinella was transferred to the British puppet Punch. See Miklaševskij, op. cit., p. 54. According to the *Encyclopaedia Britannica*, the puppet Punch, in full Punchinello, derived from the Italian Pulcinella, with whom he shared the hook-nosed, humpback and costume. He came to be the most popular of marionettes and glove puppets in the Punch-and-Judy puppet shows. See <https://www.britannica.com/ topic/Punch-puppet-character> (last accessed 10 September 2019).

4. Elizabethan Theatre and the Italianate Influence

This chapter aims to broadly reconstruct the cultural context of the last decades of the sixteenth century, in which Elizabethan drama and theatre[1] became professionalised and were exported. In Shakespeare's time, Italian Commedia dell'Arte was already travelling and inspiring the cultural environment in Italy and abroad. The connection to popular culture as well as the international influences of Italian drama and Commedia dell'Arte appear evident when looking at the various dimensions of early modern Elizabethan theatre. Apart from the distinction between 1) *theatre* as an event and a set of performative skills and 2) *drama* as a literary play, proposed by Anne Baesecke and Richard Schechner,[2] there is the dimension of 3) *theatricality* as the ability to adapt to circumstances, which in the process of professionalisation entails a) the internal organisation and administration of the company; b) the business environment of patronage, licensing and censure; c) the physical space: venues, time and place of performance; and d) changes to the repertoire in order to respond to the environment and the audience, especially when touring (*intercultural theatricality*). These aspects will be investigated here, as has been done with Commedia dell'Arte, to detect areas of common ground wherever possible.

Comparing the historical development of professional theatre in England and Italy, it will be argued that the bloom of Elizabethan drama was connected to playwrights and specific physical spaces like playhouses, whereas Commedia dell'Arte was the vagrant product of orality, which originated from the marketplaces and flourished at court. In spite of these differences, when analysing the dramatic production of the two traditions, the Italianate influence and, more specifically, that of Commedia dell'Arte can be retraced in English theatre of the time. This was partly due to a shared network of knowledge, both on a level of erudition and in popular culture, but also to direct contact on stage. In fact, a central commonality between Italian and English popular theatre is that they entailed touring; and this itinerancy and familiarity with adaptation facilitated the exportation of their repertoire to countries like Germany and Austria.

Let us start by examining the popular roots of Elizabethan theatre within a network of shared knowledge of which Commedia dell'Arte was also a part. The earlier, not yet professionalised forms of entertainment like mummers' plays and

---

[1] In the following sections, the terms 'Elizabethan theatre and drama' include early Jacobean theatre too, as the period of Shakespeare's productivity was in-between the reigns of Elizabeth I and James I, i.e. 1558–1603 and 1603–25.

[2] See Beasecke, *Das Schauspiel der englischen Komödianten in Deutschland*, pp. 3–7, and Schechner, *Performance Theory*, p. 71. Ralf Haekel further distinguishes between *Spiel* and *Text* in the sense of 'playing' and 'play'. See Haekel, *Die Englischen Komödianten in Deutschland*, p. 99.

morality plays have already been discussed along with their integration into literature. In Elizabethan drama, the continuity in function and subject matter was closely related to popular culture, both in the ambit of theatre as a set of performative skills and as dramatic text. Rituals of devotions to rulers, national heroes and Christian champions as well as a love of legendary and historical material were all powerful forces Elizabethan playwrights borrowed from the popular, as George Kernodle states.[3] However, these borrowings were usually not acknowledged since popular theatre was kept alive by performance and passed on through oral transmission or apprenticeship. In Joel Schechter's words, "it lives in bodies and voices, in their [the performers'] memories and stage acts, and those of people who know them; [...] and in that sense among others their theatre is popular", i.e. made for the people by the people and consisting of a common popular culture.[4] In this context, Diana Henderson warns against considering pre-Shakespearean society as a unified 'people', as it was neither an ideal folk culture nor a simple mass eager to be entertained. Although Elizabethan stagecraft was indebted to popular traditions, she argues that 'popular' or 'of the people' was not a compliment in Shakespeare's day.[5] Yet the actors and playwrights drew on this resource because it appealed to the new cultural 'consumers' of professional theatre: the common people.

In conjunction with the development of Elizabethan drama in a performative and literary sense, theatre became an increasingly *commercial venture*. A first impulse in this direction was the erection of custom-built playhouses, which guaranteed a certain independence from the court because the inhabitants of the city were a larger audience than the queen's entourage. Apart from the necessary internal and external organisation, such as contracts among troupe members and a sociocultural business environment regulating public spectacles by laws, licences, etc., the dimension of theatre as *physical space* was added. This special feature of the Elizabethan stage was different from Commedia dell'Arte, which used movable scaffold stages or designated areas at court. Therefore, it is worth giving a short overview of the constituents of a typical Elizabethan playhouse, later adapted by the itinerant players on the European continent. Its circular architecture with galleries evoked both the inn yards and arena theatres. The apron stage protruding into the audience space was ornamented with columns, a canopy called 'the heavens', where machinery could be hidden, and its counterpart, a trapdoor called 'hell'. Behind the façade of the tiring-house, the backstage area admitted access to the stage through three doors and could be concealed when required. Likewise, hangings and curtains would create separate closed spaces on the otherwise completely open stage, visible from all around. The elaborate costumes worn by the actors

---

[3] Kernodle, *From Art to Theatre: Form and Convention in the Early Modern*, p. 131.
[4] Schechter, *Popular Theatre*, p. 3.
[5] See Diana E. Henderson, "From popular entertainment to literature", in Shaughnessy, ed., *The Cambridge Companion to Shakespeare and Popular Culture*, pp. 6–25, p. 13.

matched the environment and insisted more on elegance than on historical accuracy. Similarly, props and scenery did not aim for scenic illusion.[6]

Evidently, apart from costumes and scenography – both being part of the physical space – the metaphorical "theatrical space" required the audiences' imaginative power as well. Jeremy Lopez defines the latter as "space collectively shared by the audience, wherein the physical space of the stage is transformed by representation and illusion."[7] The idea of making meaning collectively may be connected to a shared knowledge which contributes to understanding and response. It also shows that audiences were aware of the limitations of the early modern stage and overcame them thanks to conventions of theatricality, such as the use of symbolic props. In general, the effort of imagination on the part of the spectators was considerable and made performances with few stage elements possible, a useful procedure that facilitated travelling and contributed to the success of English players abroad, where they could not count on a proper venue.

As far as Elizabethan theatre as *drama* is concerned, hybrid genres like tragicomedy proliferated and became increasingly literate without losing their popular roots. Influenced by the rediscovery of classical drama in the Renaissance, the Elizabethan playwrights readily took up the impulses which had seeped in from the European continent and re-interpreted subject matter from English history, biblical tales and folklore on the basis of new rules derived from the Latin classics. According to Robert N. Watson, the breakthrough of Elizabethan theatre is located in Kyd's *Spanish Tragedy* and Marlowe's tragedies, since Marlowe "liberated English drama from the complacencies of both its academic and its popular conventions. As learned and popular drama commingled, the upper and lower classes became jointly invested in theatre."[8] Indeed, the plays were promulgated by state-of-the-art companies whose growing economic and cultural force derived from the large audiences in public playhouses. The social and cultural 'commingling' in theatre supports the idea of a shared knowledge, separated into high and low culture only a posteriori. For instance, the stock characters of domestic and revenge tragedy, such as the revenger, the malcontent, or the Machiavel, were modelled on allegories like Vice in the morality play and endowed with psychological depth. This pattern occurs in *Faustus*, *Hamlet* and *Othello*, as Watson argues.[9] Likewise, the mischief-maker Vice shaped the stereotypes of universal human foibles in comedy. Such use of character 'types' is one of many aspects which early Elizabethan drama shares with Commedia dell'Arte.

---

[6] For a more detailed description see E. K. Chambers, *The Elizabethan Stage* (Oxford: Clarendon Press, 1965 [1923]), vol. 2, chapter XVI.

[7] Jeremy Lopez, *Theatrical Convention and Audience Response in Early Modern Drama* (Cambridge: CUP, 2003), p. 6.

[8] Robert N. Watson, "Tragedy", in Braunmuller and Hattaway, ed., *The Cambridge Companion to English Renaissance Drama*, pp. 301–51, p. 312.

[9] Ibid., p. 338. In Watson's view, Othello's split personality makes him easy prey to Iago, and in this sense the character constellation resembles Faustus and the Devil, while

From a historical point of view, English professional troupes underwent a similar development to Commedia dell'Arte companies since both emerged from street theatre and then became respectable at court while still entertaining the masses thanks to democratic internal organisation. In both cases, courtly affiliations gave the necessary political and economic background to elevate the amateur performances to the level of professional theatre in a very short period. However, a major difference was that the most distinguished Commedia dell'Arte troupes exploited the diplomatic connections of their noble patrons to give guest performances throughout the Italian-speaking courts of Europe and therefore did not feel the need to adapt to the language and taste of the wider public. Conversely, the English companies who escaped from the saturated market of London became acclimatised on the Continent and stimulated the professionalisation of theatre there. Thus, the reasons for travelling explain the consequent different areas of imitation and emulation by the recipients (i.e. productive reception): Commedia dell'Arte inspired the arts and literature primarily in aristocratic circles, whereas the English Comedians taught German-speaking actors and playwrights how to reach a large audience with appealing theatrical productions.

Another difference lies in Commedia dell'Arte's independence from authors. By contrast, playwrights like Kyd, Marlowe and Shakespeare contributed significantly to the success of Elizabethan drama. Still, touring reduced the differences between the two since the English companies could not take their playhouse with them, and the Commedia dell'Arte practitioners started to write down the skeletal plots of their plays to make them more exportable. A closer look reveals further similarities in the two traditions' plays, both being based on a combination of Renaissance erudition and hybridised popular elements like dances, songs and stock characters which contributed to their success. Detecting adaptations and appropriations of plots or figures from Commedia dell'Arte in Shakespearean plays shows that Elizabethan drama was already a product of amalgamation before it was fruitfully exported to Germany and Austria. It was precisely this convergence of international elements that contributed to the bloom of Italian and English popular theatre and their adaptability to new cultural contexts in which they thrived.

4.1. Professional Companies: From Courtly Patronage to Public Entertainment

The earliest forms of popular performances in England were only loosely tied to the court and, if at all, more on an economic and political than on a cultural level. Initially, most public spectacles in London took place in courtyards with balustrades, in booth stages in the squares and in bear-baiting arenas, as Robert Weimann asserts. The lack of a permanent venue forced the actors to tour the

> Hamlet shares the tragic stature of Faustus and Othello. The sympathy Hamlet evokes is given by the fact that his cause is just but was not chosen by himself and takes a terrible toll.

country when they were not engaged at court.[10] Despite these precarious conditions, in the second half of the sixteenth century wandering troupes gained growing popularity and socio-economic power thanks to an emerging entertainment industry. As the demand for plays became stronger in the population, political restrictions from municipal and royal authorities increased: companies were tied to the court by a system of patronage, licensing and censure, which reduced their autonomy but gave them the necessary prestige and financial security to establish their own public playhouses and promulgate their repertoire for a large audience. Leo Salingar argues that although the court remained a powerful protection, London's theatres were neither courtly nor academic or guild-sponsored but developed a 'national' style of performance based on various models – the Inns of Court, medieval pageant waggons and contemporary influences from the Continent.[11] Here again one sees how fragile the concept of a 'national' style is, considering that it emerged from medieval performances immersed in popular culture, and that it was influenced by other international factors. In the course of time, the growing interdependency between private and public stages, and between permanent playhouses and street performances on tour had an impact on the production and reception of plays in England and abroad. In general, professional theatre increasingly moved from courtly patronage to public entertainment.

Between 1575 and 1580, only three companies of adult players were admitted at court: those of the Earl of Sussex, the Earl of Leicester and the Earl of Warwick, which slowly prevailed over the successful boy groups drawn from choirschools.[12] After the short season of revelries from Michaelmas to 6 January, i.e. Twelfth Night, or sometimes until Lent, these companies had to make a living by touring the country just as did the other semi-professional troupes not admitted at court.[13] This means that the itinerant life was well known to companies before noble sponsoring enabled them to build their own playhouses. Even then, the provinces continued to be a vital training ground.

---

[10] See Weimann, *Shakespeare und die Tradition des Volkstheaters*, pp. 21–3.
[11] See Salingar, *Shakespeare and the Traditions of Comedy*, p. 258.
[12] For a detailed account of the adult and boy companies see E. K. Chambers, *The Elizabethan Stage*, vol. 2, chapters XII and XIII. For Peter Thomson, the enduring success of child companies consisting of choristers from Saint Paul's and the Chapel Royal was due to several factors. Firstly, when they were not performing at court, they offered sophisticated spectacles in small private indoor theatres like the Blackfriars or the Curtain with a limited number of seats. Secondly, their repertoire catered to a more cultivated audience with morality plays, pastorals, classical comedies and musical interludes in-between acts. While in the 1570s child companies were ahead of adult players, their advance came to a standstill in the 1590s. Between 1600 and 1608 they went through a period of prosperity again before dissolving in 1613 due to the court's preference for adult companies. See Peter Thomson, "Playhouses and Players in the Time of Shakespeare", in Wells, ed., *The Cambridge Companion to Shakespeare Studies*, pp. 67–84, p. 71.
[13] See J. Leeds Barroll, Alexander Leggatt, Richard Hosley, and Alvin Kernan, ed., *The Revels History of Drama in English* (London and New York: Methuen, 1975), vol. 3, p. 4.

According to Willi Flemming, there were as many as 56 wandering troupes between 1540 and 1560.[14] Queen Elizabeth might have had these figures in mind when she promulgated a document dated 3 January 1572 to only allow companies with an official patron. All others were to be considered unlawful vagabonds (i.e. neither part of a guild, nor apprentices to a master, nor in possession of any land), against whom the Vagabond Act of 29 June 1572 was addressed.[15] The social advancement at court of peripatetic troupes of adults licensed by the patronage of some lord or courtier went hand in hand with their insertion into the urban fabric as providers of entertainment either privately or more frequently in public, as Erika Fischer-Lichte explains.[16] However, their reputation was still closer to that of dangerous vagabonds than to respectable professionals, and civic authorities felt the need to restrict the popularity of touring companies for fear they would bring physical and mental contamination, such as illnesses, loose morality and social upheaval. At the same time, the Master of Revels played a decisive role in the creation and control of theatre as a political and public institution right from the beginning. He could deny permission to perform and censor plays that were not in accordance with his moral principles.[17]

Apart from the strict regulations, a further aspect that encouraged touring companies to leave the city was that fewer actors and plays were needed to entertain audiences outside London. On these occasions, larger troupes would split, leaving a proportion of their members and repertoire behind or duplicating scripts and props. The itinerant players travelled through all the cities of a region with their material possessions packed in waggons and usually remained in the same place for up to fourteen days, according to Andrew Gurr's account of Shakespearean companies.[18] On tour, plays had to be shortened to suit the smaller number of performers, and complex scenes requiring special scenery or props were omitted. In other words, the actors made use of the same adaptation processes put into practice by the English Comedians in Germany a few decades later to confront similar difficulties. When the repertoire was exhausted, companies returned to London to replenish the stocks and increase their earnings during the city's theatre season.

Performing plays in different towns and creating venues at short notice was a Tudor norm even for troupes with aristocratic affiliations because it kept them flexible and independent. Despite the advantages of patronage, such as protection, prestige and official recognition, it was still a form of control, which influenced the plays and the place of performance, and thus also the price of the tickets. By the 1590s, the companies' independence from court had increased even more as

---

[14] See Willi Flemming, ed., *Barockdrama*, vol. 3, *Das Schauspiel der Wanderbühne*, p. 50.
[15] Ibid., p. 56.
[16] See Erika Fischer-Lichte, *Geschichte des Dramas: Epochen der Identität auf dem Theater von der Antike bis zur Gegenwart* (Tübingen: Francke, 1990), vol. 1, p. 95.
[17] Ibid.
[18] See Gurr, *The Shakespearian Companies*, p. 44.

their sphere of action reached a larger audience; surprisingly, this was made possible precisely by the court.

In 1583, Queen Elizabeth consented to have her own company, the Queen's Men, under her direct control. As E. K. Chambers maintains, it consisted of twelve actors, selected from the best companies and employed by the Lord Chamberlain, Henry Carey, 1st Baron Hunsdon, who was responsible for the programme at court, together with the Master of Revels Tilney, who oversaw royal entertainment and censorship.[19] Next to the Queen's Men, there were the companies of Lord Hunsdon, later renamed the Lord Chamberlain's Servants, and the Earl of Leicester's Men, who performed at court during the season of 1585–6.[20] After the death of the famous clown Dick Tarlton in 1588, the Queen's Men languished and ultimately dissolved in 1594. This date marks a watershed as their monopoly was succeeded by a 'duopoly' comprising the Lord Admiral's Men, patronised by Charles Howard, and the Lord Chamberlain's Servants.[21] The former were managed by the actor Edward Alleyn, son-in-law of the financier Philip Henslowe, and played at the Rose from 1587 to 1593, and then at the Fortune from 1600 onwards. The Lord Chamberlain's Servants were headed by James Burbage, erector of the first purpose-built theatre, the Theatre. Later, his son Richard Burbage took over at the Globe, of which Will Kemp, Shakespeare and others were shareholders from 1597. By 1603, the leading companies were transferred from courtly to royal patronage: the Chamberlain's Servants altered their name to the King's Men, the Worcester's Men became Queen Anne's Servants, and the Admiral's Men passed into the patronage of Prince Henry.[22]

The structural changes of 1594 strongly contributed to the professionalisation of theatre as an economic venture because they granted social acceptance to recognised actors and a secure income which allowed for the subsequent construction of new suburban playhouses. By virtue of this innovation, the major companies now had a fixed venue and did not have to perform at the Inns of Court anymore or travel the country to fill the intermissions between courtly engagements. That was the secret of the success of the Lord Chamberlain's and the Lord Admiral's Men and the safeguard of their 'duopoly' – an exclusive, stable playhouse. Custom-built playhouses like the Red Lion (1567), the Theatre (1576), the Curtain (1577), the Rose (1587) and later the Swan (1595) and the Globe (1599) progressively replaced improvised stages, and the improvement of performances with a

---

[19] See E. K. Chambers, *The Elizabethan Stage*, vol. 2, p. 104.
[20] Ibid., p. 105.
[21] See Leeds Barroll et al., ed., *The Revels History of Drama in English*, vol. 3, p. 16, from which I borrowed the concept of duopoly. The idea is also confirmed by a letter of the Privy Council to the Master of Revels on 19 February 1598: "Whereas licence hath bin grautned unto two companies of stage players retained unto us, the Lord Admyral and Lord Chamberlain, to use and practise stage players […] and none suffered hereafter to plaie but those two formerlie named belonging to us." Quoted in Chambers, *The Elizabethan Stage*, vol. 4, p. 325.
[22] See Schrickx, *Foreign Envoys and Travelling Players in the Age of Shakespeare and Jonson*, p. 203.

specific set of props, scenography and costumes attracted regular audiences, as R. A. Foakes explains.[23]

Apart from architectural advantages, a theatre offered the actors a secure existence tied to a collective internal association under the guidance of the leading actor, who was usually also impresario and licence holder. This form of management was common to the first professional companies in Italy, where Commedia dell'Arte troupes adopted a similar democratic sharing system (*capocomico* model)[24] because it granted financial security at times when the lack of a patron equalled precarity. As admission fees could not cover all expenses, the members of an Elizabethan company had to contribute to the finances by buying their share when they joined a company. In addition to rent and loans, they constituted their investment in a joint stock of playing apparel, properties and play texts, as sources like Philip Henslowe's diary prove.[25] More importantly, this sum of money made the shareholders team workers with equal rights, regulated by agreements and even fines when rules were broken. All decisions were taken together, and everybody could decide on a script's worth and on the readjustments to the repertoire, with plays being added with minimal time for rehearsal to increase income. In this sense, the writing of plays was what Gurr calls a "collective exercise" of the company members and in most troupes the actors were also playwrights, as in Shakespeare's case.[26] These 'authorless' and collage-like plays recall the *canovacci* of Commedia dell'Arte and represent another trait common to early modern English and Italian theatre.

The downside of a playhouse, however, was that it could be closed due to the plague or destroyed by fire, leaving the actors unemployed. Even for actors with noble patronage, there was little wealth or recognition, and an incessant demand for new material as well as a fierce competition among the few licensed companies made things even more difficult, as Jerzy Limon asserts.[27] For these reasons, the contingencies of touring represented a chance of survival and soon the more adventurous actors crossed the Channel in the 1590s. This led to an unprecedented migration to the mainland which was so important for the genesis of professional theatre there. The actors needed what Ernest Brennecke defines as "a new *Lebensraum*", where they could provide "the art offered in excess in London but of which most of Europe was starved": vocal and instrumental music, dancing, tumbling, clowning, splendid material and skilful stage adaptations.[28] In a short period of time, professional troupes of singers, acrobats and actors replaced the

---

[23] See R. A. Foakes, "Playhouses and Players", in Braunmuller and Hattaway, ed., *The Cambridge Companion to English Renaissance Drama*, pp. 1–52, p. 40.

[24] See Henke, *Performance and Literature in the Commedia dell'Arte*, p. 10.

[25] See the introduction to *Henslowe's Diary* edited by R. A. Foakes (2nd ed. Cambridge: CUP, 2002).

[26] See Gurr, *The Shakespearian Companies*, p. 99.

[27] See Jerzy Limon, *Gentlemen of a Company: English Players in Central and Eastern Europe, 1590–1660*, p. 4.

[28] Brennecke, *Shakespeare in Germany: 1590–1700*, p. 1.

amateur dramatic productions in Denmark, the Netherlands, Germany, Austria, Bohemia, and the Baltic route towards Danzig, Konigsberg and Elbing. Notably, the English Comedians avoided the areas dominated by Commedia dell'Arte, such as Italy, France, Spain, Austria and the south of Germany, although the actors occasionally crossed paths, for example at the Frankfurt fair.

When companies started touring abroad, the difficulty of the language barrier and the lack of venues had an impact on the plays, which had to be staged afresh every time. Moreover, the actors had to flexibly adapt the performance to the understanding and liking of the public. Despite the adverse conditions, they were well received, as Fynes Moryson (1566–1630), a contemporary, observed:

> Whereof I have seen some strangling broken Companeyes that passed into Netherland and Germany, followed by the people from one town to another, though they understood not their words, only to see theire action, yea marchants at Fayres bragged more to have seene them, then of the good markets they made.[29]

Improvisation after the model of the influential Commedia dell'Arte became a necessary and vital feature of adaptation in popular theatre, both on a verbal and a non-verbal level (i.e. meaning-making mechanisms connected to gesture, movement and material elements such as the stage, scenery, costumes and props), as Moryson's quote "though they understood not their words, only to see theire action" confirms.

These intriguing aspects of negotiation between imitation and emulation, adherence to the text and extemporisation were of great importance for the itinerant players in Germany. Just as they had done on tour in their home country, the wandering troupes from England exported the most celebrated plays of their time and adapted them to the audiences and venues. It is essential to point out that what they took to the mainland was already a product of amalgamation, influenced by various literary currents and performative styles and mediated not only through a bookish elite culture but also by touring companies.

These international transformations at the beginning of the seventeenth century can be identified as part of a wide-spread change in aesthetics, described in the next section. Proceeding chronologically, I will first investigate the Italianate ascendancy on the development of Elizabethan drama, before analysing how this amalgamation was transferred onto the German stage.

4.2. The Making of a Play: Italian and English Parallels

So far, the outline of the historical context in which Elizabethan theatre became professionalised in-between courtly patronage, playhouses and (inter)national touring circuits has already revealed points in common with Commedia dell'Arte

---

[29] Charles Hughes, ed., *Shakespeare's Europe: Unpublished Chapters of Fynes Moryson's Itinerary. Being a Survey of the Conditions in Europe at the End of the 16th Century* (Manchester: Sherratt and Hughes, 1903), vol. 4, p. 476.

as to emergence, internal organisation, surrounding legislative conditions and touring practices. Moving from *how* theatricality worked to *what* was produced, the dimensions of theatre as a set of skills/performance and of drama as dramatic text will come into focus here in order to detect possible intercultural affinities. In particular, the following questions shall be examined: How did the Italianate influence contribute to English theatre? Are the two types of theatre part of a network of shared knowledge? And if so, can similar changes in Elizabethan drama and Commedia dell'Arte possibly account for an arising early modern aesthetics connected to the professionalisation of theatre? A comparison of the innovations on the Italian and English stage shall shed light on the matter.

In 1578, the Queen authorised the Master of Revels Tilney to recruit companies of adult players, from which the Queen's Men and later the successful 'duopoly' of the Lord Chamberlain's Servants and Lord Admiral's Men would ensue. Incidentally, the officialisation of these courtly companies coincided with the first advent of "one Drousiano, an Italian, a commediante, and his companye"[30] to London in January 1577. London was not the first city to host Italian performers in general,[31] but it was most probably the place where Commedia dell'Arte debuted in England with the Mantuan actor-manager Drusiano Martinelli, his wife Angelica and his brother Tristano, one of the first actors to make Arlecchino famous abroad. Even though the Vagabond Act of 1572 limited the excessive power of foreign companies by allowing only those under patronage, Drusiano's company was granted permission to play in London by the Privy Council in 1573 and again in 1578, as Kathleen Lea records.[32] Historical documents like these prove that Italian performers in England were bound by the same rules as national troupes. From the literary works of the time we can ascertain that there was an

---

[30] Quoted in Chambers, *The Elizabethan Stage*, vol. 2, p. 262.

[31] The first debut of Italian touring companies in England dates from 1546/7, as an entry of the Norwich Chamberlain's accounts states: "Itm got reward on the Sonday being sent Jamys Evyn to certen Spanyards & Ytalyans who dawnsyd antycks & played diverse other feests at the Comon Halle before Mr Mayor & coialte 13/4." From the *Norwich Chamberlain's Accounts: Henry VII-Edward VI. 1546/7*, quoted in Lea, *IPC*, vol. 1, p. 352. This shows that international itinerant players entertained not only the courts but also the cities and towns. A second trace of "Ytalyans" is found again in the provinces: in Nottingham they were paid five shillings on 4 or 14 September "for serteyne pastymes that they shewed before Maister Meare and his brethren." From the *Nottingham Chamberlain's Accounts*, quoted in Lea, *IPC*, vol. 1, p. 355. One year later, Thomas Norton remonstrated against the "unchaste, shamelesse & unnaturall tomblinges of the Italian Woemen." Quoted in Chambers, *The Elizabethan Stage*, vol. 2, p. 262. From these scarce details it is difficult to deduce with certainty whether the Italian performers were only mountebanks, musicians and dancers or also actors of Commedia dell'Arte. Nor is it certain whether the Italian tumbler – probably Soldino of Florence – documented in 1575 at the Queen's Progress in Kenilworth in Robert Laneham's description and George Gascoigne *Princely Pleasures* (1576) performed Commedia dell'Arte plays or just acrobatic feasts. See Preeshl, *Shakespeare and Commedia dell'Arte: Play by Play*, p. XIV and p. 36.

[32] See Lea, *IPC*, vol. 1, p. 357.

active reception of Italian Commedia erudita and Commedia dell'Arte in theatre and drama. Examples are George Gascoigne's 1566 translation of Ludovico Ariosto's Commedia erudita *I Suppositi* (1509) or Nicholas Udall's first 'regular' comedy in English, *Ralph Roister Doister,* written in 1552 and published in 1567. According to Artemis Preeshl, it was modelled not only on the conventions established by the University Wits such as Christopher Marlowe, John Lyly and Thomas Nashe, but also on Anglicised Italian *buffone* performances which "popularised the braggart clowns in Elizabethan plays", suggesting that Italian spectacles reached England also through travelling actors.[33] Indeed, a lively exchange with Italian culture was made possible by ambassadors, exiles, spies and merchants as well as literati, artists and touring troupes from Italy at the Tudor court.

As soon as the first national companies settled down, the Italianate influence through foreign literatures and travelling individuals was strongly felt by playwrights and actors. By the 1580s, Italian comedies and characters found their way onto the stage in the form of masques,[34] testifying to a deep impact on play production and taste in England. Contemporary evidence of a shift in audience receptivity towards the Italianate style is found, for example, in Thomas Heywood's introductory poem to his *Apology for Actors* (1612), which recalls the *theatrum mundi* metaphor combined with a catalogue of Commedia dell'Arte characters populating the English world-stage:

> The world's a theatre, the earth a stage,
> Which God and nature doth with actors fill:
> Kings have their entrance in due equipage,
> And some there [sic!] parts play well, and others ill.

[33] Preeshl, *Shakespeare and Commedia dell'Arte*, p. 4. As Andrew Grewar suggests, the contact with Italian drama took place through Commedia dell'Arte performers rather than through reading. See "The Old Man's Spectacles: Commedia and Shakespeare", in Chaffee and Crick, ed., *The Routledge Companion to Commedia dell'Arte*, pp. 300–11, p. 300. Similarly, Henry F. Salerno argues that "the most important contact [between Elizabethan drama and Commedia dell'Arte] was by way of these traveling companies." Salerno, *The Elizabethan Drama and the 'Commedia dell'Arte'* (ProQuest Dissertations, 1956), p. 1.

[34] Masques were fully developed between 1604 and 1640 as central part of the Stuart court's Christmas festivities. Masked courtiers would dance and invite members of the noble audience to join their revels, while professional actors personifying allegories expounded their roles and virtues, as David Lindley explains. By contrast, early Baroque antimasques functioned as playful foil or false masque with grotesque figures, wild music and comic gesture, rooted in popular performances like the mummers' plays and pageant wagons. See David Lindley, "The Stuart masque and its makers", in Milling and Thomson, ed., *The Cambridge History of British Theatre*, vol. 1, pp. 384–98. Further examples of plays with Italian influences are *Dead Man's Fortune* (a lost musical play recalling Italian farces with disguises, intrigues and a hoaxed husband referred to as pantaloon in a stage direction for the first time in an English context), *The Masque of Flowers* (1613), *Blurt, Master Constable* (featuring Zanies and a masked ball), and an episode in Thomas Dekker's *If this ben't a Good Play, the Divel's in't*, as Henry F. Salerno analyses in *The Elizabethan Drama and the 'Commedia dell'Arte'*, pp. 21–3.

> The best no better are (in this theatre),
> Where every humor's fitted in his kinde;
> This a true subjects acts, and that a traytor,
> The first applauded, and the last confin'd,
> This plaies an honest man, and that a knave,
> A gentle person this, and he a clowne,
> One man is ragged, and another brave:
> All men have parts, and each man acts his owne.
> She a chaste lady acteth all her life;
> A wanton curtezan another playes;
> This vovets marriage love, that nuptial strife;
> Both in continual action spend their dayes:
> Some citizens, some soldiers, borne to adventer,
> Sheepheards, and sea men.[35]

Some of the most important 'types', such as Arlecchino (clown), Capitano/bravo (soldier), Innamorati or lovers (honest man/gentle person and chaste lady) as well as elements of romance (seamen, knaves,[36] kings, brave men) and pastoral plays (shepherds) are listed as familiar characters, regardless of their provenance. Noticing a changed interest in comedy, tragicomedy and tragedy at the beginning of the seventeenth century, Heywood links it to the Commedia dell'Arte characters so in vogue at that time. One might even speak of the emergence of a new aesthetics shaped by international models, especially of Italian origin, adapted to the English stage or appropriated by it.

In this new aesthetics, the functioning principles shared by Italian and English theatre in the making of a play are connected to the parameters used for the textual analysis in this work, notably to memorialisation and hybridisation. With the increase of touring companies, the other two parameters, adaptation and visualisation, gained more importance due to the different performative circumstances and audiences. For instance, Winifred Smith conjectures that during their stay in England, Drusiano Martinelli's company presented improvised pantomime in public performances while at court, but where Italian was spoken, they opted for literary pastorals and interludes. This adjustment of the repertoire to the cultural context of the spectators in the sense of Genette's "proximization", i.e. a temporal, geographic and social bringing closer of a text,[37] explains the almost antithetic opinions on Commedia dell'Arte spectacles of English authors, who either

---

[35] Thomas Heywood, *An Apology for Actors: In Three Books, from the Edition of 1612, Compared with That of W. Cartwright, with an Introduction and Notes* (London: Shakespeare Society, 1841), p. 13.

[36] Peter Thomson defines knaves as boyish characters devoted to mischief, roguery, and sexual curiosity. Usually played by young actors, they gradually replaced the fool in Jacobean theatre. See Thomson, "Clowns, fools and knaves: stages in the evolution of acting", in Milling and Thomson, ed., *The Cambridge History of British Theatre*, vol. 1, pp. 407–23, p. 420.

[37] *Palimpsests*, p. 304.

despised the characters' rudeness or praised their versatility.[38] Evidently, the aesthetic taste determining what is successful in theatre was shaped by the recipients as much as by the producers, in the sense of actors and authors. Since the role of the recipients is difficult to grasp, the focus here is set on the contribution of the producers in transforming the aesthetics from the precepts of Humanism towards a popular entertainment for the masses that occurred with the professionalisation of theatre in Italy and England.

A first point in common between English and Italian playwrights was the practice of dramatising *novelle*, myths, public events, and historical or biblical narrations or mixing plots with appealing strands from previous ones. The use of ancient as well as contemporary literature as the basis for new dramas is a form of salvaging memorialisation, although it goes through a series of transformations before it can be presented on stage. Reusing plots and characters was common in the Renaissance for comedies, tragedies and for the new genres of tragicomedy and pastoral, which were favoured by Elizabethan playwrights, Commedia erudita and Commedia dell'Arte. This recycling of material in a different context was a widespread form of hybridisation, or of what Marvin Carlson calls "ghosting" in *The Haunted Stage* – former works of literature are taken up and modified in the process of emulation to obtain a greater scenic effect or to meet the taste of the time. If the borrowed elements are still recognisable for an audience conversant with the sources, *ghosting* takes place.[39] For Carlson, *ghosting* entails a duality of perception: the material seen or known in the past must be remembered in a present event to obtain recognition and enjoyment. This renders double plotlines and complementary perspectives possible, for example when subplots work as parallel comic versions of the main plot or even as parodies. Recognising the frequent doubling of parts in Elizabethan theatre or remembering the previous roles played by an actor on stage are other instances of *ghosting* that add alternatives to the reception.[40] Shakespeare and his contemporaries made important innovations in performance by making it more theatrical and consciously playing with newly established conventions. Since these conventions shape the audiences' expectations and regulate their response, the recognition of an emulated or parodied source has different results according to their "horizon of expectations"[41] and their

---

[38] See Smith, *The Commedia dell'Arte: A Study in Italian Popular Comedy* (New York: Columbia UP, 1912), p. 176. Among the detractors of Commedia dell'Arte Smith mentions Thomas Nashe, Thomas Coryat, George Whetstone and Stephen Gosson, while Philip Sidney and Thomas Heywood supported it.
[39] See Marvin Carlson, *The Haunted Stage: The Theatre as Memory Machine*, p. 36.
[40] Ibid., pp. 37–9.
[41] This concept was coined by Hans Robert Jauss, "What is and for what purpose does one study literary history?". Lecture at Constance held in April 1967, p. 24, quoted in Holub, *Reception Theory: A Critical Introduction*, p. 60.

awareness of *ghosting*. In general, the pleasure of recognition is a "collective, historical, and mnemonic act"[42] that needs a common knowledge to work, otherwise new solutions in the field of adaptation are required.

A second point of contact between Commedia dell'Arte and Elizabethan theatre lies in their ability to reach and please both the courts and the commoners. Adaptation is necessarily tied to audiences first, and not to rules, according to A. R. Braunmuller.[43] Since language – in combination with gestures and kinesics – is a predominant channel for reaching any audience, he argues that a central aspect of change on the Elizabethan stage was rhetoric. Dramaturgy progressively became not only textual, but also more predominantly "auricular, appealing powerfully to the listener-spectator's rhythmic and auditory sensibilities", as he explains, with the heavily patterned verbal rhetoric typical of English drama in the 1590s.[44] The scarcity of props and illusionistic settings inherent to street theatre or theatre on tour imposed additional requirements on the art of speaking, i.e. rhetoric, to stimulate the audience's imagination with verbal scenery. Moreover, language helped to distinguish characters by ways of speaking, a method comparable to the use of different dialects by the Commedia dell'Arte 'types' like Venetian for Pantalone, Bolognese for Dottore and the dialect of Bergamo for Arlecchino. Especially in comedy, tricks of style and vocabulary added to the characters' personalities or even functioned as trademarks of certain actors.

In Elizabethan drama, the variation and stratification of language reflected the variety of the audience, which was diversified from a regional as well as from a social point of view. For this reason, Shakespeare resorted to writing plays "on two or more levels, complicated plots for the educated elite and double-entendre dialogues to amuse the middle classes and groundlings", as Amy Drake argues.[45] The stratagem of performing on various levels was also common to Commedia dell'Arte, which could flexibly adapt to diverse socio-cultural contexts due to improvisation, as the example of Drusiano Martinelli conforming his repertoire to the court and to the town squares in England shows. Generally, adapting plays to heterogeneous audiences was a fundamental trait of early modern professional theatre, moving between royal and public stages; and this became even more complex abroad as performers could not rely on language as the primary means of theatrical address. Both Italian actors in England and English Comedians in Germany played alternatively for aristocrats who mainly understood their language, and in marketplaces and at fairs where they had to resort to non-verbal gesture and kinesics to reach their audience. Thence, performing on multiple levels was the norm as far as theatre as a set of performative skills is concerned.

[42] Carlson, *The Haunted Stage: The Theatre as Memory Machine*, p. 51.
[43] A. R. Braunmuller, "The arts of the dramatist", in Braunmuller and Hattaway, ed., *The Cambridge Companion to English Renaissance Drama*, pp. 53–92, pp. 54–5.
[44] Ibid., p. 63.
[45] Drake, "Commedia dell'Arte Influences on Shakespearean Plays: *The Tempest, Love's Labor's Lost*, and *The Taming of the Shrew*", *Selected Papers of the Ohio Valley Shakespeare Conference* 6:3 (2013), pp. 11–30, p. 14.

In a like manner, the open absorption of theatrical traditions and the vibrant interaction with the most effective dramaturgical elements of popular theatre were frequent phenomena of adaptation in Elizabethan drama. Authors like Heywood and Shakespeare engaged with the characters and structures so favourably introduced by Italian actors. Audiences used to such intercultural permeations and aware of them would recognise *ghosting* elements, but they had to be trained first by the playwrights and performers. The 'producers' in turn depended on the spectators' understanding and approval as well as on current literary trends and material conditions of playing and staging. This leads back to the question of who shapes the taste of the time, the 'producers' or the recipients? Both are involved in the creation of a new aesthetics and as soon as the context changes, the leading principles must adapt too. Since the audiences of Commedia dell'Arte in Italy and of Elizabethan drama were familiar with professional and conventionalised theatrical performances, attention was given to diverse memorialised sources, hybridised with *ghosting* elements. By contrast, in Germany where dramatic development had not yet reached this stage, the actors had to return to previous phases of theatricality and rely more on adaptation and visualisation, as we shall see.

Summing up, the impact of Italian culture on the professionalisation of theatre in England and the ensuing similarities can be seen as part of a larger trend of creating a new aesthetics with comparable principles: firstly, memorialisation of shared materials; secondly, hybridisation in dramaturgy with a special attention to rhetoric; and thirdly, adaptation of newly established conventions to audiences from varying social, cultural and religious backgrounds for financial gain.

4.3. Shakespeare and Commedia dell'Arte – A Brief Survey

In order to evince the possible impact of Commedia dell'Arte on Shakespeare, some of his plays will briefly be compared to similar *scenari*. The emergence of analogous plots and standard characters with identifying features can be attributed to the Italianate influence, despite the different cultural context. As Charles S. Felver puts it, in Commedia dell'Arte each 'type's' personality triumphs over the individualised characters of Elizabethan drama, the spoken and embodied word triumphs over the written text, and the action triumphs over the play.[46] Still, there are some points in common, as Kathleen M. Lea and Henry F. Salerno have demonstrated.[47] To their excellent studies I would like to add the present focus on correlations in memorialisation and hybridisation, which show how adaptation of the same sources achieved different results.

Just as Commedia dell'Arte was a product of amalgamation of Commedia erudita, carnival traditions, *buffoni* and popular performers, Elizabethan drama

---

[46] See Charles S. Felver, "The Commedia dell'Arte and English Drama in the Sixteenth and Early Seventeenth Centuries", *Renaissance Drama, A Report on Research Opportunities* 6 (1963), pp. 24–34, p. 29.

[47] See Lea, *IPC*, and Salerno, *The Elizabethan Drama and the 'Commedia dell'Arte'*.

was shaped by Renaissance culture, the medieval heritage and international influences. The Italian traces in many Shakespearean plays were due to a variety of common oral and literary sources which were part of both learned culture, like Greco-Roman material, and popular knowledge, such as romance and tales. For instance, as soon as translated versions of *novelle* began to travel, Giovanni Boccaccio and Giovanni Fiorentino were plundered for their romantic adventures, while Matteo Bandello and Giovanni Battista Giraldi aka Cinthio provided tales of passion and tragedy, as Madeleine Doran points out.[48] In *Twelfth Night, The Merchant of Venice, The Taming of the Shrew, Romeo and Juliet, Measure for Measure* and *All's Well that Ends Well*, literary drama and *novelle* represent a decisive model with motifs like supposed poison or death, cross-dressing of girls as boys, disguise, madness, substitutions and the use of double plots.[49] This fruitful combination of tales, dramatised according to the principles of antiquity and enlivened by characters from Roman popular comedy, was adopted not only by English playwrights like Shakespeare; Commedia dell'Arte exploited the same conglomeration and was at the same time a repository of ancient themes and motifs, almost a "literary ragbag, a kind of Harlequin's suit in itself", in Winifred Smith's words.[50] Or we could speak of memorialisation on two levels, immersed in the same network of shared knowledge used by Elizabethan drama.

Several Commedia dell'Arte *scenari* from the first generation, i.e. edited by Flaminio Scala (1611), Basilio Locatelli (1628/32) and contained in the Corsinian miscellany (1621–42), correlate with some of Shakespeare's early plays, especially as concerns the cohesive structure of plots, the 'type'-like character relations, the situational outcomes and the *lazzi* included as subplots. In addition, both Shakespeare and Commedia dell'Arte *scenari* make use of hybrid genres like tragicomedy with pastoral, mythological, historical or romance elements. In the adaptation process, however, the same subject matter was treated differently since Commedia dell'Arte was an acting style rather than a literary genre and Shakespeare had his individual way of creating and combining sources, influenced by the cultural environment, theory *and* practice. Even if the memorialised sources were similar and hybridisation followed comparable aesthetic principles

---

[48] For more details see Madeleine Doran, *Endeavors of Art: A Study of Form in Elizabethan Drama* (Madison, Wisconsin: University of Wisconsin Press, 1972 [1954]), pp. 131–3. In addition, Alberto Martino points out that at least 27 Elizabethan comedies and tragedies are indebted to Bandello's novelle, before the subject matter was introduced and popularised in Germany by the English Comedians. See Alberto Martino, *Die italienische Literatur im deutschen Sprachraum*, p. 374.

[49] According to Leo Salingar, *Shakespeare and the Traditions of Comedy*, pp. 189–90, Shakespeare was one of the first English dramatists to borrow characteristic traits of the Commedia erudita such as the double plot with confusions of identity and ensuing complications. These borrowings are recognisable in five of the twelve comedies written between 1592 and 1604: *Love's Labour's Lost, A Midsummer Night's Dream, All's Well, The Merchant of Venice, Much Ado* and *Measure for Measure*.

[50] Smith, *The Commedia dell'Arte: A Study in Italian Popular Comedy*, p. 197.

derived from the classics, it was adaptation to the audience that made the material appealing and unique. In turn, the conventions underlying the creation of a play would also shape the audience's taste.

In the case of Shakespeare's obscure biography, it is difficult to reconstruct how exactly he availed himself of the neoclassical elements common to Italian plays or to identify mutual influences with certainty, because Commedia dell'Arte was so tied to orality. Still, there are some (textual) commonalities attributable not just to the same source on the page but to direct contact on the stage of touring companies. As there is historical evidence that Italian performers were in London in Shakespeare's time, it might be supposed that Shakespeare saw them or was at least familiar with the characters and plots, as some selected plays confirm.

Firstly, the figure of Falstaff is an instance of a Commedia dell'Arte method unusual for Shakespeare. The fact that he inserted the same darling of the public into different plays, namely *Henry IV (Parts 1 and 2)*, *Henry V* and *The Merry Wives of Windsor* is commonly imputed to the Queen's notorious preference for the character but also recalls the fixed characters of moralities and the 'types' of Commedia dell'Arte.[51] In *The Merry Wives of Windsor* (1597/1601), the comic figure Falstaff resembles the boasting Capitano turned into a fooled Zanni in the washtub incident. In a pivotal episode in Act 3.3, Falstaff is dishonourably tricked into hiding in a washtub full of dirty laundry and almost dumped into a river for his indecent proposals to the merry wives of Windsor, who prepare a sort of play-within-the-play to teach him a lesson.[52] In terms of memorialisation, there is a stockpile of medieval stories and *novelle* about unwelcome suitors forced to hide in ridiculous places.[53] Since Commedia dell'Arte drew on novelistic sources too,

---

[51] K. M. Lea puts forward the hypothesis that in *The Merry Wives of Windsor* Shakespeare drew fully from foreign sources without altering them significantly because of the short time of composition he was given for the play, namely fourteen days. Since the Queen reportedly wished to see more of Falstaff, possibly a love comedy, old plays had to function as foundation. See Lea, *IPC*, vol. 2, p. 433.

[52] "MISTRESS PAGE Your husband's coming hither, woman [i.e. Mrs Ford], with all the / officers in Windsor, to search for a gentleman that / he says is here now in the house by your consent, to / take an ill advantage of his assence: you are undone. [...] Look, here / is a basket: if he be of any reasonable stature, he / may creep in here; and throw foul linen upon him, as / if it were going to bucking: or-- it is whiting-time / --send him by your two men to Datchet-mead. MISTRESS FORD He's too big to go in there. What shall I do? FALST. [*Coming forward*] Let me see't, let me see't, O, let / me see't! I'll in, I'll in. Follow your friend's / counsel. I'll in. MISTRESS PAGE What, Sir John Falstaff! Are these your letters, knight? FALST. I love thee. Help me away. Let me creep in here. / I'll never-- [*Gets into the basket; they cover him with foul linen*]." *The Merry Wives of Windsor* 3.3.89–92 and 109–20.

[53] Duped wooers like Falstaff are present more than once in Boccaccio, as Geoffrey Bullough recounts: in tale VIII.7 of the *Decameron*, a foolish scholar in pursuit of sexual adventures is locked into a courtyard all night, while in IX.1 two unwanted suitors are forced to spend the night in a new grave. Bullough also mentions several sixteenth-century Italian *novelle* involving the opposite motif of a lover hiding in strange places after

it is not surprising that an almost analogous fate should befall Pantalone in the *scenario Li tre becchi* ('The Three Cuckolds' of the Corsinian collection, 1621–42): while Pantalone hides in a basket of clothes to commit adultery with Zanni's wife, Zanni assists Coviello with seducing Pantalone's wife.[54] Similarly, in *La innocentia rinvenuta* ('Innocence Recovered') edited by Basilio Locatelli (1628/32), Fabrizio is smuggled into Doralice's house in a chest to make Orazio, her husband-to-be, believe she was unfaithful, but is ultimately exposed by Pedrolino. Locatelli took up the motif again in *Il Zanni becco* ('Zanni the Cuckold'): Pantalone and Gratiano hide in a sack to get to Zanni's wife Isabella. When they find out they are victims of a *burla* or prank by Zanni, they decide to exact revenge by tying him up in a sack and throwing him into the river.[55] These analogies do not imply that Shakespeare was directly indebted to the plays but support the argument of shared material adapted flexibly in a variety of dramatic performances and contexts.

Secondly, *The Comedy of Errors* (1594) is a direct borrowing from Plautus' *Menaechmi* theme, which was a ubiquitous comic motif in Renaissance plays. While Basilio Locatelli's *Li duo simili di Plauto* ('The Two Look-Alikes by Plautus' 1628/32) was still close to the original plot about two twins mistaken for each other without knowing about the existence of the respective brother, Flaminio Scala and Carlo Goldoni gave their own rendition in *Li duo Capitani simili* 'The Two Similar Captains/Capitani' (1611) and in *Due gemelli veneziani*, 'Two Venetian Twins' (1747).[56] Mistaken identities and cross-dressed twins are central elements of Shakespeare's *Comedy of Errors* and *Twelfth Night* too, and since the Latin source was widely read and well known at the time owing to Gascoigne's translation of Ariosto's Commedia erudita *I Suppositi* (1509), it was surely the ultimate model. Henry Salerno argues that the addition of the Duke, the

> a successful adultery to make fun of the cuckold. The duped husband motif is also present in Giovanni Fiorentino's *Il Pecorone* ('The Simpleton' 1378) I.2, where a young student learns the art of love from a professor and unknowingly tires it out on the latter's wife. Or in Giovanni Francesco Straparola's *novella* IV.4 from *Le Tredici piacevoli notti* ('Thirteen Delightful Nights' of 1550–3, translated into French in 1560), Nerino of Portugal hides from a jealous husband in three different places. In addition, Bullough explains that the motif of the foolish suitor might be indebted to an English collection of tales, namely *Tarlton's Newes out of Purgatorie* (1590), posthumously attributed to the famous clown. The 'Tale of the Two Lovers of Pisa, and why they were whipt in Purgatorie with Nettles' is modelled on Straparola's Nerino. See Bullough, vol. 2, pp. 5–6.

[54] The play was translated by Lea in *Italian Popular Comedy*, vol. 2.

[55] To make things more complicated, just in that moment the Capitano enters Zanni's house disguised as a servant in order to sleep with Isabella and the two *vecchi* mistake him for Zanni. In the end, they discover their mistake and also that the Capitano is Pantalone's lost son. Both skeletal plots are contained in Testaverde, ed., *I canovacci della Commedia dell'Arte*, pp. 185–92 and pp. 231–8.

[56] See Testaverde, ed., op. cit., pp. 269–78 for Locatelli's text and pp. 67–76 for Scala's. Hinck provides an analysis of these two plays in *Das deutsche Lustspiel des 17. und 18. Jahrhunderts*, pp. 20–38.

Abbess, Aegeon, Lucinda as confidante and wife, and the twin slaves seem to be based on Commedia dell'Arte reworkings, though the individuality of the characters in Shakespeare surpasses the 'type'-pattern by far.[57]

Thirdly, *The Tempest*'s (1618) magical setting on an island, the character constellation and the plot are reminiscent of Arcadian plays. Pastorals in the Greco-Roman fashion flourished in many currents of Renaissance literature, from poetry to drama, and were reworked on a popular level, for instance in Commedia dell'Arte pastoral tragicomedies. In this case, the material was usually simplified and constructed around the love plot in an enchanted atmosphere with shepherds, nymphs, satyrs and magicians, sometimes even parodying the classical world.[58] Lea convincingly compares Shakespeare's *The Tempest* to a late *scenario* called *L'Arcadia Incantata* ('Enchanted Arcadia' from the Neapolitan collection edited by Placido Adriani in 1734), which testifies to the longevity of mutual influence. In Prospero she sees the established 'type' of the ill-treated magician living on an island, in Caliban a meek satyr or a rustic, and the relationship between Trinculo and Stephano echoes typical patterns connected to buffoons like Coviello and Pulcinella.[59] Compared to *L'Arcadia incantata*, in *The Tempest* the rival lover is substituted by the schemes of Prospero, but *A Midsummer Night's Dream* maintains the vicious circle of enchanted lovers bedazzled by a flower. This motif, in turn, is common to *La nave* ('The Ship', Corsinian collection of 1621–42) and the aforementioned *L'Arcadia incantata*, in which a magician puts a spell on two flower wreaths to produce love and hate, while in *Il gran mago* ('The Great Magician' edited by Locatelli) a floral wreath makes the wearer appear as the object of desire to any person who sees him or her.[60] According to Allardyce Nicoll, these similarities make it "virtually impossible not to believe that Shakespeare had witnessed the performance of an improvised pastoral of this

---

[57] See Salerno, *The Elizabethan Drama and the 'Commedia dell'Arte'*, p. 50. Salerno offers a thorough analysis of parallel features between Commedia dell'Arte and *The Comedy of Errors, Love's Labour's Lost, Romeo and Juliet, Henry VI, Part 2, A Midsummer Night's Dream, The Taming of the Shrew, Henry IV, Part 1 and 2, The Merchant of Venice, Much Ado about Nothing, As You Like It, Twelfth Night, Hamlet, The Merry Wives of Windsor, All's Well That Ends Well, Cymbeline, The Winter's Tale*, and *The Tempest*.

[58] The *scenario Li tre satiri* ('The Three Satyrs', Corsinian collection 1621–42) is an example of parodied pastoral. Firstly, the magic is bawdy; for instance, Zanni is turned into a stone and can be freed only if someone urinates on him. Secondly, ancient mythology is ridiculed by Pantalone, Zanni and Sardellino, who dress up as gods with funny attributes after having eaten all the food left as an offer in the temple. See Testaverde, ed., pp. 433–40 for the text.

[59] For a precise analysis see Lea, *IPC*, vol. 2, pp. 448–50.

[60] See *La nave* and *L'Arcadia incantata* in Testaverde, ed., pp. 465–73 and pp.751–5. Additionally, in *Il gran mago* ('The Great Magician', contained in ibid., pp. 375–84) Pantalone is turned into an ass recalling Bottom's donkey head in Shakespeare's *A Midsummer Night's Dream*. After drinking from an enchanted fountain, the same fate befalls Gratiano in *Li tre satiri* ('The Three Satyrs' of the Corsinian collection 1621–42, see ibid., pp. 433–40), while Franceschina is turned into a cow.

kind."[61] Since this cannot be proved conclusively, it is more cautious to assume that he at least had contact with the European theatrical community by word of mouth or shared with them a network of popular culture.[62] In fact, even if the *scenari* were published after the date of performance of most Shakespearean works, the plays were in circulation decades before being printed, making contact possible on the itinerant stage.

The genre of the pastoral gives further insights into the amalgamation and permeation of learned and popular culture in literature beyond the early modern period. Indeed, the fantastic, superstition and magic are linking points between an ancient, popular knowledge and a new form of representing it on stage in tragicomedy. Analysing structural elements of the Commedia dell'Arte plays edited by Flaminio Scala and Basilio Locatelli, Walter Hinck distinguishes between the "concentration-type" and the "fantastic-type".[63] The first concerns satiric comedies or tragicomedies with fixed scenery, few additions of minor characters and motifs of mistaken identities, intrigues and final discoveries. The second is characterised by the traditional 'types' in exotic or Arcadian settings with the addition of mythological or allegoric heroes of the pastoral like shepherds, nymphs and magical beings, who intervene in the storyline as threatening or protective powers.[64] The receptive history of these two forms makes Molière, Carlo Goldoni and Johann Nestroy advocates of the "concentration-type", and Shakespeare (for example in *The Tempest*), Carlo Gozzi (*Le fiabe teatrali* 1761–5) and Ferdinand Raimund (*Alpenkönig und Menschenfeind* 1828) adherents to the "fantastic-type", which ultimately prevailed.[65] The common practice for achieving the greatest possible effect seems to have been the intermingling of material from scholarly education with rituals, festivities, beliefs, stock characters, pranks and comic effects from popular theatre and culture, which travelled not only through print but also thanks to wandering troupes.

As has been shown, in England, theatre as professional entertainment both for the court and for the masses reached its apogee a little in advance of the rest of Europe. This early development was due to historical, economic and cultural factors that made England predominant but not independent of the European continent. The newly established, formally recognised companies of actors between

---

[61] Nicoll, *The World of Harlequin: A Critical Study of the Commedia dell'Arte*, p. 119.
[62] Culture travelled beyond the page, for instance through travelling individuals like the English Thomas Coryat. He described a Commedia dell'Arte performance seen in St. Mark's Square in Venice during his stay in the city from 24 June to 8 August 1608. He then published his impressions for an English readership in *Coryats Crudities | Hastily gobled up in five | Moneths trauells In France, | Sauoy, Italy, Rhetia commonly | called the Grison country, Hel- | uetia aliàs Switzerland, some | parts of high Germany, and the | Netherlands. London, Printed by W. S. Anno Domini 1611.*
[63] See Hinck, *Das deutsche Lustspiel des 17. und 18. Jahrhunderts und die italienische Komödie*, p. 19–20.
[64] Ibid., p. 115.
[65] Ibid., pp. 115–16.

the late 1570s and the late 1590s were no longer forced to tour the country for "reputation and profit",[66] at least until the watershed date of 1594. Once they entertained a regular audience in permanent theatres under royal patronage, they faced a staggering and continuing demand for new material. As far as drama is concerned, the sources of many dramatic texts were drawn from the vast repertoire of international literatures. This led to the creation of a professional entertainment industry with its own aesthetic conventions. In this chapter, it has been argued that early modern drama in Italy and England derived its formal principles from the rediscovery of the classics combined with contemporary subject matters and popular styles of performance and characters in theatre. From this network of shared knowledge, interesting subject matters had to be carefully adapted and presented with performative artistry to reach large and multifaceted audiences in the context of their time and culture, even more so on tour. Among other international influences, Italian literature, erudite drama and popular Commedia dell'Arte were fruitfully inserted into Elizabethan plays – especially Shakespeare's – and then exported to Germany, where they were amalgamated again with other theatrical elements. While the aesthetics in Elizabethan drama and Commedia dell'Arte was based on memorialisation and hybridisation, including *ghosting* and changes in rhetoric, as soon as the plays were transferred to a different context, the tastes of the audience had to be met with adaptation, requiring a step back in the evolutionary process of theatre ('backwards involution'). In particular, the non-verbal dimension of visualisation, sound and movement increased in importance as language was not always intelligible.

[66] *Hamlet*, 2.2.306.

5. The English Comedians in Germany and Austria

Before introducing the companies of English Comedians that toured northern and central Europe from the 1580s, it is necessary to give a brief outline of the conditions they found, especially in Germany.[1] As shall be argued, the resounding success of the English troupes and the impact they had on the development of theatre is due to two major factors: firstly, the absence of national forms of professional theatre on their arrival, and secondly, the effective adaptation and naturalisation of their plays. Unlike the rivalling Italian and French troupes, they did not simply transfer the repertoire in their original language but merged it with pre-existing traditions and made use of shared elements. Their ambitious venture was thus not only an "invasion in real force" but more importantly a "genuine awakening", as Ernest Brennecke defines it.[2] However, it would be wrong to assume that there were no German theatre traditions before the arrival of the English wandering troupes or that a mutual influence did not exist prior to the sixteenth century[3] – for an awakening, something must be dormant.

On the level of academic culture and at court, early modern theatre in Germany and Austria was usually performed by amateurs either as political representation

---

[1] In the following overview of English itinerant companies in Germany and Austria I rely on Albert Cohn, *Shakespeare in Germany in the Sixteenth and Seventeenth Centuries* (Wiesbaden: Dr. Martin Sändig oHG., 1967 [1865]); Wilhelm Creizenach, *Die Schauspiele der englischen Komödianten* (Berlin, Stuttgart: W. Spemann, 1889); Emil Herz, *Englische Schauspieler und englisches Schauspiel zur Zeit Shakespeares in Deutschland* (Nendeln: Kraus Reproduktion, 1977 [1903]); Willi Flemming, ed., *Barockdrama*, vol. 3, *Das Schauspiel der Wanderbühne* (Leipzig: Reclam, 1931); and Johannes Meissner, *Die englischen Comoedianten zur Zeit Shakespeares in Österreich* (Vienna: Carl Konegen, 1884).

[2] Brennecke, *Shakespeare in Germany: 1590–1700*, p. 3.

[3] According to Albert Cohn, the first documented contact with English actors in German territories is attested during the Council of Constance in 1417. However, this event was unique and not connected to any sort of regular activity on the Continent. In turn, there was a lively exchange of music and drama from the mainland under Henry VI, who hosted itinerant actors and musicians, also from Austria and Germany. Henry VIII had German minstrels at his court in 1516 and Queen Elizabeth, his daughter, cultivated this connection by inviting many exponents of the German nobility to pay visits of pleasure to England, where theatres were blooming. For example, in August 1592, Count Frederik of Mompelgard visited 'cousin' Elizabeth and saw *The Merry Wives of Windsor*. See Cohn, p. XI-XII. Ludwig of Anhalt, who travelled to England in 1596, mentioned going to the theatre there, too, as did Paul Hentzner in his *Itinerarium Germaniae, Galliae, Angliae, Italiae* (1610). Hentzner also noticed many Germans living in London. Moreover, the intellectual connection between England and Germany was not only literary; many scholars visited Oxford, Cambridge, or London. Consequently, English literature and theatre were well known and appreciated among German noblemen, and their courts welcomed itinerant actors (see ibid., p. XVII).

of the sovereign's power in the Baroque *Caesarei* at court,[4] or as school drama with a moralistic and didactic function – in both cases, it did not reach the wide public.[5] Renaissance school drama was a form of pedagogical entertainment limited to students who would exercise their linguistic and rhetorical skills by declaiming plays in Latin. Aware of its ideological potential, Martin Luther (1483–1546) fostered Protestant school drama to propagate his *propaganda fidei*, to which the Catholic Counter-Reformation answered with the opulence of Jesuit school drama. Despite differences in religious content, according to Manfred Brauneck the structure of these two forms of school theatre was similar because it followed classical drama: to begin with, a German argumentum or summary for those unable to understand Latin, then a prologue, and finally a poetic epilogue.[6] The German summary of plays performed in a foreign language was a method adopted by the first English Comedians too, as we shall see.

On the level of popular culture, German-speaking countries developed their own theatrical forms and genres moulded on medieval performances, which antedated the Renaissance discovery of ancient theatre by far. The first plays in German vernacular appeared in the fourteenth century and had mainly ecclesiastical content. In the course of time, the use of satiric and humorous passages in Passion plays and mysteries led to an increasing departure from religion towards more mundane topics.[7] By the mid-fifteenth century, the components of comic dialogues, political satire, grotesque farces, masks, music and dances re-emerged as lay Shrovetide plays or *Fastnachtspiele*.[8] Hereby Eckehard Catholy distinguishes between the early *Reihenspiel* (sequence play), an unstructured sequence of gross monologues about sex, gluttony and bodily functions, and the more elaborate and

---

[4] See Brauneck, *Die Welt als Bühne,* vol. 1, p. 515. In 1502, Konrad Celtis organised such a school drama spectacle for the future Emperor Maximilian I of Habsburg.

[5] The same elitism applies to the fifteenth-century translations of literary works into German: Heinrich Schlüsselfelder of Nuremberg translated Boccaccio's *Decameron* in 1472, while Albrecht von Eyb transposed the plays by Plautus and Terence for a larger but still erudite German readership. See J. G. Robertson, *A History of German Literature* (Edinburgh and London: W. Blackwood and Sons Ldt., 1949), p. 173.

[6] See Brauneck, *Die Welt als Bühne,* vol. 1, p. 538.

[7] Dieter Wuttke argues that the Passion play as an autonomous form of popular theatre did not emerge in continuity with antiquity but as a religious display which preannounced early modern drama with extended comic scenes. For instance, in a 1381 text from Innsbruck, a merry Andrew or clown figure named Robin/Rubin and his servant Henekin/Hans (later Hanswurst) or Harlekin (Arlecchino) make their appearance in the additions to the gospels such as the Mercator or Chandler scene. The comic potential of the skits inserted in the Passion of Christ was increased through puns, songs and beatings. See Dieter Wuttke, "Harlekins Verwandlungen", in Denzler, Glatzel and Lehmann, ed., *Commedia dell'Arte: Harlekin auf den Bühnen Europas*, pp. 52–66, p. 64.

[8] *Fastnachtspiele* describe farces with masks put on at Shrovetide, i.e. the three days preceding Ash Wednesday. According to J. G. Robertson, they have ritual origins, as they derive from the *Maskenlauf* with *Schembartläufer* representing the conflict between Winter and Spring. See Robertson, *A History of German Literature*, p. 185.

less obscene *Handlungsspiel* (plot play), a dramatisation of *Schwankliteratur* and *novelle* in verse, for example by Hans Rosenblut and Hans Foltz.[9]

In the early sixteenth century, Shrovetide plays matured a greater variety of characters and themes despite their brevity and salaciousness. Both in the marketplaces and at court they were so diffused that the term soon became a synonym for secular theatre. Rudolph Genée claims that the development of semi-literary Shrovetide plays was initially faster in Germany than in England, at least up to the appearance of the great reformer of the *Fastnachtspiel,* the cobbler and Meistersinger Hans Sachs (1494–1576).[10] Next to his prose dialogues, intended to propagate the new Reformatory doctrine of Luther, in his *Bürgerspiele* (citizens' plays) and *Schwänke* (short, facetious, anecdote-like dialogues) this prolific author from Nuremberg attenuated the crude tone of the Shrovetide plays into amusing teachings of virtue.[11] For Albert Cohn, Sachs had the merit of introducing national and foreign sources such as the recently translated tales from the *Decameron* and the popular heritage of jest literature (*Schwankliteratur*) in his tragedies and comedies with classical echoes;[12] however, he failed to produce the necessary improvement of the dramatic art, such as a division into acts and all-round characters acting out the plot instead of narrating it. Therefore, his works could not keep up with the skills and repertoire of professional actors from abroad – especially from England.

Several elements of *Fastnachtspiel* are rooted in popular culture and embedded in a network of shared knowledge. On the one hand, the ribaldry and the tirades of abuse (*Schimpftirade*) of the 'type'-like characters recall the comicality of Commedia dell'Arte; on the other hand, the final dance is comparable to the English jigs. In addition, the most effective ways of provoking laughter, namely exaggeration, repetition and contrast, are common to all three traditions. These points of contact were exploited by the touring companies from England in order to adapt their repertoire to the taste of their audiences and to shape a new aesthetics in

---

[9] See Eckehard Catholy, *Das deutsche Lustspiel: Vom Mittelalter bis zum Ende der Barockzeit* (Darmstadt: Wissenschaftliche Buchgesellschaft, 1968), pp. 24–33. As Karl Goedecke explains, the *Schwank* is usually translated as jest literature, fools' literature or simply comic literature. However, this denomination does not render justice to a popular genre thriving in German – and European – literature from the Middle Ages. It usually designates a funny episode about everyday themes with a surprising turn, enriched with bawdy or even obscene jokes. In the sixteenth century, these facetious stories were collected in *Schwankbücher* (jest books) and were frequently dramatised. See the introduction to Karl Goedecke, ed., *Schwänke des sechzehnten Jahrhunderts* (Leipzig: Brockhaus, 1880).

[10] See Rudolph Genée, *Geschichte der Shakespeare'schen Dramen in Deutschland* (Hildesheim: Georg Olms, 1969 [1870]), p. 6.

[11] See Robertson, *A History of German Literature*, p. 192. Nuremberg was the home of the Meistersinger who trained a special kind of chanted poetry, bound by strict rules and exhibited in singing contests reminiscent of the Latin *disputationes*. See ibid., p. 81.

[12] Alberto Martino recognises traces of Boccaccio in 51 *Meistersänge*, 31 *Spruchgedichte*, thirteen *Fastnachtspiele*, six comedies and two tragedies by Hans Sachs. See Martino, *Die italienische Literatur im deutschen Sprachraum*, p. 371.

Germany, including the Baltic territories, where drama was only recited by students and artisans in the late sixteenth century.[13]

In Austria, the English 'invasion' arrived a little later because the stages there had already been conquered by Italian companies. Due to the close geo-political ties of the Habsburg dynasty with Italian aristocrats like the Gonzaga of Mantua,[14] physicians, architects, sculptors, poets, dance masters, artists, musicians and actors were regularly exchanged among Catholic courts in Italy, Austria and southern Germany.[15] Pierre Louis Duchartre documents the presence of the comedians Giovanni Tabarino and a certain Flaminio at the court of Maximilian II in Linz and Vienna in 1568, and in Innsbruck in 1569, almost three decades before the English troupes reached Austria.[16] Since the Italian competition acted as a strong deterrent, the English Comedians remained in the northern plains and rarely embarked on the burdensome journey towards the more profitable markets of Vienna or Graz, controlled by Commedia dell'Arte actors.

In general, *theatre* as a set of performative skills held a more powerful appeal than *drama* as text, which accounts for the immediate success of Commedia dell'Arte and of the English Comedians despite the initial difficulties. As Catholy argues, Commedia dell'Arte arrived earlier and captivated the audiences by means of a textless performance style, rendered comprehensible by universal characters and a foregrounding of gesture over words. Furthermore, the Italians had actresses, a novelty in German-speaking lands, where *Fastnachtspiele* and school drama were always played by male amateurs.[17] By contrast, the English Comedians could not boast a female presence on stage until later and had to gradually shift the focus from literary drama to theatre as performance. Still, these initial disadvantages forced them to assimilate the language and culture of their host countries to such an extent that it ultimately had more far-reaching repercussions:

---

[13] In Cohn's words: "At a time when England was already traversed in all directions by innumerable troops of travelling players, and dramatic art had attained a high stage of development, Germany could not yet boast of any actors by profession" (Cohn, p. VII), so the first contact aroused great curiosity.

[14] For a detailed account of the Commedia dell'Arte troupes at the Habsburg court see Otto G. Schindler, "Comici dell'Arte alle corti austriache degli Asburgo", in Martino and De Michele, ed., *La ricezione della Commedia dell'Arte nell'Europa centrale 1568–1769*, pp. 96–144.

[15] Famous examples of Italian artists in Prague and Vienna are the painter, musician and costume designer Giuseppe Arcimboldo (1526–93), the architect and builder Pietro Ferrabosco (1512–75?), and the sculptor Lorenzo Mattielli (1687–1748). Moreover, European aristocracy travelled to France, Spain and Italy so frequently that most courts in southern Germany and Austria used Italian and French as predominant languages, as Orlene Murad explains in *The English Comedians at the Habsburg Court in Graz 1607–1608* (Elizabethan and Renaissance Studies, ed., by Dr. James Hogg, Salzburg: Institut für Anglistik und Amerikanistik, 1978), pp. 7–10.

[16] See Duchartre, *The Italian Comedy*, p. 86. The first presence of English Comedians in Austria is attested in 1607, at the court of Emperor Ferdinand II of Habsburg in Graz.

[17] See Catholy, *Das deutsche Lustspiel*, p. 115.

their adapted stage versions of international literature with popular additions like Pickelhering initiated German professional theatre and stimulated dramatic art.

On the level of *theatre*, the first plays of the English itinerant players in Germany hinged on mimicry, dancing, singing, music, acrobatics and clowning to make up for the language constraints – at least for those audiences who were not familiar with English from a courtly education or trade relations. On the level of *drama*, the actors had to renounce high literary standards and recast the Elizabethan plays considerably to meet the different cultural conditions. Thus, the plays by Shakespeare and his contemporaries entered the German territories in the form of translations, adaptations or extracted key episodes, presented as separate plays or incorporated into other plays. As translations of English plays into German did not appear until after the time span analysed in this study,[18] I shall focus on the other forms of adaptation to provide a general idea of the mediation done by the English Comedians abroad, before analysing the collection of 1620.

Adaptations often maintained the plots but changed some ideas or functions to suit the actors, the venue or the audience. A frequent method of intercultural theatricality in the plays of *Engelische Comedien and Tragedien* (1620) was to reduce the subject matter for the sake of simplicity and clarity. Using Genette's terminology, subplots and secondary characters were either "excised" or "condensed",[19] for instance when two similar roles merged into one to reduce the number of actors. Moreover, the actors relied on an impactful sequence of crucial scenes reduced to action, adventure and horror to convey the message; the rest of the plot would be summarised in narrative passages, for instance monologues, commentaries and self-characterisations closer to epic genres than to theatre. The priority was always to maintain the suspense and to make the content accessible to the audience with an abundance of emotional effects. On the one hand, the consequent qualitative inferiority compared to the English originals is usually ascribed to the lack of language skills necessary to translate the text properly on the part of the actors. On the other hand, the audience and the venues made a direct transfer almost impossible, hence the focus was set on effective entertainment. For this reason, each company had its own German-speaking clown who attracted the spectators with music, dance and antics during the intervals or translated the salient points of the plot.[20]

---

[18] One wonders why translations of plays appeared so late, since there were enough accomplished writers who could have given a rendition of English drama. Apparently, what was common practice among literati was not yet available for the popular stage, nor was it necessary: in the first phases public and courtly audiences were more eager to be entertained with music, dances, and pantomime than with literature and poetry.

[19] See Genette, *Palimpsests*, pp. 228–37.

[20] See Julius Tittmann, *Die Schauspiele der englischen Komödianten in Deutschland* (Leipzig: Brockhaus, 1880), p. 7. The *argumentum* was in use with Latin school comedies too, which needed a German summary of the play performed in Latin. In a like manner, Commedia dell'Arte *scenari* have an *argomento* with the salient points of the action.

Apart from the reduction of the plot, a few general considerations can be made about the categories most affected by adaptation in the repertoire of the English Comedians: language, characters and style.

Firstly, in the extant plays the language ranges from realistic and close to the spectators' common speech in comic scenes, to rhetorical and formulaic for serious passages. The original verse form was probably retained during the early English-speaking period, but long monologues or dialogues unaccompanied by action were omitted to leave place for improvisation and farces instead, as Lawrence M. Price notices.[21]

Secondly, in the plays of revenge, love, or semi-historical facts imbued with fairy-tale and magical elements, the personages are mostly devoid of a complex inner life and limited to their social status or a predominant psychological trait. To a certain degree, these universal human archetypes resonate with Commedia dell'Arte and the allegories of the moralities.

Thirdly, the difficulties in finding an appropriate style suggest that the English Comedians knew many plays by heart and tried to transpose them into German as best they could. It is difficult to speculate how well these comedians spoke German, as the texts of the collections are based on prompt-copies, and even in the early phases, their oral language knowledge was probably better than their written proficiency.[22] Had they been aided by an expert translator, the result might have been more literary, but not necessarily more suited to the audience.

Thinking back to Anna Baesecke's theory of theatre as a progression of single stages of complexity, in the case of the itinerant players in German territories it would be appropriate to speak of a 'backwards involution'.[23] English drama had already reached a complex and literary form, leaving behind the conditions still present in Germany when the first itinerant players arrived. As shall be argued, the English Comedians adapted their repertoire and artistry with impressive rapidity not only because of the linguistic vicinity of English to German, but more importantly because they could rely on previous stages of development already outdated in England but still present on the popular stage of their host countries. Instead of deploring the alleged weakness of their language and style, attention

---

[21] See Lawrence Marsden Price, *The Reception of English Literature in Germany* (New York and London: Benjamin Bloom, 1968 [1932]), p. 18.

[22] From extant letters of petition, it can be deduced that the English Comedians had a good command of the German language, provided that they wrote them themselves.

[23] See Baesecke, *Das Schauspiel der englischen Komödianten in Deutschland*, p. 10. Similarly, Friedrich Gundolf points out that: "They [the English Comedians] went the opposite way as the English drama. Their major effects are: 1) separation of theatre from literature and the pathos of the times [,] 2) augmentation of the subject matter and the sensual means of entertainment, 3) disruption of language, exchange of verse through prose in theatrical productions." My translation from Friedrich Gundolf, *Shakespeare und der deutsche Geist* (Bad Godesberg: Küpper, 1947), p. 43. His "opposite way" is comparable to my more positive 'backwards involution'.

should be drawn to the effectiveness of their adaptations. For instance, by simplifying the plots and highlighting emotion, gesture and improvisation as in Commedia dell'Arte, the English players came close to the *Fastnachtspiele* familiar to their audience. Once they had taken an 'evolutionary step back' to rediscover the force of popular oral elements over the literary dramatic text, their success grew steadily until the Thirty Years' War made touring too dangerous and thus gave the emerging German companies the opportunity to replace their English rivals. The establishment of professional theatre in German-speaking countries, as well as the protagonists of this enterprise, are the topics of the next sections.

5.1. The Four Phases of Influence

Scholarship generally identifies three to four distinct moments in the development of English companies in central Europe: the last decades of the sixteenth century, the two decades before the Thirty Years' War, the time of the war, and its aftermath.[24] On the basis of this timeframe, I have modified these phases to give attention to the progressive transformations each wave of influx brought, notably 'adaptation', 'amalgamation', 'literarisation' and 'naturalisation'. These categories provide the structure for describing the socio-cultural context of the companies active in each period.

Adaptation Phase (1585–1600)

The first years of dramatic activity from 1585 to 1600 were characterised by small, poorly equipped companies of 'pioneers', who performed abridged versions of English plays at the courts of their patrons in north-eastern Germany and in the major trading towns. Noble patronage enabled and fostered the initially slow reception of wandering troupes from England. By virtue of this system of protection, the English Comedians set up their headquarters at a patron's palace, where, according to Jerzy Limon, they received a good salary for their performances and other expenses such as costumes, props and scenery. Other privileges included the opportunity to organise tours with a backup plan in case of financial or political difficulties, the guarantee of a regular audience at court and the necessary funds to rehearse, advertise and stage a state-of-the-art play.[25] The most important patrons in this period were Duke Heinrich Julius of Brunswick-Wolfenbüttel and Landgrave Moritz 'the Learned' of Hessen-Kassel, who started the European vogue of receiving itinerant players from England and other countries.[26] Landgrave Moritz, for instance, employed not only the English *Hessische Komödianten* ('Hessian Comedians') from 1593, but also Italian Commedia

---

[24] See Limon, *Gentlemen of a Company*, pp. 29–31, and Hoffmeister, "The English Comedians in Germany", in Hoffmeister, ed., *German Baroque Literature*, pp. 142–58.
[25] See Limon, p. 10.
[26] "The Duke of Brunswicke and the Landgrave of Hessen retaine in their courts certaine of ours of the same quality." Thomas Heywood, *Apology for Actors*, 1612 (London: Shakespeare Society, 1841), p. 40.

dell'Arte actors in 1597/8, as an account of his household testifies.[27] Although there is no evidence of it, the actors probably met and exchanged experiences.

In this first phase, a direct transposition of Elizabethan drama was hindered by the language barrier, so theatre focused more on performance than on texts. The plays were usually reduced to episodic actions interspersed with interludes of the German-speaking clown, who also functioned as translator of the main plot in-between acts. A report about a sojourn of English Comedians – presumably Browne's troupe – in the chronicles of the city of Munster at the end of the adaptation phase reads as follows:

> Den 26. Novembris [1601] sindt alhir angekommen elven Engellender, so alle iunge und rasche gesellen waren, ausgenommen einer, so tzemliches althers war, der alle dinge regerede. Diesolbige agerden vif dage uf den rädthuse achtereinanderen vif verscheiden comedien *in ihrer engelscher sprache*. Sie hetten bi sich vielle *verschieden instrumente*, dar sie uf speleden, als luten, zitteren, fiolen, pipen und dergelichen; sie *dantzeden vielle neuwe und frömmede dentze* (so hir zu lande nicht gepruechlich) in anfange und ende der comedien. Sie hetten bei sich einen *schalkes narren, so in deuscher sprache vielle bötze und geckerie machede* under den ageren, wan sie einen neuwen actum wolten anfangen und sich umbkledden, darmidt ehr das volck lachent machede. Sie waren von den rade vergeliedet nicht lenger als ses taghe. Do die umb waren, mosten sie wedder wichen. Sie kregen in den vif taghen von den, so es sehen und hören wolten, vielle geldes; dan ein ieder moste ihnen geben zu ieder reise einen schillinck.[28]

By 1601, the troupes already counted eleven actors – equivalent to the number of a typical London company or a Commedia dell'Arte troupe – including a manager, who organised the tour and applied to the town council for a licence to perform. During the five days of their stay, five different plays with musical interludes and postludes, probably jigs, were performed to keep the local audience entertained. These points all coincide with touring practices in England and did not represent a novelty to the itinerant players. What was new is that they spoke a different

---

[27] "Dem welschen Jan und seiner Bereitern zweimal, summa 150 Thlr" ('150 thaler given twice to the Italian Jan and his entourage'). Quoted in Cohn, p. 445.

[28] Johannes Janssen, ed., *Die Münsterischen Chroniken von Röchell, Stevermann und Corfey*. Munster, 1856, p. 175, quoted in Schrickx, *Foreign Envoys and Travelling Players in the Age of Shakespeare and Jonson*, p. 331, my emphases. Cohn, p. CXXXIV-V, offers this translation: 'On the 26th of November [1601] there arrived here eleven Englishmen, all young and lively fellows, with the exception of one, an elderly man, who had everything under his management [Robert Browne?]. They acted on five successive days five different comedies in their own English tongue. They carried with them various musical instruments, such as lutes, zithers, violas, pipes, and such like; they danced many new and foreign dances (not usual in this country) at the beginning and at the end of their comedies. They had with them a clown, who, when they wanted to begin a new act and had to change their costume, made many antics and pranks in German during the performance, by which he brought the people to laughter. They were licensed by the Town-Council for six days only, after which time they had to depart. During those five days they took a great deal of money from those who wished to hear and see them, for everyone had to give them one shilling for the journey.'

language to that of their spectators and had to resort to translated summaries, clowning, dances and music. Considering the effort of rendering the imported English dramas accessible, this phase is characterised by adaptation to the logistic, administrative and linguistic conditions.

Firstly, the touring companies had to adapt to the haphazard venues, as they could not expect to find purpose-built playhouses like in London. Instead, they contented themselves with "town-squares, inn yards, tennis-courts and palaces", performing on "temporary structures created anywhere an audience might be found", as Peter Holland states.[29] Since this situation was not unlike the conditions found outside London for travelling troupes, the adaptation process was smooth. Symbolic stage props, sumptuous costumes, clearly identifiable attributes and over-explicit gestures made sure the message was conveyed.

Secondly, the itinerant players had to travel continuously, since even court affiliations did not secure full-time employment. They would either visit other courts, accepting the invitation of some acquaintance of their supporter, or tour the country with their patron's leave to play at annual fairs and in town halls, as historical documents prove.[30] Adapting to the administrative regulations of the city councils required tact and diplomacy. According to Ralf Haekel's reconstructions, the companies had to submit an eloquent petition, which represents one of the most important and direct sources about the English Comedians' activity on the Continent. Even with a letter of recommendation by a noble patron, the repertoire underwent preventive censorship in the form of obligatory previews. If the permission to play in a certain municipal area was granted at all, it did not last for more than two weeks and had to be extended with a new petitioning. In addition, a high tax was imposed on the financial rewards, which diminished the profit.[31] Another considerable expense was tied to the publicity, with printed bills and musical parades, rendered necessary by the presence of competing entertainers at big occasions like annual fairs.[32] Again, these conditions were customary in England

---

[29] Peter Holland, "Shakespeare abbreviated", in Shaughnessy, ed., *The Cambridge Companion to Shakespeare and Popular Culture*, pp. 26–45, p. 31.

[30] See Haekel, *Die Englischen Komödianten in Deutschland*, pp. 50–1, where he quotes a letter of recommendation by Landgrave Moritz, written to the city council of Frankfurt on 17 March 1606: "[…] es haben uns gegenwerttige vnsere Comoedianten, vnndt liebe getrewen vnderthenig ersuchet, weill die Franckfurther meß herzue nahete, das wir Ihnen nicht allein gnedig erlauben, damit sie diselbe besuchenn, vnnd daselbst Comoedien spiellen, sondernn sie auch an euch vorbitlich verschreiben wolten, damit sie desto mehrere beforderung in diesem Ihren Vorhabenn erlangen möchtten […]." In this letter, the Landgrave explains that the comedians at his service have asked him for permission to visit the Frankfurt fair and perform there, but also to recommed them to the city council in order to be well-accepted.

[31] For more information about taxes see ibid., p. 55.

[32] See Flemming, ed., *Barockdrama*, vol. 3, *Das Schauspiel der Wanderbühne*, pp. 6–9. Once the wandering troupes were more established, they abandoned blatant processions and instead introduced booklets giving information about the plot and special effects to attract a larger audience.

too, so the itinerant companies could use their experience to their advantage. Nonetheless, it was virtually impossible to make a living without a continuous engagement at court.[33]

Thirdly, there was the complex aspect of adapting the repertoire to a different cultural context. Rather than translating the plays word by word, it mostly sufficed to roughly transfer the main plot into German to entertain the audiences. Lengthy monologues, minor characters and dispensable scenes were excised or replaced by narrative sequences, and physical enactment underlined what was said on stage. According to Cohn, the repertoire comprised (pre-)Shakespearean tragedies, comedies, jigs and scriptural dramas with a strong connecting factor, because the content was already known to the spectators beforehand and could easily be inferred.[34] Particular attention, of course, was given to the comic scenes and pantomime of the clown, even in tragedies.

The use of English as the predominant language persisted throughout the first phase, although many lead actors like Sackville and Browne spoke German. A petitioning from 1596 furnishes evidence that the English Comedians performed in German at the end of this phase to facilitate their reception in the major trading towns.[35] Moreover, the cultural transfer was aided by native authors like Duke Heinrich Julius of Brunswick-Wolfenbüttel, patron of the Browne-Sackville company, who imitated and adapted the English plots, stage characters and theatrical techniques in his amateur dramas, published in 1594. This creative reception is another instance of adaptation, this time tending to cultural appropriation or – to express it neutrally – naturalisation.

Amalgamation Phase (1600–18)

The second phase covers the time span from the turn of the century to 1618, i.e. the period before the ravages of the Thirty Years' War. It is called the 'amalgamation' phase to describe the dynamic combination of foreign and autochthonous influences on the German stage in this period. The seed of Robert Browne's mainland tours with professional actors from England fell on fertile ground. Many of his colleagues soon founded their own companies and the English influence increased steadily in central Europe thanks to courtly patronage and regular visits to fairs. From these two sources, substantial sums of money were at the actors' disposal, which enhanced amalgamation in three different ambits: 1) geographic, because the companies expanded their sphere of action; 2) socio-economic, since the audiences became more diverse and the ensuing growing wealth had an impact

---

[33] For a detailed account of the finances of the touring companies see Charles Harris, "The English Comedians in Germany before the Thirty Years' War – The Financial Side", *PMLA* 22.3 (1907), pp. 446–64.
[34] See Cohn, p. VII.
[35] See Ralf Haekel "Neue Quellen zur Geschichte der Englischen Komödianten in Deutschland", *Shakespeare Jahrbuch* 140 (2004), pp. 180–5, p. 181. The text of the letter by Thomas Sackville is quoted in the next subchapter, at the description of this actor.

on staging; and 3) cultural, given that the competition of other English, Italian, French and partly German companies enlarged the adaptational process of *theatre* as performance with splendid staging, and of *drama* as text, pillaged from a variety of literary and popular sources.

Geographic amalgamation thrived in central Europe after 1604 due to the vogue for employing itinerant companies at court. Noble families like the Habsburgs in Austria, the Hohenzollerns in Germany and the Vasas in Poland gave patronage to English players, sometimes even setting up their own company after the model of Landgrave Moritz's 'Hessian Comedians'. Based on family connections and recommendations, the touring circuits were extended to Austria and all the territories of the Habsburg dynasty, the Netherlands, Poland and Denmark at least until the outbreak of the Thirty Years' War, as Willem Schrickx asserts.[36]

As far as socio-economic amalgamation is concerned, the rivalry among international companies led to enhanced productions, an inexhaustible supply of new plays, spectacular stage elements and superb acting to satisfy the growing demands of the audiences. As early as 1598, Robert Browne wrote a letter to his patron, Landgrave Moritz of Hessen-Kassel, asking "that we may have a stage made for our stately history, in the court yard, for that we cannot play in any house, it is so full of wars & stormes, in battell."[37] Evidently, the English Comedians set up extraordinary performances with special effects for their patrons in the early Baroque taste. It can therefore be supposed that in "appropriate conditions their staging may have been similar to that of London theatres" even at fairs, as Limon suggests.[38] To reach these standards, the itinerant players did not spare enormous expenses for travelling with waggons and caravans or for purchasing lavish properties and sumptuous costumes; expenses which could not be covered without the salary resulting from the contract with a patron, as the same letter testifies.[39]

Soon, the English Comedians were so firmly established that they could perform plays loosely based on English models with downsized content also in German. Their literary value was sufficient to encourage the printing of the first

---

[36] See Schrickx, *Foreign Envoys and Travelling Players in the Age of Shakespeare and Jonson*, p. 217.

[37] The letter was discovered by Ralf Haekel in the Hessian State Archive of Marburg (Inv. 4b, Nr. 208). See "Neue Quellen zur Geschichte der Englischen Komödianten in Deutschland", *Shakespeare Jahrbuch* 140 (2004), pp. 180–5, p. 183.

[38] Limon, p. 30.

[39] Wilhelm Creizenach calculates that the average admission charge of two or three kreuzers was considerable for the time and therefore achieved good profit margins, though the actors obtained only half a kreuzer and were thus still dependent on their patron, even on tour. See Creizenach, *Die Schauspiele der englischen Komödianten* (Berlin: W. Spemann, 1889), p. XVII. Browne's letter of 1598 to the Landgrave describes this plight: "[…] moreovr except your grace send espetiall word we shall have no coach nor foridg for us to come & (by my troth my good lord) we ar so weake of or late travel that we cannot come on foote." Quoted in Haekel, "Neue Quellen zur Geschichte der Englischen Komödianten in Deutschland", *Shakespeare Jahrbuch* 140 (2004), pp. 180–5, p. 183.

collections of plays, giving testimony of the linguistic and stylistic development of performances which went hand in hand with increasingly accomplished recipients. Even though the date of publication of *Engelische Comedien und Tragedien* (1620) falls into the next phase, the amalgamation it documents must have already taken place in the previous decades.

The initial adaptation of the English plays and staging techniques to the audience was rendered more complex by being combined with other international influences, especially from Italy and France, visible in the analysis of the repertoire. Subsequently, the English model was productively adopted by the first German companies, too, and intermingled with national forms of drama. These flexible components all converged in the emergent German theatre before they were fixed in a written form during the 'literarisation' phase.

Literarisation Phase (1620–48)

In the early phases, the focus of the English Comedians was mainly set on their performative art characterised by orality and physicality, but there was little occasion to exert the same influence upon dramatic literature. By contrast, when acting came to a standstill due to the war in Germany – while Austria and other surrounding neighbours still had active troupes touring them – drama thrived on the page, hence the name 'literarisation phase'.[40]

The first and most important collection containing the German adaptations of English plays, *Engelische Comedien und Tragedien* (subsequently abbreviated to *ECUT*), was printed anonymously in Leipzig in 1620 and reissued in 1624.[41] The publication date is relatively late compared to the earliest performances on the Continent in 1585 but it should be kept in mind that until the turn of the century, most plays were delivered in English and probably relied on abridged, summarised and adapted versions of the originals rather than on literary translations. Although not necessarily identical to the acting copies used by the acting comedians,

---

[40] Gerhart Hoffmeister speaks of an intermediary third phase from 1626 to 1648, in which a consolidation took place despite the war. His argument is based on the case of John Green's troupe, an offspring of Browne's company. After making his mark in Austria and a brief return to England, in 1626 Green became the principal of the *Chursächsische Truppe* in Dresden – "apparently the only one able to secure the patronage of a court during the Thirty Years' War." Hoffmeister, "The English Comedians in Germany", in Hoffmeister, ed., *German Baroque Literature*, pp. 142–58, p. 146. However, this case is an exception in the German panorama and arguably not enough to speak of a 'consolidation phase', especially in times of war, which curtailed English activities so much that most players returned to their home country or sought refuge in neutral regions like Poland or Prussia. Only few English players re-emerged after the war. Instead, attention should be given to the literary tide that took place during the forced hiatus of cultural production due to the war.

[41] All the plays of the collection are contained in Manfred Brauneck, ed., *Spieltexte der Wanderbühne* (Berlin and New York: W. de Gruyter, 1975), vol. 1. It will be subsequently abbreviated to *SW*, vol. 1.

the collection offers relevant information about the adaptation at work on the German stage.

After the 1620 and 1624 editions of *ECUT*, a second volume was published in 1630 by an anonymous editor with the title *Liebeskampff Oder Ander Theil Der Engelischen Comoedien und Tragoedien* ('Love Conflict or Another Part of English Comedies and Tragedies').[42] Compared to the first collection, the label 'Engelische' here is just a seal of quality to establish a sort of continuity and does not match the content, which was derived primarily from Spanish and Italian pastorals and *novelle*.[43] In the eight dramas it contains – four comedies, two *Singspiele*, a tragicomedy and a tragedy – structure, layout and style are more elaborate

---

[42] The entire title is *Liebeskampff Oder Ander Theil Der Engelischen Comoedien und Tragoedien / In welchen sehr schöne / ausserlesene Comoedien und Tragoedien zu befinden / und zuvor nie in Druck aussgegangen. Allen der Comoedi und Tragoedi Liebhabern / und andern zu liebe und gefallen / dergestalt in offenen Druck gegeben / dass sie gar leicht daraus Spielweiss wiederumb angerichtet / und zur Ergetzligkeit und Erquickung des Gemüths / gehalten werden können* ('The Love Conflict or Another Part of English Comedies and Tragedies, in which beautiful and select comedies and tragedies are to be found, never printed before. Openly published in this form for the sake and pleasure of all lovers of comedies and tragedies, so that they can easily extract plays from it and perform them to amuse and enliven the mind'). All the plays of *Liebeskampff* (1630) held at the Herzog August Bibliothek in Wolfenbüttel are contained in Brauneck, ed., *Spieltexte der Wanderbühne*, vol. 2. Only the titles shall be adduced here: *Comoedia und Macht des kleinen Knaben Cupidinis* ('Comedy and Power of the little boy Cupid') featuring the clown Hans Worst and a song of Adonis and Phyllis; *Comedia: Von den Aminta und Silvia* ('Comedy of Aminta and Silvia' after Tasso) with musical scores; *Comoedia und Prob getrewer Lieb* ('Comedy and test of truthful love'); *Comoedia von König Mantalors unrechtmessigen Liebe und derselben Straff* ('Comedy of King Mantalor's unlawful love and its punishment'); *Etliche newe SingeComoedien / so zur Lust wol agiret werden können* ('Several new musical comedies, to be played ad libitum': one connected to the 'Tragedy of inopportune impertinence' because of the motif of the basket as symbol of unrequited love, as in the German proverb 'Jemandem einen Korb geben'; one called *Der Mönch im Sacke*, i.e. 'The Monk in the Sack'; and one being a dance of satyrs to be inserted either in *Comoedia und Macht des kleinen Knaben Cupidinis* or in *Aminta und Silvia*); *Tragi Comedia* (tragicomedy without a proper title but indebted to *Decameron* II. 7 and V.3, as Alberto Martino found out in *Die italienische Literatur im deutschen Sprachraum*, p. 378); *Tragoedi. Unzeitiger Vorwitz* ('Tragedy of inopportune impertinence' after Cervantes' novella 'El curioso impertinente') with musical scores.

[43] Like *ECUT*, *Liebeskampff* is preceded by an apologetic preface which presents the plays as a "living example [...] thanks to which we can learn, see and recognise how to lead a civil, chaste, and honest life respecting all sorts of virtues and avoiding vice." (My translation of *SW*, vol. 2, p. 2: "[...] gleich lebendig Exempel [...] damit wir lernen, sehen und erkennen, welcher massen wir unser Leben Bürgerlich, züchtig und ehrlich, in erhaltung allerhand Tugenden, und meidung den Lüsten anrichten sollen"). To guarantee for the moral edification obtained by means of drama, the aristocratic patrons, dukes, kings, and emperors who approve of the comedians are adduced as examples. The anonymous author concludes with the wish that "my bad work" may please the readers and, if not, that they may still be favourably impressed by the first collection, *ECUT*, and drama in general. Despite the appropriation of the plays hidden in the pronoun *my*, the editor merely put

than in *ECUT*, the characters are described with more psychological depth, and the language abounds in rhetorical devices, anticipating the Baroque taste for embellishment. The return of long monologues in verse or intricate plots which the first English Comedians had left out in favour of emotional scenes and vivid dialogues in prose for the sake of simplicity signals that the written text moved away from its primary purpose of a lively performance. Instead, it became a literary product to be read and imitated. As if to confirm this, the plays of *Liebeskampff* do not appear in most of the extant lists of repertoires and are so loosely linked to the English Comedians that I will not analyse them in detail.

The literarisation phase witnesses a change of taste towards the Spanish and Italian 'rivals' of the English Comedians, noticeable in a preference for plots of novelistic intrigue in fantastic and pastoral settings, with comic subplots involving the clown. An explanation could be that the English Comedians directed their attention more to performing than to translating and editing their repertoire, so once they stopped touring the Continent due to the Thirty Years' war, their ascendancy declined, although their famous clown Pickelhering continued to populate the stage. Soon autochthonous troupes replaced the English precursors and drew on the literary products from Italy, Spain and France, which continued to thrive unhindered by the war. According to the theoretical precepts of Martin Opitz' *Prosodia Germanica, oder Buch von der Deutschen Poeterey* (1624 – the year when the second edition of *ECUT* was published), the German appropriation of international material moved away from the vitality of the early English performances preferring a regulated system of literary drama. Conscious of the danger of an international 'overflooding', Opitz tried to redeem German literature from foreign influences and provided the formal guidelines for its future development in the 'naturalisation' phase.

> together and revised plays of other authors and companies. For instance, *Aminta und Silvia* (1630) has its foundation in an Italian pastoral play by Torquato Tasso, *Aminta*, first presented on 31 July 1573 at the court of Ferrara under Alfonso d'Este by the famous Commedia dell'Arte company of the Comici Gelosi, as Brauneck explains in *Die Welt als Bühne*, vol. 1, p. 445. The German rendition follows the original closely and almost verbatim in certain scenes, like when Aminta wishes to die after finding Silvia's blood-stained veil – a motif taken from the tale of Pyramus and Thisbe – but renounces the pastoral setting and instead adds the comic servant Schrämgen to make the content palatable to the audience. Another example is the 'Tragedy of inopportune impertinence' after Cervantes' exemplary *novella El curioso impertinente* (first inserted in part one of *Don Quixote* in 1605, then published separately in *Novelas ejemplares* in 1613). The *novella* describes the famous love-test motif, found in numerous comic and tragic versions. Gustaf Fredén points out that despite the closeness to the Spanish original, the names of the characters were changed in the dramatisation and some scenes were added after the fashion of the English Comedians, e.g. the interweaving of comic scenes into a tragic main plot. This shows that the influence of the English itinerant players was still felt. See Fredén, *Friedrich Menius und das Repertoire der englischen Komödianten in Deutschland*, p. 192.

Naturalisation Phase (1648–70)

The final 'naturalisation phase' covers the decades from the Peace of Westphalia, in 1648, to 1670, when English activity on the European continent came to a stop. It is therefore not contained in the time span of this study and only briefly described. Gerhart Hoffmeister calls it a phase of "decline and dissolution", which is understandable from an English point of view.[44] Indeed, during this period there were only a few companies that were led by English veteran actors and enriched with newcomers both from Germany and from England, where the theatres had been closed by the Long Parliament of 1642 to 1660. Nonetheless, the dwindling of the English component went hand in hand with the foundation of a genuinely German Baroque theatre, which appropriated English and other foreign influences – hence the name 'naturalisation'. This is attested by the publication of *Schau-Bühne Englischer und Frantzösischer Comödianten* ('The Plays of the English and French Comedians' 1670), in which the English contribution is hardly recognisable, despite the title.[45] There are only some plays from *ECUT* and *Liebes-*

---

[44] Hoffmeister, "The English Comedians in Germany", in Hoffmeister, ed., *German Baroque Literature*, pp. 142–58, p. 151.

[45] The full title of the edition at the Austrian National Library is *Schau-Bühne Englischer und Frantzösischer Comödianten / Auff welcher werden vorgestellet die schönsten und neuesten Comödien / so vor wenig Jahren in Franckreich / Teutschland und andern Orten / bey Volckreicher Versamlung seynd agiret und praesentiret worden. Franckfurt / In Verlegung Johann Georg Schiele / Buch-Händlers. Im Jahr M DC LXX* ('The plays [literally: stage] of the English and French Comedians, in which the most beautiful and most recent comedies/plays are presented as they have been played and performed a few years ago in France, Germany and elsewhere in front of a populous crowd. Printed in Frankfurt by the bookseller Johann Georg Schiele in the year 1670'). Most of the plays of this collection are contained in Brauneck, ed., *Spieltexte der Wanderbühne*, vols. 3 and 4. The complete list of titles reads as follows. Volume 1: Foreword (taken from *Liebeskampff* 1630); *Comoedia Amor der Artzt* ('Comedy of Cupid, the Doctor'); *Comoedia Die Comoedie ohne Comoedie* ('Comedy of the Comedy without Comedy'); *Comoedia Die koestliche Laecherlichkeit* ('Comedy of the Delightful Ridiculousness'); *Comedia Sganarelle, Oder Der Hanrey in der Einbildung* ('Comedy of Sganarelle or The Imaginary Cuckold' – Sganarelle is the French descendant of the Zanni Brighella of the Commedia dell'Arte, created by Molière); *Comoedia Die Liebes-Geschicht deß Alcippe, und der Cephise: Oder Die Hanreyin nach der Einbildung* ('Love Comedy of Alcippe and Cephise or the imaginary female cuckold'); *Comoedia Die Eyfernde mit Ihr selbst* ('Comedy of the Bigot with herself'); *Tragi-Comoedia Antiochus* ('Tragicomedy of Antiochus'); *Comoedia die Bulhafftige Mutter* ('Comedy of the Paramour Mother'); *Comoedia Damons Triumph-Spiel / Darinnen die Laster verworffen / die Weisheit und Tugenden rühmlichst auff- und angenommen werden* ('Comedy of Damon's Triumph in which Vice is discarded and Wisdom and the Virtues are laudably received and accepted'). Volume 2 entitled *Schau-Bühnen Englischer und Frantzösischer Comödianten Ander Theil / Auff welcher sampt dem Pickelhäring werden vorgestellet die schönsten und neuesten Comödien / so vor wenig Jahren in Franckreich / Teutschland und andern Orten / bey Volckreicher Versamblung seynd agiret und praesentieret worden* ('Second part of the plays [literally: stage] of the English and French Comedians, in which the most beautiful and most recent

kampff to prove the longevity of the early English repertoire. In volume 1, eight out of nine plays are translations of French plays. In volumes 2 and 3, the plays by the Dutch playwright Isaak Vos, who drew on Spanish literature as well, and authors of French classicism like Molière and Corneille were adapted alongside Italian courtly love comedies for example by Giacinto Cicognini. Evidently, the English Comedians were not the major shapers of German drama anymore but were still a fundamental segment of the European network. In particular, the *Haupt- und Staatsaktion* (main and state action) became the favourite dramatic form of the Baroque period and shows how the influence from Italy, France and England lived on in an autochthonous early seventeenth-century German genre. As the term implies, the main action was devoted to serious topics – politics, religion, history, mythology – with intrigues of noble characters in exotic places, abounding in magniloquent rhetoric and sensationalism after the model of Italian and French drama and opera.[46] By contrast, the subplot was the domain of clown figures like the Anglo-German Pickelhering with semi-improvised sketches to entertain the audience after the manner of Commedia dell'Arte.

The remainder of this chapter presents the major English companies and their valuable contribution to German drama. Looking at the names and personalities behind the 'English Comedians' who provided the basis for the development of professional popular theatre, the concept of "ambassadors" suggested by Heinz Kindermann is highly suitable for describing their "collective transfer" of repertoire from one nation to the other in just a few decades.[47]

    comedies/plays are presented along with Pickelhering as they have been played and performed a few years ago in France, Germany and elsewhere in front of a populous crowd): Foreword (taken from *ECUT* 1620); *Kurtzweilige und lustige Comoedia, von Sidonia und Theagene* (cf. *ECUT* 1620); *Der Verliebten Kunstgriffe: Eine Comödia* ('The Artful Tricks of Lovers'); *Lustiges Pickelhärings Spiel / darinnen er mit einem Stein gar lustige Possen macht* (cf. *ECUT* 1620); *Comoedia von Fortunato / seinem Seckel und Wünschhütlein / Darinnen erstlich drey verstorbene Seelen als Geister / darnach die Tugend und Schande eingeführet werden* (cf. *ECUT* 1620); *Comoedia: Der Unbesonnene Liebhaber* ('Comedy of the imprudent Lover'); *Taliclea Die Großmüthige, Comoedia* ('The Magnanimous Taliclea, Comedy'). Volume 3 (without a foreword): *Comoedia, Von der Königin Esther und dem hoffärtigen Haman* (cf. *ECUT* 1620); *Comoedia, Von dem verlohrnen Sohn / in welcher die Verzweyflung und Hoffnung gar artig introduciret werden* (cf. *ECUT* 1620); *Comoedia, Von König Mantalors unrechtmäßigen Liebe und derselben Straff* (cf. *Liebeskampff* 1630); *Der Geitzige. Comoedia* ('The Miser'); *Comedia: Von den Aminta und Silvia* (cf. *Liebeskampff* 1630); *Macht des kleinen Knabens Cupidinis: Comoedia* (cf. *Liebeskampff* 1630); *Georg Dandin oder Der verwirrete Ehemann*: *Comoedia* ('George Dandin or the fooled husband' cf. Molière's Ballet-comedy *George Dandin ou le Mari confondu* of 1668).

[46]   See <https://www.britannica.com/topic/Haupt-und-Staatsaktionen> (last accessed 1 November 2019).

[47]   "[…] diese Englischen Komödianten waren Botschafter ihres Landes. Es gibt in der gesamten Theatergeschichte Europas nur wenige Beispiele einer derartigen Kollektiv-Übertragung von einer Nation zur anderen." Heinz Kindermann, *Theatergeschichte Europas*

5.2. The First 'Ambassadors': Kemp, Browne & Co.

There are historic records of English musicians at the Danish and Prussian courts in 1556 and 1579, but it took itinerant actors longer to map out the same routes.[48]

William Kemp

The earliest identifiable English entertainer on the Continent was William Kemp (died 1603), who arrived as part of a nobleman's entourage before touring with his own company. In 1585 the Earl of Leicester took Kemp with him on his way to the Netherlands to assist the United Provinces in rebellion against Philip II at the behest of Queen Elizabeth.[49] After a brief return to England, in 1586 Kemp travelled to Denmark with his colleagues from the Lord Chamberlain's Men, George Bryan and Thomas Pope, to entertain Frederick II (1559–88) at Elsinore.[50] Their performance pleased the Danish king so greatly that he recommended them to Christian I, Duke Elector of Saxony, who invited the whole ensemble to Berlin and Dresden for nine months.[51]

The novelty of their acting met with resounding success in post-Reformation Germany, where spectators were mainly used to amateur Shrovetide farces, per-

---

(Salzburg: Otto Müller, 1957–74) vol. 3, p. 366. Caveat: Kindermann was a notorious Nazi-inspired Austrian *Theaterwissenschaftler*. Although widely known for his *völkisch*/fascist stance, he was appointed head of the Vienna University *Theaterwissenschaft* sometime after WWII. His monumental theatre history of Europe is still a valuable source, though it must be used with caution.

[48] According to Eckehard Catholy, in northern Germany the Protestant Reformation was one of the major obstacles to the development of theatre other than doctrinal school drama, and accounts for the suspicion foreign troupes aroused. For these reasons, musicians and acrobats were usually more accepted than actors, as their performances appeared less problematic from an ideological point of view. See Catholy, op. cit., p. 116.

[49] Kemp's presence in the first Continental tour is proved by two historical records, mentioned by Cohn. Firstly, a letter by the Earl of Leicester's nephew, Philip Sidney, attests "Will the Lord of Leicester's jesting players" in his entourage. Secondly, since Kemp is mentioned among the members of the Lord Leicester's Men at Essex House in May 1585, the "Will" of the letter must be Kemp. See Cohn, p. XXII.

[50] In Heywood's words: "[…] the King of Denmarke, father to him that now reigneth, entertained into his service a company of English Comedians, commended unto him by the honourable Earle of Leicester." Thomas Heywood, *Apology for Actors*, 1612 (London: Shakespeare Society, 1841), p. 40. This is furthermore attested by Wilhelm Creizenach's quote from a register of board wages of the Danish royal household from August to September 1586, in which "Wilhelm Kempe, instrumentist" is mentioned alongside five other "instrumentister och springere" (i.e. musicians and acrobats, literally leapers). See Creizenach, p. III.

[51] As a document cited by Johannes Bolte testifies, during this period the English players delighted their audience with "Singspiele, Schauspiele, Springkunst, Musik und Tanz" (musical comedies, plays, acrobatics music and dance), i.e. the performing arts for which the expatriates would later be celebrated abroad. See Johannes Bolte, *Das Danziger Theater im 16. und 17. Jahrhundert* (Hamburg and Leipzig: Leopold Voß, 1895), p. XVI.

formances in foreign languages like Latin school drama and spectacles of wandering Italian or French troupes. The contact with these different traditions enabled the English players to learn from their competitors and bring back valuable inputs to their homeland on their return in 1587. Louis B. Wright argues that the mediation of Kemp's newly acquired Commedia dell'Arte tricks in his clowneries smoothed the path for the adoption of elements "after the manner of Italy" in Shakespeare's plays.[52]

In 1599, Kemp left the Lord Chamberlain's Men to start a successful solo career; in February and March 1600 he performed an itinerant nine-day-long Morris dance from London to Norwich, recorded in *Kemps Nine Daies Wonder* (1600).[53] Then, he undertook a last tour abroad in 1601, in which he may have crossed the Alps to Venice and intensified the connection with Commedia dell'Arte.[54] Richard Preiss provides evidence that shortly before he died, Kemp joined the Earl of Worcester's Men in 1602 and played Nobody in the play *No-body and Some-body* (printed in 1606), which was soon successfully exported to the Continent.[55]

Kemp was soon followed by more companies, marking the "transition from individual performers to teamwork", as Hoffmeister asserts.[56] Their hope was to find prosperity and less competition from rivalling troupes than on London's overcrowded stages. As a contemporary pamphlet significantly summed up: "We can be bankrupts (say the players) on this side and gentlemen of a company beyond the sea: be burst in London, and pieced up in Rotterdam. The sea is a purger, and at sea must our fortunes take physic."[57]

---

[52] On his return to England, Kemp joined the Lord Strange's Men until 1594, when he became a member of the Lord Chamberlain's Men. Wright argues that his international experience enhanced the expressive potential of his comical roles in Shakespeare's plays. Peter in *Romeo and Juliet*, Dogberry in *Much Ado About Nothing*, Lance in *The Two Gentlemen of Verona*, and Costard in *Love's Labor's Lost* are all indebted to the Commedia dell'Arte and the Zannis. See Louis B. Wright, "Will Kempe and the Commedia dell'Arte", *Modern Language Notes* 41.8 (1926), pp. 516–20, p. 520.

[53] See Richard Preiss, *Clowning and Authorship in Early Modern Theatre* (Cambridge: CUP, 2014), ch. 4, for an analysis of *Kemps Nine Daies Wonder*. In addition, Preiss points out that, unlike Armin, Kemp and Tarlton were not only clowns but also authors (see ibid., p. 146).

[54] Will Kemp's wanderings to Italy are mentioned in a diary entry by William Smith of Abdingdon on 2 September 1601: "Kemp, mimus quidam, qui peregrinatione quondam in Germaniam et Italiam instituerat, post multos errores, et infortunia sua, reversus: multa refert de Anthonio Sherley, equite aurato, quem Romae (legatum Persicum agentem) convenerat." Quoted in Chambers, *Elizabethan Stage*, vol. 2, p. 326.

[55] See Preiss, op. cit., p. 174.

[56] Hoffmeister, "The English Comedians in Germany", in Hoffmeister, ed., *German Baroque Literature*, pp. 142–58, p. 143.

[57] From the pamphlet *A Rod for Run-awayes. Gods Tokens, Of his feareful Iudgements, sundry wayes pronounced vpon this City, and on seuerall persons, both flying from it, and staying in it. Expressed in many dreadfull Examples of sudden Death, falne vpon both young and old, within this City, and the Suburbes, in the Fields, and open Streets, to the*

Robert Browne

Just a few years after Kempe, Robert Browne, a member of the Earl of Worcester's troupe and of the Lord Admiral's Men, started a series of successful tours in Europe, which paved the way for the creation of more companies and the spreading of professional entertainment in Germany. Browne's presence on the Continent is first attested in Leiden in 1590, and at the future Swedish king Karl IX's court at Nyköping in 1591–2 with a group of 'Instrumentalists'.[58] When theatres in London were closed in 1592 because of the plague, Robert Browne, John Bradstreet, Thomas Saxfield (Sackville) and Richard Jones crossed the Channel for a proper European tour. Their French passport, signed by the Lord High Admiral Charles Howard on 20 February 1592, states that:

> [...] Robert Browne, Jehan Bradstriet, Thomas Saxfield, Richard Jones, and their fellows in my [the Lord Admiral's] service thought of making a trip through Germany, planning to pass through Zeland, Holland and Frisia and going to practice, on the said voyage, their ability as musicians, actors and players of comedies, tragedies and histories in order to sustain themselves and meet their expenses on their said trip.[59]

On their way from the Netherlands to Frankfurt, these "musicians, actors and players" of the highest circles found favourable conditions at Duke Heinrich Julius of Brunswick-Wolfenbüttel's (1563–1613) court.[60] This nobleman and jurist was married to Elisabeth of Denmark and had already witnessed the English players there. Together with the Landgrave Moritz of Hessen-Kassel he was one of the first patrons to maintain a regular ensemble at court, which inspired him to write and publish several amateur plays in the 'English manner' in 1593–4.

As an accomplished actor and clever manager, Browne secured a stable foothold in different German courts by splitting up his ensemble, as was the common

---

terrour of all those who liue, and to the warning of those who are to dye, to be ready when God Almighty shall bee pleased to call them. By THO. D. (London, 1625), quoted in Cohn, op. cit., p. XCVI.

[58] See Limon, p. 3.

[59] Original text: "Messieurs, Comme les presentz porteurs, Robert Browne, Jehan Bradstriet, Thomas Saxfield, Richard Jones, avec leurs consortz estantz mes Joeuers et seruiteurs ont deliberé de faire vng voyage en Allemagne, auec Intention de passer par le païs de Zelande, Hollande et Frise. Et allantz en leur dict voyage d'exercer leurs qualitez en faict de musicque, agilitez et joeuz de commedies, Tragedies et histoires, pour s'entretenir et fournir à leurs despenses en leur dict voyage." Quoted from the General Archives in The Hague and translated by Schrickx, p. 329, who amends Cohn's incorrect transcription of the passport. Moreover, he argues that the phrase "mes Joueurs et seruiteurs" proves that they were members of the Lord Admiral's company. See ibid., pp. 184–5. Among the players were also Thomas Pope and George Bryan, two actors acquainted with Shakespeare and Kemp. Their early career was devoted to dancing, acrobatics and music before they joined the Lord Strange's Men; later Pope was part of the company of Edward Alleyn Jr. and acted in Shakespeare's plays. See Chambers, *The Elizabethan Stage*, vol. 2, p. 273.

[60] See Hanns Niedercken-Gebhart, "Neues Aktenmaterial über die Englischen Komödianten in Deutschland", *Euphorion* 21 (1914), pp. 72–85, p. 73.

habit in England: while Thomas Sackville and John Bradstreet settled down in Wolfenbüttel as court actor/clown and dance master/leaper respectively, the rest of Browne's troupe reached Frankfurt for the Easter fair in 1592. As Peter Brand and Bärbel Rudin explain, this fair was held twice a year in spring and autumn and attracted people from all over Europe interested in the sale of cloth, wine and books.[61] Although Browne's troupe could count on a few spectators from England among the international audience present on the occasion, their staging of *Gammer Gurton's Needle* and Marlowe's *Faustus* was not well received, probably because of the linguistic barrier.[62] In his multi-volume *Itinerary* (1591–1626), the Elizabethan traveller Fynes Moryson left a first-hand evidence of the event:

> Germany hath some fewe wandering Comedyans, more deseruing pity then prayse, for the serious parts are dully penned, and worse acted, and the mirth they make is ridiculous, and nothing less then witty… So as I remember that when some of our cast despised the Stage players came out of England into Germany, and played at Franckford in the tyme of the Mart, hauing nether a complete number of Actours, nor any good Apparell, nor any ornament of the Stage, yet the Germans, not vnderstanding a worde they sayde, both men and women, flocked wonderfully to see theire gesture and Action, rather than heare them, speaking English which they vnderstand not, and pronowncing peeces and Patches of English playes, which my selfe and some English men there present could not heare without great wearysomenes.[63]

The unfavourable comparison discrediting the performance as mere gesture without content, unworthy of the London standards does not consider how different

---

[61] See Peter Brand and Bärbel Rudin, "Der englische Komödiant Robert Browne (1563–ca. 1621): Zur Etablierung des Berufstheaters auf dem Kontinent", *Daphnis: Zeitschrift für Mittlere Deutsche Literatur und Kultur der Frühen Neuzeit (1400–1750)* 39 (2010), pp. 1–119, p. 67.

[62] Considering that *The Life and Death of Doctor Faustus* appeared in 1588 but was printed in 1604 (the so-called A text), its diffusion on the Continent was extremely rapid. Since the text of the English Comedians' play is not preserved, only conjectures can be made. Looking at the publication dates, Orlene Murad argues that the itinerant actors certainly relied on the more authentic A text and on Marlowe's lost manuscript transposed from memory on the German stage rather than on the B text published in 1616. See Murad, *The English Comedians at the Habsburg Court in Graz 1607–1608*, pp. 45–6. Interestingly, the roots of the legend around Faustus go back to a German chapbook published in Frankfurt in 1587 by Johann Spies. The folkloristic tale was then developed in various genres and exported to England, where it inspired Marlowe's tragedy. An exchange of communal understanding seems to have been travelling back and forth for many years before the English Comedians brought the topic back to Germany in a different and enriched form. In the eighteenth century, Goethe appropriated himself of the subject matter around Faust after having seen a representation of Marlowe's *The Life and Death of Doctor Faustus* by strolling puppeteers. Thus, the foundation of Goethe's great national drama was laid by English mediation of popular material developed and transformed throughout the centuries.

[63] Charles Hughes, ed., *Shakespeare's Europe: Unpublished Chapters of Fynes Moryson's Itinerary. Being a Survey of the Conditions in Europe at the End of the 16th Century*, vol. 4, p. 304.

the circumstances were. A spectacle in a proper playhouse with scenery, costumes and a dramatic text in a language intelligible to the audience is obviously more likely to deserve praise, but that was not the case in Germany for the first itinerant players. Instead, adaptation was required to put together "peeces and Patches" of successful plays and to foreground basic comic elements like mime, dances, acrobatics and primitive instincts over the spoken word. Although their hotchpotch repertoire was criticised by Moryson, it must have been effective, as the spectators "flocked wonderfully to see [...] rather than heare them. In a certain sense, he recognised the 'backwards involution' as something negative, while it was actually sensitive to the context. Anyway, Browne learned his lesson; at the autumn fair of the same year the focus was set on biblical stories and historical narrations that would be familiar to the non-English spectators from the shared network of (popular) knowledge.[64] Then he returned to courtly spheres.

In 1593, Landgrave Moritz of Hessen-Kassel, dilettante composer and playwright himself,[65] took Browne into his service as "Diener Comoediant unnd Musicus" in charge of the staging of comedies, tragedies and concerts. Given his experience with child companies in London, Browne was also requested to train the pupils of the Collegium Mauritianum to perform plays in Latin, written by the Landgrave, and in English, proving that English was spoken at court.[66]

[64] See Schrickx, *Foreign Envoys and Travelling Players in the Age of Shakespeare and Jonson*, p. 189.

[65] Landgrave Moritz of Hessen-Kassel tried his hand at Latin plays such as *Anglia*, an Anglicised version of Terence's *Andria*, and dramatisations of biblical and classical stories in German e.g. *Esther, Cassandra, Saul, Nabuchodonosor*, and *Holofernes*. They were probably performed by pupils of his courtly school after the model of the Jesuit drama. See Julius Tittmann, ed., *Die Schauspiele des Herzogs Heinrich Julius von Braunschweig* (Leipzig: Brockhaus, 1880), p. XIV. Moreover, in the Landgrave's entourage there was the court physician Johannes Rhenanus, who translated the English morality play *Lingua or The Combat of the Tongue and the Five Senses for Superiority*, attributed to Anthony Brewers (1607), into *Speculum aistheticum* (1610–13). This first attempt at German drama in blank verse was dedicated to Moritz with the aim to reach the English Comedians' level of excellence in composition, action, and performance. As Creizenach argues, Rhenanus was the earliest German author to realise the value of the plays introduced by the itinerant players because he was acquainted with the originals behind their adaptations. During his stay in England, he had seen that the success of English drama resided in the tight connection between playwrights and professional actors, which made writing compliant with playing, acting, and performing. See Creizenach, p. CXIV.

[66] See Hans Hartleb, *Deutschlands erster Theaterbau: Eine Geschichte des Theaterlebens und der Englischen Komödianten unter Landgraf Moritz dem Gelehrten von Hessen-Kassel* (Berlin and Leipzig: W. de Gruyter, 1936), p. 32 for the contract, from which I quote: "[...] Auch jeder Zeitt schuldig unnd bereitt sein soll, uff unser erfordernn unnd begeren neben seiner gesellschafft unns allerley Artt Lustiger Comoedien, Tragoedien, unnd Spiele wie wir dieselben enttweder selbst erfinden unnd ihme angebenn werden, oder er vor sich wissen oder erfinden wurtt [..] auch sowohl in Muscia Vocali als Intrumentali. [...] darneben soll er Auch schuldig sein unnss uff unser begeren ein oder mehr

Once settled in Kassel, Browne's company split up again: Richard Jones and a few other actors and musicians maintained the position at the Landgrave's court until they were dismissed in 1597, while the rest of the company travelled to Nuremberg and Prague, the then capital of the Holy Empire of the German Nation. After a short sojourn in England in 1596, Browne returned with the Earl of Lincoln, who had been sent to Kassel by Queen Elizabeth herself for the christening of Moritz's daughter Elizabeth.[67] This confirms not only the close diplomatic connections between Germany and England but also that Browne was chosen as a translator and guide because of his proficiency in the foreign language and his affiliations to the German courts.

According to Johannes Meissner, between 1598 and 1602 Browne's well-established company travelled to Wurttemberg, Strasbourg, Heidelberg, Munich, Linz, Cologne, Ulm, Nuremberg, Augsburg and Frankfurt.[68] The improved knowledge of the German language enabled them to add partly translated and partly adapted plays to their repertoire and become gradually naturalised. After stops in Aachen, Liège, Antwerp, Lille, Paris and Fontainebleau, where Browne played for the Dauphin Louis XIII, the troupe returned to Kassel in 1605. Their former patron Landgrave Moritz took them into his service again as *Fürstliche Hessische Komödianten* ('Princely Hessian Comedians'), one of the first official companies in Germany, as Brand and Rudin assert, and invited them to play in Germany's first permanent theatre, the Ottoneum in Kassel.[69] A few years later, the English impresario went back to England from 1607 to 1618 and the management of the

Knaben wie wir ihme dieseben jederzeit undergeben werden, es seyen gleich in oder Auslendische, Abzurichten." As the contract explains, Browne's tasks at court were to perform comedies, tragedies and other plays with his company at any time, either chosen or written by the Landgrave or composed by themselves and accompanied by music and singing. Moreover, Borwne should train the German and foreign pupils for acting. One of the pupils was the Landgrave's son Otto, namesake of the Ottoneum Theatre, who visited London in 1611.

[67] It is probable that Browne returned to London because his wife had died of the plague, as a letter by Philip Henslowe to Edward Alleyn, dated August 1593, testifies: "Robart [sic!] brownes wife in shordech & all hrér chellfren & howshowld be dead and heare dores sheat vpe." Foakes, ed., *Henslowe's Diary*, p. 277.

[68] See Meissner, *Die englischen Comoedianten zur Zeit Shakespeares in Österreich*, p. 32.

[69] See Brand and Rudin, "Der englische Komödiant Robert Browne (1563–ca. 1621)", pp. 1–119, p. 69. At the Ottoneum, the English Comedians performed amongst others 'Fortunatus', the 'Comedy of the King of England and Scotland', 'The Prodigal Son', 'Of Nobody and Somebody', 'Of the Jew' (of Venice or Malta?), all part of *ECUT* (1620), as well as *Von Vincentio Ladislao* by Heinrich Julius in 1607. For a detailed description of the plays given at the Ottoneum see June Schlueter, "English Actors in Kassel, Germany, during Shakespeare's Time", *Medieval and Renaissance Drama in England* 10 (1988), pp. 238–61, pp. 248–51.

itinerant players was divided between John Green and Ralph Reeve (also documented as Rudolph Remius or Rudolph Riveus).[70]

After a ten-year absence, in 1618 Browne founded a new company in Nuremberg with newly recruited actors, such as his son-in-law Robert Reynolds, and a replenished stock of plays. Instead of promoting the establishment of a permanent playhouse for their plays in German lands, he provided entertainment to the Protestant courts and major cities even though the approaching Thirty Years' War hampered touring. When the Catholic Ferdinand II was deposed in 1619, Browne replaced his fellow actor/rival Green in Prague and achieved a last success at the coronation of the Protestant 'Winter King' Frederick V of the Palatinate and his wife Elizabeth, daughter of King James VI.[71] Tired of a long life of vagrancy, the great pioneer died in London in 1621.

His heritage was taken up by various members of his troupes, who founded their own companies and toured Germany, Poland, Austria, the Netherlands and Denmark. As the chart shows, Browne and his colleagues cover the period 1592–1633, which marks the transition from the adaptation to the amalgamation phase. The dates in brackets refer to the period spent actively touring the Continent.

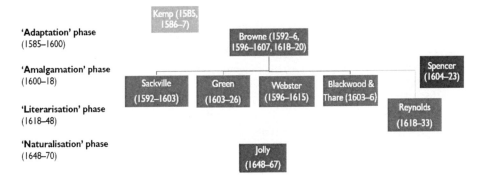

Despite the linguistic and logistic difficulties, the initial nucleus around Browne grew with every tour and brought forth numerous new splinter companies headed by Thomas Sackville, John Green, George Webster, Thomas Blackwood and John Thare. The representatives of the 'second generation' – John Green, Robert Reynolds and the last English Comedian, George Jolly – will be presented in the next subchapter; the others appear here to complete the section on Robert Browne

---

[70] According to Brand and Rudin, op. cit., pp. 1–119, p. 93–5, back in England Browne became the manager of the Children of the Queen's Revels in 1610, played for King James I, and toured the country. In 1614, he is recorded among the members of Queen Anne's company until they dissolved in 1618. Whether Browne's return to Europe caused the breakup or was a consequence of it, is not clear.

[71] The unlucky King Frederick, who contributed significantly to the outbreak of the Thirty Years' War, did not rule Bohemia for a long time, so Browne returned to Germany.

and his earlier collaborators. Only John Spencer was not part of the Browne 'enterprise'.

It should be noticed that the companies repeatedly split up and reassembled with each tour and cannot be considered as separate entities but as a network of English performers on the Continent. The strategy of independent troupes which were affiliated either to Catholic or Protestant courts proved to be a decisive political move in times of religious conflicts. Moreover, as the Italian and French competition was already strong enough, the English Comedians continued to collaborate and exchange actors and repertoire. These continuous and not consistently documented re-organisations make a precise historical reconstruction of their touring circuits complicated and provide an idea of how dynamic the development of itinerant theatre was.

Thomas Sackville aka Jahn Posset

Thomas Sackville was one of Browne's companions on the first Continental tour in 1592. In 1593, he became the principal of the newly established *Braunschweigische Hofkomödianten* ('Brunswick Courtly Comedians') at Duke Heinrich Julius's court in Wolfenbüttel and regularly toured the country during the periods of leave. A petition to the city council of Frankfurt written by Sackville reveals that plays were performed "in teutscher Sprach" (i.e. in the German language) as early as 1596. Apart from the "several lovely comedies in German language", it also advertises the "seemly music" for which the English Comedians were famous.[72]

Sackville's considerable fame rested on his stage character, the clown John/Jahn Bouschet/Bouset or Posset (either after the name of a sweet drink made of spiced beer or wine with cream, or a distorted form of the French *potage* meaning drink, or even from the old German word *Bossen*, later *Possen*, meaning jokes, fun).[73] On stage, Jahn Posset could alternatively be a wise fool or a foolish clown, depending on the situation, as Albert Cohn argues, and thus combined the grotesqueness and originality common to the two Zannis and the Shakespearean fool.[74] His ability as a singer and dancer and his peculiar mixture of German, English and Dutch to obtain a comical effect induced his patron Heinrich Julius to

---

[72] "Als M. Thomas Zackweil Engelländer vnnd *Consorten Comoedianten* Supplicirt vnnd gepetten, Inen Zuuergünstigen, dise Meß vber allerhandt lieblichen *Comoedien* In teutscher Sprach, vnnd einer zimblich musica, zu üben vnnd zu spielen, mit disem erpieten, hierinnen alle gepurende bescheidenheit Zubrauchen/. Soll man Inen willfahren, doch daß Sy mehr nit dann von einer Person ein Patz nehmen, auch mit den Kindern ein vnderscheidt haltten." City Archive of Frankfurt a.M., *Bürgermeisterbuch* ('Mayor's book') 1596, fol. 231, dated March 1596 and quoted in Ralf Haekel "Neue Quellen zur Geschichte der Englischen Komödianten in Deutschland", *Shakespeare Jahrbuch* 140 (2004), pp. 180–5, p. 181.

[73] See Meissner, *Die englischen Comoedianten zur Zeit Shakespeares in Österreich*, p. 32.

[74] See Cohn, p. XXXIII.

insert the servant Jahn/Johan/Hans Bouset into his plays and make him speak Low-German dialect to imitate Sackville.[75]

However, "Thomas Saxefiel, princely servant at Wolfenbüttel"[76] was more than a singing buffoon. In 1596, he was sent to the coronation of the Danish King with seventeen actors and musicians, among whom were Germans too, as Emil Herz states.[77] In the course of his career, he performed religious plays in English alongside the moralising German plays written by Heinrich Julius, presented Marlowe's *Doctor Faustus* in Strasbourg in 1597, and staged Shakespeare's *Romeo and Juliet* in Nördlingen (1604), for the first time ever in German.[78] Even after Sackville had left the stage in 1605 to become a mercer in the area of Wolfenbüttel, the "Engelländische Jahn Posset" was adopted by the German playwright Jacob Ayrer in his *Singspiele*, imitating the English jigs.[79]

George Webster

George Webster arrived in Germany in 1596 as part of the Earl of Lincoln's entourage and became the leader of the troupe at Landgrave Moritz's court in Kassel whilst Browne went on tour in 1598. The initial collaboration soon turned into rivalry, as Wilhelm Creizenach records: at the Frankfurt fair in 1601 Webster and his colleagues Richard Machin and Ralph Reeve outplayed Browne's troupe with elaborate costumes, special effects, and their major strength – music.[80] However, Webster's success was of short duration since in 1605 the city of Frankfurt banned his troupe on the accusation of immoral representations. After that, Ralph Reeve resumed the collaboration with Browne and was given the leadership of the 'Princely Hessian Comedians' based in Kassel.[81] They performed religious plays in Stuttgart, Nördlingen, Nuremberg and at the autumn fair in Frankfurt (1608–9) and accompanied Landgrave Moritz to the assembly summoned by Emperor Rudolf II in Prague in 1612, before dissolving in 1615.[82]

---

[75] See Tittmann, ed., *Die Schauspiele des Herzogs Heinrich Julius von Braunschweig* for all the plays.
[76] The document adducing the noble title is quoted by Cohn, p. XXXIV.
[77] See Herz, *Englische Schauspieler und englisches Schauspiel zur Zeit Shakespeares in Deutschland*, p. 33.
[78] See Karl Trautmann, "Die älteste Nachricht über eine Aufführung von Shakespeares Romeo und Julie in Deutschland (1604)", *Archiv für Literaturgeschichte* XI (1882), pp. 625–6.
[79] The main characteristics of the *Singspiel* are simple refrains accompanied by music, a bawdy and sexually explicit content, extravagant costumes and acrobatics. The *Singspiele* later evolved into eighteenth-century opera with spoken parts
[80] Creizenach explains that Richard Machin, formerly part of the 'Hessian Comedians', was taken into service by the Margrave Christian of Brandenburg in 1604. In 1611 he staged a German adaptation of the *Merchant of Venice* at the Margrave's court in Halle. See Creizenach, p. IX. This might be *Der Jud von Venedig*.
[81] Ibid., p. VI.
[82] Ibid., p. VII. These are the last traces of the 'Hessian Comedians' in Germany, while John Green toured the Catholic south and made Graz the headquarters of his troupe under the Habsburg patronage.

Thomas Blackwood and John Thare

A third splinter troupe which was established after Browne's second Continental tour was that of Thomas Blackwood and John Thare, late of the Worcester's Men, who performed independently from 1603, mainly in the south of Germany.[83] Closely connected to Sackville, their repertoire encompassed both English pieces and the Duke of Brunswick-Wolfenbüttel's plays in German.[84] By the beginning of the seventeenth century, English companies could be found everywhere in Germany and Austria, not just in their headquarters at the courts in Kassel, Brunswick, Dresden and Berlin.

John Spencer aka Hans (von) Stockfisch

The only major English company of the time not directly associated with Browne was that of John Spencer, although they were in contact. Spencer was the leader of the *Brandenburg-Sächsische Hofkomödianten* ('Courtly Comedians of Brandenburg-Saxony'), founded in 1604–5 and based in Konigsberg. As usual for that time, the patron recommended his troupe to other courts of northern Germany and city councils such as Leiden and Dresden.[85]

Spencer gained international fame both for his beloved comic stage character Hans (von) Stockfisch, a typical clown name referring to food as did Jahn Posset, and for his spectacular performances with as many as nineteen actors and sixteen musicians, specialising in opulent scenery and stunning stage effects. According to a chronicle of Nuremberg, in 1613 their repertoire comprised:

> […] von Philole und mariana, Jtem von Celido und Sedea, Auch von der Zerstörrung der Stätt Troia und Constantinopel, Vom Turcken und andere Historien mehr, neben Zierlichen täntzen, lieblicher musica und anderer lustbarkeit, Jm Halsßbrunnder Hoff alhie Jn gutter teutscher Sprache, Jn Kostlicher mascarada und Keldungen agirt und gehalten.[86]

The entry mentions several plays derived from English texts like George Peele's *The Turkish Mahomet and Hyrin the Fair Greek* ("von der Zerstörrung der Stätt Troia und Constantinopel") and John Mason's *The Turk* ("Vom Turcken"), all put on in 'good German' with excellent dancing, music and costumes. From Nuremberg, the troupe continued to Augsburg and to the Reichstag in Regensburg (part of the Habsburg territory), where their extravagant costumes and on-stage

---

[83] See Chambers, *The Elizabethan Stage*, vol. 2, p. 283.
[84] See Schrickx, *Foreign Envoys and Travelling Players*, p. 197.
[85] See Herz, *Englische Schauspieler und englisches Schauspiel zur Zeit Shakespeares in Deutschland*, p. 45.
[86] Quoted in Karl Trautmann, "Englische Komoedianten in Nürnberg (1593–1648)", *Archiv für Litteraturgeschichte* XIV (1886), pp. 113–42, p. 127. Translation: '[…] Of Philole and Mariana, Of Celido and Sedea, moreover Of the Destruction of the Cities of Troy and Constantinople, Of the Turk and other histories, alongside graceful dances, lovely music and other revelries played and performed at the Heilbronner Hof in good German, with exquisite apparel and costumes.'

settings were admired even by the Emperor Matthias himself and outshone an unspecified Italian troupe present on that occasion.[87] In 1614 and 1615 Spencer's company was recorded in Strasbourg, where on 2 July 1614 they were given permission to put on two additional plays on a Sunday for their good behaviour.[88]

Creizenach argues that Spencer hired German actors from the circle of the Nuremberg Meistersinger, which shows how intensively English and local actors collaborated in the amalgamation phase.[89] Always on the lookout for profits, Spencer is said to have become Catholic for political reasons, though he also continued to visit Protestant courts and cities with undiminished favour. It was ultimately financial trouble that put an end to his career in the first years of the war, and after 1623 records about him cease altogether.[90]

5.3. Browne's Successors and the Continental Repertoire

Returning to the direct collaborators of Robert Browne, the most enterprising heirs to his legacy were John Green[91] and Robert Reynolds.

John Green

John Green (1573–1626/8?) arrived on the Continent at the turn of the century. He is mentioned in 1603 in Cologne and later in Frankfurt in August 1606, where he signed a supplication to perform with Browne and Robert Ledbetter.[92] As the

---

[87] See Martino, "Fonti tedesche degli anni 1565–1615 per la storia della Commedia dell'Arte e per la costituzione di un repertorio dei *lazzi* dello Zanni", in Martino and De Michele, ed., *La ricezione della Commedia dell'Arte nell'Europa centrale 1568–1769*, pp. 13–68, p. 24. Martino convincingly argues that Spencer did not meet Pier Maria Cecchini on that occasion as scholars thought for decades.

[88] See Johannes Crüger, "Englische Komoedianten in Straßburg im Elsass", in *Archiv für Litteraturgeschichte* XV (1887), pp. 113–25, pp. 118–20.

[89] As Creizenach recounts, after performing at the coronation of the King of Bohemia Ferdinand II in Prague in 1617, Spencer put together a company of English and Dutch actors for Johann Sigismund in Dresden between 1617 and 1618. The expenses for this new ensemble – exorbitant 1000 thaler – had to be covered by Johann Sigismund's successor, who was not very pleased with the request. See Creizenach, p. IX.

[90] Ibid., p. X.

[91] Green's brother Thomas was a member of the Queen's Servants and a clown too, so the talent evidently ran in the family. See Eva Griffith, *A Jacobean Company and its Playhouse: The Queen's Servants at the Red Bull Theatre (c. 1605–1619)* (Cambridge: CUP, 2013), p. 187.

[92] See Meissner, *Die englischen Comoedianten zur Zeit Shakespeares in Österreich*, pp. 67–8. The 1606 supplication to play at the Easter and autumn fairs in Frankfurt provides an idea of the argumentative skills required to convince the civic authorities of the moral irreproachableness of the players: "Unterthaniglich praesentirter Intercessien schreiben in den nechst auff einander Abgewichener Jahres Ostern und Herbstmessen [...] Unsere anhero brachtte Kunstliche Tragoedias und Commoetias dem Aussländischen und Inhaimischen Volck zu exhibiren. So haben wir Zur erweysung unseres dankbaren

leader of the 'Hessian Comedians' after Browne, he took over the central role of the clown instead of his former roles of youth and woman – always interpreted by men as in the Elizabethan tradition. Emil Herz describes him as a more flexible and astute courtier than Browne, while in Lawrence M. Price's words he was "a man of coarser fiber, who judged success by financial gain. He met city councillors with effrontery and was ever ready to seek new fields when the older ones diminisht their yield."[93] In fact, after visiting the eastern cities of Elbing and Danzig in July 1607, he decided to push further south towards the territories travelled mainly by Italian companies.

Under the aegis of the Styrian branch of the Habsburg family, Green was one of the first English Comedians to perform in Austria owing to his fame as an irreprehensible entertainer and perhaps also to his 'political' conversion to Catholicism.[94] His 1608 performance at the Eggenberg Castle near Graz was vividly described in a letter by the eighteen-year-old Archduchess Maria Magdalena (1589–1631) to her brother, the future Emperor Ferdinand II (reigned 1619–37). In this

gemuths (wie in Alle weg billic gewesen) unsers Verhoffens auch uns dahin beflissen, dass niemand Durch unsere Spiel geärgert worden, Sondern Jedermann darbey Er sich Zu bespiegeln, seiner Schwacheit zu erinnern und demnächst was lasterhaffts Zu fliehen und hingegen aller Erbarkeyt und Tugend nachzujagen gelegenheit Und Ursach an die Hand gegeben, uberkahme." This extract contains a few interesting details. Firstly, it hints at the international audience present at the fairs, and indeed compatriots like Fynes Moryson would be among the spectators. Secondly, it mentions artistic tragedies and comedies 'brought here' i.e. imported from England, as if to guarantee for their excellence. Thirdly, the argument against the authorities' fear of moral corruption is that the plays teach to lead a virtuous life through reflection (*bespiegeln*). In this sense, the function of popular theatre comes close the mirror-holding clown. Also note the Anglicised form "Alle weg" for 'all-ways' instead of the more common German word *immer*.

[93] Herz, *Englische Schauspieler und englisches Schauspiel zur Zeit Shakespeares in Deutschland*, p. 72, and Price, *The Reception of English Literature in Germany*, p. 13.

[94] A letter by Archduke Ferdinand's (later Emperor Ferdinand II, 1578–1637) first wife Maria Anna, dated 11 November 1607, recounts that an unidentified troupe of actors visited the Habsburg court while the Archduke was in Regensburg: 'We have graciously ordered 300 Reichsthaler to be graciously given as payment to those particular English Comedians who came here following our gracious wish and who have several times presented their comedies for our gracious pleasure.' (My translation from Meissner, *Die englischen Comoedianten zur Zeit Shakespeares in Österreich*, p. 74). In November, the players entertained Ferdinand in Passau with two comedies: 'The Prodigal Son' and a 'Play of a Jew' (ibid., p. 130). In February 1608, the English Comedians returned to Graz. From the *Theaterbrief* about their well-received Carnival performances we know that it was Green's troupe. For this reason, Meissner and Flemming argue that the unidentified company mentioned in the letter of 1607 was Green's too, while Limon is more cautious. (See Meissner, p. 130; Flemming, p. 148; and Limon, p. 231). Furthermore, Alberto Martino observes that Ferdinand II saw a Commedia dell'Arte performance in Venice on 29 April 1598, so he was familiar with the Italian acting style. See Martino, "Fonti tedesche degli anni 1565–1615 per la storia della Commedia dell'Arte e per la costituzione di un repertorio dei *lazzi* dello Zanni", in Martino and De Michele, ed., *La ricezione della Commedia dell'Arte nell'Europa centrale 1568–1769*, pp. 13–68, p. 20.

document dated 20/22 February 1608 and usually referred to as *Theaterbrief* by scholars, she enthusiastically informs her absent brother about the two-week festivities to celebrate her engagement to Cosimo de' Medici, future Duke of Florence – another connection between England, Italy and Austria.[95] She writes that the carnival revelries encompassed masked balls, sleighrides, Italian dances, and theatre performances both by the Jesuit schoolboys and the English Comedians, which is evidence of the mutual knowledge of these different traditions. As it is one of the first records of the reception of English players in Austria, it is well worth quoting the passage at length, in a translation by Orlene Murad:

> [20 Feb.] …But I must tell EL [*Euer Liebden* i.e. your dearness] at once what plays the Englishmen put on. First of all, as they had arrived here on Wednesday after Candlemas, they rested on Thursday. On the following day, Friday, they gave the play about the *Prodigal Son*, as at Passau, but on Saturday *about a pious lady of Antwerp*, certainly an excellent and chaste play. On Sunday they had *Doctor Faustus*, on Monday *about a Duke of Florence who fell in love with a nobleman's daughter*. On Tuesday they had a play about *nobody and somebody*, which was mighty clever. On Wednesday they played *Fortunatus' purse and wishing-hat*, also very nice. On Thursday they gave the play *about the Jew* which they had also played at Passau. On Friday they and we rested. On Saturday the Jesuits gave a play about *Cipriano and Justina*, also very fine, but the boys did not act so well as usual. On Shrove Sunday the cooks had their holiday, so we had dinner at five o'clock and in the evening the English players gave another performance about the two brothers, *King Ludwig and King Friderich of Hungary*, a terrifying play because King Friederich [sic!] stabbed and murdered everybody. On mad Monday they again gave a play, about a *King of Cyprus and a Duke of Venice*, also very good. After the performance [a farce about drunken behaviour given by the Jesuits] we again had dinner at five o'clock and the English players gave another play about *the rich man and Lazarus*. I cannot tell you, my dear, how pleasurable that was, not the least bit of love-making in it, and we were all deeply moved they had acted it so well. There is no doubt about it, they really are good actors.[96]

[95] Meissner adduces the example of Hippolyt Guarinonius (1571–1654), physician at the court of Graz, who wrote a lengthy treatise about the benefits of theatre as a valid cure against melancholy in 1610 entitled *Die Grewel der Verwüstung Menschlichen Geschlechts* ('The Horrors of Corruption in Mankind'). Among the many examples of legitimate pleasures to divert and edify the mind even in times of war and political instability, there is a detailed description of a Commedia dell'Arte performance he saw during his studies at the University of Padua, with amusing "Ziarlatani" (charlatans), "Pantalon" and "Zane". See Meisser, op. cit. pp. 4–11. Since Guarinonius was in Graz when Green's troupe performed at court in 1608, he could draw a direct comparison between English and Italian theatre.

[96] The letter is preserved at the Vienna Haus-, Hof-, und Staatsarchiv, Familienkorrespondenz A, Karton 6, fols 312–15 and was reprinted and translated by Orlene Murad, *The English Comedians at the Habsburg Court in Graz 1607–1608*. Salzburg Studies in English Literature. Elizabethan and Renaissance Studies 81, Salzburg: Institut für Anglistik und Amerikanistik, Universität Salzburg, 1978, p. 6–7. My emphasis on the titles. Original text: "Brief der Erzherzogin Magdalena (Graz, Februar 1608) […] miesz E.L. gleich auch schreiben, was die Engellender für Comedi gehabt haben, alsz erstlich wie sy sein am mitwoch nach liehtmesen her khommen, haben sy am pfingstag

As in England, the period of theatrical representation was limited to the time before Christmas and during the carnival festivities, with an intense schedule.[97] Every day there were different plays: mostly comedies, but also scriptural dramas, appreciated for not having "the least bit of love-making in it", and gruesome tragedies with terrifying characters who "stabbed and murdered everybody." The repertoire of Green's company included, among others, *Niemand* ('Nobody'), *Von dem verlornen Sohn* ('The Prodigal Son'), *Fortunatus* (all printed in the collection of 1620), *Doktor Faustus* (probably an adaptation of Marlowe's tragedy, first published in 1604), *Von dem Juden* ('About the Jew', previously performed in Passau – either Marlowe's *Jew of Malta* or Shakespeare's *Merchant of Venice*, aka *Jewe of Venyce*, or even Thomas Dekker's lost *Jew of Venice*) and *Vom König von Cypern und Herzog von Venedig* ('About a King of Cyprus and a Duke of Venice').[98] The letter praises the performers' skill and their versatile repertoire which

> Donnerstag auszgerast, am Freitag nacher haben sy die Comedi von dem verlornen sohn gehabt, wie zu Passau; amb Samstag von einer frommen fraween von Antorf, ist gewiss gar fein und zuchtig gewest; am sontag haben sy gehabt von dem dockhtor Faustus; am Montag von ein herzog von florenz, der sich in eines Edelmanns tochter verliebt hat; am Erchtag [Dienstag] haben sy gehabt von Niemandts und iemand, ist gewaltig artlich gewest; am Mittwoch haben sy gehabt von des fortunatus peitl und Wünschhietel, ist auch gar schön gewest; am pfingstag [Donnerstag] haben sy die von dem Juden gehalten, die sy auch zu Passau gehalten haben. [...] am faschüng sontag haben die khöch ihre hochzeit gehabt, darnach haben mir umb 5 gessen und zu nachts nach dem essen haben die Engellender wider ein Comedi gehalten von den 2 priedern Chünig ludwig und khünig fridrich von ungern, ist ein erschröckhliche Comedi gewest, ein und so hats der khünig friderick alsz erstochen und ermördt; am unsinigen Montag haben sy wider ein Comedi gehalten von ein Chünig von Chypern und ein herzog von venedig, ist auch gar schön gewest... umb 5 sein mir nacher wider zu dem essen gangen und haben die Engellender wider ein Comedi gehalten von dem reichen man und von dem Lazarusz; ich khon E.L. nit schreiben, wie schön sy gewest ist, dann khein pissen von puellerey darin gewest ist, sy hat vnns recht bewegt, so woll haben sy aggieret; sy sein gewisz woll zu passieren für guete Comedianten." For the whole letter see Flemming, pp. 71–2, Meissner, pp. 76–80 or Schrickx, pp. 332–3, and for the translation see Orad, pp. 4–11. The letter ends with an account of a fight between a Frenchmen, a German – Lorenz – and a red-haired English actor and violin player, perhaps Green, who had red hair. The Englishman killed the Frenchman in duel and survived Lorenz's treacherous attack.

[97] The German *Fasching* differs from Shrovetide because the former refers to the weeks before the beginning of Lent, while the latter defines only the Sunday, Monday and Tuesday preceding Ash-Wednesday.

[98] Meissner argues that 'About a King of Cyprus and a Duke of Venice' is unmistakeably identical with the 1626 Dresden play *Josepho Juden von Venedigk*, which begins in Cyprus and ends in Venice. See Meissner, op. cit., p. 106. Although this explanation sounds plausible, it is not likely that the Archduchess should focus on minor characters such as the King of Cyprus and the Duke of Venice in her description of the title. Instead, in a list of plays of 1651 there is *Von dem König von Cypern und dem Fürsten aus Venetia*, which perfectly fits the title adduced by Maria Magdalena. For this reason, Creizenach puts forward the thesis that 'About a King of Cyprus and a Duke of Venice' might be an

enhanced a favourable reception also thanks to their experience in adapting to the spectators' expectation and taste. In fact, the edifying plays about princes, kings and noblemen were doubtlessly tailored to an aristocratic audience, while the clown is not mentioned at all. This tactic gained the 'virtuous' Green a long engagement at the Habsburg court in the Spanish Netherlands until 1615.[99]

After a brief stop in Wolfenbüttel and Danzig, his company was the first to visit the court of Warsaw in 1616, as Willem Schrickx states.[100] In 1617, Green performed before Emperor-Archduke Matthias with Spencer's troupe in Vienna and Prague. Such was the emperor's delight that he appointed Green *Steirischer Hofkomödiant* ('Styrian Courtly Comedian'), a position the actor maintained until the outbreak of the Thirty Years' War made him return to England.[101]

In 1626 Green reappeared in Germany with new plays and actors. Creizenach records him in Cologne in March and at the Easter fair in Frankfurt. Then he organised an extensive series of performances in Dresden from May to December with the *Chursächsische Hofkomödianten*.[102] The 'Dresden Repertoire' of 1626 is one of the most important extant lists of plays of the English Comedians and comprises a large part of Green's well-received plays in Graz, also contained in *ECUT* (and highlighted in grey in the list), along with newly imported material from England, plays with an identifiable Italian influence and religious pieces.

List of plays performed at the Dresden court in 1626[103]	
	Plays contained in *ECUT*
May 31. Dresten. haben die Engelender eine Comedia von Hertzogk von Mantua und den Hertzogk von Verona gespielt auff den steinern sahl. – 'The Englishmen played a Comedy of the Duke of Mantua and the Duke of Verona in the stone hall'	PLAYS WITH RECOGNISABLE ENGLISH MODELS
	** Plays with an Italian influence
Junius 1. Dresten. Ist eine Comedia von der Christabella gespielt worden – 'They played a Comedy of Christabella'	*Religious plays*

[99] autonomous play based on a lost play, called 'X', which served as a model for both Shakespeare's *Twelfth Night* and the German adaptation called *Tugend- und Liebesstreit* ('The Fight of Virtues and Love', 1677) combined with strands of Barnaby Riche's story of Apolonius and Silla in *Riches Farewell to the Militarie Profession* (1581). See Creizenach, p. 65.
See Cohn, p. XCV.
[100] See Schrickx, *Foreign Envoys and Travelling Players*, p. 217. Schrickx points out that the connection to Poland was mediated by the Habsburg family, as King Sigismund III Vasa was married first to Anna and then to Constanze of Austria, sisters of Maria Magdalena.
[101] See Herz, *Englische Schauspieler und englisches Schauspiel zur Zeit Shakespeares*, p. 24.
[102] See Creizenach, p. XI.
[103] Quoted at length in Cohn, p. CXV, from an Almanac published by Johannes Kretzschmer. The subdivision into four categories (plays contained in *ECUT*, plays with recognisable English models, plays with an Italian influence, religious plays) is mine. In square brackets, I added the probable sourcetexts, which are partly indebted to Chambers, *The Elizabethan Stage*, vol. 2, p. 286.

Junius 2. Dresten. IST EINE TRAGOEDIA VON ROMEO UND JULIETTA GESPIELT WORDEN – 'Tragedy of Romeo and Juliet' [Shakespeare]

Junius 4. Dresten. ** Ist eine Comoedia von Amphitrione gespielt worden – 'Comedy of Aphitruo' [by Plautus or Heywood's *The Silver Age*?]

Junius 5. Dresten. Ist eine Tragicomoedia von Hertzogk von Florentz gespielt worden – 'Tragicomedy of the Duke of Florence'

Junius 6. Dresten. IST EINE COMOEDIA VOM KÖNIG IN SPANIEN UND DEN VICE ROY IN PORTUGALL GESPIELT WORDEN – 'Comedy of the King of Spain and the Viceroy of Portugal' [Kyd's *Spanish Tragedy* or *Hieronimo Part 1*?]

Junius 8. Dresten. IST EINE TRAGOEDIA VON JULIO CESARE GESPIELT WORDEN – 'Tragedy of Julius Caesar' [Shakespeare's *Julius Caesar*]

Junius 9. Dresten. IST EINE COMOEDIA VON DER CRYSELLA GESPIELT WORDEN – 'Comedy of Crysella' [Dekker's *Patient Grisell*, based on Boccaccio and Chaucer]

Junius 11. Dresten. IST EINE COMOEDIA VON HERTZOG VON FERRARA GESPIELT WORDEN – 'Comedy of the Duke of Ferrara' [Coincident with *Annabella eines hertzogen Tochter von Ferrara* performed in Nördlingen in 1604? Similar to Martson's *Parasitaster*]

Junius 20. Dresten. IST EINE TRAGICOMOEDIA VON JEMANDT UND NIEMANDT GESPIELT WORDEN – 'Tragicomedy of Somebody and Nobody' [sometimes referred to as comedy, present in a 1608 manuscript version]

Junius 21. Dresten. IST EINE TRAGICOMOEDIA VON KÖNIG IN DENNEMARK UND DEN KÖNIG IN SCHWEDEN GESPIELT WORDEN – 'Tragicomedy of the King of Denmark and the King of Sweden' [maybe an adaptation of the anonymous *Sir Clyomon and Clamydes*]

Junius 24. Dresten. IST EINE TRAGOEDIA VON HAMLET EINEN PRINTZEN IN DENNEMARCK GESPIELT WORDEN – 'Tragedy of Hamlet, Prince of Denmark' [Shakespeare]

Junius 25. Dresten. ** Ist eine Comoedia von Orlando Furioso gespielt worden – 'Comedy of Orlando Furioso' [by Robert Green?]

Junius 27. Dresten. Ist eine Comoedia von den Koenig in Engelandt und den Koenig in Schottlandt gespielt worden – 'Comedy of the King of England and the King of Scotland'

Junius 28. Dresten. IST EINE TRAGOEDIA VON HIERONYMO MARSCHALL IN SPANIEN GESPIELT WORDEN – 'Tragedy of Hieronymo, Marshal in Spain' [Kyd][104]

Julius 3. Dresten. *Ist eine Tragicomoedia von dem Hamann undt der Koenigin Ester gespielt worden* – 'Tragicomedy of Hamann and Queen Ester'

Julius 5. Dresten. *IST EINE TRAGOEDIA VON DER MÄRTHERIN DOROTHEA GESPIELT WORDEN* – 'Tragedy of the Martyr Dorothea' [Dekker's *The Virgin Martyr*?]

Julius 7. Dresten. IST EINE TRAGOEDIA VON DR. FAUST GESPIELT WORDEN – 'Tragedy of Doctor Faustus' [Marlowe]

Julius 9. Dresten. IST EINE TRAGICOMOEDIA VON EINEM KÖNIGK IN ARRAGONA GESPIELT WORDEN – 'Tragicomedy of a King in Aragon' [Robert Green's *Alphonsus, King of Arragon*]

Julius 11. Dresten. IST EINE TRAGOEDIA VON FORTUNATO GESPIELT WORDEN – 'Tragedy of Fortunatus' [referred to as comedy in *ECUT* 1620]

Julius 13. Dresten. IST EINE COMOEDIA VON JOSEPHO JUDEN VON VENEDIGK GESPIELT WORDEN – 'Comedy of Josepho, Jew of Venice' [Shakespeare's *The Merchant of Venice*]

Julius 22. Dresten. Ist eine Tragicomoedia von den behendigen Dieb gespielt worden – 'Tragicomedy of the dexterous thief'

---

[104] Held at the Herzog August Bibliothek in Wolfenbüttel.

> Julius 23. Dresten. Ist eine Tragicomoedia von einem Hertzogk von Venedig gespielt worden – 'Tragicomedy of a Duke in Venice' [*Tugend- und Liebesstreit?*]
> Julius 31. Dresten. IST EINE TRAGOEDIA VON BARRABAS, JUDEN VON MALTA GESPIELT WORDEN – 'Tragedy of Barrabas, Jew of Malta' [Marlowe]
>
> Augustus 2. Dresten. Ist eine Tragicomoedia von dem alten proculo gespielt worden – 'Tragicomedy of the Old Proculo'
> Augustus 29. Dresten. Ist eine Tragoedia von Barrabas, Juden von Malta gespielt worden – 'Tragedy of Barrabas, Jew of Malta'
>
> Sept. 4. Dresten. Ist eine Comoedia von Hertzogk von Mantua und den Hertzogk von Verona gespielt worden – 'Comedy of the Duke of Mantua and the Duke of Verona'
> Sept. 6. Dresten. Ist eine Tragicomoedia von dem alten proculo gespielt worden – 'Tragicomedy of the Old Proculus'
> Sept. 15. Dresten. Ist eine Tragicomoedia von Hertzogk von Florentz gespielt worden – 'Tragicomedy of the Duke of Florence'
> Sept. 17. Dresten. Ist eine Tragicomoedia von den behendigen Dieb gespielt worden – 'Tragicomedy of the dexterous thief'
> Sept. 19. Dresten. Ist eine Comoedia von König in Spanien und Vice Roy in Portugall gespielt worden – 'Comedy of the King of Spain and the Viceroy of Portugal'
> Sept. 22. Dresten. Ist eine Tragicomoedia von den behendigen Dieb gespielt worden – 'Tragicomedy of the dexterous thief'
> Sept. 24. Dresten. Ist eine Comoedia von Hertzogk von Ferrara gespielt worden – 'Comedy of the Duke of Ferrara'
> Sept. 26. Dresten. IST EINE TRAGOEDIA VON LEAR, KÖNIG IN ENGELANDT GESPIELT WORDEN – 'Tragedy of Lear, King in England' [Shakespeare]
> Sept. 29. Dresten. Ist eine Tragoedia von Romeo und Julietta gespielt worden – 'Tragedy of Romeo and Juliet'
>
> Oct. 1. Dresten. Ist eine Tragoedia von der Märtherin Dorothea gespielt worden – 'Tragedy of the Martyr Dorothea'
> Oct. 4. Dresten. *Ist eine Tragicomoedia von Gevatter gespielt worden* – 'Tragicomedy of the God-father'
> Oct. 19. Dresten. *Ist eine Comoedia von verlohren Sohn gespielt worden* – 'Comedy of the Prodigal Son'
> Oct. 22. Dresten. Ist eine Comoedia von den Koenig in Engelandt und den König in Schottlandt gespielt worden – 'Comedy of the King of England and the King of Scotland'
> Oct. 29. Dresten. Ist eine Comoedia von den Graffen von Angiers gespielt worden – 'Comedy of the Count of Angiers'
>
> Nov. 5. Dresten. Ist eine Comoedia von Josepho Juden von Venedigk gespielt worden – 'Comedy of Josepho, Jew of Venice'
>
> Decemb. 4. Dresten. *Ist eine Tragoedia vom reichen Mann gespielt worden* – 'Tragedy of the rich man' [Ayrer's *Tragedia vom Reichen Mann und Armen Lazaro?*]

Although the text of most of the plays is missing, the selection comprises the favourite authors of the time, not only in their home country but also abroad. Among the 29 plays performed in a short period, only four are religious or biblical in content (marked in italics in the list) such as 'the Prodigal Son' and 'Esther'. Unsurprisingly, the vast majority echo English models (capitalised in the list) such as Shakespeare's *Romeo and Juliet*, *The Merchant of Venice*, *Hamlet*, *King Lear* and *Julius Caesar*. Further mentioned playwrights are Marlowe, Kyd, Dekker and Heywood. The other plays are based either on classical and Italian sources (marked with two asterisks in the list, like Ariosto's *Orlando Furioso* adapted by Robert Greene – not to be confused with John Green, the actor) or on tales, chapbooks and romance. The exciting fate of noble characters in exotic settings seems to be the favourite entertainment at the time, no matter if with a happy or tragic ending or with a religious background, as long as there was a clown.

Despite Green's great contribution to exporting English dramatic literature to Germany, his death is shrouded in mystery. The fact that his troupe played under the leadership of his collaborator and successor Robert Reynolds at the 1628 autumn fair in Frankfurt corroborates the hypothesis of Green's death in 1628 put forward by Herz, whereas Schrickx argues that he died in 1626.[105]

Robert Reynolds aka Pickelhering

The name of Robert Reynolds (fl. 1610–33) is generally associated with the indisputable star of Green's troupe: the clown Pickelhering, introduced in 1615 by his colleague George Vincent (died 1647) and further developed by Reynolds.[106] After marrying Browne's daughter Jane in 1615, Reynolds left the Queen Anne's Men and followed his father-in-law to the Continent in 1618, where he joined Green's company. In 1626, he succeeded Green as leading actor and clown of the *Chursächsische Hofkomödianten* at the Dresden court of the Elector of Saxony John George I (1585–1656) until 1631. It is in this period that his first appearance as Pickelhering is documented, namely in 1627 in Torgau.[107] Between 1631 and 1632, Reynolds and his *Pickelhering compagnia* continued touring Cologne, Frankfurt, Riga and Denmark, despite the war and the growing German competition. After his death in 1633, he was succeeded by William Roe, and some of his fellow actors are still mentioned as late as 1671 under the name of *Alt-Engelische Commedianten* ('Old-English Comedians').[108]

The Clown Pickelhering's Creation and Reception

During Reynolds's career, the sobriquet Pickelhering became the epitome of the English clown. The fact that he was the product of amalgamation might explain why he contributed so greatly to the development of the *Lustspiel* and even outlived the other English clowns on the German stage.

---

[105] See Herz, *Englische Schauspieler und englisches Schauspiel zur Zeit Shakespeares in Deutschland*, p. 31 and p. 132, and Schrickx, *Foreign Envoys*, pp. 218–9.
[106] For more information about George Vincent see Schrickx, op. cit., pp. 227–30.
[107] See Creizenach, *Die Schauspiele der englischen Komödianten*, p. XCIV.
[108] See Brand and Rudin, "Der englische Komödiant Robert Browne (1563–ca. 1621)", pp. 1–119, p. 117.

Firstly, the name meaning pickled herring recalled a common food among the lower classes. Likewise, his comic roles of peasant and servant made him a representative of this societal group and their problems. With this name echoing food, Vincent and Reynolds were perhaps following the model set by Sackville's clown Jahn Posset and Spencer's clown Hans Stockfisch, but also inserted themselves into an older tradition of the English mummers' play, as François Laroque observes.[109] In this sense, Pickelhering was rooted in the English clowning tradition and in popular culture.

Secondly, like Sackville's Jahn Posset, Reynolds's stage character combined Dutch and German songs with English jigs, which would become the successful genres of *Pickelheringspiel* and *Singspiel.* In these musical comedies with rhyming lyrics sung to well-known (German) tunes, adaptation and amalgamation worked together to create a new hybrid.

Thirdly, Pickelhering made use of two key elements of the clowning tradition and of Commedia dell'Arte – physicality and improvisation – as a contemporary source proves: in his travel journal of 1608–67, the merchant and traveller Peter Mundy writes that Reynolds made the audience roar with laughter because he could so "frame his face and countenance that to one half of the people on one side he would seem heartily to laugh and to those on the other side bitterly to weep and shed tears."[110] Non-verbal pantomime was evidently still more effective in the mid-seventeenth century than verbal expressions. In many of the plays of the 1620 collection, such as *Fortunatus*, the part of Pickelhering is not transcribed; rather there is just a reference to his appearance: "*Allhier agiret PICKELHERING*" ('Pickelhering acts here').[111] Since the clown was the chief character and was mostly played by the company leader as in the *capocomico* model, it is highly probable that his text was improvised and adapted to the occasion, without the need to print it word by word. This habit resonates with the *extempore* technique of English clowns like Tarlton and with the Commedia dell'Arte.

What is known of Pickelhering's looks and the imagery connected to him? The most important pictorial documents representing the English Pickelhering are two satiric pamphlets issued in 1621. In this same period, we witness the printing of *ECUT*, the heyday of Green's company and the outbreak of the Thirty Years' War. The reference to the war is clearly visible both in the images and in the texts which accompany them.

---

[109] François Laroque explains that mummers' plays were usually performed by seven dancers on the basis of a dramatised sword-dance. In one of these plays, Pickle-Herring is one of the five sons of the madman, a grotesque figure who introduces the play and then fights a Hobby horse and a dragon, before he is killed by his sons. By stamping his feet in the ground, Pickle-Herring brings his father back to life, and the joyful event is celebrated with sword-dances and a Morris dance. Moreover, Peter Pickled-Herring appears as the godfather of the deadly sin Gluttony in Marlowe's *The Life and Death of Doctor Faustus* (2.2). See Laroque, *Shakespeare's Festive World*, p. 53.

[110] Peter Mundy, *The Travels of Peter Mundy in Europe and Asia, 1608–1667* (London: R.C. Temple, 1974), vol. 4, *Travels in Europe*, p. 181.

[111] *SW*, vol. 1, p. 154.

The first pamphlet from 1621, held at the City Archive of Ulm, depicts the *Englischer Pickelhäring, jetzo vornehmer Eisenhändler, mit Aext, Beil, Barten gen Prag jubilirend*, i.e. 'The English Pickelhering, now noble ironmonger, with hatchets, axes, adzes, rejoicing on his way to Prague'. In the engraving, Pickelhering is carrying a big basket on his back so full of axes of various sizes that a few have already fallen on the ground, and he must hold some of them, especially an exaggeratedly heavy poleaxe, in his hands. He also has a bag filled with sticks, stones or bread and – judging from the melancholic expression on his bearded face – he is rather fatigued. Still, he rubs his hands in expectation of the good profits in Prague.

Figure 5: *Englischer Pickelhäring, jetzo vornehmer Eisenhändler, mit Aext, Beil, Barten gen Prag jubilirend* (1621).

In einem Buch auf einem Blatt
Steht: Varietas delectat.
Das heißt so viel als: bleiben nicht
Was man gewesen, macht lustig.
[...]
  Das weiß ich, drum ichs practicir,
  Und mich damit gar sehr lustier,
  Ihr kennt mich wohl, und wißt wer ich

Gewesen bin, wißt aber nicht
Wer ich jetzund im neuen Jahr
Bin worden, jetzt bin ich andrer Haar.
Vorm Jahr war ich nicht gering
Ein aus der Maßen gut Pickelhäring
Mein Antlitz in tausend Manieren
Konnt ich holdselig figuriren,
Alles was ich hab vorgebracht,
Das hat man ja stattlich belacht.
Ich war der Niemand, kennt ihr mich?
Ein andrer Herr jetzund bin ich
Comödi mögen andre spieln.
Das Ding thut mich jetzund vervieln,
Jetzund bin ich ein groß Merchant,
Ein Kaufmannskramer ins Böhmerland,
Ich handle nicht, wie andre Narren
Mit theuren welschen seidnen Waaren [...]
Holzaxten, Hauen, Beile, Barten,
Auf die man da gar sehr thut warten,
Trage ich jetzunder in meiner Butt
Gen Prag, das ist ein Waare gut.
Dran werd ich haben groß Profit,
Mein Rechnung kann mir fehlen nit,
Denn Aexte, Hauen, Beile, Barten,
Muß man da haben scharf ohn Scharten,
Daß man da mache U für X,
Und haue um all Crucifix. [...]
Gleichwohl ists Schade, daß daraus
Soll in der Kirch, als Gottes Haus,
Fischholz werden gehauen klein,
Keine Erbarmung wird da seyn. [...]
Ein Reformirter, ohne Zweifel
Ist einer wie der andre Teufel. [...]
Ich aber helfe dazu nicht,
Verkaufe nur, wie man hie sicht,
Die Aexte, Beil und Haun dazu.
Fürwahr, weiter ich gar nichts thu,
Das sind nur bloße Instrument,

Daß sie die brauchen zu dem End,
Da mögen sie für sich zusehen,
Wie sie es könn' verantworten. [...]. [112]

As he says at the beginning of the poem, the readers will certainly recognise in him the 'exceptionally good' and successful Pickelhering, famous for his expressiveness ("Mein Antlitz in tausend Manieren / Konnt ich holdselig figuriren") and stage roles such as Nobody, also contained in *ECUT*, but they may not know what he is now: an ironmonger. To mark the very recent change of profession, his costume still belongs to the stage. In fact, his large, feathered hat, the ruff around his neck, the tight jacket with very large round buttons and the pounding pace all recall a dancing court jester rather than an ironmonger. He explains that this change is due to the altered circumstances around him and because "Varietas delectat", meaning that variety is the spice of life or, in other words, that one must make the best of the difficult situation of the war.

It might seem a little odd to present a famous stage character and clown as merchant of weapons on his way to Prague, the city where the Thirty Years' War began. After the momentous defenestration and the rebellion of the Bohemian estates against the Habsburg monarchy in May 1618, the Protestant Frederick V of the Palatinate was crowned there on 31 October 1619. In an excess of religious fervour, the Calvinist iconoclasts saluted their new king by destroying the religious images of the St Vitus Cathedral as a sign of religious purgation after the Catholic dominion.[113] This event is criticised in the satiric pamphlet.

---

[112] Poem from the 1621 pamphlet *Englischer Pickelhäring, jetzo vornehmer Eisenhändler, mit Aext, Beil, Barten gen Prag jubilirend*, in Johann Scheible, ed., *Die Fliegenden Blätter des XVI. und XVII. Jahrhunderts, in sogenannten Einblatt-Drucken mit Kupferstichen und Holzschnitten; zunächst aus dem Gebiete der politischen und religiösen Caricatur* (Stuttgart, 1850), pp. 86–91. Translation: 'On a page of a book it says: "Varietas delectat", which means that it is pleasurable to become something different from what one used to be. [...] I know that and therefore I act accordingly to have fun. You know me and know who I used to be, but you do not know who I have become in the new year – now I am changed. A year ago, I was nothing less than a very good Pickelhering. I could set up my appearance and my movements admirably. Whatever I did was always good for a laugh. I was Nobody, do you know me? Now I am another person, others may play comedy. That occupation repulses me now, now I am a great merchant, a tradesman on my way to Bohemia. I do not trade with expensive Italian goods like other fools. [...] In my basket I carry hatchets, axes, clubs and adzes to Prague, where they are expected and where the merchandise is valuable. I will surely make good profit out of it, my expectations will not fall short, because sharp and flawless hatchets, axes, clubs, adzes are needed to pull the wool over the others' eyes and tear down all crucifixes. [...] Still, it is a pity that [the statues] in the Church, as the Lord's house, should be smashed to driftwood, without mercy. [...] Doubtlessly, a Reformed is a devil like any other. [...] But I do not contribute to that [war / destruction], I only sell, as you can see here, the necessary hatchets, axes, adzes. Forsooth, I do nothing more than that, these are but the means and those who use them for a precise end must see for themselves how they can answer for that.'

[113] See Peter H. Wilson, *Europe's Tragedy: A History of the Thirty Years War* (London: Allen Lane, 2009) for a complete overview.

The comparison with other merchant-actors trading silk from Italy ("Ich handle nicht, wie andre Narren / Mit theuren welschen seidnen Waaren") might be an allusion to Sackville, who retired from the stage to work as a merchant of fabrics, as Creizenach suggests,[114] or it could be a metaphor for the theatrical goods of the Italian Commedia dell'Arte. With the outbreak of the war, Pickelhering has abandoned the acting profession to become an arms supplier to the insurgent Bohemians. In this new role, he provides the instruments for an absurd spectacle, which he observes from a detached and ironic position. Although he feels sorry for the destroyed religious works of art in the name of a manipulative doctrine ("Daß man da mache U für X, / Und haue um all Crucifix") and labels both the Calvinists and the Protestants "einer wie der andere Teufel", he does not show any intention of taking responsibility for what the people do with the weapons he sells ("Da mögen sie für sich zusehen, / Wie sie es könn' verantworten"). Even in this unusual martial setting Pickelhering displays the typical nature of the opportunistic fool/clown who takes advantage of any situation, even war, in a seemingly naive way. Who, if not an inconsiderate fool, would rejoice in providing the enemy with arms only to make money? However, by raising the issue of responsibility, he invites readers to reflect on the senselessness of arms if they are misused as improper means to a disastrous end, in this case the outbreak of the war.

The second polemic pamphlet of 1621 portrays Pickelhering in almost identical terms with direct pictorial and intertextual references to the first pamphlet.

Figure 6: *Engelländischen Pickelhäring, welcher jetzund als ein vornehmer Händler und Jubilirer mit allerlei Judenspießen nach Frankfurt in die Meß zeucht* (1621).

---

[114] See Creizenach, p. CIII.

Here, too, the clown is carrying lances and halberds on his back and a basket full of arrows as well as a cord with rings in his left hand. His hat is flatter than in the first pamphlet and pierced by an arrow (in the poem he says that he did that on purpose to amuse his customers),[115] the ruff is replaced by a short cape, and the longer jacket covers the upper half of his elegant trousers. The posture of leaning on a lance and the pounding pace are maintained, but this time he is smiling, though still in a tired or ironic way. The very detailed background depicts a market scene: numerous stalls with arms have already been erected on the square near the busy blacksmith's shop on the left where either rings are punched out or money is minted, and many people are looking at the goods, transporting merchandise on foot or on carriages and filling up sacks with newly minted coins.

As the title *Engelländischen Pickelhäring, welcher jetzund als ein vornehmer Händler und Jubilirer mit allerlei Judenspießen nach Frankfurt in die Meß zeucht* ('The English Pickelhering, on his arrival at the Frankfurt fair as a noble and satisfied merchant selling all kinds of Jew-spears/skewers') reveals, the English Pickelhering is heading for the Frankfurt fair, this time not as an actor, but as a money-grabbing merchant. Again, the incipit of the poem expresses his imperturbable attitude towards the tragic circumstances around him and his ability to adapt to any situation: "Ein alt Sprüchwort: besser verdorben / Sey zehenmal, denn eins gestorben, / Ist wahr, ich hab es selbst probirt, / Aus meiner Kunst, die ich studirt, / Man darf auf einmal nicht verzagen."[116] He mentions his art or profession of clown as source of his resilience and his motto: better profligate than dead. In the continuation, the poem narrates what happened to Pickelhering after he sold his weapons in Prague. After a brief experience as a 'seller of lies' in newspapers and pamphlets – a short excursus to attack the media of his times – he returned to the business of ironmonger. Although he is still selling arms to both friend and foe without distinction, he expressly suggests using the spears against Jews. The poem explains his antisemitic attitude, known also from the stage, for example in the later play *Der Jud von Venedig*, as follows: Pickelhering is concerned that the prosperous Jewish community of Frankfurt might deprive him of his profit, so he uses his arms, i.e. weapons and satire, against them. At the same

---

[115] "Ein breit Barett stünd excellent, / wie ich denn auch zu diesem End / Für mein Person eins aufgesetzt, / Darauf ein Spießlein scharf gewetzt, / Euch Herren damit zu erquicken." From the pamphlet *Engelländischen Pickelhäring, welcher jetzund als ein vornehmer Händler und Jubilirer mit allerlei Judenspießen nach Frankfurt in die Meß zeucht* (1621), reprinted in Scheible, ed., *Die Fliegenden Blätter des XVI. und XVII. Jahrhunderts*, Stuttgart, 1850, p. 85. Translation: 'A braod barret would suit everyone well, therefore I have put on one myself and pierced it with a sharpened arrow to amuse your lordship.'

[116] First lines of the poem *Engelländischen Pickelhäring, welcher jetzund als ein vornehmer Händler und Jubilirer mit allerlei Judenspießen nach Frankfurt in die Meß zeucht* (1621). Taken from Scheible, ed., *Die Fliegenden Blätter des XVI. und XVII. Jahrhunderts*, pp. 81–6. Translation: 'An old saying goes: it is ten times better to be profligate than dead. That is true, I have experienced it myself, in my art, which I have studied: do not give up all at once.'

time, his excessive fear of being robbed by those he is putting in danger with his business and the usurious prices he is putting on his wares render the situation absurd and laughable.

Thus, both pamphlets give a similar picture of Pickelhering: under the naive façade of the country bumpkin there is an opportunistic, sly and ironic nature with almost evil traits, attenuated by his ridiculous behaviour, which offers the opportunity to reflect on serious themes like war, the media and economy. In this sense, the clown plays just the part assigned to him on stage and resembles both his German and Italian counterparts, Hanswurst and Zanni. Apart from these two engravings, there are no pictorial records of Pickelhering's costume and role in the early seventeenth century.

Considering the scarcity of first-hand reactions to the wandering troupes, the report by the pastor and playwright Johann Rist (1607–67) about an unknown English company performing *Pyramus and Thisbe*, presumably in his hometown of Hamburg, is most valuable. Although it was printed in 1666, the spectacle dates from his youth, therefore anytime between 1625 and 1650, when Reynolds was still active. In it, the "esteemed Monsieur Pickelherring" (sic!) is described as follows:

> He was rather fat and stout, although short, wore a nightcap with ear-flaps [typical of the fool] and a paper ruff from cheap haberdashery around his neck. His coat was barely two spans long, his coat half yellow, half red, and for the rest, his entire costume was so contrived that one could hardly look at the esteemed Pickelherring without laughing.[117]

Apart from the ridiculously short jacket, this description of a stout fellow with an exaggerated hat and a ruff around the neck matches the earlier engraving of Pickelhering. In addition, the colourful dress mentioned by Rist recalls Arlecchino. The fact that these same attributes were perpetuated even after the Thirty Years' War is testified by a later German play called *Pickelhärings Hochzeit, oder Der lustige singende Harlequin* ('Pickelhering's Wedding or the Merry Singing Harlequin') of 1652, in which Pickelhering wears a bombastic hat, an elegant cape, a longish jacket and a pair of full, embroidered trousers. By virtue of his recognisable and colourful costume, his singing and his comic role, in this play the Anglo-German clown is put on a par with a singing Harlequin, his Italo-French alter ego.[118]

---

[117] Johann Rist, *An Account of a Performance of the Burlesque Comedy of* Pyramus and Thisbe, *as performed by the English Comedians in a well known German town* [probably Hamburg], printed in Frankfurt in 1666 and translated by Brennecke, *Shakespeare in Germany: 1590–1700*, pp. 56–8.

[118] A manuscript version of the play is held at the Austrian National Library in Vienna, Cod. 13.287.

Figure 7: Detail from the title page of *Pickelhärings Hochzeit, oder Der lustig singende Harlequin* (1652).

Unlike the pamphlets of the first half of the seventeenth century, the later portraits of Pickelhering lack the polemic tone and the grotesque reference to political events. Instead, they present a stage character, still comic in his appearance and gesture, but more refined and elegant. The brutish traits have been replaced by buffoonery to please the audience with light entertainment, and perhaps make them forget the atrocities of the war. Only the club remains of the weapons carried by Pickelhering during the war; the clown can still beat his opponents, but with verbal rather with physical force only.

These later changes appear to be indebted to Italian and French influences, but the original Pickelhering created by Reynolds surpassed the popularity of his Italian rivals, who were comprehensible only to courtly audiences, mainly because he spoke German.[119] With the acceptance of local actors in English troupes and the subsequent formation of genuinely German companies after the war, the English repertoire and clown were appropriated and enriched with (inter)national features. A brief digression shall illustrate this process of expansion and the role the English and Italian models played in it.

---

[119] See Herz, *Englische Schauspieler und englisches Schauspiel zur Zeit Shakespeares in Deutschland*, p. 3.

Hans Mühlgraf & co.

An early German competitor of Reynolds was the goldsmith and dance-master Hans Mühlgraf (1588–1632) of Nuremberg, one of the few native impresarios who instituted an amateur acting company able to stand its ground against the English supremacy.[120] To achieve this, he adopted the most successful elements of the English Comedians and tailored them to his troupe so well that they outshone Reynolds in Frankfurt in 1626.[121] The dance-master Mühlgraf boasted professional dancers trained by himself, excellent musicians led by his musical half-brother Heinrich Flemming, a repertoire of demure religious plays well regarded by municipal authorities, and a German clown figure, Peter Leberwurst i.e. 'Peter Liver sausage', an equivalent to Pickelhering.

Figure 8: Stage portrait of the engraver Hans Ammon, who played the clown Peter Leberwurst in Mühlgraf's company until 1632.

The portrait of the engraver and actor Hans Ammon dressed as Peter Leberwurst places the character somewhere in-between the Anglo-German Pickelhering and the German Hanswurst, with a whiff of the Capitano of Commedia dell'Arte.

---

[120] For a detailed biography of Hans Mühlgraf, rarely mentioned in other secondary sources, see Bärbel Rudin, "Hans Mühlgraf & Co., Sitz Nürnberg: Ein deutsches Bühnenunternehmen im Dreißigjährigen Krieg", *Kleine Schriften der Gesellschaft für Theatergeschichte* 29/30 (1978), pp. 15–30.

[121] See ibid., p. 22.

Firstly, his name recalls both Hanswurst (whose name connects the diffused name Hans to a common food, the sausage) and all the other English clowns with names involving food found on the German stage, like Posset, Stockfish and Pickelhering. Secondly, although the exact date of origin of the etching is unknown, it is strikingly similar to the two representations of Pickelhering in the pamphlets of 1621, almost to the point that it seems plausible that they took inspiration from each other. Peter Leberwurst wears the same large, feathered hat and buttoned jacket, and carries a long walking stick, on which he leans while performing the same pounding dance steps as the ironmonger Pickelhering, with the noticeable accessories of a beer beaker and a sausage in his bag. The sausage, in turn, connects him to the German Hans*wurst*, a close relative of Leber*wurst*. However, the goatee and the opulent elegance of the dress, which clashes with the torn shoes, are not present in the depictions of Pickelhering and instead might echo the vacuous pomp of the Capitano of Commedia dell'Arte.

There is a further, more concrete detail pointing at the Italian influence on Mühlgraf and his collaborators. Two years after the breakthrough in 1626, Mühlgraf tried to promote his troupe in Kassel by offering newly translated Italian comedies to the audience, who had grown weary of the English plays.[122] This attempt at gaining attention shows a change of strategy in the German impresario: as soon as he could not beat the Englishmen with their own arms anymore, he resorted to a different and equally renowned model – the Italians. His plan allowed him to perform in the newly established playhouse in Nuremberg in 1628. This example shows that mutual influences were at work simultaneously in oral and written form, although the French and Italian ascendancy supplanted the significance of English sources when the activity of the itinerant players from England ceased.

George Jolly

George Jolly (1610/12–73) is usually referred to as the last English-born comedian on the Continent. His wanderings as principal of the remnants of the old Browne-Green troupe took him from the Netherlands, where he became renowned under the name of Joris Joliphous/Joliphus, to all the major cities of the empire after the Peace of Westphalia in 1648: Frankfurt, Nuremberg, Strasbourg, Regensburg, Vienna, plus Cologne in 1649 and Danzig in 1650.[123] From 1650 Jolly's Dutch-English company performed in German, also thanks to German-speaking actors such as Christoph Blümel and Johann Martin aka Laurentius von Schnüffis.

---

[122] "[…] er [lasse] auch auß Italia der berümbsten comedienschreiber ihre comedien hiehero bringen unnd inn Teutsch ubersetzen unndt transferiren." Quoted in Creizenach, p. LXV. Interestingly, Mühlgraf's translations of Italian plays, which he claims were given to him by the best authors to 'transfer' (i.e. adapt) into German, appeared only a few years after the second edition of *ECUT* (1624) and represent another instance of literarisation.
[123] See Limon, p. 124.

According to Robert J. Alexander, Jolly gained fame for being the first English Comedian to introduce women acting on stage – a novelty in Germany and England, but not for Commedia dell'Arte. Furthermore, his variegated repertoire proves how far advanced the co-existence and interconnectedness of various literary traditions already was.[124] For instance, the plays performed at the 1658 Frankfurt fair include Anglo-German favourites like the parable *Vom verlornen Sohn* ('The Prodigal Son'), the adaptation of Marlowe's *Faustus*, *Singspiele*, Italian pastoral plays, a translation of Corneille's *Cid* and contemporary German school drama plays such as the *Friedensspiele* (1653) by Johann Rist.[125]

A few years later, the English principal's notorious bad temper caused a breakup in the company. The German members led by Hans Ernst Hoffmann and Peter Schwartz founded their own troupe called *Hochteutsche Comoedianten* ('High German Comedians') in 1654 but still collaborated with their former colleagues on special occasions, for example in 1657 in Frankfurt.[126] After Jolly's return to England in 1667, national companies like the *Hochteutsche Comoedianten*, later called *Insprugger Comoedianten* ('Innsbruck Comedians' 1662–67), took over with an almost seamless transition, and in less than a century the foreign staging techniques and plays became naturalised.[127]

Two members of Jolly's company, Christoph Blümel and Johann Martin aka Laurentius von Schnüffis (part of the company from 1652 onwards), made use of their scholarly education to rework the English repertoire and combine it with new elements taken from Dutch, Spanish, Italian and French drama as well as motifs from the German *Wanderbühne* (itinerant stage/theatre) in a wonderful instance of adaptation as part of intercultural theatricality. In fact, in the second half of the seventeenth century, Blümel (born around 1630) published *Der Jude von Venetien* ('The Jew of Venetia'),[128] based on Shakespeare's *Merchant of Venice* with elements indebted to Commedia dell'Arte, which shall be discussed in chapter 7.1.

According to Ruth Gstach, *Der Jude von Venetien* was performed around 1669 by an unknown company, as was Johann Martin's play.[129] Better known by his religious name Laurentius von Schnüffis (1633–1702), Blümel's fellow-actor Martin wrote a pastoral tragicomedy entitled *Die Liebes Verzeiffelung* ('Love's

---

[124] See Robert J. Alexander, "George Jolly [Joris Joliphus] der wandernde Player und Manager / Neues zu seiner Tätigkeit in Deutschland (1648–1660)", *Kleine Schriften der Gesellschaft für Theatergeschichte* 29/30 (1978), pp. 31–48, p. 31.
[125] See ibid., p. 32.
[126] See Crüger, *Englische Komödianten in Strassburg*, pp. 113–25, pp. 124–5.
[127] For instance, one of the first German *Wandertruppen*, the *Hochtetusche Hofcomödianten*, led by Carl Andreas Paulsen (1620–78) with former members of Jolly's troupe, continued to perform jigs, which they inherited from the English Comedians and added as postludes to their autochthonous plays. See Hinck, *Das deutsche Lustspiel des 17. und 18. Jahrhunderts und die italienische Komödie*, p. 78.
[128] For the plays see Flemming, *Barockdrama*, vol. 3, *Das Schauspiel der Wanderbühne*, pp. 204–76.
[129] See Gstach, *Die Liebes Verzweiffelung*, p. 161.

Despair') between 1655 and 1662, before becoming a Capuchin monk and author of religious Baroque poetry.[130] This dramatisation of the legend of Daphnis and Chloe in German also recalls Shakespeare's *A Winter's Tale*, because the protagonist Amoena is kidnapped as a child and abandoned on an island, where she grows up among shepherds like Perdita. However, in the peasant-clown Dymas, who tries to seduce Amoena despite her noble origin, one recognises a trait alien to the Shakespearean fool and more in line with the sexual appetite and boorishness of the English Comedians' Pickelhering and of the Zannis in the Commedia dell'Arte. Thus, the two plays share a similar amalgamation of a Shakespearean plot with 'types' and patterns from Commedia dell'Arte, which accounts for the effectiveness of this combination of currents well into the seventeenth century.

The Continental Repertoire

Considering the obstacles which the first itinerant players had to face, the scale and scope of their travels is admirable. The highly skilled professionals not only overcame the financial, logistic and linguistic problems, but also set new standards of theatre and drama in central Europe.

Although the term *drama* is used for dramatic texts, all the plays associated with the English Comedians are merely acting scripts and "must be treated like a palimpsest of decades of informal transmission", as Joel B. Lande states.[131] This oral transmission makes a reconstruction of the wandering companies' repertoire difficult. For the time prior to the first collection printed in 1620, one must rely on reports contained in letters, diaries, expense accounts at court, public records about performances in different cities or the laws and incidents connected to them. The most useful sources are official applications for licences, sometimes supplemented with lists of plays delivered to the authorities in advance, of which circa fifteen are still extant – probably only a fraction of the Continental repertoire, as Price argues.[132] The most important lists will be presented on the following pages. However, they must be handled with caution since they aimed to promote the company in the eyes of the potentates with excessive professions of morality, ostentatious numbers of plays without references to authors or originals, and few indications about the troupe.[133]

---

[130] For a detailed analysis of the plays see Gstach, op. cit.; the text of the tragicomedy can be found on pp. 10–100.

[131] Joel B. Lande, *Persistence of Folly*, p. 33.

[132] See Price, op. cit., pp. 15–16 for all the lists of titles including adapted versions of plays by Beaumont, Chapman, Chettle, Davenport, Dekker, Ford, Glapthorne, Greene, Heywood, Houghton and Day, Kyd, Machin, Marlowe, Marston, Mason, Massinger, Peele, Shakespeare, Pseudo-Shakespeare, Sharpe, Shirley, Still, Wilmot and anonymous authors.

[133] Ralf Haekel justly points out that it would have been counterproductive for the itinerant companies to give away their repertoire as it represented their means of existence. Consequently, most lists can be attributed to German ensembles imitating them. See Haekel, *Die Englischen Komödianten in Deutschland*, p. 108.

The first detailed account of the English Comedians' repertoire dates from the end of the adaptation phase in 1597, so little is known about their plays before that. On 23 July 1597, an unidentified company – presumably Sackville's – submitted a petition to the city council of Strasbourg, which is contained in the diary of the Czech Baron Waldstein (1581–1623). It adduces the following translated titles: "*A Duke of Ferrari* (sic!), *Of a Man who was cheated by the Devil, The Prodigal Son, Judith, Susanna, The Rich Jew* (of Malta?), *Faustus, Of an Old Man who mistrusted his wife, Esther,* and *Errasto*".[134] Among these biblical and secular pieces, there are a few that recur in *ECUT* 1620, namely *The Prodigal Son* and *Esther. Of an Old Man who mistrusted his wife* is probably close or identical to *Ein lustig Pickelherings Spiel / von der schönen Maria und alten Hanrey* ('A merry Pickelhering play, of the beautiful Maria and the old cuckold' contained in *ECUT* too). Moreover, *Susanna* might be the drama written by Heinrich Julius between 1593 and 1594.

A second important list refers to Sackville and Thare's company in Nördlingen and was retrieved by Karl Trautmann.[135] The petition submitted on 20 January 1604 praises the moral edification the spectators and especially the young spectators will experience by attending the tasteful performances in German.[136] The ten plays mentioned can be grouped as follows: 1) biblical stories of Daniel in the Lion's Den (*Auß dem Buch Danielis 6. Capitel (Erlösung aus der Löwengrube)* and titles from the 1597 list like *vonn der kheüschen Susanna*, i.e. 'The Chaste Susanna' (probably by Duke Heinrich Julius, as is the also adduced *vonn Vincentio Ladislao Satrapa a Mantua*) and *vonn dem verlohrnen Sohn*, i.e. the Prodigal Son; 2) historic material mixed with folklore, like *Nobody and Somebody, vonn dem weisen urtheil Carolj des hertzogen Aus Burgund* ('Of the wise judgement of Carl, duke of Burgundy') and *von einem ungehorsammen Khauffmans Sohn* ('About the disobedient son of a merchant'); 3) Roman stories such as *vonn Thisbes undt Pyramo* ('Pyramus and Thisbe') and *vonn Botzarhio einem Alten Römer* ('Of Botzarhius, an old Roman); 4) adaptations of Shakespeare such as *Von Romeo und Julitha* ('Romeo and Juliet' mentioned for the first time in Germany in this

---

[134] Quoted in Schrickx, *Foreign Envoys and Travelling Players,* p. 197 and taken from G. W. Groos, ed., *The Diary of Baron Waldstein: A Traveller in Elizabethan England* (New York: Thames and Hudson, 1981).

[135] See Karl Trautmann, "Die älteste Nachricht über eine Aufführung von Shakespeares Romeo und Julie in Deutschland (1604)", *Archiv für Literaturgeschichte* XI (1882), pp. 625–6.

[136] Quoted from ibid.: "Demnach wirr unss ein Zeitlangg den Geistlichen vnndt weltlichen Historien (welche dann Inn deutscher Spraach vnnd Zierichem Habit vonn unss persönlich Comoed: unnd Tragoediweis agiert werden unnd den Zuhörenden sonnderlich aber der Jugendt Zur Forcht unndt Ehr Gottes, Auch gehorsamm Ihrer Eltern, Feine Exempla Fürstellen) Gebrauchen Lassen." Translation: 'With this petition we ask for the temporary permission to perform spiritual and worldly histories (which, both comedies and tragedies, shall be played in German and with elegant costumes by us in person to provide the audience and especially the youths with fine examples of fear and honour of God and also of obedience to their parents.'

list); and 5) the unidentified *Von Annabella eines hertzogen tochter von Ferrara* ('Of Annabella, a Duke's daughter from Ferrara').[137] Assuming that there ever was a written dramatic text for each of these titles, the greater proportion is missing. Apart from the plays later collected and published in German, such as *Susanna* and *Von Vincentio Ladislao* by Heinrich Julius (1593–4) and *Jemand und Niemandt* (extant in a manuscript version of 1608 and in a printed version in *ECUT* 1620), there are only a few manuscripts, one-off prints or synopses in theatre bills of some of the other titles mentioned in the catalogues; the rest was lost or, at best, adapted by German playwrights like Heinrich Julius, Jacob Ayrer and Andreas Gryphius.

A further list of the plays performed by Green in Graz in 1608 is contained in the already-mentioned *Theaterbrief* by the Archduchess Maria Magdalena.[138] However, the precise identification of the dramatised material from the Bible, chapbooks and Elizabethan plays presents some difficulties since denominations are vague and, at times, limited to misleading capsule synopses (for example 'About the Jew'). A reason for the change of titles might be that the adaptations were felt to be detached from the English original because they were not faithful translations but concocted creations with borrowings from other plays and genres, used as a virtually anonymous resource of plot materials without heeding authorship or copyright. The result was a communal amalgamation that in the eyes of the German recipients – mostly unaware of a literary tradition or the great names of English literature – was a genuine invention of the itinerant players.

In this context, Peter Holland points out that despite the considerable number of plays by Shakespeare on the German stage, there is no reference to the author in any of the lists of performances or published adaptations.[139] Next to *Romeo and Juliet* of the 1604 list, there are condensed versions of *Hamlet*, *King Lear*, *Julius Caesar*, *The Merchant of Venice* (all part of the 'Dresden Repertoire'), *Titus Andronicus* (printed in *ECUT* 1620), *Othello, The Moor of Venice* (documented

---

[137] Ibid. Trautmann also mentions two lists of plays submitted in Rothenburg in 1604 and 1606 with the same handwriting and almost overlapping titles, although it is still controversial whether they were really performed by an English company – most probably Thare's. "1604: 1) *Auß dem Buch Danielis 6 Kapitel.* 2) *vonn Melone, Einem vertriebnen Khönige Auß Dalmatia.* 3) *vonn Ludovico, Einem Khönige auß Hispania.* 4) *vonn Celinde unndt Sedea.* 5) *Von Pyramo unnd Thysbe.* 6) *von Annabella, Eines Markgraffen tochter von Montferrat.* 1606: 1) *vonn dem weisen Uhrteil Carolj, des hertzogen Auß Burgundt, wegen Zwayer Riter.* 2) *vonn der kheüschen Susanna.* 3) *vonn dem verlohrnen Sohn,* 4) *von Einem ungehorsammen khauffmans Sohn,* 5) *vonn Eynem Alten Römer, so seinen Sohn wegen Eines Jungen weibes des guts enterben wollen.* 6) *vonn Einem wunderbahrlichen khempffer Vincentio Ladislav Satrapa von Mantua genandt.*" Quoted from "Englische Komödianten in Rotheburg ob der Tauber", *Zeitschrift für vergleichende Litteraturgeschichte* 7 (1894), p. 61.

[138] Held at the Vienna Haus-, Hof-, und Staatsarchiv, Familienkorrespondenz A, Karton 6, fols 312–15 and reprinted in Flemming, pp. 71–2, Meissner, pp. 76–80 or Schrickx, pp. 332–3. For the translation see Orad, pp. 4–11.

[139] See Peter Holland, "Shakespeare abbreviated", in Shaughnessy, ed., *The Cambridge Companion to Shakespeare and Popular Culture*, pp. 26–45, p. 31.

in Dresden on 26 February 1661 as "Tragi-Comoedie vom Moor von Venedig"), *The Taming of the Shrew* (extant in two versions: *Kunst über alle Künste, ein bös Weib gut zu machen*, Rapperschweyl 1672, and *Comoedia von der zornigen Catharine*, Dresden 1678), *The Comedy of Errors, Henry IV,* and the play-within-the-play about Pyramus and Thisbe from *A Midsummer Night's Dream*.[140] Although Shakespeare's paternity remained unacknowledged for a long time, the adapted versions of his plays entered Germany almost a century and a half before they entered any other nation, as Cohn states;[141] and a good part of the credit for this early reception must go to the itinerant players.

Later lists from 1630, 1631, 1646, 1651 and 1660[142] still feature the old successful stock of English plays but show less influence from newer English models. Instead, German drama took over, marking the transition from amalgamation to naturalisation, for instance in the plays by Gryphius discussed in chapter 7. Before that, chapter 6 shall offer a detailed analysis of the English Comedians' repertoire in order to illustrate the multifaceted parameters at work in the adaptation process.

---

[140] See Simon Williams, *Shakespeare on the German stage*, vol. 1, *1586–1914* (Cambridge: CUP, 1990), p. 221.

[141] See Cohn, p. LXXVI.

[142] Contained in Creizenach, pp. XXVIII–IX. I will only quote the titles of the lists of 1630 and 1631, because they still belong to the time span covered in this study: "1630, Januar und Februar, Aufführungen in Dresden: 1) Vom Ritter Arsidos. 2) Von der Agrippina. 3) Von der Isabella, Königin in Klein-Britannien. 4) Von Prinz Celadon von Valentia." and "1631, März und April, Aufführungen in Dresden: 1) Vom Königreich Portugal. 2) Vom Könige aus Graecia. 3) Vom Könige aus Frankreich. 4) Vom Königreiche Valentia. 5) Vom Könige in Engelland. 6) Von der Constantia, Königs in Arragonien Tochter. 7) Vom Prinzen Serale und der Hyppolita [a peculiar mixture of *Von eines Königes Sohne* and *Von Julio und Hyppolita* contained in *ECUT* 1620]. 8) Julius Caesar."

6. Intercultural Theatricality in *Engelische Comedien und Tragedien*

The oldest existing German play performed by the English itinerant players is the 1608 manuscript of *Niemand und Jemand* ('Nobody and Somebody'), preserved at the Cistercian monastery at Rein near Graz (MS 128).[1] Apart from that, there are only lists of titles without the actual plays to document the theatrical activity of the English wandering companies during the adaptation and amalgamation phases that run from 1585 to 1620. The first publication of an acting stock associated with the English Comedians in Germany, *ECUT*, in 1620, is therefore a valuable source for studying the itinerant players' repertoire, performance and early reception. The purpose of this chapter is to analyse this collection.

The best-preserved original print of *ECUT* is held at the Herzog August Library at Wolfenbüttel. The 384 unpaginated pages in small octavo (48 sheets A-Bbb), printed by Gottfried Große in Leipzig in 1620, i.e. at the beginning of the literarisation phase, are available in a reprint edited by Manfred Brauneck, *Spieltexte der Wanderbühne*, vol. 1 (1975), from which I quote. The full title of *ECUT* reads:

> *Engelische Comedien und / Tragedien / Das ist: / Sehr Schöne, / herrliche und ausserlesene, / geist- und weltliche Comedi und / Tragedi Spiel, / Sampt dem / Pickelhering, welche wegen ihrer artigen / INVENTIONEN, kurzweiligen auch theils / wahrhafftigen Geschicht halber, von den Engelländern / in Deutschland an Königlichen, Chur- und Fürst- / lichen Höfen, auch in vornehmen Reichs- See- und Handel Städten seynd Agiret und gehalten / worden, und zuvor nie in Druck auss- / gangen / An jetzo, / Allen der Comedi und Tragedi Lieb- / habern, und Anderen zu lieb und gefallen, der Gestalt / in offenen Druck gegeben, dass sie gar leicht darauss / Spielweis wiederumb angerichtet, und zur Ergetzligkeit und / Erquickung des Gemüths gehalten wer- / den können. / Gedruckt im Jahr M.DC.XX.*[2]

---

[1] The fact that *Jemand und Niemand* was presented by English players in 1608 is attested by the Archduchess Maria Magdalena's *Theaterbrief*: "[…] am Erchtag [Dienstag] haben sy gehabt von Niemandts und iemand, ist gewaltig artlich gewest." See Flemming, pp. 71–2, Meissner, pp. 76–80 or Schrickx, pp. 332–3, and for the translation see Orad, pp. 4–11. I have visited the library of the Rein monastery to see the manuscript, but will only briefly compare it to *ECUT*, as it has already been studied at length by Willi Flemming, ed., *Barockdrama*, vol. 3, *Das Schauspiel der Wanderbühne*, Gustaf Fredén, *Friedrich Menius und das Repertoire der englischen Komödianten in Deutschland* (Stockholm: Palmers, 1939), and Julian K. Hilton, *The 'Englische Komödianten' in German-speaking States, 1592–1620: A Generation of Touring Performers as Mediators between English and German Cultures* (Oxford University: Dissertation, 1984).

[2] Translation: 'English Comedies and Tragedies, i.e. very fine, beautiful and select, spiritual and worldly Comedy and Tragedy plays, with Pickelhering, which due to their fanciful inventions, entertaining and partly true histories, have been acted and given by the Englishmen in Germany at Royal, Electoral, and Princely courts, as well as in the principal Imperial, Sea, and Commercial towns, never before printed but now published to

Figure 9: Title page of the 1620 edition of *Engelische Comedien und Tragedien*, Herzog August Library at Wolfenbüttel.

This lengthy title, on the one hand, advertises the various genres that are contained in the collection – spiritual and worldly comedies and tragedies, Pickelhering's buffooneries and at least partly true stories. On the other, it legitimises the cultural and moral value of the printed edition, sanctioned by the official authorities such as kings, electors, princes and city councils who supported the English players. Its practical utility lies in the fact that the plays could be acted by amateur troupes or read to delight lovers of theatre. The insistence on the numerous benefits offered by this collection almost sounds like an apology on the part of the unknown editor, who in Gustaf Fredén's view might be the scholar Friedrich Menius.[3]

---

[3] please all lovers of Comedies and Tragedies, and others, and in such a manner as to be fit to be easily acted for the delight and recreation of the mind. Printed in the year 1620.' Willem Schrickx observes that this title adduces the first mention ever of Pickelhering in a printed document. See *Foreign Envoys and Travelling Players in the Age of Shakespeare and Jonson*, p. 225.

See Gustaf Fredén, *Friedrich Menius und das Repertoire der englischen Komödianten in Deutschland*. Friedrich Menius (1593/4–1659) was a Mecklenburg-born scholar. After studies at the University of Rostock and in Greifswald, he stayed at the Pomeranian court until he was appointed Professor of History at the University of Dorpat (today Tartu in Estonia) in 1632. According to Fredén, during his stay at the court of Philipp Julius of Pommern-Wolgast, he may have met the English Comedians Browne, Green, and

Although Fredén's assumption cannot be proved, in all probability the editor was a well-educated German who used a literary language shaped by the Bible and chapbooks.

A reason for keeping the identity of the editor secret might be that this acting library of the English Comedians was presumably the result of unauthorised piracy of texts by multiple authors, which would also explain its erratic style, incomplete content and incohesive structure. According to Wilhelm Creizenach, the hypothesis of a simultaneous transcription during the performances, put forward by Albert Cohn[4] to explain the recurring mistakes, is unrealistic because the text is detailed, structured in rudimentary acts and even contains stage directions and songs with tunes.[5] Following this line of argument, Willi Flemming claims that the collection originated after the dissolution of John Green's troupe, when the provisional scripts of the English Comedians were printed without being edited.[6] Still, the plots are detailed enough to be performed. They contain useful clues for the reconstruction of Elizabethan plays with various versions, and their incompleteness indicates the oral circulation of the repertoire and the many readjustments it went through before it was fixed in print. Evidently, the pieces were considered as loose templates that did not demand fidelity from the actors but allowed for improvisation.

Since the English Comedians were not just 'strolling players' but professionals of the highest rank with a good command of German, as the examples of Robert Browne, Thomas Sackville and John Green show, a lack of acting or linguistic skills alone cannot explain the often-criticised quality of the texts. Even if their German was not sufficient to transpose the plays, would it not have been easier to translate them instead of cutting and distorting them? Or was the unknown editor responsible for the blunders and inconsistencies (for example, misspelling of names, incomplete lines, or characters that disappear in the course of the play)?[7]

Reynolds in Rostock in 1620. Fredén and Lawrence M. Price support the hypothesis that Menius printed their plays by pointing out that, although the editor used his judgement freely as far as stage directions and form are concerned, the solid knowledge of the Bible, the comedies of Terence and Plautus, German school drama and popular theatre would prove his identity. In 1637, Menius was imprisoned for his semi-heretic treatise *Consensus Hermetico-Mosaicus.* See Fredén, chapter 1, and Price, *The Reception of English Literature in Germany*, pp. 16–17. Until irrefutable proof is found, the editorship remains a mystery.

4   See Cohn, p. CV.
5   See Creizenach, p. LXXV.
6   See Flemming, p. 34.
7   The presence of errors in print was a common standard in the early modern period due to the involvement of many participants apart from the author in the publishing process. As Julie Stone Peters argues: "It is, however, clear that, of the various people responsible for textual production (printers, authors and editors, compositors, correctors), there were many who *were* careless in significant details: in the attribution of speeches, the names of minor characters, press correction; in the things necessary to make sense of a play (hence the notorious haphazardness – at times unintelligibility – of so many early plays)."

One could also assume that the mediocre style is due to the mediocrity of the spectators, but the thriving cultural environment in Germany and Austria and the quick reception and assimilation of the foreign influence confute this hypothesis. To avoid hasty qualitative judgements, it is important to stress that *ECUT* is not a finalised dramatic text but a theatrical text. More precisely, it must be regarded as a snapshot of an ongoing adaptation process and should be examined as such.

The 1620 collection begins with a short preface, aimed at ennobling the reputation of the actors with three examples taken from the Roman historians Livy and Macrobius.[8] Even though in ancient Rome actors were excluded from public offices, their art was appreciated in the highest circles: Sextus Roscius Amerinus enjoyed substantial rewards from the dictator Silla; his colleague Aespus' wealth was proverbial; and the actor Publius Cirus (a misspelling of Syrus) made a good reputation for himself with the emperor.[9] By indirectly comparing the status of the Roman actors to that of the comedians of his day, the editor implies that the art of theatre should be esteemed as highly as it was in the past. He then declares his intention to establish a form of professional theatre in Germany based on the model of the English 'inventiveness', 'gracefulness' and 'elegance' (my translation) in performance and style, as the following quote states:[10]

> Wenn dann zu unsern Zeiten die Englischen COMOEDIANTEN, theils wegen artiger INVENTION, theils wegen Anmuthigkeit ihrer Geberden / auch offters Zierligkeit im Reden bey hohen und Niderstands Personen mit grosses Lob erlangen / und dadurch viel

---

[7] *Theatre of the Book, 1480–1880: Print, Text, and Performance in Europe* (Oxford: OUP, 2000), p. 39.

[8] Gustaf Fredén was the first to notice that the prologue's argumentation is an approximate translation of Tomaso Garzoni's *La piazza universale di tutte le professioni del mondo e nobili e ignobili* (Venice: Giovanni Battista Somasco, 1585). In line with the Renaissance procedure of imitating and adapting content to the respective purpose, the model itself is a collage of references to authors of Greco-Roman antiquity, brought together by Garzoni (1549?–89) to describe 'all the professions of the world', as the title states. For further details see Fredén, *Friedrich Menius und das Repertoire der englischen Komödianten in Deutschland*, pp. 8–14. A German collection of plays attributed to the English Comedians that starts with a reference to an Italian scholar whose work was not translated into German until 1639 (see Frank-Rutger Hausmann, *Bibliographie der deutschen Übersetzungen aus dem Italienischen von den Anfängen bis 1730*, Tübingen: Max Niemeyer, 1992, vol. 1, pp. 522–3), testifies to the interconnectedness of Italian, English and German culture. This amalgamation also pervades *ECUT* from the foreword to the very last play.

[9] *SW*, vol. 1, pp. 1–2.

[10] The text of the plays is quoted from Brauneck's reprint of *ECUT* in *Spieltexte der Wanderbühne*, vol. 1 (subsequently abbreviated to *SW*, vol. 1), based on the print at the Herzog August library at Wolfenbüttel, A: 105 Eth. (1). In the transcription, the slashes indicate either a missing punctuation mark, which I added in my translations, or the end of a line in the original manuscript. Moreover, as was usual at the time, the words of Latin origin are capitalised, e.g. "INVENTIONEN". The abbreviation *SW*, vol. 6 refers to Brauneck, ed., *Spieltexte der Wanderbühne*, vol. 6, which contains the footnotes and comments to the preceding volumes.

hurtige und wackere INGENIA zu dergleichen INVENTIONEN lust und beliebung haben /sich darin zu üben / Also hat man ihnen hierinnen willfahren / und diese COMOEDIEN und TRAGEDIEN ihnen zum besten in öffentlichen Druck geben wollen / da man nun vermercken wird / daß sie ihnen lieb und angenemb / sollen derselben bald mehr darauff folgen / unter dessen wollen sie diese nützlich und wol gebrauchen / und ihnen gefallen lassen.[11]

Due to the great success of the English actors, German writers and companies started to emulate them, and the demand for written models increased. As Julie Stone Peters points out, the word *öffentlich* "indicate[s] the public nature of both acting and printing plays (people have undertaken 'publicly to *act* and *recite*' the comedies and tragedies, and those producing the volume now 'wish to offer them in public in Print')."[12] It also indicates the common understanding of written texts and especially drama as public domain. The anticipation that more plays 'shall follow' became reality four years later with the publication of the almost identical *Engelische Comedien und Tragedien. Zum Anderen mal gedruckt und corrigirt. Gedruckt im Jahr M.DC.XXIV* ('English Comedies and Tragedies. Reprinted and corrected. Printed in 1624'), which proves the positive reception of the first collection.

The following grid contains the titles of the fifteen plays plus a dance of the collection. To show how well balanced the internal subdivision is, I grouped them according to their genre and main features, which are added on the right.

List of contents of *Engelische Comedien und Tragedien* (1620)[13]	Genres
I. Comoedia Von der Königin Esther und hoffertigen Haman – 'Comedy of Queen Esther and haughty Haman'	Religious plays
II. Comoedia Von dem verlornen Sohn in welcher die Verzweiffelung und Hoffnung gar artig introduciret werden – 'Comedy of the Prodigal Son in which Despair and Hope are cleverly introduced'	

---

[11] *SW*, vol. 1, p. 2. Cohn offers this translation: 'As then in our times the English Comedians, partly by their pretty inventions, partly by the gracefulness of their gestures, often also by their elegance in speaking, obtain great praise from persons both of high and low condition, and thus active clever minds take a delight in and a fancy for such inventions, to exercise themselves therein, therefore have we been desirous to gratify them in this matter, and to print and publish these comedies and tragedies for their benefit; and as we shall perceive that they are agreeable and acceptable to them, more of the same shall soon follow them. In the meantime, we hope they may be willing to make good and profitable use of these and be contented with them.' (Cohn, pp. CIV-V). Fredén observes that even this seemingly more original part is indebted to Garzoni's description of the Greek actor Polo. See *Friedrich Menius und das Repertoire der englischen Komödianten in Deutschland*, pp. 11–12.

[12] Stone Peters, *Theatre of the Book, 1480–1880*, p. 238.

[13] See *SW*, vol. 1 for all the plays.

III. Comoedia Von Fortunato und seinem Seckel und Wünschhütlein, / Darinnen erstlich drey verstrorbenen Seelen als Geister, darnach die Tugend und Schande eingeführet werden – 'Comedy of Fortunatus and his purse and wishing cap, in which appear three dead souls as spirits, and afterwards Virtue and Shame' IV. Eine schöne lustig triumphirende Comoedia von eines Königes Sohne auß Engellandt und des Königes Tochter auß Schottlandt – 'A beautiful, merry, triumphant Comedy of a King's son from England and the King's daughter from Scotland' [Serule and Astrea]	Comedies with fantastic / pastoral elements
V. Eine kurtzweilige lustige Comoedia von Sidonia und Theagene – 'An entertaining, merry Comedy of Sidonia and Theagenes' VI. Eine schöne lustige Comedia / von Jemand und Niemandt – 'A beautiful merry Comedy of Somebody and Nobody'	Comedies with 'types'
VII. Tragaedia Von Julio und Hyppolita – 'Tragedy of Julius and Hyppolita' VIII. Eine sehr klägliche Tragaedia von Tito Andronico und der hoffertigen / Kaeyserin / darinnen denckwürdige Actiones zu befinden – 'A very lamentable tragedy of Titus Andronicus and the haughty Empress containing memorable scenes'	Tragedies based on Shakespeare
IX. Ein lustig Pickelherings Spiel / von der schönen Maria und alten Hanrey – 'A merry Pickelhering play of the beautiful Maria and the old cuckold' X. Ein ander lustig Pickelherings Spiel / darinnen er mit einen Stein gar lustige Possen machet – 'Another merry Pickelhering play, in which he makes merry pastime with a stone'	Farces with the clown Pickelhering
Nachfolgende Engelische Auffzüge / können nach Beliebung zwischen die Comoedien agiret werden – 'The following English interludes may be acted at pleasure between the comedies' XI. Actus I [Wife, Husband, Pickelhering, Boy, Soldier] XII. Aliud [Woman, Husband, Pickelhering, Youth/Servant, Soldier] XIII. Den Windelwäscher zu agiren mit drey Personen – 'The Nappy-washer to be played with three characters' [Husband, Wife, Neighbour] XIV. F. Fraw P. Pickelhering M. Magd M. Magister S. Studiosus – 'Wife, Pickelhering, Maid, Magister, Student' XV. Action 4. Person – 'A sketch with 4 characters' [Nobleman, Pickelhering, Wife, Husband]	Musical interludes / jigs in verse with musical scores
XVI. Curante	A French dance

The choice of plays offers a great variety of genres performed by the itinerant players: from religious plays to comedies with 'types', tragedies (both reworkings of Shakespeare), *Pickelheringspiele, Singspiele* and the musical scores of a dance. Unfortunately, the introduction does not give any information about the selection criteria. It is possible that they were the only plays available to the editor, or perhaps the most frequently staged ones.

The content, style and staging of all the plays will be analysed in detail, especially of those that can be recognised as German counterparts of English plays or at least bear an unmistakable similarity. The network of shared knowledge was indeed international and multidirectional, as the intercultural theatricality at work in *ECUT* shows. To date, the collection has chiefly been studied to identify lost sources used by Shakespeare and transferred to the Continent in the form of corrupted English plays, without giving much attention to the non-Shakespearean comedies and jigs. Although German scholars like Cohn, Creizenach, Fredén, Julian K. Hilton and Ralf Haekel insisted on the merits of the English Comedians in exporting Elizabethan drama, none of them analysed the full repertoire systematically, especially not in reference to Commedia dell'Arte.[14] My aim is to discuss all the plays of the 1620 collection from the perspective of adaptation theory to trace the interconnectedness of common sources and traditions which merged in the adaptation process. This will be done by applying the parameters of 1) memorialisation, 2) hybridisation, 3) adaptation of themes, motifs and characters, and 4) visualisation, sound and movement.

In the following subchapters, I shall summarise the content of each play, compare it to the major memorialised sources and analyse how they are connected to other plots and genres in terms of hybridisation. Due to the large number of plays, the comparison with extant pre-texts is limited to the most important parallels. My focus will be on adaptations of typical motifs and 'types', primarily from Commedia dell'Arte. The possible techniques of stagecraft and performance (visualisation) shall be pointed out scene by scene, based on the stage directions and any revealing textual reference. Whenever relevant, I shall also address other collections with original or alternative versions of the plays contained in *ECUT*, such as Jacob Ayrer's *Opus Theatricum* (1618),[15] some *canovacci* of the Commedia dell'Arte[16] and Elizabethan plays by Shakespeare, Kyd and Dekker. Each critical summary is rounded off with a short review, which addresses commonalities with

---

[14] See Cohn, *Shakespeare in Germany in the Sixteenth and Seventeenth Centuries* (1865); Creizenach, *Die Schauspiele der englischen Komödianten* (1889); Fredén, *Friedrich Menius und das Repertoire der englischen Komödianten in Deutschland* (1939); Hilton, *The 'Englische Komödianten' in German-speaking States, 1592–1620: A Generation of Touring Performers as Mediators between English and German Cultures* (1984); and Haekel, *Die Englischen Komödianten in Deutschland: Eine Einführung in die Ursprünge des deutschen Berufsschauspiels* (2004).

[15] Reprinted by Adelbert von Keller, ed., *Ayrers Dramen* (Hildesheim and New York: Georg Olms, 1973 [1865]). 8 vols.

[16] Contained in Anna Maria Testaverde, ed., *I canovacci della Commedia dell'Arte* (Torino: Einaudi, 2007).

other traditions and the role of the clown. In this context, Joel B. Lande's concepts of "fiction-internal communication" on stage *for* the audience and of "fiction-external communication" directed *at* the audience are relevant for the analysis of the clown in *ECUT*.[17] The last subchapter offers a systematic overview of the whole collection and draws conclusions on the scope of the parameters at work in the text.

6.1. The Religious Plays: *Esther* and *Von dem verlornen Sohn*

The first two plays of *ECUT*, *Comoedia von der Königin Esther und hoffertigen Haman* ('Comedy of the Queen Esther and the haughty Haman') and *Von dem verlornen Sohn* ('Of the Prodigal Son'), are dramatisations of the most favoured biblical stories since the Middle Ages, one from the Old Testament and the other from the New Testament.

Esther

The tale of Esther is memorialised in numerous renditions in Germany, such as Hans Sachs's *Comedia von der Hester* of 1536, but also in England. According to Henslowe's diary, a joint company of the Lord Chamberlain's and the Lord Admiral's Men performed *Heaster & Asheweros* on 3 June 1594.[18] This play probably formed the basis of *A newe Enterlude drawen oute of the holy Scripture, of godly Queen Hester, very necessary, newly made and imprinted this present Yere 1561, at London by Wyllyam Pickerynge and Thomas Hacket*, as Cohn argues.[19] Karl Goedecke suggests that the version in *ECUT* might be based on an English model now lost, or on a lost dramatisation of the tale by Landgrave Moritz, because it does not bear any resemblance to Hans Sachs's rendition nor to the many German plays about the same topic circulating between 1539 and 1623.[20] Hence, *The Book of Esther* in the Old Testament is the most direct source available for comparison.

The play begins with a long and solemn monologue by the Persian King Ahasuerus during a sumptuous feast, taken almost verbatim from the Scripture.

> KÖNIG. Ich König Ahasuerus Regierer und Gebieter von India, biß in Mohren / uber 123. Länder / habe euch meine liebe Fürsten und Obristen des Landes zeigen wollen die

---

[17] See Joel B. Lande, *Persistence of Folly*, p. 70. "Fiction-external communication" functions like an aside – in the sense that it is addressed to the audience and not heard by the other characters – but is not marked as such. The fact that the other characters on stage do not react to e.g. an impertinent comment of the clown allows to classify such an expression as "fiction-external".
[18] See *Henslowe's Diary*, edited by R. A. Foakes, p. 21.
[19] See Cohn, p. CIX.
[20] See Karl Goedecke and Edmund Goetze, ed., *Grundriß zur Geschichte der deutschen Dichtung* (Dresden: L. Ehlermann, 1886), vol. 2, p. 167.

Pracht und Herrligkeit unser Majestät / damit ihr aber den grossen / unzehlichen und unaußsprechlichen Reichtumb recht sehen möchtet / habe dazu berordnet 180. Tage / in dero Tagen ihr die Pracht anschawen möchtet. [...] Nun habt ihr allunser Reichtumb / Silber, Goldt und edele Kleinodien gesehen / aber eins haben wir noch / das ubertrifft diese alle / welches wir euch jetzt wollen sehen lassen. BIGTHAN und THERES gehen alsobald hin und holet unsere schöne Königin VASTHI mit ihrer Königlichen Krone / denn ihre Schöne und Krone müssen wir auch vor allem Volck zeigen.[21]

This narrative monologue is typical of the early plays of the English Comedians in Germany, in which remnants of epic sources supplied the characterisation, context and verbal scenery on stage. By 'verbal scenery' I mean the descriptions concerning time, space and background of the action, when physical props and scenography could not supply this information. We can imagine that in the later phases, when the wandering troupes were more established, lavish costumes and on-stage settings would display the riches mentioned in the description. Despite its simplicity, the monologue contains a metatheatrical device which requires a certain familiarity with dramatic conventions on the part of the audience: the king wants his counsellors to present his most valuable treasure, i.e. his wife Vasthi

---

[21] SW, vol. 1, p. 5. Translation: 'I, King Ahasuerus, ruler and disposer over 123 countries from India to Africa, wanted to show you, my dear lords and officers of the country, the magnificence and splendour of our majesty. In order that you may behold the great, immeasurable and inexpressible wealth, I have ordered a feast of 180 days, in which you might look upon the magnificence. [...] Now you have seen all our riches, silver gold and precious treasures but we still have one that surpasses them all, which we want you to see now. Bigthan and Theres, go at once and fetch the beautiful queen Vasthi with her royal crown because we want to present her beauty and crown to all the people as well.' Cf. *The Book of Esther*, King James Version (subsequently abbreviated to KJV, 1:2–11: "[1] Now it came to pass in the days of Ahasuerus, (this is Ahasuerus which reigned, from India even unto Ethiopia, over an hundred and seven and twenty provinces:) [2] That in those days, when the king Ahasuerus sat on the throne of his kingdom, which was in Shushan the palace, [3] In the third year of his reign, he made a feast unto all his princes and his servants; the power of Persia and Media, the nobles and princes of the provinces, being before him: [4] When he shewed the riches of his glorious kingdom and the honour of his excellent majesty many days, even an hundred and fourscore days. [5] And when these days were expired, the king made a feast unto all the people that were present in Shushan the palace, both unto great and small, seven days, in the court of the garden of the king's palace; [6] Where were white, green, and blue, hangings, fastened with cords of fine linen and purple to silver rings and pillars of marble: the beds were of gold and silver, upon a pavement of red, and blue, and white, and black, marble. [7] And they gave them drink in vessels of gold, (the vessels being diverse one from another,) and royal wine in abundance, according to the state of the king. [8] And the drinking was according to the law; none did compel: for so the king had appointed to all the officers of his house, that they should do according to every man's pleasure. [9] Also Vashti the queen made a feast for the women in the royal house which belonged to king Ahasuerus. [10] On the seventh day, when the heart of the king was merry with wine, he commanded Mehuman, Biztha, Harbona, Bigthan, and Abagtha, Zethar, and Carcas, the seven chamberlains that served in the presence of Ahasuerus the king, [11] To bring Vashti the queen before the king with the crown royal, to shew the people and the princes her beauty: for she was fair to look on."

(Vashti in the Bible) with her precious crown to his 'subjects', referring to the spectators.

While the chamberlain Bigthan goes to fetch the queen, Ahasuerus states that all his power and wealth are due to his faithful advisor Haman, the slayer of his enemies. Hearing that the queen refuses to come, Haman suggests repudiating her, as she would otherwise set a bad example for all other women in the realm. In *The Book of Esther*, a minister named Memucan gives this advice, while Haman is introduced later.[22] To serve the economy of staging, Memucan is left out and Haman is the accredited counsellor of the king right from the beginning.

The exemplary punishment of the queen is comically mirrored in the first entrance of the hen-pecked husband Hans Knapkäse, equally punished by his bossy wife. To atone for his coming home late the previous evening, the clown – whose name literally means 'short cheese' like the food-derived names of other famous clowns, from Pickelhering to Stockfish – must carry a heavy basket and endure her blows. Compared to the royal consorts, the power relations in this couple are turned on their head with comic effect. Moreover, like the king, Hans has an advisor, notably his neighbour, who pities him for the ill-treatment and suggests hitting the woman even harder to make her docile. The plan appears difficult to carry out, but the neighbour insists that it worked perfectly well with his own wife and adds that even the king issued the order that all noncompliant women were to be reprimanded, thus connecting the farce to the main plot. The clown expresses his satisfaction with typical expressions like "potz schlepperment" (goodness gracious) or extenuated curses like "Das dich ein Entzian [hole]" (meaning 'the gentian take you' instead of "Dass dich der Teufel hole" – 'the devil take you') and plucks up the courage to beat his wife by getting drunk. The scene is characterised by a back and forth of short dialogues in a colloquial tone, which make the characters lively and more entertaining than those in the main plot.

In the second act, the protagonist of the play, Esther, is introduced. In an unnaturally explicit narrative dialogue, the wise Jew Mardocheus tells the girl about her own life, informing her that she has been his foster-child since she was left an orphan. When Bigthan and Haman seek out beautiful Esther as the king's new wife, Mardocheus entreats her to keep her Jewish origin a secret. After a long preparation with scents and cosmetics – a passage very close to the Bible[23] –

---

[22] See *The Book of Esther*, KJV, 1:13.
[23] Cf. *The Book of Esther*, KJV, 2:12: "Now when every maid's turn was come to go in to king Ahasuerus, after that she had been twelve months, according to the manner of the women, (for so were the days of their purifications accomplished, to wit, six months with oil of myrrh, and six months with sweet odours, and with other things for the purifying of the women;)" and the text of the play: "HAMAN. Großmächtiger König / 10. Monat ist sie nun gewesen im Frawenzimmer / nemblich 6. Monat mit Balsam und Myrrhen / und 4. Monat mit guten Specereyen." *SW*, vol. 1, p. 19. Translation: 'HAMAN. Mighty king / she has been in the women's chambers for ten months now, of which six months with balsam and myrrh and four months with good spices.' Although the number of months for the purifying ritual is not the same, the unguents coincide.

Esther's modesty so pleases the king that he marries her immediately. Grateful for Haman's services, Ahasuerus makes him the most powerful man after himself. His unfair predilection for Haman, however, leads the envious councillors Bigthan and Theres to conspire against the king. Thanks to Esther and Mardocheus' intervention, they are put to death and Haman rises even higher in his lord's esteem.

Without any connection to the main plot, apart from the parodic reversal, the subplot is taken up again. Hans Knapkäse's plan has worked out and he proudly presents his transmuted wife to his neighbour. In an absurd scene echoing Shakespeare's *Taming of the Shrew*, he even makes her declare that the milk-soup they are eating is black, just to prove her absolute obedience.

> HANS. [...] Aber Fraw warumb ist die Milch so schwartz?
> WEIB. Mein lieber Mann es deucht euch nur / denn die Milch ist ja weiß.
> HANS. *Schlägt sie.* Ich sage die Milch ist schwartz.
> WEIB. Wor zum Teuffel schlagt ihr mich? Nachbar ich bitte sehet ihr / ist die Milch schwartz.
> NACHBAR. Wor zum Teuffel sol die Milch schwartz seyn. Nachbar Hans bistu toll / die Milch ist ja Schneeweiß.
> HANS. Potz schlapperment / ich will es jetzo haben / daß die Milch sol schwartz seyn. Fraw ist sie nicht schwartz?
> NACHBAR. Nachbäwrin last euch derhalben nicht schlagen / saget lieber sie ist schwartz.
> HANS. Fraw ist die Milch schwartz oder weiß?
> FRAW. O mein lieber Mann sie ist Pechschwartz.[24]

---

[24] *SW*, vol. 1, pp. 32–3. Translation: 'HANS. [...] But wife, why is the milk so black? WIFE. My dear husband, it just looks like that to you; the milk is white. HANS. *Beats her*. I say the milk is black. WIFE. Why the hell do you beat me? Neighbour, I pray you, look if the milk is black. NEIGHBOUR. Why the hell should the milk be black? Neighbour Hans, are you crazy? The milk is indeed as white as snow. HANS. Goodness gracious, I want the milk to be black now. Wife, is it not black? NEIGHBOUR. Neighbour, do not make him beat you and rather say it is black. HANS. Wife, is the milk black or white? WIFE/WOMAN. O my dear husband, it is as black as tar.' Note the sketchy editing of the collection in the jumbled reference to the wife as "Fraw" and "Weib". The discussion on whether the milk is white or black could be an indirect intertextual reference to Shakespeare's *Taming of the Shrew* (1590/2), when Catherine is drilled by Petruchio to say the sun is the moon as an act of absolute submission, especially when the neighbour bids the wife to comply as does Hortensio with Katharina. Cf. *The Taming of the Shrew* (4.5.1–22): "PETRUCHIO. Come on, i' God's name; once more toward our father's. Good Lord, how bright and goodly shines the moon! KATHARINA. The moon! the sun: it is not moonlight now. PETR. I say it is the moon that shines so bright. KATH. I know it is the sun that shines so bright. PETR. Now, by my mother's son, and that's myself, It shall be moon, or star, or what I list, Or ere I journey to your father's house. Go on, and fetch our horses back again. Evermore cross'd and cross'd; nothing but cross'd! HORTENSIO. Say as he says, or we shall never go. KATH. Forward, I pray, since we have come so far, And be it moon, or sun, or what you please: And if you please to call it a rush-candle, Henceforth I vow it shall be so for me. PETR. I say it is the moon. KATH. I know it is the moon. PETR. Nay, then you lie: it is the blessed sun. KATH. Then, God be bless'd, it is the blessed sun: But sun it is not, when you say it is not; And the moon changes even

Exalted by his neighbour's admiration, Hans exaggerates his abuse and is promptly toppled from his position of master of the house in the next scene. His son Nickel returns from a journey to France, where he has learned to make a living by jumping through a hoop. An acrobatic actor or leaper would have exhibited his skills in this scene, contrary to clumsy Hans, who remains stuck in the narrow hoop. In this ridiculous position, he is at the mercy of his wife, who beats him up and makes him promise to be her servant. In terms of intercultural theatricality, this juxtaposition of silly clown and elegant leaper recalls the bipartition of the Zannis into sly and foolish. The hoop motif, however, is uncommon and must be an English invention, as Julius Tittmann argues.[25] It might also be a legacy of the Italianate influence, since Gustaf Fredén quotes a passage from Ben Jonson's *Every Man Out of His Humour* (1599), in which a clown imitates a tumbler to amuse the audience: "Hee's like a Zani to a Tumbler, / That tries trickes after him to make men laugh" (5.1).[26] The fact that the clown is called Zani and the similarity of the scene to the hoop incident in *Esther* further attest an indebtedness to both Italian and English influences.

In the third act of this long play, Haman has become so overbearing that he expects everyone to worship him as a divinity. Since Mardocheus will not kneel before anyone but his God, Haman swears revenge on the Jewish people. The motive for his hatred is clearly stated in the Bible: being the son of Hammedatha the Agagite, a tribe hostile to the Jews, Haman is particularly keen on ruining them. In the play, the ideological reason is replaced by haughtiness, as stated in the title of the comedy. Such a simple characterisation by status or a particular trait would make comprehension easier for the audience and exploit their familiarity with the conventions of popular theatre genres, like the morality play. Not only do the characters embody allegories of virtue and vices, but the central conflict of the play also recalls the structure of a morality play with the king being torn between the virtuous Esther and the wicked Haman. Under the latter's evil influence, the manipulated king consents to slay all the Jews, not knowing that this will include his wife as well.

While Mardocheus dresses in sackcloth and ashes as a penance for having brought about the Persian king's wrath, Esther bravely intercedes for her kin during a royal banquet held for Haman. The advisor's joy about this special treatment is only disturbed by the vision of the penitent Mardocheus and he orders the Jew to be hanged the next morning. A clownish carpenter called Hans (apparently a distinct character from Hans Knapkäse in the list of dramatis personae) is called to build a gallows of 50 cubits high. Among many antics, Hans asks to take measurements of Haman since he is erecting it 'for him' – an ambiguous expression

---

as your mind. What you will have it named, even that it is; And so it shall be so for Katharina."

[25] See Tittmann, *Die Schauspiele der englischen Komödianten in Deutschland*, p. XXIII.
[26] See Fredén, *Friedrich Menius und das Repertoire der Englischen Komödianten in Deutschland*, p. 220.

which could mean 'because of him' or 'intended for him', foreshadowing of the end of the play. Some aspects faintly recall the scene of the clown-gravedigger in *Hamlet*, Act 5 and are a fine instance of gallows humour in the truest sense of the word.

> HAMAN. Gehe du alber Narr / und seum dich nicht.
> HANS. Nein ich werde [nicht] seumen vor euch ein Galgen zu bawen.
> HAMAN. Du grober Esel / sehe ich deine Allberkeit und Unverstandt nicht an / so müstu erst daran gehencket werden. Die Götter werden mich vor den Galgen behüten.
> HANS. O ja / o ja / aber vorr ewrem Halß wil ich nicht schweren.[27]

Back in the palace, the king is reminded of Mardocheus' good services and appoints Haman of all people to think of a proper way of honouring a benefactor. Under the wrong impression that he is to be honoured, Haman suggests a horse and a magnificent apparel, and is promptly disillusioned. Angered by his enemy's victory, he contritely returns home to his wife Seres, who is only named here, while in the Bible Zeresh has an active role in promoting the idea of Mardocheus' hanging on a gallows "of 50 cubits high."[28]

During the banquet in the fourth and final act, Esther reveals her identity and Haman's mischievous plan to kill those who saved the king's life. Ahasuerus sentences Haman to death by hanging, just as the clown had predicted. In vain Haman asks for mercy; he is taken up a ladder and pushed down with a rope around his neck by Hans Knapkäse, who then cuts the rope off in a dramatic gesture. The stage direction "*Kömpt Hans Knapkäse und Haman gebunden*"[29] raises the question of whether the carpenter/hangman Hans is the same person as the clown, or if it is just a typographical error in the edition. Either way, it gives insight into the staging practice of the time: on the makeshift stages of the itinerant players, there probably was a wooden structure representing the gallows, and a ladder with an exit at the top to jump behind the scenes would have sufficed to enact the difficult

---

[27] *SW*, vol. 1, pp. 57–8. Translation: 'HAMAN. Go, you fool, and do not dawdle. HANS. No, I will not forget to build a gibbet for you. HAMAN. Rude ass, would I not consider your foolishness and lack of judgement, you should be hanged. The gods will preserve me from these gallows. HANS. Yes, yes, but I would not swear on your neck.' Cf. *Hamlet* (5.1.118–36): "HAMLET. Whose grave's this, sirrah? FIRST CLOWN. Mine, sir. HAMLET. I think it be thine, indeed; for thou liest in't. FIRST CLOWN. You lie out on't, sir, and therefore it is not yours: for my part, I do not lie in't, and yet it is mine. HAMLET. Thou dost lie in't, to be in't and say it is thine: 'tis for the dead, not for the quick; therefore thou liest. FIRST CLOWN. 'Tis a quick lie, sir; 'twill away gain, from me to you. HAMLET. What man dost thou dig it for? FIRST CLOWN. For no man, sir. HAMLET. What woman, then? FIRST CLOWN. For none, neither. HAMLET. Who is to be buried in't? FIRST CLOWN. One that was a woman, sir; but, rest her soul, she's dead."

[28] "Then said Zeresh his wife and all his friends unto him, Let a gallows be made of fifty cubits high, and to morrow speak thou unto the king that Mordecai may be hanged thereon: then go thou in merrily with the king unto the banquet. And the thing pleased Haman; and he caused the gallows to be made." *The Book of Esther*, KJV, 5:14.

[29] *SW*, vol. 1, p. 68. Translation: 'Enter Hans Knapkäse with the handcuffed Haman.'

scene of the villain's plunge to his death, dangling from a rope. This hypothesis is supported by the already mentioned picture of a booth stage at a village fair by Pieter Brueghel the Younger (1632), in which a ladder is leaning against the back wall.[30]

Figure 10: Detail from Pieter Brueghel the Younger's *A Village Festival in Honour of St Hubert and St Anthony* (1632). The Fitzwilliam Museum, Cambridge.

The moral ending teaches the audience not to be blinded by haughtiness or else they will partake in Haman's bitter destiny. Just as in the Bible, Mardocheus takes Haman's place, the order of slaying the Jews is not revoked but altered in such a way that they can defend themselves, and Esther orders Haman's ten sons to be killed to complete the revenge. Eventually, the subplot is inserted into the main plot when the king settles the dispute between Hans Knapkäse and his wife. He tells Hans to be his servant while his wife shall be the queen's maid, so they will not fight any more. When the irreconcilable brawlers realise that this solution would mean a separation at night too, they ask for permission to sleep together. Thus, sex happily wins over despondency.

This dramatisation of a semi-historical episode from the Bible was received very favourably, for example by the German imitators Jacob Ayrer and Johann Rist.[31] Brauneck observes that this success might be due to the political context

---

[30] See chapter 2.1. of this study for a further reference to the painting.
[31] The German playwright Johann Rist took up the name of the clown Hans Knapkäse in his tragedy *Perseus* (1634). See Johann Rist, *Perseus. Das ist: Eine newe Tragœdia, welche*

of the persecution of the Jews, which can be read as a metaphor for the confessional conflicts destabilising Europe during the Reformation and Counterreformation period. The conciliatory ending pleads for a tolerant and respectful coexistence of different religions and is likely to have met with the approval of contemporary audiences.[32] This comment is certainly true, but in my opinion the play's strongest appeal lies in the clever hybridisation of the well-known tale from the Old Testament with a farcical subplot around the clown Hans Knapkäse and his tyrannical wife. The bipartite arrangement with the addition of comical byplays was a strategy already devised by medieval amateur actors of ecclesiastical folk drama to make the scriptural topics palatable. The hen-pecked husband motif, in particular, has been a laughingstock ever since the fourteenth-century pageants, like that of Chester and Wakefield about the Deluge.[33] It was therefore maintained in humorous plays and interludes, for example *Den Windelwäscher* about a husband forced by his wife to wash the nappies, also contained in *ECUT*. Until the last act, the two unconnected strands are held together only by a distorted reflection of the main action in the subplot, as in many other instances of Elizabethan drama or Commedia dell'Arte. While the queen Vasthi is repudiated for not obeying her lord and replaced by meek Esther, in the parodic reversal of the marital conflict, Hans is tricked into submission by his imperious wife. Thus, patriarchy is subverted until the king intervenes. Moreover, the *Psychomachia* to win the king's favour, which recalls the central conflict of the morality play, is caricatured on a lower comic level in the physical fights for the domination over the household.

As far as the adaptation of characters and themes is concerned, the subjugated husband Hans Knapkäse – probably playing the gawky hangman too – is surrounded by characters echoing the 'types' of Commedia dell'Arte, such as his despondent wife, the silly neighbour and the acrobatic son. One might find a faint resemblance between the subdued Hans and Pantalone, who takes the questionable advice of his know-all neighbour/Dottore and is fooled by Nickel/ Arlecchino with the hoop prank (*burla*). In addition, some roles recall characters of Shakespeare, like the shrew Catherine or the foolish gravedigger in *Hamlet*.

The enactment (visualisation) of passages set in the past, such as Esther's youth, or too difficult to perform, like the feast of the king, are mentioned rather than visualised on stage. By contrast, vivid scenes like the hanging or the war of the sexes are acted out and enriched with acrobatic skills, physical excesses – bordering violence – and the reversal of order, all meant to evoke laughter.

---

in Beschreibunge theils warhaffter Geschichten / theils lustiger vnd anmuhtiger Gedichten / einen Sonnenklahren Welt- vnd Hoffspiegel jedermänniglichen præsentiret vnd vorstellet (1634), in Eberhard Mannack, ed., *Johann Rist: Sämtliche Werke* (Berlin und New York: W. de Gruyter, 1972).

[32] See *SW*, vol. 1, p. 7.
[33] See *The Chester Pageant of the Water-leaders and Drawers of the Dee concerning Noah's Deluge*, contained in Rhys, ed., *Everyman and Other Old Religious Plays*.

Von dem verlornen Sohn

The second biblical play of the collection, the *Comoedia Von dem verlornen Sohn in welcher die Verzweiffelung und Hoffnung gar artig introduciret werden* ('Comedy of the Prodigal Son in which Despair and Hope are cleverly introduced'), is based on the parable of the Prodigal Son from the Gospel according to Luke. Brauneck argues that it is the most frequently dramatised parable of the sixteenth century, not only in numerous English adaptations but also in German school drama, and enjoyed considerable success for its clearly defined characters, solid structure and strong religious message.[34] For Lawrence M. Price, the English Comedians' version adduced in the *Theaterbrief* by Maria Magdalena about Green's 1608 performance might have been based on two English sources: a morality play entitled *The Contention between Liberality and Prodigality*, acted at court in 1568 and printed in 1602, or a play called *The London Prodigal*.[35] An influence of previous German adaptations is not excluded either, as Anna Baesecke suggests;[36] however, compared to the pre-texts, the accomplished actors from England increased the psychological depth of the characters in added scenes with allegorical characters and 'types' alien to the gospel. For instance, the tavern scene vividly visualises the sinful behaviour of the son. Likewise, the crucial moment of his repentance is embedded in a morality play structure with the allegories of *Verzweiffelung* (Despair) and *Hoffnung* (Hope), advertised in the title to attract the attention of the audience. The 1620 *Comoedia Von dem verlornen Sohn* thus became a well-received hybrid, somewhere in-between didactic morality play, Bible play and popular comedy, with instances of Elizabethan drama techniques and Commedia dell'Arte 'types'.

To point out the parallels between the source and the adaptation, the parable from the Gospel according to Luke will be quoted in full:

> [11] And he [Jesus] said, a certain man had two sons: [12] And the younger of them said to his father, Father, give me the portion of goods that falleth to me. And he divided unto them his living. [13] And not many days after the younger son gathered all together, and took his

---

[34] Brauneck lists all the German dramatisations of the parable of the Prodigal Son. In 1527, the Protestant Burkard Waldis treated this subject matter in the first German drama with acts, followed by Johann Ackermann (1537), Hans Salat (1537), Jörg Wickram (1540), Hans Sachs (1556), Johann Nensdorf (1608), Nikolaus Loccius (1619) and many others. In particular, Nendorf's school drama *Asotus, Das ist: Comoedia Vom Verlohrnen Sohn* makes use of typical features of the English Comedians' techniques appropriated by the German stage. For instance, the clown Johan Clant speaks Low-German dialect like in Duke Heinrich Julius's plays. Although there are some correspondences between *Asotus* (1608) and *Von dem verlornen Sohn* (*ECUT* 1620), the itinerant players had already performed the play in Nördlingen in 1604, in Passau in 1607, and in Graz in 1608 with Green's troupe, as Brauneck argues, therefore they must have had an earlier text different from Nendorf's. See *SW*, vol. 6, pp. 11–12. For a detailed comparison between Waldis, Ackermann, Nendorf and the *ECUT* play see Fredén, op. cit., chapter 20.

[35] See Price, *The Reception of English Literature in Germany*, p. 15.

[36] See Baesecke, *Das Schauspiel der englischen Komödianten in Deutschland*, p. 23.

journey into a far country, and there wasted his substance with riotous living. ¹⁴ And when he had spent all, there arose a mighty famine in that land; and he began to be in want. ¹⁵ And he went and joined himself to a citizen of that country; and he sent him into his fields to feed swine. ¹⁶ And he would fain have filled his belly with the husks that the swine did eat: and no man gave unto him. ¹⁷ And when he came to himself, he said, How many hired servants of my father's have bread enough and to spare, and I perish with hunger! ¹⁸ I will arise and go to my father, and will say unto him, Father, I have sinned against heaven, and before thee, ¹⁹ And am no more worthy to be called thy son: make me as one of thy hired servants. ²⁰ And he arose, and came to his father. But when he was yet a great way off, his father saw him, and had compassion, and ran, and fell on his neck, and kissed him. ²¹ And the son said unto him, Father, I have sinned against heaven, and in thy sight, and am no more worthy to be called thy son. ²² But the father said to his servants, Bring forth the best robe, and put it on him; and put a ring on his hand, and shoes on his feet: ²³ And bring hither the fatted calf, and kill it; and let us eat, and be merry: ²⁴ For this my son was dead, and is alive again; he was lost, and is found. And they began to be merry. ²⁵ Now his elder son was in the field: and as he came and drew nigh to the house, he heard musick and dancing. ²⁶ And he called one of the servants, and asked what these things meant. ²⁷ And he said unto him, Thy brother is come; and thy father hath killed the fatted calf, because he hath received him safe and sound. ²⁸ And he was angry, and would not go in: therefore came his father out, and intreated him. ²⁹ And he answering said to his father, Lo, these many years do I serve thee, neither transgressed I at any time thy commandment: and yet thou never gavest me a kid, that I might make merry with my friends: ³⁰ But as soon as this thy son was come, which hath devoured thy living with harlots, thou hast killed for him the fatted calf. ³¹ And he said unto him, Son, thou art ever with me, and all that I have is thine. ³² It was meet that we should make merry, and be glad: for this thy brother was dead, and is alive again; and was lost, and is found.³⁷

Before delving into the content of the dramatisation in *ECUT*, a grid with the characters from the biblical tale and those in the play gives an idea of the addition of morality play patterns and of forms of popular theatre like Commedia dell'Arte. They will be explained in the analysis.

Characters of the parable of the Prodigal Son from the Gospel according to Luke (KJV, 15:11–32)	Dramatis personae in *Comoedia Von dem verlornen Sohn*³⁸
Man / Father	Father of the Prodigal Son
Younger son	Prodigal Son
Elder son	Brother of the Prodigal Son
---	[Servant of the Prodigal Son, not mentioned in the list but acting in the plot]
---	Landlord
---	Landlady or wife
---	Daughter of the Landlord
---	Despair
---	Hope
A citizen	A citizen

[37] *The Gospel According to Luke*, King James Version, 15:11–32.
[38] The list of characters is taken from *SW*, vol. 1, p. 79. My translation.

Like the parable, *Von dem verlornen Sohn* begins in medias res with the younger son expressing his wish to try his luck in different countries and return as an admired man after all his adventures. The worried father warns him that many a youth has set out with good intentions like these but ended up in misery and damnation after squandering their patrimony "mit leichtfertigem Gesinde / auch mit Huren und Buben."[39] The father's monologue with narrative traits contains numerous moralistic teachings in line with the didactic aim of the religious play and preannounces what will happen to the Prodigal Son. As the audience was probably familiar with the plot, this foreshadowing appears redundant. However, and this is an original addition to the plot, in a soliloquy the Prodigal Son makes the strict education and stinginess of the father indirectly responsible for his subsequent aberrations:

> SOHN. [...] Hie wolte ich nicht länger geblieben seyn / es were unmüglich / dann war ich hier bey Gesellschafft / bey schönen Frawen und Jungfrawen / und meynte es würde kein Mensche in der gantzen Stadt wissen / ja so bald ich aer zu Hause kam / wuste es mein Vater / da gieng es an ein schelten / ich meynte daß ich wol geplaget ward. Sagt ich zu meinem Vater / ich bin jung / und gerne bey der Welt / gab er mir allzeit zur Antwort / ja mein Sohn es kostet aber viele Geldt [...].[40]

This speech implies that the young man might not have felt the urge to ignore the paternal and fraternal cautioning, had the parent been less controlling. So, he takes his share of the patrimony, sings and dances with joy and then departs with his servant to the blare of trumpets. Since the stage direction "*Tantzet und singet*" indicates dancing and singing, Brauneck's assumption that the rhymed quartet at the end of Act 1 – "ADE ich reite in die Welt / Ich thu und hauß wie mirs gefelt. / Dir Vater / Muttr [sic!] Bruder mein / Mügen GOtt wol befohlen seyn"[41] – was sung and followed by a musical interlude seems plausible.[42] Music and dancing at this point would give the actors time to change the scenery for the next act, while keeping the audience entertained.

Act 2 turns the short biblical description of how the son "wasted his substance with riotous living" into a detailed dramatic episode at the tavern. While the *Book of Esther* was reduced as far as characters and minor plot turns are concerned ("concision" and "condensation" in Genette's terms), the synthetic Biblical parable was amplified ("extension")[43] and hybridised with new scenes and roles. In

---

[39] *SW*, vol. 1, p. 83. Translation: '[...] with the frivolous rabble and with whores and knaves.'
[40] Ibid. Translation: 'SON. I do not want to stay here any longer, it is impossible. Whenever I used to be in company here, with women and maids, and thought nobody in town would know, my father knew it as soon as I got home. Then he would start scolding and pestering me severely. If I told my father that I am young and want to be a man of the world, he always answered: I know, my son, but it costs a lot of money.'
[41] Ibid., p. 85. Translation: 'Goodbye, I ride out into the world and live as I please. May God bless my father, mother and brother.'
[42] See *SW*, vol. 6, p. 13.
[43] See Genette, *Palimpsests*, pp. 228–37.

the tavern scene, the son's silly servant plays a decisive role although he is not mentioned in the list of dramatis personae, probably because he was played by the omnipresent clown. Upon their arrival in a new city, the servant runs into an innkeeper who has been driven almost crazy ("närrisch")[44] by his financial distress, as he declares in a typical example of self-characterisation. Hearing that the foreigners are rich, the host seizes the opportunity to make some money and calls his wife and daughter from inside. As the scene unfolds, the play makes a remarkable use of Commedia dell'Arte patterns, motifs and characters. The greedy wife takes the servant aside, promises to sleep with him and offers her young daughter to his master, should they stay at their inn.[45] The foolish servant is so tempted by a sexual adventure with the landlady that he becomes the intermediary between his master and the innkeepers in an interesting instance of adaptation of 'types'. In fact, his poor judgement, lust and gluttony recall attributes of the simpleton Zanni, while the avid host is made a cuckold by his wife like Pantalone. Moreover, they all engage in an intrigue in line with numerous Commedia dell'Arte *scenari* and *Singspiele* of the 1620 collection. Baesecke argues that the host and his family function as allegories of sins such as greed, gluttony, lust and gambling,[46] however they cannot simply be categorised as good or evil, as was the case in *Esther* or in the morality play tradition. Due to the augmented psychological depth and motives of the characters' actions, the audience understands that they are all driven by necessity and make wrong but plausible decisions, just like the 'types' of the Commedia dell'Arte, who evolved from allegorical figures to comic stereotypes.

Regarding staging techniques of visualisation, the scene features a subdivision of the stage into groups of characters who speak without being heard by the others. On the one side, the servant praises the charms of the innkeeper's daughter to his master. On the other side, the host and his wife instigate the girl to repress her feelings of love for the elegant youth and be his concubine, revealing that she has worked as a prostitute for years. Attracted by her charms, the naive son enters the tavern after a short romantic exchange, which echoes the lovemaking of the Innamorati. From a socio-historical point of view, Brauneck points out that the destitution of the host, which leads to criminality and prostitution, and the repeated complaints about the increase in prices might be interpreted as references to the plights that came along with the Thirty Years' War.[47] Allusions to contemporary events like these contribute to the "proximization" ('bringing closer') of topics.[48]

---

[44] *SW*, vol. 1, p. 89.
[45] According to R. Pascal, the technique of placing characters in different parts of the stage to present dialogues that are independent from each other is akin to the *Fastnaschspiel* and the "*décor simultané* of the mysteries." See R. Pascal, "The Stage of the 'Englische Komödianten' – Three Problems", *The Modern Language Review* 35 (1940), pp. 367–76, p. 369. If we apply this idea to the tavern scene of *Von dem verlornen Sohn*, an additional layer of adaptation to pre-existing traditions emerges.
[46] See Baesecke, op. cit., p. 25.
[47] See *SW*, vol. 6, p. 13.
[48] Genette, op. cit., p. 304.

Still, the plays were in circulation well before the outbreak of the war, and address common social problems even in times of peace.

The third act visualises the gradual downfall of the protagonist with a series of episodes alien to the biblical parable. The landlord prepares an overpriced banquet with good company, lively music – thus integrated in the play[49] – and plenty of alcohol. As a stage direction reveals, the astute host keeps refilling the glass of his guest but only drinks in little sips from his own ("*der* WIRTH *trincket seines immer halb auß*" i.e. 'the host drinks up only half of his glass').[50] Not content with the money he has won from the drunk adversary, he instructs his daughter to steal the rest while the young man is asleep.

Act 4 is comparatively short and represents the disillusion of the son. Noticing that his purse is gone, he blames the theft on his lover. This angers the hypocritical hosts so much that they strip him of his clothes, beat and rout him. Deserted by his servant, the destitute protagonist is left alone.

The function of the fifth act, according to Julius Tittmann, is to make the feelings that lead to repentance visible and thus more powerful.[51] Forced to beg at several doors, the sinner must suffer from hunger, poverty and despair before he can be pardoned. As the stage direction says, he simply knocks at the background wall to beg and from behind a voice sends him away. This is a clever solution to reduce the number of actors on stage while still visualising a scene. In line with the morality play structure, the protagonist is torn between the allegories of Despair/Satan, who suggests ending his plight by committing suicide, and angelic Hope, who encourages him to repent. Eventually, Hope drives Satan away with his own sword, perhaps a legacy of the Saint George folk play. Now the son is ready to do penance for his sins and enters the service of a townsman as the gospel says: "He went and joined himself to a citizen of that country."

Despair returns to the fray in Act 6, when the half-starved protagonist is about to feel abandoned by God. Again, Hope vigorously chases Despair away with a sword and takes the Prodigal Son to his father's house. In the biblical parable, the son makes up his mind by himself, while in the play it takes the allegorical figures to guide the erring soul. This choice follows the generic requirements of the morality play and the general tendency to make feelings, thoughts and allusions explicit in the English Comedians' adaptations. The unconditioned welcome of the lost son, the order to "bring hither the fatted calf", the remonstrance of the older son and the subsequent explanation follow the Scripture. Both in the parable and in the play, the last words come from the father and almost coincide with the Bi-

---

[49] The stage directions are precise and state when the music should start, stop or play so softly, that the actors may still be heard. E.g. "*Die Spielleute fangen wider an / geigen gar submissè, also daß man dabey reden kann.*" *SW*, vol. 1, p. 100.
[50] Ibid., p. 102.
[51] See Tittmann, *Die Schauspiele der englischen Komödianten in Deutschland*, p. 58.

ble: "dieser dein Bruder war todt / und ist wieder lebendig worden / er war verlohren / und ist wieder gefunden worden",[52] which in Christian terms is a reference to the death and resurrection of Jesus and of those who believe in him. Such quotations might indicate that the English Comedians resorted to a German translation of the Scripture to make up for their lack of linguistic knowledge, or that the editor was a pious and well-read Protestant, as suggested by Fredén.[53]

A brief comparison with an earlier German adaptation, namely *Der verlorn Sohn* by Hans Sachs (1556), shows the merits the English Comedians had in rendering epic narratives increasingly dramatic. Narrations of events were frequent in medieval drama for clarity and simplicity, and Jesuit school drama relied heavily on monologues, too, to train the pupils' rhetoric skills, as Baesecke explains.[54] In Sachs, both the sins of the Prodigal Son and his repentance are only narrated, whereas the biblical play in *ECUT* allows the spectators to *see* the fall from grace of the Prodigal Son with the insertion of the misadventures at the inn. In particular, the mischievous host and his family come to life by using character patterns reminiscent of Commedia dell'Arte and vivid dialogues instead of narrative monologues. The use of the morality play structure is another incidence of hybridisation: the allegories of Hope and Despair fight over the protagonist's soul and ultimately lead him to repentance. Owing to effective psychological and dramaturgic features acquired from the Elizabethan stage, the itinerant players heighten the pathos of the already theatrical parable by visualising the narrated parts with added roles, such as Hope and Despair, and scenes like that in the tavern. As distinct from *Esther* and all the other plays in *ECUT*, the clown is notably absent in this play but perhaps took up the role of the silly servant.

The amalgamation of popular forms of entertainment, Elizabethan drama and Commedia dell'Arte is even more conspicuous in the next two plays of the collection.

6.2. Fantastic and Pastoral Comedies: *Von Fortunato, Von eines Königes Sohne*

The comedies *Comoedia Von Fortunato* and *Comoedia von eines Königes Sohne* are grouped together because they share fantastic and pastoral elements. The sixteenth-century European vogue around the pastoral had an impact on popular theatre too, which started to draw from this imagery and create new and fascinating hybrids, especially in tragicomedy.[55] The pastiche of magicians,

---

[52] *SW*, vol. 1, p. 127. Translation: 'For this thy brother was dead, and is alive again; and was lost, and is found.'

[53] See *Friedrich Menius und das Repertoire der englischen Komödianten in Deutschland*, chapter 1.

[54] See Baesecke, op. cit., p. 24.

[55] As Robert Weimann explains, pastoral poetry and drama had their origins in Greco-Roman literature, e.g. in the novel *Daphnis and Chloe* by Longus (II century AD), and were

spirits or fairies mixed with mythological figures of the pastoral like shepherds, satyrs and gods in Arcadian settings can be observed both in later "fantastic-type" Commedia dell'Arte, as Walter Hinck calls the pastoral *scenari*,[56] and in Shakespeare's mature plays *A Midsummer Night's Dream* and *The Tempest* (although magic sleeping potions, enchanted handkerchiefs and witches appear in the tragedies *Romeo and Juliet*, *Othello* and *Macbeth* too). Relevant examples in the Italian context are *Il gran mago* ('The Great Magician' edited by Basilio Locatelli in 1628/32), where the traditional 'types' are flanked by specifically pastoral figures called Filli, Clori and Selvaggio; or *Li tre satiri* ('The Three Satyrs' of the Corsinian collection, 1621–43), which parodies the conventions of the pastoral.[57] The points of contact between Italy and England in these plays have already been discussed; this section investigates how the English Comedians worked with magic, spirits and pastoral settings on the German stage.

Von Fortunato

The *Comoedia Von Fortunato und seinem Seckel und Wünschhütlein, / Darinnen erstlich drey verstrorbenen Seelen als Geister, darnach die Tugendt und Schande eingeführet werden* ('Comedy of Fortunatus and his purse and wishing cap, in which three dead souls as spirits appear first, and afterwards Virtue and Shame') was performed in Graz in 1608 by John Green's company, as the *Theaterbrief* of the Archduchess Maria Magdalena testifies.[58] It also appears in the 'Dresden Repertoire' on 11 July 1626 as *Tragoedia von Fortunato*, always connected to Green.[59] Despite the similar titles, the comedy contained in *ECUT* 1620 is categorised as a tragedy in the 'Dresden Repertoire'. This seeming contradiction can be solved by looking at the memorialisation at work in the text.

re-vitalised in the age of Humanism by Petrach (1304–1374) on the basis of Virgil's *Eclogues*. During the Renaissance, the pastoral novel about idyllic settings detached from socio-political issues became an international vogue indicating a change of taste in fiction to which Germany conformed tardily. Jacopo Sannazaro's novel *Arcadia* (1504) set the standard, soon followed by Jorge de Montemayor's *Diana* (1524), Honoré D'Ufré's *L'Astrée* (1607–25; the name Astrea appears in a play of *ECUT* 1620), and Philip Sidney's *The Countess of Pembroke's Arcadia* (1580). In drama, Angelo Poliziano's *Fabula d'Orfeo* (1480) was imitated in Arcadian comedies like Torquato Tasso's *Aminta* (1573) and Giovanni Battista Guarini's *Pastor fido* (1590). See *Shakespeare und die Tradition des Volkstheaters*, p. 279.

[56] Hinck, *Das deutsche Lustspiel des 17. und 18. Jahrhunderts und die italienische Komödie*, pp. 19–20.

[57] For the *canovacci* of *Il gran mago* and *Li tre satiri* see Testaverde, ed., pp. 375–84 and pp. 433–40. Other *scenari* involving a magician are *La cometa*, *La pazzia di Doralice*, *Le grandezze di Zanni*, *Il fonte incantato*, *La nave*, and *Il creduto Principe*.

[58] "[…] am Mittwoch haben sy gehabt von des fortunatus peitl und Wünschhietel, ist auch gar schön gewest." For the *Theaterbrief* see Flemming, pp. 71–2, Meissner, pp. 76–80 or Schrickx, pp. 332–3 and for the translation Orad, pp. 4–11.

[59] Quoted in Cohn, p. CXV.

Its primary source is a German chapbook (*Volksbuch*) printed in Augsburg in 1509 by Johann Otmar and found circulating in numerous issues throughout sixteenth-century Europe. The proto-novel divides the story into two separate parts, a comic narration of Fortunatus' adventures with his purse and wishing cap, and a tragic sequel about the bad use his descendants make of the gifts.[60] If one limits the dramatisation of the chapbook to the episodes about the lucky charms, the designation as comedy appears legitimate. However, the lack of insight and the death of all the main characters in the second part accounts for the frequent reference to the subject as tragedy, for example in Hans Sachs's *Tragedia mit 22 Personen, der Fortunatus mit dem wunschseckel, uundt hat 5 actus* ('Tragedy with 22 characters, Fortunatus and his wishing purse, and has five acts' 1553).

Other adaptations prove a strong interest existed in the adventurous plot even in England. After a first anonymous English version of "fortunatus" or "ffortunatus" cited in Henslowe's Diary on 10 and 20 February 1595,[61] Thomas Dekker's *The Pleasant Comedie of Old Fortunatus: As it was plaied before the Queenes Maiestie this Christmas, by the Right Honourable the Earle of Nottingham, Lord high Admirall of England his Seruants* was printed in London in 1600. Dekker reduced the role of Fortunatus to a few key episodes, meant to explain how the gifts got to him and his descendants, and devoted the rest of the play to his sons' misuse of the gifts. These innovative elements are present in *Von Fortunato* too and thus prove that *Old Fortunatus* directly inspired the version of *ECUT*, as Brauneck explains.[62] The comparison of the list of dramatis personae reveals a closeness to the English play, as only minor characters were omitted while all the main roles coincide and even maintain the same names as in the English play.

Dramatis personae in Thomas Dekker's *The Pleasant Comedie of Old Fortunatus* (1600)[63]	Dramatis personae in Comoedia *Von Fortunato und seinem Seckel und Wünschhütlein*[64]
ATHELSTANE, *King of England*	King
The Soldan of Egypt	Soldan
The Prince of Cyprus	---

---

[60] For an analysis of the genesis and circulation of *Fortunatus* see Hans-Gert Roloff, ed., *Fortunatus: Studienausgabe nach der Editio Princeps von 1509* (Stuttgart: Reclam, 1981).

[61] See *Henslowe's Diary*, edited by R. A. Foakes, pp. 34–5.

[62] See *SW*, vol. 6, p. 16. Comparing the version of *ECUT* 1620 and an earlier anonymous drama manuscript found in Kassel, the *Kassler Fortunatusdrama* (1610–20) based on Hans Sachs, Brauneck demonstrates that the English Comedians produced a compilation of a no longer extant German rendition of Dekker's *The Pleasant Comedie of Old Fortunatus* (London: Printed by S. S[tafford] for William Aspley, dwelling in Paules Church-yard at the signe of the Tygers head, 1600) enriched with text passages taken from the 1509 prose proto-novel.

[63] Quoted from the online version of Dekker's *The Pleasant Comedy of Old Fortunatus* available at <https://quod.lib.umich.edu/e/eebo/A20076.0001.001/1:3?rgn=div1;view=fulltext> (last accessed 14 August 2020).

[64] *SW*, vol. 1, p. 129. My translation.

CORNWALL	---
CHESTER and LINCOLN, *English Nobles*	Two Nobles
MONTROSE and GALLOWAY, *Scotch Nobles*	---
ORLEANS, *French Noble* LONGAVILLE, *French Noble*	---
INSULTADO, a *Spanish Lord*	---
FORTUNATUS	FORTUNATUS
[ECHO, not mentioned, but present in the play]	ECHO
AMPEDO, *Son of* FORTUNATUS	AMPEDO
ANDELOCIA, *Son of* FORTUNATUS	ANDELOSIA
SHADOW, *Servant to* AMPEDO *and* ANDELOCIA	[Servant, not mentioned in the list, but present in the play]
Kings, Nobles, Soldiers, Satyrs, a Carter, a Tailor, a Monk, a Shepherd, Chorus, Boys and other Attendants	Boy
AGRIPYNE, *Daughter of* ATHELSTANE	AGRIPPINA
FORTUNE, *Goddess*	FORTUNA
VIRTUE, *Goddess.*	Virtue
VICE, *Goddess*	Vice
The Three Destinies	Three Ghosts/Spirit
Nymphs, Ladies, &c.	---

Intertextual references and a similar insistence on the moral teaching through a negative example show that the English Comedians adapted Dekker's comedy or a German translation of it, instead of drawing on the tragedy by Hans Sachs.[65] Nevertheless, an audience acquainted with the chapbook and its German dramatisation would have recognised some *ghosting* elements. And even if they remained unnoticed, the reception would have been facilitated due to structural elements of the morality play, as the synopsis shall illustrate.

Act 1 introduces the poverty-stricken knight Fortunatus from Famagusta. The protagonist's name means 'the lucky one' and indeed he is lucky enough to meet the blindfolded goddess/allegory Fortuna after wandering for days in the woods without any company other than his own echo.[66] As the following comparison of the incipits shows, *Von Fortunato* followed Dekker's *Old Fortunatus* closely but was shortened and simplified as far as the philosophic musing and the wordplays are concerned.

---

[65] For a comparison between the chapbook and its English and German dramatisations see Paul Harms, *Die deutschen Fortunatus-Dramen und ein Kassler Dichter des 17. Jahrhunderts* (Hamburg and Leipzig: Leopold Voß, 1891) and Julian K. Hilton, *The 'Englische Komödianten' in German-speaking States, 1592–1620*, ch. 4.

[66] The scenic effect of the echo in *Fortunatus* resonates also with the pastoral *scenario Il gran mago* ('The Great Magician', contained in the collection by Locatelli), in which Pantalone does the *lazzo* of the voice/echo after a shipwreck on a lonely island. The *scenario* is contained in Testaverde, ed., *I canovacci della Commedia dell'Arte*, pp. 375–84.

Echo scene in Dekker's *Old Fortunatus*

FORTUNATUS.
Enter Fortunatus meanely attired, hee walkes ere he speake once or twice about cracking Nuts.
SD. ho, ho, ho, ho.
ECCHO. *within*, Ho, ho, ho, ho,
FORTUNATUS. There boy.
ECCHO. There boy.
FORTUNATUS. And thou bee'st a goodfellow, tel me how thou cal'st this wood.
ECCHO. This wood.
FORTUNATUS. I this wood, & which is my best way out.
ECCHO. Best way out. [...]
FORTUNATUS. [...] In the meane time to tell truth here will I lie. Farwell foole.
ECCHO. farwell foole.
FORTUNATUS. Are not these comfortable words to a wise man? All haile Signior trée, by your leane ile sléepe vnder your leaues, I pray bow to me, and ile bend to you, for your backe and my browes must, I doubt, haue a game or two at Noddie erre I wake againe: downe great heart, downe. Hey, ho, well, well.[67]

Echo scene in *Von Fortunato* (*ECUT*)

FORTUNATUS.
Kömpt herauß mit zerrissenen Kleidern und spricht:
Ach ich armer / Elender Mensch bin so voller Trübsal / daß ich nicht weiß wo ich mich lassen soll / den 2. Tage bin ich schon in diesem Walde irre gegangen / und kan keinen Weg für mir finden / bin also verschmachtet / daß ich kein Tritt mehr kan fort gehen / von meinen Eltern bin ich gezogen / weil sie gar verarmet / auff daß ich mein Glück unter Fremden möge suchen. Ach / ach, Hungers werde ich sterben müssen / so ich nicht auß diesen verirreten ungehewren Walde komme. Ist hie den kein Mensch / der mich dadurch helffen könne/ Holla.
ECHO. Lah
FORTUNATUS. Wer bistu?
ECHO. Stu?
FORTUNATUS. Komm zu mir.
ECHO. Mir.
FORTUNATUS. O es ist nur ein Widerschall / neben diesen grünen Zweigen wil ich mich schlaffen legen / und der Allmächtige Gott thu mich bewahren für Schädlichkeit der wilden Thieren.[68]

Dekker's Fortunatus appears to be more self-mocking and disillusioned about the unfortunate situation than the distressed protagonist of the German play, who laments his fatigue ("bin also verschmachtet") and his fear of dying. While the first text plays with the echo ("FORTUNATUS. Farwell foole. ECCHO. farwell foole. FORTUNATUS. Are not these comfortable words to a wise man?"), the latter is

---

[67] Thomas Dekker, *The Pleasant Comedie of Old Fortunatus*. London, 1600. Quoted from the online version of Dekker's *The Pleasant Comedy of Old Fortunatus* available at <https://quod.lib.umich.edu/e/eebo/A20076.0001.001/1:3?rgn=div1;view=fulltext> (last accessed 14 August 2020).

[68] *SW*, vol. 1, pp. 131–2. Translation: 'FORT. *Enters with torn clothes and says*: O what a poor and wretched being I am, I am so dejected that I do not know what to do: I have been erring in these woods for two days and cannot find a way out. I am so exhausted that I cannot take a single step further. I set forth from my destitute parents to seek luck among strangers. Alas, alas, I will die of hunger unless I get out of this intricate, immense wood. Is there anybody who could help me? Hello? ECHO Lo. FORT. Who are you? ECHO. You? FORT. Come here to me. ECHO. Me. FORT. O it is only an echo. I will lie down to sleep next to these green boughs. May God the Almighty protect me from the dangerous wild animals.'

disappointed in finding out it is not a real person ("O es ist nur ein Widerschall"). Still, the general structure of the scenes is the same and as such proves a debt of *Von Fortunato* to Dekker.

Returning to the plot in *ECUT*, the goddess Fortuna takes pity on Fortunatus and allows him to choose one of her gifts: wisdom, fortitude, beauty, wealth, health or a long life. While he reflects on the advantages and disadvantages connected to each choice, three ghosts or spirits (the German word *Geist* can mean both) warn him not to take anything, because they have been betrayed by the gifts of Fortune and are now reduced to an eternity in chains. The importance attributed to this scene, alien to the chapbook and indebted to Dekker,[69] is attested by the mention of the ghosts in the title, alongside the allegories of Virtue and Shame. Fortuna replies that it is everyone's own responsibility to use the endowments wisely and thus already sets the moral tone, mystified by magic, inherent to the play. Fortunatus picks wealth in the form of a magical purse that fills up with ten ducats whenever he or his kin put a hand into it. Fortuna comments on his choice dryly: "Es ist mir gleich / aber du alber Narr / kuntest nicht Weißheit für Reichhumb erwehlen."[70] In exchange, he is requested to behave virtuously.

The act is closed by Pickelhering, who is merely introduced as an acting character without any lines: "*Allhier agiret PICKELHERING*".[71] This scant stage direction is unusual, since the rest of the play has precise descriptions of what the actors are to do, for example "*Er [Fortunatus] leget sich nieder / entschläfft / nicht lang darnach kömpt die GÖTTIN FORTUNA mit verbunden Augen / und spricht [...]*".[72] As in the *canovacci* of the Commedia dell'Arte, it implies that the actor playing the clown would have known which scenes and antics to present. Apart from entertaining the audience with acrobatics and pranks, the extemporised interlude might have functioned as translation or summary of the previous act. Another way of reading this stage direction could be to insert any of the *Singspiele* contained at the end of the collection at this point, if needed. None of the other plays in *ECUT* have the clown appear so often without a text.

In one of the frequent leaps in time and space imputable to the episodic nature of the chapbook, the second act shows how Fortunatus has come into possession of his second magical accessory. Spectators are told neither when nor how Fortunatus got to the palace in Cairo, the Sultan simply appears on stage and boasts

---

[69] In Dekker, Fortuna is accompanied by numerous allegorical figures among whom are four kings with broken crowns and sceptres as symbols of their lost power. The stage direction says: "*Enter a Gardiner, a Smith, a Monke, a Shepheard all crown'd, a Nimph with a Globe, another with Fortunes wheele, then Fortune: After her fowre Kings with broken Crownes and Scepters, chained in siluer Giues and led by her.*" Dekker, *The Pleasant Comedie of Old Fortunatus*.

[70] *SW*, vol. 1, p. 135. Translation: 'I do not care but, you silly fool, you could have chosen wisdom instead of wealth.'

[71] Ibid., p. 154. Translation: 'Pickelhering acts here.'

[72] Ibid., p. 132. Translation: 'He [Fortunatus] lies down, falls asleep. Shortly afterwards, the blindfolded Goddess Fortuna enters and says [...].'

about his prodigious hat, which can take its wearer anywhere in the world in the blink of an eye. Fortunatus "*hat schöne Kleider an*"[73] to visualise his prosperity, but nonetheless performs a classical *burla*/prank on the Sultan to trick him out of his precious felt hat: he asks to test the hat's weight and immediately disappears with it. This mischievous behaviour does not fulfil the condition of virtuosity imposed by the goddess Fortuna, and consequently she punishes Fortunatus with death.[74] The repentant sinner's last words to his sons are to use the gifts wisely in a scene echoing the appearance of the ghosts. While judicious Ampedo mourns, greedy Andolosia seizes the purse with the intent to disobey his father's wish. Again, Pickelhering puts an end to the act.

In Act 3, Andolosia travels to England with the inexhaustible purse to woo the beautiful princess Agrippina. Pickelhering is called on stage, this time to indicate a change of scene and not to conclude an act. From the point of view of visualisation, the same props that marked the Sultan's palace were probably reused for the English court, where Andolosia's haughtiness displeases the English king so greatly that he prohibits the sale of wood in order to boycott the newcomer's banquet. However, Andolosia circumvents the ban by using costly cinnamon and other spices purchased with his marvellous purse. After another change of scene marked by Pickelhering, the next intrigue is spun. Like the money-grabbing host in *Von dem verlornen Sohn*, the king induces his daughter to steal the purse from Andolosia while he is intoxicated by a sleeping potion. Pickelhering enters to introduce a new scene, in which Andolosia wakes up, notices the fraud, and sombrely asks the musicians to stop playing: "O ihr lieblichen MUSICANTEN höret auff mit MUSICIREN und spielen / den meine Seele ist betrübet biß in den Todt."[75] This reveals that the scene was accompanied by music. Then, he returns to his brother and confesses his inconsiderate conduct during the past ten years, but instead of heeding Ampedo's admonition, quoted verbatim from the chapbook, as Brauneck notices,[76] Andolosia snatches the wishing hat. In a narrative monologue, he declares that he shall recover his purse by magically travelling to Venice

---

[73] Ibid., p. 138. Translation of the stage direction: 'Wears beautiful clothes.'
[74] The stage direction says "FORTUNA *Gehet weg / bald kömpt sie wieder mit einem weissen Hembde / hat ein Stöcklein in der Hand / damit stosset sie ihn auff die Brust / gehet darnach wieder davon*" meaning 'FORTUNA exits, soon returns dressed in a white shirt. She has a stick in her hand with which she pokes him on the chest and the exits again.' Ibid., p. 142.
[75] *SW*, vol. 1, p. 161. Translation: 'Oh dear musicians, stop the music and playing for my soul is sick at heart.'
[76] In *SW*, vol. 6, p. 16, Brauneck compares the passage in the play "AMPEDO. Man saget im Sprichworte: Wer sein Gut verleurt / der veleurt auch den Sinn / das Spüre ich jetzt an dir wol / so du umb das Gut gebracht hast / so wollestu uns auch umb den Hut ringen / zwar mit meinen Willen / so laß ich dich nicht mitfahren / sonsten wil ich dir ihn wol thun / und vergönnen damit Kurtzweil zu haben" (*SW*, vol. 1, p. 165) with that in the chapbook "Ampedo sprach / man sagt wer sein gut verlürt der verleürt auch die sinn / das spüre ich an dir wol / so du uns umb das gutt bracht hast / so woltestu uns auch umb das hutlin

to buy jewels and then selling them in England disguised as a merchant. From the point of view of visualisation, this solution replaces a complicated change of setting and scenery and raises expectations in the audience.

Interestingly, prior to Act 4 Pickelhering is not called on stage. A reason could be that here the allegories of Shame/Vice and Virtue function as a sort of interlude which supersedes the clown's antics and explicitly places the play in the morality tradition. Apart from hybridising genres, this scene memorialises Dekker's *Old Fortunatus* with a few adaptations. Firstly, the order of events is different, because in Dekker the allegories – called Vice and Virtue, not Shame and Virtue as in the German rendition – accompany Fortuna at the beginning of the play and are thus part of the main plot. Secondly, in Dekker's play Vice puts a magic spell on the fruits of a tree to make those who eat them grow horns. Virtue responds that she shall give back their original shape to those who follow her path. In the German offshoot, each allegory plants a magical apple tree, one with beneficial and one with harmful powers. In a remarkable back and forth, Shame mockingly calls Virtue a fool because of her funny hat and her ridiculous hope that many people may eat the fruits from her tree. Virtue self-assuredly replies that since most wrongdoers hold virtue for folly, she really has something in common with a fool.[77] Although this remnant of Dekker's subplot appears less connected to the main plot

[77] bringen / zwar mitt meinem gunst unnd willen / so laß ich dich es nit hynweg furen / Ich will dir wol vergunnen kurtzweil darmitt zu haben" (Roloff, ed., *Fortunatus*, p. 146).
"SCHANDE. Wer wolt dich und deine Früchte lieben / sieh welch ein gering Kleidt du anträgest / und darzu hastu einen Narrenhut / muß derhalben etwas uber dich lachen. TUGENDT. Ja lache nur immer hin Schande und Laster / ich habe gleich unter tausendten noch einen so meine Früchte liebet [...] Werde nunmehro geschütz die Göttin mit der Narrenkap / denn Tugendt von den deinen vor Narrenwerck gehalten wird." *SW*, vol. 1, p. 167. Translation: 'SHAME. Who could prefer you and your fruits? Look at your simple dress and fool's cap! They make me laugh at you. VIRTUE. Keep laughing Shame and Vice, I am sure to find among thousands someone who loves my fruits [...] Nowadays I am considered the goddess with the fool's cap since many of your supporters deem virtue foolish.' In Dekker, the whole sequence is in verse form:
VICE. Stay, Fortune, whilst within this Groue we dwel,
If my Angelicall and Saint-like forme
Can win some amorous foole to wanton here,
And taste the fruite of this alluring trée,
Thus shall his sawcie browes adorned bée, *Makes hornes.*
To make vs laugh. [...]
VERTUE. Foule hel-bred fiend, Uertue shall striue with you,
If any be enamoured of thine eyes,
Their loue must néedes beget deformities.
Men are transformed to beastes, feasting with sinne;
But if (in spite of thee) their soules I winne,
To taste this fruite, though thou disguise their head,
Their shapes shall be re-metamorphosed.
(Dekker, *The Pleasant Comedie of Old Fortunatus*).

than in the English play, the episode had to be maintained in the English Comedians' version for the progression of the story.
In fact, Andolosia disguised as a merchant abducts Agrippina and takes her into a deep forest, close to the trees planted earlier by the allegorical figures. While he picks some apples for the hungry princess, she inadvertently puts on the magic hat and returns home with both gifts. To add insult to injury, Andolosia grows horrible horns after eating the apples of Shame, but Fortuna tells him to eat from the tree of Virtue as a remedy. In Dekker's *Old Fortunatus*, it is Virtue who transforms him back by purging him from his vicious behaviour with the bitter fruits of her tree.[78]

In Act 5, Andolosia sells the bad apples to exact revenge from the English court. As soon as Agrippina and other aristocrats grow horns, Andolosia dresses up as a doctor (the second disguise) and promises to heal them in exchange for his hat and purse. Having recovered the gifts, he leaves the horned princess in a Spanish convent to hide her shame and returns to his brother. The change of setting is so frequent in this act – and no longer marked by the presence of Pickelhering – that verbal scenery alone must suffice to follow the intricate plot of this overlong play. For instance, in Act 3, Andolosia simply says "Nun bin ich zu Lunden" and a little later in the same act "Nun bin ich kommen in die Häuptstadt Lunden / und komme gefahren von VENETIA."[79]

Moved by Ampedo's honesty, and not morally amended by Virtue like in Dekker, Andolosia decides to free the princess from her curse and return the wishing hat for good. Right when Andolosia seems to have learned from his mistakes, he is tortured to death by two counts who were deeply offended by the trick with the horns. Hearing this, Ampedo burns the cursed hat and dies of grief, while in Dekker the brothers die together in an English prison. In the end, the murderers are punished by the king, and Fortuna recovers the purse and promises to protect the kingdom in exchange. Although order is restored, one might ask why a play in which all the main characters apart from the evil king and his daughter are killed should be termed a comedy. Probably, the most important aspect for a happy ending is that Virtue prevails over Vice and that Fortuna teaches a moral lesson to the audience: wealth without wisdom is a curse.

The hybridisation at work in the *ECUT* play makes it a tragicomedy with allegorical elements from moralities and magical folklore. It appears plausible that

---

[78] The device of enchanted foods and drinks, typical of fairy tales and pastoral plays, is present in some Commedia dell'Arte *scenari* as well, and represents an instance of adaptation and intercultural theatricality. For example, *Il gran mago* features a fountain that turns those who drink from it into animals. Moreover, Marlowe's Faustus punishes a knight who maligns his magical power with deer's antlers (*The Life and Death of Doctor Faustus*, 4.1.77). As the play was part of the English Comedians' repertoire, they might have recycled the scene.

[79] *SW*, vol. 1, p. 150 and p. 168. Translation: 'Now I am in London' and 'Now I have arrived in London and I come from Venice.'

the English Comedians resorted to the *Volksbuch* primarily for linguistic borrowings and the main content, while Dekker served as model for the dramatisation. *Von Fortunato*'s indebtedness to Dekker is revealed not only by the same generic definition as a comedy and the almost specular arrangement of scenes, but also by dramatic motifs like the echo and the allegories of Vice/Shame and Virtue, reminiscent of the morality play tradition.

Still, the German play presents some differences in content arising from adaptation. Firstly, there is the usual reduction of the plot and the characters. For instance, the scene of Virtue and Vice is cut down to a moral interlude, vaguely connected to the main plot by the final moral message. Secondly, narrative passages render leaps in time and sudden changes of setting more comprehensible whereas other scenes that could have remained allusions are physically acted out, for example the story of how Fortunatus received the magical items. The detailed stage directions in the German play allow a reconstruction of the visualisation strategies, such as Pickelhering's improvisations in-between acts and music on stage. Despite the flatness of the characters and the emphasis on the moral message, the fact that the play was performed often testifies to both the performers' commendable ability to stage such a complicated plot and the audience's interest in this popular tale.

Comoedia von eines Königes Sohne

Magic also pervades *Eine schöne lustig triumphirende Comoedia von eines Königes Sohne auß Engellandt und des Königes Tochter auß Schottlandt* ('A beautiful, merry, triumphant Comedy of a King's son from England and the King's daughter from Scotland'), although it seems to be more influenced by pastoral comedies than by the legacy of folk tradition. For instance, the heroine's name, Astrea, might refer to Honoré D'Ufré's pastoral novel *L'Astrée* (France 1607–25). Apart from this faint connection, it is difficult to identify with certainty the sources memorialised here, as there is no other play comparable to it. Based on some inconsistencies in the plot, Wilhelm Creizenach and Julius Tittmann hypothesise that a lost English original was adapted for the German stage.[80] A version of this play was presumably performed by Robert Browne's troupe before Landgrave Moritz in Kassel in March 1607[81] and then abridged. It is also recorded as part of the 'Dresden Repertoire' in June and October 1626 and later in 1631 at

---

[80] See Creizenach, p. LVII, and Tittmann, *Die Schauspiele der englischen Komödianten in Deutschland*, p. LIII.

[81] June Schlueter mentions a letter by the official Johann Eckel to Landgrave Moritz dated 1 March 1607, in which he speaks of the English Comedians' plan to stage 'Of the Two British Kings at War, of Whom the One Takes the Son of the Other, but the Latter the Daughter of the Former, Prisoner.' See Schlueter, "English Actors in Kassel, Germany, during Shakespeare's Time", *Medieval and Renaissance Drama in England* 10 (1988), pp. 238–61, p. 247. Although the kings are both British, the thumbnail synopsis contained in the title resembles *Von eines Königes Sohne* so strongly that identification is almost certain.

the Court of Saxony as *Comoedia von den Koenig in Engelandt und den Koenig in Schottlandt* ('Comedy of the King of England and the King of Scotland') with the addition of Pickelhering, who is not present in the *ECUT* play.[82]

The plot reworks the renowned romance of Romeo and Juliet in an idyllic setting like that of *The Tempest*, making the play a hybrid tragicomedy with pastoral elements such as the magician in the woods with his enchanted mirror. Such bucolic surroundings and magic are also typical of the "fantastic-type" Commedia dell'Arte,[83] for instance the *scenario La nave* or in *Il fonte incantato* ('The Ship' and 'The Magic Fountain' of the Corsinian collection, 1621–42).[84] Moreover, the play's constellation of two lovers hindered by their parents and engaging in intrigues with the help of their servants recalls the core conflict of countless *scenari*.

The first act starts as a *Haupt- und Staatsaktion*: since the King of England lays claim to the throne of Scotland, his son Serule offers to resolve the conflict in a duel with the Scottish king. However, Venus prevails over Mars the moment he sees his enemy's daughter, Astrea. At first, the self-willed Scottish princess does not believe his passionate professions of love, but after a short exchange she returns his affection. The lovers negotiate an armistice of one year to gain time for their secret meetings despite their parents' hostility.

In Act 2, Serule and his servant travel to Scotland, disregarding the fact that they are forbidden from making any contact with the Scots, and hide in the woods where the magician Barrabas lives. Serule knows that the king often seeks advice from the magician and asks his servant to become the necromancer's apprentice while he inveigles himself into the court in disguise.

The third act introduces the magician to the audience. Like Marlowe's Faustus in his study, he enters the stage with a book of spells and invokes twelve spirits in his magic circle. Interrupted by Serule's servant, he entreats his new apprentice not to misuse the power of magic like his former pupil, who abducted the princess of Spain and brought her to a Sultan against her father's will.[85] After this long third-person narration, typical of the English Comedians' playing techniques, the magician swears vengeance and promises to restore order. In the list of dramatis personae and in many stage directions, the necromancer is called Runcifax Doctor (recalling the devil Runcifall in Jacob Ayrer's *Comedia von der schönen Sidea*, 1618),[86] but he introduces himself as Barrabas and is addressed by this name by

---

[82] See Creizenach, p. LVIII.
[83] Hinck, *Das deutsche Lustspiel des 17. und 18. Jahrhunderts und die italienische Komödie*, pp. 19–20.
[84] See Testaverde, ed., *I canovacci della Commedia dell'Arte*, pp. 465–73 and pp. 491–6 for the text.
[85] In the comic subplot of Marlowe's *Faustus*, the clown Robin becomes Wagner's apprentice too but is later transformed into an ape by Mephistopheles for abusing his magical power (*The Life and Death of Doctor Faustus*, 3.2). Whether this intertextual reference was conscious or not, is left to discussion.
[86] Contained in *Ayrers Dramen*, edited by Adelbert von Keller, vol. 4, pp. 2177–222.

the other characters. Apparent oversights of the editor like these are valuable clues pointing to a more elaborate version of the comedy, prior to 1620.

Contrary to most comedies in the collection, this play does not feature a clown/Pickelhering. Instead, the protagonist, a serious part, wears disguise to take on the role of a fool and see the princess incognito. To make sure the audience understands, the prince explains his plan and dresses up on stage, another instance of overexplicitness frequently found in the collection. Still, this play-within-the play is a clever metatheatrical strategy to portray the typical elements of the clown and to poke fun at the deceived king. In fact, the King of Scotland does not recognise his enemy in the fool riding a hobbyhorse. Amused by the fool's witty horseplay – in the truest sense of the word – and his preoccupation with food, which are typical traits of the clown, the king takes him into his service. He even engages in a funny dialogue with Serule and appeases his worries that the princess will not give him as much food as the king by jokingly swapping roles with his daughter:

> *Jetzt kömpt der* SOHN *und reitet auff einen Stecken.* [...]
> KÖNIG SCHOTTLANDT. So vernehme ich / daß du grosse Lust zu essen hast / uund bey mir bleiben und sein wolst? Gar wohl du solt allhier bleiben. Hertzliebe Tochter / dieser Narr gefelt mir auß dermassen wol / derhalben wil ich ihn dir verehren / daß du unterweilen deine Kurzweil an ihn siehest. [...]
> NARR. Dem kleinen Ding Diener auffwarten? Ich halt es gleich. Aber Herr König sagt mir / was es von einer ist / und ob sie auch wol so viel essen hat denn du?
> KÖNIG. Es is meine Tochter die Princessin / uund hat eben so viel essen denn ich.
> NARR. Ich weiß jetzunder nicht was ich thun soll / ob ich ihr oder dir diene / weil sie kein König ist wie du. Denn der Herr in meinen Hause sagte / du hattest das meiste essen.
> KÖNIG. Diesen Sachen wollen wir bald Rath schaffen / hör Narr / weil du ja einen Könige lust zu dienen hast / derhalben weil er das meiste essen hat / so wil ich diener halben nicht mehr König seyn / und weil ich dich meiner Tochter verehre / so sol sie König seyn / und ich will Pirncessin werden / auff daß sie also das meiste essen bekommen / und du nicht verhungerst. [...]
> NARR. O das ist recht / daß ist das allerbest / nun werde ich essen / nun werde ich trincken / so viel wie ich meine tage nit genossen habe /.[87]

---

[87] *SW*, vol. 1, pp. 235–7. Translation: '*Enter the* SON, *riding on a stick* [...] KING OF SCOTLAND. I understand you have a great wish to eat and want to stay with me? Then you shall stay here. Dearest daughter, I like this fool excessively, therefore I want to bestow him onto you so that you may enjoy his jests. [...] FOOL. I, a servant to that little creature? It is all the same for me. But lord, tell me of what kind she [literally: it] is and if she has as much food as you? KING. It is my daughter, the princess, and has as much food as I. FOOL. Now I do not know what to do, should I serve her or you, even if she is not a king like you? Because the lord in my house told me that you possess the greatest amount of food. KING. That shall be settled soon. Listen, fool, since you want to serve a king because he has the greatest amount of food, to please you I do not want to be king anymore and since I bestow you upon my daughter, she shall be king and I princess, so that she possesses the greatest amount of food, and you shall not starve. [...] FOOL. O

In the final stage direction of this act, the King of Scotland tells two mysterious personages, Duglus and Tinax, neither mentioned in the list of characters nor anywhere else, to disport themselves with the fool during his absence: "*Gehen hinein* DUGLUS, TINAX. *Der* KÖNIG *sagt sie sollen kurtzweilen mit den* NARREN *dann er verreisen werde*".[88] Since the king repeatedly muses about his future son-in-law, it appears plausible that these two minor characters are his daughter's suitors, who probably played a role in an earlier version of the play and only remain as names in this adaptation. Perhaps their function was also to provide a funny interlude with the fool before the next act.

In Act 4, the disguised prince tests Astrea's feelings for her absent lover, a typical motif of novelistic literature which is also present in another play of the collection, the *Pickelheringspiel* 'Of the beautiful Maria and the old cuckold', although with a negative outcome. Satisfied with her reaction, Serule reveals his identity but remains incognito to the king, who tells his enemy to keep his daughter company while he consults the magician Barrabas about her future husband. The irony of the situation would certainly make a hilarious scene.

On his way to the necromancer, the king recounts how the incident involving the Sultan and the Spanish princess was solved by the magician. This narrative passage may be a remnant of an excised subplot to reflect the difficult marriage negotiations of Serule and Astrea. In the woods, Barrabbas shows the sovereign a magical mirror which foretells the identity of his future son-in-law. As the king looks into it, the stage direction says that his daughter and the fool appear on stage and dance to the sound of violins, visualising the reflection for the audience: "*Der* KÖNIG *sieht in den Spiegel / wird gegeiget / der* NARR *tantzt mit der* PRINCESSIN *darvon.*"[89] Although this presage angers the king, he would be even more enraged were he able to recognise the son of his worst enemy under the fool's cap. In the meantime, the prince escapes, alarmed by his servant.

The comic effects of Act 4 are repeated with slight alterations in Act 5. This time, Serule dresses up as an Ethiopian merchant, a *Morian* ('Moor'), which allows two intertextual parallels within the collection. On the one hand, this disguise recalls Andolosia's merchant costume to take revenge on the English court in *Von Fortunato*. On the other hand, the exotic reference to Ethiopia echoes the mischievous Morian in the adapted version of *Titus Andronicus* presented in chapter 6.4. As in the previous act, the prince is left alone with his lover while the king calls on the magician to have another glimpse at the magical mirror. Again, the spectators take part in the king's vision of the Morian/Serule and Astrea dancing on stage accompanied by music: "*Nimpt den Spiegel wieder / alsßbald wir auffgegegiget /*

---

that is good, that is excellent, now I will eat, now I will drink more than I have ever done in my entire life.'

[88] *SW*, vol. 1, p. 238.
[89] Ibid., p. 245. Translation: 'The KING looks into the mirror, violin music, the FOOL dances with the PRINCESS.'

MORIAN *und die* PRINCESSIN *tantzen wieder"*;[90] when he is not gazing into the looking glass, they disappear. The ingenious expedient of the mirror combined with a series of intrigues represents such a powerful tool of dramatic irony that it is deployed twice: the first time, the king sees the fool and the princess dancing in the mirror, while the audience sees them on stage; the second time, he sees her with the *Morian*. Whereas the spectators have enough background to understand that the enchanted mirror truthfully shows the man Astrea is going to marry, namely Serule, the king's flawed perception renders him unable to interpret the vision correctly. These repeated scenes owe much to the comic potential of the hoaxed king.

In Act 6 Serule cannot make up his mind to leave the woods around the Scottish castle after the truce of one year; Astrea follows him into the forest just as the kings resume fighting. In doing so, they both fall into their respective enemy's hands. The English king proposes an exchange of prisoners, but the obstinate King of Scotland disavows his disobedient daughter and forces the prince to drink a poison. In a scene similar to Romeo's death, the young man bids the world farewell, asks death to come swiftly and then swallows the potion.

SOHN. [...] Nun Todt der du in diesen Gläßlein bist / gar unerschrocken bin ich vor dir. Nun ade ade / Todt trinck ich jetzt in mir. *Trinket er auß / der Vater stehet gar bestürtzet.* Nun Todt du bist nahe den Hertzen / mache nit lang mit mir. O wie mächtiglich wircket er / ich muß jetzt meinen Geist auffgeben / awe awe. *Felt Todt darnieder.*[91]	ROMEO. *(kisses Juliet, takes out the poison)* Come, bitter conduct, come, unsavoury guide. Thou desperate pilot, now at once run on The dashing rocks thy seasick, weary bark. Here's to my love! *(drinks the poison)* O true apothecary, Thy drugs are quick. Thus with a kiss I die. ROMEO *dies.*[92]

The similarity between the scenes and the quotes is indeed striking and might point to an indebtedness of this play to *Romeo and Juliet*. Wishing to partake in her lover's fate, Astrea runs to kiss Serule one last time, just like Juliet, who kisses Romeo before she stabs herself. In the last moment, however, tragedy is averted

---

[90] *SW*, vol. 1, p. 255. Translation: 'He takes the mirror again, violins start playing, the MORIAN and the PRINCESS dance again.'

[91] Ibid., pp. 265–6. Translation: 'SON. Now Death, I am fearless of you in this little glass. Now farewell, farewell, I drink Death. *He drinks, his father stands dismayed.* Now you are close to my heart, Death, do not keep me waiting. O how strongly it [literally: he] works, I must resign my spirit now. *He drops down dead.*'

[92] *Romeo and Juliet*, 5.3.125–31.

since Serule was only given a sleeping potion,[93] and wakes up before Astrea kills herself. Relieved, the fathers set aside their hatred and the lovers can marry at last.

As to memorialisation and hybridisation, the parallels to *Romeo and Juliet* are so numerous that it is likely that some parts of it were recycled in *Von eines Königes Sohne*, since the Shakespearean play was part of the English Comedians' repertoire and performed as early as 1604. Not only does the comedy employ the motif of the star-crossed lovers and their feuding families, but the idea of the potion is present in Shakespeare as well. Other hybridised elements like the magician recall *The Tempest*, while the flight to the wood resonates with *A Midsummer Night's Dream* but also with the tragicomedy *Li ritratti* ('The Portraits') from Locatelli's collection of 1628/32, in which the daughter of the King of Scotland flees into the woods disguised as a shepherd.[94] Remnants of an earlier, unidentified source like the suitors, the servant and the magician with two names lead us to assume that there probably was a longer version of the play, which was shortened in *ECUT*. Capable actors familiar with the whole plot would have had the chance to extemporise these excised strands even without a precise text if they wanted to perform a more complete rendition.

Von eines Königes Sohne, a play without a direct correspondent in English literature, is a fine example of the work done by the English Comedians. Apart from the usual instances of narrative passages, verbal scenery, self-characterisations and over-explicitness, there are some intriguing details, like the play-within-the-play with a fool played by a serious personage and the frequent disguises, which add to the visual force of this play. Visualisation is particularly sophisticated in the mirror scene, in which the reflection magically comes to life with music and dancing.

In both *Von Fortunato* and *Von eines Königes Sohne*, the woods are the home of magical powers and fairies, gods and allegorical figures, mostly good-natured but also mischievous or even dangerous. As in the pastoral plays of Commedia dell'Arte or Commedia erudita, the green world is a place of change and metamorphosis, where the forces of youth and love are reinvigorated by nature to prevail over the older authorities.[95] The green world in drama is part of the heritage of popular culture insofar as it is alive with creatures of folklore and superstition. As Erika Fischer-Lichte argues, it represents the 'other' world, the place where the carnivalesque reversal of societal rules takes place and where the characters go

---

[93] The frequent novelistic plot device of a sleeping potion that makes somebody look dead can also be found in the *scenario Il Marito* ('The Husband') edited by Flaminio Scala (1611). Due to an unhappy love, Franceschina feigns her death by means of a sleeping potion but eventually all ends well. See Testaverde, ed., op. cit., pp. 47–56 for the text.

[94] For the text see Testaverde, ed., op. cit., pp. 415–32.

[95] As François Laroque puts it, "the green world thus symbolises a different style of life – contemplation instead of actions, happy harmonies of music and love instead of the metallic clash of arms and the discordances of conspiracy." *Shakespeare's Festive World*, p. 193.

through the archetypal rite of passage.[96] This reference to popular culture leads to the next section about comedies with stock characters, emblematic of popular theatre.

6.3. Comedies with 'Types': *Von Sidonia und Theagene, Jemand und Niemandt*

The comedies *Von Sidonia und Theagene* and *Jemand und Niemandt* ('Somebody and Nobody') are characterised by the use of 'types' and share patterns of the "concentration-type" Commedia dell'Arte. According to Walter Hinck, this subcategory of Commedia dell'Arte refers to satiric comedies or tragicomedies with stock characters and motifs of intrigues and mistaken identities revealed in the end,[97] all of which can be found in these two plays. However, the deployed characters derive from different sources: *Jemand und Niemandt* originates from an English history play with the allegorical figures of Nobody and Somebody in the comic subplot, whereas *Von Sidonia und Theagene* features recurrent figures of Plautian comedy, which were subsequently resumed by Commedia erudita and Commedia dell'Arte. Contrary to Ralf Haekel's thesis that the English Comedians' theatre was not a "Typentheater",[98] the English, German and Italian lineage of the 'types' shall come into focus in the synopses.

Von Sidonia und Theagene

Eine kurtzweilige lustige Comoedia von Sidonia und Theagene ('An entertaining, merry Comedy of Sidonia and Theagenes') is the only play of the collection adapted from a recognisable German original, namely *Amantes amentes. Das ist: Ein anmutiges Spiel von der blinden Liebe, aber wie man deutsch nennt von der Leffeley u.f.w.* ('Foolish Lovers, i.e. a charming comedy about blind love, or as it is called in German, flirtatious liaison', 1609) by Gabriel Rollenhagen (15831629?), a lawyer, playwright and poet from Magdeburg.[99] Among his numerous literary works, the bawdy comedy *Amantes amentes* elicited the greatest success and was imitated by other playwrights and players. One such adaptation is *Von Sidonia und Theagene*, attributed to the English Comedians although the title does not occur in the principal lists of their repertoire. It follows

---

[96] See Fischer-Lichte, *Geschichte des Dramas: Epochen der Identität auf dem Theater von der Antike bis zur Gegenwart*, vol. 1, p. 258.

[97] See Hinck, *Das deutsche Lustspiel des 17. und 18. Jahrhunderts und die italienische Komödie*, pp. 19–20.

[98] Ralf Haekel, *Die Englischen Komödianten in Deutschland: Eine Einführung in die Ursprünge des deutschen Berufsschauspiels*, p. 12.

[99] For the biography see Karl Theodor Gaedertz, *Gabriel Rollenhagen: Sein Leben und seine Werke; Beitrag zur Geschichte der deutschen Litteratur des deutschen Dramas und der niederdeutschen Dialektdichtung nebst bibliographischem Anhang* (Leipzig: Hirzel, 1881).

Rollenhagen's model in a desultory way and alters his verse form to prose, probably to match the other plays in *ECUT*, as Fredén argues.[100] Apart from the change of form, the only substantial differences are the new title and the modified names of all the characters, excluding Aleke. According to Tittmann, the new names were taken from Heliodor of Emessa's Hellenistic tale of *Thyeagenes and Chariklea*, contained in the romance *Aethiopica* (around 300 AD).[101] A homonymous English dramatisation of this narrative, played at court in London in 1574 and mentioned by Cohn, might have served as a model for the adaptation.[102] Indeed, the frequent inconsistencies give reason to presume the content was taken from a previous, lost version, or translated and adopted inaccurately from the German model, as were the unusual subdivision of the acts into scenes and the detailed stage directions in Latin.

Both in *Amantes amentes* and *Von Sidonia und Theagene*, the classical affiliation is visible in the use of stock characters, probably taken from Plautian comedy and similar to Commedia dell'Arte, as the following comparative grid shows.[103]

Dramatis personae of *Amantes amentes*[104]	Dramatis personae of *Von Sidonia und Theagene*[105]	Plautian stock characters/ Commedia dell'Arte 'types'[106]
SIMON, *father*	CALARISIS, *the girl's father*	*Senex* / Pantalone (father)
VETULA, *mother*	CHRASILLA, *the girl's mother*	*Matrona* / wife, mother
LUCRETIA, *daughter*	SIDONIA, *girl/virgin*	*Virgo* / Innamorata
ALEKE, *her maid*	ALEKE, *maid*	*Ancilla* / Servetta
HANS, *farmhand*	CNEMON, *peasant*	*Parasitus* / Zanni
EURIALUS, *beau*	THEAGENES, *youth*	*Adulescens* / Innamorato
LENA, *courtesan*	----	
GRATIANUS, *Doctor of Law*	NAUSICLES, *old wooer*	*Senex* / partly Pantalone, partly Dottor Gratiano
PROLOGUE & EPILOGUE, *played by the same person*	----	

---

[100] See Fredén, *Friedrich Menius und das Repertoire der Englischen Komödianten in Deutschland*, p. 268.
[101] See Tittmann *Die Schauspiele der englischen Komödianten in Deutschland*, p. XII.
[102] See Cohn, p. CX.
[103] This was noticed by Fredén as well, but he does not go into detail and merely states the correspondence between the roles. See *Friedrich Menius und das Repertoire der Englischen Komödianten in Deutschland*, p. 261.
[104] The characters are taken and translated from a print of *Amantes amentes* held at the Herzog August library in Wolfenbüttel and accessible online, <http://diglib.hab.de/drucke/lo-6495/start.htm> (last accessed 29 July 2019).
[105] *SW*, vol. 1, p. 269.
[106] The comparison between Latin comedy and Commedia dell'Arte characters is based on Wolfgang Thiele, "Commedia dell'Arte: Stegreiftheater aus Italien und Frankreich", in G. Denzler, N. Glatzel and J. Lehmann, ed., *Commedia dell'Arte: Harlekin auf den Bühnen Europas*, pp. 1–20, p. 16.

All roles from Rollenhagen were maintained in the adaptation of *ECUT*, apart from the prologue and epilogue, which are reminiscent of the Shrovetide play and usually not present in the repertoire of the English Comedians. As in the *scenari* of Commedia dell'Arte, the simple plot is marked by a symmetrical arrangement of characters and scenes to provide comic relief through repetition and reversal. Sidonia's parents Calarisis and Chrasilla/Grasilla (both names occur in the play, another instance of blunders due to incomplete editing) wish to save their daughter from the dangers of juvenile passion. Their plan of finding a suitable husband for her ironically produces exactly the opposite result: Sidonia turns down the suitors they choose and falls in love with a young beau instead. The first to propose is the rich old wooer Nausicles, favoured by Sidonia's father Calarisis. These two old men, the suitor and the father, combine the major roles connected to Pantalone in Commedia dell'Arte: Calarisis is the suspicious father, outsmarted by the young lovers, while Nausicles plays the spurned paramour with the magniloquence of the Dottore – in Rollenhagen's version he even bears the name Doctor Gratianus, which can hardly be a coincidence. Nausicles' eloquence is instantly inhibited at the sight of Sidonia's sneering indifference towards him. The outspoken girl wilfully misunderstands his conventional metaphors in a parodic reversal of dramatic courtship, found in more than one play of the collection.[107] For instance, when the old suitor laments that his heart is sinking into despair, she jeeringly remarks that it cannot sink like a ship, because there is no hole to be seen in it, and dryly suggests he should be hospitalised for his love sickness.

> NAUSICLES. Ach lasset doch mein betrübtes Hertz nicht gar so versinken.
> SIDONIA. Solches dürffet ihr euch nicht befahren / sehe ich doch kein Loch für euch.
> NAUSICLES. [...] Betrachtet doch / wie mein Hertz gegen euch biß auf den Todt verwundt / und mein gantzer Leib von Lieb darzu schwach und kranck ist.
> SIDONIA. *Scopticè*. Kranck? So könt ihr euch in ein Spittal begeben.[108]

Ultimately, she calls Nausicles an old donkey, whom she denies both a wreath in sign of affection and her hand on the grounds that she needs a young and valiant husband – also in sexual terms. To add insult to injury, the rejected suitor is derided by the peasant Cnemon.[109]

---

[107] For example Maria in the *Pickelheringspiel* IX or the sardonic maid of the *Singspiel* XIV of the 1620 collection, and Ancilletta in *Der Jud von Venedig*, presented further on.

[108] *SW*, vol. 1, p. 279. Translation: 'NAUSICLES. Oh, do not let my heart sink into sadness like this. SIDONIA. That will not happen for sure, I do not see a hole in it. NAUSICLES. [...] Oh can't you see that my heart is wounded to death and my body is made weak and sick by love? SIDONIA. *Jeering*. Sick? Then go to the hospital.'

[109] In Rollenhagen's play, the peasant is called Hans and his parts are written in Low-German dialect. This linguistic distinction marks his lower social status and echoes the use of dialects in Commedia dell'Arte. Whether the English Comedians, if indeed they ever performed this play, would have this clown speak English, high German or a German dialect is difficult to demonstrate. However, Rudolph Genée points out that Duke Heinrich Julius

This clownish character tries his luck with Sidonia as her second wooer, mirroring and distorting the attempt made by Nausicles with a proposal peppered with "potz schlapperment", sexual explicitness and inappropriate culinary comparisons. For instance, he declares that he would speak words as sweet as fat mutton with turnips if only he was allowed to possess the girl in her comfortable bed.[110] When he starts to molest her, Sidonia turns him down because he is too boorish to 'pick a flower' (a sexual metaphor for the girl's virginity) intended for a nobleman. Like the Plautian sly servant or Zanni/Arlecchino, Cnemon combines the features of a bawdy simpleton and a witty opportunist. In fact, the scorned clown does not go away empty-handed like Nausicles but takes the opportunity to flirt with Sidonia's maid/Servetta Aleke, in a typical Commedia dell'Arte turn.

In the second act, the young Theagenes is introduced with a highly rhetorical outburst of love for Sidonia, presented to the audience in the form of a letter. To create a comic contrast, the romantic lyricism of the Innamorato is reversed on a lower social level in Cnemon's verbally and physically explicit proposal to the maid Aleke in the following scene. While the business-minded woman tests his financial resources, the clown answers in such an ambiguous way that she understands the opposite of what is true and revealed to the audience in the skilfully interwoven asides.

> ALEKE. Wenn mir aber nun Hochzeit haben gehabt / was fangen wir darnach an / womit wollen wir uns ernehren?
> CNEMON. Das will ich bald sagen / höre nur zu / ich haben einen gantzen Hut voll Gelt.
> *Submisse ad spectat[ores].*
> Einen Fingerhut meyn ich ["fiction external communication"]. Ein Weinberg der wegt alle Jahr Sieben Funder
> *Ad spectatores* Steine ["fiction external"] so / speise ich auch alle Tage 10. Gericht. Zwene Hering creutzweise uber den andern gelegt / daß sein 10 ["fiction external communication" from "zwene Hering" onwards]. [...]
> ALEKE. Je das geht wol hin / was vermag aber eure Barschafft.
> CNEMON. Ich möchte etwan noch ein tausent Gülden haben / ohne was in Schulden.
> *Ad spectat[ores]*
> Ich möcht sie wohl haben / ich hab sie aber nit ["fiction external"].[111]

---

[110] had his clown characters speak Low German after the model set by Sackville's Jahn Posset. See *Geschichte der Shakespeare'schen Dramen in Deutschland*, p. 10.
"CNEMON. Ach wie sollte es sich so fein schlaffen / ewer Bettchen ist so fein weich / ach wenn ich euch nur einmal hette / ich wollte euch so gute süsse Wort geben / wie fett Schöpsen Fleisch mit Rüben." *SW*, vol. 1, p. 287.

[111] *SW*, vol. 1, p. 292. Translation: 'ALEKE. What shall we live on once we have had our wedding? CNEMON. I will tell you at once, just listen. I have a hat full of money. *Silently, to the audience.* I mean a thimble [in German it is literally called 'fingerhat' and produces a funny wordplay]. A vineyard that bears seven waggonloads *To the audience* of stones. Thus, I eat ten courses every day, two herrings put like a cross on a plate look like a Roman 10 [X]. ALEKE. Well, that sounds wonderful. But what about your ready money? CNEMON. I should have about a thousand guilders free of debt. *To the audience* I should, but I don't.'

Thanks to a way of communicating on two levels, one "fiction-internal" and one "fiction-external",[112] marked in the quote, the spectators are aware that he only possesses a thimble full of money but pretends it is a great amount, a vineyard that produces seven waggonloads of stones, not grapes, and that the ten courses he eats are just symbolised by the Roman number 10, i.e. X, formed by crossing two herrings on a plate. In conclusion, he boasts that he should have about a thousand guilders free of debt and then adds that he does not, but in Aleke's eyes he is quite an eligible suitor. The reversal from high romance to low sexuality and the device of letting the audience know the grim reality behind the courtship on stage produces a comic effect, which was as successful in Commedia dell'Arte plays as on the English and German stage.

In Act 3, Sidonia receives the letter from Theagenes and immediately feels pierced by Cupid's arrow. This is a rare lyric exploit of an otherwise coarse character, as if her lover's courteous manners had a positive effect on her. In response, she sends Aleke with the wreath she withheld from Nausicles and is given a ring in return. A foil to this romantic exchange is provided once again by the drunk clown Cnemon, who rants about women and sings a gross love song to Aleke, until he is admitted into the house. By contrast, Nausicles performs a musical serenade immediately after him, mirroring the previous scene in serious tones and with a different outcome: he is rejected by Sidonia with rude words, even when he threatens to die of grief. This scene abounds in music, singing and the non-verbal humour of physicality.

Act 4 presents the young lovers' secret rendezvous in the absence of the girl's father. As in many fairy tales, three is a magic number and, indeed, the third suitor finally seems to be the perfect match for Sidonia: neither a dodderer nor a boor, but a handsome youth. In a romantic dialogue with typical motifs such as the love sickness and the testing of love, they seal their mutual affection:

> THEAGENES. Ach ich bin euch von Hertzen hold / wenn ihr es nur erkennen wolt.
> SIDONIA. O ihr falsche Kröte / ihr untrewes Hertz / jetzt jaget ihr mir eine Röte ab / ich trawe euch nicht es seynd nur blosse Wort derer ich mein Tage viel gehört.
> THEAGENES. Ach fühlet mein Hertz in meinem Leibe / ob es nicht solche Wort zum Mund raus zwinget / ach SIDONIA ohne euch werde ich nimmer gesundt.
> SIDONIA. Mein Hertzchen ich wolte euch nur probiren / ob es ewr ernst wer [...]
> THEAGENES. So Hertzchen / meyne ichs falsch / so hole mich der Geyer.[113]

Their skirmish recalls the Innamorati's lyricism, though style and language are undoubtedly less poetic. At first, Sidonia calls him a 'false toad' and pretends she

---

[112] These concepts are borrowed from Joel B. Lande, *Persistence of Folly*, p. 70.
[113] *SW*, vol. 1, p. 319. Translation: 'THEAGENES. Oh, I love you dearly, if only you would see it. SIDONIA. Oh, you false toad, you unfaithful heart, you just want to make me blush! I do not believe you; these are just empty phrases I have often heard in my life. THEAGENES. Alas, feel the heart in my chest which urges me to utter these words, oh Sidonia, without you I can never recover. SIDONIA. My love, I just wanted to see if you were speaking in earnest. [...] THEAGENES. Ah, my love, if I lie, stone the crows.'

does not believe his vain profession of love, which is curiously rhyming ("hold–wolt"). Using two common motifs, he passionately answers that his words are dictated by his heart and that he can only recover from his love sickness thanks to her, at which she calls him "Hertzchen" and admits it was only a test. He immediately takes up the sweet epithet "Hertzchen" and unromantically reiterates the truthfulness of his love with a colloquial curse.

Aware of her daughter's feelings, the mother plans to invite the youth to lunch so that they may settle the affair and secure a wedding. Unfortunately, when the father returns unexpectedly and surprises the mother, Theagenes, Sidonia, Aleke and Cnemon over lunch, he reacts furiously and calls Theagenes a mean seducer. However, after a tearful lamentation in line with Pantalone's *tirate*, he follows his wife's advice and consents to a double wedding between Sidonia and Theagenes and Cnemon and Aleke in the final act. The clown humorously concludes the play by telling the audience to leave as they are not invited to the celebration.

From the point of view of memorialisation and hybridisation, the version attributed to the English Comedians' acting stock is similar to Rollenhagen's original, although many incomplete scenes give room for extemporisation, especially for the clown. In no other play of the collection is the adaptation of characters and motifs so close to Commedia dell'Arte patterns: there is the sly and foolish servant, the unrequited old lover with his vain rhetoric, the parallel relationship between masters and servants as well as the romantic intrigue spun by the young lovers, to which the deceived father ultimately yields. The mediation might have taken place through the German model of the play, which borrowed the stock characters from Plautus and was then enlivened by Commedia dell'Arte devices.

The predominant role of the clown gives further insight into the comic potential exploited by the English Comedians, which was not too different from Commedia dell'Arte. Like the Zannis, Cnemon is at once clever and silly in his pursuit of physical love. His speech is composed of scatological humour, unveiled sexual allusions and constant references to food; he even sings a drunk serenade, in which acrobatic skills could be shown. In his *lazzi*, he mirrors and parodies the behaviour of the serious characters of the main plot, comments on their actions and tricks the others with a web of wordplays while letting the audience know the truth in a series of asides. All these elements point to the typical traits of the professional clown derived from Roman comedy and updated via Commedia dell'Arte on the Anglo-German stage.

Jemand und Niemandt

The second comedy with 'type'-like characters contained in the 1620 collection is *Eine schöne lustige Comedia / von Jemand und Niemandt* ('A beautiful merry Comedy of Somebody and Nobody'), one of the most successful adaptations of English material on the German stage. It is also the only play of which two different German versions are still extant, one dated 1608 and one present in the 1620 collection. Although my focus lies on the latter, the 1608 text delivers insight into some dramatic transformations from the amalgamation to the literarisation phase.

The title also occurs among the 'Dresden Repertoire' (1626) associated with Green, who could have performed either the 1608 or the 1620 rendition.

Both adaptations are based on the English play *No-body and Some-body, with the true Chronicle History of Elydure, who was fortunately three several times crowned Kinge of England*, entered in the Stationers' Register on 12 March 1606 and published the same year, but already performed between 1603 and 1605 by the Queen's Servants, according to E. K. Chambers.[114]

Figure 11: First and last page of *No-body and Some-body: with the true chronicle historie of Elydure, who was fortunately three severall times crowned King of England* (1606). Nobody, on the left, has literally no body but only trousers up to his neck, whereas Somebody has an overly long torso and very short legs.

As the title reveals, this combination of old English history, satire and allegory has a bipartite structure: the comic subplot of Somebody and Nobody is inserted into a semi-historical court intrigue, in which the rulers Archigallo and Elydure are alternately deposed. Julius Tittmann suggests that the memorialised source of the play was drawn from old chronicles about the ancient kings of Britain.[115] Both Monmouth's *Historia regum Britanniae* (1136) and Holinshed's *Chronicles of England, Scotland and Ireland* (1577) mention the deposition of the despotic King Archigallus in favour of his wise brother Elidurus, who is more devoted to philosophy than to politics. On the pretext of being ill, the new king transfers his power back to Archigallus, who turns into a good ruler. After the king's death, his

---

[114] See *The Elizabethan Stage*, vol. 2, p. 37. A digital version of the print is available at <https://collections.library.yale.edu/catalog/10191169> (last accessed 16 December 2020). For more details about the play see Schrickx, op. cit., p. 231.

[115] See Tittmann, *Die Schauspiele der englischen Komödianten in Deutschland*, p. XLII.

brothers Vigenius and Peredurus claim the throne and imprison their rival, Elidurus, even though he is still reluctant to wear the crown.[116] In the English dramatisation, these events are hybridised with new plot turns, like the conspiring courtiers or the quarrel between the envious queens, to heighten the theatrical effect. Moreover, the subplot of Somebody and Nobody transforms the sombre chronicle into a political comedy with a satiric meta-level. In fact, it humorously mirrors the court intrigue on a lower level and denounces the injustice of society with a sustained wordplay given by the personified pronouns: whenever Somebody is in the wrong, he says it was Nobody even though Nobody is honest, and Somebody is to blame.[117]

Compared to the English original, the renditions associated with the English Comedians noticeably expanded the comic subplot, probably due to the favour it enjoyed with the audience. Lawrence M. Price observes that the satiric minor action makes up about a third of the English play, while in the German adaptation of 1608 it rises to a half, reaching two thirds in the version of 1620.[118] Interestingly, the clown of the English text was excised in both German adaptations.

Before analysing the *Jemand und Niemandt* contained in *ECUT*, it is worth saying a few words about the earlier version performed in Graz in 1608, *Niemand und Jemand. Ein wahrhafftige unndt glaubwirdige History unndt Geschicht, wie es sich vor villen Jarrn in Englandt mit Khunig Arznagall und seine dreyen Prüder zu getragen* ('Somebody and Nobody. A true and trustworthy history and story as happened many years ago in England with king Arznagall and his three brothers'). The manuscript of this play is preserved at the Cistercian monastery of Rein near Graz (Codex 128) and was reissued by Willi Flemming in 1931.[119] According to Orlene Murad, it is the only extant text of the ten plays mentioned in Archduchess Maria Magdalena's letter.[120] After the performance of 1608 in Graz in the presence of Archduke Ferdinand, it was roughly transcribed and dedicated to the Archduke Maximilian, brother of Maria Magdalena, by Joannes Grün aka John Green.[121]

---

[116] Ibid.
[117] In this context, Fredén observes that the character Nemo was already known to the German-speaking audience from early sixteenth-century pamphlets and satiric poems, e.g. *Nemo*, in Latin, by Ulrich von Hutten (1518). Likewise, in England there was a ballad about *Little John Nobody* (1550), proving how deep-rooted this personage was in popular culture. See *Friedrich Menius und das Repertoire der englischen Komödianten in Deutschland*, pp. 313–5. Anston Bosman adds the information that the literary character of Nemo became associated with the fool in the early sixteenth century, when a barber from Strasbourg named Jörg Schan published a pamphlet with the image of a beggar-fool and the inscription "Niemandts hais ich, was jeder man tut, das zücht man mich ('Nobody is my name, I bear everybody's blame'). See Bosman, "Renaissance Intertheater and the Staging of *Nobody*", *ELH* 71 (2004), pp. 555–85, p. 571.
[118] See Price, *The Reception of English Literature in Germany*, p. 20.
[119] See Flemming, ed., *Barockdrama*, vol. 3, *Das Schauspiel der Wanderbühne*, pp. 73–131.
[120] See Murad, *The English Comedians at the Habsburg Court in Graz 1607–1608*, p. 30.
[121] Ibid. The encomiastic dedication in Latin verse is reproduced in Flemming, op. cit., pp. 73–4. In verse 21, Green reveals his name: "Haec tibi Joannes Grün, sacratissime

Whether Green was also the author of the play or just of the dedication and the postscript is impossible to assert, but he most certainly played the part of Nobody, as the beautiful portrait adorning the manuscript implies.

Figure 12: Picture of John Green – with noticeably red hair – as Nemo, i.e. Nobody. The image is preserved at the Cistercian monastery at Rein near Graz (MS 128). Nemo's feathered hat and large blue pantaloons reach from his knees to his neck and function as a visual pun about the character Nobody having literally no body. Since this reference to the absence of a body in the name 'No-body' makes sense only in English, the coloured picture might be an English original or inspired by the many representations of Nobody in England, such as the woodcut of the play performed by the Queen's Servants. The rosary and sacred book in his hands are symbols of the virtuosity of the personage, which were cleverly adapted to the Austrian Catholic environment. Both the portrait and the Latin inscription "Neminis virtus ubique laudabilis" ('Nobody's virtue is always praiseworthy') infer that Nobody is laudable and prays.

The Rein manuscript of 1608 is close to the English play and some scenes coincide almost literally. Perhaps Green possessed an English copy or a translation of it and either adapted it himself or gave it to an expert editor, responsible for some changes. In the earlier phases, it was not unusual for the English model to still be predominant, and alterations concerned mainly simplification and foregrounding

princeps, / Dedicat agrestic condita scripta sono", which also recurs at the end as signature: "Studiosissimus / Joannes Grün / Nob. Anglus" and in the colophone "Johanneß Grüen. m.pr."

of emotions and comedy. Compared to the later rendition in *ECUT* 1620, there are considerable differences.

Firstly, the title *Eine schöne lustige Comedia von Jemand und Niemandt* ('A Beautiful Merry Comedy of Somebody and Nobody' 1620) is shorter than that of the 1608 variant, renounces the subtitle 'A true and trustworthy history and story as happened many years ago in England with king Arznagall and his three brothers' and foregrounds Somebody in the title, who appears first and not second as in the English model and the version of 1608. Secondly, some characters have different names or no name at all, like King Arcial's wife. Thirdly, as far as structure is concerned, the 1620 play is divided into five acts, whereas the older version indicates neither acts nor scenes, but is generally faithful to the structure of the English model. Moreover, dialogues and the sequence of scenes are altered to such a degree that a comparison is difficult to draw. For example, the later version starts in medias res, recounting the injustice of tyrannical Arcial towards the counts Marsianus and Carniel in a dialogic flashback, and omits the prequel of the 1608 manuscript. In exchange, the fight of the queens is augmented with violent details in the 1620 rendition. It can therefore be stated that the two variants belong to two different periods of the itinerant players' activity, marking the transition from the amalgamation to the literarisation phase. Despite these changes, the salient points of the plot coincide. A detailed analysis of the *ECUT* version with occasional references to the English model and the 1608 version illustrate what adaptation-in-progress entailed.

The first act of *Jemand und Niemandt* (1620) starts with the conspiracy of two counts determined to depose the unjust tyrant Arcial in favour of his wise brother Ellidor. They are supported by Ellidoris/Elliodoria, wife of Ellidor, who seeks revenge on Arcial's haughty wife – simply called queen Arcial – because the latter's parasite servant humiliated her verbally and physically.[122] After the coup d'état, Ellidor is urged to accept the crown and modestly accepts only for the welfare of the state.

In strong contrast to this disinterested character, in the following scene the malevolent Somebody tells the audience of his disgraceful conduct in every respect, from theft to adultery and murder, which he always blames on the innocent Nobody in order to slander his name. The original, indirect characterisation in the form of a dialogue between the envious courtier Somebody and his conspiring servant is reduced to a monological self-characterisation on the part of the villain Jemand in the 1620 version. By contrast, the 1608 manuscript maintains the dialogue but simplifies the misdoings from financial speculation to arson, rape and drunkenness. These aspects are heightened in Jemand's speech in *ECUT*, in which the plan to defame Nobody becomes a wish to see him dead.

---

[122] The incorrect or missing names are an instance of imprecise editing as are the stage directions sometimes in Latin, sometimes in German, and the fact that the parasite courtier is not mentioned in the list of dramatis personae although he plays an important part.

Somebody and his servant scheming against Nobody in the English play (1606)	The dialogue in the Rein manuscript (1608)	Jemand's self-characterisation and evil plan in *ECUT* (1620)
Enter Somebody with two or three Seruaunts. [...] *Somb.* The slaues ambitious and his life I hate. *Seru.* How shall we bring his name in publick scandall? *Somb.* This it shall be, vse my direction. In Court and country I am *Somebody*, And therefore apt and fit to be employed: Goe thou in secrete being a subtle knaue, And sowe seditious slaunders through the Land, Oppresse the poore, suppresse the fatherlesse, Deny the widdowes foode, and the staru'd releefe, And when the wretches shall complaine their wrongs, Being cald in questions, sweare twas *Nobody*, Racke rents, raise prises, Buy up the best and choise commodities And the best had, then keepe them tll their prises Be lifted to their height, and double are, and when the raisers of this dearth are sought Though *Somebody* doe this, protest and sweare Twas *Nobody* fore Iudge and Magistrate.[123]	*Jemandts khambt ein und sein Jung.* [...] JEMANDT. Den Schellm will ich mit Haß vervolgen, dan sein Preiß khan ich nicht leiden. JUNG. Aber genediger Herr, wie sollen wir eß zuwegen bringen, daz wir sein Schandtmechten verursachen; dan ich wolt gern daz die ganze Welt Niemandtß haßet. JEMANDT. Ja, eß war guet, aber ich forcht, eß ist unmiglich, Jung; In dem Hof und in dem Ladt bin ich Jemantß genenet uund in groß Genadt bei Jedermann; du solst sobalt vonhinen und in dem ganzen Landt sollstu allerley Schellmerey treiben, rauben, stellen, fluehen, schweren, ja kheische und frome Jungfraun solstu mit Gewalt bezwingen, Khirchen rauben, Heiser abbrennen, Ehebrechen und Trunkenheit solltu alczeit yben, dan Trunkenheit ist die Mueter aller Sünden; und wans gefragt wirt, wer solcheß getan hat, ob gleich woll Jemandtß und Jemandtß Diener solcheß begangen hat, doch laß unß schweren, Niemantß hat solcheß getan, und so wirt Jederman sein Nam verachten; mach dich geret, dan sein Lob ist mir vom Herzen leidt.[125]	*Jetzt kömpt JEMANDT.* Jemandt jemandt bin ich geheissen / in der Welt durch und durch wol bekandt / und ziehe durch alle Königreich und Fürstenthümber / die ärgesten Schelmstücken / bring ich zu wegen und auff die Bahn / ich bin ein heimlicher Mörder / Brenner / ein Rauber / viel Jungfrawern thu ich schenden / doch geschicht es alles Heimlich. In Summa Alle Schlmerey / so auff Erden Heimlich geschicht / darin bin ich der Autor. Es ist aber ein ander Schelm / der heist Niemand / auff den ich alle meine Schuld werffe / der muß alles was ich thue entgelten / derselb Schelm machet mir viel Unruh/ den er wil kein Schuldt haben / sondern thut sich verantworten. Derhalben geh ich jetzt allenthalben / und suche den ehrvergessenen Schelm / den Niemandt / und wo ich ihn antreffe / wil ich ihn anklagen / und an den höchsten Galgen hencken lassen. Ich hoffe ich hoffe / ich wil ihn uberteuben / und alles was ich thue sol er verbüssen.[124]

---

[123] *No-body and Some-body* (London, 1606), B3v–B4v. Quoted from <https://collections.library.yale.edu/catalog/10191169> (last accessed 16 December 2020).

[124] *SW*, vol. 1, p. 355. Translation: '*Enter* SOMEBODY. I am called Somebody and am well known in the world. I travel all kingdoms and principalities and commit the most terrible crimes: I am a covert murderer, arsonist, thief, rapist of numerous virgins, but all of it

Unlike the previous versions, Jemand in *ECUT* does not appoint his servant to slander his rival but carries out a series of capital crimes himself ("Mörder / Brenner / ein Rauber / viel Jungfrawern thu ich schenden") to seek revenge on Nobody for denouncing his burglary at the royal treasury. Thus, there is a double mirroring of plot and of characters on a lower and satiric level. On the one hand, the revenge theme occurs both among the queens and between Somebody and Nobody. On the other hand, the contrary characters Somebody and Nobody reflect the evil King Arcial and his wise brother Ellidor. This complex structure owes much to the English original but also proves that the development of plays had prospered on the German stage and was no longer limited to reduction alone.

The main plot also contains a doubling of scenes since the former abuse of Elliodora is now repeated in the opposite direction. The new queen takes the parasite into her service, although she was formerly abused by him, and orders him to mock and beat the poverty-stricken, deposed queen Archial. In other words, she returns the mean treatment back onto her enemy. This reiterated procedure can either be seen as appropriate punishment for an uncharitable behaviour or as a comic scene of physical violence against a high-ranking personage to please an audience of commoners. In this sense, the parasite adopts some traits of the Zannis, like his willingness to do anything for money, even to the point of becoming a turncoat involved in slapstick scenes.

Contrary to the vindictive queen who misuses her power to torment her rival, in the next scene Nobody and his servant Nothing-at-all (*Gar nichts*) show sympathy for the victims of Somebody's crimes – theft, seduction of a virgin, and arson – falsely ascribed to them. Instead of these episodes being shown, they are

---

[125] happens secretly. In a nutshell, every anonymous devilment on Earth is my doing. However, there is another rogue called Nobody, whom I blame for all my deeds. He must make amends for what I do. This rascal is making me uneasy, because he does not want to be considered guilty and pleads his innocence. Therefore, I am looking for this dishonourable rascal Nobody everywhere and as soon as I find him, I want to accuse him and have him hanged from the highest gallows. I hope, I hope to find him and make him pay for what I have done.'
Quoted from Flemming, ed., *Barockdrama*, vol. 3, *Das Schauspiel der Wanderbühne*, p. 83. Translation: '*Enter Somebody and his young servant.* […] SOMEBODY. I want to persecute that rascal [Nobody] with all my hate, because I cannot stand him being praised. BOY. But milord, how shall we bring about his disrepute? I wish the whole world would hate Nobody. SOMEBODY. Yes, that would be good, but I am afraid it is impossible, my boy. At court and in the country I am called Somebody and enjoy everybody's respect. Go away now and cause all kinds of mischief, rob, steal, curse, swear, violate the chaste and pious virgins, steal from churches, burn down houses, constantly devote yourself to adultery and drunkenness because drunkenness is the mother of all sins. And when they ask you who did that, even though it was Somebody and Somebody's servant, we shall swear it was Nobody. Thus everyone will hold his name in contempt. Now begone because I hate to hear him praised.'

only narrated by the victims themselves in a series of dialogues and overheard by Nobody and his attendant. Although the subplot seems detached from the main action, they are connected by a relationship of mirroring and reversal typical of popular theatre.

In Act 2, Ellidor meets his wretched brother in the woods during a hunting party. Touched by Arcial's repentance, he persuades the counts to restore him to power. Similarly, Nobody's reputation is restored and he is celebrated for rebuilding a church, freeing some prisoners and adopting Somebody's illegitimate children. All rejoice in the fact that Nobody is honest and helpful, one of the numerous wordplays with a background of socio-political critique on which the subplot is based.[126]

In Act 3, the deposed and newly anointed queen Arcial repeats the scene of abuse towards her rival. Suddenly, the roles are reversed again, as King Arcial falls ill and dies shortly after having regretted his past errors. While his vain wife is tormented once more by Elliodoris, his younger brothers, Peridorus and Edwart, lay claims to the vacant throne, provoke a civil war and kill each other in combat. Again, Ellidor is made king against his will due to the others' folly.

The senseless fight for power is mirrored in the subplot when Nobody meets a braggart soldier, resonating with the bravo or Capitano, who challenges him to a sham duel. Apart from the presence of a Commedia dell'Arte-like character, the scene is interesting because, for the first time, Nobody refers to the fact that he does not have a body, a crucial clue for the final denouement, which is also reflected in the images of No-body described earlier. During the skirmish, Nobody is imprisoned by Somebody and summoned to court.

As in *Esther*, the main plot and the subplot finally merge in the final act when King Ellidor settles the queens' quarrel and opens the trial against Nobody. During the trial, Somebody's false accusations of murder, rape and libel are cleverly unmasked by Nobody as he does not have a body, which is necessary for committing any crime, or fingers for writing the pasquils – 'ergo, it must have been Somebody with his hand'.[127] This syllogistic but convincing explanation is enforced by the stolen jewels found in Somebody's pockets while Nobody possesses only a rosary and a Bible – just as in Green's portrait. Conversely, in the English play his pockets are full of supplications from poor people and not of Catholic objects of devotion suited to the Catholic Austrian audience, a striking instance of adaptation to the socio-cultural context of performance. In the end, Somebody is sentenced to be hanged and Nobody remains at court as a councillor. This is another parallel to *Esther*.

---

[126] A similar wordplay entailing social or religious criticism is present in *Everyman* when God complains that "Everyman liveth so after his own pleasure / And yet of their life they be nothing sure." *Everyman*, in Ernest Rhys, ed., *Everyman and Other Old Religious Plays*, p. 4. In it, God refers at once to humankind in general, including the audience, and to the protagonist of the play, Everyman, who allegorically embodies this totality.

[127] My translation of "ERGO Jemandt / jemandt hat es mit seiner Handt gethan" (*SW*, vol. 1, p. 420).

As in the English original, the satire in the subplot was maintained in an instance of memorialisation. The fact that the characters speak of themselves as personified pronouns provides an amusing but also well-founded social denunciation, which might account for the long-lasting success of the play.[128] Despite the comic potential of the wordplay, its overlong use in the German adaptation diminishes the effect and makes it a little tedious.

In *Jemand und Niemandt*, satire and moralities are hybridised to show that the mirroring characters of the main plot and the subplot are as antithetic as the allegories of Virtue and Vice. The good and bad government of the two kings in the main plot is reflected in the virtuous Nobody and the vicious Somebody in the subplot. As distinct from the morality play, however, there is no soul to fight for, at least not on stage. Still, the didactic aim behind the satire would be to teach the audience a valuable moral lesson through satire and social criticism, indirectly associated with religion: wickedness will be punished, and good deeds rewarded.

The fact that the earlier German transposition from 1608 was adapted only two years after the publication of the English play *No-body and Somebody* (1606) proves that the English Comedians exported brand new material to the Continent and shaped it during their tours. While the 1608 manuscript is still close to the English model, by 1620 the changes due to immersion in oral and popular culture mark the transition to a self-confident way of performing to please the audience.

In summary, both comedies present stock characters of different provenance but with similar purposes. In *Von Sidonia und Theagene*, the characters inherited from Plautus are involved in a romantic intrigue that makes fun of social stereotypes close to the Commedia dell'Arte, like the unrequited old lover or the suspicious father. However, the clown-peasant Cnemon takes part in the plot both as an active participant and as an ironic, external commentator, whereas the universal 'type' Nobody is not really a clown. Even if he uses the expression "potz schlapperment", usually connected to Pickelhering, his function is not to mock or evoke laughter with slapstick entertainment in the manner of the rude Cnemon or the opportunistic parasite in *Jemand und Niemandt*. Instead, by mirroring the main plot, he invites the audience to reflect on the social injustice that is shown on stage and recalls Shakespeare's philosophic jester.

Shakespeare's presence among the English Comedians' repertoire is central in the next section, devoted to the adaptations of two of his plays.

---

[128] For instance, in 1645 the Dutch playwright Isaak Vos adapted the play as *Iemant en Niemant. Zinnespel* on the basis of the German rendition associated with the English Comedians. Moreover, the allegorical character of Nobody/Nemo is often found as copperplate engraving in books of the time and ballads. Even Shakespeare refers to it in *The Tempest*: "TRINCULO. This is the tune of our catch, played by the picture of No-body" (3.2.122), as Johannes Meissner points out. See *Die englischen Comoedianten zur Zeit Shakespeares in Österreich*, pp. 96–7.

6.4. The 'Shakespearean' Tragedies: *Von Julio und Hyppolita*, *Von Tito Andronico*

The only two tragedies of *ECUT* 1620, *Von Julio und Hyppolita* and *Von Tito Andronico*, are derived from Shakespeare and allow for a direct comparison with the originals in order to detect the transformations at work in the adaptations by the English Comedians. As in my reading of the other plays, particular attention will be given to abridged or expanded scenes, narrative passages, hybridisation with other theatrical traditions like Commedia dell'Arte or the morality play and, of course, the role of the clown.

Von Julio und Hyppolita

A few strands of the *Tragaedia von Julio und Hyppolita*, performed in 1626 as part of John Green's 'Dresden Repertoire', recall the main plot of Shakespeare's *The Two Gentlemen of Verona*, although the whole structure is simplified, many characters are missing, and the ending is different. Albert Cohn claims that the unusual absence of a subplot and the frequently interrupted dialogues give every reason to conjecture that it is only a fragment of a more comprehensive play, perhaps a different English pre-text not yet discovered.[129] Following this line of argument, Creizenach argues that both Shakespeare and the German adaptation drew on the same lost source, which presumably ended tragically.[130] If this is true, the German version remained faithful to the original plot of deception and revenge and Shakespeare's happy ending would be an innovative addition.

Having a look at the list of dramatis personae of the two plays, the substantial reduction of characters already gives an impression of the cuttings to be expected in the play.

Dramatis personae in Shakespeare's *The Two Gentlemen of Verona* (1589–93)	Personae in *Von Julio und Hyppolita*[131]
Duke of Milan *father to Silvia*	Duke
VALENTINE *a gentleman of Verona*	ROMULUS *a Roman*
PROTEUS *a gentleman of Verona*	JULIUS *a Roman*
ANTONIO *father to Proteus*	---
TURIO *a foolish suitor to Silvia, favoured by her father*	---
EGLAMOUR *a Milanese courtier, who assists Silvia in her escape*	---
SPEED *page to Valentine*	Servant to Romulus
LANCE *servant to Proteus, with his dog Crab*	GROBIANUS *Pickelhering or servant to Julius* [without a dog]
PANTINO *servant to Antonio*	---
Host *of the inn in Milan where Julia lodges*	---

---

[129] See Cohn, p. CXI.
[130] See Creizenach, p. LIV.
[131] Taken from *SW*, vol. 1, p. 427. My translation.

Outlaws *who elect Valentine to be their captain*	---
JULIA *a lady of Verona, beloved of Proteus*	---
SILVIA *the Duke's daughter, beloved of Valentine*	HYPPOLITA *a princely lady*
LUCETTA *waiting-woman to Julia*	---
Servants	---
Musicians	[indirectly mentioned in the text]

Since Julia does not appear in the German play at all, the pastoral love story involving Proteus, the cross-dressing and the denouement in the woods was excised entirely as it is not crucial for the central conflict between love and friendship. Julia only survives indirectly in the name of the German counterpart to Proteus, Julius. Moreover, the fact that Valentine and Proteus are changed into Roman gentlemen might have been due to the Roman setting of *Von Tito Andronico*, the tragedy following in the collection, or it could point to the supposed unknown source the English Comedians drew upon, apart from Shakespeare.

As the synopsis reveals, the plot of the Shakespearean comedy corresponds to *Von Julio und Hyppolita* vaguely but unmistakeably. Written between 1589 and 1593 but not printed before the 1623 Folio was published, *The Two Gentlemen of Verona* is one of Shakespeare's early works, characterised by narrative monologues, and was thus easier to adapt for the German stage. At the beginning of the play, Valentine seeks honour in Milan while Proteus is completely devoted to Julia. Through Valentine's servant, Speed, Proteus sends a letter to his beloved, who is so torn between curiosity and the unwillingness to admit her feelings in front of her maid Lucetta, that she rips the letter to pieces. After putting it back together, Julia rejoices in the declaration of love. This detail of a letter torn to pieces and then reassembled reappears in an altered form in *Von Julio und Hyppolita* and proves a connection between the plays.

Before the lovers can be united, Proteus is sent to Milan, where Valentine has fallen in love with the duke's daughter Silvia. Their amorous dialogue, which is reminiscent of the flowery rhetoric of the Innamorati, is parodied by the ironic asides of the clown Speed in the manner of the Commedia dell'Arte. The parodic reversal of love continues in the following scenes with a different couple and another clownish servant. On a high and serious level, Julia and Proteus exchange vows and a ring before their goodbye. Meanwhile, on a low and comic level, the clown Lance airs his grievance about going to Milan with his master in a monologue addressed to Crab, "the sourest-natured dog that lives" (*The Two Gentlemen*, 2.3.4), and sprinkled with funny malapropisms (e.g. "I have received my proportion like the prodigious son", 2.3.3, instead of 'The Prodigal Son').

In Milan, Valentine asks Proteus to help him elope with Silvia. Proteus agrees but, once alone, reveals that he is torn between loyalty to his friend and a secret love for Silvia. He resolves to betray Valentine without losing face by letting Silvia's foolish suitor Turio into the secret of the elopement, so that he may reveal it to the duke. This new passion has completely erased Julia from his thoughts, who, in turn, knows nothing of his change of heart and decides to follow Proteus disguised as a page.

After Valentine is banished from Milan, intercepted by outlaws in the woods and made their chief, Proteus becomes the confident of all other characters without revealing his true aims. Only Silvia remains hostile and plans to join her lover in the woods dressed as a boy (the second cross-dressing in the play), like Astrea in *Von eines Königes Sohne*. Since Lance's wooing is unsuccessful, Proteus sends his new page Sebastian/Julia to Silvia with a letter and the ring he had received from his former fiancée. When Silvia tears the letter apart (the second letter torn to pieces), the heartbroken Julia tells her the story of the ring.

In the woods, Silvia is rescued from the outlaws by Proteus, who then turns into a new peril, threatening to rape her. Valentine intervenes and confronts his friend with his evil scheming. Proteus' sincere repentances induces Valentine to forgive him and Julia to reveal her identity; finally, all the lovers are reunited and marry.

The synopsis of Shakespeare's comedy points to an amalgamation of pastoral conventions, like the outlaws in the woods and several cross-dressings, with frequent features of the Commedia dell'Arte, such as the romantic intrigue with mistaken identities. The closeness to Commedia dell'Arte patterns is also visible in the artificial balancing of pairs of lovers (Julia – Proteus, Silvia – Valentine) and servants (Julia – Lucetta, Valentine – Speed, Proteus – Lance) as well as in the foolish suitor Turio, reminiscent of the braggart Capitano. In addition, the clownish servants Speed and Lance are given a pre-eminent role of entertainers and commentators in the interspersed comic scenes, which reflect and parody the serious main action.

It seems a little unfair to compare the lively comedy of *The Two Gentlemen of Verona* to the German tragedy of *Von Julio und Hyppolita*, because the latter is an incomplete adaptation with editorial blunders and not a fully developed play. Nevertheless, there are some correlations in the plots and in the character constellations which reveal a debt to Shakespeare, or at least to a common source.

At the beginning of Act 1, Hyppolita and her fiancé Romulus are discussing the details of their imminent wedding with the duke, her father. Romulus' wish to visit his parents in Rome is stronger than the others' insistent requests to postpone the journey until the wedding has taken place. The duke even warns him about waiting too long in a sort of foreshadowing: "Ich bitte bedencket euch / sehet zu das ihr vorerst Hochzeit haltet."[132] To comfort his dejected fiancée, Romulus asks his brotherly friend Julius to keep her company while he is gone and promises to write letters to Hyppolita from afar – a crucial detail for the ensuing course of the tragedy. Once alone, Julius reveals his real intent in a soliloquy, just as Proteus does in the Shakespearean play. His passionate love for Hyppolita has secretly alien-

---

[132] *SW*, vol. 1, p. 430. Translation: 'I beseech you to change your mind. Make sure you marry first.'

ated him from Romulus and turned him into a scheming villain. "Practica est multiplex, nun ich muß auch eins darvon versuchen",[133] he says, echoing Proteus' statement: "If I can check my erring love, I will; / If not, to compass her I'll use my skill" (2.4.206–7). Julius' change from faithful friend to disloyal traitor calls for visualisation on stage: depending on whether he is alone or in company, he changes personality in the blink of an eye. The audience can thus observe the two sides of his ambivalent character in a sort of play-within-the-play, as in the following extract.

> *Sie gehen hinein* JULIUS *betrübt.*
> JULIUS. Wie Ungern / sehe ich dich von hinnen ziehen.
> *Felt auff die Knie.*
> O ich wolte daß du nimmer widerkemest / als den wer ich der glückseligste Mensch / und mach mir schon etc. ["fiction external communication"]
> ROMULUS *Kömpt wieder.* Warum folgestu nicht lieber Bruder? Was bedeutet / daß du auff den Knien sizet?
> JULIUS. Hertzlieber Bruder ich ruffe die Götter an / daß sie dir wollen FAVORABILES seyn / und in kurtzen wieder anhero verfügen.
> ROMULUS. O du bist mir ein getrewer Freundt / deinesgleichen an Trewheit / hab ich noch nie in der Welt funden. Derhalben befehle ich dir noch eines / ergetze meine allerliebste / in meiner ABSENTIA mit lieblichen DISCURSEN und TRACTIERE sie mir wol / denn ich weiß du bist mir der getreweste / darumb ich sie auch nur dir allein befehle.
> JULIUS. O mich getrew. *Fellet auff die Knie.* Ich schwere bey der Sonnen Monden / und Sternen etc.[134]

An "etc." puts an abrupt end to Julius' lines twice in this quote, either because the editor could not amend this mutilated version, or because the missing content could easily be completed from the context by an extemporising actor, almost like in a *canovaccio*. Julius plays his part so well that Romulus does not suspect he might be anything but faithful ("getrew"), a word that overabounds in the dialogue and is accompanied by a reiterated gesture of kneeling to visually underline his simulated devotedness. In fact, his lies and his apparent sadness about his friend's departure are unmasked as devilish joy in the asides.

In Act 2, Julius replaces the intercepted letters from Romulus with forged ones to put his rival in a bad light. His partner in crime is his servant Grobianus in the

---

[133] *SW*, vol. 1, p. 433. Translation: 'Practica est multiplex – now it is for me to try one.'
[134] Ibid., p. 432. Translation: '*They go inside, Julius is dejected.* JULIUS. How reluctant I am to let you go. *Falls onto his knees.* Oh, I wish you would never return, then I would be the happiest person alive, and I would do etc. ROMULUS *Returns.* Why aren't you coming with us, brother? Wherefore are you kneeling? JULIUS. Dearest brother, I am praying the gods that they may be benign and lead you back soon. ROMULUS. Oh, what a faithful friend you are to me! I have never found such faithfulness anywhere else. For this reason, I beseech you, keep my lover company with sweet conversations while I am gone, and treat her well, because I know you are the most faithful person I know and therefore I commit her to you alone. JULIUS. Oh, in faith. *Falls onto his knees.* I swear by the sun, the moons and the stars etc.'

role of Pickelhering, who agrees to dress up as a messenger and deliver the fake letters. The telling name Grobianus from *Grobian* (brute, churl) reveals the hideous appearance and brutish behaviour of this equivalent to Lance. In a humorous sequence, the self-willed clown enters the stage called with a whistle:

> GROBIANUS. *kompt herauß / der Herr pfeiffet. Stehet still.*
> Mein Herr muß ja meynen / daß er einen Hundt vor sich habe.
> JULIUS. *pfeiffet noch einmal.*
> GROBIANUS. Pfeiff du immer hin / ich bin dein Hundt nicht.
> JULIUS. Jung hastu nicht gehöret / daß ich dich gerufen / wornach stehestu dann?
> GROBIANUS. Nein Gnädiger Herr / ich hab kein ruffen gehört / sondern pfeiffen / und gemeinet ihr Gnaden hetten den Hundt zu sich gepfiffen.[135]

By commenting that the disrespectful practice of whistling instead of calling him by his name is more fitting for a dog than for a person, the servant proves to be more than just a simpleton. In fact, he cleverly criticises his master's behaviour and even indirectly refers to the excised dog, Crab.

The ensuing letter scene is exceptionally well-structured from the point of view of staging techniques and the creation of suspense: when Grobianus in disguise hands out the three letters to the Duke, Hyppolita and Julius, the content is not read aloud but the audience can infer it from the reactions of rage, despair and indignation of the characters. Only later, in the fourth act, will the precise text be revealed. Apparently, Romulus brags about how well he deceived them all. Deeply disappointed, Hyppolita tears the letter to pieces – like Julia does in Shakespeare, but for different reasons. Julius immediately imitates her gesture to replace his rival in her affection.

Since Hyppolita declines his love letters – perhaps because of the ill-suited messenger of love, Grobianus[136] – in Act 3 Julius convinces the duke that a marriage would serve the reason of state. The similarity to Shakespeare is given by the fact that Proteus, like Julius, insinuates himself into everybody's sympathy and even suggests to "slander Valentine / with falsehood, cowardice and poor descent" (3.2.30–1) as Julius does with the forged letters. A major departure, however, is that Silvia does not give in like Hyppolita, who agrees to marry Julius.

Informed about the betrayal, Romulus returns, finds the forged letter torn to pieces and reads it aloud, echoing Julia's assembling of Proteus' letter. Now the audience can put together the missing pieces of the puzzle: according to the false message, Romulus fell in love with another, richer woman and forfeited his

---

[135] *SW*, vol. 1, pp. 434–5. Translation: '*Enter* GROBIANUS, *his master whistles. He stands still.* Maybe my master thinks he has got a dog before him. JULIUS *whistles again.* GROBIANUS. Keep whistling, I am not your dog. JULIUS. Boy, have not you heard me call? Why are you standing there? GROBIANUS. My lord, I did not hear you calling, but whistling, and thought your lordship was whistling to his dog.'

[136] His grisly looks are revealed not only by his name but also by Hyppolita's remark: "Mich deucht nie ein grewlichern Kerl gesehen hab." *SW*, vol. 1, p. 444. Translation: 'I think I have never seen a more horrid fellow in my life.'

fiancée. Futile though it is, the motive of the breakup evidently worked since no one questioned the letter's truthfulness. Just then, the newly-weds exit the church, and the only thing left to heart-broken Romulus is revenge. He therefore dresses up as a masked dancer – the second disguise in the play, though not a cross-dressing like that of Silvia and Julia – and joins the wedding ceremony. His appearance during the dances coincides with a short silence and a change of tune, which is a compelling strategy of visualisation and sound indicated in the stage direction.

> *Jetzt fänget man an zu tantzen / da der vollnbracht kömpt ROMULUS sampt ander vermummet / und präsentiert sich vor einen Mittäntzer [...] ROMULUS schweiget still / will nicht reden / machet tieffe Reverentz.*
> ROMULUS. Gnädiger Printz / [...] wolle nun mit seiner liebsten Princessin [...] den TRAGAEDIEN Tantz auffmachen. [...]
> JULIUS. Warumb daß mein Freundt? Warumb nicht ein andern lustigen Tantz. [...] So machet auff ihr MUSICANTEN / machet auff den TRAGAEDIEN Tantz.[137]

In fact, the merry music stops to underline Romulus' entrance. Directly addressed by Julius, he wishes to perform a "TRAGAEDIEN Tantz", and although the idea seems a little odd to the groom, he orders the musicians to play a melancholic tune, setting the tone for the final catastrophe. During the gloomy dance, Romulus reveals his identity and stabs Julius before his wife's eyes, fulfilling the purpose of the macabre dance. Desperate, Hyppolita commits suicide without realising the web of lies that entangled her, as Romulus laments: "die arme Creatur hat sich erbarmlich / und unschuldig umb ihr Leben gebracht." Then he announces: "Nun nun will ich ihr in der Unschuldt unnd Tode / gleicher Gesellschafft leisten"[138] and takes his own life. In the end, the duke becomes a hermit devoted to mourning their fate.

Being a fragment, *Von Julio und Hyppolita* can hardly be put on a par with Shakespeare, but it still contains some interesting clues for better understanding the adaptation process. Firstly, the usual reduction of plot and characters focuses primarily on the conflict of love versus friendship, turned into a tragedy. Basically, the German rendition starts with Act 3 of *The Two Gentlemen of Verona*, leaving out the prequel and only briefly introducing the characters and their relationships in the exposition. The fact that the figures on stage are identified by their position and a small spectrum of personal traits makes them appear like 'types', devoid of the psychological depth of Shakespeare's characters. Romulus shares

---

[137] SW, vol. 1, p. 456–7. Translation: '*Now the dancing begins. After that, enter ROMULUS with other masked dancers and presents himself as one of them [...] ROMULUS is silent and does not want to speak; pays his respects.*
ROMULUS. Gracious prince [...] will you and your dearest princess join in a tragedy dance?
JULIUS. Why that, my friend? Why not a different, lively dance? [...] Well, play along, MUSICIANS, play a tragedy dance.'

[138] Ibid., pp. 458–9. Translation: 'The poor creature has killed herself pitifully and innocently. Now I want to keep her company in that same innocence and death.'

Valentine's credulity, and Julius resembles Proteus in his versatility, but is presented as a scheming villain right from the beginning. At least, he does not betray his former lover like Proteus, who forgets about his fiancée Julia – excised like half of the characters of the English equivalent. Even the clowns, so beloved in all the other plays of the collection, are missing here, perhaps due to the tragic ending of the adaptation. The only comparable character is the servant Grobianus, described as Pickelhering, but he plays a marginal role in the intrigue and does not contribute much to enlivening the gloomy atmosphere with his coarse remarks.

Secondly, despite the shortcomings of the content, dramatis personae and lines, the 1620 tragedy shows a refined stylistic level. The composition in five acts follows the neoclassical model without a comic interlude or subplot, and the language is enriched with poetic sequences, Latin expressions and vocatives. In the aforementioned dialogue between Romulus and Julius, for example, the vocative "Hertzlieber Bruder ich ruffe die Götter an" is followed by words of Latin origin like "absentia", "discursen" and "tractiere".[139] In addition, the detailed stage directions allow for the reconstruction of some ingenious visualisation techniques, for instance the forged letters not read out to the audience until the end, the chameleonic behaviour of Julius feigning loyalty to Romulus or the final dancing scene between Romulus in disguise and Hyppolita. The altered structure is indeed a distinctive feature of the German play since it is the sequence of scenes and the moment of the denouement that turns the comedy into a revenge tragedy: while Valentine recognises Proteus' wrongdoings in time to forgive him, Romulus returns too late. Thus, the dramatic climax of the recognition does not lead to a solution but to catastrophe.

Thirdly, there are several motifs that connect the play to Shakespeare's comedy as well as to the larger network of popular theatre. The most important commonality between the plays is the conflict between the duties of friendship and those of love. Geoffrey Bullough gives substantial evidence of the popularity of this theme in novelistic literature from Boccaccio to Chaucer and Sir Thomas Elyot.[140] In particular, he argues that Shakespeare's intricate love plot owes much to 'The Tale of Felix and Felismena', contained in Jorge de Montemayor's pastoral novel *Diana* (1524) and probably dramatised before 1585, but then lost.[141]

In his thorough analysis of sources, however, Bullough does not mention the Commedia dell'Arte as a possible influence on Shakespeare and consequently on

---

[139] Ibid., p. 432.
[140] See Bullough, vol. 1, p. 203.
[141] Ibid., p. 205. Like Julia, the heroine Felismena follows her lover Felix dressed as a page, only to find him singing a serenade to his new sweetheart, lady Celia. Celia falls in love with the cross-dressed page and Felismena is caught in a painful double bind until Celia dies of grief and the lovers are reunited. Despite some changes, Shakespeare followed the model closely for the first half of his play. The subsequent complication due to Celia's falling in love with a woman disguised as a man was not further developed but can be found in a later comedy, *Twelfth Night*. See ibid., p. 207.

the English Comedians. This is surprising because there are various *scenari* involving the commonplace contest of suitors, for instance Flaminio Scala's comedy *Flavio Tradito* ('Flavio Betrayed', 1611). The title refers to the hero betrayed by his best friend Orazio, who falls in love with Flavio's fiancée Isabella "without considering the ancient friendship that tied him to Flavio".[142] The fact that Orazio intercepts a letter meant for Flavio to convince Isabella's father that she loves him and should be his wife, closely resembles the German tragedy. As in Shakespeare's comedy, friendship ultimately triumphs over love when the fraud is discovered by the Zanni Pedrolino. These elements place the *scenario* in-between *The Two Gentlemen of Verona* and *Von Julio und Hyppolita*.

Another variation on the theme is *La innocentia rinvenuta* ('Innocence recovered', 1628/32) edited by Basilio Locatelli: Fabrizio wants to estrange his friend Orazio – incidentally the same name as the deceiver in Scala – from his fiancée Doralice. To pretend he was admitted into her bedroom, the disloyal friend is carried into her house in a chest, like Falstaff in *The Merry Wives of Windsor* and Pickelhering in the *Singspiel* 'Pickelhering in the Chest', analysed further on. Convinced of Doralice's alleged unfaithfulness by a ring Fabrizio stole from her room, Orazio orders the Zanni Burattino to kill her in the woods. Here the plot reconnects partly to *The Two Gentlemen of Verona* and partly to *The Merchant of Venice*, because Doralice escapes death by dressing as a boy and later plays the judge during the trial concerning her own murder, until the intrigue is revealed.[143]

Although it is difficult to speak of memorialisation and an ensuing hybridisation without concrete textual evidence, intercultural exchange can be detected in the field of theatricality. Further developing Cohn and Creizenach's idea of a lost tragedy prior to Shakespeare, from which strands and the 'original' tragic ending survive in *Von Julio und Hyppolita*, Italian literature and perhaps also Commedia dell'Arte might have given the comic turn to Shakespeare's play. It is striking that the two plays with the most evident derivation from Shakespeare are also the only two tragedies in *ECUT*, more precisely revenge tragedies, even if just one of them is a tragedy in the original English version. There really may be traces of a lost tragic model, or the ending was changed to better suit the taste of an audience which was as keen on revenge and bloodshed as the Elizabethan spectators were. Another explanation might be that the editor of *ECUT* chose to insert this tragedy to balance the genres within the collection.

---

[142] The translated quote is taken from Scala's *argomento* of *Flavio Tradito* in *Il teatro delle favole rappresentative* (1611): "Occorse che della giovane Isabella s'innamorò Orazio, non avendo punto riguardo all'antica amistade che con Flavio teneva." Testaverde, ed., *I canovacci della Commedia dell'Arte*, p. 23.

[143] For the whole text see Testaverde, ed., op. cit., pp. 185–92. Moreover, both the theatrical device of cross-dressing and the double plots mirroring and parodying each other is common in many *scenari* such as *Il ritratto* ('The Portrait') by Scala, in which Silvia dresses as a page called Lesbino to be close to her lover, or the pastoral *L'Arbore incantato* ('The Enchanted Tree') by Scala, in which Fillide dressed as Lisio, as well as in pastoral *novelle*.

Von Tito Andronico

The second tragedy of *ECUT*, *Eine sehr klägliche Tragaedia von Tito Andronico und der hoffertigen / Kaeyserin / darinnen denckwürdige Actiones zu befinden* ('A very lamentable tragedy of Titus Andronicus and the haughty Empress containing memorable scenes'), also derives from Shakespeare. As the title reveals and the plot confirms, it follows *The Most Lamentable Romaine Tragedie of Titus Andronicus* closely. Henslowe's entry of a "titvs" on 6 January 1592[144] provides enough reason to assume that Shakespeare's first tragedy was written before 1592, arguably in collaboration with George Peele, and published in 1600.[145] Set in the latter days of the Roman Empire, it represents a fictional cycle of revenge involving the general Titus Andronicus and Tamora, Queen of the Goths.

Compared to Shakespeare's list of dramatis personae, the German adaptation has an evident alteration in the names and a drastic reduction of the cast to twelve parts with some doubling up of actors and silent parts. Travelling companies usually could not count on more members, so minor personages such as some of Titus' sons and numerous kinsmen had to be excised, and the content was consequently stripped down to its essentials.

Dramatis personae in Shakespeare's *Titus Andronicus* (1592/1600)	Personae in *Von Tito Andronico*[146]
ROMANS	
SATURNIUS *son of the recently deceased Emperor of Rome*	Roman emperor
BASSANIUS *younger brother of Saturnius, in love with Lavinia*	Husband of Andronica
TITUS ANDRONICUS *a Roman nobleman and general against the Goths*	TITUS ANDRONICUS
MARCUS ANDRONICUS *a Tribune of the people, brother of Titus*	VICTORIADES[147]
LUCIUS *oldest son of Titus, future Emperor*	VESPASIANUS
QUINTUS, MARTIUS, MUTIUS *the other surviving sons of Titus (in descending order of age)*	[the other two sons of Titus are not presented alive on stage, only their heads]
LAVINIA *only daughter of Titus, betrothed to Bassanius*	ANDRONICA
YOUNG LUCIUS *a Boy, son of Lucius*	---
PUBLIUS *son of Marcus Andronicus*	---
SEMPRONIUS, CAIUS, VALENTINE *kinsmen*	---
EMILIUS *a Roman*	---

---

[144] See *Henslowe's Diary*, edited by R. A. Foakes, p. 19.
[145] See Jonathan Bate, ed., *The Arden Shakespeare Titus Andronicus* (London and New York: Routledge, 1995), p. 40.
[146] Taken and translated from *SW*, vol. 1, p. 460.
[147] In *SW*, vol. 6, p. 461 Brauneck defines Victoriades as Titus' son, but he is evidently the counterpart to Marcus Andronicus, his brother. In fact, in *SW*, vol. 1, p. 484, Titus addresses Victoriades with "mein hertzlieber Bruder" ('my dearest brother').

A Captain	---
A Messenger	A Messenger
A Nurse	Wise Attendant
A Clown	---
Other Romans *including Senators, Tribunes, Soldiers and Attendants*	[not mentioned in the list but in the stage directions]
GOTHS	AFRICANS
TAMORA *Queen of the Goths and later Empress of Rome by marriage to Saturnius*	AETIOPISSA *Queen from Africa* [Ethiopia?], *later Empress*
ALARBUS *oldest son of Tamora, killed by Titus*	---
DEMESTRIUS and CHIRON *younger sons of Tamora*	HELICATES and SAPHONUS *first and second son of Aetiopissa*
AARON *a Moor in service of Tamora, her lover*	MORIAN [literally: Moor]
Other Goths *forming an army*	[mentioned in the stage directions]

Shakespeare's *Titus Andronicus* will be analysed first, to allow a contrastive and detailed comparison to its adaptation on the German stage.

On his return from the war against the Goths, the victorious general Titus declines his brother Marcus' offer of becoming the new emperor in favour of Saturnius, who shall marry Lavinia and be his son-in-law. To make amends for his fallen sons, Titus "religiously" sacrifices Queen Tamora's oldest son Alarbus, despite her pleas for him to desist from this "cruel, irreligious piety" (1.1.133). New problems arise when Bassanius, brother of Saturnius, threatens to elope with Lavinia because she was promised to him earlier. Although the inconstant Saturnius prefers Queen Tamora and slights Lavinia, Titus remains loyal. To celebrate the double wedding between the emperor and Tamora, and Lavinia and Bassanius, a hunt is organised. This is the opportunity for Tamora's slave and lover Aaron to seek revenge on Titus for the past ill-treatments of the queen and her kin, all of whom become instruments of his machinations. Taking advantage of her sons' passion for Lavinia, he incites Chiron and Demetrius to rape the girl in the woods ("The woods are ruthless, dreadful, deaf and dull", 1.1.628).

On the day of the hunt, Titus mentions a bad dream that had troubled his sleep, unconsciously predicting the looming tragedy. Stirred up by Aaron, Tamora addresses Bassanius and Lavinia so provokingly that they respond in a similar tone. Chiron and Demetrius assist their mother, kill Bassanius and throw the corpse into a pit (probably the trapdoor of the Elizabethan apron stage), into which Aaron lures Titus' sons Quintus and Martius to shift the blame onto them. A forged letter and a bag of gold further attest their alleged plot to kill Bassanius. Devastated, Titus asks to be their bail. Tamora promises to intercede for him but instead promotes his doom: Lucius is banned from Rome, and Chiron and Demetrius violate Lavinia, cut out her tongue and mutilate her hands. In a later scene, the girl reveals her plight by turning the pages of Ovid's *Metamorphoses* to the tale of Philomel, who was raped and maimed like her.

Next, Titus complies with the terrible order to sacrifice his hand in exchange for his sons, but all he obtains are the heads of the decapitated sons and his amputated hand, on which he swears revenge.[148] While his exiled son Lucius organises an army of Goths ready to assault Rome, Titus sends his grandson to warn Aaron, Chiron and Demetrius with a mysterious message. In the interim, a nurse comes in with Tamora's new-born baby and asks Aaron to kill it, because its black skin would reveal the father's identity. Instead, he kills the nurse as "a deed of policy" (4.2.150) to save the baby and entreats Tamora's sons to keep the secret or else their mother's reputation will be ruined.

As they plan their attack, Titus and his kinsmen intercept a clown on his way to the tribune. Marcus suggests employing him as messenger to the emperor with a supposed supplication enveloped around a knife, i.e. a declaration of war. Thus, the unconscious clown falls victim to Saturnius' wrath and is hanged. After that, Tamora comes up with an idea to "temper him [Titus] with all the art" (4.4.108) by dressing up as the allegories of Revenge, Murder and Rape with her sons. As soon as Tamora leaves, Titus stops playing along in the travesty and slaughters Demetrius and Chiron on stage. Meanwhile in the Goths' camp, Aaron is made prisoner and forced to reveal the truth. In Rome, Titus, the emperor and his wife discuss a pretend truce over dinner. Unaware of the precedents, Saturnius answers Titus' question about what a father should do with a raped daughter by saying that "the girl should not survive her shame" (5.3.40), at which Titus stabs Lavinia. He then reveals not only what Tamora's sons did but also that the meal the empress has just enjoyed was made of their flesh. In a climax of violence, Titus kills Tamora and is stabbed by Saturnius, who is then killed by Lucius. In the end, the new emperor Lucius tells the whole story a third time, sentences Aaron to die of starvation and throws Tamora's body to the beasts as fitting punishment for a life "beastly and devoid of pity" (5.3.198).

Considering the tragic ending of Shakespeare's stoic hero, G. K. Hunter summarises the message of the play as follows: excessive social altruism comes at a high cost, especially when rational obedience is opposed to emotions.[149] Moreover, Bullough points out that the structure of *Titus Andronicus* works with a subtle balance and contrast between groups (Romans and Goths), persons (Titus – Aaron, Lavinia – Tamora) and incidents (Tamora pleads in vain for her son as Titus does later for his own offspring; the initial murder is avenged by rape and again heightened by murder and cannibalism). The only imbalance is found in Aaron's son being spared, thus showing the greater mercifulness of the Romans.[150] This inner structure of horrid events is by far less sophisticated in the German version but still partly retraceable.

---

[148] The subsequent scene involving the killing of a fly – metaphorically in lieu of Aaron and Tamora – is an addition much discussed among scholars and not present in the German play. Perhaps it did not yet exist when the itinerant players departed from England.
[149] See G. K. Hunter, "Shakespeare and the traditions of tragedy", in Wells, ed., *The Cambridge Companion to Shakespeare Studies*, pp. 123–41, p. 133.
[150] See Bullough, vol. 7, pp. 29–30.

In Act 1 of *Von Tito Andronico*, Vespasianus, son of Titus Andronicus, praises his father's valour in the recent war and suggests he should become emperor, using words that resemble those said by Marcus in Shakespeare, but with a simpler style to match the less complex psychology of the characters. While Saturnius agrees with the proposal and nobly says: "How fair the tribune [Marcus] speaks to calm my thoughts!" (*Titus Andronicus*, 1.1.46), in the German rendition the nameless emperor angrily voices his greed for power thus: "Was? solte nun TITUS ANDRONICUS die Krone für mich auff sein Häupt setzen / nein / nimmermehr muß das geschehen."[151] In both versions, the wise general refuses the crown and is recompensed with the prospect of becoming the emperor's son-in-law. However, the promise to marry Titus' daughter, conveniently called Andronica, is forgotten as soon as the new monarch sees the African queen Aetiopissa, presumably from Ethiopia as the name suggests, but nonetheless fair-skinned, who was made a prisoner together with her sons. Within her entourage there is also *Morian* – i.e. the 'Moor' without a proper name – disguised as a simple servant so as not to reveal his secret relationship with the queen. In a soliloquy with strong narrative traits, Morian expounds both his plan to take revenge on the Romans and the murky past of Aetiopissa, who poisoned her husband when the latter started to suspect her unfaithfulness.

AARON.
Now climbeth Tamora Olympus' top,
Safe out of fortune's shot; and sits aloft,
Secure of thunder's crack or lightning flash;
Advanced above pale envy's threatening reach.
As when the golden sun salutes the morn,
And, having gilt the ocean with his beams,
Gallops the zodiac in his glistering coach,
And overlooks the highest-peering hills;
So Tamora:
Upon her wit doth earthly honour wait,
And virtue stoops and trembles at her frown.
Then, Aaron, arm thy heart, and fit thy
  thoughts,
To mount aloft with thy imperial mistress,
And mount her pitch, whom thou in triumph
  long
Hast prisoner held, fetter'd in amorous chains
And faster bound to Aaron's charming eyes
Than is Prometheus tied to Caucasus.
Away with slavish weeds and servile thoughts!
I will be bright, and shine in pearl and gold,
To wait upon this new-made empress.
To wait, said I? to wanton with this queen,
This goddess, this Semiramis, this nymph,

MORIAN.
Laß mich auch nun diese alten Lumpen ablegen / weil ich sehe / daß meine heimliche Bulinne Gunst und Grad beim Keyser hat.
Ziehet den alten Rock abe.
Denn ich hoffe sie wird noch vielmehr grosser Gnad und GRATIA bey ihm erlangen / und mit ihrem schmeichel und liebkosen zu wege bringen / daß er sie lieb gewinne / und Kaeyserin in Rom werde / wenn dann das also keme / so mache ich den Keyser warlich zum Hanrey / und treib vielmehr meine Lust und Frewde mit ihr / dann der Keyser. Aber ein jeglicher meynte / ich were nur der Königinnen Diener / nein warlich / ich bin allzeit ir hemilicher Buhle gewest / und vielmehr bey ihr geschlaffen / den der König auß Morenlandt ihr Gemahl / daß er auch zuletzt Unrath an mir und der Königinnen vermercket [...] Nam derhalben VENIAM, und vergab ihme damit in ein Becher Wein / ihren König / daß ich also meinen freyen Paß wieder zu ihr hette: Ja viele / die meine Bulinne und mich nicht gerne da sahen / habe ich heimlich in ihre Schalffkammer bey Nachte ermordet / tausent

---

[151] *SW*, vol. 1, p. 463. Translation: 'What? Should Titus Andronicus wear the crown instead of me? No, that shall never happen.'

This siren, that will charm Rome's Saturnine, And see his shipwreck and his commonweal's.[152]	und tausent Schelmerey unnd Rauberey hab ich vollenbracht / und düncket mich gleichwol / daß ich noch nicht genug Schelmerey gethan habe [...].[153]

Compared to Aaron's lyrical soliloquy full of mythological references, Morian's speech is longer and more straightforward, to the point of visualising some lines that are only alluded to in Shakespeare. As June Schlueter points out, Aaron's metaphorical words "Away with slavish weeds and servile thoughts!" are acted out in a literal change of costume by Morian, as the stage direction says, "*Ziehet den alten Rock abe.*"[154] The quotes also show that the German play partly follows Shakespeare very closely and partly adds new aspects. Morian's lines "tausent und tausent Schelmerey unnd Rauberey hab ich vollenbracht / und düncket mich gleichwol / daß ich noch nicht genug Schelmerey gethan habe" are a free translation of Aaron's words "Tut, I have done a thousand dreadful things / As willingly as one would kill a fly, / And nothing grieves me heartily indeed / But that I cannot do ten thousand more."[155] It is interesting to notice that Aaron's final confession of his wickedness in the last act of *Titus Andronicus* is placed right at the beginning of the German play to introduce Morian. Moreover, the self-characterised villain neither wants to avenge the missing sacrifice of Alarbus nor the ill-treatment of the queen, but only seeks revenge out of haughtiness and the pleasure of making the emperor a cuckold.

In Act 2, passion starts to obfuscate reason, just as Morian had envisaged. The emperor marries Aetiopissa despite his prior engagement to Andronica, and her sons Helicates and Saphonus develop an insane desire to possess the girl. While Shakespeare's Aaron unfolds his wicked plan step-by-step, exploiting the others without their knowledge, Morian immediately suggests killing Andronica's husband and raping her during a hunting party organised by Titus. Apart from cuts and discrepancies like these, the plot follows Shakespeare up to this point, but the style differs, as the following description of the day of the hunt in Act 3 illustrates.

---

[152] *Titus Andronicus*, 2.1.2–27.

[153] *SW*, vol. 1, p. 467. Translation: 'MORIAN. Let me take off these old rags, because I see that my secret lover has gained favour and grace with the emperor. *He takes off the old garments*. Indeed, I hope she will obtain even more grace and favour with him and flatter and cajole him so much that he will fall in love with her and make her empress of Rome. Once that is achieved, I will make the emperor a cuckold and enjoy her body and company much more than the emperor. Everybody thinks I am just the queen's servant, but actually I have been her lover all this time and have slept with her so much more often than the King of Africa, her husband, that he ultimately grew suspicious [...] Therefore, she procured some poison and gave it to him, her king, in a goblet of wine, so that I could freely have access to her. Yeah, many who frowned upon my lover and me, I have killed at night in their bedchamber. I have compassed thousands of devilments and robberies and I think I have not done enough [...].'

[154] See June Schlueter, "English Actors in Kassel, Germany, during Shakespeare's Time", *Medieval and Renaissance Drama in England* 10 (1988), pp. 238–61, p. 251.

[155] *Titus Andronicus*, 5.1.144–7.

TITUS. The hunt is up, the morn is bright and grey
The fields are fragrant and the woods are green:
Uncouple here and let us make a bay
And wake the emperor and his lovely bride,
And rouse the prince, and ring a hunter's peal,
That all the court may echo with that noise.
Sons let it be your charge, as it is ours,
To attend the emperor's person carefully.
I have been troubled in my sleep last night,
But dawning day new comfort hath inspired.
[…]
DEMETRIUS. *(aside)* Chiron, we hunt not, we, with horse and hound,
But hope to pluck a dainty doe to ground.[156]

TITUS ANDRONICUS. O wie lieblich und freundlich singen jetzt die Vögel in den Lüfften, / ein jeglich suchet jetzt seine Nahrung / und die Jaget ist auch schon angefangen / in Frewde und Herrligkeit. Aber mein Hertz ist mir dennoch beängstiget und beschweret den ich diese vergangen Nacht / solch ein schrecklichen Traum gehabt / und nicht weiß was er mir bedeuten wirdt. Nun muss ich wiederumb zum Käyser reiten / der persönlich bey der Jagt vorhanden. […]
ANDRONICA. […] schöner unnd lustiger Jaget habe ich mein Tage nicht gesehen.[157]

Shakespeare's passage, written in iambic pentameter, is filled with figurative analogies about the hunt, taken up as a malefic metaphor in Chiron and Demetrius' intention to chase their own "dainty doe", i.e. Titus' daughter. The German prose lacks this poetic and meaningful juxtaposition but preserves the contrast between the beautiful natural environment, echoed in Andronica's words that she never saw a more delightful hunt, and the ominous dream ("schrecklichen Traum") preannouncing the immediate catastrophe. Interestingly, the singing birds mentioned by Titus in the German version are part of Tamora's lines in Shakespeare: "The birds chant melody on every bush" (2.2.13) in a sort of collage of quotations.

Andronica and her consort meet Aetiopissa alone in the woods and are fiercely attacked by her. While in Shakespeare the audience is acquainted with Bassanius and his love for Lavinia from the beginning, the German play does not explain who this husband is nor when Andronica married him, since she was still betrothed to the emperor in Act 1. It is possible that the English Comedians would orally add some information missing in the printed play. Moreover, the sequence of scenes is altered in the German adaptation since the empress is not informed beforehand by her lover about the evil plan, as in Shakespeare; instead, she meets him after the quarrel with Titus' daughter, which thus occurs without a real cause apart from her eponymous haughtiness. Enraged by Andronica's reaction to her

---

[156] *Titus Andronicus*, 2.2.1–10, 20–6.
[157] *SW*, vol. 1, p. 476. Translation: 'TITUS. Oh, how sweetly and pleasantly the birds sing in the air, each seeking its food, and the hunt has begun in joy and splendour. But still my heart is uneasy and oppressed because I had a most dreadful dream last night, and do not know what it means. Now I must ride again to the emperor, who is present at the hunt in person. […] ANDRONICA. […] I have never seen a more beautiful and entertaining hunt in my life.'

affront, she orders her sons to stab the nameless husband. After threatening to kill the girl single-handedly, the empress prefers to leave her at her sons' mercy, well knowing that they will rape her. This is an instance of heightened cruelty in the German version, because Aetiopissa shows a sadistic pleasure in torturing her rival and then, as if nothing had happened, desires to make love to Morian, who is more devoted to Mars than to Venus, just like Aaron is to Saturn.[158]

Then, the empress imprisons Titus' sons on the charge of having affronted her, replacing the false accusation of murder, which was brought about by Aaron in the excised pit episode. The rest of the scene follows Shakespeare: Morian informs Titus that his sons will be released in exchange for his hand and tells the audience in an aside that his sons are already dead. In a narrative monologue, Helicates brags about having cut Andronica's tongue and hands off so that she would not be able to reveal who raped her. The narrative solution taken from Shakespeare replaces a very difficult scene to stage, namely the rape and mutilation of the girl. Upon receiving the heads of his decapitated sons, Titus curses Aetiopissa and addresses his lamentation to his own hand, a particularly gruesome detail. His vow to obtain revenge is enforced by the sight of Andronica, although he does not know who is responsible for her rape. A reference to the girl's melodious voice, now tragically muted, is present in both versions:

| TITUS. [...] delightful engine of her thoughts That blabbed them with such pleasing eloquence, Is torn from forth that pretty hollow cage Where, like a sweet melodious bird, it sung Sweet varied notes, enchanting every ear.[159] | TITUS. [...] wenn ich aber dich gegen mich so fröhlich lauffende kommen sahe / mit deiner Lauten / mir für Frewde zu empfahen / vertriebest du mir damit meine wunderliche Schmertzen / auch durch deine liebliche Rede / erfrischetest du offte mein altes Hertze.[160] |

In Act 5, Andronica writes the names of her rapists in the sand with a stick held between her stumps – a scene requiring less knowledge of the classics on the part of the audience compared to Shakespeare's solution of the mystery, which references Ovid's *Metamorphoses*.[161] Instead, visualisation through pantomime and

---

[158] Here the play quotes Shakespeare almost verbatim. Cf. "AARON. [...] Madam, though Venus govern your desires, / Saturn is dominator over mine" (*Titus*, 2.3.33–4) and "MORIAN. Nein schöne Käyserin / ob euch jetzt wol die Göttin VENUS gewaltig thut reitzen zu ihren Spiele / so regieret / und hat mich doch wiederum eingenommen Gott MARS" (*SW*, vol. 1, p. 482). Translation: 'MORIAN. No, fair empress. Although Venus is alluring you strongly towards her pleasures, I am ruled and possessed by the god Mars.'

[159] *Titus Andronicus*, 3.1.83–87.

[160] *SW*, vol. 1, p. 492. Translation: '[...] when I saw you running joyfully to meet me with your lute, you made me forget my pain, and refreshed my old heart with your sweet innocent talk.'

[161] In Ovid's *Metamorphoses*, Book VI, Philomela is raped and rendered mute by Tereus, her sister Procne's husband. To inform her sister, she weaves the scene into a tapestry. Then the women kill Tereus' son Itys, cook him and serve him to his father like Titus does with

non-verbal communication was a more reliable narrative vehicle than language, and therefore effective for the adaptation.[162] Informed about the wrongdoers' identity, Titus swears revenge on his hand and his sons' heads, evidently still lying on stage, and declares war against the treacherous emperor with mercenaries recruited by Vespasianus.[163] Hearing the news, the emperor orders the messenger to be hanged against all military conventions. Again, the sequence of events is different: in Shakespeare, Titus does not wait for his daughter's abusers to be revealed but sends his grandson to deliver an obscure warning to Demetrius and Chiron. Later, the emperor Saturnius receives a declaration of war from an ill-used clown and has him hanged, like the ambassador in the German play. It is interesting that the clown is left out and replaced by a messenger here, given that most of the other plays in *ECUT* feature a Pickelhering. Even if there is no direct mention of a clown, he might all the same have appeared with impromptu scenes or in the interlude.

Act 6 presents the supplementary plot strand of the illegitimate child and the killed nurse already mentioned in Shakespeare and imbued with details of violence. For instance, Morian secures Helicates and Saphonus' silence by making them ashamed of their mother's excessive lust, instead of appealing to their interest in her reputation, and saves the baby not out of pity but to raise it in a devilish manner. Before he can do that, however, he is made prisoner by Vespasianus, forced to confess his guilt, and hanged, but his son is spared, anticipating Shakespeare's ending. A few details differ in the empress's scheme too: Aetiopissa

---

the empress's sons. The Shakespearean Titus even says: "For worse than Philomel you us'd my daughter, / And worse than Procne I will be reveng'd." (*Titus Andronicus*, 5.2.203–4). Before Tereus can seek revenge, the gods decide to intervene in Ovid's tale, and turn all three into birds: Procne into a swallow, Philomela into a nightingale, and Tereus into a hoopoe.

[162] The revelation of the rapists' identity in *Von Tito Andronico* does not follow Shakespeare but hybridises another tale from the *Metamorphoses* to facilitate the reception, as Brauneck points out (*SW*, vol. 6, p. 38). In Book I of the *Metamorphoses*, Io, who was turned into a heifer by Zeus, uses a similar stratagem to make herself recognised to her father: she writes her name onto the sand with her hoof.

[163] In this scene, the 1620 play helps reconstruct Shakespeare's original or at least some missing details, which were probably slightly different from the Folio edition. As Jonathan Bate observes, when the heads of Titus' sons are brought on stage in scene 3.1, Marcus utters "Alas, poor heart, that kiss is comfortless / As frozen water to a starved snake" (*Titus Andronicus*, 3.1.251–2), referring to Lavinia. The implied stage direction is not included in any quarto or folio, therefore Dr Johnson assumed that Lavinia kissed Marcus, while nineteenth-century editors changed the stage direction to '*Lavinia kisses Titus*'. What neither of them recognised is revealed in the gruesome stage direction of the German version: the tongueless woman expresses her grief by kissing the severed heads of her dead brothers and is therefore understandably pitied by Marcus. Marcus' comment makes more sense in this context than in the other interpretations, given that both Marcus and Titus might have derived some comfort from her kiss whereas the decapitated youths cannot. See the introduction to *The Arden Shakespeare Titus Andronicus*, edited by Jonathan Bate, p. 47.

sends her sons in disguise to murder Titus but does not mention dressing up as allegories or accompanying them like Tamora. Titus recognises his enemies, cuts their throats and floods the stage with blood – a scene made possible with the aid of 'special effects' taken from the Elizabethan theatre practice, like hiding a pig bladder filled with animal blood under the costumes[164] – and announces he will serve them in a pie to their mother.

In the final act, the emperor accepts Titus' invitation to a banquet, because he believes that Aetiopissa's sons convinced him to cease the war. The fact that the host is still wearing a blood-stained cloth does not bode well but this strong item of visualisation leaves the characters on stage unmoved. During the meal, Titus kills his daughter to put an end to her pain (a scene that does not make as much sense as in Shakespeare's version, where Titus elicits the suggestion to assassinate a raped daughter from the unknowing emperor), blames Aetiopissa for the deed, reveals the appalling ingredient of the pie and stabs her. The emperor thereupon kills Titus and is slain by Vespasianus, who is proclaimed new ruler, as in the English play. Differently from Shakespeare, the German play ends in Vespasianus' sorrow, whereas Lucius punishes Aaron and the empress.

It appears evident that *Eine sehr klägliche Tragaedia von Tito Andronico und der hoffertigen Kaeyserin* memorialises the Shakespearean play and is hybridised with other sources. Manfred Brauneck claims that it is an adaptation of an anonymous English play with the same title, *The Very Lamentable Tragedy of Titus Andronicus and the Haughty Empress*. This would account for some otherwise inexplicable differences, for example that the haughty Empress is not queen of the Goths, like Shakespeare's Tamora, but an Ethiopian monarch called Aetiopissa as in the anonymous pre-text. Since the empress's lover is a *Morian* ('Moor'), the provenance from an African country is already given.[165] The motive for the

---

[164] See the introduction to *The Arden Shakespeare Titus Andronicus* edited by Jonathan Bate, who offers further details on staging techniques.

[165] Jan Vos's Dutch rendition of the subject matter, entitled *Aran en Titus, of Wraak en Weerwraak* ('Aran and Titus, or Revenge and Counter-revenge' (1641), features an African queen too, though the focus is shifted from the queen to the conflict between Aaron and Titus. See W. L. Braekman, "The relationship of Shakespeare's *Titus Andronicus* to the German play of 1620 and to Jan Vos's play 'Aran en Titus'", *Studia Germanica Gandensia* 10 (1968), pp. 7–77. Being half-way between the two countries from a geographical and cultural point of view, the Netherlands had always been a first point of contact between England and Germany. Since plots for new dramas were often drawn from English, German and Dutch sources, Anston Bosman termed this mixture "intertheater". His concept to describe the theatrical system developed by the English Comedians in-between English and German theatre is based on the idea of "interlanguage", which is taken from applied linguistics and refers to an intermediary stage during language acquisition. See "Renaissance Intertheater and the Staging of *Nobody*", *ELH* 71 (2004), pp. 555–85, p. 565. In this sense, "intertheater" differs from my concept of intercultural theatricality, because it does not consider other influences apart from England and Germany, e.g. Italy.

queen's revenge is also different, because in the German versions the sacrifice of her son Alarbus is not present.[166]

On the one hand, adaptation includes the reduction of scenes and lines, and consequently also of figures. All the minor characters are missing in the German play: Alarbus is excised, Bassanius appears merely as 'Husband' in Act 2, without having been formerly introduced in any way, and only the heads of Quintus and Martius are seen on stage, in order to diminish the speaking parts and avoid the complicated plan with the pit/trapdoor devised by Shakespeare's Aaron. When refined machinery was not available to the itinerant players, such incidents had to be sacrificed in favour of narration.

On the other hand, some turning points of the plot are expanded, for instance the re-iterated insistence on the queen's sexual appetite. Other episodes, which are only alluded to verbally in Shakespeare, are visualised for the sake of clarity, like the change of clothes and status in Morian's soliloquy. The decision on whether to perform narrative monologues or merely to summarise the action in speech evidently depended on an effort and effect relationship.

Given the similar content, scenic structure and even verbatim transpositions from Shakespeare in the German play, the question arises of whether the English Comedians had the original text with them when they arrived in Germany and subsequently translated it, or if they only inserted a conglomerate of quotes into a skeletal script of the play, to which they added impromptu scenes. Either way, the physical and graphic quality of the tragedy allowed for visualisation without words, which accounts for its exportability and success. The references to physicality, such as in the scene of the gruesome banquet, and improvisation, which probably provided the information missing in the text, for example when Andronica got married, recall Commedia dell'Arte techniques. Is it therefore possible to speak of influences of Commedia dell'Arte in the German tragedy, even if the short Shakespearean subplot with the clown was excised from the German play?

A first point of contact with Commedia dell'Arte is found in the detailed stage direction right at the beginning of the German play. It describes the antecedent

---

[166] In this context, Wilhelm Creizenach points out that the German rendition could be based on an older English dramatisation of a romance, now lost, known to both Shakespeare and the Dutch playwright Jan Vos. See Creizenach, p. 4. Another option supported by Albert Cohn and E. K. Chambers could be that Shakespeare's 1623 Folio version is the result of many reworkings, one of which laid the foundation for the German rendition. See Cohn, p. CXII, and Chambers, *The Elizabethan Stage*, vol. 2, p. 126. For instance, Cohn argues that there is a piece entitled *Titus and Vespasian*, cited repeatedly by Henslowe as "Tittus and Vespacia" between 20 April 1591 and 8 May 1592, while on 23 January 1593 he mentions a "titus & ondronicus" (a misspelling of Andronicus), perhaps to distinguish it from the other play. See Cohn, p. CXII, and *Henslowe's Diary*, edited by R. A. Foakes, pp. 17–18. As there is no character named Vespasian in Shakespeare, whereas in the 1620 collection Vespasianus is the protagonist's son and one of the main characters, this play suggests itself as one possible source apart from Shakespeare.

facts, the current situation and the relationships among the characters as well as their appearance and sentiments:

> *Jetzt kömpt herauß VESPASIANUS und hat die Römische Krone in der Hand. TITUS ANDRONICUS hat ein Lorbeer Krantz auff seinem Häupte / auch kömpft der KEYSER / aber damalen war er noch nicht Römischer KEYSER. Auch die KÖNIGIN AUSS MORENLANDT / welche schön und weiß / sampt ihren zween Söhnen: und der MORIAN / welcher schwartz und geringe Gewandt uber seine prechtige Kleider gezogen / und welcher der KÖNIGINNEN Diener / und heimlich mit ihr buhlet. Diese viere aber hat TITUS ANDRONICUS gefangen genommen. Auch ist da die ANDRONICA.*[167]

While in Shakespeare the necessary background information is given through dialogues, the German play summarises the prequel in the manner of the short plot descriptions of the Commedia dell'Arte *scenari* (*argomento*) and would have been acted out without a precise text. Furthermore, the addition of Aetiopissa's promiscuity shifts the focus of Morian's revenge from destroying Titus to making the emperor a cuckold. However base, outwitting the emperor is Morian's strongest motive. This typical theme of Commedia dell'Arte comedies well-suited for a farce is then turned into a revenge tragedy.

Other elements recalling the skeletal plots are the often mutilated or missing spoken parts (simply referred to as "etc.")[168] and the unusual structure of eight acts, sometimes as short as scenes. Thus, the German tragedy bears traces of a residual improvisation practice in the early itinerant theatre, which accounts for the discrepancies between the plays, such as additions and reductions. It should not be forgotten that between the probable date of composition of *Titus Andronicus* and the publication of the German version more than twenty years had passed, during which the play travelled and went through numerous adaptations shaped to and by the circumstances.

Apart from Shakespeare's model and echoes of Commedia dell'Arte, the adapted play features both the clear-cut division into good and evil characters and the strong moral message of the moralities, although it does not present the disguised allegories which haunt the Shakespearean Titus. As in *Von Julio und Hyppolita,* the causes of the revenge in *Von Tito Andronico* are ultimately lust and

---

[167] *SW*, vol. 1, p. 461. Translation: 'Enter VESPASIANUS with the Roman crown in his hands. TITUS ANDRONICUS is wearing a laurel wreath. Enter the EMPEROR too, who was not Roman EMPEROR at that time. There is the QUEEN OF AFRICA, who is beautiful and white, with her two sons and the black MORIAN, who is wearing simple clothes over his splendid attire and who is the servant of the Queen and her secret lover. These four have been made prisoners by TITUS ANDRONICUS. Enter ANDRONICA as well.'

[168] E.g. *SW*, vol. 1, p. 484: "TITUS ANDRONICUS. O mein lieber MORIAN / wie fröhlich Botschafft bringestu mir. Ja wenn die Käyserin auch beyde Hände begehrete wolte ich sie gerne abhawen / aber jetzt wil ich meine Handt abhawen / und sie dir ubergeben. etc." Translation: 'TITUS. Oh, my dear MORIAN, what happy news you bring to me. Even if the empress desired both hands, I would cut them off gladly. But now I will chop off my hand and give it to you. Etc.'

haughtiness – a recurrent theme in the collection since haughty Haman, too, almost spells doom for Esther. This time, however, the character constellation of a contemptuous male character opposed to a modest woman is reversed. In the German tragedy, the empress is haughty while Titus is demure and does not give her a valid reason for hating him due to the excised murder of Alarbus.

Moreover, the adaptation process required innovative additions in order for scenes to be visualised. Self-characterisations were expanded in narrative sequences and motives for actions were made clearer by acting them out directly, like Morian's change of costume. Some episodes were hybridised with more 'visual' details, such as the scene of Andronica writing the names of her perpetrators like the Ovidian Io instead of identifying with Philomel. For these reasons, *Von Tito Andronico* is more than just a mutilated version of *Titus Andronicus*; it is a not fully edited theatrical script in constant transformation to meet the taste and expectations of the audience.

6.5. The Clown's Domain: *Pickelheringspiele* and *Singspiele*

Besides the six comedies and two tragedies, *ECUT* contains two *Pickelheringspiele* or Pickelhering plays and five *Singspiele* or musical interludes, simply called *Auffzüge* (acts). Both genres belong to the category of interludes or postludes in the style of Elizabethan jigs, which were not only dances but originally interrupted or followed the main action on stage with farcical plots and clownish characters. The only difference is that the *Singspiel* is completely sung as in the German Meistersinger tradition and the *Fastnachtspiele*. These sketches gave the actors, and especially the clown Pickelhering, the opportunity to display their renowned acrobatic skills accompanied by music to entertain the audience with dances, pantomime or singing that was only loosely connected to the play. According to Fredén, the frequent repetitions and occasional references to sung parts (like "fa la la" or "hum-hum") in the *Pickelheringspiele* of *ECUT* indicate that they derived from jigs and were then turned into skits in prose.[169] However, it is difficult to state from which model they derived as their content is very much removed from any recognisable original. This is also due to the fact that only few written records of English jigs remain.[170] Instead, there is a clear connection between these interludes or *lazzi*, the tales of Italian literature and the 'types' of Commedia dell'Arte, which makes this genre particularly interesting. As in numerous *scenari* and *novelle*, the most frequent themes of the *Singspiele*, and subsequently of the *Pickelheringspiele*, are: a) the adultery of an unfaithful wife with a clever beau, scholar, soldier or clown; b) foolish old men wooing a young

---

[169] See Fredén, op. cit., p. 256.
[170] Only two English jigs – *Singing Simpkin* and *The Black Man* – are preserved, as Charles Read Baskerville asserts in *The Elizabethan Jig and Related Song Drama* (Chicago: University of Chicago Press, 1929), p. 76.

woman or a prostitute supposed to be honest; and c) termagant wives domineering over their unfortunate husbands.[171]

Given their brevity, immediacy and physicality, the *Pickelheringspiele* and *Singspiele* were performed by the itinerant players from the first phase onwards. In the course of time, the prevalent orality of these genres was substituted by a wish to have them in written form during the literarisation phase, so that various troupes could draw on a vast repertoire of skits adaptable to any circumstance. Owing to the popularity of the clown, these versatile byplays soon reached the same status as regular plays or could be inserted as subplots in other plays.

Pickelheringspiele

Ein lustig Pickelherings Spiel / von der schönen Maria und alten Hanrey ('An amusing Pickelhering play of the beautiful Maria and the old cuckold') and *Ein ander lustig Pickelherings Spiel / darinnen er mit einen Stein gar lustige Possen machet* ('Another merry Pickelhering play, in which he makes merry pastime with a stone') of *ECUT* 1620 are the first farces ever written in German with Pickelhering as the main protagonist, as Willem Schrickx observes.[172] Pickelhering even gives his name to a new hybrid genre, the *Pickelheringspiel*, which makes use of a variety of motifs, themes and characters from different cultural backgrounds.

The plot of IX. *Ein lustig Pickelherings Spiel / von der schönen Maria und alten Hanrey* (subsequently abbreviated to the 'Pickelhering play of the *Hanrey*') revolves around the unfaithful Maria and her overcredulous husband, who is proved wrong by a series of love tests. In this farce, the stingy, lustful and wrongheaded doter must learn to his cost to trust his well-meaning friends rather than a seductive woman and an opportunist servant. The fact that the characters of this farce are comparable to 'types' can already be evinced from the list of dramatis personae, in which only two characters have a proper name: Maria, the bride, and Peter, the son, while the others are described by their role or principal trait: Hans Pickelhering, the old cuckold, the bride's father, the soldier and the neighbour.[173]

---

[171] Commedia dell'Arte and the *Singspiele* are further interlinked because their development occurred in parallel to 'higher' forms. As Johannes Bolte explains, the *Singspiele* were the popular equivalent of opera, as their almost contemporaneous emergence in 1594 shows, but with different functions. Whereas opera emulated the musical drama of antiquity, experienced players made use of *Singspiele* for the sake of light entertainment, i.e. stanzas sung to famous tunes dealing with low comedy and droll stories (*Schwank*), which would later evolve into operetta. See Bolte, *Die Singspiele der englischen Komödianten und ihrer Nachfolger in Deutschland, Holland und Skandinavien* (Hamburg and Leipzig: Voß, 1893), p. 1. In a similar way, Commedia dell'Arte was connected to its more serious counterpart, Commedia erudita, and functioned as simplified version of serious opera.

[172] See Schrickx, *Foreign Envoys and Travelling Players in the Age of Shakespeare and Jonson*, p. 225.

[173] See *SW*, vol. 1, p. 523.

In the short expository first act, the old cuckold tells his 'faithful' servant Hans Pickelhering to prepare everything for his imminent wedding to the 'pure virgin' Maria. The incipit of the play provides an idea of the irreverence of the clown and of the musicality of the dialogues with elements of the *Singspiel*, such as repeated phrases and short lines.

> ALTER HANREY. Holla / holla / mein getrewer Diener Hans mein Lieber Diener wo bist du?
> HANS. Hie hie alter Narr bin ich ["fiction-external communication"].
> ALTER. Wie sagstu Hans? Mein Hans wie sagstu?
> HANS. Wie solte ich sagen / ich sagte alter Herr. *Ad spectatores*. Alter Schelm.
> ALTER. Höre Hans mein getrewer Hans / morgen werd ich Hochzeit halten / ja Hochzeit werde ich halten.
> HANS. Hochzeit machen / mein Herr? O sagt mir es doch / was wird es doch für eine Braut seyn / lieber Herr?
> ALTER. Meine Braut ist noch eine reine Jungfraw / Ja eine gar schöne Jungfraw / kennestu nicht die schöne Mariam von langen Margte / daß das wird die Braut seyn / mein getrewer Hans?
> HANS. *Ad spectatores*. Ho ho die offenbahre Hure / von welcher jederman zu sagen weiß.[174]

Switching from "fiction-internal" to asides and "fiction-external communication" (marked in the quote), as Joel B. Lande calls this phenomenon,[175] the disrespectful clown informs the audience that his master is a fool to marry a renowned strumpet but keeps him in the dark about her reputation for comedy's sake. After that, Hans Pickelhering returns with the bride-to-be Maria and her father. Just as the wooer's affected declarations of sexual ardour and well-preserved youthfulness do not match his age and appearance, Maria's declarations that she is in love are contradicted by her non-verbal gesture of spitting on the ground whenever her fiancée kisses her (visualisation). The scene's humour thus derives from the clash between the old man's distorted perception of romantic love and the evident reality of which all other characters and the audience are aware, making his naive misconception the more absurd.

The longer, second act accommodates the whole dramatic development with the arrival of two new characters: the old man's son, Peter, and Maria's former

---

[174] Ibid., pp. 525–6. Translation: 'OLD CUCKOLD. Hey there, hey there, my faithful servant Hans, my dear servant, where are you? HANS. Here, here I am, old fool. OLD MAN. What do you say? My Hans, what do you say? HANS. What I should, I said 'old master'. *Aside*. Old idiot. OLD MAN. Listen Hans, my faithful Hans: Tomorrow I am going to get married, yes, I am going to get married. HANS. Get married, my lord? Oh, do tell me, who will be the bride, dear lord? OLD MAN. My spouse is still a pure virgin, yes, a beautiful virgin. Do you know the beautiful Maria from the long market? She, she will be the bride, my faithful Hans. HANS. *Aside*. Ho ho, that renowned strumpet everybody talks about.'

[175] The concept is taken from Joel B. Lande, *Persistence of Folly*, p. 70 and applied to this play to show the multiple layers of comic speech.

lover, the destitute soldier. Just returned from a long absence, Peter tries to dissuade his father from taking a notorious whore as a wife, without avail. Meanwhile, Maria is already planning to make her husband a cuckold with the homecoming soldier according to the proverb: "MARIA. Ein harte Nuß, ein stumpfer Zahn, / Ein junges Weib, ein alter Mann / Reimen sich zusammen gar nicht wohl / Ein jeder seines Gleichen freien soll",[176] which sums up the humorous message of the play: an old man should not woo a young woman. While the lovers agree to rob the cuckold and seal their relationship with kisses and dances singing "fa la la la",[177] the jealous husband attacks the soldier but is only mocked for his rusty blade by his physically superior rival in a covert allusion to his impotence. Believing Maria's lies that the stranger is her brother, the deceived husband even apologises and invites the cause of his cuckoldry to be his guest in a scene cognate with the *Singspiel* XI 'Pickelhering in the Chest', presented in the next section. What follows is a comic pantomime: the cuckold walks in front of the dancing lovers; whenever he turns around among numerous "hum-hums", they stop, only to resume their flirting as soon as he walks on.

Eventually, the old man is made suspicious and puts his wife's honesty to the test: he pretends to go on a journey and orders Pickelhering not to admit the soldier into the house. Instead, the money-grabbing servant reveals the plan to Maria, who rewards him with a larger sum than his stingy master and tells the soldier to come to the house. When the husband returns unexpectedly, Pickelhering plays the obedient guardian and sends the husband away, pretending to take him for the soldier. This trick convinces the master of his faithfulness and gains Maria time to hide her lover in a wardrobe. She then feigns to be distressed because she has burnt a bedsheet and spreads it out with Pickelhering's help to show the non-existent hole. While her husband examines it, the soldier escapes behind the sheet. Brauneck notices that this scene constitutes a theatrical challenge on the stage and indicates a certain degree of development in the acting technique of the itinerant players.[178]

Despite the favourable outcome of the first test, the cuckold is persuaded by his neighbour to simulate his own death in order to find out about the true feelings of those he trusts. Surprised to see that only the ill-treated Peter mourns for him while his wife and his servant vulgarly rejoice, the presumed dead comes back to life and scares Maria, the soldier and the drummer Pickelhering on their way to the wedding. In the end, the duped husband is reconciled with his son, forgives his unfaithful wife but beats up his mocking servant, who runs up and down the stage calling him a cuckold.

---

[176] *SW*, vol. 1, p. 532. Translation: 'MARIA. A hard nut, a stub tooth / A young woman, an old man / Do not rhyme well / Everyone should woo the likes of him/her.'
[177] Ibid., p. 535.
[178] *SW*, vol. 6, p. 41.

This *Pickelheringspiel* memorialises and hybridises numerous sources dealing with the same subject in an instance of intercultural theatricality. Firstly, the cuckold (Pantalone) unable to find the secret lover (soldier, bravo/Capitano) hidden behind or inside household items by the sly servant (Zanni) and the unfaithful wife is a plot twist present in many *novelle* by Giovanni Fiorentino and Giovanni Francesco Straparola, and in Commedia dell'Arte.[179] Furthermore, the pretend faithful servant who does not open the door to his master – for example because the lover is inside the house – and thus reverses the power relations in a carnivalesque way, is a common motif of popular theatre. For instance, in the *scenario L'abbattimento di Zanni* ('Zanni's Despodency' 1628/32), edited by Basilio Locatelli, there is a similar scene: Pantalone wants to sleep with the Capitano's wife and orders his servant Zanni to enter the house and let him in. Once inside, Zanni enjoys the woman himself and leaves Pantalone waiting outside with gross excuses, for which he is punished later.[180]

Secondly, the idea of a love test including a simulated death occurs in various forms throughout German jest literature and English jigs before the rendition of the *Pickelheringspiel*, as Fredén explains.[181] Based on the indirect references to music and dance, like the scene of Maria dancing with the soldier, he argues that this *Pickelheringspiel* derives from an earlier *Singspiel* called *Vom engellentischen Roland* ('The English Roland', 1599), probably an English jig exported to Germany by the itinerant players.[182] This well-known tune with nine rhyming stanzas, on which many German *Singspiele* are modelled, also features a 'dead' husband, but with a different purpose: knowing that Margareta has an affair with the verger Johan, Roland feigns his death to make her regret her unfaithfulness and succeeds in winning her back.[183]

Instances of visualisation, sound and movement also indicate the play's debt to the English jig. Tittmann, for example, compares Pickelhering's use of the drums to Tarlton's jigs with the same instrument.[184] Moreover, the strong visual pantomime of the dancing couple stopping when the cuckold watches them, or the adventurous escape of the lover behind the bedsheet are further examples of the physicality in this play, comparable to Commedia dell'Arte.

Thirdly, Jacob Ayrer, the first native playwright to introduce the *Singspiel* into German literature, memorialised and adapted the plot in his *Comoedia von einem alten Wucherer* ('Comedy of an Old Paramour', 1618).[185] By making the clown

---

[179] Several *novelle* treating of adultery are found, for instance, in Giovanni Fiorentino's *Il Pecorone* (1378), or in Giovanni Francesco Straparola's *Le Tredici piacevoli notti* (1550–3). The theme is also present in *Falstaff*, as discussed in ch. 4.3.
[180] For the whole text see Testaverde, ed., op. cit., pp. 223–30.
[181] See Fredén, op. cit., p. 239.
[182] Ibid.
[183] For the *Singspiel Vom engellentischen Roland* see Johannes Bolte, *Die Singspiele der englischen Komödianten und ihrer Nachfolger in Deutschland, Holland und Skandinavien*.
[184] See Tittmann, *Die Schauspiele der englischen Komödianten in Deutschland*, p. XVI.
[185] Contained in *Ayrers Dramen*, edited by Adelbert von Keller, vol. 4, pp. 2225–77.

the main protagonist in plots of bawdy intrigues and antics, Ayrer cleverly combined the English jig and Commedia dell'Arte actions on the German stage and paved the way for a long-lasting tradition of *Possen* and *Hanswurstiaden* (farces involving Hanswurst).

In contrast to the first Pickelhering play, in which the clown contributes to making someone else a cuckold, in X. *Ein ander lustig Pickelherings Spiel / darinnen er mit einen Stein gar lustige Possen machet* ('Another merry Pickelhering play, in which he makes merry pastime with a stone' subsequently abbreviated to the 'Pickelhering play with a stone'), he is the victim of a trick. In fact, the clown is made a cuckold and a fool with the eponymous stone by his wife and his neighbour Wilhelm. Thus, the audience is given the opportunity to laugh *at* the clown instead of deriding the characters *with* the clown. In particular, the double nature of Pickelhering, who can either be a foolish simpleton or a witty mischief-maker, recalls the polymorphic Zannis of Commedia dell'Arte.

As in the first *Pickelheringspiel*, the structure is bipartite. The first act supplies the exposition, whereas the prank or *burla*, indebted to Italian novelistic literature, is carried out in the second act. At the beginning of the play, the peasant Hans, a naive and gullible clown comparable to Pickelhering, is arguing with his bossy wife about an open door neither of them wants to close. They decide to play a game: the first to speak must stand up to shut the door.[186] When the miller Wilhelm, their neighbour, enters the room and invites the woman to come to his house, the obstinate game of silence is eventually lost by Hans, who entreats her to stay. This incident, added to the fact that his wife spoke of Wilhelm in her sleep, makes him suspect that she might be unfaithful. With the typical expression of rage or surprise connected to Pickelhering, "potz schlapperment", and instances of incomplete lines open to extemporisation ending in "etc.",[187] the jealous husband declares that he will resort to a magician and be transformed into Wilhelm to test his wife's faithfulness. However, the clown's plan is overheard by her and immediately revealed to Wilhelm, who dresses up as a necromancer to mock the horned husband with a trick. When Hans arrives with his request, the 'magician' is busy casting a spell:

> WILHELM *kömpt in schwartzen Rock*. Nun bin ich der Schwartzkünstler worden [...]
> *Hans kömpt /* WILHELM *macht einen Circul / creuzet / schlägt das Buch auff.* [...]
> HANS *Wil in den Circul gehen / schlägt ihn zu rück.*
> WILHELM. Ich rathe dir komme nicht in diesen CIRCULUM oder der Teuffel nimpt dich mit.[188]

---

[186] In this incident, Fredén recognises an echo of Philocles' mutism from Machin and Markham's play *The Dumbe Knight: A historicall Comedy* (London, 1608), which however is faint. See *Friedrich Menius und das Repertoire der englischen Komödianten in Deutschland*, p. 234.
[187] *SW*, vol. 1, pp. 561–2.
[188] Ibid., pp. 564–5. Translation: '*Enter WILHELM in a black robe*. Now I have become a necromancer. [...] *Enter Hans.* WILHELM *draws a circle and a cross, opens the book.*

The similarity of this scene to the encounter between the silly servant and the grumpy magician Barrabas in the play *Eine schöne lustig triumphirende Comoedia von eines Königes Sohne auß Engellandt und des Königes Tochter auß Schottlandt* (discussed in chapter 6.2.) is striking, as illustrated in the following passage from the play:

> *Jetzt kömpt der* SCHWARTZKÜNSTLER *herein / hat ein Buch in der Hand* [...] *Er macht mit den Stecken einen Circul umb sich / schlägt das Buch auff / machet viel Creutze hin und her / nicht lang kömpt des Printzen* DIENER *herauß.* [...] DIENER *Wil zu ihn gehen /* BARRABAS *schläget ihn zurück.*
> BARRABAS. Wie nun du unverschambter Kerl / bleib auß diesem Circul / oder alßbald wil ich befehlen / daß du in den Böhmer Waldt solt gesetzt werden.[189]

The gesture of the real necromancer Barrabas and that of the pretend magician Wilhelm coincide. Both draw a circle with crosses and read magic spells from a book, and both detain a foolish character from entering this magic circle with a slightly different motivation: Hans will end up in hell and the prince's servant in the Bohemian Forest if they disobey. Due to the numerous parallels, the 'Pickelhering play with a stone' suggests itself as a parodic interlude or postlude to the serious pastoral comedy *Von eines Königes Sohne*, also contained in *ECUT*.

The disguised neighbour tells Hans to walk around the churchyard at midnight and pick up a magic stone, which will give him the semblance of Wilhelm whenever he holds it to his armpit. The irony of the prank resides, on the one hand, in the fact that the husband resorts to the cause of his cuckoldry to ask for advice; on the other hand, the gesture of holding the stone to his armpit must have looked ridiculous to the spectators, especially knowing that it does not have any effect. Hans immediately tries his magic stone at home. Playing along, Wilhelm pretends to be amazed at seeing himself in another person and the wife violently rejects the flirtatious proposals of the neighbour, i.e. Hans with the stone. Appeased by her reaction and assured of his victory, the clown even reveals the source of his secret power and boasts about his 'loyal' wife to everyone.

In general, a foolish cuckold unaware of the deception and bragging about his cunning, in other words a combination of Zanni, Pantalone and Capitano, would always score laughs. In this particular case, the comic effect of the prank is augmented by the reiterated scenes of mock-transformations and the excessive amazement of the wife and the neighbour at this artifice. A similar plot can be found both in the Italian *novella* of Calandrino with the supposedly magic stone

---

[189] [...] *HANS wants to walk into the circle, he repulses him.* WILHELM. I advise you not to enter this circle or the devil will take you.'
Ibid., p. 229. Translation: '*Enter the NECROMANCER with a book in his hand* [...] *He draws a circle around himself with a stick, opens the book, makes crosses in this and that direction. Shortly after that the prince's SERVANT appears. The SERVANT wants to approach him, but BARRABAS repulses him.* BARRABAS. How now, impertinent rascal, stay away from this circle or I shall immediately order that you shall be taken to the Bohemian Forest.'

from Boccaccio's *Decameron* (VIII.3)[190] and in the *scenario Trappolino invisibile* ('Invisible Trappolino') edited by Locatelli, where the Zanni is pranked by astute merchants who sell him an allegedly money-making flute and a mantle of invisibility. Only after some beatings does Trappolino understand the *burla*.[191] In line with the international exchange of material, Ayrer inserted this short skit as an interlude in his pastoral *Comoedia vom König in Cypern* ('Comedy of the King of Cyprus', 1618).[192]

The cross-cultural dialogue continued on the German stage even after the English Comedians had left. In fact, the main constituents of the English jig (music and dancing) were further developed in the *Singspiel* with elements of the German Shrovetide play and the Commedia dell'Arte *lazzi*.

Singspiele

The *Singspiel* with strophic texts sung to traditional tunes is a genre similar to the farcical Pickelhering play, but characterised by an exclusive use of music, dancing and singing. This derivative of the English jig won unanimous approval abroad and was soon enriched with dialogic stanzas under the name of *Singspiel* in German, and *Singende Klucht* in Dutch.[193] Via short songs and pantomime, the English Comedians could be understood with greater ease and did not need a simultaneous translation with its anti-theatrical effect of breaking the illusion on stage. Moreover, as Eckehard Catholy argues, the dancing and singing clown would remind the German-speaking audience of the *Fastnachtspiele*,[194] especially if he took up familiar tunes for an effective musical "proximization".[195]

The five *Singspiele* at the end of *ECUT* can be inserted at discretion in-between the acts of the comedies, as the title of this section says: "Nachfolgende Engelische Auffzüge / können nach Beliebung zwischen die Comoedien agiret werden" ('The following English interludes may be acted at pleasure between the comedies').[196] Most of these expressly 'English' interludes do not have a title but only a list of three to five personae or 'types' (such as a woman, a soldier, a ma-

---

[190] In Boccaccio's *novella*, Bruno and Buffalmacco convince the simpleton Calandrino to look for the famous Heliotrope stone which makes its wearer invisible. While they help him search the riverbed, they pretend they cannot see him because he found the stone and kick rocks at him all the way back to Florence, where he arrives bruised due to his alleged invisibility. He, however, does not say a word because he believes in the magic power of the stone and is thus fooled twice. See *Decameron*, VIII.3.
[191] For the whole text see Testaverde, ed., op. cit., pp. 239–48.
[192] For a detailed analysis see Fredén, op. cit., p. 234.
[193] The fact that *ECUT* 1620 records both the scores and lyrics is very rare and therefore particularly valuable.
[194] See Catholy, *Das deutsche Lustspiel: Vom Mittelalter bis zum Ende der Barockzeit*, p. 138.
[195] Genette, *Palimpsests*, p. 304.
[196] *SW*, vol. 1, p. 580.

gister, a neighbour, and of course the clown Pickelhering) like the *scenari* of Commedia dell'Arte. Another point in common with Commedia dell'Arte is the use of music, which is often documented in the *canovacci* and would later lead to the development of musical *intermezzi* as simplified operas.

As Ralf Haekel explains, the form of the *Singspiele*, consisting of rhyming verse and sung couplets following the English Chevy-Chase-stanza in ballad metre, reveals that they are based on genuine English jigs, although the originals are missing.[197] Other distinctive traits of the *Singspiele* in the 1620 collection are the rudimental musical scores attached to each musical comedy, except for XI, which indicate the tune to which the stanzas should be sung. These stanzas are of irregular length, sometimes rhymed, and try to fit the rhythm of the music with a simple, everyday language. Latin and German stage directions occur rarely or are completely missing, but generally the plot is so simple that internal references in the characters' lines suffice to make the action understandable. Apart from the play *Den Windelwäscher*, which features the motif of a hen-pecked husband and his tyrannical wife, all the *Singspiele* of the collection include adultery with a spurned or triumphant clown.

The first *Singspiel* is simply entitled XI. *ACTUS 1* and features five personae: a woman, a man, Pickelhering, a youth and a soldier. It will be called 'Pickelhering in the Chest' for simplicity's sake. This interlude presents a classical adultery plot with Pickelhering in the role of the lover opposed to an added rivalling soldier. It also resonates with the 'Pickelhering play of the *Hanrey*' and is the only *Singspiel* in the collection with stage directions (in Latin). As far as the form is concerned, the lack of musical scores is compensated for by the reference to singing in the first lines of the text: "fa la la la". There are 22 stanzas of different lengths, mostly with rhyming couplets or alternate rhyme.

In the plot, the cuckold motif is treated in a familiar way: the adulterous wife has two lovers, Pickelhering and the solider. She lures the clown into her house using the common motif that she will cure his love sickness. Unexpectedly, the soldier arrives, and the first paramour must hide in a chest. While the soldier brags about his military bravery like a Capitano, in the chest Pickelhering mockingly reverses what is said/sung without being seen or heard by the other characters, i.e. what Joel B. Lande calls "fiction-external communication":[198]

> SOLDAT. Von Jugent auff in Krieg bin ich gantz aufferzogen.
> FRAW. Du bist ein wacker Cavalier:
> PICKELHERING. Mein Seel das ist erlogen.[199]

Whereas the woman believes the vainglorious soldier or at least pretends to do so to flatter him, Pickelhering sourly remarks that it is all just a lie, to ridicule his

---

[197] See Haekel, *Die Englischen Komödianten in Deutschland*, p. 130.
[198] Joel B. Lande, *Persistence of Folly*, p. 70.
[199] *SW*, vol. 1, p. 585. Translation: 'SOLDIER. I have been educated to war from my youth. / WOMAN. You are a valiant cavalier. PH. By my soul, that is a lie.'

rival in front of the audience. Suddenly, the husband returns, and the frightened soldier wants to hide in the chest too, not knowing it is already occupied by the clown. Quick-minded, the wife says that the soldier had just entered the house pursuing an enemy but could not find anyone. After the intruder's departure, the husband deduces that Pickelhering is the enemy in question. The woman's plan works out so well that he even consents to let the lover stay overnight to protect him from his pursuer. The ironic situation reaches its climax when the husband, initially naive and then greedy, states that he is not a fool since he will keep Pickelhering's money, which was meant to buy some wine. Well-aware of the man's dishonesty, the clown adds in an aside that, although the husband might deem himself superior to a fool, he is nonetheless a cuckold: "MANN. [...] Er sol kein Pfenning haben / so wahr mich Gott erschaffen / Meinstu ich bin ein Narr. / PICKELHERING. Des Hanrey muss ich lachen."[200] The play ends with Pickelhering inviting the whole audience to be godfathers within 40 weeks' time, when the offspring of his night with the woman should be born.

Ludwig Tieck was the first to notice the similarity between this *Singspiel* and the English musical comedy *Singing Simpkin*, derived from Kemp's jig performed in 1595.[201] Rather than a proper adaptation of *Singing Simpkin*, the German interlude is a simplified translation, as the following comparison of the incipits shows:

Singing Simpkin	*Pickelhering in der Kiste*
1.	I. FRAW.
WIFE. Blind Cupid hath made my heart for to bleed,	Mein Hertz is betrübt biß in den Todt / fa la la la la la.
Fa la, la, la, la, la, la, la.	2. PICKELHERING.
SIMPKIN. But I know a man, can help you at need,	Ich kenn ein Geselln / der hilfft auß Noth / fa la la la la.
With a fa, la, la, la, fa, la, la, la, la.	FRAW.
2.	Mein Mann spatzieret offtmalß hinauß / fa la la.
WIFE. My husband he often a hunting goes out.	PICKELHERING.
SIMPKIN. And brings home a great pair of horns, there's no doubt.[202]	Und bringt ein gewaltig baar Hörner zu Hauß / fa la la.[203]

---

[200] *SW*, vol. 1, p. 589. Translation: 'HUSBAND. [...] He shall not have a single penny, by God, do you think I am a fool? / PH. The cuckold makes me laugh.'

[201] Herz, *Englische Schauspieler und englisches Schauspiel zur Zeit Shakespeares in Deutschland*, pp. 134–5. For further reference see Tieck, *Deutsches Theater* (1817) and Henry Lüdeke, *Ludwig Tieck und das alte Englische Theater* (Hildesheim: Dr. H. A. Gestenberg, 1975 [1922]). Bolte maintains that the last two stanzas were composed by the actor Robert Cox and translated by the English Comedians in the 1620 collection. See Bolte, *Die Singspiele der englischen komödianten*, p. 18.

[202] Bolte, *Singspiele der englischen Komödianten*, p. 50.

[203] *SW*, vol. 1, p. 593.

Since the plots coincide, apart from some minor changes, for example the name of the clown Simpkin becomes Pickelhering, it can be assumed that the German *Singspiel* was sung to the same tune as *Singing Simpkin*. The popularity of the English jig and its melody would also explain the absence of scores. Still, there is one striking difference in the ending: Simpkin is beaten out of the chest and off the stage by the husband, while Pickelhering triumphs over the soldier and the duped husband thanks to his clever hiding-place in the chest. A lover hidden in unusual places can also be found in the *canovacci* of Commedia dell'Arte, as has been shown in chapter 4.3. Moreover, the stratagem of hiding in a piece of furniture to elude the jealous husband recurs both in the 'Pickelhering play of the *Hanrey*', where the soldier hides in a wardrobe and escapes behind a spread-out bedsheet, and in Shakespeare's Falstaff episode with the washtub (*The Merry Wives of Windsor*, 3.3). Jacob Ayrer used the motif of the hidden lover too, this time a monk in a cheese kettle, in his *Singspiel Der Mönch im Kesskorb* ('The Monk in the Cheese Kettle', 1618).[204] Incidentally, the same motif with a man in a wooden chest or washtub appears on the booth stage in the painting by Pieter Brueghel the Younger, described in chapter 2.1.

Figure 13: Detail from Pieter Brueghel the Younger's *A Village Festival in Honour of St Hubert and St Anthony* (1632). The Fitzwilliam Museum, Cambridge.

---

[204] Moreover, in the 1630 collection *Liebeskampff*, a love-making monk appears in the *Singspiel Der Mönch im Sacke* ('The Monk in the Sack'). The betrayed husband wants to tie the monk up in sack but as he demonstrates how to get in, he is made prisoner of his own device. Later, in 1648, the Dutch actor and playwright Isaak Vos adapted the plot of the clown in the chest as *Singende Klucht van Pekelharingh in de Kist*. In this female pendant to *Singing Simpkin*, there is a chaste girl and not an adulterous wife involved in the hiding. As Wilhelm Creizenach argues, the Dutchman's knowledge of the plot was mediated by the German adaptation, which was part of the travelling repertoire well into the seventeenth century. See Creizenach, pp. LXXII-III.

XII. *ALIUD* ('another [*Singspiel*]') features a clown, a woman and a nobleman and is also known as 'The Clown as Riding Horse'. With only three characters, the second *Singspiel* of *ECUT* is a short sketch with musical scores to accompany the nineteen quatrains, mostly rhyming in couplets. The verbal references to melodies like "hum hum" or "fa la la" in the text coincide with those in the 'Pickelhering play of the *Hanrey*' and support the hypothesis that the latter was originally a *Singspiel* too.[205]

The lack of stage directions makes this presumably incomplete skit difficult to understand. At the beginning, the clown Pickelhering tells the audience that he has just returned from Amsterdam and is on the lookout for his beloved. This woman might be a prostitute because she lives in a big house and is showing off the jewels she has just received from a merchant. The clown knocks at her door and starts courting her in a bawdy manner, including ironic allusions to the rhetoric of love and physical obscenity, as the following lines from stanza 7 show:

> NARR. CUPIDO hat mein Hertz geschlagen /
> FRAW. Weiß mit die Wunden so wil ichs glauben /
> NARR. Von Hertzen gern ich bins zu frieden.
> FRAW. Nessel zu / nessel zu solches kan ich nit leiden.[206]

Without stage directions, it can only be guessed what the last line "solches kan ich nicht leiden" refers to. The woman's disgust seems to be caused by the clown showing her the wound from Cupid's arrow as she requested, but being a metaphorical wound, her reaction is a little exaggerated. The missing stage directions can be reconstructed by looking at Jacob Ayrer's *Phaenicia* (1618), in which there is a funny *lazzo* of the clown pierced in the derrière by Cupid's arrow.[207] It could

---

[205] Cf. Singspiel XII: "1. PICKELH. Zu Ambsterdam bin ich gewesen / Mein Pein und Schmertz allzumassen hum hu / Aber mein Lieb find ich nicht durchauß / Ich glaub sie sey in dem Steinhauß / fa la" (*SW*, vol. 1, p. 593). Translation: 'I have been in Amsterdam. My sorrow and woe are great indeed, hum hu, but I cannot find my love. I think she might be in that house made of stone, fa la". See also *Hanrey*: "ALTER. Ach ach ach ach / fa la la la la mich zum Hanrey / wil er machen fa la la la / fa la la la." (*SW*, vol. 1, p. 535) and "ALTER. Hum / hum / hum / alle meine Nachbarn / hum hum / hum / die thun mir sagen / hum / hum / hum / wie meine Fraw Maria / hum / hum / eine lose Hure seyn" (*SW*, vol. 1, p. 539). Translation: 'OLD MAN. Alas, alas, alas, alas, fa la la la he wants to make me a cuckold, fa la la la, fa la la la' and 'OLD MAN. Hum hum hum hum, all my neighbours, hum hum hum, tell me, hum hum hum, that my wife Maria, hum hum, is a lewd whore.'

[206] *SW*, vol. 1, p. 594. Translation: 'CLOWN. Cupid has wounded my heart / WOMAN. Show me the wounds and I will believe it / CLOWN. I comply most willingly. WOMAN. Shut that nettle cloth / shut that nettle cloth / I cannot stand such a thing.'

[207] The play is contained in *Ayrers Dramen*, edited by von Keller, vol. 3. The clown's *lazzo* can be found on p. 2054: "*Jahn geht ein, ist mit einem Pfeil, der ihm noch im geseß steckt, geschossen worden, helt bede hendt für das geseß und sagt*: Auwe, Auwe meines hertzen! / Ey wie leid ich ein grosen schmertzen!" Translation: *'Jahn enters pierced by an arrow which is still stuck in his derriere, holds both hands on it and says*: Ouch, ouch, my heart! / Oh, what great pain I suffer!'

well be that this scene was borrowed from the English Comedians and that here Pickelhering would show his wounds as requested and thus shock the woman by denuding his behind on stage in an instance of comical physicality, not yet noticed in any previous analysis of the play. This would also explain what "Nessel zu" means. In fact, nettles were commonly used as cheap and coarse fibre to make clothes, in this case Pickelhering's nettle cloth/trousers, which he is requested to shut. Then, the woman rejects him on the grounds that she is lovesick for a nobleman, who appears shortly afterwards. Together they taunt the clown by treating him like a horse and threatening to put a saddle on him, from which the alternative title derives.

In this unusual treatment of the clown Johannes Bolte sees a connection to the medieval fable of Aristoteles and Phyllis. In it, the Greek philosopher is punished for trying to stand in the way of his disciple Alexander's romance with Phyllis. In revenge, the beautiful girl forces the love-crazed philosopher to put on a saddle and let her ride on his back as if he were a horse – hence the parallel to the analysed farce.[208] This instance of memorialisation and hybridisation seems plausible and is fascinating also because it harks back to a Middle High German source, inspired by classical and pseudo-historical characters and embedded in a genre developed by the English Comedians. In this case, the unrequited lover who is turned into a horse not by magic, as in the pastoral, but as a way of humiliation, provides a funny scene in which the clown could display his acrobatic skills. Unlike the previous *Singspiel,* where the clown gets away with his prank, here he is the victim of a *burla*. The same applies to the protagonist of the next play, who is denigrated by his wife and not by his rival.

XIII. *Den Windelwäscher zu agiren mit drey Personen* ('The Blanket/napkin/nappy-washer, to be played with three characters'). This interlude with three dramatis personae – husband, wife and neighbour – exceptionally bears a full title. Contrary to the quatrains in the preceding *Singspiel* in which every line or stanza is spoken by a different character (stichomythia), in this text the 26 quatrains in rhymed couplets with musical scores present instances of single lines spoken by two characters, i.e. one completes the line of the other (antilabe).

The launderer of the title is the debauched husband Fritz, punished by his wife Greth for returning home drunk. While he is asleep, she hides his hat in order to reproach him for its loss the next day. As a punishment, she forces him to carry the dirty laundry and wash the clothes instead of her, otherwise she will beat him.

6. WEIB.
Auff der Gassen du volle Saw /
Hast ihn [den Hut] verlohren / darum schaw /
Zur Straff solstu auß unserm Hauß /
Die Wäsche tragen selber raus.[209]

---

[208] Bolte, *Die Singspiele der englischen Komödianten*, p. 21.
[209] *SW*, vol. 1, p. 600. Translation: 'WOMAN. You lost it [i.e. the hat] in the streets, you drunk pig, therefore look, as a punishment you shall carry the laundry out of the house.'

The punishment is either a clever plan to avoid doing the heavy work herself or a revenge for his nightly enjoyments at the tavern. In any case, it is a humiliating chore for a man, even more so because he must do it outside, where he can be publicly ridiculed in a sort of domestic pillory. While the intimidated husband is doing the laundry, his neighbour offers to help but the woman does not permit this and remarks it is his own fault. If he had stayed at home to entertain her instead of running about at night "like a stag on heat", "drinking like a cow" and chasing other women, she would be more amiable.[210] The irony of the situation is given by the fact that the audience knows that the husband is atoning for something he never did, i.e. losing his hat, and by the reversal of gender roles which is heightened when the neighbour says he has to return home, otherwise his wife will treat him in the same way. In the end, the husband addresses the audience directly, as in the *Singspiel* XI, and asks for help with the heavy, wet laundry.

In terms of intercultural theatricality, imperious Greth recalls the subplot of *Esther*, in which the clown Hans is beaten by his wife, a topsy-turvy situation that guarantees laughter. Moreover, the hen-pecked husband, which is a motif common to the German *Fastnachtspiele* of Hans Sachs[211] and the English Comedians, probably inspired Jacob Ayrer to write the *Singspiel Von dreyen bösen Weibern, denen weder Gott noch jhre Männer recht können thun* ('Of three mean women pleased neither with God nor with their husbands' 1618), sung to the same tune as 'The English Roland' like half of his ten *Singspiele*. In it, Wolfrum fears the floggings of his wife Lisa because he has stained his shirt, despite publicly bragging about wearing the breeches at home.[212] Likewise, in Ayrer's *Eines Singets Spiel von dem Engelländischen Jahn Posset, wie er sich in seinen Diensten verhalten, In deß Rohlands Thon, mit 8 Personen* ('*Singspiel* of the English Jahn Posset, of how he behaved in service, sung to the tune of Roland with eight characters'), Posset's nasty wife Ela forces him to carry a basket and beats him.[213] These are only some instances of how different cultures shared similar devices of popular comedy.

XIV. F Fraw P Pickelhering M. Magd M. Magister S. Studiosus ('Wife, Pickelhering, Servant-maid, Magister, Student'); also called 'A Student's Luck'. This is the most complex interlude of the collection, with a large number of char-

---

[210] The quotes are translations from *SW*, vol. 1, p. 601–2: "(WEIB) 17. Thetstu daheim bey deim Weibe belibn / Thetst ihr bißweiln die Zeit vertreibn / Daß wer die bessr / dann du lieffst rumb / Als wie die Hirsch in Brunsten thun. 18. Du thust täglich wie ein Kuh sauffn / Von einer Fettl zur andern lauffn."

[211] The motif of a husband forced to carry a basket can be found, for instance, in Hans Sachs's *Fastnachtspiel Der Krämerskorb*. Moreover, in Sach's *Der böss rauch* Simon Frauenknecht (literally women's slave) complains to his neighbour that he has to do the laundry, as Fredén points out in *Friedrich Menius und das Repertoire der englischen Komödianten in Deutschland*, pp. 228–9.

[212] Contained in *Ayrers Dramen*, edited by von Keller, vol. 1, p. 6.

[213] Ibid., vol. 2, p. 22.

acters and some 'types' that do not appear in any other play, namely a magister/scholar and a studiosus/student. To match the intricate plot, the musical scores are longer than in the previous *Singspiele*, apt for accompanying the 42 stanzas in iambic octaves rhyming alternately (ababcdcd).

A married woman wants to invite a scholar to spend the night with her while her husband is out of town. Pickelhering overhears her plan and erroneously thinks she is talking about him. When she sends her maid to fetch her lover and Pickelhering understands he is not wanted, his exaggerated self-confidence is shattered but still leaves room for funny wordplays.

> 2.
> FRAW. Mein Magd sol jetzund zu ihm gehn /
>   Denn es bald wird seyn Zeit.
> PICKELHERING. Ach nein mein Mädgen bleib nur stehn /
>   Hier bin ich schon bereit.
> FRAW. Pack dich hinweg du böser Geck /
>   Odr ich wil dir Füse schaffen /
> PICKELHERING. Ja wol die kleinest Zehen nicht /
>   Könt ihr mir daran machen.[214]

Expecting the magister, the woman tells him to go away, literally 'to make feet', but the clown wilfully takes the metaphorical German expression in a literal sense for the sake of fun and answers that she will not even 'make him a toe', i.e. move him an inch from where he is. Just then, the magister appears to fix a nightly rendezvous and the woman orders the clown not to be seen ("Lass dich bey Leib nicht sehen").[215] It could well be that Pickelhering would hide somewhere, although there is no stage direction to confirm it. This assumption is further corroborated by his "fiction-external"[216] ironical comments to retort everything his rival says in the manner of the clown in 'Pickelhering in the Chest'. Disappointed by the woman's preference for the magister, Pickelhering decides to stay at the door and wait for his moment. Suddenly, a student fleeing from pursuers appears; the clown advises him to seek refuge in the house, where the maid, mistaking him for the magister, leads him up to her mistress's room. While the dazzled student takes advantage of the situation, Pickelhering courts the maid, who counters his opportunistic professions of love in a parody of the standard lyricism of lovemaking. For instance, her sardonic remark "Deines Hertzens ich gar nicht bedarff / Es seynd viel in Fleischbänken"[217] is comparable to Sidonia's answer to Nausicles,

---

[214] *SW*, vol. 1, p. 608. Translation: 'WOMAN. It is time for my maid to fetch him [the magister]. PICKELH. Good girl, you can stop here, I am all ready. WOMAN. Away with you, foolish coxcomb, or I will make you get a move on [literally: I will make you feet]. PICKELH. I dare you remove me an inch from here [literally: You could not make even a little toe].'
[215] *SW*, vol. 1, p. 608.
[216] Joel B. Lande, *Persistence of Folly*, p. 70.
[217] *SW*, vol. 1, p. 615. Translation: 'I do not need your heart; there are enough lying on the butcher's table.'

whose heart is equally unwanted.[218] Upon leaving the house, the student receives ten thaler as a gift, which he invests in some new cloth the next day. As luck would have it, he happens to buy it from the same woman he slept with and is recognised by the money rather than by his appearance. Ashamed of her mistake, she gives him the cloth for free, if only he will keep the secret. In the end, the student and Pickelhering spend the money on wine and beer, and even comment on the fine prank in a metatheatrical exchange: "STUDIOS. Hastu die ACTION gesehen/ PICKELH. Für lachen ich schier zubörstet."[219]

Although no original is known, the theme of mistaken identities is typical not only of classical comedy and the novelistic tradition[220] but also of Commedia dell'Arte and Elizabethan drama. Like the two Zannis, Pickelhering and his unwitting accomplice, the student, upset the plan devised by the unfaithful wife/Courtesan and her lover, the magister or Dottore. In a sort of parodied revenge play, which of course echoes the favourite Elizabethan dramatic genre, the Zanni/Pickelhering sends the wrong lover, a student, into the disdainful lady's house and does not miss the chance to woo her maid, without success. Although it is not clear whether Pickelhering does this to obtain satisfaction for being flouted or just for fun, he manages to pull a fine prank on the woman. Only later is the misunderstanding cleared up when the student returns to the unfaithful wife's shop. This illogical turn of events serves the purpose of comedy. The two rivals in love even make peace at the expense of the adulteress, and instead of a moral teaching, there is only merriment about a felicitous hoax or *burla*.

XV. *ACTION 4. PERSON* ('play/skit [with] four characters') features a nobleman, Pickelhering, a woman and her husband and is also referred to as 'The Nobleman's Purchase of a Horse'. A special trait of this fifth and last *Singspiel* are the three different melodies which accompany the 46 octaves in alternate rhymes. While the first and third melody have scores like all the other *Singspiele* of *ECUT* apart from XI, the second melody is simply called "like Runda Dinella" and does not present any scores. Once again, the plot treats of love and cuckoldry, with the clown helping a married wife to commit adultery with his master, a nobleman.

At first, the servant Pickelhering is summoned to polish his noble master's boots and saddle his horse but does everything wrong on purpose. For example, he polishes the boots with white chalk instead of black polish and angers the nobleman even more when he insists on having his own horse. The change of tune into a roundelay in stanza eight indicates a new scene. Pickelhering appears and tells the audience that he was allowed to sit behind his master on his horse but fell into a puddle and was forced to walk in the mud. This complicated riding scene is conveniently narrated and not visualised. In search of money, the clown offers his

---

[218] Cf. *SW*, vol. 1, p. 279.

[219] Ibid., 619. Translation: 'STUDENT. Have you seen the prank [literally the action/act]? PICKELH. I am laughing my head off.'

[220] E.g. there are slight similarities with Giovanni Fiorentino's *Il Pecorone* I.2, in which a student is preferred to a magister.

services to a married woman and presents himself as "Monsoier [sic!] Domine / Herr Pickelhering", adding the typical expression "potz schlapperment" to unmistakeably confirm his identity.[221] Again, there is a change of tune to underline the return of the nobleman seeking to purchase a horse but also interested in the woman. Hearing that he would be willing to pay 100 thaler for a ride, which refers either literally to a horse or metaphorically to sexual intercourse, the woman bids Pickelhering to negotiate an encounter. The servant breaks the news that he has found a pretty 'horse' for the nobleman to ride, an ambiguous innuendo that extends for some lines. Puzzled, his master says: "Ich glaub du willst zum Narren werden / Oder ob du schon einer bist" to which Pickelhering answers: "Ich bin kein Narr / Hans Pickelhering"[222] to assure the nobleman that he is not joking, although, ironically, the clown is a *Narr* (fool, clown) for sure. Eventually, the servant realises that his "amadisisch Deutsch" is not understood by his master and switches to "gut Bäwrisch", which is clearer and leads to a rendezvous.[223] The fact that Pickelhering, a clown of English origin, claims to speak literary German himself, only to use the 'good old' language or dialect of the peasants immediately afterwards, provides proof of the linguistic proficiency of this stage character and his closeness to the people.

As in Commedia dell'Arte, the amorous dialogue between the nobleman and the woman employs the conventional metaphor of love being an illness that can only be cured by a special doctor, the lady, with a kiss. As they start to turn words into deeds, the husband knocks at the door, a standard pivotal point. Echoing the 'Pickelhering play of the *Hanrey*', Pickelhering pretends he cannot find the key in order to gain time, while the woman hides the knight in a room and promises to come as soon as her partner falls asleep. Since the husband does not want to leave his wife alone, she feigns a sudden pain in her stomach and runs for the room where her lover is hidden – probably the toilet, in line with the scatological humour of popular theatre. The wife asks her worried consort to wait at the door and to rattle the keys so that he can cover the noise she will make inside the room. Of course, this is just an excuse, and the rattling sound is meant to cover the lovemaking occurring inside; the wife even makes fun of the cuckold unknowingly playing a serenade. When the husband suddenly feels an urge to go to relieve himself upstairs, the nobleman leaves the house unseen. The fraud ends with the sarcastic comments of Pickelhering.

As for the other *Singspiele* derived from unknown jigs, it is difficult to speak of memorialisation and hybridisation. Nevertheless, there are some parallels to the *scenario Il vecchio geloso* ('The Jealous Old Man' in Scala's collection of

---

[221] *SW*, vol. 1, p. 627.
[222] Ibid., p. 630. Translation: 'KNIGHT. […] I think you want to become a fool / or are one already. PICKELH. […] I am not a fool / [but] Hans Pickelhering.'
[223] Ibid., p. 631: "PICKELH. Versteht ihr kein amadisisch Deutsch / Daß nimpt mich leiden Wunder / Nun will ichs euch auff gut Bäwrisch / Sagen den gantzen Blunder." Translation: 'Since, unsurprisingly, you do not understand my refined German / I will tell you the whole story again in plain and honest words like a peasant.'

1611), in which Pantalone inadvertently holds the door for his young wife Isabella and her lover Orazio in a trick orchestrated by the servant Pedrolino. Later, the gardener Burattino opens the cuckold's eyes by telling him a story in which Pantalone recognises himself but does not know whom to blame.[224] By contrast, the husband of the German play remains unaware of his disgrace.

Concerning adaptation, the character constellation of an unfaithful wife, an enterprising nobleman and a sly servant collaborating to make the husband a cuckold is typical of Commedia dell'Arte and jest literature. Similarly, the motif of hiding the lover during an interrupted rendezvous is common in the genre of the *novella*. Still, of all the hiding places used in the different renditions of the motif, the toilet is certainly the least romantic because it degrades love to the same level as other bodily functions. The strong visual effect of the scene is also given by the fact that the stage could be divided in two by the door, which separated the couple from the husband and thus allowed the audience to see both scenes at the same time. Such a simple *burla* spiced up with sexual double-entendres, scatological humour and Pickelhering's antics could either function as a counterpart to a serious play or would maximise the comic effect of a plot about cuckoldry.

XVI. *CURANTE* is a French dance, the wordless scores of which conclude the collection. This suggests that the *Singspiele* were not only sung but also enriched with dances and accompanied by music. The fact that a French dance is inserted into the collection of English comedies and tragedies illustrates how international the influences were both in the field of literature and of music and dance. Thus ends *ECUT* 1620, the first and most important collection of plays attributed to the English Comedians who promulgated intercultural theatricality thanks to their proficiency in the art of adaptation.

6.6. The Parameters at Work in the Collection

Analysis of the plays in light of the four parameters of 1) memorialisation, 2) hybridisation, 3) adaptation of themes, motifs and characters, and 4) visualisation, sound and movement shows the complexity of adaptational processes at work in *ECUT*. The following summary grid allows for a few considerations about the adaptations in content and form found throughout the collection. For simplicity's sake, in the subsequent comparison I shall refer to the numbers in the grid and not to the title of each play.

Plays	Parameter 1, memorialisation	Parameter 2, hybridisation	Parameter 3, adaptation	Parameter 4, visualisation, sound and movement
I. 'Comedy of Queen Esther	Old Testament, numerous versions of the tale	Bible/morality play with subplot of war of sexes.	Hen-pecked husband/clown, reduction to flat	Visualisation: hoop motif,

[224] For the text see Testaverde, ed., *I canovacci della Commedia dell'Arte*, pp. 35–47.

and haughty Haman'	in ecclesiastic folk poetry traditions	Instances of *Hamlet* and *Shrew*	'types' e.g. Haman the villain	physical violence, narration of serious parts
II. 'Comedy of the Prodigal Son'	Parable from the New Testament, often dramatised in morality tradition and the humanist Jesuit school drama	Hybrid of didactic morality play, Bible play, Jesuit drama and popular comedy with Elizabethan pathos	Synthetic parable dramatised with rounder characters (identification). No clown	Narration of prequel vs visualisation of fall (inn) and repentance (allegories). Songs and music
III. 'Comedy of Fortunatus and his purse and wishing cap'	Chapbook dramatised by Sachs (tragedy) and Dekker (comedy with echo scene also used in *Il Mago*)	Tragicomedy with reduced plot, allegorical (moralities) and magic (pastoral) elements, Pickelhering's improvisations	Psychomachia theme from moralities, magic elements (symbolic apple)	Music on stage, frequent change of scene explained in narrative passages. Pickelhering's entre-act skits
IV. 'Comedy of a King's son from England and the King's daughter from Scotland'	No clear source, perhaps lost English play, to which some remnants point (names, subplot)	Tragicomedy with pastoral elements (magic) as in *La nave* or *Arcadia incantata*	Romeo and Juliet theme in *Tempest* setting. No clown but disguised fool and merchant	Mirror device used twice: the king misinterprets vision acted out on stage with music and dance
V. 'Comedy of Sidonia and Theagene'	Source: Rollenhagen's *Amantes amentes* (1609)	"Intermodal transmodalization" (verse to prose), names from Greek tale	'Types' from Plautus and Commedia. Motif of rejected old wooer	Letter, wreath and ring as symbols for love. Serenades with music
VI. 'Comedy of Somebody and Nobody'	English play *No-body and Some-body* based on the *Historia regum Britanniae* enriched with satiric interlude	1608 Rein manuscript differs from 1620 play by expansion of comic subplot. Shift from amalgamation to literarisation phase	'Types' of the Commedia dell'Arte and morality play denounce social injustice, not just clowns	Subplot mirrors main action, prequel told in flashback, repeated scenes of abuse between queens (fun or moral lesson)
VII. 'Tragedy of Julius and Hyppolita'	Conflict of friendship and love found in Shakespeare's *The Two Gentlemen of Verona* and novelle	Pastoral 'Tale of Felix and Felismena' by Montemayor dramatised as tragedy ("intra-/intermodal transmodalization")	Motif of testing of friendship with forged letters. Clownish servant (Zanni) inserted in main plot	False letter intrigue revealed only in the end, play-within-the-play with masked dancer at wedding with music
VIII. 'A very lamentable tragedy of	Shakespearean tragedy, anon. play and Dutch adaptation with	Excision of scenes (pit scene) and characters, different refer-	Minor roles (clown) left out. Cuckold motif	Some scenes narrated others performed (pantomime)

Titus Andronicus'	a white Ethiopian queen	ences to Ovid to reveal the rape	from Commedia dell'Arte	according to effort-effect
IX. *Pickelheringspiel* 'of the beautiful Maria and the old cuckold'	First record of farce with clown Pickelhering as protagonist written in German	Love test found in many *novelle*, German jest literature and Hans Sachs's Shrovetide plays. Later copied by Ayrer	Cuckold motif and lover hidden with the help of servant typical of *novelle* and Commedia dell'Arte	Pantomime behind cuckold's back, feigned death, and final beating of the clown are standard gags
X. *Pickelheringspiel* 'with a stone'	Plot resonates with Boccaccio *Decameron* (VIII.3) and fantastic comedies	Clown victim of a sham, not mischief-maker. Farce with a love test turned into a prank with magic	Cuckold motif and love test ridiculed by scheming wife and neighbour/ magician	Play-within-play with wife and neighbour pretending to believe in magical stone
XI. *Singspiel* aka 'Pickelhering in the Chest'	Translation of English *Singing Simpkin*, later adapted by Vos in Dutch (1642) and Ayrer	Name of clown is Pickelhering, not Simpkin. English plot combined with Italian farces of cuckoldry	Adultery plot with two lovers, one hiding in a chest, the other involved in the wife's prank	Melody (no scores) is the same as English jig. Clown fools cuckold twice (sex and money)
XII. *Singspiel* aka 'The Clown as Riding Horse'	Idea of the saddled lover echoes the fable of Aristoteles and Phyllis	Corrupt adaptation without stage directions, structure not clear	Nobleman turns rivalling clown into victim of prank with a saddle	Musical scores and tunes like "fa la la". Visual humiliation of clown-horse
XIII. *Singspiel* 'The Blanketwasher'	Only *Singspiel* of the collection with a title, no original known but the plot resembles *lazzi* and pranks	Interlude ends with a direct address to the audience as in *Singspiel* XI. Adapted by Ayrer	Hen-pecked husband motif: wife forces husband to do laundry, neighbour advises and pities him	Scores attached to the text, antilabe. Prequel narrated, plans made explicit, humiliation of clown
XIV. *Singspiel* aka 'A Student's Luck'	Original unknown, but similarities with Fiorentino's *Il Pecorone* point to *novelle* and jest literature	Revenge comedy with 'types': unfaithful wife prefers magister over clown, who sends in student and woos maid	Adulteress promises to hide lover (chest motif). Clown and maid reverse romantic lyricism	Plan not narrated but acted out. Clown active mischief-maker. Musical scores for iambic octaves
XV. *Singspiel* aka 'The Nobleman's Purchase of a Horse'	Cuckold holding door for his rival echoes the *scenario Il vecchio geloso*, although it is not modelled on it	References to *Pickelheringspiel* 'of the *Hanrey*' and *Singspiel* 'Pickelhering in the Chest'	Metaphor of love illness typical of *Innamorati*. Cuckold fooled by servant, wife and hidden lover	Different tunes for new scenes. Hoax spiced up with sexual double-entendres and scatological humour

Not surprisingly, more than half of the plays in *ECUT* memorialise English dramas (III, IV, V, VI, VII, VIII, X, XI). Other memorialised texts are Italian *novelle* or fables (VII, X, XI, XII, XIV), German plays or *Fastnachtspiele* (III, V, IX), the Bible or Bible plays (I, II; as to religion, there are interestingly more plays which name pagan gods – IV, V, VII, VIII – than direct references to a Christian god, as in I and II), chapbooks (III, VIII), jest literature (IX) and chronicles (VI). The diffused Renaissance practice of recycling, imitating and emulating was valid for all these genres, which in turn drew on the same partly popular and partly erudite sources. As models were usually considered a public domain to be freely pillaged, adapted, condensed, simplified, expanded and mixed with other storylines according to the powers of comprehension and perceptivity of the spectators, anything that would be palatable to the audience was readily inserted to facilitate the reception of a foreign repertoire.

What makes imitation unique, however, is hybridisation. None of the analysed plays is simply a translation of the original in the narrower sense. Instead, the bare outline of the plot is transferred into a new genre – a phenomenon called "intermodal transmodalization" by Gérard Genette (I, II, III, V, VII) – or changed in genre, i.e. "intramodal transmodalization" (VII).[225] The ruling principle is a reduction to approximately one fifth of the length of the English original, as Peter Holland observes,[226] in order to leave space for interludes more or less connected to the principal plot (I, II, III, V, VI, IX, X, XI) and comic subplots savaged from other sources: Commedia dell'Arte *scenari* (IV, V, XI, XIV, XV), moralities (I, II, III, VIII), or pastorals and fairy tales of magic (III, IV, VII, X). Subsequently, this creative combination of sources gave way to hybrids like the German *Singspiel* – a combination of drama and music derived from the English jig and recorded for the first time in *ECUT*.

Wherever a comic subplot is present, its protagonist is always a clownish character, mostly Pickelhering. He is absent only in one religious play (II), the two plays with pastoral elements (III, IV) and one tragedy (VIII). 'Nobody and Somebody' represents a special case because the namesakes are undoubtedly fixed 'types' but are closer to allegorical figures who are meant to instruct than to comic figures who principally amuse the audience. In the other plays, the clown produces laughter either by fooling the others or being fooled himself: in six out of

---

[225] Genette, *Palimpsests*, p. 277 and p. 284.
[226] See Holland, "Shakespeare abbreviated", in Shaughnessy, ed., *The Cambridge Companion to Shakespeare and Popular Culture*, pp. 26–45, p. 31. As he explains, the structure was reduced to become an ordered sequence of events with almost fixed turning points. Such additions to render the plot interesting were, for example, recognitions of characters thought lost and then found again (such as abducted children or twins separated at birth and later reunited with their family); intrigues based on slandering or disguise; and mistaken identities and mixing up of facts (sometimes after eavesdropping or as part of a mischievous plan). These common elements, already present in Greek and Latin drama, were taken up in the Renaissance and developed in England, France, Spain and Italy, countries which played an important role for the emergence of a national theatre tradition in Germany and Austria.

fifteen plays he actively deceives someone (I, VII, IX, XI, XIV, XV), while in four he is the victim of a prank (V, X, XII, XIII). His double nature of mischief-maker and simpleton recalls both the distinction between the Elizabethan fool and the clown, and between the two Zannis of the Commedia dell'Arte – one sly and witty, and one naive and boorish.

So great was the success of this formula that it was immediately imitated and copied by other contemporary playwrights, especially Jacob Ayrer. Thus, the clown went from a translating mediator of plots and acrobat in short semi-improvised skits in-between acts, to an independent protagonist of longer interludes as diversion from, or reversal of, the serious plays. Here, the itinerant players made the same move Elizabethan dramatists and Commedia dell'Arte improvisers had made before: they gave the clown a central role *in* the play, rather than keeping him as a marginal laughingstock. In later, more elaborate plays like those in *ECUT*, the clown Pickelhering was introduced with a proper text which used characteristic devices common to the Italian and English comedy like dialects, malapropisms, wilful misunderstandings, ill-conveyed messages, parody, and carnivalesque reversal in the "fiction-external"[227] comments on stage or in the parallel subplots. Ultimately, the English clown became a standard element of German comedies and even gave his name to a new genre sprung from the *Singspiel*, the *Pickelheringspiel*. In *ECUT*, the clown retraces all the stages of his emancipation: improvising merry-maker without a precise text (III), minor character relegated to a loosely connected subplot (I), comic figure on a par with the serious parts (IV, V, VI, VII) and protagonist of the genres devoted to him – *Pickelheringspiel* and *Singspiel* (IX-XV). The variety of roles present in the plays of the collection makes it possible to detect a co-existence of older and newer stages of development and to recognise the forces operating on them, before they were evened out by complete assimilation.

The adaptation of themes, motifs and characters is sometimes hardly distinguishable from hybridisation, especially when the direct model cannot be reconstructed. In this case, one can only detect feeble *ghosting* elements[228] of intertheatricality rather than intertextuality. Such *ghosting* elements include references to morality play patterns, like the fight between good and evil or the flat representation of characters as pure villains (I, II, III, VI, VII, VIII); real or parodied magic props or magicians (II, IV, X); and the hen-pecked husband motif common on the popular stage (I, XIII). Other motifs retraceable in the collection of 1620 and typical of the popular stage – but we might even say of popular culture, as they can be found in folklore, fairy tales, legends and myths as well – are faithful love, magnanimity and steadfastness rewarded in the end (I, IV), or hindered by misunderstandings and intrigues (VII, VIII – Hyppolita is induced to break up her engagement by a false letter and Andronica's beloved husband is killed by

---

[227] This concept is taken from Joel B. Lande, *Persistence of Folly*, p. 70.
[228] The concept of *ghosting* is borrowed from Marvin Carlson, *The Haunted Stage: The Theatre as Memory Machine*.

Aetiopissa's sons). While these same motifs connected to love contribute to the happy outcome of a fraud in the subplots of cuckoldry, in the serious main plot they bring about tragedy (as in *Von Julio und Hyppolita*). The cuckold theme, ubiquitous in the novelistic tradition and in Commedia dell'Arte, is used in many plays of *ECUT* and sometimes combined with a hidden lover (IX, XI, XIV, XV) and/or with a love test (IX, X). The cuckold theme even occurs in a tragedy, namely *Von Tito Andronico*.

As for Commedia dell'Arte, both its 'types' – derived from Roman comedy – and its patterns occur in numerous plays (IV, V, VI, IX–XV) along with the trope of love as an illness (XI, XV) and with romance either ridiculed and reversed in the servants' unpoetic sexual passion (V, VI, XIV) or complicated by rivalling lovers (V, XI, XII, XIV; in *Von Julio und Hyppolita* the rivalry turns into tragedy). Both the male and female characters in *ECUT* are mostly flat, identified by their social status (king, queen, servant, fool, peasant, father, mother, lover, etc.) or by an unchangeable ethical attitude or emotional state (haughtiness, love, envy, etc.) rather than by their personality. There is no room for development or change as the figures are always either good or evil, virtuous or vicious – never in-between or dynamic. In this sense, they can be compared to the 'types' of Commedia dell'Arte because of their role and the speech genres connected to them, for example the poetic Innamorati (found in the serious main plots of II, IV, V, XV), the hoaxed husband Pantalone (I, II, V, IX, X, XV), the boastful Capitano (VI, IX, X, XI), the know-all Dottore (I, V, XIV – often a neighbour) and, of course, the hilarious Zanni (I, IV, V, VI, VII, IX–XV). What is different, however, is that in Commedia dell'Arte one rarely finds a representation of aristocrats, kings and queens, but rather stereotypes of merchants, scholars and servants who reflected the social spheres of the Venetian republic based on a mercantile oligarchy and not on a monarchic system, as Artemis Preeshl argues.[229] In the rest of Europe, courts and sovereigns played an important political role, and therefore they were transposed on stage to be either idealised (I, IV, VII) or criticised (III, VI, VIII), as the 1620 collection demonstrates. By contrast, the plays and farces most indebted to Commedia dell'Arte (V, IX–XV) lack references to royalty. Apart from these, the court and noble personages prevail.

A closer look at the societal roles depicted in the plays allows us to draw some general conclusions about the imagery connected to power relations and the female condition at the time. Concerning the social sphere represented on stage, the relation to political and economic power is another frequent motif that can be found in numerous plays. Most of them feature good government as opposed to tyranny and oppression (I, II, III, IV, VI, VIII). To teach the audience a moral lesson, the thirst for power, often connected to arrogance, haughtiness and wickedness, is ultimately punished either with a fall from grace or with death. But even these serious motifs can be turned into farces, for example in the clown's vain attempt to outwit his rival (V, X, XIV) or to subdue his wife (I, XIII).

---

[229] See Preeshl, *Shakespeare and Commedia dell'Arte: Play by Play*, p. 63.

Speaking of the female characters in the plays, they are central for all plots, especially those concerned with love and cuckoldry, and often hold the role of female protagonists on a par with their lovers, even in the title (I, IV, V, VII, VIII, IX–XV). On the one hand, in the serious (main) plots their importance for the play's development is reflected in their representation not just as subdued daughters like Hyppolita, but as self-willed and strong women, like Esther, Astrea and Sidonia. Sometimes haughtiness and thirst for power can turn them into dangerously powerful despots, like Aetiopissa or the queens in 'Nobody and Somebody'. On the other hand, the farcical subplots reverse this image in comic and misogynist terms and caricature the cunningness, silliness, sexual appetite or violent behaviour of the female sex.

The parameter of visualisation, sound and movement involves non-verbal elements apt for enhancing understanding or provoking laughter. References to gesture, kinesics, proxemics, music, dance, pantomime and acrobatics can be extracted both from the scant stage directions in Latin and German, and from indirect hints in the text, which show how the body was skilfully employed to visualise feelings and to make characters verisimilar or ridiculous. In most adapted plays, gesture is over-emphasised to make sure the message reaches the audience, and emotional states are physically acted out by characters tearing their garments, falling on their knees, looking aghast, wringing hands, kissing, hugging, spitting and winking.

Moreover, visualisation of events works with indexical costumes and symbolic props to characterise the status and major traits of the dramatis personae. Sometimes costumes are also used as disguise, revealed in the denouement (III, VII, VIII, X). As on the Elizabethan stage, in *ECUT* the few props were generally indispensable for the play, such as the forged letters in *Von Julio und Hyppolita*, the stone in the eponymous *Pickelheringspiel*, the magical gifts in *Von Fortunato*, and the amputated hand and heads in *Von Tito Andronico*. Symbolic props mentioned in the stage directions or in the main text also give information about the mostly schematic scenery; thus, branches indicate a forest, a table symbolises the inn and a throne stands for the court.

By contrast, a complex form of imaginative visualisation is connected to narration and verbal scenery. It can be noticed that the narrative solution reminiscent of the *Fastnachtspiele* applies primarily to excised scenes, prequels or episodes too difficult to be acted but necessary for the action. An instance would be the famous pit scene of *Titus Andronicus* which could not be staged without a trapdoor. According to an effort-effect relationship, the main action is characterised by verbal communication, especially in the form of narrative passages, whereas in the comic subplots gesture, acrobatic skills and pantomime prevail to portray in detail feigned beatings, physical violence and abuse of all kinds. Gerhart Hoffmeister even speaks of a "rift between theatre and literature"[230] in

---

[230] Hoffmeister, "The English Comedians in Germany", in Hoffmeister, ed., *German Baroque Literature*, pp. 142–58, p. 153.

favour of gesture, lavish costumes, music and accentuated passions that soon dominated the German Baroque stage under the English and Italian influence.

Music and dancing are also connected with visualisation. They appear in almost every play of the collection (II, III, IV, V, VII, VIII, IX, XI–XV), proving the importance of these visual and acoustic features, for which the English Comedians were renowned from their first Continental tours. Music sets the tone for a scene, as in the episode at the inn with the Prodigal Son; it underlines the emotions displayed by the characters, for example when Andolosia realises his mistakes and asks the musicians to stop playing in *Von Fortunato*; and it accompanies dances and festivities in the play, such as the tragic wedding dance in *Von Julio und Hyppolita*. The *Singspiele* could obviously not do without music, although there is no direct reference to musicians on stage. This leads to the assumption that singing alone sometimes had to suffice, but still worked due to the annotated music scores and the familiarity of the audience with the melody.

As a preliminary conclusion to the analysis of *ECUT*, the saying 'never judge a book by its cover' seems fitting. The inconsistencies in the stage directions and in the plots bear witness to the fact that *ECUT* was not an authoritative collection of drama, but a set of theatrical scripts from which experienced actors could draw, adding characters and expanding or reducing scenes as in a *canovaccio*. Indeed, it would be wrong to deduce that the quality of the representation was directly proportional to the apparently low quality of the texts. The Romantic author Ludwig Tieck, who translated Shakespeare's oeuvre together with August Wilhelm von Schlegel in 1833, was one of the first scholars to cautiously question the ability of the English Comedians and to attribute the lack of refinement of their plays to the cultural level of the audience and to the inaccurate edition of their texts instead:

> Haben sie [die Comödianten] selber so gespielt, wie die Stücke geschrieben sind, die diese Wanderer in Deutschland heraushaben (wenn sie von den Spielern herrühren), so können wir uns keinen großen Begriff von ihrer Geschicklichkeit machen, aus ihrem Beifall sollte man schildern, daß sie viel leisten konnten, wenn die Deutschen nicht vielleicht, wegen der Neuheit der Sache, auch mit dem Unbedeutendsten sehr zufrieden waren.[231]

Thus, Tieck addressed a dilemma every scholar of the English Comedians must face ever since: Were the performances really as 'bad' as the plays? And was this 'inferiority' due to a lack of skill on the part of the actors or to the 'low' cultural level of the audience? To give theatrical itinerancy its due credit in the history of theatre, historical reconstruction must be separated from literary assessment. This

---

[231] Ludwig Tieck, ed., *Deutsches Theater*, Berlin, 1817, vol. 1, p. XXIII. Translation: 'If they performed the plays edited by these wanderers in Germany in the same way they were written (if indeed they originate with the players), then we cannot form any great idea of their ability, but from their acclamation one should deduce that they were very capable or that perhaps the Germans were so taken in by the novelty of the thing that they easily contented themselves with negligibility.'

approach leads to a reconsideration of some hypotheses brought forward by scholars who have devoted themselves to the analysis of *ECUT*.

As Fredén argues, the numerous blunders in the collection bespeak the reverse editorial procedure of writing down the plays from memory after having either read or seen them.[232] In his view, the fact that the editor Friedrich Menius collected and enriched the texts with other sources accounts for the narrative rather than dramatic style. However, this hypothesis does not explain the curious fact that some stage directions are in Latin and others in German, or other stylistic and structural inconsistencies like the random division of the texts into acts and scenes. Instead, there must have been a written basis of prompt-copies, which were not carefully edited. Still, his idea of a reverse movement ties in with the idea of a 'backwards involution' – based on Anna Baesecke's theory of theatrical development – in the sense of taking an evolutionary step back, not due to a lack of skills but as an effective method to suit the audiences' tastes in German-speaking Europe.

In a like manner, scholarship tends to misprise the plays' function due to their simplicity of style. For instance, Ralf Haekel states that the English Comedians' plays had a didactic function to promote their patrons' political interest and to warn the spectators, by means of violent and bawdy performances, against aspiring to change the status quo.[233] Analysis of the 1620 collection does not support this line of argument. Quite the contrary: the plays are not as religious and moralistic as Jesuit drama, since even *Esther* and *The Prodigal Son*'s didactic aim is attenuated by added scenes with comic characters. Nor can any political display of power on stage be attributed to the English Comedians' patrons. The fact that Duke Heinrich Julius and Landgrave Moritz allowed the companies at their service to tour the country and perform at fairs does not mean that they paid the Comedians to entertain or educate their commons. If indeed they wanted to discipline their subjects, it is questionable whether they would have chosen theatre for that purpose. The indisputably bawdy and violent scenes of the *Singspiele* and subplots should not lead to hasty qualitative conclusions. As Tieck points out, the German public was probably 'so taken in by the novelty of the thing' ("wegen der

---

[232] See Fredén, op. cit., p. 159.
[233] "Die erhaltenen Dramen machen deutlich, daß die Englischen Komödianten zumeist eine sehr einfache Funktion erfüllten. Sie waren ein didaktisches Instrument, um politische Interessen ihres Mäzens durchzusetzen. Folglich sind die Stücke auch sehr eindeutig ausgerichtet: Es sind groß angelegte Haupt- und Staatsaktionen, in denen der Beziehungsreichtum der englischen Originale zugunsten einer einfachen sozialdisziplinierenden Belehrung aufgegeben wird. Eine zentrale und handlungsbestimmende Rolle spielen dabei die Affekte beziehungsweise ihre Verteufelung als melancholische Erkrankung oder als Todsünde. Die Figuren sind hochmütig oder wollüstig, und der Held verfällt, wenn er seine Leidenschaften nicht beherrschen kann, dem Wahnsinn und führt die Katastrophe herbei. Die zum Teil sehr gewalttätigen und derben Stücke vermitteln den Zuschauern einen Moralkodex, der den *status quo* preist und jede Form der sozialen Mobilität brandmarkt." Ralf Haekel, "Neue Quellen zur Geschichte der Englischen Komödianten in Deutschland", *Shakespeare Jahrbuch* 140 (2004), pp. 180–5, pp. 182–3.

Neuheit der Sache [...] sehr zufrieden waren") and surprised to encounter theatre for theatre's sake – neither tied to special communal occasions like the Shrovetide plays, nor to religious festivities – that this intrinsic theatricality is mainly responsible for the English Comedians' success. The itinerant players' greatest achievement, for Hoffmeister, lies in "shaping a collective style of putting together pieces for the stage and in presenting them in a new way – a way that stressed theatrical effects, the entertainment of the audience above and beyond any didactic purpose."[234] *Collective style* is another term for the amalgamation of learned and popular sources at work in the adaptation process which enabled the transfer to, and appropriation of, different dramatic traditions onto and by another culture.

By interpreting these plays from perspectives of intercultural theatricality, the unique amalgamation of Elizabethan drama, Italian Commedia dell'Arte and German genres that came into being through the English Comedians will hopefully be appreciated. In particular, the actors' attention to promoting and shaping theatre according to their audience is best made visible thanks to adaptation theory.

---

[234] Hoffmeister, "The English Comedians in Germany", in Hoffmeister, ed., *German Baroque Literature*, pp. 142–58, p. 150.

7. The German and Austrian Stages as Competition and Melting Pots

This chapter offers an overview of the legacy of the English Comedians during and after their active touring phases on the Continent. It will be argued that the German and Austrian stages functioned as melting pots for theatrical traditions either introduced for the first time, revived or enriched by the itinerant players.

After the 1620 and 1624 collections of *ECUT*, the English influence flared up once more in 1626 with the 'Dresden Repertoire'. After that, it progressively faded and is hardly recognisable in the collection *Liebeskampff* of 1630, but this does not mean that it disappeared. Quite the contrary, it was assimilated along with other traditions, especially Commedia dell'Arte, as the adaptation of *Der Jud von Venedig* (performed in 1626) shows. Of course, the Italian and English influences were only two forces in an international panorama; France and Spain had a deep impact on Baroque theatre, opera and literature too, but were mediated more by a literary exchange than by travelling performers. The inclusion of Spain and France and the impact of their literatures and itinerant players would broaden the European perspective even more. Furthermore, it could help to explain the change of paradigms towards the French and Italian cultural supremacy in German-speaking countries after the English Comedians stopped touring them due to the Thirty Years' War. However, this would go beyond the focus of this study on the effects of popular theatre from Italy and England on early modern theatre in Germany and Austria. Without making any claim to completeness, a few representative examples of intercultural theatricality will be discussed here to cover three different aspects of theatre: drama, dramatists and performance.

Regarding drama, the analytical parameters of intercultural theatricality shall be applied to *Der Jud von Venedig*, reworked and printed by a German author after the Thirty Years' War, but performed many decades before. This analysis of a play beyond the *ECUT* collection introduces the section about the most important imitators of the English Comedians from the 1590s to the 1660s: Duke Heinrich Julius, Jacob Ayrer and Andreas Gryphius. Their direct contact with English and Italian itinerant players left recognisable traces of a creative reception of foreign influences merged with autochthonous forms and topics, in particular those immersed in popular culture. As to performance, a separate subchapter is devoted to the figure of the clown and to the English and Italian contribution to the *Altwiener Volkstheater*. The practical inputs and mass-market appeal of the wandering troupes proved valuable for the emergent Viennese popular theatre, struggling to break free from foreign competition and to be recognised as an autonomous form, though still indebted to other influences. A description of the Viennese Hanswurst and Kasperl and their relationship to Arlecchino and Pickelhering shall lead back to the initial question concerning possible common roots of these entertainers in popular culture.

7.1. *Der Jud von Venedig* – Synthesis beyond the 1620 Collection

A felicitous example of the amalgamation of English and Italian influences in Germany beyond *ECUT* (1620) is the *Comoedia von Josepho Juden von Venedigk*, i.e. 'Comedy of Joseph, Jew of Venice' (subsequently abbreviated to *Der Jud von Venedig*), performed as part of the 'Dresden Repertoire' by John Green's company on 13 July and 5 November 1626.[1] According to Johannes Meissner, who reissued the play in 1884, the earliest surviving manuscript of the *Comoedia Genandt Daß Wohl Gesprochene Uhrtheil Eynes Weiblichen Studenten oder der Jud von Venedig* ('Comedy called the well-spoken verdict of a female student or the Jew of Venice), written between 1680 and 1690 and held at the National Library in Vienna, is probably based on the version mentioned in the 'Dresden Repertoire' of 1626.[2] This hypothesis seems plausible since the play was certainly in circulation long before it was published, meaning that its performance took place within the time frame considered in this study. It is added to the analysis of *ECUT* to give an overview of the amalgamation of currents some 50 years after the publication of the first collection.

Compared to the earlier plays, this comedy is more sophisticated in style and structure because it appeared after the naturalisation phase, when German dramatists were more accomplished and the new cultural taste from Italy and France

---

[1] For the list of the 'Dresden Repertoire' see Cohn, p. CXV. As the *Theaterbrief* by Maria Magdalena testifies, a play 'about the Jew' ("Von dem Juden") was performed by John Green's company in Passau in late November 1607 and in Graz during the Carnival of 1608, but the title is too imprecise to state whether it was Marlowe's *Jew of Malta*, Thomas Dekker's lost *Jew of Venice*, or Shakespeare's *Merchant of Venice*. See "Brief der Erzherzogin Magdalena (Graz, Februar 1608)", preserved at the Vienna Haus-, Hof-, und Staatsarchiv, Familienkorrespondenz A, Karton 6, fols 312–15, and reprinted by Flemming, pp. 71–2, Meissner, pp. 76–80, and Schrickx, pp. 332–3. For the translation see Orad, pp. 4–11. According to Peter Holland, the same play was put on in 1611 in Magdeburg and Halle under the name "Teutsche Komedia der *Jud von Venedig*, aus dem engländischen", as Landgrave Phillipp von Bußbach reports. A later mention of the German play occurs in 1674 in Dresden, where *Josephus Jude von Venedig* was performed. See Holland, "Shakespeare abbreviated", in Shaughnessy, ed., *The Cambridge Companion to Shakespeare and Popular Culture*, pp. 26–45, p. 31.

[2] The manuscript, preserved at the National Library in Vienna (Wiener Manuskript Codex 13791*) and accessible online, <https://digital.onb.ac.at/RepViewer/viewer.faces?doc=DTL 6500765&order=1&view=SINGLE> (last accessed 7 July 2018), was reprinted by Johannes Meissner in *Die englischen Comoedianten zur Zeit Shakespeares in Österreich*, pp. 131–89. My quotes are taken from Meissner's reprint and subsequently abbreviated to *JV*. Almost the same text with the title *Comoedia Genandt Der Jude von Venetien* – 'Comedy called The Jew of Venetia' is contained in Willi Flemming, *Barockdrama. vol. 3, Das Schauspiel der Wanderbühne*, pp. 204–76. This version of the play is taken from a manuscript of the second half of the seventeenth century, which belonged to the Margrave of Baden-Baden and is now at the Landesbibliothek of Karlsruhe. Its content coincides with that of the Vienna manuscript, except for the scene of Pickelhering reading out the petitions at court in the first act, which is missing in the Karlsruhe manuscript.

had overshadowed, but not erased, the English component. The play is generally attributed to Christoph Blümel (born around 1630, date of death unknown), a scholar from Silesia, but also a man of the theatre who was part of George Jolly's company, and a representative of early modern German drama.[3] However, his authorship is brought into question by the affix "Je ne ay pas fait Cela" on the front page of the Vienna manuscript to disclaim any responsibility regarding either content or composition; or to point to the pre-existing material being derived from a variety of sources.[4]

Figure 14: Title page of the Vienna manuscript of *Der Jud von Venedig*. Notice the line on the lower half saying "Je ne ay pas fait Cela" i.e. 'I have not done that' in French. Digital scan provided by the Austrian National Library.

The title 'The Well-Spoken Verdict of a Female Student' refers to the happy outcome of the comedy, in which a young woman disguised as a male lawyer saves her beloved from sacrificing a pound of his flesh by way of a pledge for his debts. This plot and the subtitle *Der Jud von Venedig* unmistakably connect the

---

[3] The Silesian Christoph Blümel was born around 1620 in Bolkenhain, studied in Frankfurt an der Oder in 1649 and started his acting career in 1654 in Ulm. He is recorded in Nuremberg in 1657, in Innsbruck in 1660 as part of the same company as Johann Martin, and in Frankfurt a.M. in 1668. Robert J. Alexander provides evidence that Blümel was a member of George Jolly's company on the basis of a 1655 document in which Jolly is said to have wounded his fellow Blümel. Despite this episode of violence, Blümel remained with Jolly after the company split up. A further proof of their strong bond is the fact that Jolly paid for Blümel's release from prison after a brawl in Nuremberg on 8 August 1657. See Alexander, "George Jolly [Joris Joliphus] der wandernde Player und Manager / Neues zu seiner Tätigkeit in Deutschland (1648–1660)", pp. 31–48, p. 32.

[4] For the title page see *JV*, reprinted by Johannes Meissner in *Die englischen Comoedianten zur Zeit Shakespeares in Österreich*, pp. 131–89, p. 131.

play to its Shakespearean model *The Merchant of Venice* or *The Jew of Venice* (1598). As shall be argued, Blümel's addition of 'types' and patterns of Commedia dell'Arte was not only due to the dominant Italian influence on German Baroque literature but was also indebted to the Italianate taste already present in Shakespeare's play and later exported in the English Comedians' adaptation.

In *The Merchant of Venice* Shakespeare borrowed the central flesh bond motif,[5] the casket riddle[6] and the romantic intrigue around Jessica, Lorenzo and the Jew Shylock[7] from folklore and novelistic literature, while for the characters he took inspiration partly from Marlowe and partly from the Italianate influence on English drama. Although the Jew's actions are dictated by a nexus of money-religion-family similar to that in Marlowe's revenge tragedy *The Jew of Malta* (1589), the grotesque Barabas (sic!) is transformed into Shylock, "a stock character who reacts more or less consistently and predictably to the twists of the comic plot", as Jeremy Lopez observes.[8] A villain who is ultimately tricked by two women, namely his eloped daughter and the cross-dressed advocate during the trial, is not suited for a revenge tragedy and, instead, would rather be expected in an Italianate tragicomedy with stock characters, romantic intrigues, disguises and the humorous *lazzi* of the clown. Moreover, Shakespeare's drama is a tragicomedy, more specifically a revenge tragedy with a happy ending: the punishment of the villain and a double wedding. This is a revealing indicator of the combination of a favoured genre of Commedia dell'Arte and English revenge tragedies to attenuate the tone of the latter. The itinerant players then further expanded this amalgamation with other elements from Elizabethan drama and Commedia dell'Arte, as the comparative analysis of the two plays will show.

At the beginning of *The Merchant of Venice*, Bassanio needs 3000 ducats to woo beautiful Portia at Belmont. His rich friend Antonio offers to act as a guarantor for the borrowed sum, which he will pay back once his ships return from their voyage. This gives the Jewish moneylender Shylock a chance to "feed fat the ancient grudge" (1.3.39) he harbours against his detractor Antonio by sealing

---

[5] Geoffrey Bullough observes that a direct source of the flesh bond motif is Ser Giovanni Fiorentino's *novella* IV.1 from the collection *Il Pecorone*, written in 1378. See Bullough, vol. 1, p. 458. The pound of flesh offered by a friend for the protagonist's debts, the intervention of the wife dressed as a lawyer, the ring episode and the double wedding were maintained in Shakespeare, who might have read the original or the translation of Fiorentino's tale entitled *The Palace of Pleasure* by William Painter (1566–7).

[6] As Janet Clare suggests, the testing of a man's morality and the quest of a wealthy wife are examples of orally delivered traditional folk tales combined with classical elements in the play. For instance, the choice of the lead casket over gold or silver ones is taken from *Gesta Romanorum*, Boccaccio's *Decameron* X.1 and *Confessio Amantis* by John Gower. See Clare, *Shakespeare's Stage Traffic*, pp. 124–32.

[7] As Bullough argues, the Lorenzo-Jessica subplot bears resemblance to the *novella* XIV of the fifteenth-century collection of tales *Il Novellino* by Masuccio. See Bullough, vol. 1, pp. 456–7. The elopement of the rebellious daughter with the help of a servant follows the Italian original, but in Shakespeare the maid is tuned into a man, the foolish Gobbo.

[8] Lopez, *Theatrical Convention and Audience Response in Early Modern Drama*, p. 210.

a special bond: if the debtor fails to return the money in time, Antonio shall lose a pound of his flesh. Meanwhile, Portia and her maid Nerissa welcome the suitors gathered at Belmont from all over the world to solve the casket riddle that will decree the future husband of the rich lady. Portia's heart is secretly set on Bassanio, and she rejoices in the Prince of Morocco's and the Prince of Arragon's wrong choice of the gold and silver caskets. After a *lazzo* of Shylock's clownish servant Launcelot Gobbo (meaning hunchback in Italian and perhaps alluding to a physical flaw of the comic personage),[9] Bassanio takes him into his service on his way to Belmont. Before they arrive, the suitor entreats his friend Gratiano to behave properly. In a passage revealing the play's close relationship to Commedia dell'Arte, the merrymaker Gratiano assures that he will:

> [...] put on a sober habit,
> Talk with respect and swear but now and then,
> Wear prayer books in my pocket, look demurely,
> Nay more, while grace is saying, hood mine eyes
> Thus with my hat, and sigh and say 'amen',
> Use all the observance of civility
> like one well studied in a sad ostent
> To please his grandam [...].[10]

Although the role of Gratiano is generally closer to a Zanni, here he metaphorically takes up the costume and behaviour of Dottor Gratiano, who – incidentally – has the same name. In a later scene in the same act, there is another hint at an Italian mask. In fact, Shylock's depiction of his former servant Launcelot as a lazy and always hungry opportunist is reminiscent of the Zanni: "The patch[11] is kind enough, but a huge feeder, / Snail-slow in profit, and he sleeps by day / More than a wildcat" (2.6.44–6). The play's setting in Venice during the carnival season might be a further tribute to Commedia dell'Arte. These festivities give Shylock's daughter Jessica the chance to disguise herself as a boy and elope with her lover Lorenzo. Bitterly disappointed in his daughter and outraged about her squandering his fortune with a Christian, the sole consolation left to the Jew is the prospect of receiving the pound of flesh from Antonio, who turns out to be unable to meet his debt due to the loss of his ships. Just as Bassanio finally opens the leaden casket and wins Portia, while Gratiano falls in love with Nerissa, they hear that the bankrupt Antonio is in prison, exposed to the threats of Shylock. Portia urges her future husband to run to his aid and secretly follows him disguised as a young law student from Rome to intervene in the trial. Initially, the advocate Portia seems to grant Shylock the right to his pound of flesh, at which the Jew exclaims

---

[9] In the *lazzo*, Launcelot Gobbo tests his blind father's love by telling him that his son died. After this comic reversal of the love test to win Portia, Gobbo reveals his identity and is happily reunited with his old father. See *Merchant*, 2.1.

[10] *Merchant*, 2.2.161–8.

[11] "Patch" can be read as a contemptuous term for something as insignificant as a scrap of cloth or as a reference to the patched clothes he wears, and thus to Arlecchino.

"A Daniel come to judgement; yea a Daniel" (4.1.219). Then, the lawyer in disguise tries to dissuade him by offering twice the contended sum, but the creditor obstinately insists. Finally, she states that if Shylock is unable to cut the flesh without spilling a drop of blood, he must die or resign all his possessions to Antonio and the State. Antonio magnanimously bestows his part of the fortune onto Jessica and Lorenzo but requires the defeated Shylock to convert to Christianity. As a sign of gratitude, the student/Portia asks for Bassanio's ring, and his assistant/Nerissa wishes to have Gratiano's ring. Although both men are reluctant to give away their wives' love tokens, their compliance brings about the final denouement. The plot already reveals correspondences between Shakespeare's tragicomedy and Commedia dell'Arte, but these are further developed in the German play.

The German adaptation *Der Jud von Venedig* starts as a typical *Haupt- und Staatsaktion* concerning the King of Cyprus and his son's worries about the growing wealth of the Jews. While the clown Pickelhering is reading out a series of absurd petitions, among which is also a suit against the greedy Jews, the prince decides to settle the matter at once with an exemplary punishment: he will dispossess and exile the most distinguished Jew of the community, Barrabas.

As the Jew enters, Pickelhering addresses him with irreverent nicknames like "Speckfresser" (bacon eater) and offers him a pork sausage, at which Barrabas simply answers that it is not a food he eats: "JUD. nein, Pickelhäring, es is meines Essens nicht."[12] This is one of the few indirect textual references to Shakespeare, given that Shylock refuses the dinner offered by Antonio and Bassanio for similar religious reasons:

> BASSANIO. If it please you to dine with us.
> SHYLOCK. Yes – to smell pork, to eat of the habitation which your prophet the Nazarite conjured the devil into. [...] I will buy with you, sell with you, talk with you, walk with you, and so following, but I will not eat with you, drink with you, nor pray with you.[13]

The reference to pork is present in both quotes ("to smell pork" and "Speckfresser"), although the tone is very different. In the German version, the clown Pickelhering consciously provokes the Jew verbally and physically in strongly antisemitic behaviour, but Barrabas remains calm and does not take him seriously. In Shakespeare, Shylock eloquently declines a civil invitation by denigrating the Christian religion with a sense of superiority, which will be punished by the end of the play. Thus, Shakespeare presents the Jew as a negative character right from the beginning, while Barrabas is initially neutral.

In return for solving the problem with the Jews, the prince desires to travel to Venice and takes Pickelhering with him, amused by his nonsensical arguments for accompanying him. Since the king simply ignores the fact that Pickelhering

---

[12] Both quotes are from *JV*, p. 134.
[13] *Merchant*, 1.3.26–30.

turns his instruction to take care of his son into an invitation to make mischief, the clown's response appears like an instance of "fiction-external communication".[14]

> PICKELHÄRING. Ey ja, Juncker, Last mich doch mit Ziehen. Ich kan, Bin ich ein Schelm, nicht Lenger Zu hausse Bleiben.
> KÖNIG. nun, weil du nicht Bey Unss verbleiben, sondern mit gewalt hinweg wilst, so wollen wir dich auch nicht lenger auf halten, so warte dann Unsern Sohn, den Printzen, fleissig auff Und gieb fleissig Achtung, damit er nicht in Böse geselschafft gerathen mag.
> PH. ich will schon achtung geben: wan er begehren in die Kirchen Zugehen, so will ich Ihn inss hurhauss führen ["fiction external communication"].[15]

Shortly before they sail, a one-eyed soldier begs to be taken with them and so they unknowingly travel with the disguised Jew Barrabas, who seeks revenge for his ill-treatment like Marlowe's Jew of Malta.

Act 2 is set in Venice at the aristocrat Florello's house. The father of the beautiful Ancilletta cannot decide between two eligible suitors, Grimaldi and Santinelli, who mirror Portia's unsuccessful wooers, so he asks the girl to choose herself, in lieu of a casket riddle. Self-willed and witty, Ancilletta counters the romantic effusions of the two noblemen on a high rhetorical level without ever seeming disrespectful and finally obtains a year of respite on the pretext that both are equally excellent.[16]

Meanwhile, the disguised Jew, Pickelhering and the prince incognito arrive in Venice after a troublesome voyage, for Pickelhering's stomach at least: he got so drunk that he ruined a barrel of pickled herrings mistaking it for the lavatory. The crudeness and obscenity of this superbly ironic episode give a good idea of the general bawdiness of the clown's gags in this play, which come close to the scatological humour of the *lazzi*.[17]

In the city, Ancilletta and her maid Franciscina (sic!) catch the attention of the prince and Pickelhering. The juxtaposition of the nobleman's eloquent praise of

---

[14] Joel B. Lande, *Persistence of Folly*, p. 70.

[15] *JV*, p. 138. Translation: 'PH. Oh yes, Prince, let me go along. As true as I am a rogue, I cannot remain at home. KING. If you cannot stay and strongly desire to leave, then we will not detain you. But serve our son diligently and take good care he does not fall into bad company. PH. I will take care. If he wants to go to church, I will take him to the brothel.'

[16] This short exchange provides an idea of Ancilletta's tongue-in-cheek responses: "SANTINELLI. Liebe Jungfer Ancilleta [sic!]. ANCILLETTA. Wehrtester Herr Santinelli SANTINELLI. Sie weiss das anliegen meines Hertzens. ANCILLETTA. So darf mirs der Herr nicht sagen." *JV*, p. 142. Translation: 'SANTINELLI. Dearest miss Ancilletta. ANCILLETTA. Most esteemed Sir Santinelli. SANT. You know my heart's utmost concern. ANCILL. Then, Sir, you must not tell me.'

[17] Ralf Haekel points out that this *lazzo* was taken almost verbatim from the plays *Tiberius and Annabella* and from *Tugend- und Liebesstreit* in an instance of intercultural theatricality. See *Die Englischen Komödianten in Deutschland*, pp. 138–40 for a detailed comparison.

Ancilletta's beauty and the servant's explicit sexual comments about the maid creates a comic clash, which is heightened further when the clown is sent to approach the ladies. On his return to the prince, Pickelhering engages in a standard *lazzo* of Commedia dell'Arte, namely the ill-conveyed message full of puns, malapropisms and wilful distortions such as *Floh*/flea instead of Florello, *claret*, an aromatic wine, instead of *clarissimus*, i.e. a city councillor, *Zwifeletta*/little onion instead of Ancilletta, and *concubina* for Franciscina.[18]

At the beginning of Act 3, Ancilletta and her maid mirror the previous praise of their beauty in a female key as they express their interest in the noble stranger and his servant. A double date ensues, in which the domestics' coarse courtship comically contrasts with the amorous rhetoric of the Innamorati. While the prince's handsomeness is attributed to his Cypriot provenance, the mythological birthplace of Venus, Pickelhering, who is dressed in many colours like Arlecchino, woos the 'virgin' Franciscina in more down-to-earth tones:

> PH: [...] nachdem ich heut die Carfunckelstein deiner Augen in mein gesicht gestosset, ist [...] mein gesicht Verblindet, mein gehör Verschwindet, mein Bauch Thut mir Weh, mein hertz steigt mir in die Höh, meine Hände Zittern und Beben, ich kan die Beine kaum Von der Erden heben, ich kan weder trincken noch Essen, Und deiner Augenblicklich vergessen: drum liebe mich oder ich fresse dich.[19]

Both the funny content, which reverses the conventional tropes of love lyricism like the metaphor of eyes like diamonds, the love sickness and the desire to be close to the beloved one, and the rhymes ("Verblindet–Verschwindet, Weh–Höh, Beben–heben, Essen–vergessen, mich–dich") recall the structure and bawdiness of the *Singspiel*. It could even be assumed that this parodic declaration of love was sung like a serenade in Commedia dell'Arte or a *Singspiel*.

Wishing to arrange a meeting with her lover in Florello's house, Ancilletta feigns an illness that can be cured only by a mysterious French doctor who has just arrived in town and turns out to be the prince in disguise.[20] The cloaks, hats and fake beard for this role-play are provided by a rich Jew – Barrabas – who changed his identity from Barrabas of Cyprus to Josepho, the rich Jew of Venice, and is now ready to exact his revenge by poisoning the costumes. However, Pickelhering's hastiness makes Barrabas drop the evil plan. In a short interlude, the silly clown tries out the Doctor's clothes and plays a trick (*burla*) on

---

[18] See *JV*, pp. 149–50.

[19] Ibid., pp. 152–3. Translation: 'PH: After the carbuncle stone of your eyes hit my sight today, my sight is blinded, my hearing deaf, my belly aches, my heart races, my hands shake, I can hardly lift my feet from the ground, I can neither drink nor eat nor forget you at once. Therefore, love me or I'll devour you.'

[20] Ernest Brennecke states that the courtship in disguise has been a common motif ever since Menander and Plautus and is often found in Commedia dell'Arte as well as in Molière's later comedy *L'amour Médecin* of 1665. See *Shakespeare in Germany: 1590–1700*, p. 109.

Franciscina, who does not recognise him at first but then slaps him for fooling her in a classical slapstick style.

Worried about Ancilletta's poor health, in Act 4 Florello consents to call the famous French doctor, whose fake accent and strange assistant increase his suspicions. While the Innamorati flirt on one side of the stage, on the other side the clown distracts the father with a ludicrous conversation based on wordplays and wilful misunderstandings, in line with the *lazzi* of Commedia dell'Arte. For instance, Pickelhering takes everything literally, so when Florello asks 'How long will your master be here? [literally 'is your master here']', he gives his height and distorts the doctor's false name Monsieur Colicoquello into "Monsieur von der colic gequält" ('Sir tormented by the colic').[21]

Sometime after that, the prince runs out of money and sends Pickelhering to borrow 2000 ducats from Josepho, who imposes a written contract with the same special condition as Shylock: should the prince be unable to pay him back in a month's time, a pound of the debtor's flesh will be taken in exchange. Too interested in his love affair with Ancilletta to question the 'pro forma' pledge, as Josepho trivialises it, the prince readily signs the contract.

Act 5 resembles the fourth act of the *Merchant* in most parts. Since the ships from Cyprus are delayed, the prince sends Pickelhering to borrow another 1000 ducats from the Jew and thus reaches a total of 3000 ducats. This amount of money coincides with the sum that Shylock lends Antonio. As soon as the stipulated period runs out, the Jew has the insolvent debtor arrested and brought to court in a scene reversing the initial trial against Barrabas. Suddenly, the inner stage opens and the duke, Florello and other councillors appear, as the stage direction explains.[22] Like Bassanio, some noblemen offer to pay for the prince's debt, but, like Shylock, the Jew insists on his right. Ultimately, Ancilletta, dressed as a *studiosus* from Padua, solves the case like Portia does. Firstly, she pretends to comply with the Jew, who repeats Shylock's exclamation "ein anderer Daniel, ein anderer Daniel"[23] verbatim, indicating Blümel's direct knowledge of the *Merchant* either through reading or through the mediation of the English Comedians. Then, she puts forward the restrictive clause that not a drop of blood shall be spilled. The verdict against the Jew forces him to leave without money and to be beaten, but all in all, he is not punished as severely as Shylock. Despite the excision of the final ring scene, the German version still ends with an unexpected twist. The lawyer/Ancilletta asks to be taken to Cyprus in exchange for his help, and Florello gives his blessing. As soon as the father sees through the disguise, he protests vehemently until the arrival of the ships from Cyprus reveals the prince's identity,

---

[21] *JV*, p. 166 and p. 167.
[22] The stage direction says: "Die Innere Scena eröffnet sich, Sietz der Hertzog, Florello, Santinelli Und Grimaldi Zu gericht." *JV*, p. 180. The duke's ensuing remark that he is amazed anyone would sign such an unordinary contract diminishes the tragic pathos of the scene – and indeed of the whole play – compared to Shakespeare.
[23] *JV*, p. 183.

and the two pairs of lovers – Ancilletta and the prince, and Pickelhering and Franciscina – marry.

At first sight, the plots appear similar and show many parallels between Shakespeare and Commedia dell'Arte. A comparison of the dramatis personae with the help of the grid below makes visible the use of *excision* of parts and *condensation*[24] of roles to make the character constellation of the adaptation simpler. An interesting aspect is that this reduction transforms the comic characters almost into stereotypes, in which it is possible to recognise the 'types' of Commedia dell'Arte.

Dramatis personae in Shakespeare's *Merchant of Venice*	List of characters of *Der Jud von Venedig*[25]	Commedia dell'Arte 'types'
	The King of Cyprus	
	Two Councillors of the King	
The Duke of Venice	The Duke of Venice	
The Duke of Morocco, *a suitor to Portia*	GRIMALDI, *suitor to Ancilletta*	Gratiano/Dottore
The Prince of Arragon, *suitor to Portia*	SANTINELLI, *suitor to Ancilletta*	
ANTONIO, *a merchant of Venice* BASSANIO, *an Italian lord, suitor to Portia*	The Prince of Cyprus, *lover of Ancilletta*	Innamorato
SOLANIO SALARINO GRATIANO LORENZO *gentlemen of Venice, and companions with Bassanio*	Gratiano → PICKELHERING, *clown and servant to the prince*	Zanni/Arlecchino
SHYLOCK, *the rich Jew, and father of Jessica*	The Jew BARRABAS, afterwards JOSEPHO	Pantalone
	FLORELLO, *a Senator of Venice*	
TUBAL, *a Jew, Shylock's friend*		
PORTIA, *the rich Italian lady* JESSICA, *daughter to Shylock*	ANCILLETTA, *his daughter, beloved of the prince*	Innamorata
NERISSA, *Portia's waiting gentlewoman*	FRANCISCINA, *Ancilletta's maid*	Franceschina
GOBBO, *an old man, father to Launcelot*		
LAUNCELOT GOBBO, *the clown*	PICKELHERING, *clown and servant to the prince*	Zanni/Arlecchino
STEPHANO, *a messenger*		
Jailer		
SALERIO, *a messenger from Venice*		
LEONARDO, *one of Bassanio's servants*	A Steward to the prince	

[24] See Genette, *Palimpsests*, pp. 228–37.
[25] *JV*, p. 131.

BALTHAZAR members of		
Servingman Portia's		
Messenger household		
A servingman, *employed by* Antonio		
Attendants, Court officials, Magnificoes of Venice	Some gentlemen-at-arms and officials of the King	

For instance, traits of Bassanio and Antonio are welded together in the Prince of Cyprus, who plays both the lover and the debtor, and the two women in love, Portia and Jessica, merge in Ancilletta's character, who despite being a gentlewoman bears a Latin name meaning maid (*ancilla*). The only case in which one Shakespearean character is split into two is Shylock, who corresponds not only to the Jew Barrabas/Josepho in his desire for revenge, but also to Florello in the role of the possessive father outwitted by his daughter. Probably, showing Josepho as a father would have humanised the mean merchant too much, so this trait was transferred onto Florello. Moreover, the two comic figures of Gobbo and Gratiano combine in Pickelhering, whose role is not secondary as in Shakespeare but decisive to the plot and central for comedy. The foregrounding of the clown is a process common to Italian and English popular theatre which bears witness to the amalgamation of both traditions. In fact, in Commedia dell'Arte, the Zanni evolved from a secondary merrymaker to a protagonist in the limelight. This successful formula was adopted by English itinerant players in Germany.

In terms of Commedia dell'Arte, Pickelhering closely resembles the Zanni with his irreverent and scatological *lazzi* (like the incident on the ship), *burle* (like disguising himself as a doctor to prank Franciscina), topsy-turvy logic (like when Pickelhering convinces the king to let him go to Venice) and reversal of the noble characters in the main plot. Other roles in *Der Jud von Venedig* can be compared to the characters of Commedia dell'Arte, too. Ancilletta's jealous father Florello, a councillor of Venice trying to marry off his daughter, would be Pantalone, and her rejected suitors, Grimaldi and Santinelli, possess the vacuous pomp of the Dottore. As in the binary love plots of Commedia dell'Arte, the prince and Ancilletta become a couple of Innamorati, whose affected lyricism is comically contrasted with the coarse relationship between Pickelhering (Zanni) and the ugly maid, called Franciscina like the Servetta/Franceschina. Finally, the Jew Josepho represents the 'type' of the vengeful moneylender and clothes dealer recurring in some *scenari*,[26] although – in his defence – the desire for revenge is motivated by antisemitic discrimination.

Apart from the recognisable 'types', another trait in common with Commedia dell'Arte is the attention to structure and character constellations that even outdoes

---

[26] According to Kathleen M. Lea, among the tradesmen present as 'types' in the Commedia dell'Arte there are often Jews as moneylenders and clothes dealers, sometimes distinguished by proper names, e.g. in *Est Locanda* (1648), *Pantalone Bullo* (1693), *La Fantesca, Fate Voi*, and *La Mula*. See *Italian Popular Comedy*, vol. 1, p. 122.

the Italian model and proves the literary aspiration of the author. There are carefully orchestrated scenes, like the trial at the beginning and the end, and symmetrical couples (master and servant, mistress and maid, noble lovers – servant lovers, the two suitors, the Duke of Venice and the King of Cyprus, and the two fathers) opposed to the single character of the Jew, to make the total number uneven as in the asymmetrical character constellation of Commedia dell'Arte. In addition, the German play ends with an unusual list of necessary props, echoing the lists of *robbe* (props) attached to the *scenari*.

A closer look at the internal structure reveals that the plot of the German play can be subdivided into three different strands, each showing distinct instances of memorialisation and hybridisation of sources. The first strand contains the exposition of the play in Cyprus, the prince's idea of banishing and expropriating the Jew Barrabas and the subsequent travel to Venice by sea, a prequel not found in *The Merchant of Venice*, where the ill-treatment of Shylock is limited to mockery. Instead, the Jew's Cypriot provenance, the name Barrabas and the reasons for his grudge echo Marlowe's *The Jew of Malta* (1592), with its Jew Barabas who is also exiled and deprived of all his possessions, whereupon he takes up a new identity to pursue revenge, like Barrabas/Josepho.

The second strand follows the revenge plot with the pound of flesh motif. As to the characters, Shakespeare's greedy merchant Shylock is hybridised with Marlowe's tragic hero Barabas to give the exiled Jew a stronger motive for his hatred (and his original name), and with Thomas Dekker's lost *Jew of Venice*, whose protagonist was called Josephus and might have inspired the offshoot, as E. K. Chambers argues.[27]

The third strand concerns the romantic intrigue taken from Shakespeare and hybridised with Commedia dell'Arte elements such as the comic juxtaposition of romantic and sexual love and the numerous disguises (the Jew dressed as a soldier, Pickelhering parodying a scholar, the prince pretending to be a French doctor and Ancilletta disguised as a lawyer). While the ending of the trial is indebted to Shakespeare, the character constellation and the predominant comic role of Pickelhering indicate an imitation of the Italian acting style on the creative melting pot that was the German stage.

The intercultural influence is also reflected in some parallels between *Der Jud von Venedig* and the continental version of *Twelfth Night*, entitled *Tugend- und Liebesstreit* (published in 1677). As Ernest Brennecke points out, conspicuous instances of similarity are the demur from the father to the wedding, which is alien to Shakespeare's play since Portia is an orphan, and Pickelhering's foul-mouthed narration of his bodily misfortunes at sea.[28] These correspondences prove that the editors/playwrights of these texts must have known each other's work and that the German versions of the plays are often located in-between English and Italian sources, remodelled in the adaptation process.

---

[27] See *The Elizabethan Stage*, vol. 3, p. 301.
[28] See Brennecke, *Shakespeare in Germany: 1590–1700*, p. 193.

The analysis of *Der Jud von Venedig* calls into question Orlene Murad's assertion that "insofar as it is Shakespeare's *Merchant of Venice*, it is, of course, a caricature of the original, as are all German texts of English plays performed by the English Comedians."[29] This summary judgement acknowledges the debt to Shakespeare but overlooks the creative additions in the adaptations which are attributable to the material conditions of performance, the audience they were targeted at, and the international influences they were shaped by. Only if due attention is given to these aspects, can it become clear that the adapted plays' value resides not as much in literary polish as in intercultural transmission. In the case of *Der Jud von Venedig*, the combination of Commedia dell'Arte patterns with a plot dramatised by Shakespeare, but not invented by him, results in much more than a mere caricature: a well-balanced amalgamation of English and Italian theatre, which are two of the strongest influences on German drama and playwrights in the sixteenth and seventeenth centuries, as the following section exemplifies.

7.2. English and Italian Traces in Duke Heinrich Julius, Jacob Ayrer and Andreas Gryphius

Ever since the earliest phases, German authors had been drawing inspiration from the imported English plays and they soon started to freely interpret them. The most promising imitators active before the Thirty Years' War, Heinrich Julius of Brunswick-Wolfenbüttel and Jacob Ayrer, either assisted at performances by English Comedians in person or used similar sources to write their own versions of the plays in German. The creative reception of the German playwrights may not have always been faithful to the English original, but it is for this very reason more interesting to study since it shows the aspects of plot and performance that survived in transformed or alternative versions after *ECUT* 1620. While the endeavours of these two writers fall in the period of adaptation and amalgamation, i.e. between 1585 and 1620, a few decades later Andreas Gryphius was inspired indirectly by Continental adaptations of English and Italian drama and contributed to the naturalisation of these foreign influences in German literature. In retracing the evolution of German popular drama, I will initially go back in time to the earlier phases of the English influence and follow its legacy after the Thirty Years' War and well into the eighteenth century.

Duke Heinrich Julius of Brunswick-Wolfenbüttel

The impact of the first troupes of English Comedians touring Germany under Robert Browne can be retraced in the plays of their earliest imitator and patron, Duke Heinrich Julius of Brunswick-Wolfenbüttel, Bishop of Halberstadt. Born into a Protestant family in 1564, the year of Shakespeare's birth, he received a solid education in theology, law, Latin and Greek, before assuming control over the territories of Brunswick and Wolfenbüttel in 1589. With his second wife,

---

[29] Orlene Murad, *The English Comedians at the Habsburg Court in Graz 1607–1608*, p. 65.

Elisabeth of Denmark (1573–1626), daughter of Frederick II and sister-in-law of James VI of Scotland,[30] he shared an enthusiasm for the stage and made Wolfenbüttel a headquarters for the first itinerant English troupes in the 1590s.[31]

Deeply impressed by Browne and Sackville's performances at his court, the duke produced twelve German plays in just two years, from 1593 to 1594, under their direct influence. Although the German philologist Eduard Engel dismisses them as "bad" and "completely worthless",[32] they testify to the creative reception of the English Comedians' repertoire and to a lively cultural exchange. In fact, his tragedies, comedies and tragicomedies published under the cryptonym HIBELDEHA[33] were not only indebted to the English model but may also have influenced the plays of *ECUT* issued 26 years later. This assumption is supported by a similar choice of genres, the sustained use of prose instead of verse, the didactic moral function of the main plot and the centrality of the clown in the subplot. In this context, Lawrence M. Price argues that it is possible that Heinrich Julius indicated only the main action to the professional players at his disposal and relied on their improvisational talent for the performance.[34] In other words, he would produce the skeletal *scenario*, observe the mise-en-scène, and then adopt the comedians' words in his written texts, as was the practice in Commedia dell'Arte. Price's hypothesis might explain the mysterious sudden end of the duke's dramatic output after 1594, when the itinerant players moved to other courts.

---

[30] See Julius Tittmann, ed., *Die Schauspiele des Herzogs Heinrich Julius von Braunschweig*, p. X, and E. K. Chambers, *The Elizabethan Stage*, vol. 2, p. 275, who narrates that the future King of England James I attended the duke's wedding.

[31] A visit to the residence of the Dukes of Brunswick and a look at the inner court, which still preserves the aspect it had in Heinrich Julius's times, can give a lively impression of what the English Comedians found when they first arrived there. The galleries of the rectangular inner court were closed only later, while in the late sixteenth century they resembled the inns of court in London and were well apt for serving as performance space, although probably, for smaller audiences, internal rooms were a more viable option. The whole city with its colourful frame houses and the well-preserved paved streets has not changed much since the advent of the Englishmen and easily allows an imaginary travel back in time.

[32] "Er [Heinrich Julius] hat mit gutem Willen und großem Fleiß elf schlechte, oder sagen wir es unverhohlen, ganz wertlose Stücke geschrieben, auf die kein Mensch achten würde, wenn sie nicht [...] von einem regierenden Herzog herrührten." Eduard Engel, *Geschichte der Deutschen Literatur von den Anfängen bis in die Gegenwart* (Leipzig: Freytag, 1906), p. 189.

[33] The letters stand for "Henrici Julii Brunsviciensis et Lunaeburgensis ducis, ecclesiae Halberstadensis antistititis", as Julius Tittmann explains in the introduction to *Die Schauspiele des Herzogs Heinrich Julius von Braunschweig*. All the titles and plots are quoted from Tittmann's edition, which contains the full texts by Henrich Julius and further details on his works. The translation of the titles and the analysis are mine.

[34] See Price, *The Reception of English Literature in Germany*, p. 22.

As a pious Protestant, Heinrich Julius was fond of biblical themes, such as the tale of Susanna and the didactic parable of the Prodigal Son. His *Tragica Comoedia: Von der Susanna, wie dieselbe fälschlich von zweien Alten des Ehebruchs beklaget, auch unschuldig verurtheilet, aber endlich durch Schickung Gottes des Allmächtigen von Daniele errettet, und die beiden Alten zum Tode verdammt worden* ('Tragicomedy of the Chaste Susanna, how she was wrongly accused of adultery by two old men, innocently condemned, but finally saved by Daniel through God the Almighty's providence, while the two old men were sentenced to death') was preserved in different versions, one prior to the arrival of the English Comedians at Wolfenbüttel and one written after seeing them perform.[35] While the first draft is close to the style and structure of Hans Sachs and Protestant school drama, in the second attempt the itinerant players' dramatic skill obviously induced the duke to revise the long plot, omit the prequel and the detailed trial scene, drastically reduce the number of characters, and insert a subplot with the clown John Clant, as Julius Tittmann argues.[36] In later plays, John Clant was replaced by Johan Bouset, a choice probably due to the success of Sackville's Jahn Posset.

The English influence is also visible in a version of the Prodigal Son by Heinrich Julius called *Tragoedia: Von einem ungerathenen Sohn, welcher unmenschliche und unerhörte Mortdthaten begangen, auch endlich neben seinen Mitconsorten ein erbarmlich schrecklich und greulich Ende genommen hat* ('Tragedy of an Undutiful Son, who committed inhuman and outrageous murders, and finally died a wretched, appalling and horrid death with his consorts').[37] Unlike the comedy contained in the 1620 collection, this rendition is a sensationalist tragedy enriched with gruesome details, for example fourteen murders and the eating of the heart of the protagonist's illegitimate son. According to Orlene Murad, this taste for the macabre turns the conciliatory moral message of the evangelical parable into a massacre in the manner of the Elizabethan revenge tragedies.[38] In this sense, the change of genre might be indebted to the repertoire of the English Comedians, too.

Apart from religious plots, the duke tried his hand at dramatising material derived from novelistic literature and the German *Schwankliteratur*. In particular, he explored the recurrent theme of adultery both in comedy and in tragedy with a strong moralistic intent. On the one hand, in the *Comoedia: Von einem Weibe, wie dasselbige ihre Hurerei für ihren Eheman verborgen* ('Comedy about a woman who kept her adultery hidden from her husband'), an unfaithful wife comically

---

[35] The play is contained in Tittmann, ed., *Die Schauspiele des Herzogs Heinrich Julius von Braunschweig*, p. 1–32. Ralf Haekel mentions a further source, namely the Neo-Latin play about the same topic by Nicodemus Frischlin, translated into German by his brother Jacob in 1589. See Haekel, *Die Englischen Komödianten in Deutschland*, p. 143.
[36] See Tittmann, ed., *Die Schauspiele des Herzogs Heinrich Julius von Braunschweig*, p. XVIII.
[37] For the play see ibid., pp. 175–234.
[38] See Murad, *The English Comedians at the Habsburg Court in Graz 1607–1608*, p. 36 for a detailed analysis.

circumvents her half-blind husband's love test with a clever stratagem to smuggle her lover out of the house: on the pretext that she dreamt her husband could see again, she tells him to close his good eye and thus gives his rival the chance to escape unseen.[39] The devices of love tests and hoaxed cuckolds taken from jest literature were repurposed in the *Pickelheringspiel von der schönen Maria und alten Hanrey* present in *ECUT* 1620.

On the other hand, infidelity is decried in the *Tragoedia: Von einem Buhler und einer Buhlerin, wie derselben Hurerei und Unzucht, ob sie wol ein Zeitlang verborgen gewesen, gleichwol endlich an den Tag kommen und von Gott greulich gestrafet worden sei* ('Tragedy of a Male and a Female Paramour, how their fornication and bawdiness, albeit remaining secret for some time, was ultimately discovered and severely punished by God'). In this tragedy, the protagonist Pamphilus makes a pact with the devil Satyrus – a recurrent motif of folklore and chapbooks – in order to obtain Dina, despondent wife of the drunkard Joseph.[40] During their rendezvous, the drunken husband returns, and the lover hides in a chest. Rendered suspicious by the presence of musicians and the mocking comments of his servant Johan Bouset, Joseph asks Dina if she is hiding someone and goes to check in the attic, while Pamphilus escapes. Having been fooled once, the husband seeks help from his neighbour and tests Dina's faithfulness in an act of revenge: he pretends to go on a journey and then sends the guards to his house to catch the couple red-handed. On an intercultural level, the scene with the paramour hidden in a chest is comparable to the washtub episode in Shakespeare's *The Merry Wives of Windsor* (3.3)[41] and to the *Pickelheringspiel* 'Pickelhering in the Chest' of *ECUT* 1620. Unlike the *Comoedia: Von einem Weibe* and the 'Pickelhering play of the *Hanrey*' in the 1620 collection, Heinrich Julius turned the love test into a tragedy here: in the end, Pamphilus dies in a fight with the guards for supping with the devil and the adulteress kills herself racked with guilt.

Despite the evident foregrounding of the moral message to refrain from committing adultery, the clown appears often in this tragedy and provides comic relief with his Low-German gags. For instance, when he finds out that Dina has started using make-up to allure her lover, he asks her to make him more beautiful too. Laughingly, she answers that he is a fool, at which he irreverently comments that

---

[39] For the play see Tittmann, ed., op. cit., pp. 235–64.
[40] See ibid., pp. 33–76 for the text of the play.
[41] *The Merry Wives* did not appear before 1601–3, therefore Heinrich Julius must have used a different source (perhaps common to Shakespeare), which would account for the change to a tragedy as L. M. Price argues in *The Reception of English Literature in Germany*, p. 21.

she is a whore,[42] in an instance of "fiction-external communication".[43] The comic subplot was perpetuated by the duke in the following works, all of which have a comic servant characterised by the same linguistic peculiarities as Sackville's Posset and the 'types' of Commedia dell'Arte. In fact, the clown speaks in Low-German dialect to achieve a humorous effect as Sackville did with his mixture of broken German and Dutch. Other reasons for making the clown stand out linguistically were to underline his lower social extraction and his closeness to the populace, as was the case with the Zanni, or, as Rudolph Genée argues, to indicate the foreign origin of the model.[44]

The most interesting example of emulation in Duke Heinrich Julius's oeuvre is the *Comoedia: Von Vincentio Ladislao Sacrapa von Mantua, Kämpfern zu Roß und Fuß, weiland des edlen und ehrnvesten, auch manhaften und streitbaren Barbarossae Bellicosi von Mantua, Rittern zu Malta, ehelichen nachgelassenen Sohn* ('Comedy of Vincentio Ladislao Sacrapa, warrior on horseback and on foot, lawful son of the noble and worthy, but also valiant and fierce Barbarossa Bellicosi of Mantua, knight in Malta'), which shows parallels to Shakespearean drama imported by the itinerant players and interlinked with Commedia dell'Arte 'types'.[45] With all his unbelievably pretentious epithets, Vincentio Ladislao inserts himself into the long line of conceited braggarts like Plautus' *miles gloriosus*, the Capitano of the Commedia dell'Arte or Shakespeare's Falstaff, as Eckehard Catholy argues.[46] The vainglorious narcissism of this unwitting fool induces him

---

[42] The original text of the scene from Act 4 of *Tragoedia: Von einem Buhler und einer Buhlerin* reads as follows: "JOHAN BOUSET. Wel, wat seggt gy? Schminket gy au? Und ich sou gement hebben, gy weren doch so schone van Natur. DINA. Ja, Johan Bouset, damit behelfen sich viel Frauens so wol hohes als niedriges Standes, daß, wann sie vor andern durch Schönheit wollen gesehen sein, die Schminke gebrauchen [...]. JOHAN BOUSET. Ja, wat seggte gy, kan man sick so schone maken mit dat Schminke, ey, so bestriket mey doch ock ein wenig. DINA. Es ist dir kein nütz, du bist doch schöne gnug und bist ein Narr. JOHAN BOUSET. Dat is wahr, dat wet ick wel, und gy siet ein Huer." Tittmann, ed., *Die Schauspiele des Herzogs Heinrich Julius von Braunschweig*, pp. 55–6. Translation: 'JOHAN BOUSET. Well, what do you say? Are you using make up? And I thought you were a natural beauty. DINA. Yes, Johan Bouset, many women both of high and low standing recur to make-up to make others believe they are beautiful [...]. JOHAN B. Really? Are you saying make-up can make one look beautiful? Then paint my face a little too. DINA. It would be useless; you are handsome enough and you are a fool. JOHAN BOUSET. That is true, I know it well, and you are a whore.'

[43] The concept of "fiction-external communication" is taken from Joel B. Lande, *Persistence of Folly*, p. 70.

[44] See Genée, *Geschichte der Shakespeare'schen Dramen in Deutschland*, p. 10, who notices that the clown even stresses that he is from England and does not understand German well in Duke Heinrich Julius's *Tragoedia: Von einem Buhler und einer Buhlerin*: "Ich bin ein Englisch Mann, Ick en sou dat dudsch sprake niet wal westahn."

[45] For the play see Tittmann, ed., *Die Schauspiele des Herzogs Heinrich Julius von Braunschweig*, pp. 137–74.

[46] See Catholy, *Das deutsche Lustspiel: Vom Mittelalter bis zum Ende der Barockzeit*, p. 129. Catholy explains that 'Sacrapa' is a misspelling of *satrapa*, i.e. governor/deputy,

to tell unbelievable stories, if not lies, which are unmasked by the court jester, Johan Bouset, as in this hilarious dialogue:

> VINCENTIO. [...] Als wir noch ein Student waren / Wie wir uns dann von Jugendt auff die Kriege bevlissen/ Da haben wir neben andern Studenten / Welcher in der Zahl Zweyhundert und Neun und Neuntzig gewesen / Sieben Tausent Kriegsleut erlegt / und keinen gefangen genommen. [...]
> JOHAN BOUSET. Das ist war / Das habe ich gesehen / Ich war dasselbige mahl nicht weit davon / Ich sah es wohl / Das jhr dasselbige mahl drey in einem Schuß erschosset.[47]

Here we see a Commedia dell'Arte character constellation, namely the comic couple Capitano and his servant Trappola. In his function of mirror-holder, the clown reflects and parodies the protagonist by pretending to believe his fantastic fabrication while exposing the lies with even more unbelievable stories, as Trappola does with the Capitano in Commedia dell'Arte; and like the Capitano, Vincentio is easy prey to pranks or *burle*. Noticing his unrequited love for the damsel Beatrice, Johan Bouset lures the braggadocio into a supposed marriage bed, which turns out to be a keg full of water, so that everybody can laugh at the soaked fool in the end. The trick was so successful that Jacob Ayrer inserted it in his *Phaenicia* (1618), presented in the next subsection.

Before the story was developed as a comedy by the duke, the subject matter of a braggart lying about his preposterous prowess at war, magic stones glowing in the dark, people growing pomegranate trees out of their stomachs or exceptionally intelligent horses/unicorns was already circulating throughout Europe, as the tale *Vincentius Ladislaus* contained in Karl Goedecke's collection of sixteenth-century *Schwänke* shows.[48] This, in turn, would account for similarities between this play, some details of Shakespeare's *Much Ado About Nothing* (1598–9),[49] and the

---

pointing to the inconsistency of the character, which is further revealed by the fact that his father cannot be a knight of Malta, as they were an order of knights and did not marry.

[47] Heinrich Julius of Brunswick, *Von Vincentio Ladislao*, in Tittmann, ed., *Die Schauspiele des Herzogs Heinrich Julius von Braunschweig* (Leipzig: Brockhaus, 1880), pp. 154–5. Translation: 'VINCENTIO. Keen on war ever since my youth, back in my days as a student we killed 7000 soldiers with 299 other students and took no one prisoner. JOHAN BOUSET. That is true, I have seen it, I was not far from the place where it happened, I saw it well that you killed three people with one shot that time.'

[48] Karl Goedecke, ed., *Schwänke des sechzehnten Jahrhunderts* (Leipzig: Brockhaus, 1879), pp. 67–70.

[49] According to Albert Cohn, the name of lady Beatrice and the way Vincentio's prowess is ridiculed recall a scene of Shakespeare's *Much Ado About Nothing*, in which Beatrice mocks Benedick for his military ineptitude. See *Shakespeare in Germany in the Sixteenth and Seventeenth Centuries*, p. LXIII. At the beginning of *Much Ado*, the outspoken and witty Beatrice ridicules Benedick thus: "He set up his bills here in Messina, and challenged Cupid at the flight, and my uncle's fool, reading the challenge, subscribed for Cupid, and challenged him at the birdbolt" (1.1.29–31), whereby a birdbolt is "a blunt wooden-headed arrow for stunning small birds, an appropriate weapon for children or

subplot with the soaked fool in *Von Vincentio Ladislao*. Whether the common source was really known to all three playwrights or whether they drew inspiration from each other cannot be stated with certainty, although the dates of publication point to Heinrich Julius as the first author to turn this plot from German jest literature into a comedy. This is achieved by means of the English Comedians' clown Johan Bouset, adapted from Sackville's Jahn Posset, who is partly a Shakespearean jester in his verbal confrontation with the braggart, and partly a Zanni/Trappola for exposing the grotesque Capitano in a prank reminiscent of Commedia dell'Arte.

Von Vincentio Ladislao, a play written by the patron of one of the first troupes of English Comedians, proved to be a successful addition to their repertoire[50] and represents a beautiful example of the mutual influence between Italy, Germany and England. This amalgamation lived on in Andreas Gryphius's boasting captains from the *Lustspiel Horribilicribrifax Teutsch* (1647–50), while Jahn Posset was adopted by Jacob Ayrer in his *Singspiele*.

Jacob Ayrer

The Nuremberg lawyer-playwright Jacob Ayrer (1543/4–1605) wrote more than 100 comedies, tragedies, historical dramas and musical *Fastnachtspiele*, of which 30 tragedies and comedies as well as 36 Shrovetide plays written between 1595 and 1598 are contained in the posthumous *Opus Theatricum* (1618).[51] The manuscript of the Royal Library in Dresden also features ten *Singspiele* in which he foregrounded the figure of the clown after the model of the English jigs. For this reason, Cohn sees Ayrer as Hans Sachs's successor who mingled the German heritage of the Shrovetide plays of the 'local' Meistersinger with a new and 'foreign' repertoire.[52] Whereas Heinrich Julius adopted the English Comedians' prose, Ayrer remained faithful to the *Knittelvers* (doggerel verse) of Sachs but needed new material for his comedies and tragedies. Hence, he turned to the same sources as the English playwrights, especially to Boccaccio and Bandello,[53] and to the adaptations of the English repertoire on the German stage. On the one hand, Ayrer took up the independent role of the *Engelländischen* Jahn Posset from the English

---

fools, since it could do little injury to larger targets." *The Arden Shakespeare Much Ado About Nothing*, edited by F.H. Mares (Cambridge: CUP, 1988), p. 54. Although the parallels to the Shakespearean comedy are limited, the instance of Benedick "setting up his bills" and boldly "challenging" even the gods only to be unmasked by the court fool reprises Vincentio Ladislao's fate.

[50] *Von Vincentio Ladislao* is mentioned as part of Sackville and Thare's repertoire in Nördlingen in 1604. See Trautmann "Die älteste Nachricht über eine Aufführung von Shakespeares Romeo und Julie in Deutschland (1604)", *Archiv für Literaturgeschichte* XI (1882), pp. 625–6.

[51] Ayrer's plays were edited by Adelbert von Keller as *Ayrers Dramen* in 8 volumes.

[52] See Cohn, p. LXVIII.

[53] For an analysis of Ayrer's indebtedness to Boccaccio and Bandello see Alberto Martino, *Die italienische Literatur im deutschen Sprachraum*, pp. 276–7 and p. 382.

Comedians and blended it with the German *Fastnachtspiel*.[54] On the other hand, his greatest artistic achievement was to popularise the genre of the *Singspiel* in a genuinely German form based on the same *Schwänke* as the *Fastnachtspiele* but set to popular melodies in the manner of the English jigs.

As the preface to the *Opus* says, his plays are not only pleasant to read but also "arranged after the life, and so managed that (just according to the new English manner and art) everything can be acted and played in person."[55] An example of the English content or 'manner' of his plays is the *Tragedia von dem griegischen Keyser zu Constantinopel unnd seiner tochter Pelimperia mit dem gehengten Horatio* ('Tragedy of the Greek Emperor in Constantinople and His Daughter Pelimperia with the hanged Horatio').[56] The play-within-the-play, Horatio's hanging and the cutting of Malignus' tongue appear indebted to Kyd's *Spanish Tragedy*, while the clown Jahn's *lazzo* of measuring the height of the gallows on the villain was probably taken from the comic hangman Hans in *Esther* (*ECUT* 1620). Even though *ECUT* was printed two years after Ayrer's oeuvre, the correspondences with the English Comedians' repertoire reveal that he must have taken inspiration from their performances in Nuremberg prior to 1618.

Similarly, *Esther* and the *Singspiel Den Windelwäscher* contained in the 1620 collection seem to have affected the comic subplot of the *Comedia von König Edwarto dem Dritten diß Namens, König in Engelland, und Ellipsa, Herrn Wilhelm Montagii Gemahl, ein geborne Gräffin von Varucken; mit 21 Personen und hat 6 Actus* ('Comedy of King Edward III, King of England, and Elipsa, wife of Mister Wilhelm Montagii, born countess of Varucken; with 21 characters and six acts'). In it, the tyrannical wife of the clown and bird-catcher Johan Clant forces him to carry a heavy laundry basket despite the king's attempt to settle the dispute.[57] This reprisal of the hen-pecked husband motif, probably mediated by the English Comedians, shows how long-lived it was on the German stage.

In a like manner, the comedy *Von einem alten Wucherer wie es ihme auff der Bulschafft ergangen und wie er seines Weibs lieb probirt; hat 6 Actus und 12 Personen* ('Comedy of an Old Paramour and Usurer, how he wooed and tried his wife's love, in six acts with 12 characters')[58] follows the words and action of the *Pickelheringspiel von der schönen Maria und alten Hanrey*, contained in *ECUT*

---

[54] Jacob Ayrer's *Possen* with Jahn Posset are: 21) *Vom Engelländischen Jahn Posset, wie er sich in seinem dienst verhalten, mit 8 Personenn*, 22) *Eines Singets Spiel von dem Engelländischen Jahn Posset, wie er sich in seinen Diensten verhalten, In deß Rohlands Thon, mit 8 Personen* (featuring the motif of the hen-pecked husband carrying a basket), and 23) *Der verlohrn Engelländisch Jahn Posset, mit 4 Personen*. See *Ayrers Dramen*, edited by von Keller, vol. 2.

[55] My translation of "[…] alles nach dem Leben angestellt vnd dahin gerichtet, das mans (gleichsam auff die neue Englische manier vnnd art) alles Persönlich Agirn vnd Spilen kann […]." Ibid., vol. 1, p. 6.

[56] Ibid., vol. 2, pp. 883–943.

[57] Ibid., vol. 3, pp. 1927–96.

[58] Ibid., vol. 4, pp. 2225–77.

1620, but mixes it with other plays and traditions. For instance, the Latin stock characters such as *ancilla* (maid) and *amicus* (friend) instead of proper names, and the theme of an old *usuraius* (usurer) fooled by an astute woman recall frequent patterns of Commedia dell'Arte. Although the protagonist's son warns him of the bad reputation of his fiancée as in the aforementioned *Pickelheringspiel*, the greedy usurer/Pantalone is so in love that he even consents to be taken to her in a sack, echoing the hidden wooer motif present in the other Pickelhering play of the 1620 collection, 'Pickelhering in the Chest'. After the marriage, the adulteress hides the gentleman Gendelon, her lover, behind a spread-out sheet and thus outwits her jealous husband. The same trick is used by Maria in the 'Pickelhering play of the *Hanrey*', as is the feigned death of the cuckold to test his wife's fidelity. The major difference resides in the moralistic ending, in which the usurer repudiates the unfaithful woman, thus adding an original touch to this pastiche of English and Italian influences.

Another example of intercultural theatricality is the *Comedia von der schönen Sidea, wie es ihr biß zu ihrer Verheuratung ergangen, mit 16 Personen und hat 5 actus* ('Comedy of the Beautiful Sidea, recounting what happened to her prior to her wedding, with sixteen characters and five acts') which may have borrowed the female protagonist's name from a lost play called *Celido und Sedea*, performed at Nuremberg by John Spencer in 1613.[59] It can be compared to Shakespeare's *Tempest* although, according to Creizenach, it seems more probable that Ayer used a lost (German?) common source than that he knew Shakespeare's play firsthand.[60] Cohn even goes so far as to suggest that Ayer could have been Shakespeare's source of inspiration when the German play was taken back to London by the itinerant players.[61] Although Robert Browne and John Green returned to England more than once during their career, their connection to Ayrer and their effect on Shakespeare are not sufficiently documented to make this theory tenable. Since Ayrer died in 1605 and the first documented representation of *The Tempest* dates from 1618, both ideas of a pre-Shakespearean play or a German original seem plausible, as Kathleen M. Lea cautiously argues.[62] It remains a conjecture difficult to prove but fascinating as far as the mutual influence is concerned.

Doubtlessly, the plots of *Sidea* and *The Tempest* are similar: an exiled prince with magical powers leads a retired life with his daughter in a fabulous setting populated by devils/ghosts or spirits, until his enemy's son falls into his hands. In both plays, the two youths fall in love and ultimately bring about the reconciliation of the hostile fathers, albeit through a different sequence of events. There is even a striking similarity in the arrangement of specific scenes that can hardly be coin-

---

[59] For the play see ibid., vol. 4, 2177–224. The list of plays performed on that occasion can be found in Trautmann, "Englische Komoedianten in Nürnberg (1593–1648)", *Archiv für Litteraturgeschichte* XIV (1886), pp. 113–42, p. 127.
[60] See Creizenach, p. LVII.
[61] See Cohn, p. LXXI.
[62] See Lea, *IPC*, vol. 2, p. 444.

cidental, for example the attachment of the lovers after the episode of the imprisoned prince who is obliged to pile up logs of wood.[63] Although the similarities in the plots are probably ascribable to common Italian sources of *novelle* and pastorals, they cannot be the sole explanation for the evident closeness between Ayrer and Shakespeare. Therefore, some kind of contact must have occurred.

A further source of inspiration for *Sidea* not noted so far could be the comedy *Eine schöne lustig triumphirende Comoedia von eines Königes Sohne auß Engellandt und des Königes Tochter auß Schottlandt*, also known as *Serule und Astrea* (part of *ECUT* 1620). The parallels to this play which are closer to Ayrer's sphere of influence than Shakespeare go from the hindered love of the young generation in a magical setting to the name of the magician Runcifax in *Serule und Astrea*, who echoes the devil Runcifall at the service of Sidea's father. Moreover, the protagonist of the comic subplot of *Sidea*, Jahn the Miller, gets two women pregnant, pranks their fathers and escapes disguised as an old woman – a series of *lazzi* that was surely influenced by the English Comedians' clown Jahn Posset and/or Commedia dell'Arte.

Another play worth mentioning for a fortunate combination of Italian and English material is the *Spiegel weiblicher Zucht und Ehr. Comoedia von der schönen Phaenicia und Graf Tymbri von Golison auß Arragonien, wie es ihnen in ihrer ehrlichen Lieb gangen, biß sie ehelich zusammen kommen; hat 17 Personen und 6 Actus* ('The Mirror of Female Chastity and Honour. Comedy of the beautiful Phaenicia and Count Tymbre of Golison from Aragon, enacting their honest love until they were married; with seventeen characters and six acts').[64] The play opens mythologically with Venus and Cupid's plan to punish the cold-hearted Tymbor by making him lose his mind over the beautiful Phaenicia as in Ariosto's *Orlando Furioso*. This mythological setting is reversed in the subsequent interlude with the clown Jahn who is pierced by one of Cupid's arrows, not in his heart but, ironically, in the derrière. To relieve him from his pain, Jahn's friend Gerardo suggests he should sing a serenade under his beloved Anna Maria's window, but instead pranks him by dressing up as the woman and pouring water over the conceited clown. As Meissner observes, this *burla* reprises the soaked fool episode of Vincentio Ladislao dramatised earlier by Duke Heinrich Julius.[65] Moreover, Tymbor and Phaenicia's wedding is hindered by an intrigue that takes up the strand of Don John slandering Hero in *Much Ado About Nothing* (1598–9); the same trick on the balcony happens in *Phaenicia*, when the clown dresses up as Phaenicia to make Tymbor believe his fiancée is accepting someone else's sere-

---

[63] Cf. the love scene in von Keller, ed., *Ayrers Dramen*, vol. 3, p. 2200, and *The Tempest* 3.1.
[64] The play is contained in von Keller, ed., *Ayrers Dramen*, vol. 3, pp. 2051–131.
[65] See Meissner, *Die englischen Comoedianten zur Zeit Shakespeares in Österreich*, p. 33.

nade. Similarly, the feigned death of the innocent bride and her miraculous 'resurrection' are very close to the English comedy.[66] The principal reason for this resemblance may be a novelistic source known both to Shakespeare and to Ayrer and creatively combined with other influences in this play.[67]

Despite their efforts at appropriating the content and style of the English Comedians' repertoire, neither Heinrich Julius nor Ayrer managed to build a bridge for the entrance of Shakespeare's works into Germany. Instead, the plays continued to circulate in numerous adaptations without any reference to the author, until eighteenth-century translators drew attention to the name of Shakespeare, as Simon Williams explains.[68] The same unconscious or rather unacknowledged borrowings can be noticed in some plays by the most important dramatist of the Baroque period, Andreas Gryphius.

Andreas Gryphius

In the early seventeenth century, Spain was living the *siglo de oro* (golden century), Commedia dell'Arte and Commedia erudita were blooming in Italy, France was about to reach its literary apex with Molière and Racine, and England had produced masters like Marlowe and Shakespeare. Meanwhile, Germany lagged behind because the instability of the Thirty Years' War deeply affected the lives of the people and consequently the development of culture and literature. For this reason, Andreas Gryphius's (actually Greif, 1616–64) contribution to establishing German literature in the contemporary international panorama is particularly significant.

---

[66] Lawrence M. Price argues that Ayrer's play might go back to an "Ur-*Much Ado*" brought to the Continent and then turned over into a novel by Sebastian Brandt. Apart from Brandt, Ayrer was probably also inspired by a theatrical version of the English Comedians he saw in Nuremberg. See Price, *The Reception of English Literature in Germany*, p. 24.

[67] Ayrer also tried his hand at the beloved Menaechmi theme in his *Comedia von zweyen Brüdern aus Syracusa* ('Comedy of two brothers from Syracuse'), closer to the original by Plautus, as the title suggests, than to Shakespeare's *Comedy of Errors*. According to Trautmann, other supposed relations between Ayrer and the English repertoire are to be found in *Eroberung von Konstantinopel* ('Siege of Constantinople'), which owes much to the *Türkische Triumphkomödie* performed by Spencer in Nuremberg in 1613 on the basis of George Peele's *The Turkish Mahomet and Hyrin the fair Greek*. In a like manner, Trautmann argues that Ayrer's *Comedia vom König von Cypern, wie er die Königin von Frankreich bekriegen wollte und zu der Ehe bekam* ('Comedy of the King of Cyprus who set out to fight the Queen of France and ended up marrying her') is connected to Lewis Machin and Gervase Markham's *The Dumbe Knight: A historicall Comedy* (London, 1608). The knight's name, Philocles of Cyprus, recurs in the German version entitled *Philocle und Mariana oder Untreu schlegt seinen eignen Herrn* ('Philocle and Mariana or Unfaithfulness beats its own master') in Spencer's repertoire. See Karl Trautmann, "Englische Komoedianten in Nürnberg (1593–1648)", *Archiv für Litteraturgeschichte* XIV (1886), pp. 113–42, p.127. Apart from the English adaptations, Ayrer might have taken inspiration from the Italian source of the English playwrights, namely Bandello.

[68] See Simon Williams, *Shakespeare on the German stage*, vol. 1, *1586–1914*, p. 267.

Born in the year of Shakespeare's death into a Protestant family in the re-Catholicised region of Silesia, Gryphius grew up as an orphan surrounded by fighting, fires and repeated outbreaks of the plague.[69] After a long stay in Holland, where he came into contact with contemporary Dutch and Spanish literature, and travels to France and Italy, he settled down as a syndic of the principality of Gosau from 1650 to his death. His cosmopolitan education inspired the literary achievements of "the greatest German dramatist of his generation", as J. G. Robertson calls Gryphius,[70] who was able to put into practice Martin Opitz's theoretical precepts for a national literature, contained in the *Buch von der Deutschen Poeterey* (1624), with an eye to foreign influences, like the English Comedians and Commedia dell'Arte. Two plays shall briefly illustrate this convergence of currents.[71]

The reception of professional English drama is retraceable in Gryphius's *Schimpfspiel*, i.e. invective play, *Absurda Comica Oder Herr Peter Squentz* ('Absurda comica or Master Peter Squentz', 1657).[72] Initially, this satiric depiction of a village schoolmaster's attempt to perform the tragedy of Pyramus and Thisbe for a noble audience was planned as a comic interlude in a tragedy about two unhappy lovers, *Cardenio und Celinde oder Unglücklich Verliebte* ('Cardenio and Celinde or Unhappy Lovers', 1661), as Fausto De Michele asserts, but then evolved into a separate play.[73] Although the parodic connection between the main plot and the subplot was lost, the metatheatrical aspect remained as there still is a play-within-the-play recalling the artisan plot in Shakespeare's *A Midsummer Night's Dream*. Some scholars argue that Gryphius was not directly acquainted with the English play,[74] but the similarity of themes and names suggests that Shakespeare must have served as a model, adapted by the itinerant players or other writers. In fact, in the preface, Gryphius alias Philip-Gregorio Riesentod indicates

---

[69] See Robertson, *A History of German Literature*, p. 215.
[70] Ibid., p. 216.
[71] For a full appreciation of Gryphius, which would lie beyond the scope of this study, see e.g. Katja Reetz, *Andreas Gryphius: Edition, Kommentierte Übersetzung und Werkstudie mit Ausführlicher Wissensgeschichtlicher Einleitung* (Berlin: W. de Gruyter, 2019); Eberhard Mannack, *Andreas Gryphius* (Stuttgart: J.B. Metzler, 2017) and Nicola Kaminski and Robert Schütze, ed., *Gryphius-Handbuch* (Berlin: Walter de Guyter, 2016).
[72] Richard Erich Schade observes that the title *Absurda comica* is ambiguous and can be translated either as 'comical absurdities' or as 'absurd comic'. See *Studies in Early German Comedy, 1500–1650* (Columbia, SC: Camden House, 1988), p. 200. Such double meanings, malapropisms and telling names are in accordance with the Baroque linguistic playfulness.
[73] See Fausto De Michele, "Andreas Gryphius e la Commedia dell'Arte: *Horribilicribrifax Teutsch*, tra originalità e imitazione", in Martino and De Michele, ed., *La ricezione della Commedia dell'Arte nell'Europa centrale 1568–1769*, pp. 183–212, p. 184.
[74] See Barton W. Browning, "The Development of the Vernacular Drama", in Hoffmeister, ed., *German Baroque Literature*, pp. 339–56, p. 347.

the philologist Daniel Schwenter as his primary source.[75] He then declares himself to have turned Schwenter's satire on the Meistersinger and the amateur actors of the guilds into a sociocritical play-within-the-play. Since Schwenter's *Von Piramus und Thisbe* and *Von Seredin und Violandra* were lost, it can only be assumed that the similarities with Shakespeare were mediated by this obscure author or, as Ralf Haekel surmises, that Gryphius used him as a pretext to deviate from his English model.[76]

The first and most evident detail that points to the influence of Shakespeare and the English Comedians regards the transliterated names of some characters, like Peter Quince into Peter Squentz and Bully Bottom into Bullabutän. In compliance with the taste of the audience, greater importance was given to the English clown Pickelhering, who replaces Bottom in the role of Pyramus, while Squentz assumes that of master of ceremonies and Prologue. Other names like King Theodorus and Princess Violandra, not present in Shakespeare, may owe a debt to Schwenter.

Secondly, the two versions of the play-within-the-play share the same parodied Latin source, namely the tale of Pyramus and Thisbe from the "Memorium phosis", as Squentz erroneously pronounces the *Metamorphoses* attributed to the 'Doctor of the Church Ovidius' in Act 1. These quotes highlight the importance of language, juxtapositions and malapropisms in this comedy.[77] Moreover, there are numerous sideswipes at contemporary authors, plays and characters. For example, when Master Lollinger, linen-weaver and Meistersinger, suggests that Clod-George should be given the role of Thisbe because "as a boy he played Susanna",[78] he might be alluding to the applauded religious play of the English Comedians' repertoire, also dramatised by Heinrich Julius. Another intertheatrical reference in the same scene involves Pickelhering, who pokes fun at Sackville's clown when he affirms that he cannot "laugh and weep at the same time like Jehan Potage."[79]

[75] See the preface to *Peter Squentz* in Hermann Palm and Friedrich-Wilhelm Wentzlaff-Eggebert, ed., *Andreas Gryphius: Werke in drei Bänden mit Ergänzungsband*, vol. 1 (Darmstadt: Wissenschaftliche Buchgesellschaft, 1961), pp. 7–9. Hoffmeister argues that Gryphius may have been acquainted with the story of Pyramus and Thisbe precisely via Schwenter. See "The English Comedians in Germany", in Hoffmeister, ed., *German Baroque Literature*, p. 152.

[76] See Ralf Haekel, "Von Bottom zu Pickelhering. Die Kunst des komischen Schauspiels in Shakespeares *A Midsummer Night's Dream* und Gryphius' *Absurda Comica*", in Stefanie Arend, Dirk Niefanger, and Thomas Borgstedt, ed., *Anthropologie und Medialität des Komischen im 17. Jahrhundert (1580–1730)* (New York and Amsterdam: Rodopi, 2008), pp. 207–221, p. 208.

[77] "PETER SQUENTZ. […] Der heilige alte kirchen-lehrer Ovidius schreibet in seinem schönen buch Memorium phosis, das Piramus die Thisbe zu einem brunnen bestellet habe." Palm and Wentzlaff-Eggebert, ed., *Andreas Gryphius: Werke in drei Bänden mit Ergänzungsband*, vol. 1, p. 11. Translation: 'The holy Doctor of the Church Ovidius writes in his beautiful book Memrium phosis that Pyramus summoned Thisbe to a fountain.'

[78] See ibid.

[79] "PICKELHÄRING: Das ist gut! Den ich kan nicht zugleich lachen und weinen / wie Jehan Potage." Ibid., p. 18.

Between the lines, there are references to theatrical practices of the time too, like the difficult rehearsals for troupes of amateurs in their free time, the strict selection of plays to be performed before a courtly audience,[80] and the tedious discussion on wages, which in the comedy ends merrily with Squentz buying drinks for everyone. The most original trait of Gryphius's satire on ignorant schoolmasters and outdated amateur performers is to denounce the poor conditions in which drama was produced at the time through a distancing effect, whilst simultaneously celebrating the expertise of the professional players enacting the parody.

Apart from the English sources, the Italian influence was strongly felt in *Horribilicribrifax Teutsch* (1647–50). Alternatively termed *Schertzspiel* (a synonym for comedy meaning joking play) or *Lustspiel* (comedy), it revolves around Horribilicribrifax and Daradiridatumdarides, two bragging and cheating cowards in the tradition of the *miles gloriosus* by Plautus and of the Capitano of Commedia dell'Arte. Gryphius might have seen the vainglorious Capitano involved in plots of courtship, intrigue and marriage on stage during his Italian sojourn, but most of his knowledge was bookish. In fact, Alberto Martino points out that all the Italian quotations in the play lead back to *Le bravure del Capitano Spavento* by Francesco Andreini (1607/1618).[81] In any case, the playwright reworked the theme on his terms: behind the humorous satire, Hinck sees a bitterness towards the soldiers and wars, which destroyed Germany for thirty years, comparable to the function of the Capitano as an outlet for the Italian actors to express their discontent with the Spanish enemy.[82] These examples give an impression of the fruitful connection between Italian and English drama on the Baroque stage, even after the touring companies from England stopped travelling in the German lands.

As has been shown in this short overview, the three major imitators and emulators of the English Comedians from the 1590s to the mid-seventeenth century maintained some of the most effective staging techniques, plots and characters imported from England and Italy, although the way they worked with them was slightly different from the amalgamation to the naturalisation phase. At the turn of the century, Heinrich Julius wrote *for* the English actors at his service and perhaps also *with* them, which accounts for the proximity of style and content. Rather than being pure imitation, his oeuvre is the product of a creative transfer: on the

---

[80] For instance, in Act 2 of *Peter Squentz*, the principal presents a lengthy catalogue of plays to the king, which comprises evergreens of the English Comedians' repertoire such as *Esther and Haman*, *Caesar*, and *Lazarus*, only to admit later that he is able to act out just *Pyramus and Thisbe*. In addition, prior to the mechanicals' presentation of their play to the king, the Marshal assists to a preview as was common habit among city councils when the English Comedians asked for permission to play.

[81] See Martino, *Die italienische Literatur im deutschen Sprachraum*, p. 404.

[82] For a detailed analysis of the play see Hinck, *Das deutsche Lustspiel des 17. und 18. Jahrhunderts und die italienische Komödie*, chapter 4. Ralf Böckmann observes that the Capitano was the only mask of Commedia dell'Arte to be adapted as a protagonist of German Baroque drama while the other masks merely appeared in minor roles. See *Die Commedia dell'Arte und das deutsche Drama des 17. Jahrhunderts*, p. 134.

one hand, he amplified the scenic effects of the English actors to themes derived from German jest literature. On the other, he adapted the itinerant players' input to the cultural context, for example by having the clown Jahn Posset speak Low-German dialect. Still in the amalgamation phase prior to 1620, Ayrer shaped a new dramatic style which mingled the verse forms of the Meistersinger and dramatic structure of Sachs's plays with strands and characters borrowed from the English players' repertoire. When Gryphius published his comedies in the naturalisation phase after the war (1648–70), the direct impact of the English Comedians was already far removed and mediated by their successors on the stage or by their imitators on the page, so his works became genuine appropriations sensitive of the new 'national' poetic precepts and the cultural predominance of Italy and France rather than England.

7.3. Arlecchino, Pickelhering and Hanswurst/Kasperl – Rivals or Brothers?

Historical evidence and the analysis of the plays attributed to, or influenced by, the English itinerant players indicate that their immediate success was due to popular elements such as (impromptu) songs and rhymes, dancing and acrobatics. Following the model of the famous clown Richard Tarlton, clowning and music were the first forms of contact and transmission both of different acting styles and international subject matter and remained the most frequently imitated and inspiring elements on German and Austrian stages. In many respects, the clown was at the core of the Continental stage productions. For this reason, this figure represents a fascinating example of intercultural theatricality between England, Germany and Italy.

While the content of the original English plays was mostly transferred, freely translated and combined with other sources, Stockfisch and Pickelhering appear to be the first genuinely original creations of the English Comedians to meet the audiences' tastes and expectations. The spectators could easily identify with the clown figure since he recalled the peasant of the Shrovetide plays, addressed the audience directly and mediated between the spectators and the performers. Instead of imitating the philosophical style of Shakespeare's wise fool, the Anglo-German clown developed into a personage with specific characteristics and predictable ways of acting like a 'type'. As in Commedia dell'Arte, he took up simple forenames (Hans, Kasperl) combined with local dishes (Stockfisch, Pickelhering) or drinks (Posset) to underline the physical and therefore universal sphere behind his existence. So solid was the success of Stockfisch and Pickelhering in the German-speaking lands that his name overshadowed the actor playing him, whose personality merged with the persona on stage. This again, is similar to Commedia dell'Arte, in which the same actor would always play the same personage to shape the 'type' and be shaped by it.

These examples introduce the focus of this section on morphologic and genetic similarities between the Pickelhering of the English Comedians, the Austro-German Hanswurst, the Viennese Kasperl and the Italian Arlecchino of Commedia dell'Arte. Pickelhering is the starting point of this investigation, which completes the circle of this study, from the early modern fools and clowns to their subsequent development. His stature is due to several factors ascribable to the popular comic tradition and common to all clown figures, although each national clown has peculiar, non-exchangeable features.

Firstly, like most clowns from antiquity to nowadays, Pickelhering wears a funny hat, a ruff, a colourful jacket and large trousers, and carries a slapstick. His ridiculous appearance and costume are easily recognisable and recur in similar terms in extant depictions and descriptions.

Secondly, he is characterised by grotesque grimaces and by specific movements on stage, especially pantomime, acrobatic tricks and gestures alluding to sexuality, bodily functions and physical violence. These visual elements are typical of popular forms of entertainment tied to orality.

Thirdly, Pickelhering possesses a specific speech genre which includes fixed phrases like "Potz schlapperment" or "Das dich ein Enzian", direct addresses to the audience in confidential asides and "fiction-external communication",[83] excessive boasting, malapropism, a topsy-turvy logic and a tendency to (wilfully) misunderstand what is said or take everything literally. Moreover, his use of local dialects underlines his subordinate status but also his proximity to an audience of commoners.

Fourthly, his roles encompass that of the greedy, sly and hungry servant similar to the Zanni (as in *Der Jud von Venedig*), the naive yokel echoing the 'natural fool' of the Elizabethan stage (as in the *Pickelheringspiel mit einen Stein*), the rejected bawdy suitor (as in *Von Sidonia und Theagene*), the sarcastic hangman (for example in *Esther*), the subjugated and abused husband/lover (*Den Windelwäscher*) or the cuckold (*Pickelheringspiel mit einen Stein*).

These characteristics and roles of Pickelhering, derived from the analysis of *ECUT* 1620 and *Der Jud von Venedig*, are furthermore confirmed by the poem *Markschiffs-Narren* by Max Mangoldt (Frankfurt, 1597). It vividly describes the English entertainers acting in separate spheres like the Zannis of Commedia dell'Arte: the plump and ridiculous *Jan* is preoccupied with food while the elegant *Springer* performs acrobatic leaps. A personage called *Wursthänsel* (perhaps an alternative name of Hanswurst) is merely mentioned without a description.

Als die Fechtschul hatt ein Endt,	Soon as the swordsmen's play had ended
Da war nun weiter mein Intent,	I turned to something I'd intended:
Zu sehen das Englische Spiel,	To see these English players and such
Davon ich hab gehört so viel.	Of whom I'd often heard so much.
Wie der Narr drinnen, JAN gennent,	They had a Fool, they called him JAN;
Mit Bossen wer so excellent:	Rival in jesting had he none.
Welche ich auch bekenn fürwar,	And I can solemnly attest,
Daß er damit ist Meister gar.	Of all such clowns he was the best.
Verstell also sein Angesicht,	He made such all-outlandish faces,

---

[83] The concept is borrowed from Joel B. Lande, *Persistence of Folly*, p. 70.

Daß er keim Menschen gleich mehr sicht.	He'd lost all trace of human graces.
Auf Tölpisch Bossen ist sehr geschickt,	From ribald stuff he never flinched;
Hat Schuch, der keiner ihn nicht trückt.	So big his shoes, they never pinched.
In sein Hosen noch einr hett Platz,	So big his pants, that in his fly
Hat dran ein ungeheren Latz.	Another easily could lie.
Sein Truppen ihn zum Narren macht,	At table cares not how he slops
Mit der Schlappen, die er nicht acht	When in his mouth the spoon he pops.
Wenn er da fängt zu löffeln an,	His habit for a clown was made –
Und dünckt sich seyn ein fein Person.	He thinks he's quite a smart young blade.
Der WURSTHÄNSEL ist abgericht	The WURSTHÄNSEL has been described
Auch zimlicher massen, wie man sicht:	with all the traits to him ascribed,
Vetretten beyd ihr Stelle wol,	and both play their part well.
Den SPRINGER ich auch loben soll,	The TUMBLER also did us please,
Wegen seines hohen Springen,	He sprang high in the air with ease.
Und auch noch anderer Dingen:	In dancing he had not a peer,
Höfflich ist in all seinen Sitten,	A joy it was to see him near.
Im tantzen und all seinen Tritten.	His hose they fitted him so tight,
Daß solcheche fürwar ein Lust zu sehen,	His codpiece was a lovely sight.
Wie glatt die Hosen im Anstehen,	Nubile maids and lecherous dames
Welche mit fleiß so zugericht,	He kindled into lustful flames.
Daß man was zwischen Beinen sicht:	Their interest I cannot blame,
Darnach etwan pflegen zu schawen,	He was so expert in his game. […]
Glüstige Weiber und Jungfrauwen. […]	Had he the art to be invisible.
Aber ein Kunst die fehlt ihm noch,	His income he could easily triple.
Und sprengt er noch einest so hoch.	For, know that those who paid their fee
Welch wol diente zu seinen Sachen,	To witness a bright comedy,
Wann er sich kündt unsichtbar machen.	Or hear the tunes of fine musicians,
Noch mehr Gelt er verdinen möcht,	Were more entranced by the additions
Dann nicht alle, versteht mich recht,	Of bawdy jests and comic strokes,
Hineyn zu diesem Spiele gehen,	Of antics and salacious jokes,
Die lustige Comedien zsehen,	And what, with his tight-fitting hose
Oder der Music und Seiten spiel,	The well-bred tumbler did disclose.[85]
zu gefallen, sonder ihr viel	
Wegen deß Narren groben Bossen,	
Und deß Springers glatten Hosen.[84]	

Despite the ironic tone, this short poem shows some esteem for the Comedians' talent and gives insight into the different facets of the popular clown. We are informed that the audience was attracted by the boorish manners and grotesque bodily expressions of Jan – probably Sackville's stage character Jahn Posset – and his physicality ("Verstell also sein Angesicht" and "Auf Tölpisch Bossen ist sehr geschickt") as well as by his funny costume with large shoes, oversized trousers and a giant flap ("Hat Schuch, der keiner ihn nicht trückt. / In sein Hosen noch einr hett Platz, / Hat dran ein ungeheren Latz"). Because of his appearance and his constant preoccupation with food, Jan is ridiculed by the other characters on stage

---

[84] *Markschiffs-Narren* by Max Mangoldt (1597). See Creizenach, p. 325 for the full text.
[85] Translation of *Markschiffs-Narren* by Max Mangoldt (1597) provided by Ernest Brennecke, ed., S*hakespeare in Germany: 1590–1700*, p. 8

and laughed at by the audience. The "Schlappe" he wears might refer to the typical headdress worn by fools, a two-pointed cap, sometimes with bells at its end, that resembles either the devil's horns – symbol of wickedness – or donkey's ears for stupidity.[86] The other entertainer presented by Mangoldt is the courteous, handsome and acrobatic *Springer*. Apart from his elegance and agility ("Höfflich ist in all seinen Sitten, / Im tantzen und all seinen Tritten"), the predominant physical characteristic of the tumbler is his sexuality, visualised by his skin-tight and too revealing trousers ("Wie glatt die Hosen im Anstehen, [...] / Daß man was zwischen Beinen sicht"). Seen in this light, it is possible to draw a parallel to the two Zannis of Commedia dell'Arte, later combined in Arlecchino. The always hungry simpleton Zanni coincides with the description of Jan, while the acrobatic virtuosity and sexual arousal of the sly Zanni recur in the *Springer*. This does not imply that the character traits were taken from Commedia dell'Arte but corroborates the idea of a greater shared network of popular culture common to all these comic figures, regardless of their nationality. The centre-staging of the clown by the English Comedians and Commedia dell'Arte was so fruitful and solidly successful that new figures continued to develop in Germany and Austria.

An example is Hanswurst, a clownish character welded together from "the German-Austrian medieval tradition of the Shrovetide farce – the name itself first occurs in a Low-German version of Brant's Ship of Fools in 1519 – the English actors' Pickelhering, and the Italian *arlecchino*", as Gerhart Hoffmeister argues.[87] The creative interculturality and intertextuality addressed in the quote can be recognised particularly well in the multiple names used to describe the clown in the various collections of plays attributed to the English Comedians. Whereas in *ECUT* (1620) the clown is usually called Pickelhering, *Liebeskampff* (1630) features Hans Wurst alongside Pickelher(r)ing/Pickelhäring, Jean Potage/Schampitache, John Clant/Klam (a distorted form of clown?), Jahn Posset/

---

[86] Foolish asses can be found both in Italian and English theatre: Bottom unwittingly wears the head of a donkey in *A Midsummer Night's Dream* (Act 3), while Pantalone is turned into an ass in the *scenario Il gran mago* ('The Great Magician'), edited by Basilio Locatelli. For the text of *Il gran mago* see Testaverde, ed., op. cit., pp. 375–84.

[87] Hoffmeister, "The English Comedians in Germany", in Hoffmeister, ed., *German Baroque Literature*, pp. 142–58, p. 153. He further explains that the name "hans myst" first appeared in Sebastian Brant's *Narrenschiff* ('Ship of Fools'), a satiric allegory in verse published in 1494 in Basel, Switzerland. Other mentions of Hanswurst occur in a polemic pamphlet by Martin Luther called *Wider Hans Worst* ('Against Hans Worst' 1541, incidentally targeted against the Catholic grandfather of Duke Heinrich Julius of Wolfenbüttel, Heinrich V of Brunswick-Wolfenbüttel) as well as in several *Fastnachtspiele* and comedies of the sixteenth and seventeenth centuries. In 1775, Goethe paid a tribute to the national clown in a fragment entitled *Hanswursts Hochzeit oder der Lauf der Welt* ('The Wedding of Hanswurst, or the Way of the World') sometimes called *Harlequins* or *Pickelherings Hochzeit* in previous sources, proving the synonymity of the clowns' names. (See ibid.). For a study of the history of Hanswurst see Helmut G. Asper, *Hanswurst: Studien zum Lustigmachen auf dem deutschen Theater im 17. und 18. Jahrhundert* (Emsdetten: Lechte, 1980).

Bouset, or John Banser/Panzer (alluding to the *panse* i.e. belly in French and thus further expanded to Dickwanst meaning fatty). These names all point to a shift towards an assimilation of features other than those of the English clown. From the mid-seventeenth century, the German Hanswurst supplanted his English colleagues and was further expanded in Viennese popular theatre with the transition from Hanswurst to Kasperl, who eventually superseded Arlecchino. A brief description of a famous form of popular theatre in Austria, the *Altwiener Volkstheater*, and its protagonists illustrate the metamorphoses of the English and Italian influence in Austria.[88]

In this context, in "Elizabethan Comedy and the Alt-Wiener Volkstheater" W. E. Yates convincingly points out a series of traits common to English drama of the sixteenth century and Viennese popular comedy.[89] 1) These forms of entertainments wanted to amuse the audience with a minor corrective social function, a deficiency for which they were criticised by regulators like John Lyly and Johann Christoph Gottsched.[90] 2) Both made use of successful comic figures to cater to the taste of popular spectators. 3) In both countries, this "Volk" was more homogeneous than an anonymous "Publikum" insofar as the audiences were linked by comparable expectations, namely a greater interest in the speed of production than in the literary polish. In addition, they shared a similar willingness to collaborate in the creation of "theatrical drama",[91] for example by taking up the parodic reversal of generic conventions on the parts of the author or actor. Therefore, playwrights who usually wrote for established ensembles in both traditions, commonly recycled materials also in the forms of continuations of well-received plays with beloved characters like Falstaff or Hanswurst/Kasperl.[92] Although most of these aspects can be applied to Commedia dell'Arte too, Yates does not look much into its influence on the Austrian stage but stresses the fundamental distinction of the Italian acting style as "a stylised comedy of 'types' dependent largely on pantomime" versus Elizabethan drama and the *Alt-Wiener Volkstheater* as "character-comedy".[93] However, this assertion does not take into

---

[88] For an overview on the *Wiener Volkstheater* see Otto Rommel, *Die Alt-Wiener Volkskomödie: Ihre Geschichte vom barocken Welttheater bis zum Tode Nestroys* (Vienna: Schroll, 1952); Jürgen Hein, *Das Wiener Volkstheater* (Darmstadt: Wissenschaftliche Buchgesellschaft, 1997); Eva-Maria Ernst, *Zwischen Lustigmacher und Spielmacher: Die komische Zentralfigur auf dem Wiener Volkstheater im 18. Jahrhundert* (Münster: Lit-Verlag, 2003); and Johann Hüttner and Jürgen Hein, ed., *Johann Nestroy: Sämtliche Werke. historisch-kritische Ausgabe* (Vienna: Jugend & Volk, 1996).

[89] W. E. Yates, "Elizabethan Comedy and the Alt-Wiener Volkstheater", *Forum for Modern Language Studies* 3 (1967), pp. 27–35.

[90] Ibid., p. 27.

[91] Ibid., p. 28. Yates borrows the term "theatrical drama" from Muriel C. Bradbrook, *The Growth and Structure of Elizabethan Comedy* (Berkeley and Los Angeles: University of California Press, 1956), p. 11.

[92] See Yates, op. cit., p. 29.

[93] Ibid., p. 32.

account the English Comedians' mediation nor the creative contribution of itinerant troupes in shaping popular theatre in German-speaking countries. The historical development of the Viennese popular theatre and the predominance of its comic figures show that its antecedents were not only English drama but also Commedia dell'Arte.

Initially, the competition between Italian and English troupes in Vienna delayed the genesis of an autochthonous professional theatre, but as soon as the foreign influences were assimilated, they gave way to a unique combination of forces in the *Altwiener Volkstheater*. As Jürgen Hein argues, the *Altwiener Volkstheater* is a synthesis of Jesuit school drama, Baroque opera and the *Wanderbühne*. For this reason, the predominant characteristics of this trivialised sociocritical comedy coincide with those of popular theatre in general: physicality, carnality, theatricality, music, dance, a mixture of styles, local colour, sentimentalisation, exaggeration and provocation.[94] To supplant the Italian rivals, the comedian Joseph Anton Stranitzky (1670/6?–1726), formerly a marionette player, and his son-in-law and fellow-actor Gottfried Prehauser (1699–1769) developed the pre-existing German clown figure of the good-natured but also cynical Hanswurst into a genuinely Austrian comic character equivalent to Arlecchino or Zanni.[95] There are several instances that prove the foreign influence on the Viennese popular stage in the ambit both of theatre as a set of performative skills and of drama. Still, it was an original form of theatre with its own peculiar characteristics.

Firstly, as a character, Hanswurst is usually a *Sauschneider* from Salzburg, i.e. a person who castrates pigs. His costume made him as recognisable as a Commedia dell'Arte mask and immediately calls to mind the engravings of Pickelhering discussed in chapter 5. In the following stage-portrait, the famous actor Gottfried Prehauser wears the same ruff, the same long jacket, the same large trousers, but also a few new items like the pointed green hat (like the Zanni Brighella) instead of a large, feathered one, a blue flap and a pair of colourful braces with the distinctive monogram HW for Hans Wurst. In addition, there is a visible wooden sword or slapstick called *Narrenpritsche* – an old prop of jesters and clowns, with which to beat their opponents and provoke laughter.

[94] See Jürgen Hein, *Das Wiener Volkstheater* (Darmstadt: Wissenschaftliche Buchgesellschaft, 1997), pp. 5–6.
[95] In 1709, the Viennese *Kärntnertortheater* hosted a Commedia dell'Arte company with the 'Italian Pickelhering' Sebastiano di Scio instead of Hanswurst, but the audience insisted so strongly on the Austrian clown that in 1712 Stranitzy became its permanent leaseholder, as Otto G. Schindler recounts. Due to this unprecedented popular petition favouring Austrian actors over performers from abroad, Stranitzky's *Teutsche Comoedianten Banda* ('German Comedians') secured a stable stage for the national response to the stiff foreign competition. See Otto G. Schindler, "Comici dell'Arte alle corti austriache degli Asburgo", in Martino and De Michele, ed., *La ricezione della Commedia dell'Arte nell'Europa centrale 1568–1769*, pp. 96–144, p. 139.

Figure 15: Gottfried Prehauser (1699–1769) as Hanswurst. Subtitle: Inter Vienn[enses-Comico elictus Hans-Wurst.

Although a real peasant would not have worn such an impractical outfit, the traditional dress and the use of the Viennese dialect – despite the explicit reference to Prehauser's birthplace, Salzburg – connected the Viennese Hanswurst to the lower social classes. Likewise, the Zannis from Bergamo were the servants and porters of the rich Venetians, transferred onto the stage in Commedia dell'Arte. Another point in common with the Commedia dell'Arte is the use of semi-improvisation with the other 'types' who caricatured the members of contemporary Viennese society. A novelty was that Hanswurst combined the central role of solo entertainer independent from the interplay with the ensemble, like Pickelhering, with the kinetic expressiveness and the never-changing characteristics of Arlecchino. In addition, Otto Rommel observes that a typically Austrian trait of Hanswurst is the autochthonous placid common sense with which the peasant comments on the *Haupt- und Staatsaktionen* around him like the archaic and detached fool of popular culture.[96]

---

[96] Otto Rommel maintains that Hanswurst's appeal lies in the fact that his childishly naive psyche and emotions are transparent to the audience. This transparency makes the spectators take his point of view on stage. See *Die Alt-Wiener Volkskomödie: Ihre Geschichte vom barocken Welttheater bis zum Tode Nestroys* (Vienna: Schroll, 1952), p. 325.

Prehauser's repertoire comprised farcical *Possen* and *Zauberspiele* (magical plays in line with the "fantastic-type Commedia dell'Arte"[97] and Shakespeare's mature comedies), but also the *Singspiel*, a legacy of the Shrovetide tradition and of the English Comedians, which would ultimately become the *Posse mit Gesang* i.e. farce with singing, as Jürgen Hein explains.[98] In 1720, Prehauser followed in Stranitzky's footsteps as performer of the 'New Viennese Hanswurst', a bourgeois version of the clown similar to the development from Zanni to Arlecchino.[99]

This change of tone was mainly due to the fierce *Hanswurststreit* (Hanswurst dispute) started in the 1730s by the literary critic and regulator Johann Christoph Gottsched (1700–66)[100] with the help of the actress Friederike Caroline Neuber (1697–1760). The new dramatic rules introduced by Gottsched destabilised Hanswurst but could not banish him completely. In fact, in 1737 he reappeared at the Kärntnertor Theater, played by Prehauser, next to the comic figures inspired by Commedia dell'Arte: Arlecchino/Harlekin (Franz Anton Nuth), Dottore/Bernardon (Felix Kurz) und Pantalone (Johann Ernst Leinhaas).[101] Like the English professional clowns Tarlton and Kempe and the characters of Commedia dell'Arte, Hanswurst had to sacrifice some of his spontaneous extemporisation to become a fixed literary 'type'.

In a literary form, Hanswurst's spirit was revived in Kasperl, a clown figure created by Johann Laroche (1745–1806) to comply with the Gottsched requirements: less improvisation and more authority to the author. As Hein points out, Kasperl was less free ranging in speech than the sociocritical Hanswurst and

---

[97] See Hinck, *Das deutsche Lustspiel des 17. und 18. Jahrhunderts und die italienische Komödie*, pp. 19–20.

[98] See Hein, *Das Wiener Volkstheater*, p. 20.

[99] Another aspect which reveals the closeness of the performers of the *Wiener Volkstheater* to Commedia dell'Arte is the fact that on 21 and 22 April 1723 Prehauser's troupe put on a play entitled *Arlequin Cartouche* in Augsburg, based on a German translation of Luigi Riccoboni's French *canovaccio* of 1721. See Martino, *Die italienische Literatur im deutschen Sprachraum*, p. 400.

[100] The predominance of French neoclassical drama led to Hanswurst's banishment from the stage in Leipzig in 1737, since his improvisations were neither instructional nor norm compliant. Instead, in *Versuch einer Critischen Dichtkunst vor die Deutschen* (Leipzig 1730), Gottsched insisted on the rigid Aristotelian unities of time, place and action as well as on the *Ständeklausel* ('estates-clause'). See Johann Christoph Gottsched, *Versuch einer Critischen Dichtkunst vor die Deutschen* (Leipzig: Bernhard Christoph Breitkopf, 1730), p. 707. Not even Gotthold Ephraim Lessing tried to revive the popular clown, although he criticised the annihilation of the English influence on German theatre in favour of French and Italian models. See 'Den 16. Februar 1759. Siebzehnter Brief' in G. E. Lessing, *Briefe, die neueste Literatur betreffend* (Berlin and Stettin: Nicolai, 1759), pp. 97–112.

[101] See Ferdinand Raab, *Johann Joseph Felix von Kurz genannt Bernardon: Ein Beitrag zur Geschichte des deutschen Theaters im XVIII. Jahrhundert* (Frankfurt a.M.: Rütten & Loening, 1899), p. 13. Moreover, Philipp Hafner (1735–64), the father of the Viennese *Volkstheater* and the promoter of its moral value, drew inspiration from Goldoni's *Il servitore di due padroni* ('The Servant of Two Masters', 1745) in his adaptation *Hanswurst Diener zweier Herren*.

aimed more at entertainment than at social criticism with his *lazzi* full of idle talk, for which he earned the epithet *Larifari* (literally meaning absurd babble).[102] Both his costume and role reveal parallels to other comic figures and Italian 'types'. On the one hand, Kasperl's appearance maintained much of Hanswurst's peasant clothes, enriched with a red heart stitched on to his chest as an identifying feature; and like Hanswurst, he spoke the Viennese dialect peppered with slang words. On the other hand, his roles comprise that of bird-catcher (like Mozart's Papageno), innkeeper (like Pedrolino), lemon seller, gawky domestic (like Arlecchino), disguised barber and painter, as Rommel explains.[103] Kasperl also gained fame as a marionette and puppet, well known to the present day.[104]

The *Volkstheater* tradition continued until the eighteenth century, when the combination of Pickelhering, Hanswurst and Arlecchino with various names populated the *Volksstücke* of Ferdinand Raimund (1790–1836) and Johann Nestroy (1801–62).[105] Although the English influence was soon overshadowed by the Italian ascendancy, it gave a valuable contribution to initiating the Viennese *Volkstheater* and its clowns.[106]

In summary, the figure of the clown, analysed with a focus on the geographical axis of England-Germany-Austria-Italy, represents a complex example of intercultural theatricality. Although it is undeniable that Pickelhering, Jahn Posset, Hans Stockfisch, Hanswurst, Kasperl and Arlecchino are unique in their own way, each being shaped, and emotionally charged, by a diverse historical, cultural and national context, they share a surprising number of features denoting kinship, such as: 1) a recognisable costume and props; 2) a centrality of the body with references to sex and bodily functions, physical and verbal violence, ridiculed to produce a

---

[102] See Hein, *Das Wiener Volkstheater*, p. 41.
[103] See Rommel, *Die Alt-Wiener Volkskomödie*, p. 437.
[104] Subsequently, the marionette of Kasperl became the ambivalent protagonist of 40 plays by the Count Franz von Pocci (1807–76) based on fairy tales and legends.
[105] *Volksstück*, literally people's play, designates plays for and about the common people. Their aim is to educate and entertain by means of satire and pantomime (e.g. in the *Posse*), as Hein argues in *Das Wiener Volkstheater*, p. 71. The *Wiener Volkstheater* was strongly influenced by English and Italian currents, as Ferdinand Raimund's *Bauer als Millionär* and *Alpenkönig und Menschenfeind* show. These two comedies combined 'types' and fantastic scenery from Commedia dell'Arte and the Viennese rendition of the clown figure introduced by the English Comedians. *Othello*, based on the story *Un Capitano Moro* ('A Moorish Captain') by Bocaccio's disciple Giovanni Battista Giraldi or Cinthio, first published in 1565 and later transposed on the Viennese stage as *Othellerl, der Mohr von Wien oder Die geheilte Eifersucht* by Karl Meisl in 1806, is a good example of parodic reversal in popular terms of a Shakespearean tragedy. Since the intersection of English and Italian traditions with the Viennese *Volkstheater* lies beyond the scope of this study, I will not go too much into detail.
[106] For Alexander Schwarz, Kasperl, the Austrian response to Arlecchino, is an amalgamation of Pulcinella, Pickelhering, Hanswurst and the late-medieval Till Eulenspiegel, as he explains in "Strangers to Sorrow: Arlecchino and Eulenspiegel", in Martino and De Michele, ed., *La ricezione della Commedia dell'Arte nell'Europa centrale 1568–1769*, pp. 323–40, p. 326.

cathartic function; 3) involvement in scenes of carnivalesque reversal and restoration of order; 4) recognisable, predictable and universal character traits caricatured as social 'types' with distinguishable dialects and regional identities; and 5) a constant preoccupation with earthly concerns – visible also in the food-derived names – that involve the audience and disrupt the illusion by means of self-referential theatricality and mother wit.

This leads to the conclusion that the similarity of many popular features which flourished in German-speaking countries in the period of activity of the English itinerant players is ascribable to two major factors. On the one hand, to a humanist revival of Roman comedy with its stock characters and medieval traditions such as the Lord of Misrule and Vice from the moralities; and on the other hand, to contemporary currents like Commedia dell'Arte immersed in the popular oral culture of early modern Europe. A parallel function makes Arlecchino, Pickelhering and Hanswurst/Kasperl brothers, sons of the same network of shared knowledge, but with unique national features developed independently of each other.

Conclusion – A New Perspective on Early Modern Popular Theatre

The overarching aim of this work has been to outline the multidirectional movement of early modern popular theatre along a European north-south axis, in which travelling troupes brought together and rearranged cultures of different countries. Adaptation theory has been used to reconstruct the genesis of professional theatre in Italy, England, Germany and Austria and to analyse the plays associated with the English Comedians in Germany. This has produced outcomes on different levels.

1) On a historical level, early modern theatre in Germany and Austria appears to be the product of an amalgamation of 'high' and popular culture, mediated not only on the page but also on the stage by wandering troupes from Italy and England. These professional companies shared a democratic organisation, were fostered and legitimised by noble patronage and entertained public audiences. Such a twofold target audience as well as the control mechanisms of licensing and censure required a certain elasticity and adaptability on the part of the performers even before they started travelling abroad, hence the focus on adaptation theory.

As the evolution of popular theatre in Italy and in England appears similar, one might speak of increasingly complex stages of dramaturgy, using Anna Baesecke's model of theatrical development.[1] However, her model does not explain what happened when the English players ventured out to new countries and returned to previous stages of complexity. Exporting their acting style and plays alone was not enough to meet the audience's "horizon of expectations",[2] so amalgamation and adaptation were necessary preliminary steps in order to become naturalised. I have called this phenomenon 'backwards involution' and tried to draw attention to its effectiveness. In a certain sense, the intercultural theatricality of early modern theatre resulted from the professional companies' coping strategies for facing the challenges of touring abroad.

2) On a cultural level, the Italianate influence in northern Europe was interlinked with the development of plot, character and theatrical production at work in the second half of the sixteenth century in England, and then transposed on to the German stage in a continuous exchange. I argue that this amalgamation in creation and reception was facilitated by a common network of knowledge derived, on the one hand, from the ubiquitous borrowing from the classics under the aegis of the Renaissance, and on the other hand, from popular and oral performance cultures characterised by stock characters and physicality, for example *Fastnachtspiele* and Commedia dell'Arte. The influence of Commedia dell'Arte

---

[1] See Baesecke, *Das Schauspiel der englischen Komödianten in Deutschland*, p. 10.
[2] See Hans Robert Jauss, "What is and for what purpose does one study literary history?". Lecture at Constance held in April 1967, p. 24, quoted in Holub, *Reception Theory: A Critical Introduction*, p. 60.

on Elizabethan drama and, in particular, on the English Comedians has not been given enough credit so far, as the exclusion of Commedia dell'Arte from the analysis of Shakespeare's sources by Geoffrey Bullough and from the most recent study on *ECUT* by Ralf Haekel proves.[3] The sine qua non to fully understand adaptation and amalgamation is the inclusion of as many participants in the network of shared knowledge as possible.

3) On the level of theatre and drama, Commedia dell'Arte, Elizabethan drama and German Baroque theatre evolved from a mixture of popular and erudite traditions and made use of dramatic practices and subject matters derived from ancient (oral) sources. As soon as favourable conditions made acting a profession, popular elements entered the realm of 'high' culture and shaped the aesthetic taste of the time. The analysis of the major collection of plays associated with the English itinerant players in Germany, *ECUT* (1620), reveals how early modern Italian and English theatre influenced the emerging German and Austrian stages and their subsequent development as far as plot, structure, arrangement, characters and staging techniques are concerned.

4) On the level of intercultural theatricality, the study of popular culture as network of shared knowledge is a valuable and current approach to (re)discovering commonalities. Vestiges of common roots at work in the transnational effort of professionalising theatre can be found in memorialised and hybridised sources from literature – for example the Bible, Greco-Roman drama, *novelle*, chapbooks, pastoral poetry – and from oral traditions such as fairy tales and folk plays. In the adaptation process, the sources were usually reduced and condensed into effective dramatisations, able to reach a wide and diverse audience owing to universal 'types' and recurring motifs – such as the hen-pecked husband, cuckoldry or the test of faithfulness – as well as appealing staging techniques. Visualisation entails: overemphasised gesture to reflect states of mind and convey a message via nonverbal communication; music and dance to entertain the spectators and underline what was said; and a predominance of narrative monologues and self-characterisations in the serious main plots in contrast to enactment and physicality in the comic subplots. The popularity of physicality and musicality gave way to two new genres in German drama, the *Pickelheringspiel* and the *Singspiel*, derived from the *Fastnachtspiel* with influences from the English jig and the 'types' of Commedia dell'Arte.

The initial assumption that Italian and English theatre share common elements which were then transposed onto the German stage has been underpinned by similarities both in the historic development of professional theatre as economic venture and in the playing techniques, texts and their reception. An exchange of popular traditions and erudite contents was already at work in the Middle Ages and grew exponentially in the early modern period with the rediscovery of antiquity.

[3] See Geoffrey Bullough, *Narrative and Dramatic Sources of Shakespeare* (1966) and Ralf Haekel, *Die Englischen Komödianten in Deutschland: Eine Einführung in die Ursprünge des deutschen Berufsschauspiels* (2004).

Despite the later distinction into 'high' and popular culture, these two spheres were connected and inspired each other. In particular, the figure of the fool, drawn from Plautian models and shaped by Medieval figures like Vice or the Lord of Misrule, represents an example of the transition from rite to performance to paid-for spectacle in which the professional clown functioned as a mediator of content and as a representative of popular culture and theatre.

In more general terms, my approach, which has focused on the dynamics of intercultural theatricality between Elizabethan drama, Commedia dell'Arte and German theatre, also produces insights into what *popular theatre* means in the early modern period. Its most essential factor is mobility or itineracy, a movement both on the page and on the stage. Hence, the intertheatrical commonalities – derived from a comparative study of the theatre cultures at issue and extracted from the analysis of plays contained in *ECUT* – can be categorised as follows: orality, physicality, universal 'types', adaptability and professionalisation of theatre as entertainment for the masses.

Firstly, *orality* is an important common feature of popular theatre in early modern England, Italy and Germany through which traditions, acting styles and subject matters were passed on. Unlike the Renaissance tide of literarisation, popular theatre was pervaded by a predominance of the actor or character over the author or playwright, which subsequently gave way to a collaborative theatre for a diverse audience. If there was a theatrical text, it was usually minimalistic and at least partly open to improvisation.

Secondly, popular performances are generally characterised by *physicality*, i.e. by a heightened attention to gesture, facial expression and proxemics, which are more important than, or even substitute, the textual sphere. For this reason, an intertheatrical rather than a purely intertextual approach is more suitable to fully understand the cultural interactions on the stage. In performance, the centrality of the body with its functions and needs (hunger, sexuality, bodily functions of metabolism and defecation, pain and physical violence) reflects popular culture insofar as it establishes a connection with ancient rituals of fertility and allows the spectators' immediate identification with the characters on stage.

Thirdly, the appearance of *'types'* as trivialised allegories of human vices in the tradition of the morality play is a persistent feature of early modern popular theatre, of which Commedia dell'Arte is only the most renowned version. Apart from recognisable masks, costumes or props, a method to distinguish and characterise the sociolinguistic stratification of the personages is the variation of speech genres, common to England, Italy, Germany and Austria. In the performance cultures of these countries, the often-underestimated clown is a central 'type' who provides the key to understanding the play through laughter, parody and farce. The clown as representative of the people plays with the fact that any spectacle is a mirror in which the audience can see the world reflected under a different light. Likewise, he is often involved in metamorphosis and transformation: from rites of passage to carnivalesque reversals and the reconstitution of order.

Fourthly, due to the itinerant nature of early modern popular theatre, a vital principle for its creation and reception is the *adaptability* of the performance through improvisation and cross-cultural amalgamation. The itinerant companies were among the first to understand that, as commercial products, plays had to be shaped by the taste of the audience and not vice versa; despite their seemingly low intellectual value, their marketability testifies to the actors' success. Thus, the emerging economic aspect was essential for the *professionalisation* of early modern theatre.

These four principles reveal that popular theatre works as a network of shared knowledge. Influences from various traditions, such as Elizabethan drama, Shakespeare's plays, Commedia dell'Arte and Commedia erudita, old German forms of drama, and the rediscovery of the classics appear as foundations of a complex amalgamation at work in *ECUT*. Although attempts at preserving these essentially oral forms of performance in print deprived them of their spontaneity, many elements, such as the use of 'types', survived literarisation in popular theatre across cultures. The occurrence of these features is ascribable to a humanist revival of Roman and medieval traditions but also to contemporary currents passed on by word of mouth in early modern Europe. From this network of shared knowledge stem not only the Roman mimes as well as Plautus' stock characters, but also the fool in medieval Shrovetide plays, the mask of Arlecchino in Commedia dell'Arte, the Anglo-German Pickelhering and the comic characters of Hanswurst and Kasperl in the *Wiener Volkstheater*.[4]

Essentially, early modern theatre is best described as an amalgamation of "peeces and Patches", as the Elizabethan traveller Fynes Moryson critically observed,[5] that were selected by professional playwrights and actors to suit the taste of the audiences for financial gain. The itinerant players would prioritise practicability over more literary formats in order to ensure mutual comprehension by means of theatricality, and not just of drama, even if this meant returning to previous stages of theatrical and dramatic development. Instead of deploring the

---

[4] Seen in this light, the patterns of comedy in the early modern period seem to have maintained their power throughout the centuries and up to the present day. This is perhaps due to the fact that Commedia dell'Arte and Shakespeare's plays have informed expectations of the twenty-first-century audience, and their characters and plots are so familiar that they still resonate nowadays. According to Amy Drake, many modern genres are indebted to the amalgamation of Commedia dell'Arte techniques and Shakespearean plays: from Strauss and Hofmannsthal's popular opera *Ariadne auf Naxos*, a hybrid of Commedia dell'Arte 'types' and Greek mythology, to Charlie Chaplin's slapstick scenes in film. Even sitcoms like *The Big Bang Theory* reprise the fixed characters who never really change in the course of the episodes. See Drake, "Commedia dell'Arte Influences on Shakespearean Plays: *The Tempest, Love's Labor's Lost,* and *The Taming of the Shrew*", *Selected Papers of the Ohio Valley Shakespeare Conference* 6:3 (2013), pp. 11–30, p. 22.

[5] Charles Hughes, ed., *Shakespeare's Europe: Unpublished Chapters of Fynes Moryson's Itinerary. Being a Survey of the Conditions in Europe at the End of the 16th Century*, vol. 4, p. 304.

low quality of their plays, as Moryson does, critical opinion should value the strategy of a 'backwards involution' as an efficacious intercultural tool that was sensitive to the context. In an effort to adapt their plays to their German-speaking audience, the English Comedians resorted to genres and figures immersed in popular culture and thus available to all the international participants in this network, without having to classify this culture as 'high' or 'low'. Although their plays were constructed primarily with a view to stage-effectiveness, they still opened new horizons to German drama that might have developed fruitfully – as the examples of Heinrich Julius and Ayrer prove – had the Thirty Years' War not put a sudden end to cultural activity. Even scholars disavowing the English actors' contribution had to acknowledge their success but generally failed to explain it in terms of quality.[6]

This viewpoint persists not only in academia but also in Daniel Kehlmann's recent bestseller *Tyll* (2017), which premiered in Salzburg in 2019.[7] In *Tyll*, Kehlmann rewrites the biography of the legendary Renaissance fool Till Eulenspiegel (presumably died 1350) but takes the poetic liberty of inserting him in the panorama of the Thirty Years' War; for example, he has Tyll enter the service of Frederick V of the Palatinate, 'Winter King' of Bohemia and indirect cause of the conflict. The king's wife Elizabeth, daughter of James I of England, is fond of the amusement the fool provides because she misses the lavish theatrical performances of her home country. Comparing the uncouth pranks of the paltry comedians who 'wander around through the rain screaming, jumping, farting and beating each other' to the delicate and elegant plays given by Kemp, Alleyn, Burbage and Shakespeare at Whitehall, Elizabeth blames the backwardness on the disharmonious German language and thinks back to her youth with nostalgia. Once more, the merits of the travelling companies are overshadowed by the sophistication of courtly theatre. This seems contradictory in light of historical evidence which confirms that precisely these professional entertainers, namely Kemp

[6] For instance, if one looks up 'Germany' in *The Oxford Companion to Shakespeare* edited by Michael Dobson et al. (2nd ed. Oxford: OUP, 2015), it says: "Within Shakespeare's lifetime English players travelling to courts and towns of Central Europe acquainted German audiences with professional acting, performed garbled versions of some Shakespeare plays from their repertoires, and left a few literary offshoots behind, such as a play by the Duke of Brunswick-Wolfenbüttel derived from *Titus Andronicus* and A. Gryphius' farce *Peter Squenz* adapted from *A Midsummer Night's Dream*. But their migrations practically ended with the Thirty Years' War. Shakespeare's name remained unknown; an encyclopedia first mentioned it in 1682 with obvious lack of first-hand knowledge."

[7] "Das gute Theater hatte ihr am meisten gefehlt, von Anfang an, mehr noch als das genießbare Essen. In deutschen Landen kannte man kein richtiges Theater, da zogen armselige Komödianten durch den Regen und schrien und hüpften und furzten und prügelten einander […]. Sie dachte oft ans Hoftheater in Whitehall zurück. […] Dann kamen sie tief gebückt heran, Alleyn und Kemp und der große Burbage selbst, um Papas Hand zu küssen." Daniel Kehlmann, *Tyll* (Hamburg: Rowohlt, 2017), pp. 230–2. The Austrian debut of *Tyll* at the Schauspielhaus Salzburg on 18 September 2019 was directed by Maya Fanke. See <http://schauspielhaus-salzburg.at/spielplan/stuecke1/TYLL_3486> (last accessed 27 June 2020).

and close collaborators of Alleyn and Shakespeare, shaped early modern popular theatre in Germany and Austria as entertainment for the courts and for the masses. As the English Comedians' success proves, it is most likely that the quality of the extant texts was inferior to their performance and therefore one should be careful to judge their performing ability on the basis of theatrical documents like *ECUT*. It would be equally misleading to read a *canovaccio* of the Commedia dell'Arte without considering the enactment of the skeletal plot, which would give life to the bare outline.

To put things in perspective, the seal of backwardness must concede to the idea of an effective 'backwards involution'. The premise should be that *ECUT* and similar collections of plays, upon which a reconstruction of the English Comedians' dramatic activity is based, are theatrical documents immersed in orality and not finalised dramas. Therefore, an analysis – and eventual evaluation – cannot be done by using the same criteria as with literary texts. Aided by parameters which go beyond the textual sphere and include the cultural and socio-economic context in which English plays were exported to, and performed in, German-speaking lands, this study demonstrates that the multi-layered process of adaptation was more than just downsizing and corrupting Shakespeare to amuse an uneducated audience. However, as long as the pinnacle of English literature is the direct and only benchmark, the English Comedians' endeavours do not stand a chance of being acknowledged as the beginning of adapting Shakespeare and as remarkable examples of cross-cultural adaptation; and as long as the history of theatre is studied only in a national perspective, the complex network of shared knowledge underlying early modern theatre does not come into focus. My study aims to be a step in this comparative, European direction to make visible that the Renaissance "collapse of boundaries"[8] also applies to the liminality of intercultural theatricality as literature without borders of nation, genre or textual boundaries. As has been shown, the rigidity of printed texts and fixed formal structures developed only in the seventeenth and eighteenth century with Opitz, Goldoni and Gottsched. Initially, theatre, and especially itinerant popular theatre, was dynamic and characterised by improvisation and adaptation.

To conclude, intercultural theatricality on the popular stage in Italy, England, Germany and Austria offers a new perspective on how early modern theatre came into being and for what it should be appreciated; and ultimately, it shows that culture is always constituted by an amalgamation and adaptation of "peeces and Patches".

---

[8] See Chris Barker, *Cultural Studies: Theory and Praxis*, pp. 63–9.

Bibliography

Alexander, Robert. J. "George Jolly [Joris Joliphus] der wandernde Player und Manager / Neues zu seiner Tätigkeit in Deutschland (1648–1660)". *Kleine Schriften der Gesellschaft für Theatergeschichte* 29/30 (1978): 31–48.
Arend, Stefanie; Thomas Borgstedt and Dirk Niefanger, ed. *Anthropologie und Medialität des Komischen im 17. Jahrhundert (1580-1730)*. Chloe, Beihefte zu Daphnis. Amsterdam and New York: Rodopi, 2008. Web. 3 May 2019.
Asper, Helmut G. *Hanswurst: Studien zum Lustigmachen auf dem deutschen Theater im 17. und 18. Jahrhundert*. Emsdetten: Lechte, 1980.
---. *Spieltexte der Wanderbühne: Ein Verzeichnis der Dramenmanuskripte des 17. und 18. Jahrhunderts in Wiener Bibliotheken*. Vienna: Verband der wissenschaftlichen Gesellschaften Österreich, 1975.
Aust, Hugo; Peter Haida, and Jürgen Hein, eds. *Volksstück: Vom Hanswurstspiel zum sozialen Drama der Gegenwart*. Munich: C.H. Beck, 1989.
Baesecke, Anna. *Das Schauspiel der englischen Komödianten in Deutschland. Seine dramatische Form und Entwicklung*. Diss. University of Halle, 1935.
Bakhtin, Mikhail. *Rabelais and his World*. Trans. Hélène Iswolsky. Bloomington, Indiana: Indiana UP, 1996 [1940].
Barker, Chris. *Cultural Studies: Theory and Practice*. London et al.: Sage Publications Ltd, 2003.
Barthes, Roland. *Mythologies*. Trans. Annette Lavers. London: Vintage, 1996 [1972].
---. *Critical Essays*. Trans. by Richard Howard. Evanston, IL: North Western UP, 1972.
Baskerville, Charles Read. *The Elizabethan Jig and Related Song Drama*. Chicago: University of Chicago Press, 1929.
Bassnett, Susan. *Translation Studies*. 3rd ed. London and New York: Routledge, 2002.
Bate, Jonathan, ed. *The Arden Shakespeare Titus Andronicus*. London and New York: Routledge, 1995.
Ben-Amos, Dan, ed. *Folklore Genres*. Austin and London: University of Texas Press, 1976.
Bennett, Susan. *Theatre Audiences: A Theory of Production and Reception*. London and New York: Routledge, 1990.
Bevington, David M. *From Mankind to Marlowe: Growth of Structure in the Popular Drama of Tudor England*. 2nd ed. Cambridge, Massachusetts: Harvard UP, 1968.
Bloom, Harold. *Anxiety of Influence: A Theory of Poetry*. 2nd ed. Oxford: OUP, 1997.

Böckmann, Ralf. *Die Commedia dell'Arte und das deutsche Drama des 17. Jahrhunderts: Zu Ursprung und Einflussnahme der italienischen Maskenkomödie auf das literarisierte deutsche Drama*. Nordhausen: Traugott Bautz, 2010.

Bolte, Johannes. *Das Danziger Theater im 16. und 17. Jahrhundert*. Hamburg and Leipzig: Leopold Voß, 1895.

---. *Die Singspiele der englischen Komödianten und ihrer Nachfolger in Deutschland, Holland und Skandinavien*. Hamburg and Leipzig: Leopold Voß, 1893.

Bosman, Anston. "Renaissance Intertheater and the Staging of *Nobody*". *ELH* 71 (2004): 555–85. *JSTOR*. Web. 17 February 2020.

Braekman, W. L. "The relationship of Shakespeare's *Titus Andronicus* to the German play of 1620 and to Jan Vos's play 'Aran en Titus'". *Studia Germanica Gandensia* 10 (1968): 7–77. Web. 8 June 2020.

Bragaglia, Anton Giulio, ed. *Andrea Perrucci: Dell'arte rappresentativa premeditata, ed all'improviso*. 10 vols. Florence: Edizioni Sansoni Antiquariato, 1961 [1699].

Brand, Peter, and Bärbel Rudin. "Der englische Komödiant Robert Browne (1563–ca. 1621): Zur Etablierung des Berufstheaters auf dem Kontinent". *Daphnis: Zeitschrift für Mittlere Deutsche Literatur und Kultur der Frühen Neuzeit (1400-1750)* 39 (2010): 1–119.

Brauneck, Manfred. *Die Welt als Bühne: Geschichte des europäischen Theaters*. 6 vols. Stuttgart: Metzler, 2007.

---, ed. *Spieltexte der Wanderbühne*. 6 vols. Berlin and New York: Walter de Gruyter, 1975.

Braunmuller, A. R. and Michael Hattaway, ed. *The Cambridge Companion to English Renaissance Drama*. Cambridge: CUP, 1997.

Brennecke, Ernest. *Shakespeare in Germany: 1590–1700. With Translations of Five Early Plays*. Chicago and London: University of Chicago Press, 1964.

Bullough, Geoffrey. *Narrative and Dramatic Sources of Shakespeare*. 8 vols. London and New York: Routledge, 1966.

Burke, Peter. *Popular Culture in Early Modern Europe*. New York: Harper & Row, 1978.

Carlson, Marvin. *The Haunted Stage: The Theatre as Memory Machine*. Ann Arbor: University of Michigan Press, 2011.

Catholy, Eckehard. *Das deutsche Lustspiel: Vom Mittelalter bis zum Ende der Barockzeit*. Darmstadt: Wissenschaftliche Buchgesellschaft, 1968.

Chaffee, Judith and Oliver Crick, eds. *The Routledge Companion to Commedia dell'Arte*. London and New York: Routledge, 2017.

Chambers, Edmund K. *The Elizabethan Stage*. 4 vols. Oxford: Clarendon Press, 1965 [1923].

---. *The Medieval Stage*. 2 vols. Oxford: OUP, 1925.

Clare, Janet. *Shakespeare's Stage Traffic: Imitation, Borrowing and Competition in Renaissance Theatre*. Cambridge: CUP, 2014.

Clubb, Louise George. *Italian Drama and Shakespeare's Time*. New Haven and London: Yale UP, 1989.
Coelsch-Foisner, Sabine and Christopher Herzog, eds. *Visualisierung: Bildwissen – Wissensbilder*. Heidelberg: Winter, 2020.
--- and Timo Heimerdinger, eds. *Theatralisierung*. Heidelberg: Winter, 2016.
---, ed. *Memorialisation*. Heidelberg: Winter, 2015.
--- and Dorothea Flothow, eds. *High Culture and/versus Popular Culture*. Heidelberg: Winter, 2009.
---, ed. *Elizabethan Literature and Transformation*. Tübingen: Stauffenburg, 1999.
Cohn, Albert. *Shakespeare in Germany in the Sixteenth and Seventeenth Centuries: An Account of English Actors in Germany and the Netherlands and of the Plays Performed by Them During the Same Period*. Wiesbaden: Dr Martin Sändig oHG., 1967 [1865].
Creizenach, Wilhelm. *Die Schauspiele der englischen Komödianten*. Berlin and Stuttgart: W. Spemann, 1889.
Croce, Benedetto. *Poesia popolare e poesia d'arte*. Bari: Giuseppe Laterza e figli, 1957.
Crüger, Johannes. "Englische Komoedianten in Straßburg im Elsass". *Archiv für Litteraturgeschichte* XV (1887): 113–25.
Davis, Tracy C. and Thomas Postlewait, eds. *Theatricality*. Cambridge: CUP, 2003.
Dekker, Thomas. *The Pleasant Comedie of Old Fortunatus: As it was plaied before the Queenes Maiestie this Christmas, by the Right Honourable the Earle of Nottingham, Lord high Admirall of England his Seruants*. London, 1600. Web. 4 June 2018.
Denzler, Georg; Norbert Glatzel and Jacob Lehmann, eds. *Commedia dell'Arte: Harlekin auf den Bühnen Europas*. Bamberg: Bayerische Verlagsanstalt, 1981.
Dobson, Michael; Stanley Wells, Will Sharpe and Erin Sullivan, eds. *The Oxford Companion to Shakespeare*. 2nd ed. Oxford: OUP, 2015.
Doran, Madeleine. *Endeavors of Art: A Study of Form in Elizabethan Drama*. Madison, Wisconsin et. al: University of Wisconsin Press, 1972 [1954].
Drake, Amy. "Commedia dell'Arte Influences on Shakespearean Plays: *The Tempest, Love's Labor's Lost*, and *The Taming of the Shrew*". *Selected Papers of the Ohio Valley Shakespeare Conference* 6:3 (2013): 11–30. Web. 12 May 2019.
Dshiwelegow, A. K. *Commedia dell'Arte: Die italienische Volkskomödie*. Berlin: Hensche, 1958.
Duchartre, Pierre Louis. *The Italian Comedy: The Improvisation Scenarios, Lives, Attributes, Portraits and Masks of the Illustrious Characters of the Commedia dell'arte*. Trans. R. T. Weaver. New York: Dover, 1966 [1929].
Dusinberre, Juliet. *The Arden Shakespeare As You Like It*. London and New York: Routledge, 2006.

Ebelsberger, Simone. *'Everyman' und 'Jedermann': Die Wirkungsgeschichte eines mittelenglischen Morality Plays*. Diss. University of Salzburg, 2002.

Engel, Eduard. *Geschichte der Deutschen Literatur von den Anfängen bis in die Gegenwart*. Leipzig: Freytag, 1906.

Erne, Lukas and Kareen Seidler, eds. *Early Modern German Shakespeare: Hamlet and Romeo and Juliet. 'Der Bestrafte Brudermord' and 'Romio und Julieta' in Translation*. London: Bloomsbury, 2022.

---, Maria Shmygol and Florence Hazrat, eds. *Early Modern German Shakespeare: Titus Andronicus and The Taming of the Shrew. 'Tito Andronico' and 'Kunst über alle Künste, ein bös Weib gut zu machen' in Translation*. London: Bloomsbury, 2022.

Ernst, Eva-Maria. *Zwischen Lustigmacher und Spielmacher: Die komische Zentralfigur auf dem Wiener Volkstheater im 18. Jahrhundert*. Münster: Lit, 2003.

Felver, Charles S. "The Commedia dell'Arte and English Drama in the Sixteenth and Early Seventeenth Centuries". *Renaissance Drama, A Report on Research Opportunities* 6 (1963): 24–34. JSTOR. Web. 11 April 2019.

Ferrone, Sirio. *La Commedia dell'Arte: Attrici e attori italiani in Europa (XVI-XVIII secolo)*. Torino: Einaudi, 2014.

---. *Attori, mercanti, corsari: La Commedia dell'Arte in Europa tra Cinque e Seicento*. Torino: Einaudi, 2011 [1993].

Fischer-Lichte, Erika. *Geschichte des Dramas: Epochen der Identität auf dem Theater von der Antike bis zur Gegenwart*. 2 vols. Tübingen et al.: Francke, 1990.

Flemming, Willi, ed. *Barockdrama: Das Schauspiel der Wanderbühne*. Leipzig: Reclam, 1931.

Foakes, R. A., ed. *Henslowe's Diary*. 2nd ed. Cambridge: CUP, 2002.

---, ed. *The New Cambridge Shakespeare: A Midsummer Night's Dream*. Cambridge: CUP, 1995.

Frazer, James George. *The Golden Bough: A Study in Comparative Religion*. London: Macmillan, 1890.

Fredén, Gustaf. *Friedrich Menius und das Repertoire der englischen Komödianten in Deutschland*. Stockholm: Palmers, 1939.

Gaedertz, Karl Theodor. *Gabriel Rollenhagen: Sein Leben und seine Werke; Beitrag zur Geschichte der deutschen Litteratur des deutschen Dramas und der niederdeutschen Dialektdichtung nebst bibliographischem Anhang*. Leipzig: Hirzel, 1881.

Genée, Rudolph. *Geschichte der Shakespeare'schen Dramen in Deutschland*. Hildesheim: Georg Olms, 1969 [1870].

Genette, Gérard. *Palimpsests: Literature in the Second Degree*. Trans. Channa Newman and Claude Dobinsky. Lincoln: Nebraska UP, 1997 [1982].

Goedecke, Karl and Edmund Goetze, eds. *Grundriß zur Geschichte der deutschen Dichtung*. 2 vols. Dresden: Ehlermann, 1886.

---, ed. *Schwänke des sechzehnten Jahrhunderts*. Leipzig: Brockhaus, 1880.
Goldoni, Carlo. *Il teatro comico*. 1750. Milan: Mursia, 1969.
Gottsched, Johann Christoph. *Versuch einer Critischen Dichtkunst vor die Deutschen*. Leipzig: Bernhard Christoph Breitkopf, 1730. Web. 2 March 2019.
Gottwald, Herwig. *Mythos: Mythisches in der modernen Literatur*. Heidelberg: Synchron, 2004.
Gozzi, Carlo. *The Memoirs of Count Carlo Gozzi*. Trans. John Addington Symonds. London: John C. Nimmo, 1890 [1797].
Griffith, Eva. *A Jacobean Company and its Playhouse: The Queen's Servants at the Red Bull Theatre (c. 1605–1619)*. Cambridge: CUP, 2013.
Groos, G. W., ed. *The Diary of Baron Waldstein: A Traveller in Elizabethan England*. New York: Thames and Hudson, 1981.
Gstach, Ruth. *Die Liebes Verzweiffelung des Laurentius von Schnüffis: Eine bisher unbekannte Tragikomödie der frühen Wanderbühne; Mit einem Verzeichnis der erhaltenen Spieltexte*. Berlin and Boston: Walter de Gruyter, 2017.
Gundolf, Friedrich. *Shakespeare und der deutsche Geist*. Bad Godesberg: Küpper, 1947.
Gurr, Andrew. *Playgoing in Shakespeare's London*. Cambridge: CUP, 1996.
---. *The Shakespearian Playing Companies*. Oxford: Clarendon Press, 1996.
Haekel, Ralf. *Die Englischen Komödianten in Deutschland: Eine Einführung in die Ursprünge des deutschen Berufsschauspiels*. Heidelberg: Winter, 2004.
---. "Neue Quellen zur Geschichte der Englischen Komödianten in Deutschland". *Shakespeare Jahrbuch* 140 (2004): 180–5. Web. 12 March 2018.
Harms, Paul. *Die deutschen Fortunatus-Dramen und ein Kassler Dichter des 17. Jahrhunderts*. Hamburg and Leipzig: Leopold Voß, 1891.
Harris, Charles. "The English Comedians in Germany before the Thirty Years' War – The Financial Side". *PMLA* 22.3 (1907): 446–64. Web. 17 May 2020.
Hartleb, Hans. *Deutschlands erster Theaterbau: Eine Geschichte des Theaterlebens und der Englischen Komödianten unter Landgraf Moritz dem Gelehrten von Hessen-Kassel*. Berlin and Leipzig: Walter de Gruyter, 1936.
Hausmann, Frank-Rutger. *Bibliographie der deutschen Übersetzungen aus dem Italienischen von den Anfängen bis 1730*. 2 vols. Tübingen: Max Niemeyer, 1992.
Hein, Jürgen. *Das Wiener Volkstheater*. Darmstadt: Wissenschaftliche Buchgesellschaft, 1997.
---. *Theater und Gesellschaft: Das Volksstück im 19. und 20. Jahrhundert*. Düsseldorf: Bertelsmann, 1973.
Henke, Robert. *Performance and Literature in the Commedia dell'Arte*. Cambridge: CUP, 2002.
Hergemöller, Bernd-Ulrich, ed. *Rändergruppen der spätmittelalterlichen Gesellschaft*. Warendorf: Fahlbusch, 2001.
Herz, Emil. *Englische Schauspieler und englisches Schauspiel zur Zeit Shakespeares in Deutschland*. Nendeln: Kraus Reproduktion, 1977 [1903].

Heywood, Thomas. *An Apology for Actors: In Three Books, from the Edition of 1612, Compared with That of W. Cartwright, with an Introduction and Notes.* London: Shakespeare Society, 1841. Web. 8 August 2018.

Hilton, Julian K. *The 'Englische Komödianten' in German-speaking States, 1592–1620: A Generation of Touring Performers as Mediators between English and German Cultures.* Diss. University of Oxford, 1984.

Hinck, Walter. *Das deutsche Lustspiel des 17. und 18. Jahrhunderts und die italienische Komödie: Commedia dell'Arte und théâtre italien.* Stuttgart: Metzler, 1965.

Hoffmeister, Gerhart, ed. *German Baroque Literature: The European Perspective.* New York: Frederick Ungar, 1983.

Holub, Robert C. *Reception Theory: A Critical Introduction.* London and New York: Methuen, 1984.

Hughes, Charles, ed. *Shakespeare's Europe: Unpublished Chapters of Fynes Moryson's Itinerary. Being a Survey of the Conditions in Europe at the End of the 16th Century.* 6 vols. Manchester: Sherratt and Hughes, 1903.

Hunter, George K. "Italian tragicomedy on the English stage". *Renaissance Drama* 6 (1973): 123–48. *JSTOR* Web. 17 February 2020.

Hutcheon, Linda. *A Theory of Adaptation.* London and New York: Routledge, 2006.

Hüttner, Johann and Jürgen Hein, ed. *Johann Nestroy: Sämtliche Werke. Historisch-kritische Ausgabe.* 15 vols. Vienna: Jugend & Volk, 1996.

Iser, Wolfgang. *Prospecting: From Reader Response to Literary Anthropology.* Baltimore and London: The Johns Hopkins UP, 1993.

---. *Der Akt des Lesens: Theorie ästhetischer Wirkung.* München: Wilhelm Fink, 1976.

Katritzky, M. A. and Pavel Drábek, eds. *Transnational Connections in Early Modern Theatre.* Manchester: Manchester UP, 2019.

---. *The Art of Commedia: A Study in the Commedia dell'Arte 1560-1620 with Special Reference to the Visual Records.* Amsterdam: Rhodopi, 2006.

Kehlmann, Daniel. *Tyll.* Hamburg: Rowohlt, 2017.

Keller, Adelbert von, ed. *Ayrers Dramen.* 8 vols. Hildesheim and New York: Georg Olms, 1973 [1865].

Kennedy, Dennis, ed. *The Oxford Encyclopaedia of Theatre and Performance.* Oxford: OUP, 2003.

Kernodle, George R. *From Art to Theatre, Form and Convention in the Early Modern.* Chicago: University of Chicago Press, 1944.

Kindermann, Heinz. *Theatergeschichte Europas.* 10 vols. Salzburg: Otto Müller, 1957–74.

Kommerell, Max. *Dichterische Welterfahrung: Essays. Betrachtungen über Commedia dell'Arte.* Frankfurt: Vittorio Klostermann, 1952.

Kraye, Jill, ed. *The Cambridge Companion to Humanism.* Cambridge: CUP, 1996.

Lande, Joel B. *Persistence of Folly: On the Origins of German Dramatic Literature*. Ithaca and London: Cornell UP, 2018.

Laroque, François. *Shakespeare's Festive World: Elizabethan Seasonal Entertainment and the Professional Stage*. Trans. Janet Lloyd, Cambridge: CUP, 1993.

Lea, Kathleen Marguerite. *Italian Popular Comedy: A Study in the Commedia dell'arte 1520-1620, with Special Reference to the English Stage*. 2 vols. New York: Russell & Russell, 1962 [1934].

Leeds Barroll, J.; Alexander Leggatt, Richard Hosley and Alvin Kernan. *The Revels History of Drama in English*. 8 vols. London and New York: Methuen, 1975.

Lessing, Gotthold Ephraim. *Briefe, die neueste Literatur betreffend*. Berlin and Stettin: Nicolai, 1759–65. Web. 2 March 2019.

Limon, Jerzy. *Gentlemen of a Company: English Players in Central and Eastern Europe, 1590–1660*. Cambridge: CUP, 1985.

Lopez, Jeremy. *Theatrical Convention and Audience Response in Early Modern Drama*. Cambridge: CUP, 2003.

Lüdeke, Henry. *Ludwig Tieck und das alte Englische Theater*. Hildesheim: Dr. H. A. Gestenberg, 1975 [1922].

Mannack, Eberhard, ed. *Andreas Gryphius: Dramen*. Frankfurt a.M.: Deutscher Klassiker-Verlag, 1991.

---, ed. *Johann Rist: Sämtliche Werke*. Berlin und New York: Walter de Gruyter, 1972.

Mares, F. H., ed. *The Arden Shakespeare Much Ado About Nothing*. Cambridge: CUP, 1988.

Marotti, Ferruccio and Giovanna Romei. *La Commedia dell'Arte e la società barocca*. Rome: Bulzoni editore, 1991.

Martino, Alberto and Fausto De Michele, eds. *La ricezione della Commedia dell'Arte nell'Europa centrale 1568–1769: Storia, Testi, Iconografia*. Pisa and Rome: Fabrizio Serra Editore, 2010.

---, ed. *Die italienische Literatur im deutschen Sprachraum: Ergänzungen und Berichtigungen zu Frank-Rutger Hausmanns Bibliographie*. Chloe, Beihefte zu Daphnis. Amsterdam: Rodopoi, 1994.

Mayer, David and Kenneth Richards, eds. *Western Popular Theatre*. London: Methuen, 1977.

McGill, Kathleen. "Women and Performance: The Development of Improvisation by the Sixteenth-Century Commedia dell'Arte". *Theatre Journal* 43.1 (1991): 59–69. *JSTOR*. Web. 28 August 2019.

Mehnert, Henning. *Commedia dell'Arte: Struktur – Geschichte – Rezeption*. Stuttgart: Reclam, 2003.

Meissner, Johannes. *Die englischen Comoedianten zur Zeit Shakespeares in Österreich*. Vienna: Carl Konegen, 1884.

Mentzel, Elisabeth. *Geschichte der Schauspielkunst in Frankfurt a.M.* Frankfurt a.M.: Völkers, 1882.

Miklaševskij, Konstantin. *La Commedia dell'Arte o il teatro dei commedianti italiani nei secoli XVI, XVII e XVIII*. Trans. Carla Solivetti, Venice: Marsilio, 1981 [1914].

Milling, Jane and Peter Thomson, eds. *The Cambridge History of British Theatre*. 3 vols. Cambridge: CUP, 2008.

Murad, Orlene. *The English Comedians at the Habsburg Court in Graz 1607–1608*. Salzburg Studies in English Literature. Elizabethan and Renaissance Studies 81. Salzburg: Inst. f. Anglistik u. Amerikanistik, Univ. Salzburg, 1978.

Nicoll, Allardyce. *The World of Harlequin: A Critical Study of the Commedia dell'Arte*. Cambridge: CUP, 1963.

Niedercken-Gebhart, Hanns. "Neues Aktenmaterial über die Englischen Komödianten in Deutschland". *Euphorion* 21 (1914): 72–85. Web. 3 July 2019.

Oppitz-Trotman, George. *Stages of Loss: The English Comedians and Their Reception*. Oxford: OUP, 2020.

Palm, Hermann and Friedrich-Wilhelm Wentzlaff-Eggebert, eds. *Andreas Gryphius: Werke in drei Bänden mit Ergänzungsband*. Darmstadt: Wissenschaftliche Buchgesellschaft, 1961.

Pandolfi, Vito. *Il teatro del rinascimento e la Commedia dell'Arte*. Rome: Lerici Editore, 1969.

---. *Isabella comica gelosa: Avventure di maschere*. Rome: Edizioni moderne, 1960.

---. *La Commedia dell'Arte: Storia e testo*. 6 vols. Florence: Ed. Sansoni Antiquariato, 1957.

Pascal, R. "The Stage of the 'Englische Komödianten' – Three Problems". *The Modern Language Review* 35 (1940): 367–76. Web. 25 August 2019.

Pettitt, Thomas. "English Folk Drama and the Early German *Fastnachtspiele*". *Renaissance Drama, New Series* 13 (1982): 1–34. *JSTOR*. Web. 17 May 2020.

Plett, Heinrich F., ed. *Intertextuality*. Berlin and New York: Walter de Gruyter, 1991.

Potter, Robert. *The English Morality Play: Origins, History and Influence of a Dramatic Tradition*. London and New York: Routledge, 1975.

Preeshl, Artemis. *Shakespeare and Commedia dell'Arte: Play by Play*. London and New York: Routledge, 2017.

Preiss, Richard. *Clowning and Authorship in Early Modern Theatre*. Cambridge: CUP, 2014.

Price, Lawrence Marsden. *The Reception of English Literature in Germany*. New York and London: Benjamin Blom, 1968 [1932].

Raab, Ferdinand. *Johann Joseph Felix von Kurz genannt Bernardon: Ein Beitrag zur Geschichte des deutschen Theaters im XVIII. Jahrhundert*. Frankfurt a.M.: Rütten & Loening, 1899.

Rhys, Ernest, ed. *Everyman and Other Old Religious Plays with an Introduction*. London et. al.: J. M. Dent & Sons, 1909.

Richards, Jeffrey H. *The Golden Age of Pantomime: Slapstick, Spectacle and Subversion in Victorian England.* London: Tauris, 2015.

Riha, Karl. *Commedia dell'Arte: Mit den Figurinen Moritz Sands.* Frankfurt a.M.: Insel, 1980.

Robertson, J. G. *A History of German Literature.* Edinburgh and London: William Blackwood and Sons Ldt., 1949.

Roloff, Hans-Gert, ed. *Fortunatus: Studienausgabe nach der Editio Princeps von 1509.* Stuttgart: Reclam, 1981.

Rommel, Otto. *Die Alt-Wiener Volkskomödie: Ihre Geschichte vom barocken Welttheater bis zum Tode Nestroys.* Vienna: Schroll, 1952.

Rudin, Bärbel. "Hans Mühlgraf & Co., Sitz Nürnberg: Ein deutsches Bühnenunternehmen im Dreißigjährigen Krieg". *Kleine Schriften der Gesellschaft für Theatergeschichte* 29/30 (1978): 15–30.

Salerno, Henry F. *Scenarios of the Commedia dell'Arte: Flaminio Scala's 'Il Teatro delle favole rappresentative'.* New York: New York UP; London: University of London Press Limited, 1967.

---. *The Elizabethan Drama and the 'Commedia dell'Arte'.* ProQuest Dissertations and Theses, 1956. Web. 7 October 2018.

Salingar, Leo. *Shakespeare and the Traditions of Comedy.* Cambridge: CUP, 1974.

Sanders, Julie. *Adaptation and Appropriation.* London and New York: Routledge, 2006.

Schabert, Ina, ed. *Shakespeare-Handbuch: die Zeit, der Mensch, das Werk, die Nachwelt.* Stuttgart: Kröner, 1992.

Schade, Richard Erich. *Studies in Early German Comedy, 1500-1650.* Columbia, SC: Camden House, 1988.

Schechner, Richard. *Performance Theory.* London and New York: Routledge, 2003 [1988].

Schechter, Joel, ed. *Popular Theatre: A Sourcebook.* London and New York: Routledge, 2003.

Scheible, Johann, ed. *Die Fliegenden Blätter des XVI. und XVII. Jahrhunderts, in sogenannten Einblatt-Drucken mit Kupferstichen und Holzschnitten; zunächst aus dem Gebiete der politischen und religiösen Caricatur.* Stuttgart, 1850.

Schlueter, June. "English Actors in Kassel, Germany, during Shakespeare's Time". *Medieval & Renaissance Drama in England* 10 (1988): 238–61. JSTOR. Web. 17 November 2020.

Schmitz, Thomas A. *Das Volksstück.* Stuttgart: Metzler, 1990.

Schrickx, Willem. *Foreign Envoys and Travelling Players in the Age of Shakespeare and Jonson.* Wetteren: Universa, 1986.

Shaughnessy, Robert, ed. *The Cambridge Companion to Shakespeare and Popular Culture.* Cambridge: CUP, 2007.

Smith, Winifred. *The Commedia dell'Arte: A Study in Italian Popular Comedy.* New York: Columbia UP, 1912.

Stone Peters, Julie. *Theatre of the Book, 1480-1880: Print, Text, and Performance in Europe*. Oxford: OUP, 2000.

Storey, John, ed. *Cultural Theory and Popular Culture: A Reader*. Hemel Hempstead: Prentice Hall, 1998.

Stubbes, Philip. *The Anatomy of Abuses*. London, 1583. Web. 8 January 2021.

Tessari, Roberto. *Commedia dell'Arte: La Maschera e l'Ombra*. Milan: Mursia, 1981.

Testaverde, Anna Maria, ed. *I canovacci della Commedia dell'Arte*. Torino: Einaudi, 2007.

Thiele, Wolfgang, ed. *Commedia dell'Arte: Geschichte – Theorie – Praxis*. Wiesbaden: Harrassowitz, 1997.

Tittmann, Julius, ed. *Die Schauspiele der englischen Komödianten in Deutschland*. Leipzig: Brockhaus, 1880.

---, ed. *Die Schauspiele des Herzogs Heinrich Julius von Braunschweig*. Leipzig: Brockhaus, 1880.

Trautmann, Karl. "Englische Komoedianten in Nürnberg (1593–1648)". *Archiv für Litteraturgeschichte* XIV (1886): 113–42.

---. "Englische Komoedianten in Ulm (1594–1657)". *Archiv für Litteraturgeschichte* XIII (1885): 315–324.

---. "Englische Komoedianten in Frankfurt (1615)". *Archiv für Litteraturgeschichte* XII (1884): 417–8.

---. "Englische Komoedianten in München (1597, 1600, 1607)". *Archiv für Litteraturgeschichte* XII (1884): 319–20.

---. "Die älteste Nachricht über eine Aufführung von Shakespeares Romeo und Julie in Deutschland (1604)". *Archiv für Litteraturgeschichte* XI (1882): 625–6.

Treccani, Giovanni. *Enciclopedia italiana delle Scienze, Lettere ed Arti*. Rome: Istituto della Enciclopedia Italiana, 1950.

Tronstad, Ragnhild. "Could the World become a Stage? Theatricality and Metaphorical Structures". *Theatricality* 98/99. Spec. issue of *SubStance* 31.2:3 (2002): 216–24. *JSTOR*. Web. 6 July 2017.

Vianello, Daniele. *L'arte del buffone: Maschere e spettacolo tra Italia e Baviera nel XVI secolo*. Rome: Bulzoni editore, 2005.

Weber, Samuel M. *Theatricality as Medium*. New York: Fordham UP, 2004.

Weimann, Robert. *Shakespeare und die Tradition des Volkstheaters: Soziologie, Dramaturgie, Gestaltung*. Berlin: Henschel, 1967.

Wells, Stanley, ed. *The Cambridge Companion to Shakespeare Studies*. Cambridge: CUP, 1991.

Welsford, Enid. *The Fool: His Social and Literary History*. London: Faber and Faber, 1935.

Whalen, Richard. "Commedia dell'Arte in *Othello*: A Satiric Comedy Ending in Tragedy". *Brief Chronicles* 3 (2011): 71–108. *JSTOR*. Web. 21 October 2019.

Williams, Raymond. *Keywords: A Vocabulary of Culture and Society*. London: Fontana P, 1983 [1976].
Williams, Simon. *Shakespeare on the German stage, 1586–1914*. Cambridge: CUP, 1990.
Wilson, Peter H. *Europe's Tragedy: A History of the Thirty Years War*. London: Allen Lane, 2009.
Wright, Louis B. "Will Kempe and the Commedia dell'Arte". *Modern Language Notes* 41.8 (1926): 516–20. *JSTOR*. Web. 11 April 2019.
Yates, W. E. "Elizabethan Comedy and the Alt-Wiener Volkstheater". *Forum for Modern Language Studies* 3 (1967): 27–35. Web. 26 August 2020.
Zarrilli, Phillip B. and Gary Jaz Williams, eds. *Theatre Histories: An Introduction*. London and New York: Routledge, 2006.
Zorzi, Ludovico. "Struttura → fortuna della 'Fiaba' gozziana". *Chigiana Journal of Musicological Studies* XXXI (1974): 25–40. Web. 24 June 2019.

List of Illustrations

Figures 1, 10, 13: Details from Pieter Brueghel the Younger, *A Village Festival in Honour of St Hubert and St Anthony* (1632). © The Fitzwilliam Museum, Cambridge.

Figure 2: Richard Tarlton with his pipe and tabor inside the majuscule letter 'T'. In John Scottowe, *Alphabet* (around 1592). © British Library Board, MS. Harley 3885 f19.

Figure 3: Typical topic of a *canovaccio* with the (a)symmetrical arrangement of characters and masks taken from Ludovico Zorzi, "Struttura → fortuna della 'Fiaba' gozziana". *Chigiana, Journal of Musicological Studies* XXXI (1974): 25–40, p. 38. Web. 24 June 2019.

Figure 4: Pantalone and Zanni/Brighella singing a serenade. Detail from the northwest wall of the 'Narrentreppe'. DE001466 Burg Trausnitz, Landshut, Narrentreppe, R. 2, Figuren aus der Commedia dell'Arte, Padovano, 1575–9. © Bayerische Schlösserverwaltung, Wolf-Christian von der Mülbe.

Figure 5: Etching from the pamphlet *Englischer Pickelhäring, jetzo vornehmer Eisenhändler, mit Aext, Beil, Barten gen Prag jubilirend* (1621). Taken from Johann Scheible, ed., *Die Fliegenden Blätter des XVI. und XVII. Jahrhundert*s (Stuttgart, 1850), p. 86.

Figure 6: Etching from the pamphlet *Engelländischen Pickelhäring, welcher jetzund als ein vornehmer Händler und Jubilirer mit allerlei Judenspießen nach Frankfurt in die Meß zeucht* (1621). Taken from Scheible, ed., *Die Fliegenden Blätter des XVI. und XVII. Jahrhunderts*, p. 81.

Figure 7: Title page of the anonymous play *Pickelhärings Hochzeit, oder Der lustig singende Harlequin* (1652). Taken from Ernest Brennecke, ed., *Shakespeare in Germany: 1590–1700. With Translations of Five Early Plays*, p. 57.

Figure 8: Stage portrait of the engraver Hans Ammon, who played the clown Peter Leberwurst in Hans Mühlgraf's company until 1632. Etching from the Germanisches Nationalmuseum Nuremberg contained in Bärbel Rudin, "Hans Mühlgraf & Co., Sitz Nürnberg: Ein deutsches Bühnenunternehmen im Dreißigjährigen Krieg". *Kleine Schriften der Gesellschaft für Theatergeschichte* 29/30 (1978), pp. 15–30, p. 22.

Figure 9: Title page of the 1620 edition of *Engelische Comedien und Tragedien* A: 105 Eth. (1). By kind permission of the Herzog August Bibliothek Wolfenbüttel.

Figure 11: Details of the title page and last leaf verso of Anon., *No-body and Some-body*, 1606, RB62750. © The Huntington Library, San Marino, California.

Figure 12: Picture of John Green as Nobody in the 1608 manuscript of *Niemand und Jemand. Ein wahrhafftige unndt glaubwirdige History unndt Geschicht, wie es sich vor villen Jarrn in Englandt mit Khunig Arnagall und seine dreyen Prüder zu getragen* (MS 128). By kind permission of the Cistercian monastery at Rein near Graz.

Figure 14: Title page of the Vienna manuscript of *Der Jud von Venedig*. Digital scan provided by the Österreichische Nationalbibliothek, Vienna, Cod. 13791*, fol. 1r.

Figure 15: Coloured etching of Gottfried Prehauser (1699–1769) as Hanswurst. © Wienbibliothek im Rathaus, photographed by Julia Teresa Friehs.

List of Abbreviations and Glossary

ECUT: *Engelische Comedien und Tragedien* (1620). Reprinted in volume 1 of *Spieltexte der Wanderbühne*. Ed. Manfred Brauneck. 6 vols. Berlin and New York: Walter de Gruyter, 1975.

IPC: Lea, Kathleen Marguerite. *Italian Popular Comedy: A Study in the Commedia dell'arte 1520-1620, with Special Reference to the English Stage*. 2 vols. New York: Russell & Russell, 1962 [1934].

SW: Brauneck, Manfred, ed. *Spieltexte der Wanderbühne*. 6 vols. Berlin and New York: Walter de Gruyter, 1975.

(Alt-)Wiener Volkstheater: The old Viennese popular theatre is an Austrian form of theatre which was developed in the eighteenth century by Anton Stranitzky and Philipp Hafner under the influence of the German Hanswurst and Italian drama. The most illustrious representatives of mature Viennese popular theatre are Ferdinand Raimund and Johann Nestroy.

Buffone (pl. *buffoni*): A proto-professional stand-up comedian, like the English buffoon or jester, who performed at court and in public in late sixteenth-century Italy.

Burla (pl. *burle*): practical jokes or pranks typical of the Zannis in Commedia dell'Arte.

Canovaccio (pl. *canovacci*): literally 'canvas', i.e. the skeletal plot of a Commedia dell'Arte play. It usually consisted of a list of characters and props and presented the salient turns in the summarised action outline.

Fastnachtspiel (pl. *Fastnachtspiele*): Burlesque performances similar to Shrovetide plays by amateurs in fifteenth-century German-speaking countries during the carnival revelries.

Hanswurst: German clown figure of sixteenth-century popular and itinerant theatre.

Lazzo (pl. *lazzi):* miniature comic business or self-contained digressions with elaborate word plays based on puns or absurd logic typical of the Zannis in Commedia dell'Arte.

Narr: German word for (professional) fool.

Novella (pl. *novelle*): narrative prose fiction in-between the length of a short story and a novel. It originated in Renaissance Italy with the *Decameron* by Giovanni Boccaccio (1353).

Pickelheringspiel (pl. *Pickelheringspiele*): early seventeenth-century farces and skits involving the Anglo-German clown Pickelhering and characterised by puns, wordplays, acrobatics and themes like adultery.

Posse (pl. *Possen*): popular comedy or farce with parodic elements which developed as independent genre (often with songs) in the Viennese *Volkstheater* from the comic subplots of the late seventeenth-century German plays.

Scenario (pl. *scenari*): initially a synonym for *canovaccio*. After Basilio Locatelli's academic collection *Della Scena de' Soggetti Comici* (1628/32) appeared, it identified more elaborate *canovacci* closer to drama.

Schwank (pl. *Schwänke*): A popular genre thriving in German – and European – literature from the Middle Ages, often translated as jest literature, fools' literature or simply comic literature. It usually designates a funny episode with bawdy or even obscene jokes. In the sixteenth century, these facetious stories were collected in frequently dramatised *Schwankbücher* (jest books).

Singspiel (pl. *Singpsiele*): German musical comedy with rhymed stanzas sung to a well-known tune in the early seventeenth century. In the eighteenth century, it evolved into a popular counterpart of courtly opera, especially in Vienna.

'Types' in Commedia dell'Arte (Zanni/Arlecchino, Innamorati, Pantalone, Dottore, Capitano, Servetta): Italian Commedia dell'Arte is a form of popular theatre based on the improvisation between fixed characters who represent (and caricature) social stereotypes. These *tipi fissi* or 'fixed types' were recognisable by their name, masks, physical, psychological, social and linguistic attributes.